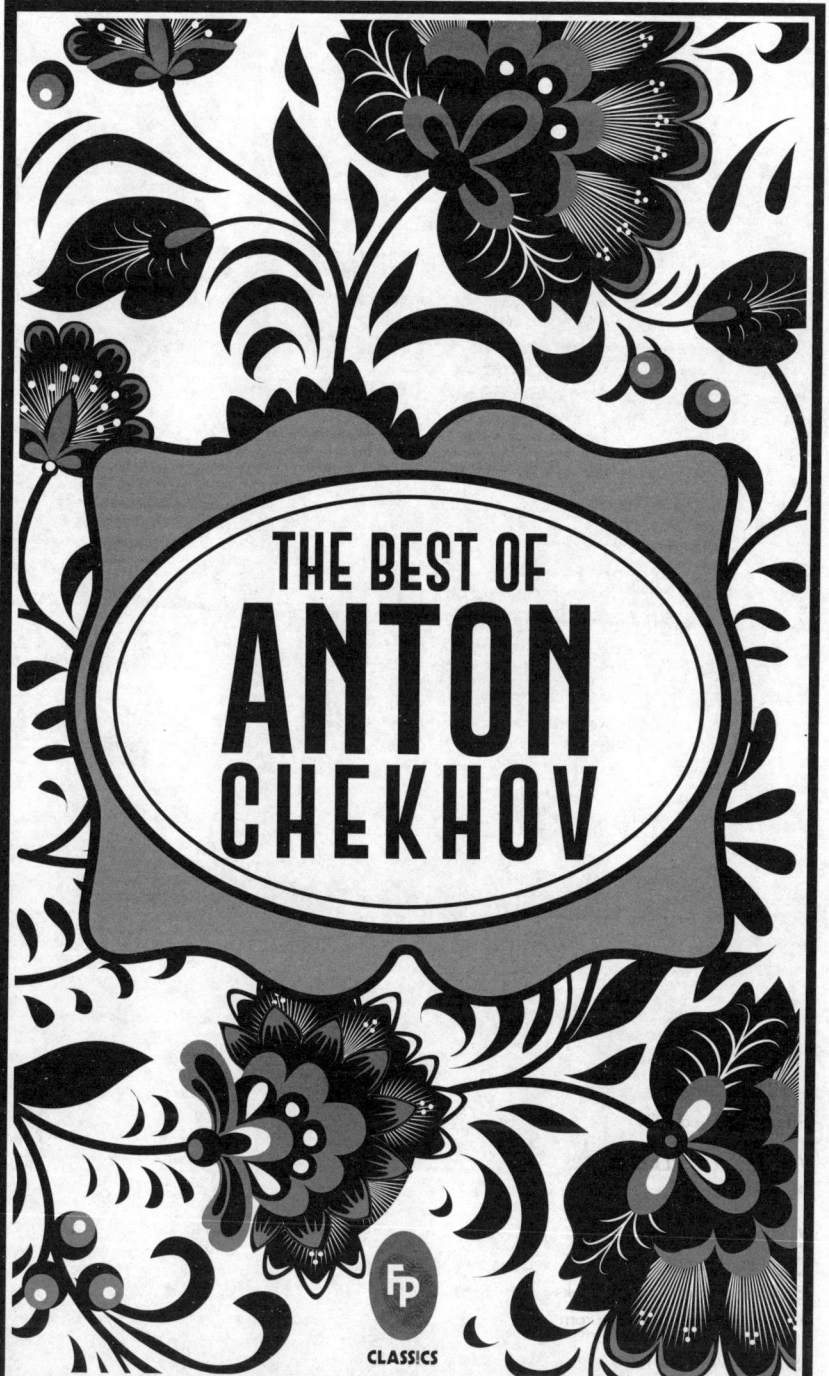

First Published 2024

FiNGERPRINT! CLASSICS
Prakash Books

Fingerprint Publishing
@FingerprintP
@fingerprintpublishingbooks
www.fingerprintpublishing.com

ISBN: 978 93 6214 130 9

"I was oppressed with a sense of vague discontent and dissatisfaction with my own life, which was passing so quickly and uninterestingly, and I kept thinking it would be a good thing if I could tear my heart out of my breast, that heart which had grown so weary of life."

Anton Chekhov, one of the greatest writers of all time, was born on January 29, 1860, in Taganrog, Russia. As a playwright and short story writer, Chekhov profoundly influenced the development of modern literature, leaving an indelible mark on both genres. Despite his relatively short life—he died of tuberculosis on July 15, 1904, at the age of 44—Chekhov's body of work is vast and varied, encompassing over 200 short stories, numerous plays, and several novellas.

Chekhov's early life was marked by hardship. He was the third of six children in a family plagued by financial difficulties. His father, Pavel Yegorovich Chekhov, was a grocer who eventually went bankrupt and fled to Moscow to escape debtors' prison. This left young Anton behind to finish his schooling while supporting himself and his family. Despite these challenges, Chekhov excelled academically, displaying a remarkable aptitude for literature and science.

In 1879, Chekhov moved to Moscow to join his family and enrolled in medical school at Moscow State University. He supported himself by writing short, humorous sketches for various magazines under pseudonyms. These early works, although light-hearted and often comedic, revealed Chekhov's keen observational skills and his ability to depict the intricacies of human nature with a sharp yet compassionate eye.

Chekhov completed his medical studies in 1884, becoming a physician. However, writing increasingly occupied his time and attention. His medical career and literary pursuits often intersected, as his experiences as a doctor provided rich material for his stories. Chekhov famously stated, "Medicine is my lawful wife, and literature is my mistress," illustrating his dual dedication to both professions.

The 1880s and 1890s were prolific years for Chekhov. During this period, he produced some of his most enduring short stories, such as "The Bet," "The Lady with the Dog," and "The Darling." These stories are characterized by their economy of language, depth of character, and exploration of themes like the futility of existence, the complexity of human relationships, and the often-painful search for meaning.

In addition to his short stories, Chekhov made significant contributions to drama. His major plays, including "Ivanov," "Three Sisters," and "The Cherry Orchard," are cornerstones of the modern theatrical canon. These plays broke away from the melodramatic conventions of the time, emphasizing character development and psychological depth over plot. They often depict the struggles of the Russian intelligentsia and the gentry, portraying their unfulfilled dreams, existential angst, and the inexorable passage of time.

Chekhov's writing style is noted for its subtlety and restraint. He often employed a technique known as "Chekhov's gun," which posits that every element in a story must be necessary, and irrelevant details should be removed. This principle of economy and precision has influenced countless writers and remains a cornerstone of effective storytelling.

Beyond his literary achievements, Chekhov was also known for his humanitarian efforts. He provided free medical care to the poor, built schools and clinics in rural areas. Despite his struggles with illness, Chekhov's later years were marked by continued literary productivity and critical acclaim. His legacy endures through his profound influence on both literature and theater. Chekhov's works continue to be read and performed worldwide, celebrated for their timeless insights into the human condition and their masterful blend of compassion, irony, and realism.

Contents

Short Stories   9

    The Lady with the Dog   11
    The Bet   29
    The Darling   37
    The Death of a Government Clerk   49

Plays   53

    Ivanov   55
    The Three Sisters   141
    The Cherry Orchard   227

Selected Letters   299

SHORT STORIES

Translated by Constance Garnett

SHORT STORIES

Translated by Constance Garnett

The Lady with the Dog

[Written in 1899 in Yalta.
First published in *Russkaya Mysl* (*Russian Thought*),
a Russian magazine, in December 1899. First published
in English in 1903. One of Chekhov's most celebrated
stories, it has been adapted for stage time and again.]

I

It was said that a new person had appeared on the sea-front: a lady with a little dog. Dmitri Dmitritch Gurov, who had by then been a fortnight at Yalta, and so was fairly at home there, had begun to take an interest in new arrivals. Sitting in Verney's pavilion, he saw, walking on the sea-front, a fair-haired young lady of medium height, wearing a *béret*; a white Pomeranian dog was running behind her.

And afterwards he met her in the public gardens and in the square several times a day. She was walking alone, always wearing the same *béret*, and always with the same white dog;

no one knew who she was, and every one called her simply "the lady with the dog."

"If she is here alone without a husband or friends, it wouldn't be amiss to make her acquaintance," Gurov reflected.

He was under forty, but he had a daughter already twelve years old, and two sons at school. He had been married young, when he was a student in his second year, and by now his wife seemed half as old again as he. She was a tall, erect woman with dark eyebrows, staid and dignified, and, as she said of herself, intellectual. She read a great deal, used phonetic spelling, called her husband, not Dmitri, but Dimitri, and he secretly considered her unintelligent, narrow, inelegant, was afraid of her, and did not like to be at home. He had begun being unfaithful to her long ago—had been unfaithful to her often, and, probably on that account, almost always spoke ill of women, and when they were talked about in his presence, used to call them "the lower race."

It seemed to him that he had been so schooled by bitter experience that he might call them what he liked, and yet he could not get on for two days together without "the lower race." In the society of men he was bored and not himself, with them he was cold and uncommunicative; but when he was in the company of women he felt free, and knew what to say to them and how to behave; and he was at ease with them even when he was silent. In his appearance, in his character, in his whole nature, there was something attractive and elusive which allured women and disposed them in his favour; he knew that, and some force seemed to draw him, too, to them.

Experience often repeated, truly bitter experience, had taught him long ago that with decent people, especially Moscow people—always slow to move and irresolute—every intimacy, which at first so agreeably diversifies life and appears a light and charming adventure, inevitably grows into a regular problem of extreme intricacy, and in the long run the situation becomes unbearable. But at every fresh meeting with an interesting woman this experience seemed to slip out of his memory, and he was eager for life, and everything seemed simple and amusing.

One evening he was dining in the gardens, and the lady in the *béret* came up slowly to take the next table. Her expression, her gait, her dress, and the way she did her hair told him that she was a lady, that she was married, that she was in Yalta for the first time and alone, and that she was dull there . . .

The stories told of the immorality in such places as Yalta are to a great extent untrue; he despised them, and knew that such stories were for the most part made up by persons who would themselves have been glad to sin if they had been able; but when the lady sat down at the next table three paces from him, he remembered these tales of easy conquests, of trips to the mountains, and the tempting thought of a swift, fleeting love affair, a romance with an unknown woman, whose name he did not know, suddenly took possession of him.

He beckoned coaxingly to the Pomeranian, and when the dog came up to him he shook his finger at it. The Pomeranian growled: Gurov shook his finger at it again.

The lady looked at him and at once dropped her eyes.

"He doesn't bite," she said, and blushed.

"May I give him a bone?" he asked; and when she nodded he asked courteously, "Have you been long in Yalta?"

"Five days."

"And I have already dragged out a fortnight here."

There was a brief silence.

"Time goes fast, and yet it is so dull here!" she said, not looking at him.

"That's only the fashion to say it is dull here. A provincial will live in Belyov or Zhidra and not be dull, and when he comes here it's 'Oh, the dulness! Oh, the dust!' One would think he came from Grenada."

She laughed. Then both continued eating in silence, like strangers, but after dinner they walked side by side; and there sprang up between them the light jesting conversation of people who are free and satisfied, to whom it does not matter where they go or what they talk about. They walked and talked of the strange light on the sea: the water was of a soft warm lilac hue, and there was a golden streak from the moon upon it. They talked of how sultry it was after a hot day. Gurov told her that he came from Moscow, that he had taken his degree in Arts, but had a post in a bank; that he had trained as an opera-singer, but had given it up, that he owned two houses in Moscow . . . And from her he learnt that she had grown up in Petersburg, but had lived in S—— since her marriage two years before, that she was staying another month in Yalta, and that her husband, who needed a holiday too, might perhaps come and fetch her. She was not sure whether her husband had a post in a Crown Department or under the Provincial

Council—and was amused by her own ignorance. And Gurov learnt, too, that she was called Anna Sergeyevna.

Afterwards he thought about her in his room at the hotel—thought she would certainly meet him next day; it would be sure to happen. As he got into bed he thought how lately she had been a girl at school, doing lessons like his own daughter; he recalled the diffidence, the angularity, that was still manifest in her laugh and her manner of talking with a stranger. This must have been the first time in her life she had been alone in surroundings in which she was followed, looked at, and spoken to merely from a secret motive which she could hardly fail to guess. He recalled her slender, delicate neck, her lovely grey eyes.

"There's something pathetic about her, anyway," he thought, and fell asleep.

II

A week had passed since they had made acquaintance. It was a holiday. It was sultry indoors, while in the street the wind whirled the dust round and round, and blew people's hats off. It was a thirsty day, and Gurov often went into the pavilion, and pressed Anna Sergeyevna to have syrup and water or an ice. One did not know what to do with oneself.

In the evening when the wind had dropped a little, they went out on the groyne to see the steamer come in. There were a great many people walking about the harbour; they had gathered to welcome some one, bringing bouquets. And two peculiarities of a well-dressed Yalta crowd were very conspicuous: the elderly ladies were dressed like young ones, and there were great numbers of generals.

Owing to the roughness of the sea, the steamer arrived late, after the sun had set, and it was a long time turning about before it reached the groyne. Anna Sergeyevna looked through her lorgnette at the steamer and the passengers as though looking for acquaintances, and when she turned to Gurov her eyes were shining. She talked a great deal and asked disconnected questions, forgetting next moment what she had asked; then she dropped her lorgnette in the crush.

The festive crowd began to disperse; it was too dark to see people's faces. The wind had completely dropped, but Gurov and Anna Sergeyevna still stood as though waiting to see someone else come from the steamer. Anna Sergeyevna was silent now, and sniffed the flowers without looking at Gurov.

"The weather is better this evening," he said. "Where shall we go now? Shall we drive somewhere?"

She made no answer.

Then he looked at her intently, and all at once put his arm round her and kissed her on the lips, and breathed in the moisture and the fragrance of the flowers; and he immediately looked round him, anxiously wondering whether any one had seen them.

"Let us go to your hotel," he said softly. And both walked quickly.

The room was close and smelt of the scent she had bought at the Japanese shop. Gurov looked at her and thought: "What different people one meets in the world!" From the past he preserved memories of careless, good-natured women, who loved cheerfully and were grateful to him for the happiness he gave them, however brief it might be; and of women like his wife who loved without any genuine feeling, with superfluous phrases, affectedly, hysterically, with an expression that suggested that it was not love nor passion, but something more significant; and of two or three others, very beautiful, cold women, on whose faces he had caught a glimpse of a rapacious expression—an obstinate desire to snatch from life more than it could give, and these were capricious, unreflecting, domineering, unintelligent women not in their first youth, and when Gurov grew cold to them their beauty excited his hatred, and the lace on their linen seemed to him like scales.

But in this case there was still the diffidence, the angularity of inexperienced youth, an awkward feeling; and there was a sense of consternation as though some one had suddenly knocked at the door. The attitude of Anna Sergeyevna—"the lady with the dog"—to what had happened was somehow peculiar, very grave, as though it were her fall—so it seemed, and it was strange and inappropriate. Her face dropped and faded, and on both sides of it her long hair hung down mournfully; she mused in a dejected attitude like "the woman who was a sinner" in an old-fashioned picture.

"It's wrong," she said. "You will be the first to despise me now."

There was a watermelon on the table. Gurov cut himself a slice and began eating it without haste. There followed at least half an hour of silence.

Anna Sergeyevna was touching; there was about her the purity of a good, simple woman who had seen little of life. The solitary candle burning on the table threw a faint light on her face, yet it was clear that she was very unhappy.

"How could I despise you?" asked Gurov. "You don't know what you are saying."

"God forgive me," she said, and her eyes filled with tears. "It's awful."

"You seem to feel you need to be forgiven."

"Forgiven? No. I am a bad, low woman; I despise myself and don't attempt to justify myself. It's not my husband but myself I have deceived. And not only just now; I have been deceiving myself for a long time. My husband may be a good, honest man, but he is a flunkey! I don't know what he does there, what his work is, but I know he is a flunkey! I was twenty when I was married to him. I have been tormented by curiosity; I wanted something better. 'There must be a different sort of life,' I said to myself. I wanted to live! To live, to live! . . . I was fired by curiosity . . . you don't understand it, but, I swear to God, I could not control myself; something happened to me: I could not be restrained. I told my husband I was ill, and came here . . . And here I have been walking about as though I were dazed, like a mad creature; . . . and now I have become a vulgar, contemptible woman whom any one may despise."

Gurov felt bored already, listening to her. He was irritated by the naïve tone, by this remorse, so unexpected and inopportune; but for the tears in her eyes, he might have thought she was jesting or playing a part.

"I don't understand," he said softly. "What is it you want?"

She hid her face on his breast and pressed close to him.

"Believe me, believe me, I beseech you . . ." she said. "I love a pure, honest life, and sin is loathsome to me. I don't know what I am doing. Simple people say: 'The Evil One has beguiled me.' And I may say of myself now that the Evil One has beguiled me."

"Hush, hush! . . ." he muttered.

He looked at her fixed, scared eyes, kissed her, talked softly and affectionately, and by degrees she was comforted, and her gaiety returned; they both began laughing.

Afterwards when they went out there was not a soul on the sea-front. The town with its cypresses had quite a deathlike air, but the sea still broke noisily on the shore; a single barge was rocking on the waves, and a lantern was blinking sleepily on it.

They found a cab and drove to Oreanda.

"I found out your surname in the hall just now: it was written on the board—Von Diderits," said Gurov. "Is your husband a German?"

"No; I believe his grandfather was a German, but he is an Orthodox Russian himself."

At Oreanda they sat on a seat not far from the church, looked down at the sea, and were silent. Yalta was hardly visible through the morning mist; white clouds stood motionless on the mountain-tops. The leaves did not stir on the trees, grasshoppers chirruped, and the monotonous hollow sound of the sea rising up from below, spoke of the peace, of the eternal sleep awaiting us. So it must have sounded when there was no Yalta, no Oreanda here; so it sounds now, and it will sound as indifferently and monotonously when we are all no more. And in this constancy, in this complete indifference to the life and death of each of us, there lies hid, perhaps, a pledge of our eternal salvation, of the unceasing movement of life upon earth, of unceasing progress towards perfection. Sitting beside a young woman who in the dawn seemed so lovely, soothed and spellbound in these magical surroundings—the sea, mountains, clouds, the open sky—Gurov thought how in reality everything is beautiful in this world when one reflects: everything except what we think or do ourselves when we forget our human dignity and the higher aims of our existence.

A man walked up to them—probably a keeper—looked at them and walked away. And this detail seemed mysterious and beautiful, too. They saw a steamer come from Theodosia, with its lights out in the glow of dawn.

"There is dew on the grass," said Anna Sergeyevna, after a silence.

"Yes. It's time to go home."

They went back to the town.

Then they met every day at twelve o'clock on the sea-front, lunched and dined together, went for walks, admired the sea. She complained that she slept badly, that her heart throbbed violently; asked the same questions, troubled now by jealousy and now by the fear that he did not respect her sufficiently. And often in the square or gardens, when there was no one near them, he suddenly drew her to him and kissed her passionately. Complete idleness, these kisses in broad daylight while he looked round in dread of some one's seeing them, the heat, the smell of the sea, and the continual passing to and fro before him of idle, well-dressed, well-fed people, made a new man of him; he told Anna Sergeyevna how beautiful she was, how fascinating. He was impatiently passionate, he would not move a step away from her, while she was often pensive and continually urged him to confess that he did not respect her, did not love her in the least, and thought of her as nothing but a common woman. Rather late almost every evening they drove somewhere out of town, to Oreanda or to the waterfall; and the expedition was always a success, the scenery invariably impressed them as grand and beautiful.

They were expecting her husband to come, but a letter came from him, saying that there was something wrong with his eyes, and he entreated his wife to come home as quickly as possible. Anna Sergeyevna made haste to go.

"It's a good thing I am going away," she said to Gurov. "It's the finger of destiny!"

She went by coach and he went with her. They were driving the whole day. When she had got into a compartment of the express, and when the second bell had rung, she said:

"Let me look at you once more . . . look at you once again. That's right."

She did not shed tears, but was so sad that she seemed ill, and her face was quivering.

"I shall remember you . . . think of you," she said. "God be with you; be happy. Don't remember evil against me. We are parting forever—it must be so, for we ought never to have met. Well, God be with you."

The train moved off rapidly, its lights soon vanished from sight, and a minute later there was no sound of it, as though everything had conspired together to end as quickly as possible that sweet delirium, that madness. Left alone on the platform, and gazing into the dark distance, Gurov listened to the chirrup of the grasshoppers and the hum of the telegraph wires, feeling as though he had only just waked up. And he thought, musing, that there had been another episode or adventure in his life, and it, too, was at an end, and nothing was left of it but a memory . . . He was moved, sad, and conscious of a slight remorse. This young woman whom he would never meet again had not been happy with him; he was genuinely warm and affectionate with her, but yet in his manner, his tone, and his caresses there had been a shade of light irony, the coarse condescension of a happy man who was, besides, almost twice her age. All the time she had called him kind, exceptional, lofty; obviously he had seemed to her different from what he really was, so he had unintentionally deceived her . . .

Here at the station was already a scent of autumn; it was a cold evening.

"It's time for me to go north," thought Gurov as he left the platform. "High time!"

III

At home in Moscow everything was in its winter routine; the stoves were heated, and in the morning it was still dark when the children were having breakfast and getting ready for school, and the nurse would light the lamp for a short time. The frosts had begun already. When the first snow has fallen, on the first day of sledge-driving it is pleasant to see the white earth, the white roofs, to draw soft, delicious breath, and the season brings back the days of one's youth. The old limes and birches, white with hoarfrost, have a good-natured expression; they are nearer to one's heart than cypresses and palms, and near them one doesn't want to be thinking of the sea and the mountains.

Gurov was Moscow born; he arrived in Moscow on a fine frosty day, and when he put on his fur coat and warm gloves, and walked along Petrovka, and when on Saturday evening he heard the ringing of the bells, his recent trip and the places he had seen lost all charm for him. Little by little he became absorbed in Moscow life, greedily read three newspapers a day, and declared he did not read the Moscow papers on principle! He already felt a longing to go to restaurants, clubs, dinner-parties, anniversary celebrations, and he felt flattered at entertaining distinguished lawyers and artists, and at playing cards with a professor at the doctors' club. He could already eat a whole plateful of salt fish and cabbage.

In another month, he fancied, the image of Anna Sergeyevna would be shrouded in a mist in his memory, and only from time to time would visit him in his dreams with a touching smile as others did. But more than a month passed, real winter had come, and everything was still clear in his memory as though he had parted with Anna Sergeyevna only the day before.

And his memories glowed more and more vividly. When in the evening stillness he heard from his study the voices of his children, preparing their lessons, or when he listened to a song or the organ at the restaurant, or the storm howled in the chimney, suddenly everything would rise up in his memory: what had happened on the groyne, and the early morning with the mist on the mountains, and the steamer coming from Theodosia, and the kisses. He would pace a long time about his room, remembering it all and smiling; then his memories passed into dreams, and in his fancy the past was mingled with what was to come. Anna Sergeyevna did not visit him in dreams, but followed him about everywhere like a shadow and haunted him. When he shut his eyes he saw her as though she were living before him, and she seemed to him lovelier, younger, tenderer than she was; and he imagined himself finer than he had been in Yalta. In the evenings she peeped out at him from the bookcase, from the fireplace, from the corner—he heard her breathing, the caressing rustle of her dress. In the street he watched the women, looking for some one like her.

He was tormented by an intense desire to confide his memories to some one. But in his home it was impossible to talk of his love, and he had no one outside; he could not talk to his tenants nor to any one at the bank. And what had he to talk of? Had he been in love, then? Had there been anything beautiful, poetical, or edifying or simply interesting in his relations with Anna Sergeyevna? And there was nothing for him but to talk vaguely of love, of woman, and no one guessed what it meant; only his wife twitched her black eyebrows, and said:

"The part of a lady-killer does not suit you at all, Dimitri."

One evening, coming out of the doctors' club with an official with whom he had been playing cards, he could not resist saying:

"If only you knew what a fascinating woman I made the acquaintance of in Yalta!"

The official got into his sledge and was driving away, but turned suddenly and shouted:

"Dmitri Dmitritch!"

"What?"

"You were right this evening: the sturgeon was a bit too strong!"

These words, so ordinary, for some reason moved Gurov to indignation, and struck him as degrading and unclean. What savage manners, what people! What senseless nights, what uninteresting, uneventful days! The rage for card-playing, the gluttony, the drunkenness, the continual talk always about the same thing. Useless pursuits and conversations always about the same things absorb the better part of one's time, the better part of one's strength, and in the end there is left a life grovelling and curtailed, worthless and trivial, and there is no escaping or getting away from it—just as though one were in a madhouse or a prison.

Gurov did not sleep all night, and was filled with indignation. And he had a headache all next day. And the next night he slept badly; he sat up in bed, thinking, or paced up and down his room. He was sick of his children, sick of the bank; he had no desire to go anywhere or to talk of anything.

In the holidays in December he prepared for a journey, and told his wife he was going to Petersburg to do something in the interests of a young friend—and he set off for S——. What for? He did not very well know himself. He wanted to see Anna Sergeyevna and to talk with her—to arrange a meeting, if possible.

He reached S—— in the morning, and took the best room at the hotel, in which the floor was covered with grey army cloth, and on the table was an inkstand, grey with dust and adorned with a figure on horseback, with its hat in its hand and its head broken off. The hotel porter gave him the necessary information; Von Diderits lived in a house of his own in Old Gontcharny Street—it was not far from the hotel: he was rich and lived in good style, and had his own horses; every one in the town knew him. The porter pronounced the name "Dridirits."

Gurov went without haste to Old Gontcharny Street and found the house. Just opposite the house stretched a long grey fence adorned with nails.

"One would run away from a fence like that," thought Gurov, looking from the fence to the windows of the house and back again.

He considered: today was a holiday, and the husband would probably be at home. And in any case it would be tactless to go into the house and upset her. If he were to send her a note it might fall into her husband's hands, and then it might ruin everything. The best thing was to trust to chance. And he kept walking up and down the street by the fence, waiting for the chance. He saw a beggar go in at the gate and dogs fly at him; then an hour later he heard a piano, and the sounds were faint and indistinct.

Probably it was Anna Sergeyevna playing. The front door suddenly opened, and an old woman came out, followed by the familiar white Pomeranian. Gurov was on the point of calling to the dog, but his heart began beating violently, and in his excitement he could not remember the dog's name.

He walked up and down, and loathed the grey fence more and more, and by now he thought irritably that Anna Sergeyevna had forgotten him, and was perhaps already amusing herself with someone else, and that that was very natural in a young woman who had nothing to look at from morning till night but that confounded fence. He went back to his hotel room and sat for a long while on the sofa, not knowing what to do, then he had dinner and a long nap.

"How stupid and worrying it is!" he thought when he woke and looked at the dark windows: it was already evening. "Here I've had a good sleep for some reason. What shall I do in the night?"

He sat on the bed, which was covered by a cheap grey blanket, such as one sees in hospitals, and he taunted himself in his vexation:

"So much for the lady with the dog . . . so much for the adventure . . . You're in a nice fix . . ."

That morning at the station a poster in large letters had caught his eye. "The Geisha" was to be performed for the first time. He thought of this and went to the theatre.

"It's quite possible she may go to the first performance," he thought.

The theatre was full. As in all provincial theatres, there was a fog above the chandelier, the gallery was noisy and restless; in the front row the local dandies were standing up before the beginning of the performance, with their hands behind them; in the Governor's box the Governor's daughter, wearing a boa, was sitting in the front seat, while the Governor himself lurked modestly behind the curtain with only his hands visible; the orchestra was a long time tuning up; the stage curtain swayed. All the time the audience were coming in and taking their seats Gurov looked at them eagerly.

Anna Sergeyevna, too, came in. She sat down in the third row, and when Gurov looked at her his heart contracted, and he understood clearly that for him there was in the whole world no creature so near, so precious, and so important to him; she, this little woman, in no way remarkable, lost in a provincial crowd, with a vulgar lorgnette in her hand, filled his whole life now, was his sorrow and his joy, the one happiness that he now desired for himself, and to the sounds of the inferior orchestra, of the wretched provincial violins, he thought how lovely she was. He thought and dreamed.

A young man with small side-whiskers, tall and stooping, came in with Anna Sergeyevna and sat down beside her; he bent his head at every step and seemed to be continually bowing. Most likely this was the husband whom at Yalta, in a rush of bitter feeling, she had called a flunkey. And there really was in his long figure, his side-whiskers, and the small bald patch on his head, something of the flunkey's obsequiousness; his smile was sugary, and in his buttonhole there was some badge of distinction like the number on a waiter.

During the first interval the husband went away to smoke; she remained alone in her stall. Gurov, who was sitting in the stalls, too, went up to her and said in a trembling voice, with a forced smile:

"Good evening."

She glanced at him and turned pale, then glanced again with horror, unable to believe her eyes, and tightly gripped the fan and the lorgnette in her hands, evidently struggling with herself not to faint. Both were silent. She was sitting, he was standing, frightened by her confusion and not venturing to sit down beside her. The violins and the flute began tuning up. He felt suddenly frightened; it seemed as though all the people in the boxes were looking at them. She got up and went quickly to the door; he followed her, and both walked senselessly along passages, and up and down stairs, and figures in legal, scholastic, and civil service uniforms, all wearing badges, flitted before their eyes. They caught glimpses of ladies, of fur coats hanging on pegs; the draughts blew on them, bringing a smell of stale tobacco. And Gurov, whose heart was beating violently, thought:

"Oh, heavens! Why are these people here and this orchestra! . . ."

And at that instant he recalled how when he had seen Anna Sergeyevna off at the station he had thought that everything was over and they would never meet again. But how far they were still from the end!

On the narrow, gloomy staircase over which was written "To the Amphitheatre," she stopped.

"How you have frightened me!" she said, breathing hard, still pale and overwhelmed. "Oh, how you have frightened me! I am half dead. Why have you come? Why?"

"But do understand, Anna, do understand . . ." he said hastily in a low voice. "I entreat you to understand . . ."

She looked at him with dread, with entreaty, with love; she looked at him intently, to keep his features more distinctly in her memory.

"I am so unhappy," she went on, not heeding him. "I have thought of nothing but you all the time; I live only in the thought of you. And I wanted to forget, to forget you; but why, oh, why, have you come?"

On the landing above them two schoolboys were smoking and looking down, but that was nothing to Gurov; he drew Anna Sergeyevna to him, and began kissing her face, her cheeks, and her hands.

"What are you doing, what are you doing!" she cried in horror, pushing him away. "We are mad. Go away today; go away at once . . . I beseech you by all that is sacred, I implore you . . . There are people coming this way!"

Some one was coming up the stairs.

"You must go away," Anna Sergeyevna went on in a whisper. "Do you hear, Dmitri Dmitritch? I will come and see you in Moscow. I have never been happy; I am miserable now, and I never, never shall be happy, never! Don't make me suffer still more! I swear I'll come to Moscow. But now let us part. My precious, good, dear one, we must part!"

She pressed his hand and began rapidly going downstairs, looking round at him, and from her eyes he could see that she really was unhappy. Gurov stood for a little while, listened, then, when all sound had died away, he found his coat and left the theatre.

IV

And Anna Sergeyevna began coming to see him in Moscow. Once in two or three months she left S——, telling her husband that she was going to consult a doctor about an internal complaint—and her husband believed her, and did not believe her. In Moscow she stayed at the Slaviansky Bazaar hotel, and at once sent a man in a red cap to Gurov. Gurov went to see her, and no one in Moscow knew of it.

Once he was going to see her in this way on a winter morning (the messenger had come the evening before when he was out). With him walked his daughter, whom he wanted to take to school: it was on the way. Snow was falling in big wet flakes.

"It's three degrees above freezing-point, and yet it is snowing," said Gurov to his daughter. "The thaw is only on the surface of the earth; there is quite a different temperature at a greater height in the atmosphere."

"And why are there no thunderstorms in the winter, father?"

He explained that, too. He talked, thinking all the while that he was going to see her, and no living soul knew of it, and probably never would know. He had two lives: one, open, seen and known by all who cared to know, full of relative truth and of relative falsehood, exactly like the lives of his friends and acquaintances; and another life running its course in secret. And through some strange, perhaps accidental, conjunction of circumstances, everything that was essential, of interest and of value to him, everything in which he was sincere and did not deceive himself, everything that made the kernel of his life, was hidden from other people; and all that was false in him, the sheath in which he hid himself to conceal the truth—such, for instance, as his work in the bank, his discussions at the club, his "lower race," his presence with his wife at anniversary festivities—all that was open. And he judged of others by himself, not believing in what he saw, and always believing that every man had his real, most interesting life under the cover of secrecy and under the cover of night. All personal life rested on secrecy, and possibly it was partly on that account that civilised man was so nervously anxious that personal privacy should be respected.

After leaving his daughter at school, Gurov went on to the Slaviansky Bazaar. He took off his fur coat below, went upstairs, and softly knocked at the door. Anna Sergeyevna, wearing his favourite grey dress, exhausted by the journey and the suspense, had been expecting him since the evening before. She was pale; she looked at him, and did not smile, and he had hardly come in when she fell on his breast. Their kiss was slow and prolonged, as though they had not met for two years.

"Well, how are you getting on there?" he asked. "What news?"

"Wait; I'll tell you directly . . . I can't talk."

She could not speak; she was crying. She turned away from him, and pressed her handkerchief to her eyes.

"Let her have her cry out. I'll sit down and wait," he thought, and he sat down in an armchair.

Then he rang and asked for tea to be brought him, and while he drank his tea she remained standing at the window with her back to him. She was crying from emotion, from the miserable consciousness that their life was so hard for them; they could only meet in secret, hiding themselves from people, like thieves! Was not their life shattered?

"Come, do stop!" he said.

It was evident to him that this love of theirs would not soon be over, that he could not see the end of it. Anna Sergeyevna grew more and more attached to him. She adored him, and it was unthinkable to say to her that it was bound to have an end some day; besides, she would not have believed it!

He went up to her and took her by the shoulders to say something affectionate and cheering, and at that moment he saw himself in the looking-glass.

His hair was already beginning to turn grey. And it seemed strange to him that he had grown so much older, so much plainer during the last few years. The shoulders on which his hands rested were warm and quivering. He felt compassion for this life, still so warm and lovely, but probably already not far from beginning to fade and wither like his own. Why did she love him so much? He always seemed to women different from what he was, and they loved in him not himself, but the man created by their imagination, whom they had been eagerly seeking all their lives; and afterwards, when they noticed their mistake, they loved him all the same. And not one of them had been happy with him. Time passed, he had made their acquaintance, got on with them, parted, but he had never once loved; it was anything you like, but not love.

And only now when his head was grey he had fallen properly, really in love—for the first time in his life.

Anna Sergeyevna and he loved each other like people very close and akin, like husband and wife, like tender friends; it seemed to them that fate itself had meant them for one another, and they could not understand why he had a wife and she a husband; and it was as though they were a pair of birds of passage, caught and forced to live in different cages. They forgave each other for what they were ashamed of in their past, they forgave everything in the present, and felt that this love of theirs had changed them both.

In moments of depression in the past he had comforted himself with any arguments that came into his mind, but now he no longer cared for arguments; he felt profound compassion, he wanted to be sincere and tender . . .

"Don't cry, my darling," he said. "You've had your cry; that's enough . . . Let us talk now, let us think of some plan."

Then they spent a long while taking counsel together, talked of how to avoid the necessity for secrecy, for deception, for living in different towns and not seeing each other for long at a time. How could they be free from this intolerable bondage?

"How? How?" he asked, clutching his head. "How?"

And it seemed as though in a little while the solution would be found, and then a new and splendid life would begin; and it was clear to both of them that they had still a long, long road before them, and that the most complicated and difficult part of it was only just beginning.

The Bet

[Written in December 1888. First published in No. 4613 issue of *Novoye Vremya*, a Russian newspaper, on January 1, 1889, titled 'Fairy tale.' The story was revised and included in *Chekhov's Collected Works* published by Adolf Marks with the title 'The Bet.']

It was a dark autumn night. The old banker was walking up and down his study and remembering how, fifteen years before, he had given a party one autumn evening. There had been many clever men there, and there had been interesting conversations. Among other things they had talked of capital punishment. The majority of the guests, among whom were many journalists and intellectual men, disapproved of the death penalty. They considered that form of punishment out of date, immoral, and unsuitable for Christian States. In the opinion of some of them the death penalty ought to be replaced everywhere by imprisonment for life.

"I don't agree with you," said their host the banker. "I have not tried either the death penalty or imprisonment for life, but if one may judge *a priori*, the death penalty is more moral and more humane than imprisonment for life. Capital punishment kills a man at once, but lifelong imprisonment kills him slowly. Which executioner is the more humane, he who kills you in a few minutes or he who drags the life out of you in the course of many years?"

"Both are equally immoral," observed one of the guests, "for they both have the same object—to take away life. The State is not God. It has not the right to take away what it cannot restore when it wants to."

Among the guests was a young lawyer, a young man of five-and-twenty. When he was asked his opinion, he said:

"The death sentence and the life sentence are equally immoral, but if I had to choose between the death penalty and imprisonment for life, I would certainly choose the second. To live anyhow is better than not at all."

A lively discussion arose. The banker, who was younger and more nervous in those days, was suddenly carried away by excitement; he struck the table with his fist and shouted at the young man:

"It's not true! I'll bet you two millions you wouldn't stay in solitary confinement for five years."

"If you mean that in earnest," said the young man, "I'll take the bet, but I would stay not five but fifteen years."

"Fifteen? Done!" cried the banker. "Gentlemen, I stake two millions!"

"Agreed! You stake your millions and I stake my freedom!" said the young man.

And this wild, senseless bet was carried out! The banker, spoilt and frivolous, with millions beyond his reckoning, was delighted at the bet. At supper he made fun of the young man, and said:

"Think better of it, young man, while there is still time. To me two millions are a trifle, but you are losing three or four of the best years of your life. I say three or four, because you won't stay longer. Don't forget either, you unhappy man, that voluntary confinement is a great deal harder to bear than compulsory. The thought that you have the right to step out in liberty at any moment will poison your whole existence in prison. I am sorry for you."

And now the banker, walking to and fro, remembered all this, and asked himself: "What was the object of that bet? What is the good of that man's losing fifteen years of his life and my throwing away two millions? Can it prove that the death penalty is better or worse than imprisonment for life? No, no. It was all nonsensical and meaningless. On my part it was the caprice of a pampered man, and on his part simple greed for money . . ."

Then he remembered what followed that evening. It was decided that the young man should spend the years of his captivity under the strictest supervision in one of the lodges in the banker's garden. It was agreed that for fifteen years he should not be free to cross the threshold of the lodge, to see human beings, to hear the human voice, or to receive letters and newspapers. He was allowed to have a musical instrument and books, and was allowed to write letters, to drink wine, and to smoke. By the terms of the agreement, the only relations he could have with the outer world were by a little window made purposely for that object. He might have anything he wanted—books, music, wine, and so on—in any quantity he desired by writing an order, but could only receive them through the window. The agreement provided for every detail and every trifle that would make his imprisonment strictly solitary, and bound the young man to stay there *exactly* fifteen years, beginning from twelve o'clock of November 14, 1870, and ending at twelve o'clock of November 14, 1885. The slightest attempt on his part to break the conditions, if only two minutes before the end, released the banker from the obligation to pay him two millions.

For the first year of his confinement, as far as one could judge from his brief notes, the prisoner suffered severely from loneliness and depression. The sounds of the piano could be heard continually day and night from his lodge. He refused wine and tobacco. Wine, he wrote, excites the desires, and desires are the worst foes of the prisoner; and besides, nothing could be more dreary than drinking good wine and seeing no one. And tobacco spoilt the air of his room. In the first year the books he sent for were principally of a light character; novels with a complicated love plot, sensational and fantastic stories, and so on.

In the second year the piano was silent in the lodge, and the prisoner asked only for the classics. In the fifth year music was audible again, and the prisoner asked for wine. Those who watched him through the window said that all that year he spent doing nothing but eating and drinking and lying on his bed, frequently yawning and angrily talking to himself. He did not read books. Sometimes at night he would sit down to write; he would spend hours writing, and in the morning tear up all that he had written. More than once he could be heard crying.

In the second half of the sixth year the prisoner began zealously studying languages, philosophy, and history. He threw himself eagerly into these studies—so much so that the banker had enough to do to get him the books he ordered. In the course of four years some six hundred volumes were procured at his request. It was during this period that the banker received the following letter from his prisoner:

"My dear Jailer, I write you these lines in six languages. Show them to people who know the languages. Let them read them. If they find not one mistake I implore you to fire a shot in the garden. That shot will show me that my efforts have not been thrown away. The geniuses of all ages and of all lands speak different languages, but the same flame burns in them all. Oh, if you only knew what unearthly happiness my soul feels now from being able to understand them!" The prisoner's desire was fulfilled. The banker ordered two shots to be fired in the garden.

Then after the tenth year, the prisoner sat immovably at the table and read nothing but the Gospel. It seemed strange to the banker that a man who in four years had mastered six hundred learned volumes should waste nearly a year over one thin book easy of comprehension. Theology and histories of religion followed the Gospels.

In the last two years of his confinement the prisoner read an immense quantity of books quite indiscriminately. At one time he was busy with the natural sciences, then he would ask for Byron or Shakespeare. There were notes in which he demanded at the same time books on chemistry, and a manual of medicine, and a novel, and some treatise on philosophy or theology. His reading suggested a man swimming in the sea among the wreckage of his ship, and trying to save his life by greedily clutching first at one spar and then at another.

* * *

The old banker remembered all this, and thought:

"Tomorrow at twelve o'clock he will regain his freedom. By our agreement I ought to pay him two millions. If I do pay him, it is all over with me: I shall be utterly ruined."

Fifteen years before, his millions had been beyond his reckoning; now he was afraid to ask himself which were greater, his debts or his assets. Desperate gambling on the Stock Exchange, wild speculation and the excitability which he could not get over even in advancing years, had by degrees led to the decline of his fortune and the proud, fearless, self-confident millionaire had become a banker of middling rank, trembling at every rise and fall in his investments. "Cursed bet!" muttered the old man, clutching his head in despair. "Why didn't the man die? He is only forty now. He will take my last penny from me, he will marry, will enjoy life, will gamble on the Exchange; while I shall look at him with envy like a beggar, and hear from him every day the same sentence: 'I am indebted to you for the happiness of my life, let me help you!' No, it is too much! The one means of being saved from bankruptcy and disgrace is the death of that man!"

It struck three o'clock, the banker listened; everyone was asleep in the house and nothing could be heard outside but the rustling of the chilled trees. Trying to make no noise, he took from a fireproof safe the key of the door which had not been opened for fifteen years, put on his overcoat, and went out of the house.

It was dark and cold in the garden. Rain was falling. A damp cutting wind was racing about the garden, howling and giving the trees no rest. The banker strained his eyes, but could see neither the earth nor the white statues, nor the lodge, nor the trees. Going to the spot where the lodge stood, he twice called the watchman. No answer followed. Evidently the watchman had sought shelter from the weather, and was now asleep somewhere either in the kitchen or in the greenhouse.

"If I had the pluck to carry out my intention," thought the old man, "suspicion would fall first upon the watchman."

He felt in the darkness for the steps and the door, and went into the entry of the lodge. Then he groped his way into a little passage and lighted a match. There was not a soul there. There was a bedstead with no bedding on it, and in the corner there was a dark cast-iron stove. The seals on the door leading to the prisoner's rooms were intact.

When the match went out the old man, trembling with emotion, peeped through the little window. A candle was burning dimly in the prisoner's room. He was sitting at the table. Nothing could be seen but his back, the hair on his head, and his hands. Open books were lying on the table, on the two easy chairs, and on the carpet near the table.

Five minutes passed and the prisoner did not once stir. Fifteen years' imprisonment had taught him to sit still. The banker tapped at the window with his finger, and the prisoner made no movement whatever in response. Then the banker cautiously broke the seals off the door and put the key in the keyhole. The rusty lock gave a grating sound and the door creaked. The banker expected to hear at once footsteps and a cry of astonishment, but three minutes passed and it was as quiet as ever in the room. He made up his mind to go in.

At the table a man unlike ordinary people was sitting motionless. He was a skeleton with the skin drawn tight over his bones, with long curls like a woman's and a shaggy beard. His face was yellow with an earthy tint in it, his cheeks were hollow, his back long and narrow, and the hand on which his shaggy head was propped was so thin and delicate that it was dreadful to look at it. His hair was already streaked with silver, and seeing his emaciated, aged-looking face, no one would have believed that he was only forty. He was asleep . . . In front of his bowed head there lay on the table a sheet of paper on which there was something written in fine handwriting.

"Poor creature!" thought the banker, "he is asleep and most likely dreaming of the millions. And I have only to take this half-dead man, throw him on the bed, stifle him a little with the pillow, and the most conscientious expert would find no sign of a violent death. But let us first read what he has written here . . ."

The banker took the page from the table and read as follows:

"Tomorrow at twelve o'clock I regain my freedom and the right to associate with other men, but before I leave this room and see the sunshine, I think it necessary to say a few words to you. With a clear conscience I tell you, as before God, who beholds me, that I despise freedom and life and health, and all that in your books is called the good things of the world.

"For fifteen years I have been intently studying earthly life. It is true I have not seen the earth nor men, but in your books I have drunk fragrant wine, I have sung songs, I have hunted stags and wild boars in the forests, have loved women . . . Beauties as ethereal as clouds, created by the magic of your poets and geniuses, have visited me at night, and have whispered in my ears wonderful tales that have set my brain in a whirl. In your books I have climbed to the peaks of Elburz and Mont Blanc, and from there

I have seen the sun rise and have watched it at evening flood the sky, the ocean, and the mountain-tops with gold and crimson. I have watched from there the lightning flashing over my head and cleaving the storm clouds. I have seen green forests, fields, rivers, lakes, towns. I have heard the singing of the sirens, and the strains of the shepherds' pipes; I have touched the wings of comely devils who flew down to converse with me of God . . . In your books I have flung myself into the bottomless pit, performed miracles, slain, burned towns, preached new religions, conquered whole kingdoms . . .

"Your books have given me wisdom. All that the unresting thought of man has created in the ages is compressed into a small compass in my brain. I know that I am wiser than all of you.

"And I despise your books, I despise wisdom and the blessings of this world. It is all worthless, fleeting, illusory, and deceptive, like a mirage. You may be proud, wise, and fine, but death will wipe you off the face of the earth as though you were no more than mice burrowing under the floor, and your posterity, your history, your immortal geniuses will burn or freeze together with the earthly globe.

"You have lost your reason and taken the wrong path. You have taken lies for truth, and hideousness for beauty. You would marvel if, owing to strange events of some sorts, frogs and lizards suddenly grew on apple and orange trees instead of fruit, or if roses began to smell like a sweating horse; so I marvel at you who exchange heaven for earth. I don't want to understand you.

"To prove to you in action how I despise all that you live by, I renounce the two millions of which I once dreamed as of paradise and which now I despise. To deprive myself of the right to the money I shall go out from here five hours before the time fixed, and so break the compact . . ."

When the banker had read this he laid the page on the table, kissed the strange man on the head, and went out of the lodge, weeping. At no other time, even when he had lost heavily on the Stock Exchange, had he felt so great a contempt for himself. When he got home he lay on his bed, but his tears and emotion kept him for hours from sleeping.

Next morning the watchmen ran in with pale faces, and told him they had seen the man who lived in the lodge climb out of the window into the garden, go to the gate, and disappear. The banker went at once with the servants to the lodge and made sure of the flight of his prisoner. To avoid arousing unnecessary talk, he took from the table the writing in which the millions were renounced, and when he got home locked it up in the fireproof safe.

The Darling

[First published in Moscow on January 3, 1899,
in *Semya* (Family) magazine.
Collected in *The Darling and Other Stories* (1916).]

Olenka, the daughter of the retired collegiate assessor, Plemyanniakov, was sitting in her back porch, lost in thought. It was hot, the flies were persistent and teasing, and it was pleasant to reflect that it would soon be evening. Dark rainclouds were gathering from the east, and bringing from time to time a breath of moisture in the air.

Kukin, who was the manager of an open-air theatre called the Tivoli, and who lived in the lodge, was standing in the middle of the garden looking at the sky.

"Again!" he observed despairingly. "It's going to rain again! Rain every day, as though to spite me. I might as well hang myself! It's ruin! Fearful losses every day."

He flung up his hands, and went on, addressing Olenka:

"There! that's the life we lead, Olga Semyonovna. It's enough to make one cry. One works and does one's utmost, one wears oneself out, getting no sleep at night, and racks one's brain what to do for the best. And then what happens? To begin with, one's public is ignorant, boorish. I give them the very best operetta, a dainty masque, first rate music-hall artists. But do you suppose that's what they want! They don't understand anything of that sort. They want a clown; what they ask for is vulgarity. And then look at the weather! Almost every evening it rains. It started on the tenth of May, and it's kept it up all May and June. It's simply awful! The public doesn't come, but I've to pay the rent just the same, and pay the artists."

The next evening the clouds would gather again, and Kukin would say with an hysterical laugh:

"Well, rain away, then! Flood the garden, drown me! Damn my luck in this world and the next! Let the artists have me up! Send me to prison!—to Siberia!—the scaffold! Ha, ha, ha!"

And next day the same thing.

Olenka listened to Kukin with silent gravity, and sometimes tears came into her eyes. In the end his misfortunes touched her; she grew to love him. He was a small thin man, with a yellow face, and curls combed forward on his forehead. He spoke in a thin tenor; as he talked his mouth worked on one side, and there was always an expression of despair on his face; yet he aroused a deep and genuine affection in her. She was always fond of some one, and could not exist without loving. In earlier days she had loved her papa, who now sat in a darkened room, breathing with difficulty; she had loved her aunt who used to come every other year from Bryansk; and before that, when she was at school, she had loved her French master. She was a gentle, soft-hearted, compassionate girl, with mild, tender eyes and very good health. At the sight of her full rosy cheeks, her soft white neck with a little dark mole on it, and the kind, naïve smile, which came into her face when she listened to anything pleasant, men thought, "Yes, not half bad," and smiled too, while lady visitors could not refrain from seizing her hand in the middle of a conversation, exclaiming in a gush of delight, "You darling!"

The house in which she had lived from her birth upwards, and which was left her in her father's will, was at the extreme end of the town, not far from the Tivoli. In the evenings and at night she could head the band playing, and the crackling and banging of fireworks, and it seemed to her that it was Kukin struggling with his destiny, storming the entrenchments of his chief foe, the indifferent public; there was a sweet thrill at her heart, she had no desire to sleep, and when he returned home at day-break, she tapped softly at her bedroom window, and showing him only her face and one shoulder through the curtain, she gave him a friendly smile . . .

He proposed to her, and they were married. And when he had a closer view of her neck and her plump, fine shoulders, he threw up his hands, and said:

"You darling!"

He was happy, but as it rained on the day and night of his wedding, his face still retained an expression of despair.

They got on very well together. She used to sit in his office, to look after things in the Tivoli, to put down the accounts and pay the wages. And her rosy cheeks, her sweet, naïve, radiant smile, were to be seen now at the office window, now in the refreshment bar or behind the scenes of the theatre. And already she used to say to her acquaintances that the theatre was the chief and most important thing in life and that it was only through the drama that one could derive true enjoyment and become cultivated and humane.

"But do you suppose the public understands that?" she used to say. "What they want is a clown. Yesterday we gave 'Faust Inside Out,' and almost all the boxes were empty; but if Vanitchka and I had been producing some vulgar thing, I assure you the theatre would have been packed. Tomorrow Vanitchka and I are doing 'Orpheus in Hell.' Do come."

And what Kukin said about the theatre and the actors she repeated. Like him she despised the public for their ignorance and their indifference to art; she took part in the rehearsals, she corrected the actors, she kept an eye on the behaviour of the musicians, and when there was an unfavourable notice in the local paper, she shed tears, and then went to the editor's office to set things right.

The actors were fond of her and used to call her "Vanitchka and I," and "the darling"; she was sorry for them and used to lend them small sums of money, and if they deceived her, she used to shed a few tears in private, but did not complain to her husband.

They got on well in the winter too. They took the theatre in the town for the whole winter, and let it for short terms to a Little Russian company, or to a conjurer, or to a local dramatic society. Olenka grew stouter, and was always beaming with satisfaction, while Kukin grew thinner and yellower, and continually complained of their terrible losses, although he had not done badly all the winter. He used to cough at night, and she used to give him hot raspberry tea or lime-flower water, to rub him with eau-de-Cologne and to wrap him in her warm shawls.

"You're such a sweet pet!" she used to say with perfect sincerity, stroking his hair. "You're such a pretty dear!"

Towards Lent he went to Moscow to collect a new troupe, and without him she could not sleep, but sat all night at her window, looking at the stars, and she compared herself with the hens, who are awake all night and uneasy when the cock is not in the hen-house. Kukin was detained in Moscow, and wrote that he would be back at Easter, adding some instructions about the Tivoli. But on the Sunday before Easter, late in the evening, came a sudden ominous knock at the gate; some one was hammering on the gate as though on a barrel—boom, boom, boom! The drowsy cook went flopping with her bare feet through the puddles, as she ran to open the gate.

"Please open," said some one outside in a thick bass. "There is a telegram for you."

Olenka had received telegrams from her husband before, but this time for some reason she felt numb with terror. With shaking hands she opened the telegram and read as follows:

"IVAN PETROVITCH DIED SUDDENLY TODAY. AWAITING IMMATE INSTRUCTIONS FUFUNERAL TUESDAY."

That was how it was written in the telegram—"fufuneral," and the utterly incomprehensible word "immate." It was signed by the stage manager of the operatic company.

"My darling!" sobbed Olenka. "Vanka, my precious, my darling! Why did I ever meet you! Why did I know you and love you! Your poor heartbroken Olenka is alone without you!"

Kukin's funeral took place on Tuesday in Moscow, Olenka returned home on Wednesday, and as soon as she got indoors, she threw herself on her bed and sobbed so loudly that it could be heard next door, and in the street.

"Poor darling!" the neighbours said, as they crossed themselves. "Olga Semyonovna, poor darling! How she does take on!"

Three months later Olenka was coming home from mass, melancholy and in deep mourning. It happened that one of her neighbours, Vassily Andreitch Pustovalov, returning home from church, walked back beside her. He was the manager at Babakayev's, the timber merchant's. He wore

The Darling

a straw hat, a white waistcoat, and a gold watch-chain, and looked more a country gentleman than a man in trade.

"Everything happens as it is ordained, Olga Semyonovna," he said gravely, with a sympathetic note in his voice; "and if any of our dear ones die, it must be because it is the will of God, so we ought have fortitude and bear it submissively."

After seeing Olenka to her gate, he said goodbye and went on. All day afterwards she heard his sedately dignified voice, and whenever she shut her eyes she saw his dark beard. She liked him very much. And apparently she had made an impression on him too, for not long afterwards an elderly lady, with whom she was only slightly acquainted, came to drink coffee with her, and as soon as she was seated at table began to talk about Pustovalov, saying that he was an excellent man whom one could thoroughly depend upon, and that any girl would be glad to marry him. Three days later Pustovalov came himself. He did not stay long, only about ten minutes, and he did not say much, but when he left, Olenka loved him—loved him so much that she lay awake all night in a perfect fever, and in the morning she sent for the elderly lady. The match was quickly arranged, and then came the wedding.

Pustovalov and Olenka got on very well together when they were married. Usually he sat in the office till dinner-time, then he went out on business, while Olenka took his place, and sat in the office till evening, making up accounts and booking orders.

"Timber gets dearer every year; the price rises twenty per cent," she would say to her customers and friends. "Only fancy we used to sell local timber, and now Vassitchka always has to go for wood to the Mogilev district. And the freight!" she would add, covering her cheeks with her hands in horror. "The freight!"

It seemed to her that she had been in the timber trade for ages and ages, and that the most important and necessary thing in life was timber; and there was something intimate and touching to her in the very sound of words such as "baulk," "post," "beam," "pole," "scantling," "batten," "lath," "plank," etc.

At night when she was asleep she dreamed of perfect mountains of planks and boards, and long strings of wagons, carting timber somewhere far away. She dreamed that a whole regiment of six-inch beams forty feet high, standing on end, was marching upon the timber-yard; that logs, beams, and boards knocked together with the resounding crash of dry wood, kept falling and getting up again, piling themselves on each other. Olenka cried out in her sleep, and Pustovalov said to her tenderly: "Olenka, what's the matter, darling? Cross yourself!"

Her husband's ideas were hers. If he thought the room was too hot, or that business was slack, she thought the same. Her husband did not care for entertainments, and on holidays he stayed at home. She did likewise.

"You are always at home or in the office," her friends said to her. "You should go to the theatre, darling, or to the circus."

"Vassitchka and I have no time to go to theatres," she would answer sedately. "We have no time for nonsense. What's the use of these theatres?"

On Saturdays Pustovalov and she used to go to the evening service; on holidays to early mass, and they walked side by side with softened faces as they came home from church. There was a pleasant fragrance about them both, and her silk dress rustled agreeably. At home they drank tea, with fancy bread and jams of various kinds, and afterwards they ate pie. Every day at twelve o'clock there was a savoury smell of beet-root soup and of mutton or duck in their yard, and on fast-days of fish, and no one could pass the gate without feeling hungry. In the office the samovar was always boiling, and customers were regaled with tea and cracknels. Once a week the couple went to the baths and returned side by side, both red in the face.

"Yes, we have nothing to complain of, thank God," Olenka used to say to her acquaintances. "I wish every one were as well off as Vassitchka and I."

When Pustovalov went away to buy wood in the Mogilev district, she missed him dreadfully, lay awake and cried. A young veterinary surgeon in the army, called Smirnin, to whom they had let their lodge, used sometimes to come in in the evening. He used to talk to her and play cards with her, and this entertained her in her husband's absence. She was particularly interested in what he told her of his home life. He was married and had a little boy, but was separated from his wife because she had been unfaithful to him, and now he hated her and used to send her forty roubles a month for the maintenance of their son. And hearing of all this, Olenka sighed and shook her head. She was sorry for him.

"Well, God keep you," she used to say to him at parting, as she lighted him down the stairs with a candle. "Thank you for coming to cheer me up, and may the Mother of God give you health."

The Darling

And she always expressed herself with the same sedateness and dignity, the same reasonableness, in imitation of her husband. As the veterinary surgeon was disappearing behind the door below, she would say:

"You know, Vladimir Platonitch, you'd better make it up with your wife. You should forgive her for the sake of your son. You may be sure the little fellow understands."

And when Pustovalov came back, she told him in a low voice about the veterinary surgeon and his unhappy home life, and both sighed and shook their heads and talked about the boy, who, no doubt, missed his father, and by some strange connection of ideas, they went up to the holy ikons, bowed to the ground before them and prayed that God would give them children.

And so the Pustovalovs lived for six years quietly and peaceably in love and complete harmony.

But behold! one winter day after drinking hot tea in the office, Vassily Andreitch went out into the yard without his cap on to see about sending off some timber, caught cold and was taken ill. He had the best doctors, but he grew worse and died after four months' illness. And Olenka was a widow once more.

"I've nobody, now you've left me, my darling," she sobbed, after her husband's funeral. "How can I live without you, in wretchedness and misery! Pity me, good people, all alone in the world!"

She went about dressed in black with long "weepers," and gave up wearing hat and gloves for good. She hardly ever went out, except to church, or to her husband's grave, and led the life of a nun. It was not till six months later that she took off the weepers and opened the shutters of the windows. She was sometimes seen in the mornings, going with her cook to market for provisions, but what went on in her house and how she lived now could only be surmised. People guessed, from seeing her drinking tea in her garden with the veterinary surgeon, who read the newspaper aloud to her, and from the fact that, meeting a lady she knew at the post-office, she said to her:

"There is no proper veterinary inspection in our town, and that's the cause of all sorts of epidemics. One is always hearing of people's getting infection from the milk supply, or catching diseases from horses and cows. The health of domestic animals ought to be as well cared for as the health of human beings."

She repeated the veterinary surgeon's words, and was of the same opinion as he about everything. It was evident that she could not live a year without some attachment, and had found new happiness in the lodge. In any one else this would have been censured, but no one could think ill of Olenka; everything she did was so natural. Neither she nor the veterinary surgeon said anything to other people of the change in their relations, and tried, indeed, to conceal it, but without success, for Olenka could not keep a secret. When he had visitors, men serving in his regiment, and she poured out tea or served the supper, she would begin talking of the cattle plague, of the foot and mouth disease, and of the municipal slaughterhouses. He was dreadfully embarrassed, and when the guests had gone, he would seize her by the hand and hiss angrily:

"I've asked you before not to talk about what you don't understand. When we veterinary surgeons are talking among ourselves, please don't put your word in. It's really annoying."

And she would look at him with astonishment and dismay, and ask him in alarm: "But, Voloditchka, what am I to talk about?"

And with tears in her eyes she would embrace him, begging him not to be angry, and they were both happy.

But this happiness did not last long. The veterinary surgeon departed, departed for ever with his regiment, when it was transferred to a distant place—to Siberia, it may be. And Olenka was left alone.

Now she was absolutely alone. Her father had long been dead, and his armchair lay in the attic, covered with dust and lame of one leg. She got thinner and plainer, and when people met her in the street they did not look at her as they used to, and did not smile to her; evidently her best years were over and left behind, and now a new sort of life had begun for her, which did not bear thinking about. In the evening Olenka sat in the porch, and heard the band playing and the fireworks popping in the Tivoli, but now the sound stirred no response. She looked into her yard without interest, thought of nothing, wished for nothing, and afterwards, when night came on she went to bed and dreamed of her empty yard. She ate and drank as it were unwillingly.

And what was worst of all, she had no opinions of any sort. She saw the objects about her and understood what she saw, but could not form any opinion about them, and did not know what to talk about. And how awful it is not to have any opinions! One sees a bottle, for instance, or the rain, or a peasant driving in his cart, but what the bottle is for, or the rain, or the peasant, and what is the meaning of it, one can't say, and could not even for a thousand roubles. When she had Kukin, or Pustovalov, or the veterinary surgeon, Olenka could explain everything, and give her opinion about anything you like, but now there was the same emptiness in her brain and in her heart as there was in her yard outside. And it was as harsh and as bitter as wormwood in the mouth.

Little by little the town grew in all directions. The road became a street, and where the Tivoli and the timber-yard had been, there were new turnings and houses. How rapidly time passes! Olenka's house grew dingy, the roof got rusty, the shed sank on one side, and the whole yard was overgrown with docks and stinging-nettles. Olenka herself had grown plain and elderly; in summer she sat in the porch, and her soul, as before, was empty and dreary and full of bitterness. In winter she sat at her window and looked at the snow. When she caught the scent of spring, or heard the chime of the church bells, a sudden rush of memories from the past came over her, there was a tender ache in her heart, and her eyes brimmed over with tears; but this was only for a minute, and then came emptiness again and the sense of the futility of life. The black kitten, Briska, rubbed against her and purred softly, but Olenka was not touched by these feline caresses. That was not what she needed. She wanted a love that would absorb her whole being, her whole soul and reason—that would give her ideas and an object in life, and would warm her old blood. And she would shake the kitten off her skirt and say with vexation:

"Get along; I don't want you!"

And so it was, day after day and year after year, and no joy, and no opinions. Whatever Mavra, the cook, said she accepted.

One hot July day, towards evening, just as the cattle were being driven away, and the whole yard was full of dust, some one suddenly knocked at the gate. Olenka went to open it herself and was dumbfounded when she looked out: she saw Smirnin, the veterinary surgeon, grey-headed, and dressed as a civilian. She suddenly remembered everything. She could not help crying and letting her head fall on his breast without uttering a word, and in the violence of her feeling she did not notice how they both walked into the house and sat down to tea.

"My dear Vladimir Platonitch! What fate has brought you?" she muttered, trembling with joy.

"I want to settle here for good, Olga Semyonovna," he told her. "I have resigned my post, and have come to settle down and try my luck on my own account. Besides, it's time for my boy to go to school. He's a big boy. I am reconciled with my wife, you know."

"Where is she?' asked Olenka.

"She's at the hotel with the boy, and I'm looking for lodgings."

"Good gracious, my dear soul! Lodgings? Why not have my house? Why shouldn't that suit you? Why, my goodness, I wouldn't take any rent!" cried Olenka in a flutter, beginning to cry again. "You live here, and the lodge will do nicely for me. Oh dear! how glad I am!"

Next day the roof was painted and the walls were whitewashed, and Olenka, with her arms akimbo walked about the yard giving directions. Her face was beaming with her old smile, and she was brisk and alert as though she had waked from a long sleep. The veterinary's wife arrived—a thin, plain lady, with short hair and a peevish expression. With her was her little Sasha, a boy of ten, small for his age, blue-eyed, chubby, with dimples in his cheeks. And scarcely had the boy walked into the yard when he ran after the cat, and at once there was the sound of his gay, joyous laugh.

"Is that your puss, auntie?" he asked Olenka. "When she has little ones, do give us a kitten. Mamma is awfully afraid of mice."

Olenka talked to him, and gave him tea. Her heart warmed and there was a sweet ache in her bosom, as though the boy had been her own child. And when he sat at the table in the evening, going over his lessons, she looked at him with deep tenderness and pity as she murmured to herself: "You pretty pet! . . . my precious! . . . Such a fair little thing, and so clever."

"'An island is a piece of land which is entirely surrounded by water,'" he read aloud.

"An island is a piece of land," she repeated, and this was the first opinion to which she gave utterance with positive conviction after so many years of silence and dearth of ideas.

Now she had opinions of her own, and at supper she talked to Sasha's parents, saying how difficult the lessons were at the high schools, but that yet the high school was better than a commercial one, since with a high-school education all careers were open to one, such as being a doctor or an engineer.

Sasha began going to the high school. His mother departed to Harkov to her sister's and did not return; his father used to go off every day to inspect cattle, and would often be away from home for three days together, and it seemed to Olenka as though Sasha was entirely abandoned, that he was not wanted at home, that he was being starved, and she carried him off to her lodge and gave him a little room there.

And for six months Sasha had lived in the lodge with her. Every morning Olenka came into his bedroom and found him fast asleep, sleeping noiselessly with his hand under his cheek. She was sorry to wake him.

"Sashenka," she would say mournfully, "get up, darling. It's time for school."

He would get up, dress and say his prayers, and then sit down to breakfast, drink three glasses of tea, and eat two large cracknels and a half a buttered roll. All this time he was hardly awake and a little ill-humoured in consequence.

"You don't quite know your fable, Sashenka," Olenka would say, looking at him as though he were about to set off on a long journey. "What a lot of trouble I have with you! You must work and do your best, darling, and obey your teachers."

"Oh, do leave me alone!" Sasha would say.

Then he would go down the street to school, a little figure, wearing a big cap and carrying a satchel on his shoulder. Olenka would follow him noiselessly.

"Sashenka!" she would call after him, and she would pop into his hand a date or a caramel. When he reached the street where the school was, he would feel ashamed of being followed by a tall, stout woman, he would turn round and say:

"You'd better go home, auntie. I can go the rest of the way alone."

She would stand still and look after him fixedly till he had disappeared at the school-gate.

Ah, how she loved him! Of her former attachments not one had been so deep; never had her soul surrendered to any feeling so spontaneously, so disinterestedly, and so joyously as now that her maternal instincts were aroused. For this little boy with the dimple in his cheek and the big school cap, she would have given her whole life, she would have given it with joy and tears of tenderness. Why? Who can tell why?

When she had seen the last of Sasha, she returned home, contented and serene, brimming over with love; her face, which had grown younger during the last six months, smiled and beamed; people meeting her looked at her with pleasure.

"Good morning, Olga Semyonovna, darling. How are you, darling?"

"The lessons at the high school are very difficult now," she would relate at the market. "It's too much; in the first class yesterday they gave him a fable to learn by heart, and a Latin translation and a problem. You know it's too much for a little chap."

And she would begin talking about the teachers, the lessons, and the school books, saying just what Sasha said.

At three o'clock they had dinner together: in the evening they learned their lessons together and cried. When she put him to bed, she would stay a long time making the Cross over him and murmuring a prayer; then she would go to bed and dream of that faraway misty future when Sasha would finish his studies and become a doctor or an engineer, would have a big house of his own with horses and a carriage, would get married and have children ... She would fall asleep still thinking of the same thing, and tears would run down her cheeks from her closed eyes, while the black cat lay purring beside her: "Mrr, mrr, mrr."

Suddenly there would come a loud knock at the gate.

Olenka would wake up breathless with alarm, her heart throbbing. Half a minute later would come another knock.

"It must be a telegram from Harkov," she would think, beginning to tremble from head to foot. "Sasha's mother is sending for him from Harkov ... Oh, mercy on us!"

She was in despair. Her head, her hands, and her feet would turn chill, and she would feel that she was the most unhappy woman in the world. But another minute would pass, voices would be heard: it would turn out to be the veterinary surgeon coming home from the club.

"Well, thank God!" she would think.

And gradually the load in her heart would pass off, and she would feel at ease. She would go back to bed thinking of Sasha, who lay sound asleep in the next room, sometimes crying out in his sleep:

"I'll give it you! Get away! Shut up!"

The Death of a Government Clerk

[First published with the subtitle 'The Incident' in
Oskolki (*Fragments*), a Russian literary weekly, on July 2, 1883.
Published in *Motley Stories* (1886) without the subtitle.
Collected in *Love and Other Stories* (1922).]

One fine evening, a no less fine government clerk called Ivan Dmitritch Tchervyakov was sitting in the second row of the stalls, gazing through an opera glass at the *Cloches de Corneville*. He gazed and felt at the acme of bliss. But suddenly . . . In stories one so often meets with this "But suddenly." The authors are right: life is so full of surprises! But suddenly his face puckered up, his eyes disappeared, his breathing was arrested . . . he took the opera glass from his eyes, bent over and . . . "Aptchee!!" he sneezed as you perceive. It is not reprehensible for anyone to sneeze anywhere. Peasants sneeze and so do police superintendents, and sometimes even privy councillors. All men sneeze. Tchervyakov was not in the least confused, he wiped his face with his handkerchief, and like a polite man, looked round to see whether he had disturbed any one by his sneezing. But then he was overcome with confusion. He saw that an old gentleman sitting in front of him in the first row of the stalls was carefully wiping his bald head and his neck with his glove and muttering something to himself. In the old gentleman, Tchervyakov recognised Brizzhalov, a civilian general serving in the Department of Transport.

"I have spattered him," thought Tchervyakov, "he is not the head of my department, but still it is awkward. I must apologise."

Tchervyakov gave a cough, bent his whole person forward, and whispered in the general's ear.

"Pardon, your Excellency, I spattered you accidentally..."

"Never mind, never mind."

"For goodness sake excuse me, I... I did not mean to."

"Oh, please, sit down! let me listen!"

Tchervyakov was embarrassed, he smiled stupidly and fell to gazing at the stage. He gazed at it but was no longer feeling bliss. He began to be troubled by uneasiness. In the interval, he went up to Brizzhalov, walked beside him, and overcoming his shyness, muttered:

"I spattered you, your Excellency, forgive me... you see... I didn't do it to..."

"Oh, that's enough... I'd forgotten it, and you keep on about it!" said the general, moving his lower lip impatiently.

"He has forgotten, but there is a fiendish light in his eye," thought Tchervyakov, looking suspiciously at the general. "And he doesn't want to talk. I ought to explain to him... that I really didn't intend... that it is the law of nature or else he will think I meant to spit on him. He doesn't think so now, but he will think so later!"

On getting home, Tchervyakov told his wife of his breach of good manners. It struck him that his wife took too frivolous a view of the incident; she was a little frightened, but when she learned that Brizzhalov was in a different department, she was reassured.

"Still, you had better go and apologise," she said, "or he will think you don't know how to behave in public."

"That's just it! I did apologise, but he took it somehow queerly... he didn't say a word of sense. There wasn't time to talk properly."

Next day Tchervyakov put on a new uniform, had his hair cut and went to Brizzhalov's to explain; going into the general's reception room he saw there a number of petitioners and among them the general himself, who was beginning to interview them. After questioning several petitioners the general raised his eyes and looked at Tchervyakov.

"Yesterday at the *Arcadia*, if you recollect, your Excellency," the latter began, "I sneezed and ... accidentally spattered ... Exc ..."

"What nonsense ... It's beyond anything! What can I do for you," said the general addressing the next petitioner.

"He won't speak," thought Tchervyakov, turning pale; "that means that he is angry ... No, it can't be left like this ... I will explain to him."

When the general had finished his conversation with the last of the petitioners and was turning towards his inner apartments, Tchervyakov took a step towards him and muttered:

"Your Excellency! If I venture to trouble your Excellency, it is simply from a feeling I may say of regret! ... It was not intentional if you will graciously believe me."

The general made a lachrymose face, and waved his hand.

"Why, you are simply making fun of me, sir," he said as he closed the door behind him.

"Where's the making fun in it?" thought Tchervyakov, "there is nothing of the sort! He is a general, but he can't understand. If that is how it is I am not going to apologise to that *fanfaron* any more! The devil take him. I'll write a letter to him, but I won't go. By Jove, I won't."

So thought Tchervyakov as he walked home; he did not write a letter to the general, he pondered and pondered and could not make up that letter. He had to go next day to explain in person.

"I ventured to disturb your Excellency yesterday," he muttered, when the general lifted enquiring eyes upon him, "not to make fun as you were pleased to say. I was apologising for having spattered you in sneezing ... And I did not dream of making fun of you. Should I dare to make fun of you, if we should take to making fun, then there would be no respect for persons, there would be ..."

"Be off!" yelled the general, turning suddenly purple, and shaking all over.

"What?" asked Tchervyakov, in a whisper turning numb with horror.

"Be off!" repeated the general, stamping.

Something seemed to give way in Tchervyakov's stomach. Seeing nothing and hearing nothing he reeled to the door, went out into the street, and went staggering along . . . Reaching home mechanically, without taking off his uniform, he lay down on the sofa and died.

PLAYS

PLAYS

IVANOV

IVANOV

Characters

NICHOLAS IVANOFF, perpetual member of the Council of Peasant Affairs
ANNA, his wife. Nee Sarah Abramson
MATTHEW SHABELSKI, a count, uncle of Ivanoff
PAUL LEBEDIEFF, President of the Board of the Zemstvo
ZINAIDA, his wife
SASHA, their daughter, twenty years old
LVOFF, a young government doctor
MARTHA BABAKINA, a young widow, owner of an estate and daughter of a rich merchant
KOSICH, an exciseman
MICHAEL BORKIN, a distant relative of Ivanoff, and manager of his estate
AVDOTIA NAZAROVNA, an old woman
GEORGE, lives with the Lebedieffs
FIRST GUEST   SECOND GUEST   THIRD GUEST   FOURTH GUEST
PETER, a servant of Ivanoff
GABRIEL, a servant of Lebedieff
GUESTS OF BOTH SEXES
The play takes place in one of the provinces of central Russia

ACT I

The garden of IVANOFF'S country place. On the left is a terrace and the facade of the house. One window is open. Below the terrace is a broad semicircular lawn, from which paths lead to right and left into a garden. On the right are several garden benches and tables. A lamp is burning on one of the tables. It is evening. As the curtain rises sounds of the piano and violoncello are heard.

    IVANOFF is sitting at a table reading.
    BORKIN, in top-boots and carrying a gun, comes in from the rear of the garden. He is a little tipsy. As he sees IVANOFF he comes toward him on tiptoe, and when he comes opposite him he stops and points the gun at his face.

IVANOFF.

    [Catches sight of BORKIN. Shudders and jumps to his feet] Misha! What are you doing? You frightened me! I can't stand your stupid jokes when I am so nervous as this. And having frightened me, you laugh! [He sits down.]

BORKIN.
: [Laughing loudly] There, I am sorry, really. I won't do it again. Indeed I won't. [Take off his cap] How hot it is! Just think, my dear boy, I have covered twelve miles in the last three hours. I am worn out. Just feel how my heart is beating.

IVANOFF.
: [Goes on reading] Oh, very well. I shall feel it later!

BORKIN.
: No, feel it now. [He takes IVANOFF'S hand and presses it against his breast] Can you feel it thumping? That means that it is weak and that I may die suddenly at any moment. Would you be sorry if I died?

IVANOFF.
: I am reading now. I shall attend to you later.

BORKIN.
: No, seriously, would you be sorry if I died? Nicholas, would you be sorry if I died?

IVANOFF.
: Leave me alone!

BORKIN.
: Come, tell me if you would be sorry or not.

IVANOFF.
: I am sorry that you smell so of vodka, Misha, it is disgusting.

BORKIN.
: Do I smell of vodka? How strange! And yet, it is not so strange after all. I met the magistrate on the road, and I must admit that we did drink about eight glasses together. Strictly speaking, of course, drinking is very harmful. Listen, it is harmful, isn't it? Is it? Is it?

IVANOFF.
: This is unendurable! Let me warn you, Misha, that you are going too far.

BORKIN.
: Well, well, excuse me. Sit here by yourself then, for heaven's sake, if it amuses you. [Gets up and goes away] What extraordinary people one meets in the world. They won't even allow themselves to be spoken to. [He comes back] Oh, yes, I nearly forgot. Please let me have eighty-two roubles.

IVANOFF.
    Why do you want eighty-two roubles?
BORKIN.
    To pay the workmen to-morrow.
IVANOFF.
    I haven't the money.
BORKIN.
    Many thanks. [Angrily] So you haven't the money! And yet the workmen must be paid, mustn't they?
IVANOFF.
    I don't know. Wait till my salary comes in on the first of the month.
BORKIN.
    How is it possible to discuss anything with a man like you? Can't you understand that the workmen are coming to-morrow morning and not on the first of the month?
IVANOFF.
    How can I help it? I'll be hanged if I can do anything about it now. And what do you mean by this irritating way you have of pestering me whenever I am trying to read or write or——
BORKIN.
    Must the workmen be paid or not, I ask you? But, good gracious! What is the use of talking to you! [Waves his hand] Do you think because you own an estate you can command the whole world? With your two thousand acres and your empty pockets you are like a man who has a cellar full of wine and no corkscrew. I have sold the oats as they stand in the field. Yes, sir! And to-morrow I shall sell the rye and the carriage horses. [He stamps up and down] Do you think I am going to stand upon ceremony with you? Certainly not! I am not that kind of a man!

    ANNA appears at the open window.

ANNA.
    Whose voice did I hear just now? Was it yours, Misha? Why are you stamping up and down?
BORKIN.
    Anybody who had anything to do with your Nicholas would stamp up and down.

ANNA.
>   Listen, Misha! Please have some hay carried onto the croquet lawn.

BORKIN.
>   [Waves his hand] Leave me alone, please!

ANNA.
>   Oh, what manners! They are not becoming to you at all. If you want to be liked by women you must never let them see you when you are angry or obstinate. [To her husband] Nicholas, let us go and play on the lawn in the hay!

IVANOFF.
>   Don't you know it is bad for you to stand at the open window, Annie? [Calls] Shut the window, Uncle!
>   [The window is shut from the inside.]

BORKIN.
>   Don't forget that the interest on the money you owe Lebedieff must be paid in two days.

IVANOFF.
>   I haven't forgotten it. I am going over to see Lebedieff today and shall ask him to wait.
>   [He looks at his watch.]

BORKIN.
>   When are you going?

IVANOFF.
>   At once.

BORKIN.
>   Wait! Wait! Isn't this Sasha's birthday? So it is! The idea of my forgetting it. What a memory I have. [Jumps about] I shall go with you! [Sings] I shall go, I shall go! Nicholas, old man, you are the joy of my life. If you were not always so nervous and cross and gloomy, you and I could do great things together. I would do anything for you. Shall I marry Martha Babakina and give you half her fortune? That is, not half, either, but all—take it all!

IVANOFF.
>   Enough of this nonsense!

BORKIN.
>   No, seriously, shan't I marry Martha and halve the money with you?

But no, why should I propose it? How can you understand? [Angrily] You say to me: "Stop talking nonsense!" You are a good man and a clever one, but you haven't any red blood in your veins or any—well, enthusiasm. Why, if you wanted to, you and I could cut a dash together that would shame the devil himself. If you were a normal man instead of a morbid hypochondriac we would have a million in a year. For instance, if I had twenty-three hundred roubles now I could make twenty thousand in two weeks. You don't believe me? You think it is all nonsense? No, it isn't nonsense. Give me twenty-three hundred roubles and let me try. Ofsianoff is selling a strip of land across the river for that price. If we buy this, both banks will be ours, and we shall have the right to build a dam across the river. Isn't that so? We can say that we intend to build a mill, and when the people on the river below us hear that we mean to dam the river they will, of course, object violently and we shall say: If you don't want a dam here you will have to pay to get us away. Do you see the result? The factory would give us five thousand roubles, Korolkoff three thousand, the monastery five thousand more—

IVANOFF.
All that is simply idiotic, Misha. If you don't want me to lose my temper you must keep your schemes to yourself.

BORKIN.
[Sits down at the table] Of course! I knew how it would be! You never will act for yourself, and you tie my hands so that I am helpless.
Enter SHABELSKI and LVOFF.

SHABELSKI.
The only difference between lawyers and doctors is that lawyers simply rob you, whereas doctors both rob you and kill you. I am not referring to any one present. [Sits down on the bench] They are all frauds and swindlers. Perhaps in Arcadia you might find an exception to the general rule and yet—I have treated thousands of sick people myself in my life, and I have never met a doctor who did not seem to me to be an unmistakable scoundrel.

BORKIN.
[To IVANOFF] Yes, you tie my hands and never do anything for yourself, and that is why you have no money.

SHABELSKI.

As I said before, I am not referring to any one here at present; there may be exceptions though, after all—[He yawns.]

IVANOFF.

[Shuts his book] What have you to tell me, doctor?

LVOFF.

[Looks toward the window] Exactly what I said this morning: she must go to the Crimea at once. [Walks up and down.]

SHABELSKI.

[Bursts out laughing] To the Crimea! Why don't you and I set up as doctors, Misha? Then, if some Madame Angot or Ophelia finds the world tiresome and begins to cough and be consumptive, all we shall have to do will be to write out a prescription according to the laws of medicine: that is, first, we shall order her a young doctor, and then a journey to the Crimea. There some fascinating young Tartar——

IVANOFF.

[Interrupting] Oh, don't be coarse! [To LVOFF] It takes money to go to the Crimea, and even if I could afford it, you know she has refused to go.

LVOFF.

Yes, she has. [A pause.]

BORKIN.

Look here, doctor, is Anna really so ill that she absolutely must go to the Crimea?

LVOFF.

[Looking toward the window] Yes, she has consumption.

BORKIN.

Whew! How sad! I have seen in her face for some time that she could not last much longer.

LVOFF.

Can't you speak quietly? She can hear everything you say. [A pause.]

BORKIN.

[Sighing] The life of man is like a flower, blooming so gaily in a field. Then, along comes a goat, he eats it, and the flower is gone!

SHABELSKI.

Oh, nonsense, nonsense. [Yawning] Everything is a fraud and a swindle. [A pause.]

BORKIN.

Gentlemen, I have been trying to tell Nicholas how he can make some money, and have submitted a brilliant plan to him, but my seed, as usual, has fallen on barren soil. Look what a sight he is now: dull, cross, bored, peevish——

SHABELSKI.

[Gets up and stretches himself] You are always inventing schemes for everybody, you clever fellow, and telling them how to live; can't you tell me something? Give me some good advice, you ingenious young man. Show me a good move to make.

BORKIN.

[Getting up] I am going to have a swim. Goodbye, gentlemen. [To Shabelski] There are at least twenty good moves you could make. If I were you I should have twenty thousand roubles in a week.

[He goes out; SHABELSKI follows him.]

SHABELSKI.

How would you do it? Come, explain.

BORKIN.

There is nothing to explain, it is so simple. [Coming back] Nicholas, give me a rouble.

IVANOFF silently hands him the money

BORKIN.

Thanks. Shabelski, you still hold some trump cards.

SHABELSKI follows him out.

SHABELSKI.

Well, what are they?

BORKIN.

If I were you I should have thirty thousand roubles and more in a week. [They go out together.]

IVANOFF.

[After a pause] Useless people, useless talk, and the necessity of answering stupid questions, have wearied me so, doctor, that I am ill. I have become so irritable and bitter that I don't know myself. My head aches for days at a time. I hear a ringing in my ears, I can't sleep, and yet there is no escape from it all, absolutely none.

LVOFF.
Ivanoff, I have something serious to speak to you about.
IVANOFF.
What is it?
LVOFF.
It is about your wife. She refuses to go to the Crimea alone, but she would go with you.
IVANOFF.
[Thoughtfully] It would cost a great deal for us both to go, and besides, I could not get leave to be away for so long. I have had one holiday already this year.
LVOFF.
Very well, let us admit that. Now to proceed. The best cure for consumption is absolute peace of mind, and your wife has none whatever. She is forever excited by your behaviour to her. Forgive me, I am excited and am going to speak frankly. Your treatment of her is killing her. [A pause] Ivanoff, let me believe better things of you.
IVANOFF.
What you say is true, true. I must be terribly guilty, but my mind is confused. My will seems to be paralysed by a kind of stupor; I can't understand myself or any one else. [Looks toward the window] Come, let us take a walk, we might be overheard here. [They get up] My dear friend, you should hear the whole story from the beginning if it were not so long and complicated that to tell it would take all night. [They walk up and down] Anna is a splendid, an exceptional woman. She has left her faith, her parents and her fortune for my sake. If I should demand a hundred other sacrifices, she would consent to every one without the quiver of an eyelid. Well, I am not a remarkable man in any way, and have sacrificed nothing. However, the story is a long one. In short, the whole point is, my dear doctor—[Confused] that I married her for love and promised to love her forever, and now after five years she loves me still and I—[He waves his hand] Now, when you tell me she is dying, I feel neither love nor pity, only a sort of loneliness and weariness. To all appearances this must seem horrible, and I cannot understand myself what is happening to me. [They go out.]
SHABELSKI comes in.

SHABELSKI.

[Laughing] Upon my word, that man is no scoundrel, but a great thinker, a master-mind. He deserves a memorial. He is the essence of modern ingenuity, and combines in himself alone the genius of the lawyer, the doctor, and the financier. [He sits down on the lowest step of the terrace] And yet he has never finished a course of studies in any college; that is so surprising. What an ideal scoundrel he would have made if he had acquired a little culture and mastered the sciences! "You could make twenty thousand roubles in a week," he said. "You still hold the ace of trumps: it is your title." [Laughing] He said I might get a rich girl to marry me for it! [ANNA opens the window and looks down] "Let me make a match between you and Martha," says he. Who is this Martha? It must be that Balabalkina—Babakalkina woman, the one that looks like a laundress.

ANNA.

Is that you, Count?

SHABELSKI.

What do you want?

ANNA laughs.

SHABELSKI.

[With a Jewish accent] Vy do you laugh?

ANNA.

I was thinking of something you said at dinner, do you remember? How was it—a forgiven thief, a doctored horse.

SHABELSKI.

A forgiven thief, a doctored horse, and a Christianised Jew are all worth the same price.

ANNA.

[Laughing] You can't even repeat the simplest saying without ill-nature. You are a most malicious old man. [Seriously] Seriously, Count you are extremely disagreeable, and very tiresome and painful to live with. You are always grumbling and growling, and everybody to you is a blackguard and a scoundrel. Tell me honestly, Count, have you ever spoken well of any one?

SHABELSKI.

Is this an inquisition?

ANNA.
> We have lived under this same roof now for five years, and I have never heard you speak kindly of people, or without bitterness and derision. What harm has the world done to you? Is it possible that you consider yourself better than any one else?

SHABELSKI.
> Not at all. I think we are all of us scoundrels and hypocrites. I myself am a degraded old man, and as useless as a cast-off shoe. I abuse myself as much as any one else. I was rich once, and free, and happy at times, but now I am a dependent, an object of charity, a joke to the world. When I am at last exasperated and defy them, they answer me with a laugh. When I laugh, they shake their heads sadly and say, "The old man has gone mad." But oftenest of all I am unheard and unnoticed by every one.

ANNA.
> [Quietly] Screaming again.

SHABELSKI.
> Who is screaming?

ANNA.
> The owl. It screams every evening.

SHABELSKI.
> Let it scream. Things are as bad as they can be already. [Stretches himself] Alas, my dear Sarah! If I could only win a thousand or two roubles, I should soon show you what I could do. I wish you could see me! I should get away out of this hole, and leave the bread of charity, and should not show my nose here again until the last judgment day.

ANNA.
> What would you do if you were to win so much money?

SHABELSKI.
> [Thoughtfully] First I would go to Moscow to hear the Gipsies play, and then—then I should fly to Paris and take an apartment and go to the Russian Church.

ANNA.
> And what else?

SHABELSKI.
> I would go and sit on my wife's grave for days and days and think. I would sit there until I died. My wife is buried in Paris. [A pause.]

ANNA.
How terribly dull this is! Shall we play a duet?
SHABELSKI.
As you like. Go and get the music ready. [ANNA goes out.]
IVANOFF and LVOFF appear in one of the paths.
IVANOFF.
My dear friend, you left college last year, and you are still young and brave. Being thirty-five years old I have the right to advise you. Don't marry a Jewess or a bluestocking or a woman who is queer in any way. Choose some nice, common-place girl without any strange and startling points in her character. Plan your life for quiet; the greyer and more monotonous you can make the background, the better. My dear boy, do not try to fight alone against thousands; do not tilt with windmills; do not dash yourself against the rocks. And, above all, may you be spared the so-called rational life, all wild theories and impassioned talk. Everything is in the hands of God, so shut yourself up in your shell and do your best. That is the pleasant, honest, healthy way to live. But the life I have chosen has been so tiring, oh, so tiring! So full of mistakes, of injustice and stupidity! [Catches sight of SHABELSKI, and speaks angrily] There you are again, Uncle, always under foot, never letting one have a moment's quiet talk!
SHABELSKI.
[In a tearful voice] Is there no refuge anywhere for a poor old devil like me? [He jumps up and runs into the house.]
IVANOFF.
Now I have offended him! Yes, my nerves have certainly gone to pieces. I must do something about it, I must——
LVOFF.
[Excitedly] Ivanoff, I have heard all you have to say and——and——I am going to speak frankly. You have shown me in your voice and manner, as well as in your words, the most heartless egotism and pitiless cruelty. Your nearest friend is dying simply because she is near you, her days are numbered, and you can feel such indifference that you go about giving advice and analysing your feelings. I cannot say all I should like to; I have not the gift of words, but——but I can at least say that you are deeply antipathetic to me.

IVANOFF.
> I suppose I am. As an onlooker, of course you see me more clearly than I see myself, and your judgment of me is probably right. No doubt I am terribly guilty. [Listens] I think I hear the carriage coming. I must get ready to go. [He goes toward the house and then stops] You dislike me, doctor, and you don't conceal it. Your sincerity does you credit. [He goes into the house.]

LVOFF.
> [Alone] What a confoundedly disagreeable character! I have let another opportunity slip without speaking to him as I meant to, but I simply cannot talk calmly to that man. The moment I open my mouth to speak I feel such a commotion and suffocation here [He puts his hand on his breast] that my tongue sticks to the roof of my mouth. Oh, I loathe that Tartuffe, that unmitigated rascal, with all my heart! There he is, preparing to go driving in spite of the entreaties of his unfortunate wife, who adores him and whose only happiness is his presence. She implores him to spend at least one evening with her, and he cannot even do that. Why, he might shoot himself in despair if he had to stay at home! Poor fellow, what he wants are new fields for his villainous schemes. Oh, I know why you go to Lebedieff's every evening, Ivanoff! I know.
>
> Enter IVANOFF, in hat and coat, ANNA and SHABELSKI

SHABELSKI.
> Look here, Nicholas, this is simply barbarous You go away every evening and leave us here alone, and we get so bored that we have to go to bed at eight o'clock. It is a scandal, and no decent way of living. Why can you go driving if we can't? Why?

ANNA.
> Leave him alone, Count. Let him go if he wants to.

IVANOFF.
> How can a sick woman like you go anywhere? You know you have a cough and must not go out after sunset. Ask the doctor here. You are no child, Annie, you must be reasonable. And as for you, what would you do with yourself over there?

SHABELSKI.
> I am ready to go anywhere: into the jaws of a crocodile, or even into the jaws of hell, so long as I don't have to stay here. I am horribly

bored. I am stupefied by this dullness. Every one here is tired of me. You leave me at home to entertain Anna, but I feel more like scratching and biting her.

ANNA.

Leave him alone, Count. Leave him alone. Let him go if he enjoys himself there.

IVANOFF.

What does this mean, Annie? You know I am not going for pleasure. I must see Lebedieff about the money I owe him.

ANNA.

I don't see why you need justify yourself to me. Go ahead! Who is keeping you?

IVANOFF.

Heavens! Don't let us bite one another's heads off. Is that really unavoidable?

SHABELSKI.

[Tearfully] Nicholas, my dear boy, do please take me with you. I might possibly be amused a little by the sight of all the fools and scoundrels I should see there. You know I haven't been off this place since Easter.

IVANOFF.

[Exasperated] Oh, very well! Come along then! How tiresome you all are!

SHABELSKI.

I may go? Oh, thank you! [Takes him gaily by the arm and leads him aside] May I wear your straw hat?

IVANOFF.

You may, only hurry, please.

SHABELSKI runs into the house.

IVANOFF.

How tired I am of you all! But no, what am I saying? Annie, my manner to you is insufferable, and it never used to be. Well, good-bye, Annie. I shall be back by one.

ANNA.

Nicholas! My dear husband, stay at home to-night!

IVANOFF.

[Excitedly] Darling, sweetheart, my dear, unhappy one, I implore you to let me leave home in the evenings. I know it is cruel and unjust to ask this, but let me do you this injustice. It is such torture for me to stay. As soon as the sun goes down my soul is overwhelmed by the most horrible despair. Don't ask me why; I don't know; I swear I don't. This dreadful melancholy torments me here, it drives me to the Lebedieff's and there it grows worse than ever. I rush home; it still pursues me; and so I am tortured all through the night. It is breaking my heart.

ANNA.

Nicholas, won't you stay? We will talk together as we used to. We will have supper together and read afterward. The old grumbler and I have learned so many duets to play to you. [She kisses him. Then, after a pause] I can't understand you any more. This has been going on for a year now. What has changed you so?

IVANOFF.

I don't know.

ANNA.

And why don't you want me to go driving with you in the evening?

IVANOFF.

As you insist on knowing, I shall have to tell you. It is a little cruel, but you had best understand. When this melancholy fit is on me I begin to dislike you, Annie, and at such times I must escape from you. In short, I simply have to leave this house.

ANNA.

Oh, you are sad, are you? I can understand that! Nicholas, let me tell you something: won't you try to sing and laugh and scold as you used to? Stay here, and we will drink some liqueur together, and laugh, and chase away this sadness of yours in no time. Shall I sing to you? Or shall we sit in your study in the twilight as we used to, while you tell me about your sadness? I can read such suffering in your eyes! Let me look into them and weep, and our hearts will both be lighter. [She laughs and cries at once] Or is it really true that the flowers return with every spring, but lost happiness never returns? Oh, is it? Well, go then, go!

IVANOFF.

Pray for me, Annie! [He goes; then stops and thinks for a moment] No, I can't do it. [IVANOFF goes out.]

ANNA.

Yes, go, go—[Sits down at the table.]

LVOFF.
[Walking up and down] Make this a rule, Madam: as soon as the sun goes down you must go indoors and not come out again until morning. The damp evening air is bad for you.

ANNA.
Yes, sir!

LVOFF.
What do you mean by "Yes, sir"? I am speaking seriously.

ANNA.
But I don't want to be serious. [She coughs.]

LVOFF.
There now, you see, you are coughing already.

SHABELSKI comes out of the house in his hat and coat.

SHABELSKI.
Where is Nicholas? Is the carriage here yet? [Goes quickly to ANNA and kisses her hand] Good-night, my darling! [Makes a face and speaks with a Jewish accent] I beg your bardon! [He goes quickly out.]

LVOFF.
Idiot!

A pause; the sounds of a concertina are heard in the distance.

ANNA.
Oh, how lonely it is! The coachman and the cook are having a little ball in there by themselves, and I—I am, as it were, abandoned. Why are you walking about, Doctor? Come and sit down here.

LVOFF.
I can't sit down.

[A pause.]

ANNA.
They are playing "The Sparrow" in the kitchen. [She sings]

> "*Sparrow, Sparrow, where are you?*
> *On the mountain drinking dew.*"

[A pause] Are your father and mother living, Doctor?

LVOFF.
My mother is living; my father is dead.

ANNA.
    Do you miss your mother very much?
LVOFF.
    I am too busy to miss any one.
ANNA.
    [Laughing] The flowers return with every spring, but lost happiness never returns. I wonder who taught me that? I think it was Nicholas himself. [Listens] The owl is hooting again.
LVOFF.
    Well, let it hoot.
ANNA.
    I have begun to think, Doctor, that fate has cheated me. Other people who, perhaps, are no better than I am are happy and have not had to pay for their happiness. But I have paid for it all, every moment of it, and such a price! Why should I have to pay so terribly? Dear friend, you are all too considerate and gentle with me to tell me the truth; but do you think I don't know what is the matter with me? I know perfectly well. However, this isn't a pleasant subject—[With a Jewish accent] "I beg your bardon!" Can you tell funny stories?
LVOFF.
    No, I can't.
ANNA.
    Nicholas can. I am beginning to be surprised, too, at the injustice of people. Why do they return hatred for love, and answer truth with lies? Can you tell me how much longer I shall be hated by my mother and father? They live fifty miles away, and yet I can feel their hatred day and night, even in my sleep. And how do you account for the sadness of Nicholas? He says that he only dislikes me in the evening, when the fit is on him. I understand that, and can tolerate it, but what if he should come to dislike me altogether? Of course that is impossible, and yet—no, no, I mustn't even imagine such a thing. [Sings]

        "Sparrow, Sparrow, where are you?"

[She shudders] What fearful thoughts I have! You are not married, Doctor; there are many things that you cannot understand.

LVOFF.
>You say you are surprised, but—but it is you who surprise me. Tell me, explain to me how you, an honest and intelligent woman, almost a saint, could allow yourself to be so basely deceived and dragged into this den of bears? Why are you here? What have you in common with such a cold and heartless—but enough of your husband! What have you in common with these wicked and vulgar surroundings? With that eternal grumbler, the crazy and decrepit Count? With that swindler, that prince of rascals, Misha, with his fool's face? Tell me, I say, how did you get here?

ANNA.
>[laughing] That is what he used to say, long ago, oh, exactly! Only his eyes are larger than yours, and when he was excited they used to shine like coals—go on, go on!

LVOFF.
>[Gets up and waves his hand] There is nothing more to say. Go into the house.

ANNA.
>You say that Nicholas is not what he should be, that his faults are so and so. How can you possibly understand him? How can you learn to know any one in six months? He is a wonderful man, Doctor, and I am sorry you could not have known him as he was two or three years ago. He is depressed and silent now, and broods all day without doing anything, but he was splendid then. I fell in love with him at first sight. [Laughing] I gave one look and was caught like a mouse in a trap! So when he asked me to go with him I cut every tie that bound me to my old life as one snips the withered leaves from a plant. But things are different now. Now he goes to the Lebedieff's to amuse himself with other women, and I sit here in the garden and listen to the owls. [The WATCHMAN'S rattle is heard] Tell me, Doctor, have you any brothers and sisters?

LVOFF.
>No.

>ANNA sobs.

LVOFF.
>What is it? What is the matter?

ANNA.
>   I can't stand it, Doctor, I must go.

LVOFF.
>   Where?

ANNA.
>   To him. I am going. Have the horses harnessed. [She runs into the house.]

LVOFF.
>   No, I certainly cannot go on treating any one under these conditions. I not only have to do it for nothing, but I am forced to endure this agony of mind besides. No, no, I can't stand it. I have had enough of it. [He goes into the house.]

>   *The curtain falls.*

ACT II

The drawing-room of LEBEDIEFF'S house. In the centre is a door leading into a garden. Doors open out of the room to the right and left. The room is furnished with valuable old furniture, which is carefully protected by linen covers. The walls are hung with pictures. The room is lighted by candelabra. ZINAIDA is sitting on a sofa; the elderly guests are sitting in arm-chairs on either hand. The young guests are sitting about the room on small chairs. KOSICH, AVDOTIA NAZAROVNA, GEORGE, and others are playing cards in the background. GABRIEL is standing near the door on the right. The maid is passing sweetmeats about on a tray. During the entire act guests come and go from the garden, through the room, out of the door on the left, and back again. Enter MARTHA through the door on the right. She goes toward ZINAIDA.

ZINAIDA.
  [Gaily] My dearest Martha!

MARTHA.

How do you do, Zinaida? Let me congratulate you on your daughter's birthday.

ZINAIDA.

Thank you, my dear; I am delighted to see you. How are you?

MARTHA.

Very well indeed, thank you. [She sits down on the sofa] Good evening, young people!

The younger guests get up and bow.

FIRST GUEST.

[Laughing] Young people indeed! Do you call yourself an old person?

MARTHA.

[Sighing] How can I make any pretense to youth now?

FIRST GUEST.

What nonsense! The fact that you are a widow means nothing. You could beat any pretty girl you chose at a canter.

GABRIEL brings MARTHA some tea.

ZINAIDA.

Why do you bring the tea in like that? Go and fetch some jam to eat with it!

MARTHA.

No thank you; none for me, don't trouble yourself. [A pause.]

FIRST GUEST.

[To MARTHA] Did you come through Mushkine on your way here?

MARTHA.

No, I came by way of Spassk. The road is better that way.

FIRST GUEST.

Yes, so it is.

KOSICH.

Two in spades.

GEORGE.

Pass.

AVDOTIA.

Pass.

SECOND GUEST.

Pass.

MARTHA.
The price of lottery tickets has gone up again, my dear. I have never known such a state of affairs. The first issue is already worth two hundred and seventy and the second nearly two hundred and fifty. This has never happened before.

ZINAIDA.
How fortunate for those who have a great many tickets!

MARTHA.
Don't say that, dear; even when the price of tickets is high it does not pay to put one's capital into them.

ZINAIDA.
Quite true, and yet, my dear, one never can tell what may happen. Providence is sometimes kind.

THIRD GUEST.
My impression is, ladies, that at present capital is exceedingly unproductive. Shares pay very small dividends, and speculating is exceedingly dangerous. As I understand it, the capitalist now finds himself in a more critical position than the man who——

MARTHA.
Quite right.

FIRST GUEST yawns.

MARTHA.
How dare you yawn in the presence of ladies?

FIRST GUEST.
I beg your pardon! It was quite an accident.

ZINAIDA gets up and goes out through the door on the right.

GEORGE.
Two in hearts.

SECOND GUEST.
Pass.

KOSICH.
Pass.

MARTHA.
[Aside] Heavens! This is deadly! I shall die of ennui.

Enter ZINAIDA and LEBEDIEFF through the door on the right.

ZINAIDA.

Why do you go off by yourself like a prima donna? Come and sit with our guests!

[She sits down in her former place.]

LEBEDIEFF.

[Yawning] Oh, dear, our sins are heavy! [He catches sight of MARTHA] Why, there is my little sugar-plum! How is your most esteemed highness?

MARTHA.

Very well, thank you.

LEBEDIEFF.

Splendid, splendid! [He sits down in an armchair] Quite right—Oh, Gabriel!

GABRIEL brings him a glass of vodka and a tumbler of water. He empties the glass of vodka and sips the water.

FIRST GUEST.

Good health to you!

LEBEDIEFF.

Good health is too much to ask. I am content to keep death from the door. [To his wife] Where is the heroine of this occasion, Zuzu?

KOSICH.

[In a plaintive voice] Look here, why haven't we taken any tricks yet? [He jumps up] Yes, why have we lost this game entirely, confound it?

AVDOTIA.

[Jumps up angrily] Because, friend, you don't know how to play it, and have no right to be sitting here at all. What right had you to lead from another suit? Haven't you the ace left? [They both leave the table and run forward.]

KOSICH.

[In a tearful voice] Ladies and gentlemen, let me explain! I had the ace, king, queen, and eight of diamonds, the ace of spades and one, just one, little heart, do you understand? Well, she, bad luck to her, she couldn't make a little slam. I said one in no-trumps———*

---

* The game played is vint, the national card-game of Russia and the direct ancestor of auction bridge, with which it is almost identical. [translator's note]

AVDOTIA.
> [Interrupting him] No, I said one in no-trumps; you said two in no-trumps——

KOSICH.
> This is unbearable! Allow me—you had—I had—you had—[To LEBEDIEFF] But you shall decide it, Paul: I had the ace, king, queen, and eight of diamonds——

LEBEDIEFF.
> [Puts his fingers into his ears] Stop, for heaven's sake, stop!

AVDOTIA.
> [Yelling] I said no-trumps, and not he!

KOSICH.
> [Furiously] I'll be damned if I ever sit down to another game of cards with that old cat!
> He rushes into the garden. The SECOND GUEST follows him. GEORGE is left alone at the table.

AVDOTIA.
> Whew! He makes my blood boil! Old cat, indeed! You're an old cat yourself!

MARTHA.
> How angry you are, aunty!

AVDOTIA.
> [Sees MARTHA and claps her hands] Are you here, my darling? My beauty! And was I blind as a bat, and didn't see you? Darling child! [She kisses her and sits down beside her] How happy this makes me! Let me feast my eyes on you, my milk-white swan! Oh, oh, you have bewitched me!

LEBEDIEFF.
> Why don't you find her a husband instead of singing her praises?

AVDOTIA.
> He shall be found. I shall not go to my grave before I have found a husband for her, and one for Sasha too. I shall not go to my grave— [She sighs] But where to find these husbands nowadays? There sit some possible bridegrooms now, huddled together like a lot of half-drowned rats!

THIRD GUEST.

    A most unfortunate comparison! It is my belief, ladies, that if the young men of our day prefer to remain single, the fault lies not with them, but with the existing, social conditions!

LEBEDIEFF.

    Come, enough of that! Don't give us any mo re philosophy; I don't like it!

Enter SASHA. She goes up to her father.

SASHA.

How can you endure the stuffy air of this room when the weather is so beautiful?

ZINAIDA.

    My dear Sasha, don't you see that Martha is here?

SASHA.

    I beg your pardon.

[She goes up to MARTHA and shakes hands.]

MARTHA.

    Yes, here I am, my dear little Sasha, and proud to congratulate you. [They kiss each other] Many happy returns of the day, dear!

SASHA.

    Thank you! [She goes and sits down by her father.]

LEBEDIEFF.

    As you were saying, Avdotia Nazarovna, husbands are hard to find. I don't want to be rude, but I must say that the young men of the present are a dull and poky lot, poor fellows! They can't dance or talk or drink as they should do.

AVDOTIA.

    Oh, as far as drinking goes, they are all experts. Just give them—give them——

LEBEDIEFF.

    Simply to drink is no art. A horse can drink. No, it must be done in the right way. In my young days we used to sit and cudgel our brains all day over our lessons, but as soon as evening came we would fly off on some spree and keep it up till dawn. How we used to dance and flirt, and drink, too! Or sometimes we would sit and chatter and discuss everything under the sun until we almost wagged our tongues off. But now—[He waves his hand] Boys are a puzzle to me. They are not willing either to give a candle to God or a pitchfork to the devil! There is only one young fellow in the country who is worth a penny, and he is married. [Sighs] They say, too, that he is going crazy.

MARTHA.
Who is he?

LEBEDIEFF.
Nicholas Ivanoff.

MARTHA.
Yes, he is a fine fellow, only [Makes a face] he is very unhappy.

ZINAIDA.
How could he be otherwise, poor boy! [She sighs] He made such a bad mistake. When he married that Jewess of his he thought of course that her parents would give away whole mountains of gold with her, but, on the contrary, on the day she became a Christian they disowned her, and Ivanoff has never seen a penny of the money. He has repented of his folly now, but it is too late.

SASHA.
Mother, that is not true!

MARTHA.
How can you say it is not true, Sasha, when we all know it to be a fact? Why did he have to marry a Jewess? He must have had some reason for doing it. Are Russian girls so scarce? No, he made a mistake, poor fellow, a sad mistake. [Excitedly] And what on earth can he do with her now? Where could she go if he were to come home some day and say: "Your parents have deceived me; leave my house at once!" Her parents wouldn't take her back. She might find a place as a house-maid if she had ever learned to work, which she hasn't. He worries and worries her now, but the Count interferes. If it had not been for the Count, he would have worried her to death long ago.

AVDOTIA.
They say he shuts her up in a cellar and stuffs her with garlic, and she eats and eats until her very soul reeks of it. [Laughter.]

SASHA.
But, father, you know that isn't true!

LEBEDIEFF.

What if it isn't, Sasha? Let them spin yarns if it amuses them. [He calls] Gabriel!

GABRIEL brings him another glass of vodka and a glass of water.

ZINAIDA.

His misfortunes have almost ruined him, poor man. His affairs are in a frightful condition. If Borkin did not take such good charge of his estate he and his Jewess would soon be starving to death. [She sighs] And what anxiety he has caused us! Heaven only knows how we have suffered. Do you realise, my dear, that for three years he has owed us nine thousand roubles?

MARTHA.

[Horrified] Nine thousand!

ZINAIDA.

Yes, that is the sum that my dear Paul has undertaken to lend him. He never knows to whom it is safe to lend money and to whom it is not. I don't worry about the principal, but he ought to pay the interest on his debt.

SASHA.

[Hotly] Mamma, you have already discussed this subject at least a thousand times!

ZINAIDA.

What difference does it make to you? Why should you interfere?

SASHA.

What is this mania you all have for gossiping about a man who has never done any of you any harm? Tell me, what harm has he done you?

THIRD GUEST.

Let me say two words, Miss Sasha. I esteem Ivanoff, and have always found him an honourable man, but, between ourselves, I also consider him an adventurer.

SASHA.

I congratulate you on your opinion!

THIRD GUEST.

In proof of its truth, permit me to present to you the following facts, as they were communicated to me by his secretary, or shall I say rather, by his factotum, Borkin. Two years ago, at the time of the cattle plague, he bought some cattle and had them insured—

ZINAIDA.

Yes, I remember hearing' of that.

THIRD GUEST.

He had them insured, as you understand, and then inoculated them with the disease and claimed the insurance.

SASHA.

Oh, what nonsense, nonsense, nonsense! No one bought or inoculated any cattle! The story was invented by Borkin, who then went about boasting of his clever plan. Ivanoff would not forgive Borkin for two weeks after he heard of it. He is only guilty of a weak character and too great faith in humanity. He can't make up his mind to get rid of that Borkin, and so all his possessions have been tricked and stolen from him. Every one who has had anything to do with Ivanoff has taken advantage of his generosity to grow rich.

LEBEDIEFF.

Sasha, you little firebrand, that will do!

SASHA.

Why do you all talk like this? This eternal subject of Ivanoff, Ivanoff, and always Ivanoff has grown insufferable, and yet you never speak of anything else. [She goes toward the door, then stops and comes back] I am surprised, [To the young men] and utterly astonished at your patience, young men! How can you sit there like that? Aren't you bored? Why, the very air is as dull as ditchwater! Do, for heaven's sake say something; try to amuse the girls a little, move about! Or if you can't talk of anything except Ivanoff, you might laugh or sing or dance——

LEBEDIEFF.

[Laughing] That's right, Sasha! Give them a good scolding.

SASHA.

Look here, will you do me a favour? If you refuse to dance or sing or laugh, if all that is tedious, then let me beg you, implore you, to summon all your powers, if only for this once, and make one witty or clever remark. Let it be as impertinent and malicious as you like, so long as it is funny and original. Won't you perform this miracle, just once, to surprise us and make us laugh? Or else you might think of some little thing which you could all do together, something to make you stir about. Let the girls admire you for once in their lives! Listen to me! I suppose you want them to like you? Then why don't try to make them do it? Oh, dear! There is something wrong with you all! You are a lot of sleepy stick-in-the-muds! I have told you so a thousand times and shall always go on repeating it; there is something wrong with every one of you; something wrong, wrong, wrong!

Enter IVANOFF and SHABELSKI through the door on the right.

SHABELSKI.

Who is making a speech here? Is it you, Sasha? [He laughs and shakes hands with her] Many happy returns of the day, my dear child. May you live as long as possible in this life, but never be born again!

ZINAIDA.

[Joyfully] My dear Count!

LEBEDIEFF.

Who can this be? Not you, Count?

SHABELSKI.

[Sees ZINAIDA and MARTHA sitting side by side] Two gold mines side by side! What a pleasant picture it makes! [He shakes hands with ZINAIDA] Good evening, Zuzu! [Shakes hands with MARTHA] Good evening, Birdie!

ZINAIDA.

I am charmed to see you, Count. You are a rare visitor here now. [Calls] Gabriel, bring some tea! Please sit down.

She gets up and goes to the door and back, evidently much preoccupied. SASHA sits down in her former place. IVANOFF silently shakes hands with every one.

LEBEDIEFF.

[To SHABELSKI] What miracle has brought you here? You have given us a great surprise. Why, Count, you're a rascal, you haven't been treating us right at all. [Leads him forward by the hand] Tell me, why don't you ever come to see us now? Are you offended?

SHABELSKI.

How can I get here to see you? Astride a broomstick? I have no horses of my own, and Nicholas won't take me with him when he goes out.

• 86 •

He says I must stay at home to amuse Sarah. Send your horses for me and I shall come with pleasure.

LEBE DIEFF.

[With a wave of the hand] Oh, that is easy to say! But Zuzu would rather have a fit than lend the horses to any one. My dear, dear old friend, you are more to me than any one I know! You and I are survivors of those good old days that are gone forever, and you alone bring back to my mind the love and longings of my lost youth. Of course I am only joking, and yet, do you know, I am almost in tears?

SHABELSKI.

Stop, stop! You smell like the air of a wine cellar.

LEBEDIEFF.

Dear friend, you cannot imagine how lonely I am without my old companions! I could hang myself! [Whispers] Zuzu has frightened all the decent men away with her stingy ways, and now we have only this riff-raff, as you see: Tom, Dick, and Harry. However, drink your tea.

ZINAIDA.

[Anxiously, to GABRIEL] Don't bring it in like that! Go fetch some jam to eat with it!

SHABELSKI.

[Laughing loudly, to IVANOFF] Didn't I tell you so? [To LEBEDIEFF] I bet him driving over, that as soon as we arrived Zuzu would want to feed us with jam!

ZINAIDA.

Still joking, Count! [She sits down.]

LEBEDIEFF.

She made twenty jars of it this year, and how else do you expect her to get rid of it?

SHABELSKI.

[Sits down near the table] Are you still adding to the hoard, Zuzu? You will soon have a million, eh?

ZINAIDA.

[Sighing] I know it seems as if no one could be richer than we, but where do they think the money comes from? It is all gossip.

SHABELSKI.

Oh, yes, we all know that! We know how badly you play your cards! Tell me, Paul, honestly, have you saved up a million yet?

LEBEDIEFF.

I don't know. Ask Zuzu.

SHABELSKI.

[To MARTHA] And my plump little Birdie here will soon have a million too! She is getting prettier and plumper not only every day, but every hour. That means she has a nice little fortune.

MARTHA.

Thank you very much, your highness, but I don't like such jokes.

SHABELSKI.

My dear little gold mine, do you call that a joke? It was a wail of the soul, a cry from the heart, that burst through my lips. My love for you and Zuzu is immense. [Gaily] Oh, rapture! Oh, bliss! I cannot look at you two without a madly beating heart!

ZINAIDA.

You are still the same, Count. [To GEORGE] Put out the candles please, George. [GEORGE gives a start. He puts out the candles and sits down again] How is your wife, Nicholas?

IVANOFF.

She is very ill. The doctor said to-day that she certainly had consumption.

ZINAIDA.

Really? Oh, how sad! [She sighs] And we are all so fond of her!

SHABELSKI.

What trash you all talk! That story was invented by that sham doctor, and is nothing but a trick of his. He wants to masquerade as an Aesculapius, and so has started this consumption theory. Fortunately her husband isn't jealous. [IVANOFF makes an inpatient gesture] As for Sarah, I wouldn't trust a word or an action of hers. I have made a point all my life of mistrusting all doctors, lawyers, and women. They are shammers and deceivers.

LEBEDIEFF.

[To SHABELSKI] You are an extraordinary person, Matthew! You have mounted this misanthropic hobby of yours, and you ride it through thick and thin like a lunatic You are a man like any other, and yet, from the way you talk one would imagine that you had the pip, or a cold in the head.

SHABELSKI.
Would you have me go about kissing every rascal and scoundrel I meet?

LEBEDIEFF.
Where do you find all these rascals and scoundrels?

SHABELSKI.
Of course I am not talking of any one here present, nevertheless——

LEBEDIEFF.
There you are again with your "nevertheless." All this is simply a fancy of yours.

SHABELSKI.
A fancy? It is lucky for you that you have no knowledge of the world!

LEBEDIEFF.
My knowledge of the world is this: I must sit here prepared at any moment to have death come knocking at the door. That is my knowledge of the world. At our age, brother, you and I can't afford to worry about knowledge of the world. So then—[He calls] Oh, Gabriel!

SHABELSKI.
You have had quite enough already. Look at your nose.

LEBEDIEFF.
No matter, old boy. I am not going to be married to-day.

ZINAIDA.
Doctor Lvoff has not been here for a long time. He seems to have forgotten us.

SASHA.
That man is one of my aversions. I can't stand his icy sense of honour. He can't ask for a glass of water or smoke a cigarette without making a display of his remarkable honesty. Walking and talking, it is written on his brow: "I am an honest man." He is a great bore.

SHABELSKI.
He is a narrow-minded, conceited medico. [Angrily] He shrieks like a parrot at every step: "Make way for honest endeavour!" and thinks himself another St. Francis. Everybody is a rascal who doesn't make as much noise as he does. As for his penetration, it is simply remarkable! If a peasant is well off and lives decently, he sees at once that he must

be a thief and a scoundrel. If I wear a velvet coat and am dressed by my valet, I am a rascal and the valet is my slave. There is no place in this world for a man like him. I am actually afraid of him. Yes, indeed, he is likely, out of a sense of duty, to insult a man at any moment and to call him a knave.

IVANOFF.
I am dreadfully tired of him, but I can't help liking him, too, he is so sincere.

SHABELSKI.
Oh, yes, his sincerity is beautiful! He came up to me yesterday evening and remarked absolutely apropos of nothing: "Count, I have a deep aversion to you!" It isn't as if he said such things simply, but they are extremely pointed. His voice trembles, his eyes flash, his veins swell. Confound his infernal honesty! Supposing I am disgusting and odious to him? What is more natural? I know that I am, but I don't like to be told so to my face. I am a worthless old man, but he might have the decency to respect my grey hairs. Oh, what stupid, heartless honesty!

LEBEDIEFF.
Come, come, you have been young yourself, and should make allowances for him.

SHABELSKI.
Yes, I have been young and reckless; I have played the fool in my day and have seen plenty of knaves and scamps, but I have never called a thief a thief to his face, or talked of ropes in the house of a man who had been hung. I knew how to behave, but this idiotic doctor of yours would think himself in the seventh heaven of happiness if fate would allow him to pull my nose in public in the name of morality and human ideals.

LEBEDIEFF.
Young men are all stubborn and restive. I had an uncle once who thought himself a philosopher. He would fill his house with guests, and after he had had a drink he would get up on a chair, like this, and begin: "You ignoramuses! You powers of darkness! This is the dawn of a new life!" And so on and so on; he would preach and preach——

SASHA.
And the guests?

LEBEDIEFF.

They would just sit and listen and go on drinking. Once, though, I challenged him to a duel, challenged my own uncle! It came out of a discussion about Sir Francis Bacon. I was sitting, I remember, where Matthew is, and my uncle and the late Gerasim Nilitch were standing over there, about where Nicholas is now. Well, Gerasim Nilitch propounded this question——

Enter BORKIN. He is dressed like a dandy and carries a parcel under his arm. He comes in singing and skipping through the door on the right. A murmur of approval is heard.

THE GIRLS.

Oh, Michael Borkin!

LEBEDIEFF.

Hallo, Misha!

SHABELSKI.

The soul of the company!

BORKIN.

Here we are! [He runs up to SASHA] Most noble Signorina, let me be so bold as to wish to the whole world many happy returns of the birthday of such an exquisite flower as you! As a token of my enthusiasm let me presume to present you with these fireworks and this Bengal fire of my own manufacture. [He hands her the parcel] May they illuminate the night as brightly as you illuminate the shadows of this dark world. [He spreads them out theatrically before her.]

SASHA.

Thank you.

LEBEDIEFF.

[Laughing loudly, to IVANOFF] Why don't you send this Judas packing?

BORKIN.

[To LEBEDIEFF] My compliments to you, sir. [To IVANOFF] How are you, my patron? [Sings] Nicholas voila, hey ho hey! [He greets everybody in turn] Most highly honoured Zinaida! Oh, glorious Martha! Most ancient Avdotia! Noblest of Counts!

SHABELSKI.

[Laughing] The life of the company! The moment he comes in the air fe els livelier. Have you noticed it?

BORKIN.
> Whew! I am tired! I believe I have shaken hands with everybody. Well, ladies and gentlemen, haven't you some little tidbit to tell me; something spicy? [Speaking quickly to ZINAIDA] Oh, aunty! I have something to tell you. As I was on my way here—[To GABRIEL] Some tea, please Gabriel, but without jam—as I was on my way here I saw some peasants down on the river-bank pulling the bark off the trees. Why don't you lease that meadow?

LEBEDIEFF.
> [To IVANOFF] Why don't you send that Judas away?

ZINAIDA.
> [Startled] Why, that is quite true! I never thought of it.

BORKIN.
> [Swinging his arms] I can't sit still! What tricks shall we be up to next, aunty? I am all on edge, Martha, absolutely exalted. [He sings] "Once more I stand before thee!"

ZINAIDA.
> Think of something to amuse us, Misha, we are all bored.

BORKIN.
> Yes, you look so. What is the matter with you all? Why are you sitting there as solemn as a jury? Come, let us play something; what shall it be? Forfeits? Hide-and-seek? Tag? Shall we dance, or have the fireworks?

THE GIRLS.
> [Clapping their hands] The fireworks! The fireworks! [They run into the garden.]

SASHA.
> [To IVANOFF] What makes you so depressed today?

IVANOFF.
> My head aches, little Sasha, and then I feel bored.

SASHA.
> Come into the sitting-room with me.

They go out through the door on the right. All the guests go into the garden and ZINAIDA and LEBEDIEFF are left alone.

ZINAIDA.
> That is what I like to see! A young man like Misha comes into the room and in a minute he has everybody laughing. [She puts out the large

lamp] There is no reason the candles should burn for nothing so long as they are all in the garden. [She blows out the candles.]

LEBEDIEFF.
[Following her] We really ought to give our guests something to eat, Zuzu!

ZINAIDA.
What crowds of candles; no wonder we are thought rich.

LEBEDIEFF.
[Still following her] Do let them have something to eat, Zuzu; they are young and must be hungry by now, poor things—Zuzu!

ZINAIDA.
The Count did not finish his tea, and all that sugar has been wasted. [Goes out through the door on the left.]

LEBEDIEFF.
Bah! [Goes out into the garden.]

Enter IVANOFF and SASHA through the door on the right.

IVANOFF.
This is how it is, Sasha: I used to work hard and think hard, and never tire; now, I neither do anything nor think anything, and I am weary, body and soul. I feel I am terribly to blame, my conscience leaves me no peace day or night, and yet I can't see clearly exactly what my mistakes are. And now comes my wife's illness, our poverty, this eternal backbiting, gossiping, chattering, that foolish Borkin—My home has become unendurable to me, and to live there is worse than torture. Frankly, Sasha, the presence of my wife, who loves me, has become unbearable. You are an old friend, little Sasha, you will not be angry with me for speaking so openly. I came to you to be cheered, but I am bored here too, something urges me home again. Forgive me, I shall slip away at once.

SASHA.
I can understand your trouble, Nicholas. You are unhappy because you are lonely. You need some one at your side whom you can love, someone who understands you.

IVANOFF.
What an idea, Sasha! Fancy a crusty old badger like myself starting a love affair! Heaven preserve me from such misfortune! No, my little

sage, this is not a case for romance. The fact is, I can endure all I have to suffer: sadness, sickness of mind, ruin, the loss of my wife, and my lonely, broken old age, but I cannot, I will not, endure the contempt I have for myself! I am nearly killed by shame when I think that a strong, healthy man like myself has become—oh, heaven only knows what—by no means a Manfred or a Hamlet! There are some unfortunates who feel flattered when people call them Hamlets and cynics, but to me it is an insult. It wounds my pride and I am tortured by shame and suffer agony.

SASHA.

[Laughing through her tears] Nicholas, let us run away to America together!

IVANOFF.

I haven't the energy to take such a step as that, and besides, in America you—[They go toward the door into the garden] As a matter of fact, Sasha, this is not a good place for you to live. When I look about at the men who surround you I am terrified for you; whom is there you could marry? Your only chance will be if some passing lieutenant or student steals your heart and carries you away.

Enter ZINAIDA through the door on the right with a jar of jam.

IVANOFF.

Excuse me, Sasha, I shall join you in a minute.

SASHA goes out into the garden.

IVANOFF.

[To ZINAIDA] Zinaida, may I ask you a favour?

ZINAIDA.

What is it?

IVANOFF.

The fact is, you know, that the interest on my note is due day after to-morrow, but I should be more than obliged to you if you will let me postpone the payment of it, or would let me add the interest to the capital. I simply cannot pay it now; I haven't the money.

ZINAIDA.

Oh, Ivanoff, how could I do such a thing? Would it be business-like? No, no, don't ask it, don't torment an unfortunate old woman.

IVANOFF.
    I beg your pardon. [He goes out into the garden.]

ZINAIDA.
    Oh, dear! Oh, dear! What a fright he gave me! I am trembling all over. [Goes out through the door on the right.]
    Enter KOSICH through the door on the left. He walks across the stage.

KOSICH.
    I had the ace, king, queen, and eight of diamonds, the ace of spades, and one, just one little heart, and she—may the foul fiend fly away with her,—she couldn't make a little slam!
    Goes out through the door on the right. Enter from the garden AVDOTIA and FIRST GUEST.

AVDOTIA.
    Oh, how I should like to get my claws into her, the miserable old miser! How I should like it! Does she think it a joke to leave us sitting here since five o'clock without even offering us a crust to eat? What a house! What management!

FIRST GUEST.
    I am so bored that I feel like beating my head against the wall. Lord, what a queer lot of people! I shall soon be howling like a wolf and snapping at them from hunger and weariness.

AVDOTIA.
    How I should like to get my claws into her, the old sinner!

FIRST GUEST.
    I shall get a drink, old lady, and then home I go! I won't have anything to do with these belles of yours. How the devil can a man think of love who hasn't had a drop to drink since dinner?

AVDOTIA.
    Come on, we will go and find something.

FIRST GUEST.
    Sh! Softly! I think the brandy is in the sideboard in the dining-room. We will find George! Sh!
    They go out through the door on the left. Enter ANNA and LVOFF through the door on the right.

ANNA.
>No, they will be glad to see us. Is no one here? Then they must be in the garden.

LVOFF.
>I should like to know why you have brought me into this den of wolves. This is no place for you and me; honourable people should not be subjected to such influences as these.

ANNA.
>Listen to me, Mr. Honourable Man. When you are escorting a lady it is very bad manners to talk to her the whole way about nothing but your own honesty. Such behaviour may be perfectly honest, but it is also tedious, to say the least. Never tell a woman how good you are; let her find it out herself. My Nicholas used only to sing and tell stories when he was young as you are, and yet every woman knew at once what kind of a man he was.

LVOFF.
>Don't talk to me of your Nicholas; I know all about him!

ANNA.
>You are a very worthy man, but you don't know anything at all. Come into the garden. He never said: "I am an honest man; these surroundings are too narrow for me." He never spoke of wolves' dens, called people bears or vultures. He left the animal kingdom alone, and the most I have ever heard him say when he was excited was: "Oh, how unjust I have been to-day!" or "Annie, I am sorry for that man." That's what he would say, but you—

ANNA and LVOFF go out. Enter AVDOTIA and FIRST GUEST through the door on the left.

FIRST GUEST.
>There isn't any in the dining-room, so it must be somewhere in the pantry. We must find George. Come this way, through the sitting-room.

AVDOTIA.
>Oh, how I should like to get my claws into her!

They go out through the door on the right. MARTHA and BORKIN run in laughing from the garden. SHABELSKI comes mincing behind them, laughing and rubbing his hands.

MARTHA.

Oh, I am so bored! [Laughs loudly] This is deadly! Every one looks as if he had swallowed a poker. I am frozen to the marrow by this icy dullness. [She skips about] Let us do something!

BORKIN catches her by the waist and kisses her cheek.

SHABELSKI.
[Laughing and snapping his fingers] Well, I'll be hanged! [Cackling] Really, you know!

MARTHA.
Let go! Let go, you wretch! What will the Count think? Stop, I say!

BORKIN.
Angel! Jewel! Lend me twenty-three hundred roubles.

MARTHA.
Most certainly not! Do what you please, but I'll thank you to leave my money alone. No, no, no! Oh, let go, will you?

SHABELSKI.
[Mincing around them] The little birdie has its charms! [Seriously] Come, that will do!

BORKIN.
Let us come to the point, and consider my proposition frankly as a business arrangement. Answer me honestly, without tricks and equivocations, do you agree to do it or not? Listen to me; [Pointing to Shabelski] he needs money to the amount of at least three thousand a year; you need a husband. Do you want to be a Countess?

SHABELSKI.
[Laughing loudly] Oh, the cynic!

BORKIN.
Do you want to be a Countess or not?

MARTHA.
[Excitedly] Wait a minute; really, Misha, these things aren't done in a second like this. If the Count wants to marry me, let him ask me himself, and—and—I don't see, I don't understand—all this is so sudden——

BORKIN.
Come, don't let us beat about the bush; this is a business arrangement. Do you agree or not?

SHABELSKI.
[Chuckling and rubbing his hands] Supposing I do marry her, eh? Hang

it, why shouldn't I play her this shabby trick? What do you say, little puss? [He kisses her cheek] Dearest chick-a-biddy!

MARTHA.
Stop! Stop! I hardly know what I am doing. Go away! No—don't go!

BORKIN.
Answer at once: is it yes or no? We can't stand here forever.

MARTHA.
Look here, Count, come and visit me for three or four days. It is gay at my house, not like this place. Come to-morrow. [To BORKIN] Or is this all a joke?

BORKIN.
[Angrily] How could I joke on such a serious subject?

MARTHA.
Wait! Stop! Oh, I feel faint! A Countess! I am fainting, I am falling!

BORKIN and SHABELSKI laugh and catch her by the arms. They kiss her cheeks and lead her out through the door on the right. IVANOFF and SASHA run in from the garden.

IVANOFF.
[Desperately clutching his head] It can't be true! Don't Sasha, don't! Oh, I implore you not to!

SASHA.
I love you madly. Without you my life can have no meaning, no happiness, no hope.

IVANOFF.
Why, why do you say that? What do you mean? Little Sasha, don't say it!

SASHA.
You were the only joy of my childhood; I loved you body and soul then, as myself, but now—Oh, I love you, Nicholas! Take me with you to the ends of the earth, wherever you wish; but for heaven's sake let us go at once, or I shall die.

IVANOFF.
[Shaking with wild laughter] What is this? Is it the beginning for me of a new life? Is it, Sasha? Oh, my happiness, my joy! [He draws her to him] My freshness, my youth!

Enter ANNA from the garden. She sees her husband and SASHA, and stops as if petrified.

IVANOFF.
> Oh, then I shall live once more? And work?
>
> IVANOFF and SASHA kiss each other. After the kiss they look around and see ANNA.

IVANOFF.
> [With horror] Sarah!

The curtain falls.

ACT III

Library in IVANOFF'S house. On the walls hang maps, pictures, guns, pistols, sickles, whips, etc. A writing-table. On it lie in disorder knick-knacks, papers, books, parcels, and several revolvers. Near the papers stand a lamp, a decanter of vodka, and a plate of salted herrings. Pieces of bread and cucumber are scattered about. SHABELSKI and LEBEDIEFF are sitting at the writing-table. BORKIN is sitting astride a chair in the middle of the room. PETER is standing near the door.

LEBEDIEFF.
   The policy of France is clear and definite; the French know what they want: it is to skin those German sausages, but the Germans must sing another song; France is not the only thorn in their flesh.
SHABELSKI.
   Nonsense! In my opinion the Germans are cowards and the French are the same. They are showing their teeth at one another, but you can take my word for it, they will not do more than that; they'll never fight!

BORKIN.
  Why should they fight? Why all these congresses, this arming and expense? Do you know what I would do in their place? I would catch all the dogs in the kingdom and inoculate them with Pasteur's serum, then I would let them loose in the enemy's country, and the enemies would all go mad in a month.

LEBEDIEFF.
  [Laughing] His head is small, but the great ideas are hidden away in it like fish in the sea!

SHABELSKI.
  Oh, he is a genius.

LEBEDIEFF.
  Heaven help you, Misha, you are a funny chap. [He stops laughing] But how is this, gentlemen? Here we are talking Germany, Germany, and never a word about vodka! Repetatur! [He fills three glasses] Here's to you all! [He drinks and eats] This herring is the best of all relishes.

SHABELSKI.
  No, no, these cucumbers are better; every wise man since the creation of the world has been trying to invent something better than a salted cucumber, and not one has succeeded. [To PETER] Peter, go and fetch some more cucumbers. And Peter, tell the cook to make four little onion pasties, and see that we get them hot.

  PETER goes out.

LEBEDIEFF.
  Caviar is good with vodka, but it must be prepared with skill. Take a quarter of a pound of pressed caviar, two little onions, and a little olive oil; mix them together and put a slice of lemon on top—so! Lord! The very perfume would drive you crazy!

BORKIN.
  Roast snipe are good too, but they must be cooked right. They should first be cleaned, then sprinkled with bread crumbs, and roasted until they will crackle between the teeth—crunch, crunch!

SHABELSKI.
  We had something good at Martha's yesterday: white mushrooms.

LEBEDIEFF.
  You don't say so!

SHABELSKI.
And they were especially well prepared, too, with onions and bay-leaves and spices, you know. When the dish was opened, the odour that floated out was simply intoxicating!

LEBEDIEFF.
What do you say, gentlemen? Repetatur! [He drinks] Good health to you! [He looks at his watch] I must be going. I can't wait for Nicholas. So you say Martha gave you mushrooms? We haven't seen one at home. Will you please tell me, Count, what plot you are hatching that takes you to Martha's so often?

SHABELSKI.
[Nodding at BORKIN] He wants me to marry her.

LEBEDIEFF.
Wants you to marry her! How old are you?

SHABELSKI.
Sixty-two.

LEBEDIEFF.
Really, you are just the age to marry, aren't you? And Martha is just suited to you!

BORKIN.
This is not a question of Martha, but of Martha's money.

LEBEDIEFF.
Aren't you moonstruck, and don't you want the moon too?

SHABELSKI.
Borkin here is quite in earnest about it; the clever fellow is sure I shall obey orders, and marry Martha.

BORKIN.
What do you mean? Aren't you sure yourself?

SHABELSKI.
Are you mad? I never was sure of anything. Bah!

BORKIN.
Many thanks! I am much obliged to you for the information. So you are trying to fool me, are you? First you say you will marry Martha and then you say you won't; the devil only knows which you really mean, but I have given her my word of honour that you will. So you have changed your mind, have you?

SHABELSKI.
He is actually in earnest; what an extraordinary man!
BORKIN.
[losing his temper] If that is how you feel about it, why have you turned an honest woman's head? Her heart is set on your title, and she can neither eat nor sleep for thinking of it. How can you make a jest of such things? Do you think such behaviour is honourable?
SHABELSKI.
[Snapping his fingers] Well, why not play her this shabby trick, after all? Eh? Just out of spite? I shall certainly do it, upon my word I shall! What a joke it will be!
Enter LVOFF.
LEBEDIEFF.
We bow before you, Aesculapius! [He shakes hands with LVOFF and sings]

"Doctor, doctor, save, oh, save me,
I am scared to death of dying!"

LVOFF.
Hasn't Ivanoff come home yet?
LEBEDIEFF.
Not yet. I have been waiting for him myself for over an hour.
LVOFF walks impatiently up and down.
LEBEDIEFF.
How is Anna to-day?
LVOFF.
Very ill.
LEBEDIEFF.
[Sighing] May one go and pay one's respects to her?
LVOFF.
No, please don't. She is asleep, I believe.
LEBEDIEFF.
She is a lovely, charming woman. [Sighing] The day she fainted at our house, on Sasha's birthday, I saw that she had not much longer to live, poor thing. Let me see, why did she faint? When I ran up, she was lying

on the floor, ashy white, with Nicholas on his knees beside her, and Sasha was standing by them in tears. Sasha and I went about almost crazy for a week after that.

SHABELSKI.
[To LVOFF] Tell me, most honoured disciple of science, what scholar discovered that the frequent visits of a young doctor were beneficial to ladies suffering from affections of the chest? It is a remarkable discovery, remarkable! Would you call such treatment Allopathic or Homeopathic?

LVOFF tries to answer, but makes an impatient gesture instead, and walks out of the room.

SHABELSKI.
What a withering look he gave me!

LEBEDIEFF.
Some fiend must prompt you to say such things! Why did you offend him?

SHABELSKI.
[Angrily] Why does he tell such lies? Consumption! No hope! She is dying! It is nonsense, I can't abide him!

LEBEDIEFF.
What makes you think he is lying?

SHABELSKI.
[Gets up and walks up and down] I can't bear to think that a living person could die like that, suddenly, without any reason at all. Don't let us talk about it!

KOSICH runs in panting.

KOSICH.
Is Ivanoff at home? How do you do? [He shakes hands quickly all round] Is he at home?

BORKIN.
No, he isn't.

KOSICH.
[Sits down and jumps up again] In that case I must say goodbye; I must be going. Business, you know. I am absolutely exhausted; run off my feet!

LEBEDIEFF.
Where did you blow in from?

KOSICH.

From Barabanoff's. He and I have been playing cards all night; we have only just stopped. I have been absolutely fleeced; that Barabanoff is a demon at cards. [In a tearful voice] Just listen to this: I had a heart and he [He turns to BORKIN, who jumps away from him] led a diamond, and I led a heart, and he led another diamond. Well, he didn't take the trick. [To LEBEDIEFF] We were playing three in clubs. I had the ace and queen, and the ace and ten of spades—

LEBEDIEFF.

[Stopping up his ears] Spare me, for heaven's sake, spare me!

KOSICH.

[To SHABELSKI] Do you understand? I had the ace and queen of clubs, the ace and ten of spades.

SHABELSKI.

[Pushes him away] Go away, I don't want to listen to you!

KOSICH.

When suddenly misfortune overtook me. My ace of spades took the first trick—

SHABELSKI.

[Snatching up a revolver] Leave the room, or I shall shoot!

KOSICH.

[Waving his hands] What does this mean? Is this the Australian bush, where no one has any interests in common? Where there is no public spirit, and each man lives for himself alone? However, I must be off. My time is precious. [He shakes hands with LEBEDIEFF] Pass!

General laughter. KOSICH goes out. In the doorway he runs into AVDOTIA.

AVDOTIA.

[Shrieks] Bad luck to you, you nearly knocked me down.

ALL.

Oh, she is always everywhere at once!

AVDOTIA.

So this is where you all are? I have been looking for you all over the house. Good-day to you, boys!

[She shakes hands with everybody.]

LEBEDIEFF.
   What brings you here?
AVDOTIA.
   Business, my son. [To SHABELSKI] Business connected with your highness. She commanded me to bow. [She bows] And to inquire after your health. She told me to say, the little birdie, that if you did not come to see her this evening she would cry her eyes out. Take him aside, she said, and whisper in his ear. But why should I make a secret of her message? We are not stealing chickens, but arranging an affair of lawful love by mutual consent of both parties. And now, although I never drink, I shall take a drop under these circumstances.
LEBEDIEFF.
   So shall I. [He pours out the vodka] You must be immortal, you old magpie! You were an old woman when I first knew you, thirty years ago.
AVDOTIA.
   I have lost count of the years. I have buried three husbands, and would have married a fourth if any one had wanted a woman without a dowry. I have had eight children. [She takes up the glass] Well, we have begun a good work, may it come to a good end! They will live happily ever after, and we shall enjoy their happiness. Love and good luck to them both! [She drinks] This is strong vodka!
SHABELSKI.
   [laughing loudly, to LEBEDIEFF] The funny thing is, they actually think I am in earnest. How strange! [He gets up] And yet, Paul, why shouldn't I play her this shabby trick? Just out of spite? To give the devil something to do, eh, Paul?
LEBEDIEFF.
   You are talking nonsense, Count. You and I must fix our thoughts on dying now; we have left Martha's money far behind us; our day is over.
SHABELSKI.
   No, I shall certainly marry her; upon my word, I shall!
   Enter IVANOFF and LVOFF.
LVOFF.
   Will you please spare me five minutes of your time?

LEBEDIEFF.

Hallo, Nicholas! [He goes to meet IVANOFF] How are you, old friend? I have been waiting an hour for you.

AVDOTIA.

[Bows] How do you do, my son?

IVANOFF.

[Bitterly] So you have turned my library into a bar-room again, have you? And yet I have begged you all a thousand times not to do so! [He goes up to the table] There, you see, you have spilt vodka all over my papers and scattered crumbs and cucumbers everywhere! It is disgusting!

LEBEDIEFF.

I beg your pardon, Nicholas. Please forgive me. I have something very important to speak to you about.

BORKIN.

So have I.

LVOFF.

May I have a word with you?

IVANOFF.

[Pointing to LEBEDIEFF] He wants to speak to me; wait a minute. [To LEBEDIEFF] Well, what is it?

LEBEDIEFF.

[To the others] Excuse me, ladies and gentlemen, I want to speak to him in private.

SHABELSKI goes out, followed by AVDOTIA, BORKIN, and LVOFF.

IVANOFF.

Paul, you may drink yourself as much as you choose, it is your weakness, but I must ask you not to make my uncle tipsy. He never used to drink at all; it is bad for him.

LEBEDIEFF.

[Startled] My dear boy, I didn't know that! I wasn't thinking of him at all.

IVANOFF.

If this old baby should die on my hands the blame would be mine, not yours. Now, what do you want? [A pause.]

LEBEDIEFF.

The fact is, Nicholas—I really don't know how I can put it to make it seem less brutal—Nicholas, I am ashamed of myself, I am blushing, my tongue sticks to the roof of my mouth. My dear boy, put yourself in my place; remember that I am not a free man, I am as putty in the hands of my wife, a slave—forgive me!

IVANOFF.

What does this mean?

LEBEDIEFF.

My wife has sent me to you; do me a favour, be a friend to me, pay her the interest on the money you owe her. Believe me, she has been tormenting me and going for me tooth and nail. For heaven's sake, free yourself from her clutches!

IVANOFF.

You know, Paul, that I have no money now.

LEBEDIEFF.

I know, I know, but what can I do? She won't wait. If she should sue you for the money, how could Sasha and I ever look you in the face again?

IVANOFF.

I am ready to sink through the floor with shame, Paul, but where, where shall I get the money? Tell me, where? There is nothing I can do but to wait until I sell my wheat in the autumn.

LEBEDIEFF.

[Shrieks] But she won't wait! [A pause.]

IVANOFF.

Your position is very delicate and unpleasant, but mine is even worse. [He walks up and down in deep thought] I am at my wit's end, there is nothing I can sell now.

LEBEDIEFF.

You might go to Mulbach and get some money from him; doesn't he owe you sixty thousand roubles?

IVANOFF makes a despairing gesture.

LEBEDIEFF.

Listen to me, Nicholas, I know you will be angry, but you must forgive an old drunkard like me. This is between friends; remember I am your friend. We were students together, both Liberals; we had the same interests and ideals; we studied together at the University of Moscow. It is our Alma Mater. [He takes out his purse] I have a private fund here; not a soul at home knows of its existence. Let me lend it to you. [He takes out the money and lays it on the table] Forget your pride; this is between friends! I should take it from you, indeed I should! [A pause] There is the money, one hundred thousand roubles. Take it; go to her yourself and say: "Take the money, Zinaida, and may you choke on it." Only, for heaven's sake, don't let her see by your manner that you got it from me, or she would certainly go for me, with her old jam! [He looks intently into IVANOFF'S face] There, there, no matter. [He quickly takes up the money and stuffs it back into his pocket] Don't take it, I was only joking. Forgive me! Are you hurt?

IVANOFF waves his hand.

LEBEDIEFF.

Yes, the truth is—[He sighs] This is a time of sorrow and pain for you. A man, brother, is like a samovar; he cannot always stand coolly on a shelf; hot coals will be dropped into him some day, and then—fizz! The comparison is idiotic, but it is the best I can think of. [Sighing] Misfortunes wring the soul, and yet I am not worried about you, brother. Wheat goes through the mill, and comes out as flour, and you will come safely through your troubles; but I am annoyed, Nicholas, and angry with the people around you. The whole countryside is buzzing with gossip; where does it all start? They say you will be soon arrested for your debts, that you are a bloodthirsty murderer, a monster of cruelty, a robber.

IVANOFF.

All that is nothing to me; my head is aching.

LEBEDIEFF.

Because you think so much.

IVANOFF.

I never think.

LEBEDIEFF.

Come, Nicholas, snap your fingers at the whole thing, and drive over to visit us. Sasha loves and understands you. She is a sweet, honest, lovely girl; too good to be the child of her mother and me! Sometimes, when

I look at her, I cannot believe that such a treasure could belong to a fat old drunkard like me. Go to her, talk to her, and let her cheer you. She is a good, true-hearted girl.

IVANOFF.
Paul, my dear friend, please go, and leave me alone.

LEBEDIEFF.
I understand, I understand! [He glances at his watch] Yes, I understand. [He kisses IVANOFF] Good-bye, I must go to the blessing of the school now. [He goes as far as the door, then stops] She is so clever! Sasha and I were talking about gossiping yesterday, and she flashed out this epigram: "Father," she said, "fire-flies shine at night so that the night-birds may make them their prey, and good people are made to be preyed upon by gossips and slanderers." What do you think of that? She is a genius, another George Sand!

IVANOFF.
[Stopping him as he goes out] Paul, what is the matter with me?

LEBEDIEFF.
I have wanted to ask you that myself, but I must confess I was ashamed to. I don't know, old chap. Sometimes I think your troubles have been too heavy for you, and yet I know you are not the kind to give in to them; you would not be overcome by misfortune. It must be something else, Nicholas, but what it may be I can't imagine.

IVANOFF.
I can't imagine either what the matter is, unless—and yet no—[A pause] Well, do you see, this is what I wanted to say. I used to have a workman called Simon, you remember him. Once, at threshing-time, to show the girls how strong he was, he loaded himself with two sacks of rye, and broke his back. He died soon after. I think I have broken my back also. First I went to school, then to the university, then came the cares of this estate, all my plans—I did not believe what others did; did not marry as others did; I worked passionately, risked everything; no one else, as you know, threw their money away to right and left as I did. So I heaped the burdens on my back, and it broke. We are all heroes at twenty, ready to attack anything, to do everything, and at thirty are worn-out, useless men. How, oh, how do you account for this weariness? However, I may be quite wrong; go away, Paul, I am boring you.

LEBEDIEFF.

    I know what is the matter with you, old man: you got out of bed on the wrong side this morning.

IVANOFF.

    That is stupid, Paul, and stale. Go away!

LEBEDIEFF.

    It is stupid, certainly. I see that myself now. I am going at once. [LEBEDIEFF goes out.]

IVANOFF.

    [Alone] I am a worthless, miserable, useless man. Only a man equally miserable and suffering, as Paul is, could love or esteem me now. Good God! How I loathe myself! How bitterly I hate my voice, my hands, my thoughts, these clothes, each step I take! How ridiculous it is, how disgusting! Less than a year ago I was healthy and strong, full of pride and energy and enthusiasm. I worked with these hands here, and my words could move the dullest man to tears. I could weep with sorrow, and grow indignant at the sight of wrong. I could feel the glow of inspiration, and understand the beauty and romance of the silent nights which I used to watch through from evening until dawn, sitting at my worktable, and giving up my soul to dreams. I believed in a bright future then, and looked into it as trustfully as a child looks into its mother's eyes. And now, oh, it is terrible! I am tired and without hope; I spend my days and nights in idleness; I have no control over my feet or brain. My estate is ruined, my woods are falling under the blows of the axe. [He weeps] My neglected land looks up at me as reproachfully as an orphan. I expect nothing, am sorry for nothing; my whole soul trembles at the thought of each new day. And what can I think of my treatment of Sarah? I promised her love and happiness forever; I opened her eyes to the promise of a future such as she had never even dreamed of. She believed me, and though for five years I have seen her sinking under the weight of her sacrifices to me, and losing her strength in her struggles with her conscience, God knows she has never given me one angry look, or uttered one word of reproach. What is the result? That I don't love her! Why? Is it possible? Can it be true? I can't understand. She is suffering; her days are numbered; yet I fly like a contemptible coward from her white face, her sunken chest, her pleading eyes. Oh, I am ashamed, ashamed! [A pause] Sasha, a young girl, is sorry for me in my misery. She confesses to me that she loves me; me, almost an old man! Whereupon I lose my head, and exalted as if by music, I yell: "Hurrah for a new life and new happiness!" Next day I believe in this new life and happiness as little as I believe in my happiness at home. What is the matter with me? What is this pit I am wallowing in? What is the cause of this weakness? What does this nervousness come from? If my sick wife wounds my pride, if a servant makes a mistake, if my gun misses fire, I lose my temper and get violent and altogether unlike myself. I can't, I can't understand it; the easiest way out would be a bullet through the head!

Enter LVOFF.

LVOFF.
I must have an explanation with you, Ivanoff.

IVANOFF.
If we are going to have an explanation every day, doctor, we shall neither of us have the strength to stand it.

LVOFF.
Will you be good enough to hear me?

IVANOFF.
I have heard all you have told me every day, and have failed to discover yet what you want me to do.

LVOFF.
I have always spoken plainly enough, and only an utterly heartless and cruel man could fail to understand me.

IVANOFF.
I know that my wife is dying; I know that I have sinned irreparably; I know that you are an honest man. What more can you tell me?

LVOFF.
The sight of human cruelty maddens me. The woman is dying and she has a mother and father whom she loves, and longs to see once more before she dies. They know that she is dying and that she loves them still, but with diabolical cruelty, as if to flaunt their religious zeal, they refuse to see her and forgive her. You are the man for whom she has sacrificed her home, her peace of mind, everything. Yet you unblushingly go gadding to the Lebedieffs' every evening, for reasons that are absolutely unmistakable!

IVANOFF.

Ah me, it is two weeks since I was there!

LVOFF.

[Not listening to him] To men like yourself one must speak plainly, and if you don't want to hear what I have to say, you need not listen. I always call a spade a spade; the truth is, you want her to die so that the way may be cleared for your other schemes. Be it so; but can't you wait? If, instead of crushing the life out of your wife by your heartless egoism, you let her die naturally, do you think you would lose Sasha and Sasha's money? Such an absolute Tartuffe as you are could turn the girl's head and get her money a year from now as easily as you can to-day. Why are you in such a hurry? Why do you want your wife to die now, instead of in a month's time, or a year's?

IVANOFF.

This is torture! You are a very bad doctor if you think a man can control himself forever. It is all I can do not to answer your insults.

LVOFF.

Look here, whom are you trying to deceive? Throw off this disguise!

IVANOFF.

You who are so clever, you think that nothing in the world is easier than to understand me, do you? I married Annie for her money, did I? And when her parents wouldn't give it to me, I changed my plans, and am now hustling her out of the world so that I may marry another woman, who will bring me what I want? You think so, do you? Oh, how easy and simple it all is! But you are mistaken, doctor; in each one of us there are too many springs, too many wheels and cogs for us to judge each other by first impressions or by two or three external indications. I can not understand you, you cannot understand me, and neither of us can understand himself. A man may be a splendid doctor, and at the same time a very bad judge of human nature; you will admit that, unless you are too self-confident.

LVOFF.

Do you really think that your character is so mysterious, and that I am too stupid to tell vice from virtue?

IVANOFF.

It is clear that we shall never agree, so let me beg you to answer me now without any more preamble: exactly what do you want me to do? [Angrily] What are you after anyway? And with whom have I the honour of speaking? With my lawyer, or with my wife's doctor?

LVOFF.
I am a doctor, and as such I demand that you change your conduct toward your wife; it is killing her.

IVANOFF.
What shall I do? Tell me! If you understand me so much better than I understand myself, for heaven's sake tell me exactly what to do!

LVOFF.
In the first place, don't be so unguarded in your behaviour.

IVANOFF.
Heaven help me, do you mean to say that you understand yourself? [He drinks some water] Now go away; I am guilty a thousand times over; I shall answer for my sins before God; but nothing has given you the right to torture me daily as you do.

LVOFF.
Who has given you the right to insult my sense of honour? You have maddened and poisoned my soul. Before I came to this place I knew that stupid, crazy, deluded people existed, but I never imagined that any one could be so criminal as to turn his mind deliberately in the direction of wickedness. I loved and esteemed humanity then, but since I have known you—

IVANOFF.
I have heard all that before.

LVOFF.
You have, have you?

He goes out, shrugging his shoulders. He sees SASHA, *who comes in at this moment dressed for riding.*

LVOFF.
Now, however, I hope that we can understand one another!

IVANOFF.
[Startled] Oh, Sasha, is that you?

SASHA.
Yes, it is I. How are you? You didn't expect me, did you? Why haven't you been to see us?

IVANOFF.
Sasha, this is really imprudent of you! Your coming will have a terrible effect on my wife!

SASHA.
She won't see me; I came in by the back entrance; I shall go in a minute. I am so anxious about you. Tell me, are you well? Why haven't you been to see us for such a long time?

IVANOFF.
My wife is offended already, and almost dying, and now you come here; Sasha, Sasha, this is thoughtless and unkind of you.

SASHA.
How could I help coming? It is two weeks since you were at our house, and you have not answered my letters. I imagined you suffering dreadfully, or ill, or dead. I have not slept for nights. I am going now, but first tell me that you are well.

IVANOFF.
No, I am not well. I am a torment to myself, and every one torments me without end. I can't stand it! And now you come here. How morbid and unnatural it all is, Sasha. I am terribly guilty.

SASHA.
What dreadful, pitiful speeches you make! So you are guilty, are you? Tell me, then, what is it you have done?

IVANOFF I don't know; I don't know!

SASHA.
That is no answer. Every sinner should know what he is guilty of. Perhaps you have been forging money?

IVANOFF.
That is stupid.

SASHA.
Or are you guilty because you no longer love your wife? Perhaps you are, but no one is master of his feelings, and you did not mean to stop loving her. Do you feel guilty because she saw me telling you that I love you? No, that cannot be, because you did not want her to see it—

IVANOFF.
[Interrupting her] And so on, and so on! First you say I love, and then

you say I don't; that I am not master of my feelings. All these are commonplace, worn-out sentiments, with which you cannot help me.

SASHA.
It is impossible to talk to you. [She looks at a picture on the wall] How well those dogs are drawn! Were they done from life?

IVANOFF.
Yes, from life. And this whole romance of ours is a tedious old story; a man loses heart and begins to go down in the world; a girl appears, brave and strong of heart, and gives him a hand to help him to rise again. Such situations are pretty, but they are only found in novels and not in real life.

SASHA.
No, they are found in real life too.

IVANOFF.
Now I see how well you understand real life! My sufferings seem noble to you; you imagine you have discovered in me a second Hamlet; but my state of mind in all its phases is only fit to furnish food for contempt and derision. My contortions are ridiculous enough to make any one die of laughter, and you want to play the guardian angel; you want to do a noble deed and save me. Oh, how I hate myself to-day! I feel that this tension must soon be relieved in some way. Either I shall break something, or else—

SASHA.
That is exactly what you need. Let yourself go! Smash something; break it to pieces; give a yell! You are angry with me, it was foolish of me to come here. Very well, then, get excited about it; storm at me; stamp your feet! Well, aren't you getting angry?

IVANOFF.
You ridiculous girl!

SASHA.
Splendid! So we are smiling at last! Be kind, do me the favour of smiling once more!

IVANOFF.
[Laughing] I have noticed that whenever you start reforming me and saving my soul, and teaching me how to be good, your face grows naive, oh so naive, and your eyes grow as wide as if you were looking

at a comet. Wait a moment; your shoulder is covered with dust. [He brushes her shoulder] A naive man is nothing better than a fool, but you women contrive to be naive in such a way that in you it seems sweet, and gentle, and proper, and not as silly as it really is. What a strange way you have, though, of ignoring a man as long as he is well and happy, and fastening yourselves to him as soon as he begins to whine and go down-hill! Do you actually think it is worse to be the wife of a strong man than to nurse some whimpering invalid?

SASHA.
Yes, it is worse.

IVANOFF.
Why do you think so? [Laughing loudly] It is a good thing Darwin can't hear what you are saying! He would be furious with you for degrading the human race. Soon, thanks to your kindness, only invalids and hypochondriacs will be born into the world.

SASHA.
There are a great many things a man cannot understand. Any girl would rather love an unfortunate man than a fortunate one, because every girl would like to do something by loving. A man has his work to do, and so for him love is kept in the background. To talk to his wife, to walk with her in the garden, to pass the time pleasantly with her, that is all that love means to a man. But for us, love means life. I love you; that means that I dream only of how I shall cure you of your sadness, how I shall go with you to the ends of the earth. If you are in heaven, I am in heaven; if you are in the pit, I am in the pit. For instance, it would be the greatest happiness for me to write all night for you, or to watch all night that no one should wake you. I remember that three years ago, at threshing time, you came to us all dusty and sunburnt and tired, and asked for a drink. When I brought you a glass of water you were already lying on the sofa and sleeping like a dead man. You slept there for half a day, and all that time I watched by the door that no one should disturb you. How happy I was! The more a girl can do, the greater her love will be; that is, I mean, the more she feels it.

IVANOFF.
The love that accomplishes things—hm—that is a fairy tale, a girl's dream; and yet, perhaps it is as it should be. [He shrugs his shoulders] How

can I tell? [Gaily] On my honour, Sasha, I really am quite a respectable man. Judge for yourself: I have always liked to discuss things, but I have never in my life said that our women were corrupt, or that such and such a woman was on the down-hill path. I have always been grateful, and nothing more. No, nothing more. Dear child, how comical you are! And what a ridiculous old stupid I am! I shock all good Christian folk, and go about complaining from morning to night. [He laughs and then leaves her suddenly] But you must go, Sasha; we have forgotten ourselves.

SASHA.
Yes, it is time to go. Good-bye. I am afraid that that honest doctor of yours will have told Anna out of a sense of duty that I am here. Take my advice: go at once to your wife and stay with her. Stay, and stay, and stay, and if it should be for a year, you must still stay, or for ten years. It is your duty. You must repent, and ask her forgiveness, and weep. That is what you ought to do, and the great thing is not to forget to do right.

IVANOFF.
Again I feel as if I were going crazy; again!

SASHA.
Well, heaven help you! You must forget me entirely. In two weeks you must send me a line and I shall be content with that. But I shall write to you—

BORKIN looks in at the door.

BORKIN.
Ivanoff, may I come in? [He sees SASHA] I beg your pardon, I did not see you. Bonjour! [He bows.]

SASHA.
[Embarrassed] How do you do?

BORKIN.
You are plumper and prettier than ever.

SASHA.
[To IVANOFF] I must go, Nicholas, I must go. [She goes out.]

BORKIN.
What a beautiful apparition! I came expecting prose and found poetry instead. [Sings]
"You showed yourself to the world as a bird——"

IVANOFF walks excitedly up and down.

BORKIN.

[Sits down] There is something in her, Nicholas, that one doesn't find in other women, isn't there? An elfin strangeness. [He sighs] Although she is without doubt the richest girl in the country, her mother is so stingy that no one will have her. After her mother's death Sasha will have the whole fortune, but until then she will only give her ten thousand roubles and an old flat-iron, and to get that she will have to humble herself to the ground. [He feels in his pockets] Will you have a smoke? [He offers IVANOFF his cigarette case] These are very good.

IVANOFF.

[Comes toward BORKIN stifled with rage] Leave my house this instant, and don't you ever dare to set foot in it again! Go this instant! BORKIN gets up and drops his cigarette.

IVANOFF.

Go at once!

BORKIN.

Nicholas, what do you mean? Why are you so angry?

IVANOFF.

Why! Where did you get those cigarettes? Where? You think perhaps that I don't know where you take the old man every day, and for what purpose?

BORKIN.

[Shrugs his shoulders] What business is it of yours?

IVANOFF.

You blackguard, you! The disgraceful rumours that you have been spreading about me have made me disreputable in the eyes of the whole countryside. You and I have nothing in common, and I ask you to leave my house this instant.

BORKIN.

I know that you are saying all this in a moment of irritation, and so I am not angry with you. Insult me as much as you please. [He picks up his cigarette] It is time though, to shake off this melancholy of yours; you're not a schoolboy.

IVANOFF.

What did I tell you? [Shuddering] Are you making fun of me?
Enter ANNA.

BORKIN.
>   There now, there comes Anna! I shall go.
>
>   IVANOFF stops near the table and stands with his head bowed.

ANNA.
>   [After a pause] What did she come here for? What did she come here for, I ask you?

IVANOFF.
>   Don't ask me, Annie. [A pause] I am terribly guilty. Think of any punishment you want to inflict on me; I can stand anything, but don't, oh, don't ask questions!

ANNA.
>   [Angrily] So that is the sort of man you are? Now I understand you, and can see how degraded, how dishonourable you are! Do you remember that you came to me once and lied to me about your love? I believed you, and left my mother, my father, and my faith to follow you. Yes, you lied to me of goodness and honour, of your noble aspirations and I believed every word——

IVANOFF.
>   I have never lied to you, Annie.

ANNA.
>   I have lived with you five years now, and I am tired and ill, but I have always loved you and have never left you for a moment. You have been my idol, and what have you done? All this time you have been deceiving me in the most dastardly way——

IVANOFF.
>   Annie, don't say what isn't so. I have made mistakes, but I have never told a lie in my life. You dare not accuse me of that!

ANNA.
>   It is all clear to me now. You married me because you expected my mother and father to forgive me and give you my money; that is what you expected.

IVANOFF.
>   Good Lord, Annie! If I must suffer like this, I must have the patience to bear it. [He begins to weep.]

ANNA.
>   Be quiet! When you found that I wasn't bringing you any money, you

tried another game. Now I remember and understand everything. [She begins to cry] You have never loved me or been faithful to me—never!

IVANOFF.
Sarah! That is a lie! Say what you want, but don't insult me with a lie!

ANNA.
You dishonest, degraded man! You owe money to Lebedieff, and now, to escape paying your debts, you are trying to turn the head of his daughter and betray her as you have betrayed me. Can you deny it?

IVANOFF.
[Stifled with rage] For heaven's sake, be quiet! I can't answer for what I may do! I am choking with rage and I—I might insult you!

ANNA.
I am not the only one whom you have basely deceived. You have always blamed Borkin for all your dishonest tricks, but now I know whose they are.

IVANOFF.
Sarah, stop at once and go away, or else I shall say something terrible. I long to say a dreadful, cruel thing [He shrieks] Hold your tongue, Jewess!

ANNA.
I won't hold my tongue! You have deceived me too long for me to be silent now.

IVANOFF.
So you won't be quiet? [He struggles with himself] Go, for heaven's sake!

ANNA.
Go now, and betray Sasha!

IVANOFF.
Know then that you—are dying! The doctor told me that you are dying.

ANNA.
[Sits down and speaks in a low voice] When did he

IVANOFF.
[Clutches his head with both hands] Oh, how guilty I am—how guilty! [He sobs.]

The curtain falls.

About a year passes between the third and fourth acts.

ACT IV

A sitting-room in LEBEDIEFF'S house. In the middle of the wall at the back of the room is an arch dividing the sitting-room from the ballroom. To the right and left are doors. Some old bronzes are placed about the room; family portraits are hanging on the walls. Everything is arranged as if for some festivity. On the piano lies a violin; near it stands a violoncello. During the entire act guests, dressed as for a ball, are seen walking about in the ball-room.

Enter LVOFF, looking at his watch.

LVOFF.

It is five o'clock. The ceremony must have begun. First the priest will bless them, and then they will be led to the church to be married. Is this how virtue and justice triumph? Not being able to rob Sarah, he has tortured her to death; and now he has found another victim whom he will deceive until he has robbed her, and then he will get rid of her as he got rid of poor Sarah. It is the same old sordid story. [A pause] He will live to a fine old age in the seventh heaven of happiness, and will die with a clear conscience. No, Ivanoff, it shall not be! I shall drag your villainy to light! And when I tear off that accursed mask of yours and show you to the world as the blackguard you are, you shall come plunging down headfirst from your seventh heaven, into a pit so deep that the devil himself will not be able to drag you out of it! I am a man of honour; it is my duty to interfere in such cases as yours, and to open the eyes of the blind. I shall fulfil my mission, and to-morrow will find me far away from this accursed place. [Thoughtfully] But what shall I do? To have an explanation with Lebedieff would be a hopeless task. Shall I make a scandal, and challenge Ivanoff to a duel? I am as excited as a child, and have entirely lost the power of planning anything. What shall I do? Shall I fight a duel?

Enter KOSICH. He goes gaily up to LVOFF.

KOSICH.

I declared a little slam in clubs yesterday, and made a grand slam! Only that man Barabanoff spoilt the whole game for me again. We were playing—well, I said "No trumps" and he said "Pass." "Two in clubs," he passed again. I made it two in hearts. He said "Three in clubs," and just imagine, can you, what happened? I declared a little slam and he never showed his ace! If he had showed his ace, the villain, I should have declared a grand slam in no trumps!

LVOFF.

Excuse me, I don't play cards, and so it is impossible for me to share your enthusiasm. When does the ceremony begin?

KOSICH.

At once, I think. They are now bringing Zuzu to herself again. She is bellowing like a bull; she can't bear to see the money go.

LVOFF.

And what about the daughter?

KOSICH.

No, it is the money. She doesn't like this affair anyway. He is marrying her daughter, and that means he won't pay his debts for a long time. One can't sue one's son-in-law.

MARTHA, very much dressed up, struts across the stage past LVOFF and KOSICH. The latter bursts out laughing behind his hand. MARTHA looks around.

MARTHA.
   Idiot!
   KOSICH digs her in the ribs and laughs loudly.
MARTHA.
   Boor!
KOSICH.
   [Laughing] The woman's head has been turned. Before she fixed her eye on a title she was like any other woman, but there is no coming near her now! [Angrily] A boor, indeed!
LVOFF.
   [Excitedly] Listen to me; tell me honestly, what do you think of Ivanoff?
KOSICH.
   He's no good at all. He plays cards like a lunatic. This is what happened last year during Lent: I, the Count, Borkin and he, sat down to a game of cards. I led a——
   LVOFF [Interrupting him] Is he a good man?
KOSICH.
   He? Yes, he's a good one! He and the Count are a pair of trumps. They have keen noses for a good game. First, Ivanoff set his heart on the Jewess, then, when his schemes failed in that quarter, he turned his thoughts toward Zuzu's money-bags. I'll wager you he'll ruin Zuzu in a year. He will ruin Zuzu, and the Count will ruin Martha. They will gather up all the money they can lay hands on, and live happily ever after! But, doctor, why are you so pale to-day? You look like a ghost.
LVOFF.
   Oh, it's nothing. I drank a little too much yesterday.
   Enter LEBEDIEFF with SASHA.
LEBEDIEFF.
   We can have our talk here. [To LVOFF and KOSICH] Go into the ball-room, you two old fogies, and talk to the girls. Sasha and I want to talk alone here.
KOSICH.
   [Snapping his fingers enthusiastically as he goes by SASHA] What a picture! A queen of trumps!

LEBEDIEFF.

Go along, you old cave-dweller; go along.

KOSICH and LVOFF go out.

LEBEDIEFF.

Sit down, Sasha, there—[He sits down and looks about him] Listen to me attentively and with proper respect. The fact is, your mother has asked me to say this, do you understand? I am not speaking for myself. Your mother told me to speak to you.

SASHA.

Papa, do say it briefly!

LEBEDIEFF.

When you are married we mean to give you fifteen thousand roubles. Please don't let us have any discussion about it afterward. Wait, now! Be quiet! That is only the beginning. The best is yet to come. We have allotted you fifteen thousand roubles, but in consideration of the fact that Nicholas owes your mother nine thousand, that sum will have to be deducted from the amount we mean to give you. Very well. Now, beside that——

SASHA.

Why do you tell me all this?

LEBEDIEFF.

Your mother told me to.

SASHA.

Leave me in peace! If you had any respect for yourself or me you could not permit yourself to speak to me in this way. I don't want your money! I have not asked for it, and never shall.

LEBEDIEFF.

What are you attacking me for? The two rats in Gogol's fable sniffed first and then ran away, but you attack without even sniffing.

SASHA.

Leave me in peace, and do not offend my ears with your two-penny calculations.

LEBEDIEFF.

[Losing his temper] Bah! You all, every one of you, do all you can to make me cut my throat or kill somebody. One of you screeches and fusses all day and counts every penny, and the other is so clever and humane and emancipated that she cannot understand her own father! I offend your ears, do I? Don't you realise that before I came here to offend your ears I was being torn to pieces over there, [He points to the door] literally drawn and quartered? So you cannot understand? You two have addled my brain till I am utterly at my wits' end; indeed I am! [He goes toward the door, and stops] I don't like this business at all; I don't like any thing about you—

SASHA.

What is it, especially, that you don't like?

LEBEDIEFF.

Everything, everything!

SASHA.

What do you mean by everything?

LEBEDIEFF.

Let me explain exactly what I mean. Everything displeases me. As for your marriage, I simply can't abide it. [He goes up to SASHA and speaks caressingly] Forgive me, little Sasha, this marriage may be a wise one; it may be honest and not misguided, nevertheless, there is something about the whole affair that is not right; no, not right! You are not marrying as other girls do; you are young and fresh and pure as a drop of water, and he is a widower, battered and worn. Heaven help him. I don't understand him at all. [He kisses his daughter] Forgive me for saying so, Sasha, but I am sure there is something crooked about this affair; it is making a great deal of talk. It seems people are saying that first Sarah died, and then suddenly Ivanoff wanted to marry you. [Quickly] But, no, I am like an old woman; I am gossiping like a magpie. You must not listen to me or any one, only to your own heart.

SASHA.

Papa, I feel myself that there is something wrong about my marriage. Something wrong, yes, wrong! Oh, if you only knew how heavy my heart is; this is unbearable! I am frightened and ashamed to confess this; Papa darling, you must help me, for heaven's sake. Oh, can't you tell me what I should do?

LEBEDIEFF.

What is the matter, Sasha, what is it?

SASHA.

I am so frightened, more frightened than I have ever been before. [She glances around her] I cannot understand him now, and I never shall. He has not smiled or looked straight into my eyes once since we have been engaged. He is forever complaining and apologising for something; hinting at some crime he is guilty of, and trembling. I am so tired! There are even moments when I think—I think—that I do not love him as I should, and when he comes to see us, or talks to me, I get so tired! What does it mean, dear father? I am afraid.

LEBEDIEFF.

My darling, my only child, do as your old father advises you; give him up!

SASHA.

[Frightened] Oh! How can you say that?

LEBEDIEFF.

Yes, do it, little Sasha! It will make a scandal, all the tongues in the country will be wagging about it, but it is better to live down a scandal than to ruin one's life.

SASHA.

Don't say that, father. Oh, don't. I refuse to listen! I must crush such gloomy thoughts. He is good and unhappy and misunderstood. I shall love him and learn to understand him. I shall set him on his feet again. I shall do my duty. That is settled.

LEBEDIEFF.

This is not your duty, but a delusion—

SASHA.

We have said enough. I have confessed things to you that I have not dared to admit even to myself. Don't speak about this to any one. Let us forget it.

LEBEDIEFF.

I am hopelessly puzzled, and either my mind is going from old age or else you have all grown very clever, but I'll be hanged if I understand this business at all.

Enter SHABELSKI.

SHABELSKI.

Confound you all and myself, too! This is maddening!

LEBEDIEFF.

What do you want?

SHABELSKI Seriously, I must really do something horrid and rascally, so that not only I but everybody else will be disgusted by it. I certainly shall find something to do, upon my word I shall! I have already told Borkin to announce that I am to be married. [He laughs] Everybody is a scoundrel and I must be one too!

LEBEDIEFF.

I am tired of you, Matthew. Look here, man you talk in such a way that, excuse my saying so, you will soon find yourself in a lunatic asylum!

SHABELSKI.

Could a lunatic asylum possibly be worse than this house, or any other? Kindly take me there at once. Please do! Everybody is wicked and futile and worthless and stupid; I am an object of disgust to myself, I don't believe a word I say——

LEBEDIEFF.

Let me give you a piece of advice, old man; fill your mouth full of tow, light it, and blow at everybody. Or, better still, take your hat and go home. This is a wedding, we all want to enjoy ourselves and you are croaking like a raven. Yes, really.

SHABELSKI leans on the piano and begins to sob.

LEBEDIEFF.

Good gracious, Matthew, Count! What is it, dear Matthew, old friend? Have I offended you? There, forgive me; I didn't mean to hurt you. Come, drink some water.

SHABELSKI.

I don't want any water. [Raises his head.]

LEBEDIEFF.

What are you crying about?

SHABELSKI.

Nothing in particular; I was just crying.

LEBEDIEFF.

Matthew, tell me the truth, what is it? What has happened?

SHABELSKI.

I caught sight of that violoncello, and—and—I remembered the Jewess.

LEBEDIEFF.
What an unfortunate moment you have chosen to remember her. Peace be with her! But don't think of her now.
SHABELSKI.
We used to play duets together. She was a beautiful, a glorious woman.
SASHA sobs.
LEBEDIEFF.
What, are you crying too? Stop, Sasha! Dear me, they are both howling now, and I—and I—Do go away; the guests will see you!
SHABELSKI.
Paul, when the sun is shining, it is gay even in a cemetery. One can be cheerful even in old age if it is lighted by hope; but I have nothing to hope for—not a thing!
LEBEDIEFF.
Yes, it is rather sad for you. You have no children, no money, no occupation. Well, but what is there to be done about it? [To SASHA] What is the matter with you, Sasha?
SHABELSKI.
Paul, give me some money. I will repay you in the next world. I would go to Paris and see my wife's grave. I have given away a great deal of money in my life, half my fortune indeed, and I have a right to ask for some now. Besides, I am asking a friend.
LEBEDIEFF.
[Embarrassed] My dear boy, I haven't a penny. All right though. That is to say, I can't promise anything, but you understand—very well, very well. [Aside] This is agony!
Enter MARTHA.
MARTHA.
Where is my partner? Count, how dare you leave me alone? You are horrid! [She taps SHABELSKI on the arm with her fan]
SHABELSKI.
[Impatiently] Leave me alone! I can't abide you!
MARTHA.
[Frightened] How? What?
SHABELSKI.
Go away!

MARTHA.
  [Sinks into an arm-chair] Oh! Oh! Oh! [She bursts into tears.]
  Enter ZINAIDA crying.
ZINAIDA.
  Some one has just arrived; it must be one of the ushers. It is time for the ceremony to begin.
SASHA.
  [Imploringly] Mother!
LEBEDIEFF.
  Well, now you are all bawling. What a quartette! Come, come, don't let us have any more of this dampness! Matthew! Martha! If you go on like this, I—I—shall cry too. [Bursts into tears] Heavens!
ZINAIDA.
  If you don't need your mother any more, if you are determined not to obey her, I shall have to do as you want, and you have my blessing.
  Enter IVANOFF, dressed in a long coat, with gloves on.
  LEBEDIEFF This is the finishing touch! What do you want?
SHABELSKI.
  Why are you here?
IVANOFF.
  I beg your pardon, you must allow me to speak to Sasha alone.
LEBEDIEFF.
  The bridegroom must not come to see the bride before the wedding. It is time for you to go to the church.
IVANOFF.
  Paul, I implore you.
  LEBEDIEFF shrugs his shoulders. LEBEDIEFF, ZINAIDA, SHABELSKI, and MARTHA go out.
SASHA.
  [Sternly] What do you want?
IVANOFF.
  I am choking with anger; I cannot speak calmly. Listen to me; as I was dressing just now for the wedding, I looked in the glass and saw how grey my temples were. Sasha, this must not be! Let us end this senseless comedy before it is too late. You are young and pure; you have all your life before you, but I——

SASHA.

The same old story; I have heard it a thousand times and I am tired of it. Go quickly to the church and don't keep everybody waiting!

IVANOFF.

I shall go straight home, and you must explain to your family somehow that there is to be no wedding. Explain it as you please. It is time we came to our senses. I have been playing the part of Hamlet and you have been playing the part of a noble and devoted girl. We have kept up the farce long enough.

SASHA.

[Losing her temper] How can you speak to me like this? I won't have it.

IVANOFF.

But I am speaking, and will continue to speak.

SASHA.

What do you mean by coming to me like this? Your melancholy has become absolutely ridiculous!

IVANOFF.

No, this is not melancholy. It is ridiculous, is it? Yes, I am laughing, and if it were possible for me to laugh at myself a thousand times more bitterly I should do so and set the whole world laughing, too, in derision. A fierce light has suddenly broken over my soul; as I looked into the glass just now, I laughed at myself, and nearly went mad with shame. [He laughs] Melancholy indeed! Noble grief! Uncontrollable sorrow! It only remains for me now to begin to write verses! Shall I mope and complain, sadden everybody I meet, confess that my manhood has gone forever, that I have decayed, outlived my purpose, that I have given myself up to cowardice and am bound hand and foot by this loathsome melancholy? Shall I confess all this when the sun is shining so brightly and when even the ants are carrying their little burdens in peaceful self-content? No, thanks. Can I endure the knowledge that one will look upon me as a fraud, while another pities me, a third lends me a helping hand, or worst of all, a fourth listens reverently to my sighs, looks upon me as a new Mahomet, and expects me to expound a new religion every moment? No, thank God for the pride and conscience he has left me still. On my way here I laughed at myself, and it seemed to me that the flowers and birds were laughing mockingly too.

SASHA.

    This is not anger, but madness!

IVANOFF.

    You think so, do you? No, I am not mad. I see things in their right light now, and my mind is as clear as your conscience. We love each other, but we shall never be married. It makes no difference how I rave and grow bitter by myself, but I have no right to drag another down with me. My melancholy robbed my wife of the last year of her life. Since you have been engaged to me you have forgotten how to laugh and have aged five years. Your father, to whom life was always simple and clear, thanks to me, is now unable to understand anybody. Wherever I go, whether hunting or visiting, it makes no difference, I carry depression, dulness, and discontent along with me. Wait! Don't interrupt me! I am bitter and harsh, I know, but I am stifled with rage. I cannot speak otherwise. I have never lied, and I never used to find fault with my lot, but since I have begun to complain of everything, I find fault with it involuntarily, and against my will. When I murmur at my fate every one who hears me is seized with the same disgust of life and begins to grumble too. And what a strange way I have of looking at things! Exactly as if I were doing the world a favour by living in it. Oh, I am contemptible.

SASHA.

    Wait a moment. From what you have just said, it is obvious that you are tired of your melancholy mood, and that the time has come for you to begin life afresh. How splendid!

IVANOFF.

    I don't see anything splendid about it. How can I lead a new life? I am lost forever. It is time we both understood that. A new life indeed!

SASHA.

    Nicholas, come to your senses. How can you say you are lost? What do you mean by such cynicism? No, I won't listen to you or talk with you. Go to the church!

IVANOFF.

    I am lost!

SASHA.

    Don't talk so loud; our guests will hear you!

IVANOFF.

If an intelligent, educated, and healthy man begins to complain of his lot and go down-hill, there is nothing for him to do but to go on down until he reaches the bottom—there is no hope for him. Where could my salvation come from? How can I save myself? I cannot drink, because it makes my head ache. I never could write bad poetry. I cannot pray for strength and see anything lofty in the languor of my soul. Laziness is laziness and weakness weakness. I can find no other names for them. I am lost, I am lost; there is no doubt of that. [Looking around] Some one might come in; listen, Sasha, if you love me you must help me. Renounce me this minute; quickly!

SASHA.

Oh, Nicholas! If you only knew how you are torturing me; what agony I have to endure for your sake! Good thoughtful friend, judge for yourself; can I possibly solve such a problem? Each day you put some horrible problem before me, each one more difficult than the last. I wanted to help you with my love, but this is martyrdom!

IVANOFF.

And when you are my wife the problems will be harder than ever. Understand this: it is not love that is urging you to take this step, but the obstinacy of an honest nature. You have undertaken to reawaken the man in me and to save me in the face of every difficulty, and you are flattered by the hope of achieving your object. You are willing to give up now, but you are prevented from doing it by a feeling that is a false one. Understand yourself!

SASHA.

What strange, wild reasoning! How can I give you up now? How can I? You have no mother, or sister, or friends. You are ruined; your estate has been destroyed; every one is speaking ill of you—

IVANOFF.

It was foolish of me to come here; I should have done as I wanted to—

Enter LEBEDIEFF.

SASHA.

[Running to her father] Father! He has rushed over here like a madman, and is torturing me! He insists that I should refuse to marry him; he says he doesn't want to drag me down with him. Tell him that I won't accept his generosity. I know what I am doing!

LEBEDIEFF.
I can't understand a word of what you are saying. What generosity?

IVANOFF.
This marriage is not going to take place.

SASHA.
It is going to take place. Papa, tell him that it is going to take place.

LEBEDIEFF.
Wait! Wait! What objection have you to the marriage?

IVANOFF.
I have explained it all to her, but she refuses to understand me.

LEBEDIEFF.
Don't explain it to her, but to me, and explain it so that I may understand. God forgive you, Nicholas, you have brought a great deal of darkness into our lives. I feel as if I were living in a museum; I look about me and don't understand anything I see. This is torture. What on earth can an old man like me do with you? Shall I challenge you to a duel?

IVANOFF.
There is no need of a duel. All you need is a head on your shoulders and a knowledge of the Russian language.

SASHA.
[Walks up and down in great excitement] This is dreadful, dreadful! Absolutely childish.

LEBEDIEFF.
Listen to me, Nicholas; from your point of view what you are doing is quite right and proper, according to the rules of psychology, but I think this affair is a scandal and a great misfortune. I am an old man; hear me out for the last time. This is what I want to say to you: calm yourself; look at things simply, as every one else does; this is a simple world. The ceiling is white; your boots are black; sugar is sweet. You love Sasha and she loves you. If you love her, stay with her; if you don't, leave her. We shan't blame you. It is all perfectly simple. You are two healthy, intelligent, moral young people; thank God, you both

have food and clothing—what more do you want? What if you have no money? That is no great misfortune—happiness is not bought with wealth. Of course your estate is mortgaged, Nicholas, as I know, and you have no money to pay the interest on the debt, but I am Sasha's father. I understand. Her mother can do as she likes—if she won't give any money, why, confound her, then she needn't, that's all! Sasha has just said that she does not want her part of it. As for your principles, Schopenhauer and all that, it is all folly. I have one hundred thousand roubles in the bank. [Looking around him] Not a soul in the house knows it; it was my grandmother's money. That shall be for you both. Take it, give Matthew two thousand—

[The guests begin to collect in the ball-room].

IVANOFF.
It is no use discussing it any more, I must act as my conscience bids me.

SASHA.
And I shall act as my conscience bids me—you may say what you please; I refuse to let you go! I am going to call my mother.

LEBEDIEFF.
I am utterly puzzled.

IVANOFF.
Listen to me, poor old friend. I shall not try to explain myself to you. I shall not tell you whether I am honest or a rascal, healthy or mad; you wouldn't understand me. I was young once; I have been eager and sincere and intelligent. I have loved and hated and believed as no one else has. I have worked and hoped and tilted against windmills with the strength of ten—not sparing my strength, not knowing what life was. I shouldered a load that broke my back. I drank, I worked, I excited myself, my energy knew no bounds. Tell me, could I have done otherwise? There are so few of us and so much to do, so much to do! And see how cruelly fate has revenged herself on me, who fought with her so bravely! I am a broken man. I am old at thirty. I have submitted myself to old age. With a heavy head and a sluggish mind, weary, used up, discouraged, without faith or love or an object in life, I wander like a shadow among other men, not knowing why I am alive or what it is that I want. Love seems to me to be folly, caresses false. I see no sense in working or playing, and

all passionate speeches seem insipid and tiresome. So I carry my sadness with me wherever I go; a cold weariness, a discontent, a horror of life. Yes, I am lost for ever and ever. Before you stands a man who at thirty-five is disillusioned, wearied by fruitless efforts, burning with shame, and mocking at his own weakness. Oh, how my pride rebels against it all! What mad fury chokes me! [He staggers] I am staggering—my strength is failing me. Where is Matthew? Let him take me home.

[Voices from the ball-room] The best man has arrived!

Enter SHABELSKI.

SHABELSKI.

In an old worn-out coat—without gloves! How many scornful glances I get for it! Such silly jokes and vulgar grins! Disgusting people.

Enter BORKIN quickly. He is carrying a bunch of flowers and is in a dress-coat. He wears a flower in his buttonhole.

BORKIN.

This is dreadful! Where is he? [To IVANOFF] They have been waiting for you for a long time in the church, and here you are talking philosophy! What a funny chap you are. Don't you know you must not go to church with the bride, but alone, with me? I shall then come back for her. Is it possible you have not understood that? You certainly are an extraordinary man!

Enter LVOFF.

LVOFF.

[To IVANOFF] Ah! So you are here? [Loudly] Nicholas Ivanoff, I denounce you to the world as a scoundrel!

IVANOFF.

[Coldly] Many thanks!

BORKIN.

[To LVOFF] Sir, this is dastardly! I challenge you to a duel!

LVOFF.

Monsieur Borkin, I count it a disgrace not only to fight with you, but even to talk to you! Monsieur Ivanoff, however, can receive satisfaction from me whenever he chooses!

SHABELSKI.

Sir, I shall fight you!

SASHA.

[To LVOFF] Why, oh why, have you insulted him? Gentlemen, I beg you, let him tell me why he has insulted him.

LVOFF.

Miss Sasha, I have not insulted him without cause. I came here as a man of honour, to open your eyes, and I beg you to listen to what I have to tell you.

SASHA.

What can you possibly have to tell me? That you are a man of honour? The whole world knows it. You had better tell me on your honour whether you understand what you have done or not. You have come in here as a man of honour and have insulted him so terribly that you have nearly killed me. When you used to follow him like a shadow and almost keep him from living, you were convinced that you were doing your duty and that you were acting like a man of honour. When you interfered in his private affairs, maligned him and criticised him; when you sent me and whomever else you could, anonymous letters, you imagined yourself to be an honourable man! And, thinking that that too was honourable, you, a doctor, did not even spare his dying wife or give her a moment's peace from your suspicions. And no matter what violence, what cruel wrong you committed, you still imagined yourself to be an unusually honourable and clear-sighted man.

IVANOFF.

[Laughing] This is not a wedding, but a parliament! Bravo! Bravo!

SASHA.

[To LVOFF] Now, think it over! Do you see what sort of a man you are, or not? Oh, the stupid, heartless people! [Takes IVANOFF by the hand] Come away from here Nicholas! Come, father, let us go!

IVANOFF.

Where shall we go? Wait a moment. I shall soon put an end to the whole thing. My youth is awake in me again; the former Ivanoff is here once more.

[He takes out a revolver.]

SASHA.

[Shrieking] I know what he wants to do! Nicholas, for God's sake!

IVANOFF.
I have been slipping down-hill long enough. Now, halt! It is time to know what honour is. Out of the way! Thank you, Sasha!
SASHA.
[Shrieking] Nicholas! For God's sake hold him!
IVANOFF.
Let go! [He rushes aside, and shoots himself.]

The curtain falls.

THE THREE SISTERS

Translated by Julius West

THE THREE SISTERS

Translated by Julius West

Characters

ANDREY SERGEYEVITCH PROSOROV
NATALIA IVANOVA (NATASHA), his fiancée, later his wife (28)
His sisters:
OLGA
MASHA
IRINA
FEODOR ILITCH KULIGIN, high school teacher, married to MASHA (20)
ALEXANDER IGNATEYEVITCH VERSHININ, lieutenant-colonel in charge of a battery (42)
NICOLAI LVOVITCH TUZENBACH, baron, lieutenant in the army (30)
VASSILI VASSILEVITCH SOLENI, captain
IVAN ROMANOVITCH CHEBUTIKIN, army doctor (60)
ALEXEY PETROVITCH FEDOTIK, sub-lieutenant
VLADIMIR CARLOVITCH RODE, sub-lieutenant
FERAPONT, door-keeper at local council offices, an old man
ANFISA, nurse (80)
The action takes place in a provincial town.
[Ages are stated in brackets.]

ACT I

In PROSOROV'S house. A sitting-room with pillars; behind is seen a large dining-room. It is midday, the sun is shining brightly outside. In the dining-room the table is being laid for lunch.

[OLGA, in the regulation blue dress of a teacher at a girl's high school, is walking about correcting exercise books; MASHA, in a black dress, with a hat on her knees, sits and reads a book; IRINA, in white, stands about, with a thoughtful expression.]

OLGA.
It's just a year since father died last May the fifth, on your name-day, Irina. It was very cold then, and snowing. I thought I would never survive it, and you were in a dead faint. And now a year has gone by and we are already thinking about it without pain, and you are wearing a white dress and your face is happy. [Clock strikes twelve] And the clock struck just the same way then. [Pause] I remember that there was music at the funeral, and they fired a volley in the cemetery. He was a general in

command of a brigade but there were few people present. Of course, it was raining then, raining hard, and snowing.

IRINA.

Why think about it!

[BARON TUZENBACH, CHEBUTIKIN and SOLENI appear by the table in the dining-room, behind the pillars.]

OLGA.

It's so warm to-day that we can keep the windows open, though the birches are not yet in flower. Father was put in command of a brigade, and he rode out of Moscow with us eleven years ago. I remember perfectly that it was early in May and that everything in Moscow was flowering then. It was warm too, everything was bathed in sunshine. Eleven years have gone, and I remember everything as if we rode out only yesterday. Oh, God! When I awoke this morning and saw all the light and the spring, joy entered my heart, and I longed passionately to go home.

CHEBUTIKIN.

Will you take a bet on it?

TUZENBACH.

Oh, nonsense.

[MASHA, lost in a reverie over her book, whistles softly.]

OLGA.

Don't whistle, Masha. How can you! [Pause] I'm always having headaches from having to go to the High School every day and then teach till evening. Strange thoughts come to me, as if I were already an old woman. And really, during these four years that I have been working here, I have been feeling as if every day my strength and youth have been squeezed out of me, drop by drop. And only one desire grows and gains in strength . . .

IRINA.

To go away to Moscow. To sell the house, drop everything here, and go to Moscow . . .

OLGA.

Yes! To Moscow, and as soon as possible.

[CHEBUTIKIN and TUZENBACH laugh.]

IRINA.
I expect Andrey will become a professor, but still, he won't want to live here. Only poor Masha must go on living here.
OLGA.
Masha can come to Moscow every year, for the whole summer.
[MASHA is whistling gently.]
IRINA.
Everything will be arranged, please God. [Looks out of the window] It's nice out to-day. I don't know why I'm so happy: I remembered this morning that it was my name-day, and I suddenly felt glad and remembered my childhood, when mother was still with us. What beautiful thoughts I had, what thoughts!
OLGA.
You're all radiance to-day, I've never seen you look so lovely. And Masha is pretty, too. Andrey wouldn't be bad-looking, if he wasn't so stout; it does spoil his appearance. But I've grown old and very thin, I suppose it's because I get angry with the girls at school. To-day I'm free. I'm at home. I haven't got a headache, and I feel younger than I was yesterday. I'm only twenty-eight. . . . All's well, God is everywhere, but it seems to me that if only I were married and could stay at home all day, it would be even better. [Pause] I should love my husband.
TUZENBACH.
[To SOLENI] I'm tired of listening to the rot you talk. [Entering the sitting-room] I forgot to say that Vershinin, our new lieutenant-colonel of artillery, is coming to see us to-day. [Sits down to the piano.]
OLGA.
That's good. I'm glad.
IRINA.
Is he old?
TUZENBACH.
Oh, no. Forty or forty-five, at the very outside. [Plays softly] He seems rather a good sort. He's certainly no fool, only he likes to hear himself speak.
IRINA.
Is he interesting?

TUZENBACH.

Oh, he's all right, but there's his wife, his mother-in-law, and two daughters. This is his second wife. He pays calls and tells everybody that he's got a wife and two daughters. He'll tell you so here. The wife isn't all there, she does her hair like a flapper and gushes extremely. She talks philosophy and tries to commit suicide every now and again, apparently in order to annoy her husband. I should have left her long ago, but he bears up patiently, and just grumbles.

SOLENI.

[Enters with CHEBUTIKIN from the dining-room] With one hand I can only lift fifty-four pounds, but with both hands I can lift 180, or even 200 pounds. From this I conclude that two men are not twice as strong as one, but three times, perhaps even more. . . .

CHEBUTIKIN.

[Reads a newspaper as he walks] If your hair is coming out . . . take an ounce of naphthaline and hail a bottle of spirit . . . dissolve and use daily. . . . [Makes a note in his pocket diary] When found make a note of! Not that I want it though. . . . [Crosses it out] It doesn't matter.

IRINA.

Ivan Romanovitch, dear Ivan Romanovitch!

CHEBUTIKIN.

What does my own little girl want?

IRINA.

Ivan Romanovitch, dear Ivan Romanovitch! I feel as if I were sailing under the broad blue sky with great white birds around me. Why is that? Why?

CHEBUTIKIN.

[Kisses her hands, tenderly] My white bird. . . .

IRINA.

When I woke up to-day and got up and dressed myself, I suddenly began to feel as if everything in this life was open to me, and that I knew how I must live. Dear Ivan Romanovitch, I know everything. A man must work, toil in the sweat of his brow, whoever he may be, for that is the meaning and object of his life, his happiness, his enthusiasm. How fine it is to be a workman who gets up at daybreak and breaks stones in the street, or a shepherd, or a schoolmaster, who teaches children, or an engine-driver on the railway. . . . My God, let alone a man, it's better to be an ox, or just a horse, so long as it can work, than a young woman who wakes up at twelve o'clock, has her coffee in bed, and then spends two hours dressing. . . . Oh it's awful! Sometimes when it's hot, your thirst can be just as tiresome as my need for work. And if I don't get up early in future and work, Ivan Romanovitch, then you may refuse me your friendship.

CHEBUTIKIN.
[Tenderly] I'll refuse, I'll refuse. . . .

OLGA.
Father used to make us get up at seven. Now Irina wakes at seven and lies and meditates about something till nine at least. And she looks so serious! [Laughs.]

IRINA.
You're so used to seeing me as a little girl that it seems queer to you when my face is serious. I'm twenty!

TUZENBACH.
How well I can understand that craving for work, oh God! I've never worked once in my life. I was born in Petersburg, a chilly, lazy place, in a family which never knew what work or worry meant. I remember that when I used to come home from my regiment, a footman used to have to pull off my boots while I fidgeted and my mother looked on in adoration and wondered why other people didn't see me in the same light. They shielded me from work; but only just in time! A new age is dawning, the people are marching on us all, a powerful, health-giving storm is gathering, it is drawing near, soon it will be upon us and it will drive away laziness, indifference, the prejudice against labour, and rotten dullness from our society. I shall work, and in twenty-five or thirty years, every man will have to work. Every one!

CHEBUTIKIN.
I shan't work.

TUZENBACH.
You don't matter.

SOLENI.
In twenty-five years' time, we shall all be dead, thank the Lord. In two or three years' time apoplexy will carry you off, or else I'll blow your

brains out, my pet. [Takes a scent-bottle out of his pocket and sprinkles his chest and hands.]
CHEBUTIKIN.
[Laughs] It's quite true, I never have worked. After I came down from the university I never stirred a finger or opened a book, I just read the papers.... [Takes another newspaper out of his pocket] Here we are.... I've learnt from the papers that there used to be one, Dobrolubov [Note: Dobroluboy (1836-81), in spite of the shortness of his career, established himself as one of the classic literary critics of Russia], for instance, but what he wrote—I don't know ... God only knows.... [Somebody is heard tapping on the floor from below] There.... They're calling me downstairs, somebody's come to see me. I'll be back in a minute ... won't be long.... [Exit hurriedly, scratching his beard.]
IRINA.
He's up to something.
TUZENBACH.
Yes, he looked so pleased as he went out that I'm pretty certain he'll bring you a present in a moment.
IRINA.
How unpleasant!
OLGA.
Yes, it's awful. He's always doing silly things.
MASHA.

"There stands a green oak by the sea.
And a chain of bright gold is around it ...
And a chain of bright gold is around it...."

[Gets up and sings softly.]
OLGA.
You're not very bright to-day, Masha. [MASHA sings, putting on her hat] Where are you off to?
MASHA.
Home.
IRINA.
That's odd....

TUZENBACH.
    On a name-day, too!
MASHA.
    It doesn't matter. I'll come in the evening. Good-bye, dear. [Kisses MASHA] Many happy returns, though I've said it before. In the old days when father was alive, every time we had a name-day, thirty or forty officers used to come, and there was lots of noise and fun, and to-day there's only a man and a half, and it's as quiet as a desert . . . I'm off . . . I've got the hump to-day, and am not at all cheerful, so don't you mind me. [Laughs through her tears] We'll have a talk later on, but good-bye for the present, my dear; I'll go somewhere.
IRINA.
    [Displeased] You are queer. . . .
OLGA.
    [Crying] I understand you, Masha.
SOLENI.
    When a man talks philosophy, well, it is philosophy or at any rate sophistry; but when a woman, or two women, talk philosophy—it's all my eye.
MASHA.
    What do you mean by that, you very awful man?
SOLENI.
    Oh, nothing. You came down on me before I could say . . . help!
    [Pause.]
MASHA.
    [Angrily, to OLGA] Don't cry!
    [Enter ANFISA and FERAPONT with a cake.]
ANFISA.
    This way, my dear. Come in, your feet are clean. [To IRINA] From the District Council, from Mihail Ivanitch Protopopov . . . a cake.
IRINA.
    Thank you. Please thank him. [Takes the cake.]
FERAPONT.
    What?
IRINA.
    [Louder] Please thank him.

OLGA.

> Give him a pie, nurse. Ferapont, go, she'll give you a pie.

FERAPONT.

> What?

ANFISA.

> Come on, gran'fer, Ferapont Spiridonitch. Come on. [Exeunt.]

MASHA.

> I don't like this Mihail Potapitch or Ivanitch, Protopopov. We oughtn't to invite him here.

IRINA.

> I never asked him.

MASHA.

> That's all right.
> [Enter CHEBUTIKIN followed by a soldier with a silver samovar; there is a rumble of dissatisfied surprise.]

OLGA.

> [Covers her face with her hands] A samovar! That's awful! [Exit into the dining-room, to the table.]

IRINA.

> My dear Ivan Romanovitch, what are you doing!

TUZENBACH.

> [Laughs] I told you so!

MASHA.

> Ivan Romanovitch, you are simply shameless!

CHEBUTIKIN.

> My dear good girl, you are the only thing, and the dearest thing I have in the world. I'll soon be sixty. I'm an old man, a lonely worthless old man. The only good thing in me is my love for you, and if it hadn't been for that, I would have been dead long ago.... [To IRINA] My dear little girl, I've known you since the day of your birth, I've carried you in my arms... I loved your dead mother....

MASHA.

> But your presents are so expensive!

CHEBUTIKIN.

> [Angrily, through his tears] Expensive presents.... You really, are!...

[To the orderly] Take the samovar in there. . . . [Teasing] Expensive presents!
[The orderly goes into the dining-room with the samovar.]
ANFISA.
[Enters and crosses stage] My dear, there's a strange Colonel come! He's taken off his coat already. Children, he's coming here. Irina darling, you'll be a nice and polite little girl, won't you. . . . Should have lunched a long time ago. . . . Oh, Lord. . . . [Exit.]
TUZENBACH.
It must be Vershinin. [Enter VERSHININ] Lieutenant-Colonel Vershinin!
VERSHININ.
[To MASHA and IRINA] I have the honour to introduce myself, my name is Vershinin. I am very glad indeed to be able to come at last. How you've grown! Oh! oh!
IRINA.
Please sit down. We're very glad you've come.
VERSHININ.
[Gaily] I am glad, very glad! But there are three sisters, surely. I remember—three little girls. I forget your faces, but your father, Colonel Prosorov, used to have three little girls, I remember that perfectly, I saw them with my own eyes. How time does fly! Oh, dear, how it flies!
TUZENBACH.
Alexander Ignateyevitch comes from Moscow.
IRINA.
From Moscow? Are you from Moscow?
VERSHININ.
Yes, that's so. Your father used to be in charge of a battery there, and I was an officer in the same brigade. [To MASHA] I seem to remember your face a little.
MASHA.
I don't remember you.
IRINA.
Olga! Olga! [Shouts into the dining-room] Olga! Come along! [OLGA enters from the dining-room] Lieutenant Colonel Vershinin comes from Moscow, as it happens.

VERSHININ.
I take it that you are Olga Sergeyevna, the eldest, and that you are Maria . . . and you are Irina, the youngest. . . .
OLGA.
So you come from Moscow?
VERSHININ.
Yes. I went to school in Moscow and began my service there; I was there for a long time until at last I got my battery and moved over here, as you see. I don't really remember you, I only remember that there used to be three sisters. I remember your father well; I have only to shut my eyes to see him as he was. I used to come to your house in Moscow. . . .
OLGA.
I used to think I remembered everybody, but . . .
VERSHININ.
My name is Alexander Ignateyevitch.
IRINA.
Alexander Ignateyevitch, you've come from Moscow. That is really quite a surprise!
OLGA.
We are going to live there, you see.
IRINA.
We think we may be there this autumn. It's our native town, we were born there. In Old Basmanni Road. . . . [They both laugh for joy.]
MASHA.
We've unexpectedly met a fellow countryman. [Briskly] I remember: Do you remember, Olga, they used to speak at home of a "lovelorn Major." You were only a Lieutenant then, and in love with somebody, but for some reason they always called you a Major for fun.
VERSHININ.
[Laughs] That's it . . . the lovelorn Major, that's got it!
MASHA.
You only wore moustaches then. You have grown older! [Through her tears] You have grown older!
VERSHININ.
Yes, when they used to call me the lovelorn Major, I was young and in love. I've grown out of both now.

OLGA.
   But you haven't a single white hair yet. You're older, but you're not yet old.
VERSHININ.
   I'm forty-two, anyway. Have you been away from Moscow long?
IRINA.
   Eleven years. What are you crying for, Masha, you little fool.... [Crying] And I'm crying too.
MASHA.
   It's all right. And where did you live?
VERSHININ.
   Old Basmanni Road.
OLGA.
   Same as we.
VERSHININ.
   Once I used to live in German Street. That was when the Red Barracks were my headquarters. There's an ugly bridge in between, where the water rushes underneath. One gets melancholy when one is alone there. [Pause] Here the river is so wide and fine! It's a splendid river!
OLGA.
   Yes, but it's so cold. It's very cold here, and the midges....
VERSHININ.
   What are you saying! Here you've got such a fine healthy Russian climate. You've a forest, a river . . . and birches. Dear, modest birches, I like them more than any other tree. It's good to live here. Only it's odd that the railway station should be thirteen miles away.... Nobody knows why.
SOLENI.
   I know why. [All look at him] Because if it was near it wouldn't be far off, and if it's far off, it can't be near. [An awkward pause.]
TUZENBACH.
   Funny man.
OLGA.
   Now I know who you are. I remember.
VERSHININ.
   I used to know your mother.

CHEBUTIKIN.
>She was a good woman, rest her soul.

IRINA.
>Mother is buried in Moscow.

OLGA.
>At the Novo-Devichi Cemetery.

MASHA.
>Do you know, I'm beginning to forget her face. We'll be forgotten in just the same way.

VERSHININ.
>Yes, they'll forget us. It's our fate, it can't be helped. A time will come when everything that seems serious, significant, or very important to us will be forgotten, or considered trivial. [Pause] And the curious thing is that we can't possibly find out what will come to be regarded as great and important, and what will be feeble, or silly. Didn't the discoveries of Copernicus, or Columbus, say, seem unnecessary and ludicrous at first, while wasn't it thought that some rubbish written by a fool, held all the truth? And it may so happen that our present existence, with which we are so satisfied, will in time appear strange, inconvenient, stupid, unclean, perhaps even sinful. . . .

TUZENBACH.
>Who knows? But on the other hand, they may call our life noble and honour its memory. We've abolished torture and capital punishment, we live in security, but how much suffering there is still!

SOLENI.
>[In a feeble voice] There, there. . . . The Baron will go without his dinner if you only let him talk philosophy.

TUZENBACH.
>Vassili Vassilevitch, kindly leave me alone. [Changes his chair] You're very dull, you know.

SOLENI.
>[Feebly] There, there, there.

TUZENBACH.
>[To VERSHININ] The sufferings we see to-day—there are so many of them!—still indicate a certain moral improvement in society.

VERSHININ.
    Yes, yes, of course.
CHEBUTIKIN.
    You said just now, Baron, that they may call our life noble; but we are very petty.... [Stands up] See how little I am. [Violin played behind.]
MASHA.
    That's Andrey playing—our brother.
IRINA.
    He's the learned member of the family. I expect he will be a professor some day. Father was a soldier, but his son chose an academic career for himself.
MASHA.
    That was father's wish.
OLGA.
    We ragged him to-day. We think he's a little in love.
IRINA.
    To a local lady. She will probably come here to-day.
MASHA.
    You should see the way she dresses! Quite prettily, quite fashionably too, but so badly! Some queer bright yellow skirt with a wretched little fringe and a red bodice. And such a complexion! Andrey isn't in love. After all he has taste, he's simply making fun of us. I heard yesterday that she was going to marry Protopopov, the chairman of the Local Council. That would do her nicely.... [At the side door] Andrey, come here! Just for a minute, dear! [Enter ANDREY.]
OLGA.
    My brother, Andrey Sergeyevitch.
VERSHININ.
    My name is Vershinin.
ANDREY.
    Mine is Prosorov. [Wipes his perspiring hands] You've come to take charge of the battery?
OLGA.
    Just think, Alexander Ignateyevitch comes from Moscow.
ANDREY.
    That's all right. Now my little sisters won't give you any rest.

VERSHININ.
> I've already managed to bore your sisters.

IRINA.
> Just look what a nice little photograph frame Andrey gave me to-day. [Shows it] He made it himself.

VERSHININ.
> [Looks at the frame and does not know what to say] Yes. . . . It's a thing that . . .

IRINA.
> And he made that frame there, on the piano as well. [Andrey waves his hand and walks away.]

OLGA.
> He's got a degree, and plays the violin, and cuts all sorts of things out of wood, and is really a domestic Admirable Crichton. Don't go away, Andrey! He's got into a habit of always going away. Come here! [MASHA and IRINA take his arms and laughingly lead him back.]

MASHA.
> Come on, come on!

ANDREY.
> Please leave me alone.

MASHA.
> You are funny. Alexander Ignateyevitch used to be called the lovelorn Major, but he never minded.

VERSHININ.
> Not the least.

MASHA.
> I'd like to call you the lovelorn fiddler!

IRINA.
> Or the lovelorn professor!

OLGA.
> He's in love! little Andrey is in love!

IRINA.
> [Applauds] Bravo, Bravo! Encore! Little Andrey is in love.

CHEBUTIKIN.
> [Goes up behind ANDREY and takes him round the waist with both arms] Nature only brought us into the world that we should love!

[Roars with laughter, then sits down and reads a newspaper which he takes out of his pocket.]

ANDREY.

That's enough, quite enough. . . . [Wipes his face] I couldn't sleep all night and now I can't quite find my feet, so to speak. I read until four o'clock, then tried to sleep, but nothing happened. I thought about one thing and another, and then it dawned and the sun crawled into my bedroom. This summer, while I'm here, I want to translate a book from the English. . . .

VERSHININ.

Do you read English?

ANDREY.

Yes father, rest his soul, educated us almost violently. It may seem funny and silly, but it's nevertheless true, that after his death I began to fill out and get rounder, as if my body had had some great pressure taken off it. Thanks to father, my sisters and I know French, German, and English, and Irina knows Italian as well. But we paid dearly for it all!

MASHA.

A knowledge of three languages is an unnecessary luxury in this town. It isn't even a luxury but a sort of useless extra, like a sixth finger. We know a lot too much.

VERSHININ.

Well, I say! [Laughs] You know a lot too much! I don't think there can really be a town so dull and stupid as to have no place for a clever, cultured person. Let us suppose even that among the hundred thousand inhabitants of this backward and uneducated town, there are only three persons like yourself. It stands to reason that you won't be able to conquer that dark mob around you; little by little as you grow older you will be bound to give way and lose yourselves in this crowd of a hundred thousand human beings; their life will suck you up in itself, but still, you won't disappear having influenced nobody; later on, others like you will come, perhaps six of them, then twelve, and so on, until at last your sort will be in the majority. In two or three hundred years' time life on this earth will be unimaginably beautiful and wonderful. Mankind needs such a life, and if it is not ours to-day then we must look ahead for it, wait, think, prepare for it. We must see and know more than our fathers and grandfathers saw and knew. [Laughs] And you complain that you know too much.

MASHA.

[Takes off her hat] I'll stay to lunch.

IRINA.

[Sighs] Yes, all that ought to be written down.

[ANDREY has gone out quietly.]

TUZENBACH.

You say that many years later on, life on this earth will be beautiful and wonderful. That's true. But to share in it now, even though at a distance, we must prepare by work. . . .

VERSHININ.

[Gets up] Yes. What a lot of flowers you have. [Looks round] It's a beautiful flat. I envy you! I've spent my whole life in rooms with two chairs, one sofa, and fires which always smoke. I've never had flowers like these in my life. . . . [Rubs his hands] Well, well!

TUZENBACH.

Yes, we must work. You are probably thinking to yourself: the German lets himself go. But I assure you I'm a Russian, I can't even speak German. My father belonged to the Orthodox Church. . . . [Pause.]

VERSHININ.

[Walks about the stage] I often wonder: suppose we could begin life over again, knowing what we were doing? Suppose we could use one life, already ended, as a sort of rough draft for another? I think that every one of us would try, more than anything else, not to repeat himself, at the very least he would rearrange his manner of life, he would make sure of rooms like these, with flowers and light . . . I have a wife and two daughters, my wife's health is delicate and so on and so on, and if I had to begin life all over again I would not marry. . . . No, no!

[Enter KULIGIN in a regulation jacket.]

KULIGIN.

[Going up to IRINA] Dear sister, allow me to congratulate you on the day sacred to your good angel and to wish you, sincerely and from the bottom of my heart, good health and all that one can wish for a girl of your years. And then let me offer you this book as a present. [Gives it to her] It is the history of our High School during the last fifty years, written by myself. The book is worthless, and written because I had nothing to do, but read it all the same. Good day, gentlemen! [To VERSHININ] My name is Kuligin, I am a master of the local High School. [Note: He adds that he is a Nadvorny Sovetnik (almost the same as a German Hofrat), an undistinguished civilian title with no English equivalent.] [To IRINA] In this book you will find a list of all those who have taken the full course at our High School during these fifty years. Feci quod potui, faciant meliora potentes. [Kisses MASHA.]

IRINA.
But you gave me one of these at Easter.

KULIGIN.
[Laughs] I couldn't have, surely! You'd better give it back to me in that case, or else give it to the Colonel. Take it, Colonel. You'll read it some day when you're bored.

VERSHININ.
Thank you. [Prepares to go] I am extremely happy to have made the acquaintance of . . .

OLGA.
Must you go? No, not yet?

IRINA.
You'll stop and have lunch with us. Please do.

OLGA.
Yes, please!

VERSHININ.
[Bows] I seem to have dropped in on your name-day. Forgive me, I didn't know, and I didn't offer you my congratulations. [Goes with OLGA into the dining-room.]

KULIGIN.
To-day is Sunday, the day of rest, so let us rest and rejoice, each in a manner compatible with his age and disposition. The carpets will have to be taken up for the summer and put away till the winter . . . Persian powder or naphthaline. . . . The Romans were healthy because they knew both how to work and how to rest, they had mens sana

in corpore sano. Their life ran along certain recognized patterns. Our director says: "The chief thing about each life is its pattern. Whoever loses his pattern is lost himself"— and it's just the same in our daily life. [Takes MASHA by the waist, laughing] Masha loves me. My wife loves me. And you ought to put the window curtains away with the carpets. . . . I'm feeling awfully pleased with life to-day. Masha, we've got to be at the director's at four. They're getting up a walk for the pedagogues and their families.

MASHA.
I shan't go.
KULIGIN.
[Hurt] My dear Masha, why not?
MASHA.
I'll tell you later. . . . [Angrily] All right, I'll go, only please stand back. . . . [Steps away.]
KULIGIN.
And then we're to spend the evening at the director's. In spite of his ill-health that man tries, above everything else, to be sociable. A splendid, illuminating personality. A wonderful man. After yesterday's committee he said to me: "I'm tired, Feodor Ilitch, I'm tired!" [Looks at the clock, then at his watch] Your clock is seven minutes fast. "Yes," he said, "I'm tired." [Violin played off.]
OLGA.
Let's go and have lunch! There's to be a masterpiece of baking!
KULIGIN.
Oh my dear Olga, my dear. Yesterday I was working till eleven o'clock at night, and got awfully tired. To-day I'm quite happy. [Goes into dining-room] My dear . . .
CHEBUTIKIN.
[Puts his paper into his pocket, and combs his beard] A pie? Splendid!
MASHA.
[Severely to CHEBUTIKIN] Only mind; you're not to drink anything to-day. Do you hear? It's bad for you.
CHEBUTIKIN.
Oh, that's all right. I haven't been drunk for two years. And it's all the same, anyway!

MASHA.
>   You're not to dare to drink, all the same. [Angrily, but so that her husband should not hear] Another dull evening at the Director's, confound it!

TUZENBACH.
>   I shouldn't go if I were you. . . . It's quite simple.

CHEBUTIKIN.
>   Don't go.

MASHA.
>   Yes, "don't go. . . ." It's a cursed, unbearable life. . . . [Goes into dining-room.]

CHEBUTIKIN.
>   [Follows her] It's not so bad.

SOLENI.
>   [Going into the dining-room] There, there, there. . . .

TUZENBACH.
>   Vassili Vassilevitch, that's enough. Be quiet!

SOLENI.
>   There, there, there. . . .

KULIGIN.
>   [Gaily] Your health, Colonel! I'm a pedagogue and not quite at home here. I'm Masha's husband. . . . She's a good sort, a very good sort.

VERSHININ.
>   I'll have some of this black vodka. . . . [Drinks] Your health! [To OLGA] I'm very comfortable here!
>   [Only IRINA and TUZENBACH are now left in the sitting-room.]

IRINA.
>   Masha's out of sorts to-day. She married when she was eighteen, when he seemed to her the wisest of men. And now it's different. He's the kindest man, but not the wisest.

OLGA.
>   [Impatiently] Andrey, when are you coming?

ANDREY.
>   [Off] One minute. [Enters and goes to the table.]

TUZENBACH.
>   What are you thinking about?

IRINA.
I don't like this Soleni of yours and I'm afraid of him. He only says silly things.

TUZENBACH.
He's a queer man. I'm sorry for him, though he vexes me. I think he's shy. When there are just the two of us he's quite all right and very good company; when other people are about he's rough and hectoring. Don't let's go in, let them have their meal without us. Let me stay with you. What are you thinking of? [Pause] You're twenty. I'm not yet thirty. How many years are there left to us, with their long, long lines of days, filled with my love for you. . . .

IRINA.
Nicolai Lvovitch, don't speak to me of love.

TUZENBACH.
[Does not hear] I've a great thirst for life, struggle, and work, and this thirst has united with my love for you, Irina, and you're so beautiful, and life seems so beautiful to me! What are you thinking about?

IRINA.
You say that life is beautiful. Yes, if only it seems so! The life of us three hasn't been beautiful yet; it has been stifling us as if it was weeds . . . I'm crying. I oughtn't. . . . [Dries her tears, smiles] We must work, work. That is why we are unhappy and look at the world so sadly; we don't know what work is. Our parents despised work. . . .

[Enter NATALIA IVANOVA; she wears a pink dress and a green sash.]

NATASHA.
They're already at lunch . . . I'm late . . . [Carefully examines herself in a mirror, and puts herself straight] I think my hair's done all right. . . . [Sees IRINA] Dear Irina Sergeyevna, I congratulate you! [Kisses her firmly and at length] You've so many visitors, I'm really ashamed. . . . How do you do, Baron!

OLGA.
[Enters from dining-room] Here's Natalia Ivanovna. How are you, dear! [They kiss.]

NATASHA.
Happy returns. I'm awfully shy, you've so many people here.

· 164 ·

OLGA.
All our friends. [Frightened, in an undertone] You're wearing a green sash! My dear, you shouldn't!

NATASHA.
Is it a sign of anything?

OLGA.
No, it simply doesn't go well . . . and it looks so queer.

NATASHA.
[In a tearful voice] Yes? But it isn't really green, it's too dull for that. [Goes into dining-room with OLGA.]
[They have all sat down to lunch in the dining-room, the sitting-room is empty.]

KULIGIN.
I wish you a nice fiancée, Irina. It's quite time you married.

CHEBUTIKIN.
Natalia Ivanovna, I wish you the same.

KULIGIN.
Natalia Ivanovna has a fiancé already.

MASHA.
[Raps with her fork on a plate] Let's all get drunk and make life purple for once!

KULIGIN.
You've lost three good conduct marks.

VERSHININ.
This is a nice drink. What's it made of?

SOLENI.
Blackbeetles.

IRINA.
[Tearfully] Phoo! How disgusting!

OLGA.
There is to be a roast turkey and a sweet apple pie for dinner. Thank goodness I can spend all day and the evening at home. You'll come in the evening, ladies and gentlemen. . . .

VERSHININ.
And please may I come in the evening!

IRINA.
  Please do.
NATASHA.
  They don't stand on ceremony here.
CHEBUTIKIN.
  Nature only brought us into the world that we should love! [Laughs.]
ANDREY.
  [Angrily] Please don't! Aren't you tired of it?
  [Enter FEDOTIK and RODE with a large basket of flowers.]
FEDOTIK.
  They're lunching already.
RODE.
  [Loudly and thickly] Lunching? Yes, so they are....
FEDOTIK.
  Wait a minute! [Takes a photograph] That's one. No, just a moment....
  [Takes another] That's two. Now we're ready!
  [They take the basket and go into the dining-room, where they have a noisy reception.]
RODE.
  [Loudly] Congratulations and best wishes! Lovely weather to-day, simply perfect. Was out walking with the High School students all the morning. I take their drills.
FEDOTIK.
  You may move, Irina Sergeyevna! [Takes a photograph] You look well to-day. [Takes a humming-top out of his pocket] Here's a humming-top, by the way. It's got a lovely note!
IRINA.
  How awfully nice!
MASHA.

  "There stands a green oak by the sea,
  And a chain of bright gold is around it ...
  And a chain of bright gold is around it ..."

  [Tearfully] What am I saying that for? I've had those words running in my head all day....

KULIGIN.
> There are thirteen at table!

RODE.
> [Aloud] Surely you don't believe in that superstition? [Laughter.]

KULIGIN.
> If there are thirteen at table then it means there are lovers present. It isn't you, Ivan Romanovitch, hang it all.... [Laughter.]

CHEBUTIKIN.
> I'm a hardened sinner, but I really don't see why Natalia Ivanovna should blush....
> [Loud laughter; NATASHA runs out into the sitting-room, followed by ANDREY.]

ANDREY.
> Don't pay any attention to them! Wait... do stop, please....

NATASHA.
> I'm shy... I don't know what's the matter with me and they're all laughing at me. It wasn't nice of me to leave the table like that, but I can't... I can't. [Covers her face with her hands.]

ANDREY.
> My dear, I beg you. I implore you not to excite yourself. I assure you they're only joking, they're kind people. My dear, good girl, they're all kind and sincere people, and they like both you and me. Come here to the window, they can't see us here.... [Looks round.]

NATASHA.
> I'm so unaccustomed to meeting people!

ANDREY.
> Oh your youth, your splendid, beautiful youth! My darling, don't be so excited! Believe me, believe me... I'm so happy, my soul is full of love, of ecstasy.... They don't see us! They can't! Why, why or when did I fall in love with you—Oh, I can't understand anything. My dear, my pure darling, be my wife! I love you, love you... as never before....
> [They kiss.]
> [Two officers come in and, seeing the lovers kiss, stop in astonishment.]

Curtain falls.

ACT II

Scene as before. It is 8 p.m. Somebody is heard playing a concertina outside in' the street. There is no fire. NATALIA IVANOVNA enters in indoor dress carrying a candle; she stops by the door which leads into ANDREY'S room.

NATASHA.
What are you doing, Andrey? Are you reading? It's nothing, only I. . . . [She opens another door, and looks in, then closes it] Isn't there any fire. . . .

ANDREY.
[Enters with book in hand] What are you doing, Natasha?

NATASHA.
I was looking to see if there wasn't a fire. It's Shrovetide, and the servant is simply beside herself; I must look out that something doesn't happen. When I came through the dining-room yesterday midnight, there was a candle burning. I couldn't get her to tell me who had lighted it. [Puts down her candle] What's the time?

ANDREY.
> [Looks at his watch] A quarter past eight.

NATASHA.
> And Olga and Irina aren't in yet. The poor things are still at work. Olga at the teacher's council, Irina at the telegraph office. . . . [Sighs] I said to your sister this morning, "Irina, darling, you must take care of yourself." But she pays no attention. Did you say it was a quarter past eight? I am afraid little Bobby is quite ill. Why is he so cold? He was feverish yesterday, but to-day he is quite cold . . . I am so frightened!

ANDREY.
> It's all right, Natasha. The boy is well.

NATASHA.
> Still, I think we ought to put him on a diet. I am so afraid. And the entertainers were to be here after nine; they had better not come, Audrey.

ANDREY.
> I don't know. After all, they were asked.

NATASHA.
> This morning, when the little boy woke up and saw me he suddenly smiled; that means he knew me. "Good morning, Bobby!" I said, "good morning, darling." And he laughed. Children understand, they understand very well. So I'll tell them, Andrey dear, not to receive the entertainers.

ANDREY.
> [Hesitatingly] But what about my sisters. This is their flat.

NATASHA.
> They'll do as I want them. They are so kind. . . . [Going] I ordered sour milk for supper. The doctor says you must eat sour milk and nothing else, or you won't get thin. [Stops] Bobby is so cold. I'm afraid his room is too cold for him. It would be nice to put him into another room till the warm weather comes. Irina's room, for instance, is just right for a child: it's dry and has the sun all day. I must tell her, she can share Olga's room. It isn't as if she was at home in the daytime, she only sleeps here. . . . [A pause] Andrey, darling, why are you so silent?

ANDREY.
> I was just thinking. . . . There is really nothing to say. . . .

NATASHA.
> Yes . . . there was something I wanted to tell you. . . . Oh, yes. Ferapont has come from the Council offices, he wants to see you.

ANDREY.
> [Yawns] Call him here.

[NATASHA goes out; ANDREY reads his book, stooping over the candle she has left behind. FERAPONT enters; he wears a tattered old coat with the collar up. His ears are muffled.]

ANDREY.
> Good morning, grandfather. What have you to say?

FERAPONT.
> The Chairman sends a book and some documents or other. Here. . . . [Hands him a book and a packet.]

ANDREY.
> Thank you. It's all right. Why couldn't you come earlier? It's past eight now.

FERAPONT.
> What?

ANDREY.
> [Louder]. I say you've come late, it's past eight.

FERAPONT.
> Yes, yes. I came when it was still light, but they wouldn't let me in. They said you were busy. Well, what was I to do. If you're busy, you're busy, and I'm in no hurry. [He thinks that ANDREY is asking him something] What?

ANDREY.
> Nothing. [Looks through the book] To-morrow's Friday. I'm not supposed to go to work, but I'll come—all the same . . . and do some work. It's dull at home. [Pause] Oh, my dear old man, how strangely life changes, and how it deceives! To-day, out of sheer boredom, I took up this book—old university lectures, and I couldn't help laughing. My God, I'm secretary of the local district council, the council which has Protopopov for its chairman, yes, I'm the secretary, and the summit of my ambitions is—to become a member of the council! I to be a member of the local district council, I, who dream every night that I'm a professor of Moscow University, a famous scholar of whom all Russia is proud!

FERAPONT.

    I can't tell . . . I'm hard of hearing. . . .

ANDREY.

    If you weren't, I don't suppose I should talk to you. I've got to talk to somebody, and my wife doesn't understand me, and I'm a bit afraid of my sisters—I don't know why unless it is that they may make fun of me and make me feel ashamed . . . I don't drink, I don't like publichouses, but how I should like to be sitting just now in Tyestov's place in Moscow, or at the Great Moscow, old fellow!

FERAPONT.

    Moscow? That's where a contractor was once telling that some merchants or other were eating pancakes; one ate forty pancakes and he went and died, he was saying. Either forty or fifty, I forget which.

ANDREY.

    In Moscow you can sit in an enormous restaurant where you don't know anybody and where nobody knows you, and you don't feel all the same that you're a stranger. And here you know everybody and everybody knows you, and you're a stranger . . . and a lonely stranger.

FERAPONT.

    What? And the same contractor was telling—perhaps he was lying—that there was a cable stretching right across Moscow.

ANDREY.

    What for?

FERAPONT.

    I can't tell. The contractor said so.

ANDREY.

    Rubbish. [He reads] Were you ever in Moscow?

FERAPONT.

    [After a pause] No. God did not lead me there. [Pause] Shall I go?

ANDREY.

    You may go. Good-bye. [FERAPONT goes] Good-bye. [Reads] You can come to-morrow and fetch these documents. . . . Go along. . . . [Pause] He's gone. [A ring] Yes, yes. . . . [Stretches himself and slowly goes into his own room.]

[Behind the scene the nurse is singing a lullaby to the child. MASHA and VERSHININ come in. While they talk, a maidservant lights candles and a lamp.]

MASHA.
I don't know. [Pause] I don't know. Of course, habit counts for a great deal. After father's death, for instance, it took us a long time to get used to the absence of orderlies. But, apart from habit, it seems to me in all fairness that, however it may be in other towns, the best and most-educated people are army men.

VERSHININ.
I'm thirsty. I should like some tea.

MASHA.
[Glancing at her watch] They'll bring some soon. I was given in marriage when I was eighteen, and I was afraid of my husband because he was a teacher and I'd only just left school. He then seemed to me frightfully wise and learned and important. And now, unfortunately, that has changed.

VERSHININ.
Yes . . . yes.

MASHA.
I don't speak of my husband, I've grown used to him, but civilians in general are so often coarse, impolite, uneducated. Their rudeness offends me, it angers me. I suffer when I see that a man isn't quite sufficiently refined, or delicate, or polite. I simply suffer agonies when I happen to be among schoolmasters, my husband's colleagues.

VERSHININ.
Yes. . . . It seems to me that civilians and army men are equally interesting, in this town, at any rate. It's all the same! If you listen to a member of the local intelligentsia, whether to civilian or military, he will tell you that he's sick of his wife, sick of his house, sick of his estate, sick of his horses. . . . We Russians are extremely gifted in the direction of thinking on an exalted plane, but, tell me, why do we aim so low in real life? Why?

MASHA.
Why?

VERSHININ.

Why is a Russian sick of his children, sick of his wife? And why are his wife and children sick of him?

MASHA.

You're a little downhearted to-day.

VERSHININ.

Perhaps I am. I haven't had any dinner, I've had nothing since the morning. My daughter is a little unwell, and when my girls are ill, I get very anxious and my conscience tortures me because they have such a mother. Oh, if you had seen her to-day! What a trivial personality! We began quarrelling at seven in the morning and at nine I slammed the door and went out. [Pause] I never speak of her, it's strange that I bear my complaints to you alone. [Kisses her hand] Don't be angry with me. I haven't anybody but you, nobody at all.... [Pause.]

MASHA.

What a noise in the oven. Just before father's death there was a noise in the pipe, just like that.

VERSHININ.

Are you superstitious?

MASHA.

Yes.

VERSHININ.

That's strange. [Kisses her hand] You are a splendid, wonderful woman. Splendid, wonderful! It is dark here, but I see your sparkling eyes.

MASHA.

[Sits on another chair] There is more light here.

VERSHININ.

I love you, love you, love you ... I love your eyes, your movements, I dream of them.... Splendid, wonderful woman!

MASHA.

[Laughing] When you talk to me like that, I laugh; I don't know why, for I'm afraid. Don't repeat it, please.... [In an undertone] No, go on, it's all the same to me.... [Covers her face with her hands] Somebody's coming, let's talk about something else.

[IRINA and TUZENBACH come in through the dining-room.]

TUZENBACH.
My surname is really triple. I am called Baron Tuzenbach-Krone-Altschauer, but I am Russian and Orthodox, the same as you. There is very little German left in me, unless perhaps it is the patience and the obstinacy with which I bore you. I see you home every night.

IRINA.
How tired I am!

TUZENBACH.
And I'll come to the telegraph office to see you home every day for ten or twenty years, until you drive me away. [He sees MASHA and VERSHININ; joyfully] Is that you? How do you do.

IRINA.
Well, I am home at last. [To MASHA] A lady came to-day to telegraph to her brother in Saratov that her son died to-day, and she couldn't remember the address anyhow. So she sent the telegram without an address, just to Saratov. She was crying. And for some reason or other I was rude to her. "I've no time," I said. It was so stupid. Are the entertainers coming to-night?

MASHA.
Yes.

IRINA.
[Sitting down in an armchair] I want a rest. I am tired.

TUZENBACH.
[Smiling] When you come home from your work you seem so young, and so unfortunate.... [Pause.]

IRINA.
I am tired. No, I don't like the telegraph office, I don't like it.

MASHA.
You've grown thinner.... [Whistles a little] And you look younger, and your face has become like a boy's.

TUZENBACH.
That's the way she does her hair.

IRINA.
I must find another job, this one won't do for me. What I wanted, what I hoped to get, just that is lacking here. Labour without poetry, without ideas.... [A knock on the floor] The doctor is knocking.

[To TUZENBACH] Will you knock, dear. I can't . . . I'm tired. . . . [TUZENBACH knocks] He'll come in a minute. Something ought to be done. Yesterday the doctor and Andrey played cards at the club and lost money. Andrey seems to have lost 200 roubles.

MASHA.

[With indifference] What can we do now?

IRINA.

He lost money a fortnight ago, he lost money in December. Perhaps if he lost everything we should go away from this town. Oh, my God, I dream of Moscow every night. I'm just like a lunatic. [Laughs] We go there in June, and before June there's still . . . February, March, April, May . . . nearly half a year!

MASHA.

Only Natasha mustn't get to know of these losses.

IRINA.

I expect it will be all the same to her.

[CHEBUTIKIN, who has only just got out of bed—he was resting after dinner—comes into the dining-room and combs his beard. He then sits by the table and takes a newspaper from his pocket.]

MASHA.

Here he is. . . . Has he paid his rent?

IRINA.

[Laughs] No. He's been here eight months and hasn't paid a copeck. Seems to have forgotten.

MASHA.

[Laughs] What dignity in his pose! [They all laugh. A pause.]

IRINA.

Why are you so silent, Alexander Ignateyevitch?

VERSHININ.

I don't know. I want some tea. Half my life for a tumbler of tea: I haven't had anything since morning.

CHEBUTIKIN.

Irina Sergeyevna!

IRINA.

What is it?

CHEBUTIKIN.
   Please come here, Venez ici. [IRINA goes and sits by the table] I can't do without you. [IRINA begins to play patience.]
VERSHININ.
   Well, if we can't have any tea, let's philosophize, at any rate.
TUZENBACH.
   Yes, let's. About what?
VERSHININ.
   About what? Let us meditate . . . about life as it will be after our time; for example, in two or three hundred years.
TUZENBACH.
   Well? After our time people will fly about in balloons, the cut of one's coat will change, perhaps they'll discover a sixth sense and develop it, but life will remain the same, laborious, mysterious, and happy. And in a thousand years' time, people will still be sighing: "Life is hard!"—and at the same time they'll be just as afraid of death, and unwilling to meet it, as we are.
VERSHININ.
   [Thoughtfully] How can I put it? It seems to me that everything on earth must change, little by little, and is already changing under our very eyes. After two or three hundred years, after a thousand—the actual time doesn't matter—a new and happy age will begin. We, of course, shall not take part in it, but we live and work and even suffer to-day that it should come. We create it—and in that one object is our destiny and, if you like, our happiness.
   [MASHA laughs softly.]
TUZENBACH.
   What is it?
MASHA.
   I don't know. I've been laughing all day, ever since morning.
VERSHININ.
   I finished my education at the same point as you, I have not studied at universities; I read a lot, but I cannot choose my books and perhaps what I read is not at all what I should, but the longer I love, the more I want to know. My hair is turning white, I am nearly an old man now, but I know so little, oh, so little! But I think I know the things that

matter most, and that are most real. I know them well. And I wish I could make you understand that there is no happiness for us, that there should not and cannot be.... We must only work and work, and happiness is only for our distant posterity. [Pause] If not for me, then for the descendants of my descendants.

[FEDOTIK and RODE come into the dining-room; they sit and sing softly, strumming on a guitar.]

TUZENBACH.

According to you, one should not even think about happiness! But suppose I am happy!

VERSHININ.

No.

TUZENBACH.

[Moves his hands and laughs] We do not seem to understand each other. How can I convince you? [MASHA laughs quietly, TUZENBACH continues, pointing at her] Yes, laugh! [To VERSHININ] Not only after two or three centuries, but in a million years, life will still be as it was; life does not change, it remains for ever, following its own laws which do not concern us, or which, at any rate, you will never find out. Migrant birds, cranes for example, fly and fly, and whatever thoughts, high or low, enter their heads, they will still fly and not know why or where. They fly and will continue to fly, whatever philosophers come to life among them; they may philosophize as much as they like, only they will fly....

MASHA.

Still, is there a meaning?

TUZENBACH.

A meaning.... Now the snow is falling. What meaning? [Pause.]

MASHA.

It seems to me that a man must have faith, or must search for a faith, or his life will be empty, empty.... To live and not to know why the cranes fly, why babies are born, why there are stars in the sky.... Either you must know why you live, or everything is trivial, not worth a straw. [A pause.]

VERSHININ.

Still, I am sorry that my youth has gone.

MASHA.
Gogol says: life in this world is a dull matter, my masters!
TUZENBACH.
And I say it's difficult to argue with you, my masters! Hang it all.
CHEBUTIKIN.
[Reading] Balzac was married at Berdichev. [IRINA is singing softly] That's worth making a note of. [He makes a note] Balzac was married at Berdichev. [Goes on reading.]
IRINA.
[Laying out cards, thoughtfully] Balzac was married at Berdichev.
TUZENBACH.
The die is cast. I've handed in my resignation, Maria Sergeyevna.
MASHA.
So I heard. I don't see what good it is; I don't like civilians.
TUZENBACH.
Never mind. . . . [Gets up] I'm not handsome; what use am I as a soldier? Well, it makes no difference . . . I shall work. If only just once in my life I could work so that I could come home in the evening, fall exhausted on my bed, and go to sleep at once. [Going into the dining-room] Workmen, I suppose, do sleep soundly!
FEDOTIK.
[To IRINA] I bought some coloured pencils for you at Pizhikov's in the Moscow Road, just now. And here is a little knife.
IRINA.
You have got into the habit of behaving to me as if I am a little girl, but I am grown up. [Takes the pencils and the knife, then, with joy] How lovely!
FEDOTIK.
And I bought myself a knife . . . look at it . . . one blade, another, a third, an ear-scoop, scissors, nail-cleaners.
RODE.
[Loudly] Doctor, how old are you?
CHEBUTIKIN.
I? Thirty-two. [Laughter]
FEDOTIK.
I'll show you another kind of patience. . . . [Lays out cards.]

[A samovar is brought in; ANFISA attends to it; a little later NATASHA enters and helps by the table; SOLENI arrives and, after greetings, sits by the table.]

VERSHININ.
   What a wind!

MASHA.
   Yes. I'm tired of winter. I've already forgotten what summer's like.

IRINA.
   It's coming out, I see. We're going to Moscow.

FEDOTIK.
   No, it won't come out. Look, the eight was on the two of spades. [Laughs] That means you won't go to Moscow.

CHEBUTIKIN.
   [Reading paper] Tsitsigar. Smallpox is raging here.

ANFISA.
   [Coming up to MASHA] Masha, have some tea, little mother. [To VERSHININ] Please have some, sir . . . excuse me, but I've forgotten your name. . . .

MASHA.
   Bring some here, nurse. I shan't go over there.

IRINA.
   Nurse!

ANFISA.
   Coming, coming!

NATASHA.
   [To SOLENI] Children at the breast understand perfectly. I said "Good morning, Bobby; good morning, dear!" And he looked at me in quite an unusual way. You think it's only the mother in me that is speaking; I assure you that isn't so! He's a wonderful child.

SOLENI.
   If he was my child I'd roast him on a frying-pan and eat him. [Takes his tumbler into the drawing-room and sits in a corner.]

NATASHA.
   [Covers her face in her hands] Vulgar, ill-bred man!

MASHA.
>He's lucky who doesn't notice whether it's winter now, or summer. I think that if I were in Moscow, I shouldn't mind about the weather.

VERSHININ.
>A few days ago I was reading the prison diary of a French minister. He had been sentenced on account of the Panama scandal. With what joy, what delight, he speaks of the birds he saw through the prison windows, which he had never noticed while he was a minister. Now, of course, that he is at liberty, he notices birds no more than he did before. When you go to live in Moscow you'll not notice it, in just the same way. There can be no happiness for us, it only exists in our wishes.

TUZENBACH.
>[Takes cardboard box from the table] Where are the pastries?

IRINA.
>Soleni has eaten them.

TUZENBACH.
>All of them?

ANFISA.
>[Serving tea] There's a letter for you.

VERSHININ.
>For me? [Takes the letter] From my daughter. [Reads] Yes, of course... I will go quietly. Excuse me, Maria Sergeyevna. I shan't have any tea. [Stands up, excited] That eternal story....

MASHA.
>What is it? Is it a secret?

VERSHININ.
>[Quietly] My wife has poisoned herself again. I must go. I'll go out quietly. It's all awfully unpleasant. [Kisses MASHA'S hand] My dear, my splendid, good woman... I'll go this way, quietly. [Exit.]

ANFISA.
>Where has he gone? And I'd served tea.... What a man.

MASHA.
>[Angrily] Be quiet! You bother so one can't have a moment's peace....
>[Goes to the table with her cup] I'm tired of you, old woman!

ANFISA.
    My dear! Why are you offended!
ANDREY'S VOICE.
    Anfisa!
ANFISA.
    [Mocking] Anfisa! He sits there and . . . [Exit.]
MASHA.
    [In the dining-room, by the table angrily] Let me sit down! [Disturbs the cards on the table] Here you are, spreading your cards out. Have some tea!
IRINA.
    You are cross, Masha.
MASHA.
    If I am cross, then don't talk to me. Don't touch me!
CHEBUTIKIN.
    Don't touch her, don't touch her. . . .
MASHA.
    You're sixty, but you're like a boy, always up to some beastly nonsense.
NATASHA.
    [Sighs] Dear Masha, why use such expressions? With your beautiful exterior you would be simply fascinating in good society, I tell you so directly, if it wasn't for your words. Je vous prie, pardonnez moi, Marie, mais vous avez des manières un peu grossières.
TUZENBACH.
    [Restraining his laughter] Give me . . . give me . . . there's some cognac, I think.
NATASHA.
    Il parait, que mon Bobick déjà ne dort pas, he has awakened. He isn't well to-day. I'll go to him, excuse me . . . [Exit.]
IRINA.
    Where has Alexander Ignateyevitch gone?
MASHA.
    Home. Something extraordinary has happened to his wife again.
TUZENBACH.
    [Goes to SOLENI with a cognac-flask in his hands] You go on sitting by yourself, thinking of something—goodness knows what. Come

and let's make peace. Let's have some cognac. [They drink] I expect I'll have to play the piano all night, some rubbish most likely . . . well, so be it!

SOLENI.
Why make peace? I haven't quarrelled with you.

TUZENBACH.
You always make me feel as if something has taken place between us. You've a strange character, you must admit.

SOLENI.
[Declaims] "I am strange, but who is not? Don't be angry, Aleko!"

TUZENBACH.
And what has Aleko to do with it? [Pause.]

SOLENI.
When I'm with one other man I behave just like everybody else, but in company I'm dull and shy and . . . talk all manner of rubbish. But I'm more honest and more honourable than very, very many people. And I can prove it.

TUZENBACH.
I often get angry with you, you always fasten on to me in company, but I like you all the same. I'm going to drink my fill to-night, whatever happens. Drink, now!

SOLENI.
Let's drink. [They drink] I never had anything against you, Baron. But my character is like Lermontov's [In a low voice] I even rather resemble Lermontov, they say. . . . [Takes a scent-bottle from his pocket, and scents his hands.]

TUZENBACH.
I've sent in my resignation. Basta! I've been thinking about it for five years, and at last made up my mind. I shall work.

SOLENI.
[Declaims] "Do not be angry, Aleko . . . forget, forget, thy dreams of yore. . . ."
[While he is speaking ANDREY enters quietly with a book, and sits by the table.]

TUZENBACH.
I shall work.

CHEBUTIKIN.

[Going with IRINA into the dining-room] And the food was also real Caucasian onion soup, and, for a roast, some chehartma.

SOLENI.

Cheremsha [Note: A variety of garlic.] isn't meat at all, but a plant something like an onion.

CHEBUTIKIN.

No, my angel. Chehartma isn't onion, but roast mutton.

SOLENI.

And I tell you, chehartma—is a sort of onion.

CHEBUTIKIN.

And I tell you, chehartma—is mutton.

SOLENI.

And I tell you, cheremsha—is a sort of onion.

CHEBUTIKIN.

What's the use of arguing! You've never been in the Caucasus, and never ate any chehartma.

SOLENI.

I never ate it, because I hate it. It smells like garlic.

ANDREY.

[Imploring] Please, please! I ask you!

TUZENBACH.

When are the entertainers coming?

IRINA.

They promised for about nine; that is, quite soon.

TUZENBACH.

[Embraces ANDREY]

"Oh my house, my house, my new-built house."

ANDREY.

[Dances and sings] "Newly-built of maple-wood."

CHEBUTIKIN.

[Dances]

"Its walls are like a sieve!" [Laughter.]

TUZENBACH.

[Kisses ANDREY] Hang it all, let's drink. Andrey, old boy, let's drink with you. And I'll go with you, Andrey, to the University of Moscow.

SOLENI.
Which one? There are two universities in Moscow.
ANDREY.
There's one university in Moscow.
SOLENI.
Two, I tell you.
ANDREY.
Don't care if there are three. So much the better.
SOLENI.
There are two universities in Moscow! [There are murmurs and "hushes"] There are two universities in Moscow, the old one and the new one. And if you don't like to listen, if my words annoy you, then I need not speak. I can even go into another room.... [Exit.]
TUZENBACH.
Bravo, bravo! [Laughs] Come on, now. I'm going to play. Funny man, Soleni.... [Goes to the piano and plays a waltz.]
MASHA.
[Dancing solo] The Baron's drunk, the Baron's drunk, the Baron's drunk!
[NATASHA comes in.]
NATASHA.
[To CHEBUTIKIN] Ivan Romanovitch!
[Says something to CHEBUTIKIN, then goes out quietly; CHEBUTIKIN touches TUZENBACH on the shoulder and whispers something to him.]
IRINA.
What is it?
CHEBUTIKIN.
Time for us to go. Good-bye.
TUZENBACH.
Good-night. It's time we went.
IRINA.
But, really, the entertainers?
ANDREY.
[In confusion] There won't be any entertainers. You see, dear, Natasha says that Bobby isn't quite well, and so.... In a word, I don't care, and it's absolutely all one to me.

IRINA.
[Shrugging her shoulders] Bobby ill!

MASHA.
What is she thinking of! Well, if they are sent home, I suppose they must go. [To IRINA] Bobby's all right, it's she herself.... Here! [Taps her forehead] Little bourgeoise!
[ANDREY goes to his room through the right-hand door, CHEBUTIKIN follows him. In the dining-room they are saying good-bye.]

FEDOTIK.
What a shame! I was expecting to spend the evening here, but of course, if the little baby is ill ... I'll bring him some toys to-morrow.

RODE.
[Loudly] I slept late after dinner to-day because I thought I was going to dance all night. It's only nine o'clock now!

MASHA.
Let's go into the street, we can talk there. Then we can settle things.
(Good-byes and good nights are heard. TUZENBACH'S merry laughter is heard. [All go out] ANFISA and the maid clear the table, and put out the lights. [The nurse sings] ANDREY, wearing an overcoat and a hat, and CHEBUTIKIN enter silently.)

CHEBUTIKIN.
I never managed to get married because my life flashed by like lightning, and because I was madly in love with your mother, who was married.

ANDREY.
One shouldn't marry. One shouldn't, because it's dull.

CHEBUTIKIN.
So there I am, in my loneliness. Say what you will, loneliness is a terrible thing, old fellow.... Though really ... of course, it absolutely doesn't matter!

ANDREY.
Let's be quicker.

CHEBUTIKIN.
What are you in such a hurry for? We shall be in time.

ANDREY.
I'm afraid my wife may stop me.

CHEBUTIKIN.
   Ah!
ANDREY.
   I shan't play to-night, I shall only sit and look on. I don't feel very well. . . . What am I to do for my asthma, Ivan Romanovitch?
CHEBUTIKIN.
   Don't ask me! I don't remember, old fellow, I don't know.
ANDREY.
   Let's go through the kitchen. [They go out.]
   [A bell rings, then a second time; voices and laughter are heard.]
IRINA.
   [Enters] What's that?
ANFISA.
   [Whispers] The entertainers! [Bell.]
IRINA.
   Tell them there's nobody at home, nurse. They must excuse us.
   [ANFISA goes out. IRINA walks about the room deep in thought; she is excited. SOLENI enters.]
SOLENI.
   [In surprise] There's nobody here. . . . Where are they all?
IRINA.
   They've gone home.
SOLENI.
   How strange. Are you here alone?
IRINA.
   Yes, alone. [A pause] Good-bye.
SOLENI.
   Just now I behaved tactlessly, with insufficient reserve. But you are not like all the others, you are noble and pure, you can see the truth. . . . You alone can understand me. I love you, deeply, beyond measure, I love you.
IRINA.
   Good-bye! Go away.
SOLENI.
   I cannot live without you. [Follows her] Oh, my happiness! [Through his tears] Oh, joy! Wonderful, marvellous, glorious eyes, such as I have never seen before. . . .

IRINA.

[Coldly] Stop it, Vassili Vassilevitch!

SOLENI.

This is the first time I speak to you of love, and it is as if I am no longer on the earth, but on another planet. [Wipes his forehead] Well, never mind. I can't make you love me by force, of course . . . but I don't intend to have any more-favoured rivals. . . . No . . . I swear to you by all the saints, I shall kill my rival. . . . Oh, beautiful one!

[NATASHA enters with a candle; she looks in through one door, then through another, and goes past the door leading to her husband's room.]

NATASHA.

Here's Andrey. Let him go on reading. Excuse me, Vassili Vassilevitch, I did not know you were here; I am engaged in domesticities.

SOLENI.

It's all the same to me. Good-bye! [Exit.]

NATASHA.

You're so tired, my poor dear girl! [Kisses IRINA] If you only went to bed earlier.

IRINA.

Is Bobby asleep?

NATASHA.

Yes, but restlessly. By the way, dear, I wanted to tell you, but either you weren't at home, or I was busy . . . I think Bobby's present nursery is cold and damp. And your room would be so nice for the child. My dear, darling girl, do change over to Olga's for a bit!

IRINA.

[Not understanding] Where?

[The bells of a troika are heard as it drives up to the house.]

NATASHA.

You and Olga can share a room, for the time being, and Bobby can have yours. He's such a darling; to-day I said to him, "Bobby, you're mine! Mine!" And he looked at me with his dear little eyes. [A bell rings] It must be Olga. How late she is! [The maid enters and whispers to NATASHA] Protopopov? What a queer man to do such a thing. Protopopov's come and wants me to go for a drive with him in his troika. [Laughs] How funny these men are. . . . [A bell rings] Somebody has come. Suppose I did go and have half an hour's drive. . . . [To the maid] Say I shan't be long. [Bell rings] Somebody's ringing, it must be Olga. [Exit.]

[The maid runs out; IRINA sits deep in thought; KULIGIN and OLGA enter, followed by VERSHININ.]

KULIGIN.
Well, there you are. And you said there was going to be a party.

VERSHININ.
It's queer; I went away not long ago, half an hour ago, and they were expecting entertainers.

IRINA.
They've all gone.

KULIGIN.
Has Masha gone too? Where has she gone? And what's Protopopov waiting for downstairs in his troika? Whom is he expecting?

IRINA.
Don't ask questions . . . I'm tired.

KULIGIN.
Oh, you're all whimsies. . . .

OLGA.
My committee meeting is only just over. I'm tired out. Our chairwoman is ill, so I had to take her place. My head, my head is aching. . . . [Sits] Andrey lost 200 roubles at cards yesterday . . . the whole town is talking about it. . . .

KULIGIN.
Yes, my meeting tired me too. [Sits.]

VERSHININ.
My wife took it into her head to frighten me just now by nearly poisoning herself. It's all right now, and I'm glad; I can rest now. . . . But perhaps we ought to go away? Well, my best wishes, Feodor Ilitch, let's go somewhere together! I can't, I absolutely can't stop at home. . . . Come on!

KULIGIN.
I'm tired. I won't go. [Gets up] I'm tired. Has my wife gone home?

IRINA.

I suppose so.

KULIGIN.

[Kisses IRINA'S hand] Good-bye, I'm going to rest all day to-morrow and the day after. Best wishes! [Going] I should like some tea. I was looking forward to spending the whole evening in pleasant company and—o, fallacem hominum spem! . . . Accusative case after an interjection. . . .

VERSHININ.

Then I'll go somewhere by myself. [Exit with KULIGIN, whistling.]

OLGA.

I've such a headache . . . Andrey has been losing money. . . . The whole town is talking. . . . I'll go and lie down. [Going] I'm free to-morrow. . . . Oh, my God, what a mercy! I'm free to-morrow, I'm free the day after. . . . Oh my head, my head. . . . [Exit.]

IRINA.

[alone] They've all gone. Nobody's left.

[A concertina is being played in the street. The nurse sings.]

NATASHA.

[in fur coat and cap, steps across the dining-room, followed by the maid] I'll be back in half an hour. I'm only going for a little drive. [Exit.]

IRINA.

[Alone in her misery] To Moscow! Moscow! Moscow!

Curtain falls.

ACT III

The room shared by OLGA and IRINA. Beds, screened off, on the right and left. It is past 2 a.m. Behind the stage a fire-alarm is ringing; it has apparently been going for some time. Nobody in the house has gone to bed yet. MASHA is lying on a sofa dressed, as usual, in black. Enter OLGA and ANFISA.

ANFISA.
  Now they are downstairs, sitting under the stairs. I said to them, "Won't you come up," I said, "You can't go on like this," and they simply cried, "We don't know where father is." They said, "He may be burnt up by now." What an idea! And in the yard there are some people . . . also undressed.

OLGA.
  [Takes a dress out of the cupboard] Take this grey dress. . . . And this . . . and the blouse as well. . . . Take the skirt, too, nurse. . . . My God! How awful it is! The whole of the Kirsanovsky Road seems to have burned down. Take this . . . and this. . . . [Throws clothes into her hands]

The poor Vershinins are so frightened. . . . Their house was nearly burnt. They ought to come here for the night. . . . They shouldn't be allowed to go home. . . . Poor Fedotik is completely burnt out, there's nothing left. . . .

ANFISA.

Couldn't you call Ferapont, Olga dear. I can hardly manage. . . .

OLGA.

[Rings] They'll never answer. . . . [At the door] Come here, whoever there is! [Through the open door can be seen a window, red with flame: a fire-engine is heard passing the house] How awful this is. And how I'm sick of it! [FERAPONT enters] Take these things down. . . . The Kolotilin girls are down below . . . and let them have them. This, too.

FERAPONT.

Yes'm. In the year twelve Moscow was burning too. Oh, my God! The Frenchmen were surprised.

OLGA.

Go on, go on. . . .

FERAPONT.

Yes'm. [Exit.]

OLGA.

Nurse, dear, let them have everything. We don't want anything. Give it all to them, nurse. . . . I'm tired, I can hardly keep on my legs. . . . The Vershinins mustn't be allowed to go home. . . . The girls can sleep in the drawing-room, and Alexander Ignateyevitch can go downstairs to the Baron's flat . . . Fedotik can go there, too, or else into our dining-room. . . . The doctor is drunk, beastly drunk, as if on purpose, so nobody can go to him. Vershinin's wife, too, may go into the drawing-room.

ANFISA.

[Tired] Olga, dear girl, don't dismiss me! Don't dismiss me!

OLGA.

You're talking nonsense, nurse. Nobody is dismissing you.

ANFISA.

[Puts OLGA'S head against her bosom] My dear, precious girl, I'm working, I'm toiling away . . . I'm growing weak, and they'll all say go away! And where shall I go? Where? I'm eighty. Eighty-one years old. . . .

OLGA.
You sit down, nurse dear.... You're tired, poor dear.... [Makes her sit down] Rest, dear. You're so pale!
[NATASHA comes in.]
NATASHA.
They are saying that a committee to assist the sufferers from the fire must be formed at once. What do you think of that? It's a beautiful idea. Of course the poor ought to be helped, it's the duty of the rich. Bobby and little Sophy are sleeping, sleeping as if nothing at all was the matter. There's such a lot of people here, the place is full of them, wherever you go. There's influenza in the town now. I'm afraid the children may catch it.
OLGA.
[Not attending] In this room we can't see the fire, it's quiet here.
NATASHA.
Yes ... I suppose I'm all untidy. [Before the looking-glass] They say I'm growing stout ... it isn't true! Certainly it isn't! Masha's asleep; the poor thing is tired out.... [Coldly, to ANFISA] Don't dare to be seated in my presence! Get up! Out of this! [Exit ANFISA; a pause] I don't understand what makes you keep on that old woman!
OLGA.
[Confusedly] Excuse me, I don't understand either ...
NATASHA.
She's no good here. She comes from the country, she ought to live there.... Spoiling her, I call it! I like order in the house! We don't want any unnecessary people here. [Strokes her cheek] You're tired, poor thing! Our head mistress is tired! And when my little Sophie grows up and goes to school I shall be so afraid of you.
OLGA.
I shan't be head mistress.
NATASHA.
They'll appoint you, Olga. It's settled.
OLGA.
I'll refuse the post. I can't ... I'm not strong enough.... [Drinks water] You were so rude to nurse just now ... I'm sorry. I can't stand it ... everything seems dark in front of me....

NATASHA.
> [Excited] Forgive me, Olga, forgive me . . . I didn't want to annoy you.
> [MASHA gets up, takes a pillow and goes out angrily.]

OLGA.
> Remember, dear . . . we have been brought up, in an unusual way, perhaps, but I can't bear this. Such behaviour has a bad effect on me, I get ill . . . I simply lose heart!

NATASHA.
> Forgive me, forgive me. . . . [Kisses her.]

OLGA.
> Even the least bit of rudeness, the slightest impoliteness, upsets me.

NATASHA.
> I often say too much, it's true, but you must agree, dear, that she could just as well live in the country.

OLGA.
> She has been with us for thirty years.

NATASHA.
> But she can't do any work now. Either I don't understand, or you don't want to understand me. She's no good for work, she can only sleep or sit about.

OLGA.
> And let her sit about.

NATASHA.
> [Surprised] What do you mean? She's only a servant. [Crying] I don't understand you, Olga. I've got a nurse, a wet-nurse, we've a cook, a housemaid . . . what do we want that old woman for as well? What good is she? [Fire-alarm behind the stage.]

OLGA.
> I've grown ten years older to-night.

NATASHA.
> We must come to an agreement, Olga. Your place is the school, mine—the home. You devote yourself to teaching, I, to the household. And if I talk about servants, then I do know what I am talking about; I do know what I am talking about . . . And to-morrow there's to be no more of that old thief, that old hag . . . [Stamping] that witch! And don't you dare to annoy me! Don't you dare! [Stopping short]

Really, if you don't move downstairs, we shall always be quarrelling. This is awful.

[Enter KULIGIN.]

KULIGIN.

Where's Masha? It's time we went home. The fire seems to be going down. [Stretches himself] Only one block has burnt down, but there was such a wind that it seemed at first the whole town was going to burn. [Sits] I'm tired out. My dear Olga . . . I often think that if it hadn't been for Masha, I should have married you. You are awfully nice. . . . I am absolutely tired out. [Listens.]

OLGA.

What is it?

KULIGIN.

The doctor, of course, has been drinking hard; he's terribly drunk. He might have done it on purpose! [Gets up] He seems to be coming here. . . . Do you hear him? Yes, here. . . . [Laughs] What a man . . . really . . . I'll hide myself. [Goes to the cupboard and stands in the corner] What a rogue.

OLGA.

He hadn't touched a drop for two years, and now he suddenly goes and gets drunk. . . .

[Retires with NATASHA to the back of the room. CHEBUTIKIN enters; apparently sober, he stops, looks round, then goes to the washstand and begins to wash his hands.]

CHEBUTIKIN.

[Angrily] Devil take them all . . . take them all. . . . They think I'm a doctor and can cure everything, and I know absolutely nothing, I've forgotten all I ever knew, I remember nothing, absolutely nothing. [OLGA and NATASHA go out, unnoticed by him] Devil take it. Last Wednesday I attended a woman in Zasip—and she died, and it's my fault that she died. Yes . . . I used to know a certain amount five-and-twenty years ago, but I don't remember anything now. Nothing. Perhaps I'm not really a man, and am only pretending that I've got arms and legs and a head; perhaps I don't exist at all, and only imagine that I walk, and eat, and sleep. [Cries] Oh, if only I didn't exist! [Stops crying; angrily] The devil only knows. . . . Day before yesterday they were talking in the club; they said, Shakespeare, Voltaire . . . I'd never read, never read at all, and I put on an expression as if I had read. And so did the others. Oh, how beastly! How petty! And then I remembered the woman I killed on Wednesday . . . and I couldn't get her out of my mind, and everything in my mind became crooked, nasty, wretched. . . . So I went and drank. . . .

[IRINA, VERSHININ and TUZENBACH enter; TUZENBACH is wearing new and fashionable civilian clothes.]

IRINA.
Let's sit down here. Nobody will come in here.
VERSHININ.
The whole town would have been destroyed if it hadn't been for the soldiers. Good men! [Rubs his hands appreciatively] Splendid people! Oh, what a fine lot!
KULIGIN.
[Coming up to him] What's the time?
TUZENBACH.
It's past three now. It's dawning.
IRINA.
They are all sitting in the dining-room, nobody is going. And that Soleni of yours is sitting there. [To CHEBUTIKIN] Hadn't you better be going to sleep, doctor?
CHEBUTIKIN.
It's all right . . . thank you. . . . [Combs his beard.]
KULIGIN.
[Laughs] Speaking's a bit difficult, eh, Ivan Romanovitch! [Pats him on the shoulder] Good man! In vino veritas, the ancients used to say.
TUZENBACH.
They keep on asking me to get up a concert in aid of the sufferers.
IRINA.
As if one could do anything. . . .
TUZENBACH.
It might be arranged, if necessary. In my opinion Maria Sergeyevna is an excellent pianist.
KULIGIN.
Yes, excellent!

IRINA.
She's forgotten everything. She hasn't played for three years . . . or four.
TUZENBACH.
In this town absolutely nobody understands music, not a soul except myself, but I do understand it, and assure you on my word of honour that Maria Sergeyevna plays excellently, almost with genius.
KULIGIN.
You are right, Baron, I'm awfully fond of Masha. She's very fine.
TUZENBACH.
To be able to play so admirably and to realize at the same time that nobody, nobody can understand you!
KULIGIN.
[Sighs] Yes. . . . But will it be quite all right for her to take part in a concert? [Pause] You see, I don't know anything about it. Perhaps it will even be all to the good. Although I must admit that our Director is a good man, a very good man even, a very clever man, still he has such views. . . . Of course it isn't his business but still, if you wish it, perhaps I'd better talk to him.
[CHEBUTIKIN takes a porcelain clock into his hands and examines it.]
VERSHININ.
I got so dirty while the fire was on, I don't look like anybody on earth. [Pause] Yesterday I happened to hear, casually, that they want to transfer our brigade to some distant place. Some said to Poland, others, to Chita.
TUZENBACH.
I heard so, too. Well, if it is so, the town will be quite empty.
IRINA.
And we'll go away, too!
CHEBUTIKIN.
[Drops the clock which breaks to pieces] To smithereens!
[A pause; everybody is pained and confused.]
KULIGIN.
[Gathering up the pieces] To smash such a valuable object—oh, Ivan Romanovitch, Ivan Romanovitch! A very bad mark for your misbehaviour!

IRINA.

That clock used to belong to our mother.

CHEBUTIKIN.

Perhaps. . . . To your mother, your mother. Perhaps I didn't break it; it only looks as if I broke it. Perhaps we only think that we exist, when really we don't. I don't know anything, nobody knows anything. [At the door] What are you looking at? Natasha has a little romance with Protopopov, and you don't see it. . . . There you sit and see nothing, and Natasha has a little romance with Protopovov. . . . [Sings] Won't you please accept this date. . . . [Exit.]

VERSHININ.

Yes. [Laughs] How strange everything really is! [Pause] When the fire broke out, I hurried off home; when I get there I see the house is whole, uninjured, and in no danger, but my two girls are standing by the door in just their underclothes, their mother isn't there, the crowd is excited, horses and dogs are running about, and the girls' faces are so agitated, terrified, beseeching, and I don't know what else. My heart was pained when I saw those faces. My God, I thought, what these girls will have to put up with if they live long! I caught them up and ran, and still kept on thinking the one thing: what they will have to live through in this world! [Fire-alarm; a pause] I come here and find their mother shouting and angry. [MASHA enters with a pillow and sits on the sofa] And when my girls were standing by the door in just their underclothes, and the street was red from the fire, there was a dreadful noise, and I thought that something of the sort used to happen many years ago when an enemy made a sudden attack, and looted, and burned. . . . And at the same time what a difference there really is between the present and the past! And when a little more time has gone by, in two or three hundred years perhaps, people will look at our present life with just the same fear, and the same contempt, and the whole past will seem clumsy and dull, and very uncomfortable, and strange. Oh, indeed, what a life there will be, what a life! [Laughs] Forgive me, I've dropped into philosophy again. Please let me continue. I do awfully want to philosophize, it's just how I feel at present. [Pause] As if they are all asleep. As I was saying: what a life there will be! Only just imagine. . . . There are

only three persons like yourselves in the town just now, but in future generations there will be more and more, and still more, and the time will come when everything will change and become as you would have it, people will live as you do, and then you too will go out of date; people will be born who are better than you. . . . [Laughs] Yes, to-day I am quite exceptionally in the vein. I am devilishly keen on living. . . . [Sings.]
"The power of love all ages know,
From its assaults great good does grow." [Laughs.]

MASHA.
   Trum-tum-tum . . .
VERSHININ.
   Tum-tum . . .
MASHA.
   Tra-ra-ra?
VERSHININ.
   Tra-ta-ta. [Laughs.]
   [Enter FEDOTIK.]
FEDOTIK.
   [Dancing] I'm burnt out, I'm burnt out! Down to the ground! [Laughter.]
IRINA.
   I don't see anything funny about it. Is everything burnt?
FEDOTIK.
   [Laughs] Absolutely. Nothing left at all. The guitar's burnt, and the photographs are burnt, and all my correspondence. . . . And I was going to make you a present of a note-book, and that's burnt too.
   [SOLENI comes in.]
IRINA.
   No, you can't come here, Vassili Vassilevitch. Please go away.
SOLENI.
   Why can the Baron come here and I can't?
VERSHININ.
   We really must go. How's the fire?
SOLENI.
   They say it's going down. No, I absolutely don't see why the Baron can, and I can't? [Scents his hands.]

VERSHININ.
>   Trum-tum-tum.

MASHA.
>   Trum-tum.

VERSHININ.
>   [Laughs to SOLENI] Let's go into the dining-room.

SOLENI.
>   Very well, we'll make a note of it. "If I should try to make this clear, the geese would be annoyed, I fear." [Looks at TUZENBACH] There, there, there. . . . [Goes out with VERSHININ and FEDOTIK.]

IRINA.
>   How Soleni smelt of tobacco. . . . [In surprise] The Baron's asleep! Baron! Baron!

TUZENBACH.
>   [Waking] I am tired, I must say. . . . The brickworks. . . . No, I'm not wandering, I mean it; I'm going to start work soon at the brickworks . . . I've already talked it over. [Tenderly, to IRINA] You're so pale, and beautiful, and charming. . . . Your paleness seems to shine through the dark air as if it was a light. . . . You are sad, displeased with life. . . . Oh, come with me, let's go and work together!

MASHA.
>   Nicolai Lvovitch, go away from here.

TUZENBACH.
>   [Laughs] Are you here? I didn't see you. [Kisses IRINA'S hand] good-bye, I'll go . . . I look at you now and I remember, as if it was long ago, your name-day, when you, cheerfully and merrily, were talking about the joys of labour. . . . And how happy life seemed to me, then! What has happened to it now? [Kisses her hand] There are tears in your eyes. Go to bed now; it is already day . . . the morning begins. . . . If only I was allowed to give my life for you!

MASHA.
>   Nicolai Lvovitch, go away! What business . . .

TUZENBACH.
>   I'm off. [Exit.]

MASHA.
>   [Lies down] Are you asleep, Feodor?

KULIGIN.

Eh?

MASHA.

Shouldn't you go home.

KULIGIN.

My dear Masha, my darling Masha. . . .

IRINA.

She's tired out. You might let her rest, Fedia.

KULIGIN.

I'll go at once. My wife's a good, splendid . . . I love you, my only one. . . .

MASHA.

[Angrily] Amo, amas, amat, amamus, amatis, amant.

KULIGIN.

[Laughs] No, she really is wonderful. I've been your husband seven years, and it seems as if I was only married yesterday. On my word. No, you really are a wonderful woman. I'm satisfied, I'm satisfied, I'm satisfied!

MASHA.

I'm bored, I'm bored, I'm bored. . . . [Sits up] But I can't get it out of my head. . . . It's simply disgraceful. It has been gnawing away at me . . . I can't keep silent. I mean about Andrey. . . . He has mortgaged this house with the bank, and his wife has got all the money; but the house doesn't belong to him alone, but to the four of us! He ought to know that, if he's an honourable man.

KULIGIN.

What's the use, Masha? Andrey is in debt all round; well, let him do as he pleases.

MASHA.

It's disgraceful, anyway. [Lies down]

KULIGIN.

You and I are not poor. I work, take my classes, give private lessons . . . I am a plain, honest man . . . Omnia mea mecum porto, as they say.

MASHA.

I don't want anything, but the unfairness of it disgusts me. [Pause] You go, Feodor.

KULIGIN.
 [Kisses her] You're tired, just rest for half an hour, and I'll sit and wait for you. Sleep. . . . [Going] I'm satisfied, I'm satisfied, I'm satisfied. [Exit.]
IRINA.
 Yes, really, our Andrey has grown smaller; how he's snuffed out and aged with that woman! He used to want to be a professor, and yesterday he was boasting that at last he had been made a member of the district council. He is a member, and Protopopov is chairman. . . . The whole town talks and laughs about it, and he alone knows and sees nothing. . . . And now everybody's gone to look at the fire, but he sits alone in his room and pays no attention, only just plays on his fiddle. [Nervily] Oh, it's awful, awful, awful. [Weeps] I can't, I can't bear it any longer! . . . I can't, I can't! . . . [OLGA comes in and clears up at her little table. IRINA is sobbing loudly] Throw me out, throw me out, I can't bear any more!
OLGA.
 [Alarmed] What is it, what is it? Dear!
IRINA.
 [Sobbing] Where? Where has everything gone? Where is it all? Oh my God, my God! I've forgotten everything, everything . . . I don't remember what is the Italian for window or, well, for ceiling . . . I forget everything, every day I forget it, and life passes and will never return, and we'll never go away to Moscow . . . I see that we'll never go. . . .
OLGA.
 Dear, dear. . . .
IRINA.
 [Controlling herself] Oh, I am unhappy . . . I can't work, I shan't work. Enough, enough! I used to be a telegraphist, now I work at the town council offices, and I have nothing but hate and contempt for all they give me to do . . . I am already twenty-three, I have already been at work for a long while, and my brain has dried up, and I've grown thinner, plainer, older, and there is no relief of any sort, and time goes and it seems all the while as if I am going away from the real, the beautiful life, farther and farther away, down some precipice. I'm in despair and I can't understand how it is that I am still alive, that I haven't killed myself.

OLGA.
Don't cry, dear girl, don't cry ... I suffer, too.
IRINA.
I'm not crying, not crying.... Enough.... Look, I'm not crying any more. Enough ... enough!
OLGA.
Dear, I tell you as a sister and a friend if you want my advice, marry the Baron. [IRINA cries softly] You respect him, you think highly of him.... It is true that he is not handsome, but he is so honourable and clean ... people don't marry from love, but in order to do one's duty. I think so, at any rate, and I'd marry without being in love. Whoever he was, I should marry him, so long as he was a decent man. Even if he was old....
IRINA.
I was always waiting until we should be settled in Moscow, there I should meet my true love; I used to think about him, and love him.... But it's all turned out to be nonsense, all nonsense....
OLGA.
[Embraces her sister] My dear, beautiful sister, I understand everything; when Baron Nicolai Lvovitch left the army and came to us in evening dress, [Note: I.e. in the correct dress for making a proposal of marriage.] he seemed so bad-looking to me that I even started crying.... He asked, "What are you crying for?" How could I tell him! But if God brought him to marry you, I should be happy. That would be different, quite different.
[NATASHA with a candle walks across the stage from right to left without saying anything.]
MASHA.
[Sitting up] She walks as if she's set something on fire.
OLGA.
Masha, you're silly, you're the silliest of the family. Please forgive me for saying so. [Pause.]
MASHA.
I want to make a confession, dear sisters. My soul is in pain. I will confess to you, and never again to anybody ... I'll tell you this minute. [Softly] It's my secret but you must know everything ... I can't be

silent.... [Pause] I love, I love ... I love that man.... You saw him only just now.... Why don't I say it ... in one word. I love Vershinin.

OLGA.

[Goes behind her screen] Stop that, I don't hear you in any case.

MASHA.

What am I to do? [Takes her head in her hands] First he seemed queer to me, then I was sorry for him ... then I fell in love with him ... fell in love with his voice, his words, his misfortunes, his two daughters.

OLGA.

[Behind the screen] I'm not listening. You may talk any nonsense you like, it will be all the same, I shan't hear.

MASHA.

Oh, Olga, you are foolish. I am in love—that means that is to be my fate. It means that is to be my lot.... And he loves me.... It is all awful. Yes; it isn't good, is it? [Takes IRINA'S hand and draws her to her] Oh, my dear.... How are we going to live through our lives, what is to become of us.... When you read a novel it all seems so old and easy, but when you fall in love yourself, then you learn that nobody knows anything, and each must decide for himself.... My dear ones, my sisters ... I've confessed, now I shall keep silence.... Like the lunatics in Gogol's story, I'm going to be silent ... silent ...

[ANDREY enters, followed by FERAPONT.]

ANDREY.

[Angrily] What do you want? I don't understand.

FERAPONT.

[At the door, impatiently] I've already told you ten times, Andrey Sergeyevitch.

ANDREY.

In the first place I'm not Andrey Sergeyevitch, but sir. [Note: Quite literally, "your high honour," to correspond to Andrey's rank as a civil servant.]

FERAPONT.

The firemen, sir, ask if they can go across your garden to the river. Else they go right round, right round; it's a nuisance.

ANDREY.

All right. Tell them it's all right. [Exit FERAPONT] I'm tired of them. Where is Olga? [OLGA comes out from behind the screen] I came to you for the key of the cupboard. I lost my own. You've got a little key. [OLGA gives him the key; IRINA goes behind her screen; pause] What a huge fire! It's going down now. Hang it all, that Ferapont made me so angry that I talked nonsense to him. . . . Sir, indeed. . . . [A pause] Why are you so silent, Olga? [Pause] It's time you stopped all that nonsense and behaved as if you were properly alive. . . . You are here, Masha. Irina is here, well, since we're all here, let's come to a complete understanding, once and for all. What have you against me? What is it?

OLGA.

Please don't, Audrey dear. We'll talk to-morrow. [Excited] What an awful night!

ANDREY.

[Much confused] Don't excite yourself. I ask you in perfect calmness; what have you against me? Tell me straight.

VERSHININ'S VOICE.

Trum-tum-tum!

MASHA.

[Stands; loudly] Tra-ta-ta! [To OLGA] Goodbye, Olga, God bless you. [Goes behind screen and kisses IRINA] Sleep well. . . . Goodbye, Andrey. Go away now, they're tired . . . you can explain to-morrow. . . . [Exit.]

ANDREY.

I'll only say this and go. Just now. . . . In the first place, you've got something against Natasha, my wife; I've noticed it since the very day of my marriage. Natasha is a beautiful and honest creature, straight and honourable—that's my opinion. I love and respect my wife; understand it, I respect her, and I insist that others should respect her too. I repeat, she's an honest and honourable person, and all your disapproval is simply silly . . . [Pause] In the second place, you seem to be annoyed because I am not a professor, and am not engaged in study. But I work for the zemstvo, I am a member of the district council, and I consider my service as worthy and as high as the service of science. I am a member of the district council, and I am proud of it, if you want to know. [Pause] In the third place, I have still this to say . . . that I have mortgaged the house without obtaining your permission. . . . For that I am to blame, and ask to be forgiven. My debts led me into doing it . . .

thirty-five thousand . . . I do not play at cards any more, I stopped long ago, but the chief thing I have to say in my defence is that you girls receive a pension, and I don't . . . my wages, so to speak. . . . [Pause.]

KULIGIN.

[At the door] Is Masha there? [Excitedly] Where is she? It's queer. . . . [Exit.]

ANDREY.

They don't hear. Natasha is a splendid, honest person. [Walks about in silence, then stops] When I married I thought we should be happy . . . all of us. . . . But, my God. . . . [Weeps] My dear, dear sisters, don't believe me, don't believe me. . . . [Exit.]

[Fire-alarm. The stage is clear.]

IRINA.

[behind her screen] Olga, who's knocking on the floor?

OLGA.

It's doctor Ivan Romanovitch. He's drunk.

IRINA.

What a restless night! [Pause] Olga! [Looks out] Did you hear? They are taking the brigade away from us; it's going to be transferred to some place far away.

OLGA.

It's only a rumour.

IRINA.

Then we shall be left alone. . . . Olga!

OLGA.

Well?

IRINA.

My dear, darling sister, I esteem, I highly value the Baron, he's a splendid man; I'll marry him, I'll consent, only let's go to Moscow! I implore you, let's go! There's nothing better than Moscow on earth! Let's go, Olga, let's go!

Curtain falls

ACT IV

The old garden at the house of the PROSOROVS. There is a long avenue of firs, at the end of which the river can be seen. There is a forest on the far side of the river. On the right is the terrace of the house: bottles and tumblers are on a table here; it is evident that champagne has just been drunk. It is midday. Every now and again passers-by walk across the garden, from the road to the river; five soldiers go past rapidly. CHEBUTIKIN, in a comfortable frame of mind which does not desert him throughout the act, sits in an armchair in the garden, waiting to be called. He wears a peaked cap and has a stick. IRINA, KULIGIN with a cross hanging from his neck and without his moustaches, and TUZENBACH are standing on the terrace seeing off FEDOTIK and RODE, who are coming down into the garden; both officers are in service uniform.

TUZENBACH.
    [Exchanges kisses with FEDOTIK] You're a good sort, we got on so well together. [Exchanges kisses with RODE] Once again. . . . Good-bye, old man!

IRINA.
> Au revoir!

FEDOTIK.
> It isn't au revoir, it's good-bye; we'll never meet again!

KULIGIN.
> Who knows! [Wipes his eyes; smiles] Here I've started crying!

IRINA.
> We'll meet again sometime.

FEDOTIK.
> After ten years—or fifteen? We'll hardly know one another then; we'll say, "How do you do?" coldly.... [Takes a snapshot] Keep still.... Once more, for the last time.

RODE.
> [Embracing TUZENBACH] We shan't meet again.... [Kisses IRINA'S hand] Thank you for everything, for everything!

FEDOTIK.
> [Grieved] Don't be in such a hurry!

TUZENBACH.
> We shall meet again, if God wills it. Write to us. Be sure to write.

RODE.
> [Looking round the garden] Good-bye, trees! [Shouts] Yo-ho! [Pause] Good-bye, echo!

KULIGIN.
> Best wishes. Go and get yourselves wives there in Poland.... Your Polish wife will clasp you and call you "kochanku!" [Note: Darling.] [Laughs.]

FEDOTIK.
> [Looking at the time] There's less than an hour left. Soleni is the only one of our battery who is going on the barge; the rest of us are going with the main body. Three batteries are leaving to-day, another three to-morrow and then the town will be quiet and peaceful.

TUZENBACH.
> And terribly dull.

RODE.
> And where is Maria Sergeyevna?

KULIGIN.
> Masha is in the garden.

FEDOTIK.
> We'd like to say good-bye to her.

RODE.
> Good-bye, I must go, or else I'll start weeping. . . . [Quickly embraces KULIGIN and TUZENBACH, and kisses IRINA'S hand] We've been so happy here. . . .

FEDOTIK.
> [To KULIGIN] Here's a keepsake for you . . . a note-book with a pencil. . . . We'll go to the river from here. . . . [They go aside and both look round.]

RODE.
> [Shouts] Yo-ho!

KULIGIN.
> [Shouts] Good-bye!
> [At the back of the stage FEDOTIK and RODE meet MASHA; they say good-bye and go out with her.]

IRINA.
> They've gone. . . . [Sits on the bottom step of the terrace.]

CHEBUTIKIN.
> And they forgot to say good-bye to me.

IRINA.
> But why is that?

CHEBUTIKIN.
> I just forgot, somehow. Though I'll soon see them again, I'm going to-morrow. Yes . . . just one day left. I shall be retired in a year, then I'll come here again, and finish my life near you. I've only one year before I get my pension. . . . [Puts one newspaper into his pocket and takes another out] I'll come here to you and change my life radically . . . I'll be so quiet . . . so agree . . . agreeable, respectable. . . .

IRINA.
> Yes, you ought to change your life, dear man, somehow or other.

CHEBUTIKIN.
> Yes, I feel it. [Sings softly.] "Tarara-boom-deay. . . ."

KULIGIN.
> We won't reform Ivan Romanovitch! We won't reform him!

CHEBUTIKIN.
> If only I was apprenticed to you! Then I'd reform.

IRINA.
> Feodor has shaved his moustache! I can't bear to look at him.

KULIGIN.
> Well, what about it?

CHEBUTIKIN.
> I could tell you what your face looks like now, but it wouldn't be polite.

KULIGIN.
> Well! It's the custom, it's modus vivendi. Our Director is clean-shaven, and so I too, when I received my inspectorship, had my moustaches removed. Nobody likes it, but it's all one to me. I'm satisfied. Whether I've got moustaches or not, I'm satisfied. . . . [Sits.]

[At the back of the stage ANDREY is wheeling a perambulator containing a sleeping infant.]

IRINA.
> Ivan Romanovitch, be a darling. I'm awfully worried. You were out on the boulevard last night; tell me, what happened?

CHEBUTIKIN.
> What happened? Nothing. Quite a trifling matter. [Reads paper] Of no importance!

KULIGIN.
> They say that Soleni and the Baron met yesterday on the boulevard near the theatre. . . .

TUZENBACH.
> Stop! What right . . . [Waves his hand and goes into the house.]

KULIGIN.
> Near the theatre . . . Soleni started behaving offensively to the Baron, who lost his temper and said something nasty. . . .

CHEBUTIKIN.
> I don't know. It's all bunkum.

KULIGIN.
> At some seminary or other a master wrote "bunkum" on an essay, and the student couldn't make the letters out—thought it was a Latin word

"luckum." [Laughs] Awfully funny, that. They say that Soleni is in love with Irina and hates the Baron. . . . That's quite natural. Irina is a very nice girl. She's even like Masha, she's so thoughtful. . . . Only, Irina your character is gentler. Though Masha's character, too, is a very good one. I'm very fond of Masha. [Shouts of "Yo-ho!" are heard behind the stage.]

IRINA.

[Shudders] Everything seems to frighten me today. [Pause] I've got everything ready, and I send my things off after dinner. The Baron and I will be married to-morrow, and to-morrow we go away to the brickworks, and the next day I go to the school, and the new life begins. God will help me! When I took my examination for the teacher's post, I actually wept for joy and gratitude. . . . [Pause] The cart will be here in a minute for my things. . . .

KULIGIN.

Somehow or other, all this doesn't seem at all serious. As if it was all ideas, and nothing really serious. Still, with all my soul I wish you happiness.

CHEBUTIKIN.

[With deep feeling] My splendid . . . my dear, precious girl. . . . You've gone on far ahead, I won't catch up with you. I'm left behind like a migrant bird grown old, and unable to fly. Fly, my dear, fly, and God be with you! [Pause] It's a pity you shaved your moustaches, Feodor Ilitch.

KULIGIN.

Oh, drop it! [Sighs] To-day the soldiers will be gone, and everything will go on as in the old days. Say what you will, Masha is a good, honest woman. I love her very much, and thank my fate for her. People have such different fates. There's a Kosirev who works in the excise department here. He was at school with me; he was expelled from the fifth class of the High School for being entirely unable to understand ut consecutivum. He's awfully hard up now and in very poor health, and when I meet him I say to him, "How do you do, ut consecutivum." "Yes," he says, "precisely consecutivum . . ." and coughs. But I've been successful all my life, I'm happy, and I even have a Stanislaus Cross, of the second class, and now I myself teach others that ut consecutivum. Of course, I'm a clever man, much cleverer than many, but happiness doesn't only lie in that. . . .

["The Maiden's Prayer" is being played on the piano in the house.]

IRINA.

    To-morrow night I shan't hear that "Maiden's Prayer" any more, and I shan't be meeting Protopopov. . . . [Pause] Protopopov is sitting there in the drawing-room; and he came to-day . . .

KULIGIN.

    Hasn't the head-mistress come yet?

IRINA.

    No. She has been sent for. If you only knew how difficult it is for me to live alone, without Olga. . . . She lives at the High School; she, a head-mistress, busy all day with her affairs and I'm alone, bored, with nothing to do, and hate the room I live in. . . . I've made up my mind: if I can't live in Moscow, then it must come to this. It's fate. It can't be helped. It's all the will of God, that's the truth. Nicolai Lvovitch made me a proposal. . . . Well? I thought it over and made up my mind. He's a good man . . . it's quite remarkable how good he is. . . . And suddenly my soul put out wings, I became happy, and light-hearted, and once again the desire for work, work, came over me. . . . Only something happened yesterday, some secret dread has been hanging over me. . . .

CHEBUTIKIN.

    Luckum. Rubbish.

NATASHA.

    [At the window] The head-mistress.

KULIGIN.

    The head-mistress has come. Let's go. [Exit with IRINA into the house.]

CHEBUTIKIN.

    "It is my washing day. . . . Tara-ra . . . boom-deay."

    [MASHA approaches, ANDREY is wheeling a perambulator at the back.]

MASHA.

    Here you are, sitting here, doing nothing.

CHEBUTIKIN.

    What then?

MASHA.

    [Sits] Nothing. . . . [Pause] Did you love my mother?

CHEBUTIKIN.
  Very much.
MASHA.
  And did she love you?
CHEBUTIKIN.
  [After a pause] I don't remember that.
MASHA.
  Is my man here? When our cook Martha used to ask about her gendarme, she used to say my man. Is he here?
CHEBUTIKIN.
  Not yet.
MASHA.
  When you take your happiness in little bits, in snatches, and then lose it, as I have done, you gradually get coarser, more bitter. [Points to her bosom] I'm boiling in here. . . . [Looks at ANDREY with the perambulator] There's our brother Andrey. . . . All our hopes in him have gone. There was once a great bell, a thousand persons were hoisting it, much money and labour had been spent on it, when it suddenly fell and was broken. Suddenly, for no particular reason. . . . Andrey is like that. . . .
ANDREY.
  When are they going to stop making such a noise in the house? It's awful.
CHEBUTIKIN.
  They won't be much longer. [Looks at his watch] My watch is very old-fashioned, it strikes the hours. . . . [Winds the watch and makes it strike] The first, second, and fifth batteries are to leave at one o'clock precisely. [Pause] And I go to-morrow.
ANDREY.
  For good?
CHEBUTIKIN.
  I don't know. Perhaps I'll return in a year. The devil only knows . . . it's all one. . . . [Somewhere a harp and violin are being played.]
ANDREY.
  The town will grow empty. It will be as if they put a cover over it. [Pause] Something happened yesterday by the theatre. The whole town knows of it, but I don't.

CHEBUTIKIN.
>   Nothing. A silly little affair. Soleni started irritating the Baron, who lost his temper and insulted him, and so at last Soleni had to challenge him. [Looks at his watch] It's about time, I think. . . . At half-past twelve, in the public wood, that one you can see from here across the river. . . . Piff-paff. [Laughs] Soleni thinks he's Lermontov, and even writes verses. That's all very well, but this is his third duel.

MASHA.
>   Whose?

CHEBUTIKIN.
>   Soleni's.

MASHA.
>   And the Baron?

CHEBUTIKIN.
>   What about the Baron? [Pause.]

MASHA.
>   Everything's all muddled up in my head. . . . But I say it ought not to be allowed. He might wound the Baron or even kill him.

CHEBUTIKIN.
>   The Baron is a good man, but one Baron more or less—what difference does it make? It's all the same! [Beyond the garden somebody shouts "Co-ee! Hallo!"] You wait. That's Skvortsov shouting; one of the seconds. He's in a boat. [Pause.]

ANDREY.
>   In my opinion it's simply immoral to fight in a duel, or to be present, even in the quality of a doctor.

CHEBUTIKIN.
>   It only seems so. . . . We don't exist, there's nothing on earth, we don't really live, it only seems that we live. Does it matter, anyway!

MASHA.
>   You talk and talk the whole day long. [Going] You live in a climate like this, where it might snow any moment, and there you talk. . . . [Stops] I won't go into the house, I can't go there. . . . Tell me when Vershinin comes. . . . [Goes along the avenue] The migrant birds are already on the wing. . . . [Looks up] Swans or geese. . . . My dear, happy things. . . . [Exit.]

ANDREY.
>   Our house will be empty. The officers will go away, you are going, my sister is getting married, and I alone will remain in the house.

CHEBUTIKIN.
>   And your wife?
>   [FERAPONT enters with some documents.]

ANDREY.
>   A wife's a wife. She's honest, well-bred, yes; and kind, but with all that there is still something about her that degenerates her into a petty, blind, even in some respects misshapen animal. In any case, she isn't a man. I tell you as a friend, as the only man to whom I can lay bare my soul. I love Natasha, it's true, but sometimes she seems extraordinarily vulgar, and then I lose myself and can't understand why I love her so much, or, at any rate, used to love her....

CHEBUTIKIN.
>   [Rises] I'm going away to-morrow, old chap, and perhaps we'll never meet again, so here's my advice. Put on your cap, take a stick in your hand, go ... go on and on, without looking round. And the farther you go, the better.
>   [SOLENI goes across the back of the stage with two officers; he catches sight of CHEBUTIKIN, and turns to him, the officers go on.]

SOLENI.
>   Doctor, it's time. It's half-past twelve already. [Shakes hands with ANDREY.]

CHEBUTIKIN.
>   Half a minute. I'm tired of the lot of you. [To ANDREY] If anybody asks for me, say I'll be back soon.... [Sighs] Oh, oh, oh!

SOLENI.
>   "He didn't have the time to sigh. The bear sat on him heavily." [Goes up to him] What are you groaning about, old man?

CHEBUTIKIN.
>   Stop it!

SOLENI.
>   How's your health?

CHEBUTIKIN.
>   [Angry] Mind your own business.

SOLENI.
 The old man is unnecessarily excited. I won't go far, I'll only just bring him down like a snipe. [Takes out his scent-bottle and scents his hands] I've poured out a whole bottle of scent to-day and they still smell . . . of a dead body. [Pause] Yes. . . . You remember the poem

> "But he, the rebel seeks the storm,
> As if the storm will bring him rest . . ."?

CHEBUTIKIN.
 Yes.

> "He didn't have the time to sigh,
> The bear sat on him heavily."

[Exit with SOLENI.]
[Shouts are heard. ANDREY and FERAPONT come in.]
FERAPONT.
 Documents to sign. . . .
ANDREY.
 [Irritated]. Go away! Leave me! Please! [Goes away with the perambulator.]
FERAPONT.
 That's what documents are for, to be signed. [Retires to back of stage.]
[Enter IRINA, with TUZENBACH in a straw hat; KULIGIN walks across the stage, shouting "Co-ee, Masha, co-ee!"]
TUZENBACH.
 He seems to be the only man in the town who is glad that the soldiers are going.
IRINA.
 One can understand that. [Pause] The town will be empty.
TUZENBACH.
 My dear, I shall return soon.
IRINA.
 Where are you going?
TUZENBACH.
 I must go into the town and then . . . see the others off.

IRINA.

It's not true . . . Nicolai, why are you so absentminded to-day? [Pause] What took place by the theatre yesterday?

TUZENBACH.

[Making a movement of impatience] In an hour's time I shall return and be with you again. [Kisses her hands] My darling . . . [Looking her closely in the face] it's five years now since I fell in love with you, and still I can't get used to it, and you seem to me to grow more and more beautiful. What lovely, wonderful hair! What eyes! I'm going to take you away to-morrow. We shall work, we shall be rich, my dreams will come true. You will be happy. There's only one thing, one thing only: you don't love me!

IRINA.

It isn't in my power! I shall be your wife, I shall be true to you, and obedient to you, but I can't love you. What can I do! [Cries] I have never been in love in my life. Oh, I used to think so much of love, I have been thinking about it for so long by day and by night, but my soul is like an expensive piano which is locked and the key lost. [Pause] You seem so unhappy.

TUZENBACH.

I didn't sleep at night. There is nothing in my life so awful as to be able to frighten me, only that lost key torments my soul and does not let me sleep. Say something to me [Pause] say something to me. . . .

IRINA.

What can I say, what?

TUZENBACH.

Anything.

IRINA.

Don't! don't! [Pause.]

TUZENBACH.

It is curious how silly trivial little things, sometimes for no apparent reason, become significant. At first you laugh at these things, you think they are of no importance, you go on and you feel that you haven't got the strength to stop yourself. Oh don't let's talk about it! I am happy. It is as if for the first time in my life I see these firs, maples, beeches, and they all look at me inquisitively and wait. What beautiful trees and how beautiful, when one comes to think of it, life must be near them! [A shout of Co-ee! in the distance] It's time I went. . . . There's a tree which has dried up but it still sways in the breeze with the others. And so it seems to me that if I die, I shall still take part in life in one way or another. Good-bye, dear. . . . [Kisses her hands] The papers which you gave me are on my table under the calendar.

IRINA.

I am coming with you.

TUZENBACH.

[Nervously] No, no! [He goes quickly and stops in the avenue] Irina!

IRINA.

What is it?

TUZENBACH.

[Not knowing what to say] I haven't had any coffee to-day. Tell them to make me some. . . . [He goes out quickly.]

[IRINA stands deep in thought. Then she goes to the back of the stage and sits on a swing. ANDREY comes in with the perambulator and FERAPONT also appears.]

FERAPONT.

Andrey Sergeyevitch, it isn't as if the documents were mine, they are the government's. I didn't make them.

ANDREY.

Oh, what has become of my past and where is it? I used to be young, happy, clever, I used to be able to think and frame clever ideas, the present and the future seemed to me full of hope. Why do we, almost before we have begun to live, become dull, grey, uninteresting, lazy, apathetic, useless, unhappy. . . . This town has already been in existence for two hundred years and it has a hundred thousand inhabitants, not one of whom is in any way different from the others. There has never been, now or at any other time, a single leader of men, a single scholar, an artist, a man of even the slightest eminence who might arouse envy or a passionate desire to be imitated. They only eat, drink, sleep, and then they die . . . more people are born and also eat, drink, sleep, and so as not to go silly from boredom, they try to make life many-sided with their beastly backbiting, vodka, cards, and litigation. The wives deceive their husbands, and the husbands lie, and pretend they see nothing and hear nothing, and the evil influence irresistibly oppresses the children and the divine spark in them is extinguished, and they become just as pitiful corpses and just as much like one another as their fathers and mothers. . . . [Angrily to FERAPONT] What do you want?

FERAPONT.
What? Documents want signing.

ANDREY.
I'm tired of you.

FERAPONT.
[Handing him papers] The hall-porter from the law courts was saying just now that in the winter there were two hundred degrees of frost in Petersburg.

ANDREY.
The present is beastly, but when I think of the future, how good it is! I feel so light, so free; there is a light in the distance, I see freedom. I see myself and my children freeing ourselves from vanities, from kvass, from goose baked with cabbage, from after-dinner naps, from base idleness. . . .

FERAPONT.
He was saying that two thousand people were frozen to death. The people were frightened, he said. In Petersburg or Moscow, I don't remember which.

ANDREY.
[Overcome by a tender emotion] My dear sisters, my beautiful sisters! [Crying] Masha, my sister. . . .

NATASHA.
[At the window] Who's talking so loudly out here? Is that you, Andrey? You'll wake little Sophie. Il ne faut pas faire du bruit, la Sophie est dormée deja. Vous êtes un ours. [Angrily] If you want to talk, then give the perambulator and the baby to somebody else. Ferapont, take the perambulator!

FERAPONT.
Yes'm. [Takes the perambulator.]

ANDREY.
[Confused] I'm speaking quietly.

NATASHA.
> [At the window, nursing her boy] Bobby! Naughty Bobby! Bad little Bobby!

ANDREY.
> [Looking through the papers] All right, I'll look them over and sign if necessary, and you can take them back to the offices. . . .
> [Goes into house reading papers; FERAPONT takes the perambulator to the back of the garden.]

NATASHA.
> [At the window] Bobby, what's your mother's name? Dear, dear! And who's this? That's Aunt Olga. Say to your aunt, "How do you do, Olga!" [Two wandering musicians, a man and a girl, are playing on a violin and a harp. VERSHININ, OLGA, and ANFISA come out of the house and listen for a minute in silence; IRINA comes up to them.]

OLGA.
> Our garden might be a public thoroughfare, from the way people walk and ride across it. Nurse, give those musicians something!

ANFISA.
> [Gives money to the musicians] Go away with God's blessing on you. [The musicians bow and go away] A bitter sort of people. You don't play on a full stomach. [To IRINA] How do you do, Arisha! [Kisses her] Well, little girl, here I am, still alive! Still alive! In the High School, together with little Olga, in her official apartments . . . so the Lord has appointed for my old age. Sinful woman that I am, I've never lived like that in my life before. . . . A large flat, government property, and I've a whole room and bed to myself. All government property. I wake up at nights and, oh God, and Holy Mother, there isn't a happier person than I!

VERSHININ.
> [Looks at his watch] We are going soon, Olga Sergeyevna. It's time for me to go. [Pause] I wish you every . . . every. . . . Where's Maria Sergeyevna?

IRINA.
> She's somewhere in the garden. I'll go and look for her.

VERSHININ.
> If you'll be so kind. I haven't time.

ANFISA.
> I'll go and look, too. [Shouts] Little Masha, co-ee! [Goes out with IRINA down into the garden] Co-ee, co-ee!

VERSHININ.
> Everything comes to an end. And so we, too, must part. [Looks at his watch] The town gave us a sort of farewell breakfast, we had champagne to drink and the mayor made a speech, and I ate and listened, but my soul was here all the time. . . . [Looks round the garden] I'm so used to you now.

OLGA.
> Shall we ever meet again?

VERSHININ.
> Probably not. [Pause] My wife and both my daughters will stay here another two months. If anything happens, or if anything has to be done . . .

OLGA.
> Yes, yes, of course. You need not worry. [Pause] To-morrow there won't be a single soldier left in the town, it will all be a memory, and, of course, for us a new life will begin. . . . [Pause] None of our plans are coming right. I didn't want to be a head-mistress, but they made me one, all the same. It means there's no chance of Moscow. . . .

VERSHININ.
> Well . . . thank you for everything. Forgive me if I've . . . I've said such an awful lot—forgive me for that too, don't think badly of me.

OLGA.
> [Wipes her eyes] Why isn't Masha coming . . .

VERSHININ.
> What else can I say in parting? Can I philosophize about anything? [Laughs] Life is heavy. To many of us it seems dull and hopeless, but still, it must be acknowledged that it is getting lighter and clearer, and it seems that the time is not far off when it will be quite clear. [Looks at his watch] It's time I went! Mankind used to be absorbed in wars, and all its existence was filled with campaigns, attacks, defeats, now we've outlived all that, leaving after us a great waste place, which there is nothing to fill with at present; but mankind is looking for something, and will certainly find it. Oh, if it only happened more quickly. [Pause]

If only education could be added to industry, and industry to education. [Looks at his watch] It's time I went....

OLGA.

Here she comes.

[Enter MASHA.]

VERSHININ.

I came to say good-bye....

[OLGA steps aside a little, so as not to be in their way.]

MASHA.

[Looking him in the face] Good-bye. [Prolonged kiss.]

OLGA.

Don't, don't. [MASHA is crying bitterly]

VERSHININ.

Write to me.... Don't forget! Let me go.... It's time. Take her, Olga Sergeyevna... it's time... I'm late...

[He kisses OLGA'S hand in evident emotion, then embraces MASHA once more and goes out quickly.]

OLGA.

Don't, Masha! Stop, dear.... [KULIGIN enters.]

KULIGIN.

[Confused] Never mind, let her cry, let her.... My dear Masha, my good Masha.... You're my wife, and I'm happy, whatever happens... I'm not complaining, I don't reproach you at all.... Olga is a witness to it. Let's begin to live again as we used to, and not by a single word, or hint...

MASHA.

[Restraining her sobs] "There stands a green oak by the sea,
And a chain of bright gold is around it....
And a chain of bright gold is around it...."
I'm going off my head... "There stands... a green oak... by the sea."...

OLGA.

Don't, Masha, don't... give her some water....

MASHA.

I'm not crying any more....

KULIGIN.
   She's not crying any more . . . she's a good . . . [A shot is heard from a distance.]
MASHA.
   "There stands a green oak by the sea,
   And a chain of bright gold is around it . . .
   An oak of green gold. . . ."

   I'm mixing it up. . . . [Drinks some water] Life is dull . . . I don't want anything more now . . . I'll be all right in a moment. . . . It doesn't matter. . . . What do those lines mean? Why do they run in my head? My thoughts are all tangled.
   [IRINA enters.]
OLGA.
   Be quiet, Masha. There's a good girl. . . . Let's go in.
MASHA.
   [Angrily] I shan't go in there. [Sobs, but controls herself at once] I'm not going to go into the house, I won't go. . . .
IRINA.
   Let's sit here together and say nothing. I'm going away to-morrow. . . .
   [Pause.]
KULIGIN.
   Yesterday I took away these whiskers and this beard from a boy in the third class. . . . [He puts on the whiskers and beard] Don't I look like the German master. . . . [Laughs] Don't I? The boys are amusing.
MASHA.
   You really do look like that German of yours.
OLGA.
   [Laughs] Yes. [MASHA weeps.]
IRINA.
   Don't, Masha!
KULIGIN.
   It's a very good likeness. . . .
   [Enter NATASHA.]

NATASHA.

[To the maid] What? Mihail Ivanitch Protopopov will sit with little Sophie, and Andrey Sergeyevitch can take little Bobby out. Children are such a bother.... [To IRINA] Irina, it's such a pity you're going away to-morrow. Do stop just another week. [Sees KULIGIN and screams; he laughs and takes off his beard and whiskers] How you frightened me! [To IRINA] I've grown used to you and do you think it will be easy for me to part from you? I'm going to have Andrey and his violin put into your room—let him fiddle away in there!—and we'll put little Sophie into his room. The beautiful, lovely child! What a little girlie! To-day she looked at me with such pretty eyes and said "Mamma!"

KULIGIN.

A beautiful child, it's quite true.

NATASHA.

That means I shall have the place to myself to-morrow. [Sighs] In the first place I shall have that avenue of fir-trees cut down, then that maple. It's so ugly at nights.... [To IRINA] That belt doesn't suit you at all, dear.... It's an error of taste. And I'll give orders to have lots and lots of little flowers planted here, and they'll smell.... [Severely] Why is there a fork lying about here on the seat? [Going towards the house, to the maid] Why is there a fork lying about here on the seat, I say? [Shouts] Don't you dare to answer me!

KULIGIN.

Temper! temper! [A march is played off; they all listen.]

OLGA.

They're going.

[CHEBUTIKIN comes in.]

MASHA.

They're going. Well, well.... Bon voyage! [To her husband] We must be going home.... Where's my coat and hat?

KULIGIN.

I took them in ... I'll bring them, in a moment.

OLGA.

Yes, now we can all go home. It's time.

CHEBUTIKIN.

Olga Sergeyevna!

OLGA.

What is it? [Pause] What is it?

CHEBUTIKIN.

Nothing... I don't know how to tell you.... [Whispers to her.]

OLGA.

[Frightened] It can't be true!

CHEBUTIKIN.

Yes... such a story... I'm tired out, exhausted, I won't say any more.... [Sadly] Still, it's all the same!

MASHA.

What's happened?

OLGA.

[Embraces IRINA] This is a terrible day... I don't know how to tell you, dear....

IRINA.

What is it? Tell me quickly, what is it? For God's sake! [Cries.]

CHEBUTIKIN.

The Baron was killed in the duel just now.

IRINA.

[Cries softly] I knew it, I knew it....

CHEBUTIKIN.

[Sits on a bench at the back of the stage] I'm tired.... [Takes a paper from his pocket] Let 'em cry.... [Sings softly] "Tarara-boom-deay, it is my washing day...." Isn't it all the same!

[The three sisters are standing, pressing against one another.]

MASHA.

Oh, how the music plays! They are leaving us, one has quite left us, quite and for ever. We remain alone, to begin our life over again. We must live ... we must live....

IRINA.

[Puts her head on OLGA's bosom] There will come a time when everybody will know why, for what purpose, there is all this suffering, and there will be no more mysteries. But now we must live ... we must work, just work! To-morrow, I'll go away alone, and I'll teach and give my whole life to those who, perhaps, need it. It's autumn now, soon it will be winter, the snow will cover everything, and I shall be working, working....

OLGA.

[Embraces both her sisters] The bands are playing so gaily, so bravely, and one does so want to live! Oh, my God! Time will pass on, and we shall depart for ever, we shall be forgotten; they will forget our faces, voices, and even how many there were of us, but our sufferings will turn into joy for those who will live after us, happiness and peace will reign on earth, and people will remember with kindly words, and bless those who are living now. Oh dear sisters, our life is not yet at an end. Let us live. The music is so gay, so joyful, and, it seems that in a little while we shall know why we are living, why we are suffering. . . . If we could only know, if we could only know!

[The music has been growing softer and softer; KULIGIN, smiling happily, brings out the hat and coat; ANDREY wheels out the perambulator in which BOBBY is sitting.]

CHEBUTIKIN.

[Sings softly] "Tara . . . ra-boom-deay. . . . It is my washing-day." . . .

[Reads a paper] It's all the same! It's all the same!

OLGA.

If only we could know, if only we could know!

Curtain falls.

THE CHERRY ORCHARD

Translated by Julius West

THE CHERRY ORCHARD

Translated by Julius West

Characters

LUBOV ANDREYEVNA RANEVSKY (Mme. RANEVSKY), a landowner
ANYA, her daughter, aged seventeen
VARYA (BARBARA), her adopted daughter, aged twenty-seven
LEONID ANDREYEVITCH GAEV, Mme. Ranevsky's brother
ERMOLAI ALEXEYEVITCH LOPAKHIN, a merchant
PETER SERGEYEVITCH TROFIMOV, a student
BORIS BORISOVITCH SIMEONOV-PISCHIN, a landowner
CHARLOTTA IVANOVNA, a governess
SIMEON PANTELEYEVITCH EPIKHODOV, a clerk
DUNYASHA (AVDOTYA FEDOROVNA), a maidservant
FIERS, an old footman, aged eighty-seven
YASHA, a young footman
A TRAMP
A STATION-MASTER
POST-OFFICE CLERK
GUESTS
A SERVANT
The action takes place on Mme. RANEVSKY'S estate

ACT I

A room which is still called the nursery. One of the doors leads into ANYA'S room. It is close on sunrise. It is May. The cherry-trees are in flower but it is chilly in the garden. There is an early frost. The windows of the room are shut. DUNYASHA comes in with a candle, and LOPAKHIN with a book in his hand.

LOPAKHIN.
>The train's arrived, thank God. What's the time?

DUNYASHA.
>It will soon be two. [Blows out candle] It is light already.

LOPAKHIN.
>How much was the train late? Two hours at least. [Yawns and stretches himself] I have made a rotten mess of it! I came here on purpose to meet them at the station, and then overslept myself . . . in my chair. It's a pity. I wish you'd wakened me.

DUNYASHA.
>I thought you'd gone away. [Listening] I think I hear them coming.

LOPAKHIN.

[Listens] No. . . . They've got to collect their luggage and so on. . . . [Pause] Lubov Andreyevna has been living abroad for five years; I don't know what she'll be like now. . . . She's a good sort—an easy, simple person. I remember when I was a boy of fifteen, my father, who is dead—he used to keep a shop in the village here—hit me on the face with his fist, and my nose bled. . . . We had gone into the yard together for something or other, and he was a little drunk. Lubov Andreyevna, as I remember her now, was still young, and very thin, and she took me to the washstand here in this very room, the nursery. She said, "Don't cry, little man, it'll be all right in time for your wedding." [Pause] "Little man". . . . My father was a peasant, it's true, but here I am in a white waistcoat and yellow shoes . . . a pearl out of an oyster. I'm rich now, with lots of money, but just think about it and examine me, and you'll find I'm still a peasant down to the marrow of my bones. [Turns over the pages of his book] Here I've been reading this book, but I understood nothing. I read and fell asleep. [Pause.]

DUNYASHA.

The dogs didn't sleep all night; they know that they're coming.

LOPAKHIN.

What's up with you, Dunyasha . . . ?

DUNYASHA.

My hands are shaking. I shall faint.

LOPAKHIN.

You're too sensitive, Dunyasha. You dress just like a lady, and you do your hair like one too. You oughtn't. You should know your place.

EPIKHODOV.

[Enters with a bouquet. He wears a short jacket and brilliantly polished boots which squeak audibly. He drops the bouquet as he enters, then picks it up] The gardener sent these; says they're to go into the dining-room. [Gives the bouquet to DUNYASHA.]

LOPAKHIN.

And you'll bring me some kvass.

DUNYASHA.

Very well. [Exit.]

EPIKHODOV.

There's a frost this morning—three degrees, and the cherry-trees are all in flower. I can't approve of our climate. [Sighs] I can't. Our climate is indisposed to favour us even this once. And, Ermolai Alexeyevitch, allow me to say to you, in addition, that I bought myself some boots two days ago, and I beg to assure you that they squeak in a perfectly unbearable manner. What shall I put on them?

LOPAKHIN.

Go away. You bore me.

EPIKHODOV.

Some misfortune happens to me every day. But I don't complain; I'm used to it, and I can smile. [DUNYASHA comes in and brings LOPAKHIN some kvass] I shall go. [Knocks over a chair] There. . . . [Triumphantly] There, you see, if I may use the word, what circumstances I am in, so to speak. It is even simply marvellous. [Exit.]

DUNYASHA.

I may confess to you, Ermolai Alexeyevitch, that Epikhodov has proposed to me.

LOPAKHIN.

Ah!

DUNYASHA.

I don't know what to do about it. He's a nice young man, but every now and again, when he begins talking, you can't understand a word he's saying. I think I like him. He's madly in love with me. He's an unlucky man; every day something happens. We tease him about it. They call him "Two-and-twenty troubles."

LOPAKHIN.

[Listens] There they come, I think.

DUNYASHA.

They're coming! What's the matter with me? I'm cold all over.

LOPAKHIN.

There they are, right enough. Let's go and meet them. Will she know me? We haven't seen each other for five years.

DUNYASHA.

[Excited] I shall faint in a minute. . . . Oh, I'm fainting!

[Two carriages are heard driving up to the house. LOPAKHIN and DUNYASHA quickly go out. The stage is empty. A noise begins in the next room. FIERS, leaning on a stick, walks quickly across the stage; he has just been to meet LUBOV ANDREYEVNA. He wears an old-fashioned livery and a tall hat. He is saying something to himself, but not a word of it can be made out. The noise behind the stage gets louder and louder. A voice is heard: "Let's go in there." Enter LUBOV ANDREYEVNA, ANYA, and CHARLOTTA IVANOVNA with a little dog on a chain, and all dressed in travelling clothes, VARYA in a long coat and with a kerchief on her head. GAEV, SIMEONOV-PISCHIN, LOPAKHIN, DUNYASHA with a parcel and an umbrella, and a servant with luggage—all cross the room.]

ANYA.
 Let's come through here. Do you remember what this room is, mother?

LUBOV.
 [Joyfully, through her tears] The nursery!

VARYA.
 How cold it is! My hands are quite numb. [To LUBOV ANDREYEVNA] Your rooms, the white one and the violet one, are just as they used to be, mother.

LUBOV.
 My dear nursery, oh, you beautiful room.... I used to sleep here when I was a baby. [Weeps] And here I am like a little girl again. [Kisses her brother, VARYA, then her brother again] And Varya is just as she used to be, just like a nun. And I knew Dunyasha. [Kisses her.]

GAEV.
 The train was two hours late. There now; how's that for punctuality?

CHARLOTTA.
 [To PISCHIN] My dog eats nuts too.

PISCHIN.
 [Astonished] To think of that, now!

[All go out except ANYA and DUNYASHA.]

DUNYASHA.
 We did have to wait for you!
 [Takes off ANYA'S cloak and hat.]

ANYA.
    I didn't get any sleep for four nights on the journey. . . . I'm awfully cold.
DUNYASHA.
    You went away during Lent, when it was snowing and frosty, but now? Darling! [Laughs and kisses her] We did have to wait for you, my joy, my pet. . . . I must tell you at once, I can't bear to wait a minute.
ANYA.
    [Tired] Something else now . . .?
DUNYASHA.
    The clerk, Epikhodov, proposed to me after Easter.
ANYA.
    Always the same. . . . [Puts her hair straight] I've lost all my hairpins. . . . [She is very tired, and even staggers as she walks.]
DUNYASHA.
    I don't know what to think about it. He loves me, he loves me so much!
ANYA.
    [Looks into her room; in a gentle voice] My room, my windows, as if I'd never gone away. I'm at home! To-morrow morning I'll get up and have a run in the garden. . . .Oh, if I could only get to sleep! I didn't sleep the whole journey, I was so bothered.
DUNYASHA.
    Peter Sergeyevitch came two days ago.
ANYA.
    [Joyfully] Peter!
DUNYASHA.
    He sleeps in the bath-house, he lives there. He said he was afraid he'd be in the way. [Looks at her pocket-watch] I ought to wake him, but Barbara Mihailovna told me not to. "Don't wake him," she said. [Enter VARYA, a bunch of keys on her belt.]
VARYA.
    Dunyasha, some coffee, quick. Mother wants some.
DUNYASHA.
    This minute. [Exit.]
VARYA.
    Well, you've come, glory be to God. Home again. [Caressing her] My darling is back again! My pretty one is back again!

ANYA.
> I did have an awful time, I tell you.

VARYA.
> I can just imagine it!

ANYA.
> I went away in Holy Week; it was very cold then. Charlotta talked the whole way and would go on performing her tricks. Why did you tie Charlotta on to me?

VARYA.
> You couldn't go alone, darling, at seventeen!

ANYA.
> We went to Paris; it's cold there and snowing. I talk French perfectly horribly. My mother lives on the fifth floor. I go to her, and find her there with various Frenchmen, women, an old abbé with a book, and everything in tobacco smoke and with no comfort at all. I suddenly became very sorry for mother—so sorry that I took her head in my arms and hugged her and wouldn't let her go. Then mother started hugging me and crying. . . .

VARYA.
> [Weeping] Don't say any more, don't say any more. . . .

ANYA.
> She's already sold her villa near Mentone; she's nothing left, nothing. And I haven't a copeck left either; we only just managed to get here. And mother won't understand! We had dinner at a station; she asked for all the expensive things, and tipped the waiters one rouble each. And Charlotta too. Yasha wants his share too—it's too bad. Mother's got a footman now, Yasha; we've brought him here.

VARYA.
> I saw the wretch.

ANYA.
> How's business? Has the interest been paid?

VARYA.
> Not much chance of that.

ANYA.
> Oh God, oh God . . .

VARYA.
    The place will be sold in August.
ANYA.
    O God. . . .
LOPAKHIN.
    [Looks in at the door and moos] Moo! . . . [Exit.]
VARYA.
    [Through her tears] I'd like to. . . . [Shakes her fist.]
ANYA.
    [Embraces VARYA, softly] Varya, has he proposed to you? [VARYA shakes head] But he loves you. . . . Why don't you make up your minds? Why do you keep on waiting?
VARYA.
    I think that it will all come to nothing. He's a busy man. I'm not his affair . . . he pays no attention to me. Bless the man, I don't want to see him. . . . But everybody talks about our marriage, everybody congratulates me, and there's nothing in it at all, it's all like a dream. [In another tone] You've got a brooch like a bee.
ANYA.
    [Sadly] Mother bought it. [Goes into her room, and talks lightly, like a child] In Paris I went up in a balloon!
VARYA.
    My darling's come back, my pretty one's come back! [DUNYASHA has already returned with the coffee-pot and is making the coffee, VARYA stands near the door] I go about all day, looking after the house, and I think all the time, if only you could marry a rich man, then I'd be happy and would go away somewhere by myself, then to Kiev . . . to Moscow, and so on, from one holy place to another. I'd tramp and tramp. That would be splendid!
ANYA.
    The birds are singing in the garden. What time is it now?
VARYA.
    It must be getting on for three. Time you went to sleep, darling. [Goes into ANYA'S room] Splendid!
    [Enter YASHA with a plaid shawl and a travelling bag.]

YASHA.
> [Crossing the stage: Politely] May I go this way?

DUNYASHA.
> I hardly knew you, Yasha. You have changed abroad.

YASHA.
> Hm ... and who are you?

DUNYASHA.
> When you went away I was only so high. [Showing with her hand] I'm Dunyasha, the daughter of Theodore Kozoyedov. You don't remember!

YASHA.
> Oh, you little cucumber!
> [Looks round and embraces her. She screams and drops a saucer. YASHA goes out quickly.]

VARYA.
> [In the doorway: In an angry voice] What's that?

DUNYASHA.
> [Through her tears] I've broken a saucer.

VARYA.
> It may bring luck.

ANYA.
> [Coming out of her room] We must tell mother that Peter's here.

VARYA.
> I told them not to wake him.

ANYA.
> [Thoughtfully] Father died six years ago, and a month later my brother Grisha was drowned in the river—such a dear little boy of seven! Mother couldn't bear it; she went away, away, without looking round.... [Shudders] How I understand her; if only she knew! [Pause] And Peter Trofimov was Grisha's tutor, he might tell her....
> [Enter FIERS in a short jacket and white waistcoat.]

FIERS.
> [Goes to the coffee-pot, nervously] The mistress is going to have some food here.... [Puts on white gloves] Is the coffee ready? [To DUNYASHA, severely] You! Where's the cream?

DUNYASHA.
> Oh, dear me ...! [Rapid exit.]

FIERS.
   [Fussing round the coffee-pot] Oh, you bungler. . . . [Murmurs to himself] Back from Paris . . . the master went to Paris once . . . in a carriage. . . . [Laughs.]
VARYA.
   What are you talking about, Fiers?
FIERS.
   I beg your pardon? [Joyfully] The mistress is home again. I've lived to see her! Don't care if I die now. . . . [Weeps with joy.]
   [Enter LUBOV ANDREYEVNA, GAEV, LOPAKHIN, and SIMEONOV-PISCHIN, the latter in a long jacket of thin cloth and loose trousers. GAEV, coming in, moves his arms and body about as if he is playing billiards.]
LUBOV.
   Let me remember now. Red into the corner! Twice into the centre!
GAEV.
   Right into the pocket! Once upon a time you and I used both to sleep in this room, and now I'm fifty-one; it does seem strange.
LOPAKHIN.
   Yes, time does go.
GAEV.
   Who does?
LOPAKHIN.
   I said that time does go.
GAEV.
   It smells of patchouli here.
ANYA.
   I'm going to bed. Good-night, mother. [Kisses her.]
LUBOV.
   My lovely little one. [Kisses her hand] Glad to be at home? I can't get over it.
ANYA.
   Good-night, uncle.
GAEV.
   [Kisses her face and hands] God be with you. How you do resemble your mother! [To his sister] You were just like her at her age, Luba.

[ANYA gives her hand to LOPAKHIN and PISCHIN and goes out, shutting the door behind her.]

LUBOV.
She's awfully tired.

PISCHIN.
It's a very long journey.

VARYA.
[To LOPAKHIN and PISCHIN] Well, sirs, it's getting on for three, quite time you went.

LUBOV.
[Laughs] You're just the same as ever, Varya. [Draws her close and kisses her] I'll have some coffee now, then we'll all go. [FIERS lays a cushion under her feet] Thank you, dear. I'm used to coffee. I drink it day and night. Thank you, dear old man. [Kisses FIERS.]

VARYA.
I'll go and see if they've brought in all the luggage. [Exit.]

LUBOV.
Is it really I who am sitting here? [Laughs] I want to jump about and wave my arms. [Covers her face with her hands] But suppose I'm dreaming! God knows I love my own country, I love it deeply; I couldn't look out of the railway carriage, I cried so much. [Through her tears] Still, I must have my coffee. Thank you, Fiers. Thank you, dear old man. I'm so glad you're still with us.

FIERS.
The day before yesterday.

GAEV.
He doesn't hear well.

LOPAKHIN.
I've got to go off to Kharkov by the five o'clock train. I'm awfully sorry! I should like to have a look at you, to gossip a little. You're as fine-looking as ever.

PISCHIN.
[Breathes heavily] Even finer-looking . . . dressed in Paris fashions . . . confound it all.

LOPAKHIN.
Your brother, Leonid Andreyevitch, says I'm a snob, a usurer, but that

is absolutely nothing to me. Let him talk. Only I do wish you would believe in me as you once did, that your wonderful, touching eyes would look at me as they did before. Merciful God! My father was the serf of your grandfather and your own father, but you—you more than anybody else—did so much for me once upon a time that I've forgotten everything and love you as if you belonged to my family . . . and even more.

LUBOV.

I can't sit still, I'm not in a state to do it. [Jumps up and walks about in great excitement] I'll never survive this happiness. . . . You can laugh at me; I'm a silly woman. . . . My dear little cupboard. [Kisses cupboard] My little table.

GAEV.

Nurse has died in your absence.

LUBOV.

[Sits and drinks coffee] Yes, bless her soul. I heard by letter.

GAEV.

And Anastasius has died too. Peter Kosoy has left me and now lives in town with the Commissioner of Police. [Takes a box of sugar-candy out of his pocket and sucks a piece.]

PISCHIN.

My daughter, Dashenka, sends her love.

LOPAKHIN.

I want to say something very pleasant, very delightful, to you. [Looks at his watch] I'm going away at once, I haven't much time . . . but I'll tell you all about it in two or three words. As you already know, your cherry orchard is to be sold to pay your debts, and the sale is fixed for August 22; but you needn't be alarmed, dear madam, you may sleep in peace; there's a way out. Here's my plan. Please attend carefully! Your estate is only thirteen miles from the town, the railway runs by, and if the cherry orchard and the land by the river are broken up into building lots and are then leased off for villas you'll get at least twenty-five thousand roubles a year profit out of it.

GAEV.

How utterly absurd!

LUBOV.

I don't understand you at all, Ermolai Alexeyevitch.

LOPAKHIN.

    You will get twenty-five roubles a year for each dessiatin from the leaseholders at the very least, and if you advertise now I'm willing to bet that you won't have a vacant plot left by the autumn; they'll all go. In a word, you're saved. I congratulate you. Only, of course, you'll have to put things straight, and clean up.... For instance, you'll have to pull down all the old buildings, this house, which isn't any use to anybody now, and cut down the old cherry orchard....

LUBOV.

    Cut it down? My dear man, you must excuse me, but you don't understand anything at all. If there's anything interesting or remarkable in the whole province, it's this cherry orchard of ours.

LOPAKHIN.

    The only remarkable thing about the orchard is that it's very large. It only bears fruit every other year, and even then you don't know what to do with them; nobody buys any.

GAEV.

    This orchard is mentioned in the "Encyclopaedic Dictionary."

LOPAKHIN.

    [Looks at his watch] If we can't think of anything and don't make up our minds to anything, then on August 22, both the cherry orchard and the whole estate will be up for auction. Make up your mind! I swear there's no other way out, I'll swear it again.

FIERS.

    In the old days, forty or fifty years back, they dried the cherries, soaked them and pickled them, and made jam of them, and it used to happen that...

GAEV.

    Be quiet, Fiers.

FIERS.

    And then we'd send the dried cherries off in carts to Moscow and Kharkov. And money! And the dried cherries were soft, juicy, sweet, and nicely scented.... They knew the way....

LUBOV.

    What was the way?

FIERS.
    They've forgotten. Nobody remembers.
PISCHIN.
    [To LUBOV ANDREYEVNA] What about Paris? Eh? Did you eat frogs?
LUBOV.
    I ate crocodiles.
PISCHIN.
    To think of that, now.
LOPAKHIN.
    Up to now in the villages there were only the gentry and the labourers, and now the people who live in villas have arrived. All towns now, even small ones, are surrounded by villas. And it's safe to say that in twenty years' time the villa resident will be all over the place. At present he sits on his balcony and drinks tea, but it may well come to pass that he'll begin to cultivate his patch of land, and then your cherry orchard will be happy, rich, splendid. . . .
GAEV.
    [Angry] What rot!
    [Enter VARYA and YASHA.]
VARYA.
    There are two telegrams for you, little mother. [Picks out a key and noisily unlocks an antique cupboard] Here they are.
LUBOV.
    They're from Paris. . . . [Tears them up without reading them] I've done with Paris.
GAEV.
    And do you know, Luba, how old this case is? A week ago I took out the bottom drawer; I looked and saw figures burnt out in it. That case was made exactly a hundred years ago. What do you think of that? What? We could celebrate its jubilee. It hasn't a soul of its own, but still, say what you will, it's a fine bookcase.
PISCHIN.
    [Astonished] A hundred years. . . . Think of that!
GAEV.
    Yes . . . it's a real thing. [Handling it] My dear and honoured case! I congratulate you on your existence, which has already for more than

a hundred years been directed towards the bright ideals of good and justice; your silent call to productive labour has not grown less in the hundred years [Weeping] during which you have upheld virtue and faith in a better future to the generations of our race, educating us up to ideals of goodness and to the knowledge of a common consciousness. [Pause.]

LOPAKHIN.

Yes. . . .

LUBOV.

You're just the same as ever, Leon.

GAEV.

[A little confused] Off the white on the right, into the corner pocket. Red ball goes into the middle pocket!

LOPAKHIN.

[Looks at his watch] It's time I went.

YASHA.

[Giving LUBOV ANDREYEVNA her medicine] Will you take your pills now?

PISCHIN.

You oughtn't to take medicines, dear madam; they do you neither harm nor good. . . . Give them here, dear madam. [Takes the pills, turns them out into the palm of his hand, blows on them, puts them into his mouth, and drinks some kvass] There!

LUBOV.

[Frightened] You're off your head!

PISCHIN.

I've taken all the pills.

LOPAKHIN.

Gormandizer! [All laugh.]

FIERS.

They were here in Easter week and ate half a pailful of cucumbers. . . . [Mumbles.]

LUBOV.

What's he driving at?

VARYA.

He's been mumbling away for three years. We're used to that.

YASHA.
> Senile decay.

[CHARLOTTA IVANOVNA crosses the stage, dressed in white: she is very thin and tightly laced; has a lorgnette at her waist.]

LOPAKHIN.
> Excuse me, Charlotta Ivanovna, I haven't said "How do you do" to you yet. [Tries to kiss her hand.]

CHARLOTTA.
> [Takes her hand away] If you let people kiss your hand, then they'll want your elbow, then your shoulder, and then . . .

LOPAKHIN.
> My luck's out to-day! [All laugh] Show us a trick, Charlotta Ivanovna!

LUBOV ANDREYEVNA.
> Charlotta, do us a trick.

CHARLOTTA.
> It's not necessary. I want to go to bed. [Exit.]

LOPAKHIN.
> We shall see each other in three weeks. [Kisses LUBOV ANDREYEVNA'S hand] Now, good-bye. It's time to go. [To GAEV] See you again. [Kisses PISCHIN] Au revoir. [Gives his hand to VARYA, then to FIERS and to YASHA] I don't want to go away. [To LUBOV ANDREYEVNA]. If you think about the villas and make up your mind, then just let me know, and I'll raise a loan of 50,000 roubles at once. Think about it seriously.

VARYA.
> [Angrily] Do go, now!

LOPAKHIN.
> I'm going, I'm going. . . . [Exit.]

GAEV.
> Snob. Still, I beg pardon. . . . Varya's going to marry him, he's Varya's young man.

VARYA.
> Don't talk too much, uncle.

LUBOV.
> Why not, Varya? I should be very glad. He's a good man.

PISCHIN.

    To speak the honest truth . . . he's a worthy man. . . . And my Dashenka . . . also says that . . . she says lots of things. [Snores, but wakes up again at once] But still, dear madam, if you could lend me . . . 240 roubles . . . to pay the interest on my mortgage to-morrow . . .

VARYA.

    [Frightened] We haven't got it, we haven't got it!

LUBOV.

    It's quite true. I've nothing at all.

PISCHIN.

    I'll find it all right [Laughs] I never lose hope. I used to think, "Everything's lost now. I'm a dead man," when, lo and behold, a railway was built over my land . . . and they paid me for it. And something else will happen to-day or to-morrow. Dashenka may win 20,000 roubles . . . she's got a lottery ticket.

LUBOV.

    The coffee's all gone, we can go to bed.

FIERS.

    [Brushing GAEV'S trousers; in an insistent tone] You've put on the wrong trousers again. What am I to do with you?

VARYA.

    [Quietly] Anya's asleep. [Opens window quietly] The sun has risen already; it isn't cold. Look, little mother: what lovely trees! And the air! The starlings are singing!

GAEV.

    [Opens the other window] The whole garden's white. You haven't forgotten, Luba? There's that long avenue going straight, straight, like a stretched strap; it shines on moonlight nights. Do you remember? You haven't forgotten?

LUBOV.

    [Looks out into the garden] Oh, my childhood, days of my innocence! In this nursery I used to sleep; I used to look out from here into the orchard. Happiness used to wake with me every morning, and then it was just as it is now; nothing has changed. [Laughs from joy] It's all, all white! Oh, my orchard! After the dark autumns and the cold winters, you're young again, full of happiness, the angels of heaven haven't left you. . . . If only I could take my heavy burden off my breast and shoulders, if I could forget my past!

GAEV.

Yes, and they'll sell this orchard to pay off debts. How strange it seems!

LUBOV.

Look, there's my dead mother going in the orchard . . . dressed in white! [Laughs from joy] That's she.

GAEV.

Where?

VARYA.

God bless you, little mother.

LUBOV.

There's nobody there; I thought I saw somebody. On the right, at the turning by the summer-house, a white little tree bent down, looking just like a woman. [Enter TROFIMOV in a worn student uniform and spectacles] What a marvellous garden! White masses of flowers, the blue sky. . . .

TROFIMOV.

Lubov Andreyevna! [She looks round at him] I only want to show myself, and I'll go away. [Kisses her hand warmly] I was told to wait till the morning, but I didn't have the patience.

[LUBOV ANDREYEVNA looks surprised.]

VARYA.

[Crying] It's Peter Trofimov.

TROFIMOV.

Peter Trofimov, once the tutor of your Grisha. . . . Have I changed so much?

[LUBOV ANDREYEVNA embraces him and cries softly.]

GAEV.

[Confused] That's enough, that's enough, Luba.

VARYA.

[Weeps] But I told you, Peter, to wait till to-morrow.

LUBOV.

My Grisha . . . my boy . . . Grisha . . . my son.

VARYA.

What are we to do, little mother? It's the will of God.

TROFIMOV.

[Softly, through his tears] It's all right, it's all right.

LUBOV.

[Still weeping] My boy's dead; he was drowned. Why? Why, my friend? [Softly] Anya's asleep in there. I am speaking so loudly, making such a noise. . . . Well, Peter? What's made you look so bad? Why have you grown so old?

TROFIMOV.

In the train an old woman called me a decayed gentleman.

LUBOV.

You were quite a boy then, a nice little student, and now your hair is not at all thick and you wear spectacles. Are you really still a student? [Goes to the door.]

TROFIMOV.

I suppose I shall always be a student.

LUBOV.

[Kisses her brother, then VARYA] Well, let's go to bed. . . . And you've grown older, Leonid.

PISCHIN.

[Follows her] Yes, we've got to go to bed. . . . Oh, my gout! I'll stay the night here. If only, Lubov Andreyevna, my dear, you could get me 240 roubles to-morrow morning—

GAEV.

Still the same story.

PISCHIN.

Two hundred and forty roubles . . . to pay the interest on the mortgage.

LUBOV.

I haven't any money, dear man.

PISCHIN.

I'll give it back . . . it's a small sum. . . .

LUBOV.

Well, then, Leonid will give it to you. . . . Let him have it, Leonid.

GAEV.

By all means; hold out your hand.

LUBOV.

Why not? He wants it; he'll give it back.

[LUBOV ANDREYEVNA, TROFIMOV, PISCHIN, and FIERS go out. GAEV, VARYA, and YASHA remain.]

GAEV.
My sister hasn't lost the habit of throwing money about. [To YASHA] Stand off, do; you smell of poultry.

YASHA.
[Grins] You are just the same as ever, Leonid Andreyevitch.

GAEV.
Really? [To VARYA] What's he saying?

VARYA.
[To YASHA] Your mother's come from the village; she's been sitting in the servants' room since yesterday, and wants to see you. . . .

YASHA.
Bless the woman!

VARYA.
Shameless man.

YASHA.
A lot of use there is in her coming. She might have come tomorrow just as well. [Exit.]

VARYA.
Mother hasn't altered a scrap, she's just as she always was. She'd give away everything, if the idea only entered her head.

GAEV.
Yes. . . . [Pause] If there's any illness for which people offer many remedies, you may be sure that particular illness is incurable, I think. I work my brains to their hardest. I've several remedies, very many, and that really means I've none at all. It would be nice to inherit a fortune from somebody, it would be nice to marry our Anya to a rich man, it would be nice to go to Yaroslav and try my luck with my aunt the Countess. My aunt is very, very rich.

VARYA.
[Weeps] If only God helped us.

GAEV.
Don't cry. My aunt's very rich, but she doesn't like us. My sister, in the first place, married an advocate, not a noble. . . . [ANYA appears in the doorway] She not only married a man who was not a noble, but she

behaved herself in a way which cannot be described as proper. She's nice and kind and charming, and I'm very fond of her, but say what you will in her favour and you still have to admit that she's wicked; you can feel it in her slightest movements.

VARYA.

[Whispers] Anya's in the doorway.

GAEV.

Really? [Pause] It's curious, something's got into my right eye... I can't see properly out of it. And on Thursday, when I was at the District Court...

[Enter ANYA.]

VARYA.

Why aren't you in bed, Anya?

ANYA.

Can't sleep. It's no good.

GAEV.

My darling! [Kisses ANYA'S face and hands] My child.... [Crying] You're not my niece, you're my angel, you're my all.... Believe in me, believe...

ANYA.

I do believe in you, uncle. Everybody loves you and respects you... but, uncle dear, you ought to say nothing, no more than that. What were you saying just now about my mother, your own sister? Why did you say those things?

GAEV.

Yes, yes. [Covers his face with her hand] Yes, really, it was awful. Save me, my God! And only just now I made a speech before a bookcase... it's so silly! And only when I'd finished I knew how silly it was.

VARYA.

Yes, uncle dear, you really ought to say less. Keep quiet, that's all.

ANYA.

You'd be so much happier in yourself if you only kept quiet.

GAEV.

All right, I'll be quiet. [Kisses their hands] I'll be quiet. But let's talk business. On Thursday I was in the District Court, and a lot of us met there together, and we began to talk of this, that, and the other, and now I think I can arrange a loan to pay the interest into the bank.

VARYA.
If only God would help us!

GAEV.
I'll go on Tuesday. I'll talk with them about it again. [To VARYA] Don't howl. [To ANYA] Your mother will have a talk to Lopakhin; he, of course, won't refuse . . . And when you've rested you'll go to Yaroslav to the Countess, your grandmother. So you see, we'll have three irons in the fire, and we'll be safe. We'll pay up the interest. I'm certain. [Puts some sugar-candy into his mouth] I swear on my honour, on anything you will, that the estate will not be sold! [Excitedly] I swear on my happiness! Here's my hand. You may call me a dishonourable wretch if I let it go to auction! I swear by all I am!

ANYA.
[She is calm again and happy] How good and clever you are, uncle. [Embraces him] I'm happy now! I'm happy! All's well!
[Enter FIERS.]

FIERS.
[Reproachfully] Leonid Andreyevitch, don't you fear God? When are you going to bed?

GAEV.
Soon, soon. You go away, Fiers. I'll undress myself. Well, children, bye-bye . . .! I'll give you the details to-morrow, but let's go to bed now. [Kisses ANYA and VARYA] I'm a man of the eighties. . . . People don't praise those years much, but I can still say that I've suffered for my beliefs. The peasants don't love me for nothing, I assure you. We've got to learn to know the peasants! We ought to learn how. . . .

ANYA.
You're doing it again, uncle!

VARYA.
Be quiet, uncle!

FIERS.
[Angrily] Leonid Andreyevitch!

GAEV.
  I'm coming, I'm coming.... Go to bed now. Off two cushions into the middle! I turn over a new leaf.... [Exit. FIERS goes out after him.]
ANYA.
  I'm quieter now. I don't want to go to Yaroslav, I don't like grandmother; but I'm calm now; thanks to uncle. [Sits down.]
VARYA.
  It's time to go to sleep. I'll go. There's been an unpleasantness here while you were away. In the old servants' part of the house, as you know, only the old people live—little old Efim and Polya and Evstigney, and Karp as well. They started letting some tramps or other spend the night there—I said nothing. Then I heard that they were saying that I had ordered them to be fed on peas and nothing else; from meanness, you see.... And it was all Evstigney's doing.... Very well, I thought, if that's what the matter is, just you wait. So I call Evstigney.... [Yawns] He comes. "What's this," I say, "Evstigney, you old fool."... [Looks at ANYA] Anya dear! [Pause] She's dropped off.... [Takes ANYA'S arm] Let's go to bye-bye.... Come along!... [Leads her] My darling's gone to sleep! Come on.... [They go. In the distance, the other side of the orchard, a shepherd plays his pipe. TROFIMOV crosses the stage and stops on seeing VARYA and ANYA] Sh! She's asleep, asleep. Come on, dear.
ANYA.
  [Quietly, half-asleep] I'm so tired ... all the bells ... uncle, dear! Mother and uncle!
VARYA.
  Come on, dear, come on! [They go into ANYA'S room.]
TROFIMOV.
  [Moved] My sun! My spring!

Curtain falls.

ACT II

In a field. An old, crooked shrine, which has been long abandoned; near it a well and large stones, which apparently are old tombstones, and an old garden seat. The road is seen to GAEV'S estate. On one side rise dark poplars, behind them begins the cherry orchard. In the distance is a row of telegraph poles, and far, far away on the horizon are the indistinct signs of a large town, which can only be seen on the finest and clearest days. It is close on sunset. CHARLOTTA, YASHA, and DUNYASHA are sitting on the seat; EPIKHODOV stands by and plays on a guitar; all seem thoughtful. CHARLOTTA wears a man's old peaked cap; she has unslung a rifle from her shoulders and is putting to rights the buckle on the strap.

CHARLOTTA.

[Thoughtfully] I haven't a real passport. I don't know how old I am, and I think I'm young. When I was a little girl my father and mother used to go round fairs and give very good performances and I used to do the salto mortale and various little things. And when papa and mamma died a German lady took me to her and began to teach me. I liked it. I grew up and became a governess. And where I came from and who I am, I don't know. . . . Who my parents were—perhaps they weren't married—I don't know. [Takes a cucumber out of her pocket and eats] I don't know anything. [Pause] I do want to talk, but I haven't anybody to talk to . . . I haven't anybody at all.

EPIKHODOV.

[Plays on the guitar and sings]

> *"What is this noisy earth to me,*
> *What matter friends and foes?"*

I do like playing on the mandoline!

DUNYASHA.

That's a guitar, not a mandoline. [Looks at herself in a little mirror and powders herself.]

EPIKHODOV.

For the enamoured madman, this is a mandoline. [Sings]

> *"Oh that the heart was warmed,*
> *By all the flames of love returned!"*

[YASHA sings too.]

CHARLOTTA.

These people sing terribly. . . . Foo! Like jackals.

DUNYASHA.

[To YASHA] Still, it must be nice to live abroad.

YASHA.

Yes, certainly. I cannot differ from you there. [Yawns and lights a cigar.]

EPIKHODOV.

That is perfectly natural. Abroad everything is in full complexity.

YASHA.

That goes without saying.

EPIKHODOV.

I'm an educated man, I read various remarkable books, but I cannot understand the direction I myself want to go—whether to live or to shoot myself, as it were. So, in case, I always carry a revolver about with me. Here it is. [Shows a revolver.]

CHARLOTTA.

I've done. Now I'll go. [Slings the rifle] You, Epikhodov, are a very clever man and very terrible; women must be madly in love with you. Brrr! [Going] These wise ones are all so stupid. I've nobody to talk to. I'm always alone, alone; I've nobody at all . . . and I don't know who I am or why I live. [Exit slowly.]

EPIKHODOV.

As a matter of fact, independently of everything else, I must express my feeling, among other things, that fate has been as pitiless in her dealings with me as a storm is to a small ship. Suppose, let us grant, I am wrong; then why did I wake up this morning, to give an example, and behold an enormous spider on my chest, like that. [Shows with both hands] And if I do drink some kvass, why is it that there is bound to be something of the most indelicate nature in it, such as a beetle? [Pause] Have you read Buckle? [Pause] I should like to trouble you, Avdotya Fedorovna, for two words.

DUNYASHA.

Say on.

EPIKHODOV.

I should prefer to be alone with you. [Sighs.]

DUNYASHA.

[Shy] Very well, only first bring me my little cloak. . . . It's by the cupboard. It's a little damp here.

EPIKHODOV.

Very well . . . I'll bring it. . . . Now I know what to do with my revolver. [Takes guitar and exits, strumming.]

YASHA.

Two-and-twenty troubles! A silly man, between you and me and the gatepost. [Yawns.]

DUNYASHA.

I hope to goodness he won't shoot himself. [Pause] I'm so nervous, I'm worried. I went into service when I was quite a little girl, and now I'm not used to common life, and my hands are white, white as a lady's. I'm so tender and so delicate now; respectable and afraid of everything. . . .

I'm so frightened. And I don't know what will happen to my nerves if you deceive me, Yasha.

YASHA.

[Kisses her] Little cucumber! Of course, every girl must respect herself; there's nothing I dislike more than a badly behaved girl.

DUNYASHA.

I'm awfully in love with you; you're educated, you can talk about everything. [Pause.]

YASHA.

[Yawns] Yes. I think this: if a girl loves anybody, then that means she's immoral. [Pause] It's nice to smoke a cigar out in the open air. . . . [Listens] Somebody's coming. It's the mistress, and people with her. [DUNYASHA embraces him suddenly] Go to the house, as if you'd been bathing in the river; go by this path, or they'll meet you and will think I've been meeting you. I can't stand that sort of thing.

DUNYASHA.

[Coughs quietly] My head's aching because of your cigar.

[Exit. YASHA remains, sitting by the shrine. Enter LUBOV ANDREYEVNA, GAEV, and LOPAKHIN.]

LOPAKHIN.

You must make up your mind definitely—there's no time to waste. The question is perfectly plain. Are you willing to let the land for villas or no? Just one word, yes or no? Just one word!

LUBOV.

Who's smoking horrible cigars here? [Sits.]

GAEV.

They built that railway; that's made this place very handy. [Sits] Went to town and had lunch . . . red in the middle! I'd like to go in now and have just one game.

LUBOV.

You'll have time.

LOPAKHIN.

Just one word! [Imploringly] Give me an answer!

GAEV.

[Yawns] Really!

LUBOV.

[Looks in her purse] I had a lot of money yesterday, but there's very little to-day. My poor Varya feeds everybody on milk soup to save money, in the kitchen the old people only get peas, and I spend recklessly. [Drops the purse, scattering gold coins] There, they are all over the place.

YASHA.

Permit me to pick them up. [Collects the coins.]

LUBOV.

Please do, Yasha. And why did I go and have lunch there? . . . A horrid restaurant with band and tablecloths smelling of soap. . . . Why do you drink so much, Leon? Why do you eat so much? Why do you talk so much? You talked again too much to-day in the restaurant, and it wasn't at all to the point—about the seventies and about decadents. And to whom? Talking to the waiters about decadents!

LOPAKHIN.

Yes.

GAEV.

[Waves his hand] I can't be cured, that's obvious. . . . [Irritably to YASHA] What's the matter? Why do you keep twisting about in front of me?

YASHA.

[Laughs] I can't listen to your voice without laughing.

GAEV.

[To his sister] Either he or I . . .

LUBOV.

Go away, Yasha; get out of this. . . .

YASHA.

[Gives purse to LUBOV ANDREYEVNA] I'll go at once. [Hardly able to keep from laughing] This minute. . . . [Exit.]

LOPAKHIN.

That rich man Deriganov is preparing to buy your estate. They say he'll come to the sale himself.

LUBOV.

Where did you hear that?

LOPAKHIN.

They say so in town.

GAEV.

Our Yaroslav aunt has promised to send something, but I don't know when or how much.

LOPAKHIN.

How much will she send? A hundred thousand roubles? Or two, perhaps?

LUBOV.

I'd be glad of ten or fifteen thousand.

LOPAKHIN.

You must excuse my saying so, but I've never met such frivolous people as you before, or anybody so unbusinesslike and peculiar. Here I am telling you in plain language that your estate will be sold, and you don't seem to understand.

LUBOV.

What are we to do? Tell us, what?

LOPAKHIN.

I tell you every day. I say the same thing every day. Both the cherry orchard and the land must be leased off for villas and at once, immediately—the auction is staring you in the face: Understand! Once you do definitely make up your minds to the villas, then you'll have as much money as you want and you'll be saved.

LUBOV.

Villas and villa residents—it's so vulgar, excuse me.

GAEV.

I entirely agree with you.

LOPAKHIN.

I must cry or yell or faint. I can't stand it! You're too much for me! [To GAEV] You old woman!

GAEV.

Really!

LOPAKHIN.

Old woman! [Going out.]

LUBOV.

[Frightened] No, don't go away, do stop; be a dear. Please. Perhaps we'll find some way out!

LOPAKHIN.
   What's the good of trying to think!

LUBOV.
   Please don't go away. It's nicer when you're here. . . . [Pause] I keep on waiting for something to happen, as if the house is going to collapse over our heads.

GAEV.
   [Thinking deeply] Double in the corner . . . across the middle. . . .

LUBOV.
   We have been too sinful. . . .

LOPAKHIN.
   What sins have you committed?

GAEV.
   [Puts candy into his mouth] They say that I've eaten all my substance in sugar-candies. [Laughs.]

LUBOV.
   Oh, my sins. . . . I've always scattered money about without holding myself in, like a madwoman, and I married a man who made nothing but debts. My husband died of champagne—he drank terribly—and to my misfortune, I fell in love with another man and went off with him, and just at that time—it was my first punishment, a blow that hit me right on the head—here, in the river . . . my boy was drowned, and I went away, quite away, never to return, never to see this river again . . . I shut my eyes and ran without thinking, but he ran after me . . . without pity, without respect. I bought a villa near Mentone because he fell ill there, and for three years I knew no rest either by day or night; the sick man wore me out, and my soul dried up. And last year, when they had sold the villa to pay my debts, I went away to Paris, and there he robbed me of all I had and threw me over and went off with another woman. I tried to poison myself. . . . It was so silly, so shameful. . . . And suddenly I longed to be back in Russia, my own land, with my little girl. . . . [Wipes her tears] Lord, Lord be merciful to me, forgive me my sins! Punish me no more! [Takes a telegram out of her pocket] I had this to-day from Paris. . . . He begs my forgiveness, he implores me to return. . . . [Tears it up] Don't I hear music? [Listens.]

GAEV.
> That is our celebrated Jewish band. You remember—four violins, a flute, and a double-bass.
>
> LUBOV So it still exists? It would be nice if they came along some evening.

LOPAKHIN.
> [Listens] I can't hear. . . . [Sings quietly] "For money will the Germans make a Frenchman of a Russian." [Laughs] I saw such an awfully funny thing at the theatre last night.

LUBOV.
> I'm quite sure there wasn't anything at all funny. You oughtn't to go and see plays, you ought to go and look at yourself. What a grey life you lead, what a lot you talk unnecessarily.

LOPAKHIN.
> It's true. To speak the straight truth, we live a silly life. [Pause] My father was a peasant, an idiot, he understood nothing, he didn't teach me, he was always drunk, and always used a stick on me. In point of fact, I'm a fool and an idiot too. I've never learned anything, my handwriting is bad, I write so that I'm quite ashamed before people, like a pig!

LUBOV.
> You ought to get married, my friend.

LOPAKHIN.
> Yes . . . that's true.

LUBOV.
> Why not to our Varya? She's a nice girl.

LOPAKHIN.
> Yes.

LUBOV.
> She's quite homely in her ways, works all day, and, what matters most, she's in love with you. And you've liked her for a long time.

LOPAKHIN.
> Well? I don't mind . . . she's a nice girl. [Pause.]

GAEV.
> I'm offered a place in a bank. Six thousand roubles a year. . . . Did you hear?

LUBOV.
>   What's the matter with you! Stay where you are. . . .
>   [Enter FIERS with an overcoat.]

FIERS.
>   [To GAEV] Please, sir, put this on, it's damp.

GAEV.
>   [Putting it on] You're a nuisance, old man.
>   FIERS It's all very well. . . . You went away this morning without telling me. [Examining GAEV.]

LUBOV.
>   How old you've grown, Fiers!

FIERS.
>   I beg your pardon?

LOPAKHIN.
>   She says you've grown very old!

FIERS.
>   I've been alive a long time. They were already getting ready to marry me before your father was born. . . . [Laughs] And when the Emancipation came I was already first valet. Only I didn't agree with the Emancipation and remained with my people. . . . [Pause] I remember everybody was happy, but they didn't know why.

LOPAKHIN.
>   It was very good for them in the old days. At any rate, they used to beat them.

FIERS.
>   [Not hearing] Rather. The peasants kept their distance from the masters and the masters kept their distance from the peasants, but now everything's all anyhow and you can't understand anything.

GAEV.
>   Be quiet, Fiers. I've got to go to town tomorrow. I've been promised an introduction to a General who may lend me money on a bill.

LOPAKHIN.
>   Nothing will come of it. And you won't pay your interest, don't you worry.

LUBOV.
>   He's talking rubbish. There's no General at all.
>   [Enter TROFIMOV, ANYA, and VARYA.]

GAEV.

    Here they are.

ANYA.

    Mother's sitting down here.

LUBOV.

    [Tenderly] Come, come, my dears. . . . [Embracing ANYA and VARYA] If you two only knew how much I love you. Sit down next to me, like that. [All sit down.]

LOPAKHIN.

    Our eternal student is always with the ladies.

TROFIMOV.

    That's not your business.

LOPAKHIN.

    He'll soon be fifty, and he's still a student.

TROFIMOV.

    Leave off your silly jokes!

LOPAKHIN.

    Getting angry, eh, silly?

TROFIMOV.

    Shut up, can't you.

LOPAKHIN.

    [Laughs] I wonder what you think of me?

TROFIMOV.

    I think, Ermolai Alexeyevitch, that you're a rich man, and you'll soon be a millionaire. Just as the wild beast which eats everything it finds is needed for changes to take place in matter, so you are needed too. [All laugh.]

VARYA.

    Better tell us something about the planets, Peter.

LUBOV ANDREYEVNA.

    No, let's go on with yesterday's talk!

TROFIMOV.

    About what?

GAEV.

    About the proud man.

TROFIMOV.
Yesterday we talked for a long time but we didn't come to anything in the end. There's something mystical about the proud man, in your sense. Perhaps you are right from your point of view, but if you take the matter simply, without complicating it, then what pride can there be, what sense can there be in it, if a man is imperfectly made, physiologically speaking, if in the vast majority of cases he is coarse and stupid and deeply unhappy? We must stop admiring one another. We must work, nothing more.

GAEV.
You'll die, all the same.

TROFIMOV.
Who knows? And what does it mean—you'll die? Perhaps a man has a hundred senses, and when he dies only the five known to us are destroyed and the remaining ninety-five are left alive.

LUBOV.
How clever of you, Peter!

LOPAKHIN.
[Ironically] Oh, awfully!

TROFIMOV.
The human race progresses, perfecting its powers. Everything that is unattainable now will some day be near at hand and comprehensible, but we must work, we must help with all our strength those who seek to know what fate will bring. Meanwhile in Russia only a very few of us work. The vast majority of those intellectuals whom I know seek for nothing, do nothing, and are at present incapable of hard work. They call themselves intellectuals, but they use "thou" and "thee" to their servants, they treat the peasants like animals, they learn badly, they read nothing seriously, they do absolutely nothing, about science they only talk, about art they understand little. They are all serious, they all have severe faces, they all talk about important things. They philosophize, and at the same time, the vast majority of us, ninety-nine out of a hundred, live like savages, fighting and cursing at the slightest opportunity, eating filthily, sleeping in the dirt, in stuffiness, with fleas, stinks, smells, moral filth, and so on . . . And it's obvious that all our nice talk is only carried on to distract ourselves and others. Tell me,

where are those crèches we hear so much of? and where are those reading-rooms? People only write novels about them; they don't really exist. Only dirt, vulgarity, and Asiatic plagues really exist. . . . I'm afraid, and I don't at all like serious faces; I don't like serious conversations. Let's be quiet sooner.

LOPAKHIN.

You know, I get up at five every morning, I work from morning till evening, I am always dealing with money—my own and other people's—and I see what people are like. You've only got to begin to do anything to find out how few honest, honourable people there are. Sometimes, when I can't sleep, I think: "Oh Lord, you've given us huge forests, infinite fields, and endless horizons, and we, living here, ought really to be giants."

LUBOV.

You want giants, do you? . . . They're only good in stories, and even there they frighten one. [EPIKHODOV enters at the back of the stage playing his guitar. Thoughtfully:] Epikhodov's there.

ANYA.

[Thoughtfully] Epikhodov's there.

GAEV.

The sun's set, ladies and gentlemen.

TROFIMOV.

Yes.

GAEV [Not loudly, as if declaiming] O Nature, thou art wonderful, thou shinest with eternal radiance! Oh, beautiful and indifferent one, thou whom we call mother, thou containest in thyself existence and death, thou livest and destroyest. . . .

VARYA.

[Entreatingly] Uncle, dear!

ANYA.

Uncle, you're doing it again!

TROFIMOV.

You'd better double the red into the middle.

GAEV.

I'll be quiet, I'll be quiet.

[They all sit thoughtfully. It is quiet. Only the mumbling of FIERS is heard. Suddenly a distant sound is heard as if from the sky, the sound of a breaking string, which dies away sadly.]

LUBOV.

What's that?

LOPAKHIN.

I don't know. It may be a bucket fallen down a well somewhere. But it's some way off.

GAEV.

Or perhaps it's some bird . . . like a heron.

TROFIMOV.

Or an owl.

LUBOV.

[Shudders] It's unpleasant, somehow. [A pause.]

FIERS.

Before the misfortune the same thing happened. An owl screamed and the samovar hummed without stopping.

GAEV.

Before what misfortune?

FIERS.

Before the Emancipation. [A pause.]

LUBOV.

You know, my friends, let's go in; it's evening now. [To ANYA] You've tears in your eyes. . . . What is it, little girl? [Embraces her.]

ANYA.

It's nothing, mother.

TROFIMOV.

Some one's coming.

[Enter a TRAMP in an old white peaked cap and overcoat. He is a little drunk.]

TRAMP.

Excuse me, may I go this way straight through to the station?

GAEV.

You may. Go along this path.

TRAMP.

I thank you from the bottom of my heart. [Hiccups] Lovely weather. . . . [Declaims] My brother, my suffering brother. . . . Come out on the

Volga, you whose groans . . . [To VARYA] Mademoiselle, please give a hungry Russian thirty copecks. . . .

[VARYA screams, frightened.]

LOPAKHIN.
[Angrily] There's manners everybody's got to keep!

LUBOV.
[With a start] Take this . . . here you are. . . . [Feels in her purse] There's no silver. . . . It doesn't matter, here's gold.

TRAMP.
I am deeply grateful to you! [Exit. Laughter.]

VARYA.
[Frightened] I'm going, I'm going. . . . Oh, little mother, at home there's nothing for the servants to eat, and you gave him gold.

LUBOV.
What is to be done with such a fool as I am! At home I'll give you everything I've got. Ermolai Alexeyevitch, lend me some more! . . .

LOPAKHIN.
Very well.

LUBOV.
Let's go, it's time. And Varya, we've settled your affair; I congratulate you.

VARYA.
[Crying] You shouldn't joke about this, mother.

LOPAKHIN.
Oh, feel me, get thee to a nunnery.

GAEV.
My hands are all trembling; I haven't played billiards for a long time.

LOPAKHIN.
Oh, feel me, nymph, remember me in thine orisons.

LUBOV.
Come along; it'll soon be supper-time.

VARYA.
He did frighten me. My heart is beating hard.

LOPAKHIN.
Let me remind you, ladies and gentlemen, on August 22 the cherry orchard will be sold. Think of that! . . . Think of that! . . .

[All go out except TROFIMOV and ANYA.]

ANYA.

[Laughs] Thanks to the tramp who frightened Barbara, we're alone now.

TROFIMOV.

Varya's afraid we may fall in love with each other and won't get away from us for days on end. Her narrow mind won't allow her to understand that we are above love. To escape all the petty and deceptive things which prevent our being happy and free, that is the aim and meaning of our lives. Forward! We go irresistibly on to that bright star which burns there, in the distance! Don't lag behind, friends!

ANYA.

[Clapping her hands] How beautifully you talk! [Pause] It is glorious here to-day!

TROFIMOV.

Yes, the weather is wonderful.

ANYA.

What have you done to me, Peter? I don't love the cherry orchard as I used to. I loved it so tenderly, I thought there was no better place in the world than our orchard.

TROFIMOV.

All Russia is our orchard. The land is great and beautiful, there are many marvellous places in it. [Pause] Think, Anya, your grandfather, your great-grandfather, and all your ancestors were serf-owners, they owned living souls; and now, doesn't something human look at you from every cherry in the orchard, every leaf and every stalk? Don't you hear voices . . .? Oh, it's awful, your orchard is terrible; and when in the evening or at night you walk through the orchard, then the old bark on the trees sheds a dim light and the old cherry-trees seem to be dreaming of all that was a hundred, two hundred years ago, and are oppressed by their heavy visions. Still, at any rate, we've left those two hundred years behind us. So far we've gained nothing at all—we don't yet know what the past is to be to us—we only philosophize, we complain that we are dull, or we drink vodka. For it's so clear that in order to begin to live in the present we must first redeem the past, and that can only be done by suffering, by strenuous, uninterrupted labour. Understand that, Anya.

ANYA.

    The house in which we live has long ceased to be our house; I shall go away. I give you my word.

TROFIMOV.

    If you have the housekeeping keys, throw them down the well and go away. Be as free as the wind.

ANYA.

    [Enthusiastically] How nicely you said that!

TROFIMOV.

    Believe me, Anya, believe me! I'm not thirty yet, I'm young, I'm still a student, but I have undergone a great deal! I'm as hungry as the winter, I'm ill, I'm shaken. I'm as poor as a beggar, and where haven't I been—fate has tossed me everywhere! But my soul is always my own; every minute of the day and the night it is filled with unspeakable presentiments. I know that happiness is coming, Anya, I see it already....

ANYA.

    [Thoughtful] The moon is rising.

    [EPIKHODOV is heard playing the same sad song on his guitar. The moon rises. Somewhere by the poplars VARYA is looking for ANYA and calling, "Anya, where are you?"]

TROFIMOV.

    Yes, the moon has risen. [Pause] There is happiness, there it comes; it comes nearer and nearer; I hear its steps already. And if we do not see it we shall not know it, but what does that matter? Others will see it!

THE VOICE OF VARYA.

    Anya! Where are you?

TROFIMOV.

    That's Varya again! [Angry] Disgraceful!

ANYA.

    Never mind. Let's go to the river. It's nice there.

    TROFIMOV Let's go. [They go out.]

THE VOICE OF VARYA.

    Anya! Anya!

Curtain falls.

ACT III

A reception-room cut off from a drawing-room by an arch. Chandelier lighted. A Jewish band, the one mentioned in Act II, is heard playing in another room. Evening. In the drawing-room the grand rond is being danced. Voice of SIMEONOV PISCHIN "Promenade a une paire!" Dancers come into the reception-room; the first pair are PISCHIN and CHARLOTTA IVANOVNA; the second, TROFIMOV and LUBOV ANDREYEVNA; the third, ANYA and the POST OFFICE CLERK; the fourth, VARYA and the STATION-MASTER, and so on. VARYA is crying gently and wipes away her tears as she dances. DUNYASHA is in the last pair. They go off into the drawing-room, PISCHIN shouting, "Grand rond, balancez:" and "Les cavaliers à genou et remerciez vos dames!" FIERS, in a dress-coat, carries a tray with seltzer-water across. Enter PISCHIN and TROFIMOV from the drawing-room.

PISCHIN.

I'm full-blooded and have already had two strokes; it's hard for me to dance, but, as they say, if you're in Rome, you must do as Rome does. I've got the strength of a horse. My dead father, who liked a joke, peace to his bones, used to say, talking of our ancestors, that the ancient stock of the Simeonov-Pischins was descended from that identical horse that Caligula made a senator. . . . [Sits] But the trouble is, I've no money! A hungry dog only believes in meat. [Snores and wakes up again immediately] So I . . . only believe in money. . . .

TROFIMOV.

Yes. There is something equine about your figure.

PISCHIN.

Well . . . a horse is a fine animal . . . you can sell a horse.

[Billiard playing can be heard in the next room. VARYA appears under the arch.]

TROFIMOV.

[Teasing] Madame Lopakhin! Madame Lopakhin!

VARYA.

[Angry] Decayed gentleman!

TROFIMOV.

Yes, I am a decayed gentleman, and I'm proud of it!

VARYA.

[Bitterly] We've hired the musicians, but how are they to be paid? [Exit.]

TROFIMOV.

[To PISCHIN] If the energy which you, in the course of your life, have spent in looking for money to pay interest had been used for something else, then, I believe, after all, you'd be able to turn everything upside down.

PISCHIN.

Nietzsche . . . a philosopher . . . a very great, a most celebrated man . . . a man of enormous brain, says in his books that you can forge banknotes.

TROFIMOV.

And have you read Nietzsche?

PISCHIN.

Well . . . Dashenka told me. Now I'm in such a position, I wouldn't mind forging them . . . I've got to pay 310 roubles the day after tomorrow . . . I've got 130 already. . . . [Feels his pockets, nervously]

I've lost the money! The money's gone! [Crying] Where's the money? [Joyfully] Here it is behind the lining . . . I even began to perspire.
[Enter LUBOV ANDREYEVNA and CHARLOTTA IVANOVNA.]
LUBOV.
[Humming a Caucasian dance] Why is Leonid away so long? What's he doing in town? [To DUNYASHA] Dunyasha, give the musicians some tea.
TROFIMOV.
Business is off, I suppose.
LUBOV.
And the musicians needn't have come, and we needn't have got up this ball. . . . Well, never mind. . . . [Sits and sings softly.]
CHARLOTTA.
[Gives a pack of cards to PISCHIN] Here's a pack of cards, think of any one card you like.
PISCHIN.
I've thought of one.
CHARLOTTA.
Now shuffle. All right, now. Give them here, oh my dear Mr. Pischin. Ein, zwei, drei! Now look and you'll find it in your coat-tail pocket.
PISCHIN.
[Takes a card out of his coat-tail pocket] Eight of spades, quite right! [Surprised] Think of that now!
CHARLOTTA.
[Holds the pack of cards on the palm of her hand. To TROFIMOV] Now tell me quickly. What's the top card?
TROFIMOV.
Well, the queen of spades.
CHARLOTTA.
Right! [To PISCHIN] Well now? What card's on top?
PISCHIN.
Ace of hearts.
CHARLOTTA.
Right! [Claps her hands, the pack of cards vanishes] How lovely the weather is to-day. [A mysterious woman's voice answers her, as if from under the floor, "Oh yes, it's lovely weather, madam."] You are

so beautiful, you are my ideal. [Voice, "You, madam, please me very much too."]

STATION-MASTER.

[Applauds] Madame ventriloquist, bravo!

PISCHIN.

[Surprised] Think of that, now! Delightful, Charlotte Ivanovna . . . I'm simply in love. . . .

CHARLOTTA.

In love? [Shrugging her shoulders] Can you love? Guter Mensch aber schlechter Musikant.

TROFIMOV.

[Slaps PISCHIN on the shoulder] Oh, you horse!

CHARLOTTA.

Attention please, here's another trick. [Takes a shawl from a chair] Here's a very nice plaid shawl, I'm going to sell it. . . . [Shakes it] Won't anybody buy it?

PISCHIN.

[Astonished] Think of that now!

CHARLOTTA.

Ein, zwei, drei.

[She quickly lifts up the shawl, which is hanging down. ANYA is standing behind it; she bows and runs to her mother, hugs her and runs back to the drawing-room amid general applause.]

LUBOV.

[Applauds] Bravo, bravo!

CHARLOTTA.

Once again! Ein, zwei, drei!

[Lifts the shawl. VARYA stands behind it and bows.]

PISCHIN.

[Astonished] Think of that, now.

CHARLOTTA.

The end!

[Throws the shawl at PISCHIN, curtseys and runs into the drawing-room.]

PISCHIN.

[Runs after her] Little wretch. . . . What? Would you? [Exit.]

LUBOV.
> Leonid hasn't come yet. I don't understand what he's doing so long in town! Everything must be over by now. The estate must be sold; or, if the sale never came off, then why does he stay so long?

VARYA.
> [Tries to soothe her] Uncle has bought it. I'm certain of it.

TROFIMOV.
> [Sarcastically] Oh, yes!

VARYA.
> Grandmother sent him her authority for him to buy it in her name and transfer the debt to her. She's doing it for Anya. And I'm certain that God will help us and uncle will buy it.

LUBOV.
> Grandmother sent fifteen thousand roubles from Yaroslav to buy the property in her name—she won't trust us—and that wasn't even enough to pay the interest. [Covers her face with her hands] My fate will be settled to-day, my fate....

TROFIMOV.
> [Teasing VARYA] Madame Lopakhin!

VARYA.
> [Angry] Eternal student! He's already been expelled twice from the university.

LUBOV.
> Why are you getting angry, Varya? He's teasing you about Lopakhin, well what of it? You can marry Lopakhin if you want to, he's a good, interesting man.... You needn't if you don't want to; nobody wants to force you against your will, my darling.

VARYA.
> I do look at the matter seriously, little mother, to be quite frank. He's a good man, and I like him.

LUBOV.
> Then marry him. I don't understand what you're waiting for.

VARYA.
> I can't propose to him myself, little mother. People have been talking about him to me for two years now, but he either says nothing, or jokes about it. I understand. He's getting rich, he's busy, he can't bother about

me. If I had some money, even a little, even only a hundred roubles, I'd throw up everything and go away. I'd go into a convent.

TROFIMOV.
  How nice!

VARYA.
  [To TROFIMOV] A student ought to have sense! [Gently, in tears] How ugly you are now, Peter, how old you've grown! [To LUBOV ANDREYEVNA, no longer crying] But I can't go on without working, little mother. I want to be doing something every minute.

[Enter YASHA.]

YASHA.
  [Nearly laughing] Epikhodov's broken a billiard cue! [Exit.]

VARYA.
  Why is Epikhodov here? Who said he could play billiards? I don't understand these people. [Exit.]

LUBOV.
  Don't tease her, Peter, you see that she's quite unhappy without that.

TROFIMOV.
  She takes too much on herself, she keeps on interfering in other people's business. The whole summer she's given no peace to me or to Anya, she's afraid we'll have a romance all to ourselves. What has it to do with her? As if I'd ever given her grounds to believe I'd stoop to such vulgarity! We are above love.

LUBOV.
  Then I suppose I must be beneath love. [In agitation] Why isn't Leonid here? If I only knew whether the estate is sold or not! The disaster seems to me so improbable that I don't know what to think, I'm all at sea . . . I may scream . . . or do something silly. Save me, Peter. Say something, say something.

TROFIMOV.
  Isn't it all the same whether the estate is sold to-day or isn't? It's been all up with it for a long time; there's no turning back, the path's grown over. Be calm, dear, you shouldn't deceive yourself, for once in your life at any rate you must look the truth straight in the face.

LUBOV.
  What truth? You see where truth is, and where untruth is, but I seem

to have lost my sight and see nothing. You boldly settle all important questions, but tell me, dear, isn't it because you're young, because you haven't had time to suffer till you settled a single one of your questions? You boldly look forward, isn't it because you cannot foresee or expect anything terrible, because so far life has been hidden from your young eyes? You are bolder, more honest, deeper than we are, but think only, be just a little magnanimous, and have mercy on me. I was born here, my father and mother lived here, my grandfather too, I love this house. I couldn't understand my life without that cherry orchard, and if it really must be sold, sell me with it! [Embraces TROFIMOV, kisses his forehead]. My son was drowned here. . . . [Weeps] Have pity on me, good, kind man.

TROFIMOV.
You know I sympathize with all my soul.

LUBOV.
Yes, but it ought to be said differently, differently. . . . [Takes another handkerchief, a telegram falls on the floor] I'm so sick at heart to-day, you can't imagine. Here it's so noisy, my soul shakes at every sound. I shake all over, and I can't go away by myself, I'm afraid of the silence. Don't judge me harshly, Peter . . . I loved you, as if you belonged to my family. I'd gladly let Anya marry you, I swear it, only dear, you ought to work, finish your studies. You don't do anything, only fate throws you about from place to place, it's so odd. . . . Isn't it true? Yes? And you ought to do something to your beard to make it grow better [Laughs] You are funny!

TROFIMOV.
[Picking up telegram] I don't want to be a Beau Brummel.

LUBOV.
This telegram's from Paris. I get one every day. Yesterday and to-day. That wild man is ill again, he's bad again. . . . He begs for forgiveness, and implores me to come, and I really ought to go to Paris to be near him. You look severe, Peter, but what can I do, my dear, what can I do; he's ill, he's alone, unhappy, and who's to look after him, who's to keep him away from his errors, to give him his medicine punctually? And why should I conceal it and say nothing about it; I love him, that's plain, I love him, I love him. . . . That love is a stone round my neck; I'm going with it to the bottom, but I love that stone and can't live

without it. [Squeezes TROFIMOV'S hand] Don't think badly of me,
Peter, don't say anything to me, don't say . . .
TROFIMOV.
[Weeping] For God's sake forgive my speaking candidly, but that man
has robbed you!
LUBOV.
No, no, no, you oughtn't to say that! [Stops her ears.]
TROFIMOV.
But he's a wretch, you alone don't know it! He's a petty thief, a
nobody. . . .
LUBOV.
[Angry, but restrained] You're twenty-six or twenty-seven, and still a
schoolboy of the second class!
TROFIMOV.
Why not!
LUBOV.
You ought to be a man, at your age you ought to be able to understand
those who love. And you ought to be in love yourself, you must fall
in love! [Angry] Yes, yes! You aren't pure, you're just a freak, a queer
fellow, a funny growth . . .
TROFIMOV.
[In horror] What is she saying!
LUBOV.
"I'm above love!" You're not above love, you're just what our Fiers calls
a bungler. Not to have a mistress at your age!
TROFIMOV.
[In horror] This is awful! What is she saying? [Goes quickly up into the
drawing-room, clutching his head] It's awful . . . I can't stand it, I'll go
away. [Exit, but returns at once] All is over between us! [Exit.]
LUBOV.
[Shouts after him] Peter, wait! Silly man, I was joking! Peter! [Somebody
is heard going out and falling downstairs noisily. ANYA and VARYA
scream; laughter is heard immediately] What's that?
[ANYA comes running in, laughing.]
ANYA.
Peter's fallen downstairs! [Runs out again.]

LUBOV.
>This Peter's a marvel.
>[The STATION-MASTER stands in the middle of the drawing-room and recites "The Magdalen" by Tolstoy. He is listened to, but he has only delivered a few lines when a waltz is heard from the front room, and the recitation is stopped. Everybody dances. TROFIMOV, ANYA, VARYA, and LUBOV ANDREYEVNA come in from the front room.]

LUBOV.
>Well, Peter... you pure soul... I beg your pardon... let's dance.
>[She dances with PETER. ANYA and VARYA dance. FIERS enters and stands his stick by a side door. YASHA has also come in and looks on at the dance.]

YASHA.
>Well, grandfather?

FIERS.
>I'm not well. At our balls some time back, generals and barons and admirals used to dance, and now we send for post-office clerks and the Station-master, and even they come as a favour. I'm very weak. The dead master, the grandfather, used to give everybody sealing-wax when anything was wrong. I've taken sealing-wax every day for twenty years, and more; perhaps that's why I still live.

YASHA.
>I'm tired of you, grandfather. [Yawns] If you'd only hurry up and kick the bucket.

FIERS.
>Oh you... bungler! [Mutters.]
>[TROFIMOV and LUBOV ANDREYEVNA dance in the reception-room, then into the sitting-room.]

LUBOV.
>Merci. I'll sit down. [Sits] I'm tired.
>[Enter ANYA.]

ANYA.
>[Excited] Somebody in the kitchen was saying just now that the cherry orchard was sold to-day.

LUBOV.
>Sold to whom?

ANYA.

    He didn't say to whom. He's gone now. [Dances out into the reception-room with TROFIMOV.]

YASHA.

    Some old man was chattering about it a long time ago. A stranger!

FIERS.

    And Leonid Andreyevitch isn't here yet, he hasn't come. He's wearing a light, demi-saison overcoat. He'll catch cold. Oh these young fellows.

LUBOV.

    I'll die of this. Go and find out, Yasha, to whom it's sold.

YASHA.

    Oh, but he's been gone a long time, the old man. [Laughs.]

LUBOV.

    [Slightly vexed] Why do you laugh? What are you glad about?

YASHA.

    Epikhodov's too funny. He's a silly man. Two-and-twenty troubles.

LUBOV.

    Fiers, if the estate is sold, where will you go?

FIERS.

    I'll go wherever you order me to go.

LUBOV.

    Why do you look like that? Are you ill? I think you ought to go to bed. . . .

FIERS.

    Yes . . . [With a smile] I'll go to bed, and who'll hand things round and give orders without me? I've the whole house on my shoulders.

YASHA.

    [To LUBOV ANDREYEVNA] Lubov Andreyevna! I want to ask a favour of you, if you'll be so kind! If you go to Paris again, then please take me with you. It's absolutely impossible for me to stop here. [Looking round; in an undertone] What's the good of talking about it, you see for yourself that this is an uneducated country, with an immoral population, and it's so dull. The food in the kitchen is beastly, and here's this Fiers walking about mumbling various inappropriate things. Take me with you, be so kind!

    [Enter PISCHIN.]

PISCHIN.
　I come to ask for the pleasure of a little waltz, dear lady.... [LUBOV ANDREYEVNA goes to him] But all the same, you wonderful woman, I must have 180 little roubles from you... I must.... [They dance] 180 little roubles.... [They go through into the drawing-room.]

YASHA.
　[Sings softly] "Oh, will you understand
　My soul's deep restlessness?"
　[In the drawing-room a figure in a grey top-hat and in baggy check trousers is waving its hands and jumping about; there are cries of "Bravo, Charlotta Ivanovna!"]

DUNYASHA.
　[Stops to powder her face] The young mistress tells me to dance—there are a lot of gentlemen, but few ladies—and my head goes round when I dance, and my heart beats, Fiers Nicolaevitch; the Post-office clerk told me something just now which made me catch my breath. [The music grows faint.]

FIERS.
　What did he say to you?

DUNYASHA.
　He says, "You're like a little flower."

YASHA.
　[Yawns] Impolite.... [Exit.]

DUNYASHA.
　Like a little flower. I'm such a delicate girl; I simply love words of tenderness.

FIERS.
　You'll lose your head.
　[Enter EPIKHODOV.]

EPIKHODOV.
　You, Avdotya Fedorovna, want to see me no more than if I was some insect. [Sighs] Oh, life!

DUNYASHA.
　What do you want?

EPIKHODOV.
　Undoubtedly, perhaps, you may be right. [Sighs] But, certainly, if you regard the matter from the aspect, then you, if I may say so, and you

must excuse my candidness, have absolutely reduced me to a state of mind. I know my fate, every day something unfortunate happens to me, and I've grown used to it a long time ago, I even look at my fate with a smile. You gave me your word, and though I . . .

DUNYASHA.
Please, we'll talk later on, but leave me alone now. I'm meditating now. [Plays with her fan.]

EPIKHODOV.
Every day something unfortunate happens to me, and I, if I may so express myself, only smile, and even laugh.

[VARYA enters from the drawing-room.]

VARYA.
Haven't you gone yet, Simeon? You really have no respect for anybody. [To DUNYASHA] You go away, Dunyasha. [To EPIKHODOV] You play billiards and break a cue, and walk about the drawing-room as if you were a visitor!

EPIKHODOV.
You cannot, if I may say so, call me to order.

VARYA.
I'm not calling you to order, I'm only telling you. You just walk about from place to place and never do your work. Goodness only knows why we keep a clerk.

EPIKHODOV.
[Offended] Whether I work, or walk about, or eat, or play billiards, is only a matter to be settled by people of understanding and my elders.

VARYA.
You dare to talk to me like that! [Furious] You dare? You mean that I know nothing? Get out of here! This minute!

EPIKHODOV.
[Nervous] I must ask you to express yourself more delicately.

VARYA.
[Beside herself] Get out this minute. Get out! [He goes to the door, she follows] Two-and-twenty troubles! I don't want any sign of you here! I don't want to see anything of you! [EPIKHODOV has gone out; his voice can be heard outside: "I'll make a complaint against you."] What, coming back? [Snatches up the stick left by FIERS by the door] Go . . .

go . . . go, I'll show you. . . . Are you going? Are you going? Well, then take that. [She hits out as LOPAKHIN enters.]

LOPAKHIN.
  Much obliged.
VARYA.
  [Angry but amused] I'm sorry.
LOPAKHIN.
  Never mind. I thank you for my pleasant reception.
VARYA.
  It isn't worth any thanks. [Walks away, then looks back and asks gently] I didn't hurt you, did I?
LOPAKHIN.
  No, not at all. There'll be an enormous bump, that's all.
VOICES FROM THE DRAWING-ROOM.
  Lopakhin's returned! Ermolai Alexeyevitch!
PISCHIN.
  Now we'll see what there is to see and hear what there is to hear . . . [Kisses LOPAKHIN] You smell of cognac, my dear, my soul. And we're all having a good time.
  [Enter LUBOV ANDREYEVNA.]
LUBOV.
  Is that you, Ermolai Alexeyevitch? Why were you so long? Where's Leonid?
LOPAKHIN.
  Leonid Andreyevitch came back with me, he's coming. . . .
LUBOV.
  [Excited] Well, what? Is it sold? Tell me?
LOPAKHIN.
  [Confused, afraid to show his pleasure] The sale ended up at four o'clock. . . . We missed the train, and had to wait till half-past nine. [Sighs heavily] Ooh! My head's going round a little.
  [Enter GAEV; in his right hand he carries things he has bought, with his left he wipes away his tears.]
LUBOV.
  Leon, what's happened? Leon, well? [Impatiently, in tears] Quick, for the love of God. . . .

GAEV.

[Says nothing to her, only waves his hand; to FIERS, weeping] Here, take this.... Here are anchovies, herrings from Kertch.... I've had no food to-day.... I have had a time! [The door from the billiard-room is open; the clicking of the balls is heard, and YASHA'S voice, "Seven, eighteen!" GAEV'S expression changes, he cries no more] I'm awfully tired. Help me change my clothes, Fiers.

[Goes out through the drawing-room; FIERS after him.]

PISCHIN.

What happened? Come on, tell us!

LUBOV.

Is the cherry orchard sold?

LOPAKHIN.

It is sold.

LUBOV.

Who bought it?

LOPAKHIN.

I bought it.

[LUBOV ANDREYEVNA is overwhelmed; she would fall if she were not standing by an armchair and a table. VARYA takes her keys off her belt, throws them on the floor, into the middle of the room and goes out.]

LOPAKHIN.

I bought it! Wait, ladies and gentlemen, please, my head's going round, I can't talk.... [Laughs] When we got to the sale, Deriganov was there already. Leonid Andreyevitch had only fifteen thousand roubles, and Deriganov offered thirty thousand on top of the mortgage to begin with. I saw how matters were, so I grabbed hold of him and bid forty. He went up to forty-five, I offered fifty-five. That means he went up by fives and I went up by tens.... Well, it came to an end. I bid ninety more than the mortgage; and it stayed with me. The cherry orchard is mine now, mine! [Roars with laughter] My God, my God, the cherry orchard's mine! Tell me I'm drunk, or mad, or dreaming.... [Stamps his feet] Don't laugh at me! If my father and grandfather rose from their graves and looked at the whole affair, and saw how their Ermolai, their beaten and uneducated Ermolai, who used to run barefoot in the winter, how that very Ermolai has bought an estate, which is the most beautiful thing in the world! I've bought the estate where my grandfather and my father were slaves, where they weren't even allowed into the kitchen. I'm asleep, it's only a dream, an illusion. . . . It's the fruit of imagination, wrapped in the fog of the unknown. . . . [Picks up the keys, nicely smiling] She threw down the keys, she wanted to show she was no longer mistress here. . . . [Jingles keys] Well, it's all one! [Hears the band tuning up] Eh, musicians, play, I want to hear you! Come and look at Ermolai Lopakhin laying his axe to the cherry orchard, come and look at the trees falling! We'll build villas here, and our grandsons and great-grandsons will see a new life here. . . . Play on, music! [The band plays. LUBOV ANDREYEVNA sinks into a chair and weeps bitterly. LOPAKHIN continues reproachfully] Why then, why didn't you take my advice? My poor, dear woman, you can't go back now. [Weeps] Oh, if only the whole thing was done with, if only our uneven, unhappy life were changed!

PISCHIN.

[Takes his arm; in an undertone] She's crying. Let's go into the drawing-room and leave her by herself . . . come on. . . . [Takes his arm and leads him out.]

LOPAKHIN.

What's that? Bandsmen, play nicely! Go on, do just as I want you to! [Ironically] The new owner, the owner of the cherry orchard is coming! [He accidentally knocks up against a little table and nearly upsets the candelabra] I can pay for everything! [Exit with PISCHIN]
[In the reception-room and the drawing-room nobody remains except LUBOV ANDREYEVNA, who sits huddled up and weeping bitterly. The band plays softly. ANYA and TROFIMOV come in quickly. ANYA goes up to her mother and goes on her knees in front of her. TROFIMOV stands at the drawing-room entrance.]

ANYA.

Mother! mother, are you crying? My dear, kind, good mother, my beautiful mother, I love you! Bless you! The cherry orchard is sold, we've got it no longer, it's true, true, but don't cry mother, you've still got your life before you, you've still your beautiful pure soul . . . Come with me, come, dear, away from here, come! We'll plant a new garden, finer than this, and you'll see it, and you'll understand, and deep joy, gentle joy will sink into your soul, like the evening sun, and you'll smile, mother! Come, dear, let's go!

Curtain falls.

ACT IV

The stage is set as for Act I. There are no curtains on the windows, no pictures; only a few pieces of furniture are left; they are piled up in a corner as if for sale. The emptiness is felt. By the door that leads out of the house and at the back of the stage, portmanteaux and travelling paraphernalia are piled up. The door on the left is open; the voices of VARYA and ANYA can be heard through it. LOPAKHIN stands and waits. YASHA holds a tray with little tumblers of champagne. Outside, EPIKHODOV is tying up a box. Voices are heard behind the stage. The peasants have come to say good-bye. The voice of GAEV is heard: "Thank you, brothers, thank you."

YASHA.
　The common people have come to say good-bye. I am of the opinion, Ermolai Alexeyevitch, that they're good people, but they don't understand very much.
　[The voices die away. LUBOV ANDREYEVNA and GAEV enter. She is not crying but is pale, and her face trembles; she can hardly speak.]

GAEV.
>You gave them your purse, Luba. You can't go on like that, you can't!

LUBOV.
>I couldn't help myself, I couldn't! [They go out.]

LOPAKHIN.
>[In the doorway, calling after them] Please, I ask you most humbly! Just a little glass to say good-bye. I didn't remember to bring any from town and I only found one bottle at the station. Please, do! [Pause] Won't you really have any? [Goes away from the door] If I only knew—I wouldn't have bought any. Well, I shan't drink any either. [YASHA carefully puts the tray on a chair] You have a drink, Yasha, at any rate.

YASHA.
>To those departing! And good luck to those who stay behind! [Drinks] I can assure you that this isn't real champagne.

LOPAKHIN.
>Eight roubles a bottle. [Pause] It's devilish cold here.

YASHA.
>There are no fires to-day, we're going away. [Laughs]

LOPAKHIN.
>What's the matter with you?

YASHA.
>I'm just pleased.

LOPAKHIN.
>It's October outside, but it's as sunny and as quiet as if it were summer. Good for building. [Looking at his watch and speaking through the door] Ladies and gentlemen, please remember that it's only forty-seven minutes till the train goes! You must go off to the station in twenty minutes. Hurry up.

[TROFIMOV, in an overcoat, comes in from the grounds.]

TROFIMOV.
>I think it's time we went. The carriages are waiting. Where the devil are my goloshes? They're lost. [Through the door] Anya, I can't find my goloshes! I can't!

LOPAKHIN.
>I've got to go to Kharkov. I'm going in the same train as you. I'm going to spend the whole winter in Kharkov. I've been hanging about with

you people, going rusty without work. I can't live without working. I must have something to do with my hands; they hang about as if they weren't mine at all.

TROFIMOV.
  We'll go away now and then you'll start again on your useful labours.
LOPAKHIN.
  Have a glass.
TROFIMOV.
  I won't.
LOPAKHIN.
  So you're off to Moscow now?
TROFIMOV Yes. I'll see them into town and to-morrow I'm off to Moscow.
LOPAKHIN.
  Yes. . . . I expect the professors don't lecture nowadays; they're waiting till you turn up!
TROFIMOV.
  That's not your business.
LOPAKHIN.
  How many years have you been going to the university?
TROFIMOV.
  Think of something fresh. This is old and flat. [Looking for his goloshes] You know, we may not meet each other again, so just let me give you a word of advice on parting: "Don't wave your hands about! Get rid of that habit of waving them about. And then, building villas and reckoning on their residents becoming freeholders in time—that's the same thing; it's all a matter of waving your hands about. . . . Whether I want to or not, you know, I like you. You've thin, delicate fingers, like those of an artist, and you've a thin, delicate soul. . . ."
LOPAKHIN.
  [Embraces him] Good-bye, dear fellow. Thanks for all you've said. If you want any, take some money from me for the journey.
TROFIMOV.
  Why should I? I don't want it.
LOPAKHIN.
  But you've nothing!

TROFIMOV.
> Yes, I have, thank you; I've got some for a translation. Here it is in my pocket. [Nervously] But I can't find my goloshes!

VARYA.
> [From the other room] Take your rubbish away! [Throws a pair of rubber goloshes on to the stage.]

TROFIMOV.
> Why are you angry, Varya? Hm! These aren't my goloshes!

LOPAKHIN.
> In the spring I sowed three thousand acres of poppies, and now I've made forty thousand roubles net profit. And when my poppies were in flower, what a picture it was! So I, as I was saying, made forty thousand roubles, and I mean I'd like to lend you some, because I can afford it. Why turn up your nose at it? I'm just a simple peasant....

TROFIMOV.
> Your father was a peasant, mine was a chemist, and that means absolutely nothing. [LOPAKHIN takes out his pocket-book] No, no.... Even if you gave me twenty thousand I should refuse. I'm a free man. And everything that all you people, rich and poor, value so highly and so dearly hasn't the least influence over me; it's like a flock of down in the wind. I can do without you, I can pass you by. I'm strong and proud. Mankind goes on to the highest truths and to the highest happiness such as is only possible on earth, and I go in the front ranks!

LOPAKHIN.
> Will you get there?

TROFIMOV.
> I will. [Pause] I'll get there and show others the way. [Axes cutting the trees are heard in the distance.]

LOPAKHIN.
> Well, good-bye, old man. It's time to go. Here we stand pulling one another's noses, but life goes its own way all the time. When I work for a long time, and I don't get tired, then I think more easily, and I think I get to understand why I exist. And there are so many people in Russia, brother, who live for nothing at all. Still, work goes on without that. Leonid Andreyevitch, they say, has accepted a post in a bank; he will get sixty thousand roubles a year.... But he won't stand it; he's very lazy.

ANYA.
[At the door] Mother asks if you will stop them cutting down the orchard until she has gone away.
TROFIMOV.
Yes, really, you ought to have enough tact not to do that. [Exit.]
LOPAKHIN, All right, all right . . . yes, he's right. [Exit.]
ANYA.
Has Fiers been sent to the hospital?
YASHA.
I gave the order this morning. I suppose they've sent him.
ANYA.
[To EPIKHODOV, who crosses the room] Simeon Panteleyevitch, please make inquiries if Fiers has been sent to the hospital.
YASHA.
[Offended] I told Egor this morning. What's the use of asking ten times!
EPIKHODOV.
The aged Fiers, in my conclusive opinion, isn't worth mending; his forefathers had better have him. I only envy him. [Puts a trunk on a hat-box and squashes it] Well, of course. I thought so! [Exit.]
YASHA.
[Grinning] Two-and-twenty troubles.
VARYA.
[Behind the door] Has Fiers been taken away to the hospital?
ANYA.
Yes.
VARYA.
Why didn't they take the letter to the doctor?
ANYA.
It'll have to be sent after him. [Exit.]
VARYA.
[In the next room] Where's Yasha? Tell him his mother's come and wants to say good-bye to him.
YASHA.
[Waving his hand] She'll make me lose all patience!
[DUNYASHA has meanwhile been bustling round the luggage; now that YASHA is left alone, she goes up to him.]

DUNYASHA.

    If you only looked at me once, Yasha. You're going away, leaving me behind.

    [Weeps and hugs him round the neck.]

YASHA.

    What's the use of crying? [Drinks champagne] In six days I'll be again in Paris. To-morrow we get into the express and off we go. I can hardly believe it. Vive la France! It doesn't suit me here, I can't live here . . . it's no good. Well, I've seen the uncivilized world; I have had enough of it. [Drinks champagne] What do you want to cry for? You behave yourself properly, and then you won't cry.

DUNYASHA.

    [Looks in a small mirror and powders her face] Send me a letter from Paris. You know I loved you, Yasha, so much! I'm a sensitive creature, Yasha.

YASHA.

    Somebody's coming.

    [He bustles around the luggage, singing softly. Enter LUBOV ANDREYEVNA, GAEV, ANYA, and CHARLOTTA IVANOVNA.]

GAEV.

    We'd better be off. There's no time left. [Looks at YASHA] Somebody smells of herring!

LUBOV.

    We needn't get into our carriages for ten minutes. . . . [Looks round the room] Good-bye, dear house, old grandfather. The winter will go, the spring will come, and then you'll exist no more, you'll be pulled down. How much these walls have seen! [Passionately kisses her daughter] My treasure, you're radiant, your eyes flash like two jewels! Are you happy? Very?

ANYA.

    Very! A new life is beginning, mother!

GAEV.

    [Gaily] Yes, really, everything's all right now. Before the cherry orchard was sold we all were excited and we suffered, and then, when the question was solved once and for all, we all calmed down, and even became cheerful. I'm a bank official now, and a financier . . . red in the middle; and you, Luba, for some reason or other, look better, there's no doubt about it.

LUBOV Yes. My nerves are better, it's true. [She puts on her coat and hat] I sleep well. Take my luggage out, Yasha. It's time. [To ANYA] My little girl, we'll soon see each other again. . . . I'm off to Paris. I'll live there on the money your grandmother from Yaroslav sent along to buy the estate—bless her!—though it won't last long.

ANYA.

You'll come back soon, soon, mother, won't you? I'll get ready, and pass the exam at the Higher School, and then I'll work and help you. We'll read all sorts of books to one another, won't we? [Kisses her mother's hands] We'll read in the autumn evenings; we'll read many books, and a beautiful new world will open up before us. . . . [Thoughtfully] You'll come, mother. . . .

LUBOV.

I'll come, my darling. [Embraces her.]

[Enter LOPAKHIN. CHARLOTTA is singing to herself.]

GAEV.

Charlotta is happy; she sings!

CHARLOTTA.

[Takes a bundle, looking like a wrapped-up baby] My little baby, bye-bye. [The baby seems to answer, "Oua! Oua!"] Hush, my nice little boy. ["Oua! Oua!"] I'm so sorry for you! [Throws the bundle back] So please find me a new place. I can't go on like this.

LOPAKHIN.

We'll find one, Charlotta Ivanovna, don't you be afraid.

GAEV.

Everybody's leaving us. Varya's going away . . . we've suddenly become unnecessary.

CHARLOTTA.

I've nowhere to live in town. I must go away. [Hums] Never mind.

[Enter PISCHIN.]

LOPAKHIN.

Nature's marvel!

PISCHIN.

[Puffing] Oh, let me get my breath back. . . . I'm fagged out . . . My most honoured, give me some water. . . .

GAEV.

Come for money, what? I'm your humble servant, and I'm going out of the way of temptation. [Exit.]

PISCHIN.

I haven't been here for ever so long . . . dear madam. [To LOPAKHIN] You here? Glad to see you . . . man of immense brain . . . take this . . . take it. . . . [Gives LOPAKHIN money] Four hundred roubles. . . . That leaves 840. . . .

LOPAKHIN.

[Shrugs his shoulders in surprise] As if I were dreaming. Where did you get this from?

PISCHIN.

Stop . . . it's hot. . . . A most unexpected thing happened. Some Englishmen came along and found some white clay on my land. . . . [To LUBOV ANDREYEVNA] And here's four hundred for you . . . beautiful lady. . . . [Gives her money] Give you the rest later. . . . [Drinks water] Just now a young man in the train was saying that some great philosopher advises us all to jump off roofs. "Jump!" he says, and that's all. [Astonished] To think of that, now! More water!

LOPAKHIN.

Who were these Englishmen?

PISCHIN.

I've leased off the land with the clay to them for twenty-four years. . . . Now, excuse me, I've no time. . . . I must run off. . . . I must go to Znoikov and to Kardamonov . . . I owe them all money. . . . [Drinks] Good-bye. I'll come in on Thursday.

LUBOV.

We're just off to town, and to-morrow I go abroad.

PISCHIN.

[Agitated] What? Why to town? I see furniture . . . trunks. . . . Well, never mind. [Crying] Never mind. These Englishmen are men of immense intellect. . . . Never mind. . . . Be happy. . . . God will help you. . . . Never mind. . . . Everything in this world comes to an end. . . . [Kisses LUBOV ANDREYEVNA'S hand] And if you should happen to hear that my end has come, just remember this old . . . horse and say: "There was one such and such a Simeonov-Pischin, God bless his soul. . . ." Wonderful weather . . . yes. . . . [Exit deeply moved, but returns at once and says in the door] Dashenka sent her love! [Exit.]

LUBOV.
Now we can go. I've two anxieties, though. The first is poor Fiers [Looks at her watch] We've still five minutes. . . .

ANYA.
Mother, Fiers has already been sent to the hospital. Yasha sent him off this morning.

LUBOV.
The second is Varya. She's used to getting up early and to work, and now she's no work to do she's like a fish out of water. She's grown thin and pale, and she cries, poor thing. . . . [Pause] You know very well, Ermolai Alexeyevitch, that I used to hope to marry her to you, and I suppose you are going to marry somebody? [Whispers to ANYA, who nods to CHARLOTTA, and they both go out] She loves you, she's your sort, and I don't understand, I really don't, why you seem to be keeping away from each other. I don't understand!

LOPAKHIN.
To tell the truth, I don't understand it myself. It's all so strange. . . . If there's still time, I'll be ready at once . . . Let's get it over, once and for all; I don't feel as if I could ever propose to her without you.

LUBOV.
Excellent. It'll only take a minute. I'll call her.

LOPAKHIN.
The champagne's very appropriate. [Looking at the tumblers] They're empty, somebody's already drunk them. [YASHA coughs] I call that licking it up. . . .

LUBOV.
[Animated] Excellent. We'll go out. Yasha, allez. I'll call her in. . . . [At the door] Varya, leave that and come here. Come! [Exit with YASHA.]

LOPAKHIN.
[Looks at his watch] Yes. . . . [Pause.]

[There is a restrained laugh behind the door, a whisper, then VARYA comes in.]

VARYA.

[Looking at the luggage in silence] I can't seem to find it....

LOPAKHIN.

What are you looking for?

VARYA.

I packed it myself and I don't remember. [Pause.]

LOPAKHIN.

Where are you going to now, Barbara Mihailovna?

VARYA.

I? To the Ragulins.... I've got an agreement to go and look after their house ... as housekeeper or something.

LOPAKHIN.

Is that at Yashnevo? It's about fifty miles. [Pause] So life in this house is finished now....

VARYA.

[Looking at the luggage] Where is it? ... perhaps I've put it away in the trunk.... Yes, there'll be no more life in this house....

LOPAKHIN.

And I'm off to Kharkov at once ... by this train. I've a lot of business on hand. I'm leaving Epikhodov here ... I've taken him on.

VARYA.

Well, well!

LOPAKHIN.

Last year at this time the snow was already falling, if you remember, and now it's nice and sunny. Only it's rather cold.... There's three degrees of frost.

VARYA.

I didn't look. [Pause] And our thermometer's broken.... [Pause.]

VOICE AT THE DOOR.

Ermolai Alexeyevitch!

LOPAKHIN.

[As if he has long been waiting to be called] This minute. [Exit quickly.]
[VARYA, sitting on the floor, puts her face on a bundle of clothes and weeps gently. The door opens. LUBOV ANDREYEVNA enters carefully.]

LUBOV.

Well? [Pause] We must go.

VARYA.

[Not crying now, wipes her eyes] Yes, it's quite time, little mother. I'll get to the Ragulins to-day, if I don't miss the train. . . .

LUBOV.

[At the door] Anya, put on your things. [Enter ANYA, then GAEV, CHARLOTTA IVANOVNA. GAEV wears a warm overcoat with a cape. A servant and drivers come in. EPIKHODOV bustles around the luggage] Now we can go away.

ANYA.

[Joyfully] Away!

GAEV.

My friends, my dear friends! Can I be silent, in leaving this house for evermore?—can I restrain myself, in saying farewell, from expressing those feelings which now fill my whole being . . . ?

ANYA.

[Imploringly] Uncle!

VARYA.

Uncle, you shouldn't!

GAEV.

[Stupidly] Double the red into the middle. . . . I'll be quiet.

[Enter TROFIMOV, then LOPAKHIN.]

TROFIMOV.

Well, it's time to be off.

LOPAKHIN.

Epikhodov, my coat!

LUBOV.

I'll sit here one more minute. It's as if I'd never really noticed what the walls and ceilings of this house were like, and now I look at them greedily, with such tender love. . . .

GAEV.

I remember, when I was six years old, on Trinity Sunday, I sat at this window and looked and saw my father going to church. . . .

LUBOV.

Have all the things been taken away?

LOPAKHIN.

Yes, all, I think. [To EPIKHODOV, putting on his coat] You see that everything's quite straight, Epikhodov.

EPIKHODOV.

[Hoarsely] You may depend upon me, Ermolai Alexeyevitch!

LOPAKHIN.

What's the matter with your voice?

EPIKHODOV.

I swallowed something just now; I was having a drink of water.

YASHA.

[Suspiciously] What manners. . . .

LUBOV.

We go away, and not a soul remains behind.

LOPAKHIN.

Till the spring.

VARYA.

[Drags an umbrella out of a bundle, and seems to be waving it about. LOPAKHIN appears to be frightened] What are you doing? . . . I never thought . . .

TROFIMOV.

Come along, let's take our seats . . . it's time! The train will be in directly.

VARYA.

Peter, here they are, your goloshes, by that trunk. [In tears] And how old and dirty they are. . . .

TROFIMOV.

[Putting them on] Come on!

GAEV.

[Deeply moved, nearly crying] The train . . . the station. . . . Cross in the middle, a white double in the corner. . . .

LUBOV.

Let's go!

LOPAKHIN.

Are you all here? There's nobody else? [Locks the side-door on the left] There's a lot of things in there. I must lock them up. Come!

ANYA.

Good-bye, home! Good-bye, old life!

TROFIMOV.
  Welcome, new life! [Exit with ANYA.]
  [VARYA looks round the room and goes out slowly. YASHA and CHARLOTTA, with her little dog, go out.]
LOPAKHIN.
  Till the spring, then! Come on . . . till we meet again! [Exit.]
  [LUBOV ANDREYEVNA and GAEV are left alone. They might almost have been waiting for that. They fall into each other's arms and sob restrainedly and quietly, fearing that somebody might hear them.]
GAEV.
  [In despair] My sister, my sister. . . .
LUBOV.
  My dear, my gentle, beautiful orchard! My life, my youth, my happiness, good-bye! Good-bye!
ANYA'S VOICE.
  [Gaily] Mother!
TROFIMOV'S VOICE.
  [Gaily, excited] Coo-ee!
LUBOV.
  To look at the walls and the windows for the last time. . . . My dead mother used to like to walk about this room. . . .
GAEV.
  My sister, my sister!
ANYA'S VOICE.
  Mother!
TROFIMOV'S VOICE.
  Coo-ee!
LUBOV.
  We're coming! [They go out.]
  [The stage is empty. The sound of keys being turned in the locks is heard, and then the noise of the carriages going away. It is quiet. Then the sound of an axe against the trees is heard in the silence sadly and by itself. Steps are heard. FIERS comes in from the door on the right. He is dressed as usual, in a short jacket and white waistcoat; slippers on his feet. He is ill. He goes to the door and tries the handle.]

FIERS.
It's locked. They've gone away. [Sits on a sofa] They've forgotten about me. . . . Never mind, I'll sit here. . . . And Leonid Andreyevitch will have gone in a light overcoat instead of putting on his fur coat. . . . [Sighs anxiously] I didn't see. . . . Oh, these young people! [Mumbles something that cannot be understood] Life's gone on as if I'd never lived. [Lying down] I'll lie down. . . . You've no strength left in you, nothing left at all. . . . Oh, you . . . bungler!
[He lies without moving. The distant sound is heard, as if from the sky, of a breaking string, dying away sadly. Silence follows it, and only the sound is heard, some way away in the orchard, of the axe falling on the trees.]

Curtain falls.

SELECTED LETTERS

Translated by Constance Garnett

SELECTED LETTERS

Translated by Constance Garnett

TO HIS BROTHER MIHAIL.

TAGANROG, July 1, 1876.

DEAR BROTHER MISHA,

I got your letter when I was fearfully bored and was sitting at the gate yawning, and so you can judge how welcome that immense letter was. Your writing is good, and in the whole letter I have not found one mistake in spelling. But one thing I don't like: why do you style yourself "your worthless and insignificant brother"? You recognize your insignificance? . . . Recognize it before God; perhaps, too, in the presence of beauty, intelligence, nature, but not before men. Among men you must be conscious of your dignity. Why, you are not a rascal, you are an honest man, aren't you? Well, respect yourself as an honest man and know that an honest man is not something worthless. Don't confound "being humble" with "recognizing one's worthlessness." . . .

It is a good thing that you read. Acquire the habit of doing so. In time you will come to value that habit. Madame Beecher-

Stowe has wrung tears from your eyes? I read her once, and six months ago read her again with the object of studying her—and after reading I had an unpleasant sensation which mortals feel after eating too many raisins or currants. . . . Read "Don Quixote." It is a fine thing. It is by Cervantes, who is said to be almost on a level with Shakespeare. I advise my brothers to read—if they haven't already done so—Turgenev's "Hamlet and Don Quixote." You won't understand it, my dear. If you want to read a book of travel that won't bore you, read Gontcharov's "The Frigate Pallada."

. . . I am going to bring with me a boarder who will pay twenty roubles a month and live under our general supervision. Though even twenty roubles is not enough if one considers the price of food in Moscow and mother's weakness for feeding boarders with righteous zeal.

TO HIS COUSIN, MIHAIL CHEKHOV.

TAGANROG, May 10, 1877.

. . . If I send letters to my mother, care of you, please give them to her when you are alone with her; there are things in life which one can confide in one person only, whom one trusts. It is because of this that I write to my mother without the knowledge of the others, for whom my secrets are quite uninteresting, or, rather, unnecessary. . . . My second request is of more importance. Please go on comforting my mother, who is both physically and morally broken. She has found in you not merely a nephew but a great deal more and better than a nephew. My mother's character is such that the moral support of others is a great help to her. It is a silly request, isn't it? But you will understand, especially as I have said "moral," i.e., spiritual support. There is no one in this wicked world dearer to us than our mother, and so you will greatly oblige your humble servant by comforting his worn-out and weary mother. . . .

TO HIS UNCLE, M. G. CHEKHOV.

MOSCOW, 1885.

... I could not come to see you last summer because I took the place of a district doctor friend of mine who went away for his holiday, but this year I hope to travel and therefore to see you. Last December I had an attack of spitting blood, and decided to take some money from the Literary Fund and go abroad for my health. I am a little better now, but I still think that I shall have to go away. And whenever I go abroad, or to the Crimea, or to the Caucasus, I will go through Taganrog.

... I am sorry I cannot join you in being of service to my native Taganrog.... I am sure that if my work had been there I should have been calmer, more cheerful, in better health, but evidently it is my fate to remain in Moscow. My home and my career are here. I have work of two sorts. As a doctor I should have grown slack in Taganrog and forgotten my medicine, but in Moscow a doctor has no time to go to the club and play cards. As a writer I am no use except in Moscow or Petersburg.

My medical work is progressing little by little. I go on steadily treating patients. Every day I have to spend more than a rouble on cabs. I have a lot of friends and therefore many patients. Half of them I have to treat for nothing, but the other half pay me three or five roubles a visit. ... I need hardly say I have not made a fortune yet, and it will be a long time before I do, but I live tolerably and need nothing. So long as I am alive and well the position of the family is secure. I have bought new furniture, hired a good piano, keep two servants, give little evening parties with music and singing. I have no debts and do not want to borrow. Till quite recently we used to run an account at the butcher's and grocer's, but now I have stopped even that, and we pay cash for everything. What will come later, there is no knowing; as it is we have nothing to complain of....

TO N. A. LEIKIN.

MOSCOW, October, 1885.

... You advise me to go to Petersburg, and say that Petersburg is not China. I know it is not, and as you are aware, I have long realized the necessity of going there; but what am I to do? Owing to the fact that we are a large family, I never have a ten-rouble note to spare, and to go there, even if I did it in the most uncomfortable and beggarly way, would cost at least fifty roubles. How am I to get the money? I can't squeeze it out of my family and don't think I ought to. If I were to cut down our two courses at dinner to one, I should begin to pine away from pangs of conscience. ... Allah only knows how difficult it is for me to keep my balance, and how easy it would be for me to slip and lose my equilibrium. I fancy that if next month I should earn twenty or thirty roubles less, my balance would be gone, and I should be in difficulties. I am awfully apprehensive about money matters and, owing to this quite uncommercial cowardice in pecuniary affairs, I avoid loans and payments on account. I am not difficult to move. If I had money I should fly from one city to another endlessly.

TO A. S. SUVORIN.

MOSCOW, February 21, 1886.

... Thank you for the flattering things you say about my work and for having published my story so soon. You can judge yourself how refreshing, even inspiring, the kind attention of an experienced and gifted writer like yourself has been to me.

I agree with what you say about the end of my story which you have cut out; thank you for the helpful advice. I have been writing for the last six years, but you are the first person who has taken the trouble to advise and explain.

... I do not write very much—not more than two or three short stories weekly.

TO D. V. GRIGOROVITCH.

MOSCOW, March 28, 1886.

Your letter, my kind, fervently beloved bringer of good tidings, struck me like a flash of lightning. I almost burst into tears, I was overwhelmed, and now I feel it has left a deep trace in my soul! May God show the same tender kindness to you in your age as you have shown me in my youth! I can find neither words nor deeds to thank you. You know with what eyes ordinary people look at the elect such as you, and so you can judge what your letter means for my self-esteem. It is better than any diploma, and for a writer who is just beginning it is payment both for the present and the future. I am almost dazed. I have no power to judge whether I deserve this high reward. I only repeat that it has overwhelmed me.

If I have a gift which one ought to respect, I confess before the pure candour of your heart that hitherto I have not respected it. I felt that I had a gift, but I had got into the habit of thinking that it was insignificant. Purely external causes are sufficient to make one unjust to oneself, suspicious, and morbidly sensitive. And as I realize now I have always had plenty of such causes. All my friends and relatives have always taken a condescending tone to my writing, and never ceased urging me in a friendly way not to give up real work for the sake of scribbling. I have hundreds of friends in Moscow, and among them a dozen or two writers, but I cannot recall a single one who reads me or considers me an artist. In Moscow there is a so-called Literary Circle: talented people and mediocrities of all ages and colours gather once a week in a private room of a restaurant and exercise their tongues. If I went there and read them a single passage of your letter, they would laugh in my face. In the course of the five years that I have been knocking about from one newspaper office to another I have had time to assimilate the general view of my literary insignificance. I soon got used to looking down upon my work, and so it has gone from bad to worse. That is the first reason. The second is that I am a doctor, and am up to my ears in medical work, so that the proverb about trying to catch two hares has given to no one more sleepless nights than me.

I am writing all this to you in order to excuse this grievous sin a little before you. Hitherto my attitude to my literary work has been frivolous, heedless, casual. I don't remember a single story over which I have spent more than twenty-four hours, and "The Huntsman," which you liked, I wrote in the bathing-shed! I wrote my stories as reporters write their notes about fires, mechanically, half-unconsciously, taking no thought of the reader or myself.... I wrote and did all I could not to waste upon the story the scenes and images dear to me which—God knows why—I have treasured and kept carefully hidden.

The first impulse to self-criticism was given me by a very kind and, to the best of my belief, sincere letter from Suvorin. I began to think of writing something decent, but I still had no faith in my being any good as a writer. And then, unexpected and undreamed of, came your letter. Forgive the comparison: it had on me the effect of a Governor's order to clear out of the town within twenty-four hours—i.e., I suddenly felt an imperative need to hurry, to make haste and get out of where I have stuck....

I agree with you in everything. When I saw "The Witch" in print I felt myself the cynicism of the points to which you call my attention. They would not have been there had I written this story in three or four days instead of in one.

I shall put an end to working against time, but cannot do so just yet.... It is impossible to get out of the rut I have got into. I have nothing against going hungry, as I have done in the past, but it is not a question of myself.... I give to literature my spare time, two or three hours a day and a bit of the night, that is, time which is of no use except for short things. In the summer, when I have more time and have fewer expenses, I will start on some serious work.

I cannot put my real name on the book because it is too late: the design for the cover is ready and the book printed. Many of my Petersburg friends advised me, even before you did, not to spoil the book by a pseudonym, but I did not listen to them, probably out of vanity. I dislike my book very much. It's a hotch-potch, a disorderly medley of the poor stuff I wrote as a student, plucked by the censor and by the editors of comic papers. I am sure that many people will be disappointed when they read it. Had I known that I had readers and that you were watching me, I would not have published this book.

I rest all my hopes on the future. I am only twenty-six. Perhaps I shall succeed in doing something, though time flies fast.

Forgive my long letter and do not blame a man because, for the first time in his life, he has made bold to treat himself to the pleasure of writing to Grigorovitch.

Send me your photograph, if possible. I am so overwhelmed with your kindness that I feel as though I should like to write a whole ream to you. God grant you health and happiness, and believe in the sincerity of your deeply respectful and grateful

A. CHEKHOV.

TO N. A. LEIKIN.

MOSCOW, April 6, 1886.

... I am ill. Spitting of blood and weakness. I am not writing anything.... If I don't sit down to write to-morrow, you must forgive me—I shall not send you a story for the Easter number. I ought to go to the South but I have no money.... I am afraid to submit myself to be sounded by my colleagues. I am inclined to think it is not so much my lungs as my throat that is at fault.... I have no fever.

TO MADAME M. V. KISELYOV.

BABKINO, June, 1886.

LOVE UNRIPPLED [Parody of a feminine novel.]

(A NOVEL) Part I.

It was noon.... The setting sun with its crimson, fiery rays gilded the tops of pines, oaks, and fir-trees.... It was still; only in the air the birds were singing, and in the distance a hungry wolf howled mournfully.... The driver turned round and said:

"More snow has fallen, sir."

"What?"

"I say, more snow has fallen."

"Ah!"

Vladimir Sergeitch Tabatchin, who is the hero of our story, looked for the last time at the sun and expired.

A week passed. . . . Birds and corncrakes hovered, whistling, over a newly-made grave. The sun was shining. A young widow, bathed in tears, was standing by, and in her grief sopping her whole handkerchief. . . .

MOSCOW,
September 21, 1886.

. . . It is not much fun to be a great writer. To begin with, it's a dreary life. Work from morning till night and not much to show for it. Money is as scarce as cats' tears. I don't know how it is with Zola and Shtchedrin, but in my flat it is cold and smoky. . . . They give me cigarettes, as before, on holidays only. Impossible cigarettes! Hard, damp, sausage-like. Before I begin to smoke I light the lamp, dry the cigarette over it, and only then I begin on it; the lamp smokes, the cigarette splutters and turns brown, I burn my fingers . . . it is enough to make one shoot oneself!

. . . I am more or less ill, and am gradually turning into a dried dragon-fly.

. . . I go about as festive as though it were my birthday, but to judge from the critical glances of the lady cashier at the Budilnik, I am not dressed in the height of fashion, and my clothes are not brand-new. I go in buses, not in cabs.

But being a writer has its good points. In the first place, my book, I hear, is going rather well; secondly, in October I shall have money; thirdly, I am beginning to reap laurels: at the refreshment bars people point at me with their fingers, they pay me little attentions and treat me to sandwiches. Korsh caught me in his theatre and straight away presented me with a free pass. . . . My medical colleagues sigh when they meet me, begin to talk of literature and assure me that they are sick of medicine. And so on. . . .

September 29.

. . . Life is grey, there are no happy people to be seen. . . . Life is a nasty business for everyone. When I am serious I begin to think that people who have an aversion for death are illogical. So far as I understand the order of things, life consists of nothing but horrors, squabbles, and trivialities mixed together or alternating!

December 3.

This morning an individual sent by Prince Urusov turned up and asked me for a short story for a sporting magazine edited by the said Prince. I refused, of course, as I now refuse all who come with supplications to the foot of my pedestal. In Russia there are now two unattainable heights: Mount Elborus and myself.

The Prince's envoy was deeply disappointed by my refusal, nearly died of grief, and finally begged me to recommend him some writers who are versed in sport. I thought a little, and very opportunely remembered a lady writer who dreams of glory and has for the last year been ill with envy of my literary fame. In short, I gave him your address. . . . You might write a story "The Wounded Doe"—you remember, how the huntsmen wound a doe; she looks at them with human eyes, and no one can bring himself to kill her. It's not a bad subject, but dangerous because it is difficult to avoid sentimentality—you must write it like a report, without pathetic phrases, and begin like this: "On such and such a date the huntsmen in the Daraganov forest wounded a young doe. . . ." And if you drop a tear you will strip the subject of its severity and of everything worth attention in it.

December 13.

. . . With your permission I steal out of your last two letters to my sister two descriptions of nature for my stories. It is curious that you have quite a masculine way of writing. In every line (except when dealing with children) you are a man! This, of course, ought to flatter your vanity, for speaking generally, men are a thousand times better than women, and superior to them.

In Petersburg I was resting—i.e., for days together I was rushing about town paying calls and listening to compliments which my soul abhors. Alas and alack! In Petersburg I am becoming fashionable like Nana. While Korolenko, who is serious, is hardly known to the editors, my twaddle is being read by all Petersburg. Even the senator G. reads me. . . . It is gratifying, but my literary feeling is wounded. I feel ashamed of the public which runs after lap-dogs simply because it fails to notice elephants, and I am deeply convinced that not a soul will know me when I begin to work in earnest.

TO HIS BROTHER NIKOLAY.

MOSCOW, 1886.

... You have often complained to me that people "don't understand you"! Goethe and Newton did not complain of that.... Only Christ complained of it, but He was speaking of His doctrine and not of Himself.... People understand you perfectly well. And if you do not understand yourself, it is not their fault.

I assure you as a brother and as a friend I understand you and feel for you with all my heart. I know your good qualities as I know my five fingers; I value and deeply respect them. If you like, to prove that I understand you, I can enumerate those qualities. I think you are kind to the point of softness, magnanimous, unselfish, ready to share your last farthing; you have no envy nor hatred; you are simple-hearted, you pity men and beasts; you are trustful, without spite or guile, and do not remember evil. ... You have a gift from above such as other people have not: you have talent. This talent places you above millions of men, for on earth only one out of two millions is an artist. Your talent sets you apart: if you were a toad or a tarantula, even then, people would respect you, for to talent all things are forgiven.

You have only one failing, and the falseness of your position, and your unhappiness and your catarrh of the bowels are all due to it. That is your utter lack of culture. Forgive me, please, but veritas magis amicitiae. ... You see, life has its conditions. In order to feel comfortable among educated people, to be at home and happy with them, one must be cultured to a certain extent. Talent has brought you into such a circle, you belong to it, but ... you are drawn away from it, and you vacillate between cultured people and the lodgers vis-a-vis.

Cultured people must, in my opinion, satisfy the following conditions:
1. They respect human personality, and therefore they are always kind, gentle, polite, and ready to give in to others. They do not make a row because of a hammer or a lost piece of india-rubber; if they live with anyone they do not regard it as a favour and, going away, they do not say "nobody can live with you." They forgive noise and cold and dried-up meat and witticisms and the presence of strangers in their homes.

2. They have sympathy not for beggars and cats alone. Their heart aches for what the eye does not see. . . . They sit up at night in order to help P. . . ., to pay for brothers at the University, and to buy clothes for their mother.
3. They respect the property of others, and therefor pay their debts.
4. They are sincere, and dread lying like fire. They don't lie even in small things. A lie is insulting to the listener and puts him in a lower position in the eyes of the speaker. They do not pose, they behave in the street as they do at home, they do not show off before their humbler comrades. They are not given to babbling and forcing their uninvited confidences on others. Out of respect for other people's ears they more often keep silent than talk.
5. They do not disparage themselves to rouse compassion. They do not play on the strings of other people's hearts so that they may sigh and make much of them. They do not say "I am misunderstood," or "I have become second-rate," because all this is striving after cheap effect, is vulgar, stale, false. . . .
6. They have no shallow vanity. They do not care for such false diamonds as knowing celebrities, shaking hands with the drunken P., [Translator's Note: Probably Palmin, a minor poet.] listening to the raptures of a stray spectator in a picture show, being renowned in the taverns. . . . If they do a pennyworth they do not strut about as though they had done a hundred roubles' worth, and do not brag of having the entry where others are not admitted. . . . The truly talented always keep in obscurity among the crowd, as far as possible from advertisement. . . . Even Krylov has said that an empty barrel echoes more loudly than a full one.
7. If they have a talent they respect it. They sacrifice to it rest, women, wine, vanity. . . . They are proud of their talent. . . . Besides, they are fastidious.
8. They develop the aesthetic feeling in themselves. They cannot go to sleep in their clothes, see cracks full of bugs on the walls, breathe bad air, walk on a floor that has been spat upon, cook their meals over an oil stove. They seek as far as possible to restrain and ennoble the sexual instinct. . . . What they want in a woman is not a bed-fellow . . . They do not ask for the cleverness which shows

itself in continual lying. They want especially, if they are artists, freshness, elegance, humanity, the capacity for motherhood.... They do not swill vodka at all hours of the day and night, do not sniff at cupboards, for they are not pigs and know they are not. They drink only when they are free, on occasion.... For they want mens sana in corpore sano.

And so on. This is what cultured people are like. In order to be cultured and not to stand below the level of your surroundings it is not enough to have read "The Pickwick Papers" and learnt a monologue from "Faust."...

What is needed is constant work, day and night, constant reading, study, will.... Every hour is precious for it.... Come to us, smash the vodka bottle, lie down and read.... Turgenev, if you like, whom you have not read.

You must drop your vanity, you are not a child ... you will soon be thirty. It is time!

I expect you.... We all expect you.

TO MADAME M. V. KISELYOV.

MOSCOW, January 14, 1887.

... Even your praise of "On the Road" has not softened my anger as an author, and I hasten to avenge myself for "Mire." Be on your guard, and catch hold of the back of a chair that you may not faint. Well, I begin.

One meets every critical article with a silent bow even if it is abusive and unjust—such is the literary etiquette. It is not the thing to answer, and all who do answer are justly blamed for excessive vanity. But since your criticism has the nature of "an evening conversation on the steps of the Babkino lodge" ... and as, without touching on the literary aspects of the story, it raises general questions of principle, I shall not be sinning against the etiquette if I allow myself to continue our conversation.

In the first place, I, like you, do not like literature of the kind we are discussing. As a reader and "a private resident" I am glad to avoid it, but if you ask my honest and sincere opinion about it, I shall say that it is still an open question whether it has a right to exist, and no one has yet settled it....

Neither you nor I, nor all the critics in the world, have any trustworthy data that would give them the right to reject such literature. I do not know which are right: Homer, Shakespeare, Lopez da Vega, and, speaking generally, the ancients who were not afraid to rummage in the "muck heap," but were morally far more stable than we are, or the modern writers, priggish on paper but coldly cynical in their souls and in life. I do not know which has bad taste—the Greeks who were not ashamed to describe love as it really is in beautiful nature, or the readers of Gaboriau, Marlitz, Pierre Bobo. Like the problems of non-resistance to evil, of free will, etc., this question can only be settled in the future. We can only refer to it, but are not competent to decide it. Reference to Turgenev and Tolstoy—who avoided the "muck heap"—does not throw light on the question. Their fastidiousness does not prove anything; why, before them there was a generation of writers who regarded as dirty not only accounts of "the dregs and scum," but even descriptions of peasants and of officials below the rank of titular councillor. Besides, one period, however brilliant, does not entitle us to draw conclusions in favour of this or that literary tendency. Reference to the demoralizing effects of the literary tendency we are discussing does not decide the question either. Everything in this world is relative and approximate. There are people who can be demoralized even by children's books, and who read with particular pleasure the piquant passages in the Psalms and in Solomon's Proverbs, while there are others who become only the purer from closer knowledge of the filthy side of life. Political and social writers, lawyers, and doctors who are initiated into all the mysteries of human sinfulness are not reputed to be immoral; realistic writers are often more moral than archimandrites. And, finally, no literature can outdo real life in its cynicism, a wineglassful won't make a man drunk when he has already emptied a barrel.

2. That the world swarms with "dregs and scum" is perfectly true. Human nature is imperfect, and it would therefore be strange to see none but righteous ones on earth. But to think that the duty of literature is to unearth the pearl from the refuse heap means to reject literature itself. "Artistic" literature is only "art" in so far as it paints life as it really is. Its vocation is to be absolutely true and honest. To narrow down its function to the particular task of finding "pearls" is as deadly for it as it would be to make Levitan draw a tree without including the dirty bark and the yellow

leaves. I agree that "pearls" are a good thing, but then a writer is not a confectioner, not a provider of cosmetics, not an entertainer; he is a man bound, under contract, by his sense of duty and his conscience; having put his hand to the plough he mustn't turn back, and, however distasteful, he must conquer his squeamishness and soil his imagination with the dirt of life. He is just like any ordinary reporter. What would you say if a newspaper correspondent out of a feeling of fastidiousness or from a wish to please his readers would describe only honest mayors, high-minded ladies, and virtuous railway contractors?

To a chemist nothing on earth is unclean. A writer must be as objective as a chemist, he must lay aside his personal subjective standpoint and must understand that muck heaps play a very respectable part in a landscape, and that the evil passions are as inherent in life as the good ones.

3. Writers are the children of their age, and therefore, like everybody else, must submit to the external conditions of the life of the community. Thus, they must be perfectly decent. This is the only thing we have a right to ask of realistic writers. But you say nothing against the form and executions of "Mire." . . . And so I suppose I have been decent.

4. I confess I seldom commune with my conscience when I write. This is due to habit and the brevity of my work. And so when I express this or that opinion about literature, I do not take myself into account.

5. You write: "If I were the editor I would have returned this feuilleton to you for your own good." Why not go further? Why not muzzle the editors themselves who publish such stories? Why not send a reprimand to the Headquarters of the Press Department for not suppressing immoral newspapers?

The fate of literature would be sad indeed if it were at the mercy of individual views. That is the first thing. Secondly, there is no police which could consider itself competent in literary matters. I agree that one can't dispense with the reins and the whip altogether, for knaves find their way even into literature, but no thinking will discover a better police for literature than the critics and the author's own conscience. People have been trying to discover such a police since the creation of the world, but they have found nothing better.

Here you would like me to lose one hundred and fifteen roubles and be put to shame by the editor; others, your father among them, are delighted with the story. Some send insulting letters to Suvorin, pouring abuse on the paper and on me, etc. Who, then, is right? Who is the true judge?

6. Further you write, "Leave such writing to spiritless and unlucky scribblers such as Okrects, Pince-Nez, or Aloe."

Allah forgive you if you were sincere when you wrote those words! A condescending and contemptuous tone towards humble people simply because they are humble does no credit to the heart. In literature the lower ranks are as necessary as in the army—this is what the head says, and the heart ought to say still more.

Ough! I have wearied you with my drawn-out reflections. Had I known my criticism would turn out so long I would not have written it. Please forgive me! . . .

You have read my "On the Road." Well, how do you like my courage? I write of "intellectual" subjects and am not afraid. In Petersburg I excite a regular furore. A short time ago I discoursed upon non-resistance to evil, and also surprised the public. On New Year's Day all the papers presented me with a compliment, and in the December number of the Russkoye Bogatstvo, in which Tolstoy writes, there is an article thirty-two pages long by Obolensky entitled "Chekhov and Korolenko." The fellow goes into raptures over me and proves that I am more of an artist than Korolenko. He is probably talking rot, but, anyway, I am beginning to be conscious of one merit of mine: I am the only writer who, without ever publishing anything in the thick monthlies, has merely on the strength of writing newspaper rubbish won the attention of the lop-eared critics—there has been no instance of this before. . . . At the end of 1886 I felt as though I were a bone thrown to the dogs.

. . . I have written a play on four sheets of paper. It will take fifteen to twenty minutes to act. . . . It is much better to write small things than big ones: they are unpretentious and successful. . . . What more would you have? I wrote my play in an hour and five minutes. I began another, but have not finished it, for I have no time.

TO HIS UNCLE, M. G. CHEKHOV.

MOSCOW, January 18, 1887.

... During the holidays I was so overwhelmed with work that on Mother's name-day I was almost dropping with exhaustion.

I must tell you that in Petersburg I am now the most fashionable writer. One can see that from papers and magazines, which at the end of 1886 were taken up with me, bandied my name about, and praised me beyond my deserts. The result of this growth of my literary reputation is that I get a number of orders and invitations—and this is followed by work at high pressure and exhaustion. My work is nervous, disturbing, and involving strain. It is public and responsible, which makes it doubly hard. Every newspaper report about me agitates both me and my family.... My stories are read at public recitations, wherever I go people point at me, I am overwhelmed with acquaintances, and so on, and so on. I have not a day of peace, and feel as though I were on thorns every moment.

... Volodya [Translator's Note: He had apparently criticized the name Vladimir, which means "lord of the world."] is right.... It is true that a man cannot possess the world, but a man can be called "the lord of the world." Tell Volodya that out of gratitude, reverence, or admiration of the virtues of the best men—those qualities which make a man exceptional and akin to the Deity—peoples and historians have a right to call their elect as they like, without being afraid of insulting God's greatness or of raising a man to God. The fact is we exalt, not a man as such, but his good qualities, just that divine principle which he has succeeded in developing in himself to a high degree. Thus remarkable kings are called "great," though bodily they may not be taller than I. I. Loboda; the Pope is called "Holiness," the patriarch used to be called "Ecumenical," although he was not in relations with any planet but the earth; Prince Vladimir was called "the lord of the world," though he ruled only a small strip of ground, princes are called "serene" and "illustrious," though a Swedish match is a thousand times brighter than they are—and so on. In using these expressions we do not lie or exaggerate, but simply express our delight, just as a mother does not lie when she calls her child "my golden one." It is the feeling of beauty that speaks in us, and beauty cannot endure what is commonplace and trivial; it induces us to make comparisons which Volodya may, with his intellect, pull to pieces, but which he will understand with his heart. For instance, it is usual to compare black eyes with the night, blue with the azure of the sky, curls with waves, etc., and even the Bible likes these comparisons; for instance, "Thy womb is more spacious than heaven," or "The Sun of righteousness arises," "The rock of faith," etc. The feeling of beauty in man knows no limits or bounds. This is why a Russian prince may be called "the lord of the world"; and my friend Volodya may have the same name, for names are given to people, not for their merits, but in honour and commemoration of remarkable men of the past. . . . If your young scholar does not agree with me, I have one more argument which will be sure to appeal to him: in exalting people even to God we do not sin against love, but, on the contrary, we express it. One must not humiliate people—that is the chief thing. Better say to man "My angel" than hurl "Fool" at his head—though men are more like fools than they are like angels.

TO HIS SISTER.

TAGANROG, April 2, 1887.

The journey from Moscow to Serpuhov was dull. My fellow-travellers were practical persons of strong character who did nothing but talk of the prices of flour. . . .

. . . At twelve o'clock we were at Kursk. An hour of waiting, a glass of vodka, a tidy-up and a wash, and cabbage soup. Change to another train. The carriage was crammed full. Immediately after Kursk I made friends with my neighbours: a landowner from Harkov, as jocose as Sasha K.; a lady who had just had an operation in Petersburg; a police captain; an officer from Little Russia; and a general in military uniform. We settled social questions. The general's arguments were sound, short, and liberal; the police captain was the type of an old battered sinner of an hussar yearning for amorous adventures. He had the affectations of a governor: he opened his mouth long before he began to speak, and having said a word he gave a long growl like a dog, "er-r-r." The lady was injecting morphia, and sent the men to fetch her ice at the stations.

At Belgrade I had cabbage soup. We got to Harkov at nine o'clock. A touching parting from the police captain, the general and the others.... I woke up at Slavyansk and sent you a postcard. A new lot of passengers got in: a landowner and a railway inspector. We talked of railways. The inspector told us how the Sevastopol railway stole three hundred carriages from the Azov line and painted them its own colour.

... Twelve o'clock. Lovely weather. There is a scent of the steppe and one hears the birds sing. I see my old friends the ravens flying over the steppe.

The barrows, the water-towers, the buildings—everything is familiar and well-remembered. At the station I have a helping of remarkably good and rich sorrel soup. Then I walk along the platform. Young ladies. At an upper window at the far end of the station sits a young girl (or a married lady, goodness knows which) in a white blouse, beautiful and languid. I look at her, she looks at me.... I put on my glasses, she does the same.... Oh, lovely vision! I caught a catarrh of the heart and continued my journey. The weather is devilishly, revoltingly fine. Little Russians, oxen, ravens, white huts, rivers, the line of the Donets railway with one telegraph wire, daughters of landowners and farmers, red dogs, the trees—it all flits by like a dream.... It is hot. The inspector begins to bore me. The rissoles and pies, half of which I have not got through, begin to smell bitter.... I shove them under somebody else's seat, together with the remains of the vodka.

... I arrive at Taganrog.... It gives one the impression of Herculaneum and Pompeii; there are no people, and instead of mummies there are sleepy drishpaks and melon-shaped heads. All the houses look flattened out, and as though they had long needed replastering, the roofs want painting, the shutters are closed....

At eight o'clock in the evening my uncle, his family, Irina, the dogs, the rats that live in the storeroom, the rabbits were fast asleep. There was nothing for it but to go to bed too. I sleep on the drawing-room sofa. The sofa has not increased in length, and is as short as it was before, and so when I go to bed I have either to stick up my legs in an unseemly way or to let them hang down to the floor. I think of Procrustes and his bed....

April 6.

I wake up at five. The sky is grey. There is a cold, unpleasant wind that reminds one of Moscow. It is dull. I wait for the church bells and go to late

Mass. In the cathedral it is all very charming, decorous, and not boring. The choir sings well, not at all in a plebeian style, and the congregation entirely consists of young ladies in olive-green dresses and chocolate-coloured jackets. . . .

April 8, 9, and 10.

Frightfully dull. It is cold and grey. . . . During all my stay in Taganrog I could only do justice to the following things: remarkably good ring rolls sold at the market, the Santurninsky wine, fresh caviare, excellent crabs and uncle's genuine hospitality. Everything else is poor and not to be envied. The young ladies here are not bad, but it takes some time to get used to them. They are abrupt in their movements, frivolous in their attitude to men, run away from their parents with actors, laugh loudly, easily fall in love, whistle to dogs, drink wine, etc. . . .

On Saturday I continued my journey. At the Moskaya station the air is lovely and fresh, caviare is seventy kopecks a pound. At Rostdov I had two hours to wait, at Taganrog twenty. I spent the night at an acquaintance's. The devil only knows what I haven't spent a night on: on beds with bugs, on sofas, settees, boxes. Last night I spent in a long and narrow parlour on a sofa under a looking-glass. . . .

April 25.

. . . Yesterday was the wedding—a real Cossack wedding with music, feminine bleating, and revolting drunkenness. . . . The bride is sixteen. They were married in the cathedral. I acted as best man, and was dressed in somebody else's evening suit with fearfully wide trousers, and not a single stud on my shirt. In Moscow such a best man would have been kicked out, but here I looked smarter than anyone.

I saw many rich and eligible young ladies. The choice is enormous, but I was so drunk all the time that I took bottles for young ladies and young ladies for bottles. Probably owing to my drunken condition the local ladies found me witty and satirical! The young ladies here are regular sheep, if one gets up from her place and walks out of the room all the others follow her. One of them, the boldest and the most brainy, wishing to show that she is not a stranger to social polish and subtlety, kept slapping me on the hand and saying, "Oh, you wretch!" though her face still retained its scared expression. I taught her to say to her partners, "How naive you are!"

The bride and bridegroom, probably because of the local custom of kissing every minute, kissed with such gusto that their lips made a loud smack, and it gave me a taste of sugary raisins in my mouth and a spasm in my left calf. The inflammation of the vein in my left leg got worse through their kisses.

. . . At Zvyerevo I shall have to wait from nine in the evening till five in the morning. Last time I spent the night there in a second-class railway-carriage on the siding. I went out of the carriage in the night and outside I found veritable marvels: the moon, the limitless steppe, the barrows, the wilderness; deathly stillness, and the carriages and the railway lines sharply standing out from the dusk. It seemed as though the world were dead. . . . It was a picture one would not forget for ages and ages.

RAGOZINA BALKA,
April 30, 1887.

It is April 30. The evening is warm. There are storm-clouds about, and so one cannot see a thing. The air is close and there is a smell of grass.

I am staying in the Ragozina Balka at K.'s. There is a small house with a thatched roof, and barns made of flat stone. There are three rooms, with earthen floors, crooked ceilings, and windows that lift up and down instead of opening outwards. . . . The walls are covered with rifles, pistols, sabres and whips. The chest of drawers and the window-sills are littered with cartridges, instruments for mending rifles, tins of gunpowder, and bags of shot. The furniture is lame and the veneer is coming off it. I have to sleep on a consumptive sofa, very hard, and not upholstered . . . Ash-trays and all such luxuries are not to be found within a radius of ten versts. . . . The first necessaries are conspicuous by their absence, and one has in all weathers to slip out to the ravine, and one is warned to make sure there is not a viper or some other creature under the bushes.

The population consists of old K., his wife, Pyotr, a Cossack officer with broad red stripes on his trousers, Alyosha, Hahko (that is, Alexandr), Zoika, Ninka, the shepherd Nikita and the cook Akulina. There are immense numbers of dogs who are furiously spiteful and don't let anyone pass them by day or by night. I have to go about under escort, or there will be one writer less in Russia. . . . The most cursed of the dogs is Muhtar, an old cur on whose face dirty tow hangs instead of wool. He hates me and rushes at me with a roar every time I go out of the house.

Now about food. In the morning there is tea, eggs, ham and bacon fat. At midday, soup with goose, roast goose with pickled sloes, or a turkey, roast chicken, milk pudding, and sour milk. No vodka or pepper allowed. At five o'clock they make on a camp fire in the wood a porridge of millet and bacon fat. In the evening there is tea, ham, and all that has been left over from dinner.

The entertainments are: shooting bustards, making bonfires, going to Ivanovka, shooting at a mark, setting the dogs at one another, preparing gunpowder paste for fireworks, talking politics, building turrets of stone, etc.

The chief occupation is scientific farming, introduced by the youthful Cossack, who bought five roubles' worth of works on agriculture. The most important part of this farming consists of wholesale slaughter, which does not cease for a single moment in the day. They kill sparrows, swallows, bumblebees, ants, magpies, crows—to prevent them eating bees; to prevent the bees from spoiling the blossom on the fruit-trees they kill bees, and to prevent the fruit-trees from exhausting the ground they cut down the fruit-trees. One gets thus a regular circle which, though somewhat original, is based on the latest data of science.

We retire at nine in the evening. Sleep is disturbed, for Belonozhkas and Muhtars howl in the yard and Tseter furiously barks in answer to them from under my sofa. I am awakened by shooting: my hosts shoot with rifles from the windows at some animal which does damage to their crops. To leave the house at night one has to call the Cossack, for otherwise the dogs would tear one to bits.

The weather is fine. The grass is tall and in blossom. I watch bees and men among whom I feel myself something like a Mikluha-Maklay. Last night there was a beautiful thunderstorm.

. . . The coal mines are not far off. To-morrow morning early I am going on a one-horse droshky to Ivanovka (twenty-three versts) to fetch my letters from the post.

... We eat turkeys' eggs. Turkeys lay eggs in the wood on last year's leaves. They kill hens, geese, pigs, etc., by shooting here. The shooting is incessant.

TAGANROG,
May 11.

... From K.'s I went to the Holy Mountains. ... I came to Slavyansk on a dark evening. The cabmen refuse to take me to the Holy Mountains at night, and advise me to spend the night at Slavyansk, which I did very willingly, for I felt broken and lame with pain. ... The town is something like Gogol's Mirgorod; there is a hairdresser and a watchmaker, so that one may hope that in another thousand years there will be a telephone. The walls and fences are pasted with the advertisements of a menagerie. ... On green and dusty streets walk pigs, cows, and other domestic creatures. The houses look cordial and friendly, rather like kindly grandmothers; the pavements are soft, the streets are wide, there is a smell of lilac and acacia in the air; from the distance come the singing of a nightingale, the croaking of frogs, barking, and sounds of a harmonium, of a woman screeching. ... I stopped in Kulikov's hotel, where I took a room for seventy-five kopecks. After sleeping on wooden sofas and washtubs it was a voluptuous sight to see a bed with a mattress, a washstand. ... Fragrant breezes came in at the wide-open window and green branches thrust themselves in. It was a glorious morning. It was a holiday (May 6th) and the bells were ringing in the cathedral. People were coming out from mass. I saw police officers, justices of the peace, military superintendents, and other principalities and powers come out of the church. I bought two kopecks' worth of sunflower seeds, and hired for six roubles a carriage on springs to take me to the Holy Mountains and back (in two days' time). I drove out of the town through little streets literally drowned in the green of cherry, apricot, and apple trees. The birds sang unceasingly. Little Russians whom I met took off their caps, taking me probably for Turgenev; my driver jumped every minute off the box to put the harness to rights, or to crack his whip at the boys who ran after the carriage. ... There were strings of pilgrims along the road. On all sides there were white hills, big and small. The horizon was bluish-white, the rye was tall, oak copses were met with here and there—the only things lacking were crocodiles and rattlesnakes.

I came to the Holy Mountains at twelve o'clock. It is a remarkably beautiful and unique place. The monastery stands on the bank of the river Donets at the foot of a huge white rock covered with gardens, oaks, and ancient pines crowded together and over-hanging, one above another. It seems as if the trees had not enough room on the rock, and as if some force were driving them upwards. . . . The pines literally hang in the air and look as though they might fall any minute. Cuckoos and nightingales sing night and day.

The monks, very pleasant people, gave me a very unpleasant room with a pancake-like mattress. I spent two nights at the monastery and gathered a mass of impressions. While I was there some fifteen thousand pilgrims assembled because of St. Nicolas' Day; eight-ninths of them were old women. I did not know before that there were so many old women in the world; had I known, I would have shot myself long ago. About the monks, my acquaintance with them and how I gave medical advice to the monks and the old women, I will write to the Novoye Vremya and tell you when we meet. The services are endless: at midnight they ring for matins, at five for early mass, at nine for late mass, at three for the song of praise, at five for vespers, at six for the special prayers. Before every service one hears in the corridors the weeping sound of a bell, and a monk runs along crying in the voice of a creditor who implores his debtor to pay him at least five kopecks for a rouble:

"Lord Jesus Christ, have mercy upon us! Please come to matins!"

It is awkward to stay in one's room, and so one gets up and goes out. I have chosen a spot on the bank of the Donets, where I sit during all the services.

I have bought an ikon for Auntie. [Translator's Note: His mother's sister.] The food is provided gratis by the monastery for all the fifteen thousand: cabbage soup with dried fresh-water fish and porridge. Both are good, and so is the rye bread.

The church bells are wonderful. The choir is not up to much. I took part in a religious procession on boats.

TO V. G. KOROLENKO.

MOSCOW, October 17, 1887.

... I am extremely glad to have met you. I say it sincerely and with all my heart. In the first place, I deeply value and love your talent; it is dear to me for many reasons. In the second, it seems to me that if you and I live in this world another ten or twenty years we shall be bound to find points of contact. Of all the Russians now successfully writing I am the lightest and most frivolous; I am looked upon doubtfully; to speak the language of the poets, I have loved my pure Muse but I have not respected her; I have been unfaithful to her and often took her to places that were not fit for her to go to. But you are serious, strong, and faithful. The difference between us is great, as you see, but nevertheless when I read you, and now when I have met you, I think that we have something in common. I don't know if I am right, but I like to think it.

TO HIS BROTHER ALEXANDR.

MOSCOW, November 20, 1887.

Well, the first performance [Translator's Note: "Ivanov."] is over. I will tell you all about it in detail. To begin with, Korsh promised me ten rehearsals, but gave me only four, of which only two could be called rehearsals, for the other two were tournaments in which messieurs les artistes exercised themselves in altercation and abuse. Davydov and Glama were the only two who knew their parts; the others trusted to the prompter and their own inner conviction.

Act One.—I am behind the stage in a small box that looks like a prison cell. My family is in a box of the benoire and is trembling. Contrary to my expectations, I am cool and am conscious of no agitation. The actors are nervous and excited, and cross themselves. The curtain goes up ... the actor whose benefit night it is comes on. His uncertainty, the way that he forgets his part, and the wreath that is presented to him make the play unrecognizable to me from the first sentences. Kiselevsky, of whom I had great hopes, did not deliver a single phrase correctly—literally not a single one. He said things of his own composition. In spite of this and of the stage manager's blunders, the first act was a great success. There were many calls.

Act Two.—A lot of people on the stage. Visitors. They don't know their parts, make mistakes, talk nonsense. Every word cuts me like a knife in my back. But—o Muse!—this act, too, was a success. There were calls for all the actors, and I was called before the curtain twice. Congratulations and success.

Act Three.—The acting is not bad. Enormous success. I had to come before the curtain three times, and as I did so Davydov was shaking my hand, and Glama, like Manilov, was pressing my other hand to her heart. The triumph of talent and virtue.

Act Four, Scene One.—It does not go badly. Calls before the curtain again. Then a long, wearisome interval. The audience, not used to leaving their seats and going to the refreshment bar between two scenes, murmur. The curtain goes up. Fine: through the arch one can see the supper table (the wedding). The band plays flourishes. The groomsmen come out: they are drunk, and so you see they think they must behave like clowns and cut capers. The horseplay and pot-house atmosphere reduce me to despair. Then Kiselevsky comes out: it is a poetical, moving passage, but my Kiselevsky does not know his part, is drunk as a cobbler, and a short poetical dialogue is transformed into something tedious and disgusting: the public is perplexed. At the end of the play the hero dies because he cannot get over the insult he has received. The audience, grown cold and tired, does not understand this death (the actors insisted on it; I have another version). There are calls for the actors and for me. During one of the calls I hear sounds of open hissing, drowned by the clapping and stamping.

On the whole I feel tired and annoyed. It was sickening though the play had considerable success. . . .

Theatre-goers say that they had never seen such a ferment in a theatre, such universal clapping and hissing, nor heard such discussions among the audience as they saw and heard at my play. And it has never happened before at Korsh's that the author has been called after the second act.

November 24.

. . . It has all subsided at last, and I sit as before at my writing-table and compose stories with untroubled spirit. You can't think what it was like! . . . I have already told you that at the first performance there was such excitement in the audience and on the stage as the prompter, who has served at the theatre for thirty-two years, had never seen. They made an uproar, shouted, clapped and hissed; at the refreshment bar it almost came to fighting, and in the gallery the students wanted to throw someone out and two persons were removed by the police. The excitement was general. . . .

. . . The actors were in a state of nervous tension. All that I wrote to you and Maslov about their acting and attitude to their work must not, of course, go any further. There is much one has to excuse and understand. . . . It turned out that the actress who was doing the chief part in my play had a daughter lying dangerously ill—how could she feel like acting? Kurepin did well to praise the actors.

The next day after the performance there was a review by Pyotr Kitcheyev in the Moskovsky Listok. He calls my play impudently cynical and immoral rubbish. The Moskovskiya Vyedomosti praised it.

. . . If you read the play you will not understand the excitement I have described to you; you will find nothing special in it. Nikolay, Shehtel, and Levitan—all of them painters—assure me that on the stage it is so original that it is quite strange to look at. In reading one does not notice it.

TO D. V. GRIGOROVITCH.

MOSCOW, 1887.

I have just read "Karelin's Dream," and I am very much interested to know how far the dream you describe really is a dream. I think your description of the workings of the brain and of the general feeling of a person who is asleep is physiologically correct and remarkably artistic. I remember I read two or three years ago a French story, in which the author described the daughter of a minister., and probably without himself suspecting it, gave a correct medical description of hysteria. I thought at the time that an artist's instinct may sometimes be worth the brains of a scientist, that both have the same purpose, the same nature, and that perhaps in time, as their methods become perfect, they are destined to become one vast prodigious force which now it is difficult even to imagine. . . . "Karelin's Dream" has suggested to me similar thoughts, and to-day I willingly believe Buckle, who saw in Hamlet's musings on the dust of Alexander the Great,

Shakespeare's knowledge of the law of the transmutation of substance—i.e., the power of the artist to run ahead of the men of science.... Sleep is a subjective phenomenon, and the inner aspect of it one can only observe in oneself. But since the process of dreaming is the same in all men, every reader can, I think, judge Karelin by his own standards, and every critic is bound to be subjective. From my own personal experience this is how I can formulate my impression.

In the first place the sensation of cold is given by you with remarkable subtlety. When at night the quilt falls off I begin to dream of huge slippery stones, of cold autumnal water, naked banks—and all this dim, misty, without a patch of blue sky; sad and dejected like one who has lost his way, I look at the stones and feel that for some reason I cannot avoid crossing a deep river; I see then small tugs that drag huge barges, floating beams.... All this is infinitely grey, damp, and dismal. When I run from the river I come across the fallen cemetery gates, funerals, my school-teachers.... And all the time I am cold through and through with that oppressive nightmare-like cold which is impossible in waking life, and which is only felt by those who are asleep. The first pages of "Karelin's Dream" vividly brought it to my memory—especially the first half of page five, where you speak of the cold and loneliness of the grave.

I think that had I been born in Petersburg and constantly lived there, I should always dream of the banks of the Neva, the Senate Square, the massive monuments.

When I feel cold in my sleep I dream of people.... I happened to have read a criticism in which the reviewer blames you for introducing a man who is "almost a minister," and thus spoiling the generally dignified tone of the story. I don't agree with him. What spoils the tone is not the people but your characterization of them, which in some places interrupts the picture of the dream. One does dream of people, and always of unpleasant ones.... I, for instance, when I feel cold, always dream of my teacher of scripture, a learned priest of imposing appearance, who insulted my mother when I was a little boy; I dream of vindictive, implacable, intriguing people, smiling with spiteful glee—such as one can never see in waking life. The laughter at the carriage window is a characteristic symptom of Karelin's nightmare. When in dreams one feels the presence of some evil will, the inevitable ruin brought about by some outside force, one always hears something like such laughter. . . . One dreams of people one loves, too, but they generally appear to suffer together with the dreamer.

But when my body gets accustomed to the cold, or one of my family covers me up, the sensation of cold, of loneliness, and of an oppressive evil will, gradually disappears. . . . With the returning warmth I begin to feel that I walk on soft carpets or on grass, I see sunshine, women, children. . . . The pictures change gradually, but more rapidly than they do in waking life, so that on awaking it is difficult to remember the transitions from one scene to another. . . . This abruptness is well brought out in your story, and increases the impression of the dream.

Another natural fact you have noticed is also extremely striking: dreamers express their moods in outbursts of an acute kind, with childish genuineness, like Karelin. Everyone knows that people weep and cry out in their sleep much more often than they do in waking life. This is probably due to the lack of inhibition in sleep and of the impulses which make us conceal things.

Forgive me, I so like your story that I am ready to write you a dozen sheets, though I know I can tell you nothing new or good. . . . I restrain myself and am silent, fearing to bore you and to say something silly.

I will say once more that your story is magnificent. The public finds it "vague," but to a writer who gloats over every line such vagueness is more transparent than holy water. . . . Hard as I tried I could detect only two small blots, even those are rather farfetched!

(1) I think that at the beginning of the story the feeling of cold is soon blunted in the reader and becomes habitual, owing to the frequent repetition of the word "cold," and (2), the word "glossy" is repeated too often.

There is nothing else I could find, and I feel that as one is always feeling the need of refreshing models, "Karelin's Dream" is a splendid event in my existence as an author. This is why I could not contain myself and ventured to put before you some of my thoughts and impressions.

There is little good I can say about myself. I write not what I want to be writing, and I have not enough energy or solitude to write as you advised me. . . . There are many good subjects jostling in my head—and that is all. I am sustained by hopes of the future, and watch the present slip fruitlessly away.

Forgive this long letter, and accept the sincere good wishes of your devoted

A. CHEKHOV.

TO V. G. KOROLENKO.

MOSCOW, January 9, 1888.

Following your friendly advice I began writing a story for the *Syeverny Vyestnik*. To begin with I have attempted to describe the steppe, the people who live there, and what I have experienced in the steppe. It is a good subject, and I enjoy writing about it, but unfortunately from lack of practice in writing long things, and from fear of making it too rambling, I fall into the opposite extreme: each page turns out a compact whole like a short story, the pictures accumulate, are crowded, and, getting in each other's way, spoil the impression as a whole. As a result one gets, not a picture in which all the details are merged into one whole like stars in the heavens, but a mere diagram, a dry record of impressions. A writer—you, for instance—will understand me, but the reader will be bored and curse.

. . . Your "Sokolinets" is, I think, the most remarkable novel that has appeared of late. It is written like a good musical composition, in accordance with all the rules which an artist instinctively divines. Altogether in the whole of your book you are such a great artist, such a force, that even your worst failings, which would have been the ruin of any other writer, pass unnoticed. For instance, in the whole of your book there is an obstinate exclusion of women, and I have only just noticed it.

TO A. N. PLESHTCHEYEV.

MOSCOW, February 5, 1888.

. . . I am longing to read Korolenko's story. He is my favourite of contemporary writers. His colours are rich and vivid, his style is irreproachable, though in places rather elaborate, his images are noble. Leontyev is good too. He is not so mature and picturesque, but he is warmer than Korolenko, more peaceful and feminine. . . . But, Allah kerim, why do they both specialize? The first will not part with his convicts, and the second feeds his readers with nothing but officers. . . . I understand specialization in art such as genre, landscape, history, but I cannot admit of such specialties as convicts, officers, priests. . . . This is not specialization but partiality. In Petersburg you do not care for Korolenko, and here in Moscow we do not read Shtcheglov, but I fully believe in the future of both of them. Ah, if only we had decent critics!

February 9.

. . . You say you liked Dymov [Translator's Note: One of the characters in "The Steppe."] as a subject. Life creates such characters as the dare-devil Dymov not to be dissenters nor tramps, but downright revolutionaries. . . . There never will be a revolution in Russia, and Dymov will end by taking to drink or getting into prison. He is a superfluous man.

March 6.

It is devilishly cold, but the poor birds are already flying to Russia! They are driven by homesickness and love for their native land. If poets knew how many millions of birds fall victims to their longing and love for their homes, how many of them freeze on the way, what agonies they endure on getting home in March and at the beginning of April, they would have sung their praises long ago! . . . Put yourself in the place of a corncrake who does not fly but walks all the way, or of a wild goose who gives himself up to man to escape being frozen. . . . Life is hard in this world!

TO I. L. SHTCHEGLOV.

MOSCOW, April 18, 1888.

. . . In any case I am more often merry than sad, though if one comes to think of it I am bound hand and foot. . . . You, my dear man, have a flat, but I have a whole house which, though a poor specimen, is still a house, and one of two storeys, too! You have a wife who will forgive your having no money, and I have a whole organization which will collapse if I don't earn a sufficient number of roubles a month—collapse and fall on my shoulders like a heavy stone.

May 3.

... I have just sent a story to the Syeverny Vyestnik. I feel a little ashamed of it. It is frightfully dull, and there is so much discussion and preaching in it that it is mawkish. I didn't like to send it, but had to, for I need money as I do air. ...

I have had a letter from Leman. He tells me that "we" (that is all of you Petersburg people) "have agreed to print advertisements about each other's work on our books," invites me to join, and warns me that among the elect may be included only such persons as have a "certain degree of solidarity with us." I wrote to say that I agreed, and asked him how does he know with whom I have solidarity and with whom I have not? How fond of stuffiness you are in Petersburg! Don't you feel stifled with such words as "solidarity," "unity of young writers," "common interests," and so on? Solidarity and all the rest of it I admit on the stock-exchange, in politics, in religious affairs, etc., but solidarity among young writers is impossible and unnecessary. ... We cannot feel and think in the same way, our aims are different, or we have no aims whatever, we know each other little or not at all, and so there is nothing on to which this solidarity could be securely hooked. ... And is there any need for it? No, in order to help a colleague, to respect his personality and his work, to refrain from gossiping about him, envying him, telling him lies and being hypocritical, one does not need so much to be a young writer as simply a man. ... Let us be ordinary people, let us treat everybody alike, and then we shall not need any artificially worked up solidarity. Insistent desire for particular, professional, clique solidarity such as you want, will give rise to unconscious spying on one another, suspiciousness, control, and, without wishing to do so, we shall become something like Jesuits in relation to one another. ... I, dear Jean, have no solidarity with you, but I promise you as a literary man perfect freedom so long as you live; that is, you may write where and how you wish, you may think like Koreisha if you like, betray your convictions and tendencies a thousand times, etc., etc., and my human relations with you will not alter one jot, and I will always publish advertisements of your books on the wrappers of mine.

TO A. S. SUVORIN.

SUMY, MADAME LINTVARYOV'S ESTATE, May 30, 1888.

. . . I am staying on the bank of the Psyol, in the lodge of an old signorial estate. I took the place without seeing it, trusting to luck, and have not regretted it so far. The river is wide and deep, with plenty of islands, of fish and of crayfish. The banks are beautiful, well-covered with grass and trees. And best of all, there is so much space that I feel as if for my one hundred roubles I have obtained a right to live on an expanse of which one can see no end. Nature and life here is built on the pattern now so old-fashioned and rejected by magazine editors. Nightingales sing night and day, dogs bark in the distance, there are old neglected gardens, sad and poetical estates shut up and deserted where live the souls of beautiful women; old footmen, relics of serfdom, on the brink of the grave; young ladies longing for the most conventional love. In addition to all these things, not far from me there is even such a hackneyed cliche as a water-mill (with sixteen wheels), with a miller, and his daughter who always sits at the window, apparently waiting for someone. All that I see and hear now seems familiar to me from old novels and fairy-tales. The only thing that has something new about it is a mysterious bird, which sits somewhere far away in the reeds, and night and day makes a noise that sounds partly like a blow on an empty barrel and partly like the mooing of a cow shut up in a barn. Every Little Russian has seen this bird in the course of his life, but everyone describes it differently, which means that no one has seen it. . . . Every day I row to the mill, and in the evening I go to the islands to fish with fishing maniacs from the Haritovenko factory. Our conversations are sometimes interesting. On the eve of Whit Sunday all the maniacs will spend the night on the islands and fish all night; I, too. There are some splendid types.

My hosts have turned out to be very nice and hospitable people. It is a family worth studying. It consists of six members. The old mother, a very kind, rather flabby woman who has had suffering enough in her life; she reads Schopenhauer and goes to church to hear the Song of Praise; she conscientiously studies every number of the Vyestnik Evropi and Syeverny Vyestnik, and knows writers I have not dreamed of; attaches much importance to the fact that once the painter Makovsky stayed in her lodge and now a young writer is staying there; talking to Pleshtcheyev she feels a holy thrill all over and rejoices every minute that it has been "vouchsafed" to her to see the great poet.

Her eldest daughter, a woman doctor—the pride of the whole family and "a saint" as the peasants call her—really is remarkable. She has a tumour on the brain, and in consequence of it she is totally blind, has epileptic fits and constant headaches. She knows what awaits her, and stoically with amazing coolness speaks of her approaching death. In the course of my medical practice I have grown used to seeing people who were soon going to die, and I have always felt strange when people whose death was at hand talked, smiled, or wept in my presence; but here, when I see on the verandah this blind woman who laughs, jokes, or hears my stories read to her, what begins to seem strange to me is not that she is dying, but that we do not feel our own death, and write stories as though we were never going to die.

The second daughter, also a woman doctor, is a gentle, shy, infinitely kind creature, loving to everyone. Patients are a regular torture to her, and she is scrupulous to morbidity with them. At consultations we always disagree: I bring good tidings where she sees death, and I double the doses which she prescribes. But where death is obvious and inevitable my lady doctor feels quite in an unprofessional way. I was receiving patients with her one day at a medical centre; a young Little Russian woman came with a malignant tumour of the glands in her neck and at the back of her head. The tumour had spread so far that no treatment could be thought of. And because the woman was at present feeling no pain, but would in another six months die in terrible agony, the doctor looked at her in such a guilty way as though she were asking forgiveness for being well, and ashamed that medical science was helpless. She takes a zealous part in managing the house and estate, and understands every detail of it. She knows all about horses even. When the side horse does not pull or gets restless, she knows how to help matters and instructs the coachman. I believe she has never hurt anyone, and it seems to me that she has not been happy for a single instant and never will be.

The third daughter, who has finished her studies at Bezstuzhevka, is a vigorous, sunburnt young girl with a loud voice. Her laugh can be heard a mile away. She is a passionate Little Russian patriot. She has built a school on the estate at her own expense, and teaches the children Krylov's fables translated into Little Russian. She goes to Shevtchenko's grave as a Turk goes to Mecca. She does not cut her hair, wears stays and a bustle, looks after the housekeeping, is fond of laughing and singing.

The eldest son is a quiet, modest, intelligent, hardworking young man with no talents; he has no pretensions, and is apparently content with what life has given him. He has been dismissed from the University [Translator's Note: On political grounds, of course, is understood.] just before taking his degree, but he does not boast of it. He speaks little. He loves farming and the land and lives in harmony with the peasants.

The second son is a young man mad over Tchaikovsky's being a genius. He dreams of living according to Tolstoy.

Pleshtcheyev is staying with us. They all look upon him as a demi-god, consider themselves happy if he bestows attention on somebody's junket, bring him flowers, invite him everywhere, and so on.... And he "listens and eats," and smokes his cigars which give his admirers a headache. He is slow to move, with the indolence of old age, but this does not prevent the fair sex from taking him about in boats, driving with him to the neighbouring estates, and singing songs to him. Here he is by way of being the same thing as in Petersburg—i.e., an ikon which is prayed to for being old and for having once hung by the side of the miracle-working ikons. So far as I am concerned I regard him—not to speak of his being a very good, warm-hearted and sincere man—as a vessel full of traditions, interesting memories, and good platitudes.

... What you say about "The Lights" is quite just. You say that neither the conversation about pessimism nor Kisotcha's story in any way help to solve the question of pessimism. It seems to me it is not for writers of fiction to solve such questions as that of God, of pessimism, etc. The writer's business is simply to describe who has been speaking about God or about pessimism, how, and in what circumstances. The artist must be not the judge of his characters and of their conversations, but merely an impartial witness. I have heard a desultory conversation of two Russians about pessimism—a conversation which settles nothing—and I must report that conversation as I heard it; it is for the jury, that is, for the readers, to decide on the value of it. My business is merely to be talented—i.e., to know how to distinguish important statements from unimportant, how to throw light on the characters, and to speak their language. Shtcheglov-Leontyev blames me for finishing the story with the words, "There's no making out anything in this world." He thinks a writer who is a good psychologist ought to be able to make it out—that is what he is a psychologist for. But I don't agree with him. It is time that writers, especially those who are artists, recognized that there is no making out anything in this world, as once Socrates recognized it, and Voltaire, too. The mob thinks it knows and understands everything; and the more stupid it is the wider it imagines its outlook to be. And if a writer whom the mob believes in has the courage to say that he does not understand anything of what he sees, that alone will be something gained in the realm of thought and a great step in advance.

TO A. N. PLESHTCHEYEV.

SUMY, June 28, 1888.

... We have been to the province of Poltava. We went to the Smagins', and to Sorotchintsi. We drove with a four-in-hand, in an ancestral, very comfortable carriage. We had no end of laughter, adventures, misunderstandings, halts, and meetings on the way. ... If you had only seen the places where we stayed the night and the villages stretching eight or ten versts through which we drove! ... What weddings we met on the road, what lovely music we heard in the evening stillness, and what a heavy smell of fresh hay there was! Really one might sell one's soul to the devil for the pleasure of looking at the warm evening sky, the pools and the rivulets reflecting the sad, languid sunset. ...

... The Smagins' estate is "great and fertile," but old, neglected, and dead as last year's cobwebs. The house has sunk, the doors won't shut, the tiles in the stove squeeze one another out and form angles, young suckers of cherries and plums peep up between the cracks of the floors. In the room where I slept a nightingale had made herself a nest between the window and the shutter, and while I was there little naked nightingales, looking like undressed Jew babies, hatched out from the eggs. Sedate storks live on the barn. At the beehouse there is an old grandsire who remembers the King Goroh [Translator's Note: The equivalent of Old King Cole.] and Cleopatra of Egypt.

Everything is crumbling and decrepit, but poetical, sad, and beautiful in the extreme.

TO HIS SISTER.

FEODOSIA, July, 1888.

... The journey from Sumy to Harkov is frightfully dull. Going from Harkov to Simferopol one might well die of boredom. The Crimean steppe is depressing, monotonous, with no horizon, colourless like Ivanenko's stories, and on the whole rather like the tundra. . . . From Simferopol mountains begin and, with them, beauty. Ravines, mountains, ravines, mountains, poplars stick out from the ravines, vineyards loom dark on the mountains—all this is bathed in moonlight, is new and wild, and sets one's imagination working in harmony with Gogol's "Terrible Vengeance." Particularly fantastic are the alternating precipices and tunnels when you see now depths full of moonlight and now complete sinister darkness. It is rather uncanny and delightful. One feels it is something not Russian, something alien. I reached Sevastopol at night. The town is beautiful in itself and beautiful because it stands by a marvellous sea. The best in the sea is its colour, and that one cannot describe. It is like blue copperas. As to steamers and sailing vessels, piers and harbours, what strikes one most of all is the poverty of the Russians. Except the "popovkas," which look like Moscow merchants' wives, and two or three decent steamers, there is nothing to speak of in the bay.

... In the morning it was deadly dull. Heat, dust, thirst. . . . In the harbour there was a stench of ropes, and one caught glimpses of faces burnt brick-red, sounds of a pulley, of the splashing of dirty water, knocking, Tatar words, and all sorts of uninteresting nonsense. You go up to a steamer: men in rags, bathed in sweat and almost baked by the sun, dizzy, with tatters on their backs and shoulders, unload Portland cement; you stand and look at them and the whole scene becomes so remote, so alien, that one feels insufferably dull and uninterested. It is entertaining to get on board and set off, but it is rather a bore to sail and talk to a crowd of passengers consisting of elements all of which one knows by heart and is weary of already.... Yalta is a mixture of something European that reminds one of the views of Nice, with something cheap and shoddy. The box-like hotels in which unhappy consumptives are pining, the impudent Tatar faces, the ladies' bustles with their very undisguised expression of something very abominable, the faces of the idle rich, longing for cheap adventures, the smell of perfumery instead of the scent of the cedars and the sea, the miserable dirty pier, the melancholy lights far out at sea, the prattle of young ladies and gentlemen who have crowded here in order to admire nature of which they have no idea—all this taken together produces such a depressing effect and is so overwhelming that one begins to blame oneself for being biassed and unfair.... At five o'clock in the morning I arrived at Feodosia—a greyish-brown, dismal, and dull-looking little town. There is no grass, the trees are wretched, the soil is coarse and hopelessly poor. Everything is burnt up by the sun, and only the sea smiles—the sea which has nothing to do with wretched little towns or tourists. Sea bathing is so nice that when I got into the water I began to laugh for no reason at all....

July 22.

... Yesterday we went to Shah-Mamai Aivazovsky's estate, twenty-five versts from Feodosia. It is a magnificent estate, rather like fairyland; such estates may probably be seen in Persia. Aivazovsky [Translator's Note: The famous marine painter.] himself, a vigorous old man of seventy-five, is a mixture of a good-natured Armenian and an overfed bishop; he is full of dignity, has soft hands, and offers them like a general. He is not very intelligent, but is a complex nature worthy of attention. He combines in himself a general, a bishop, an artist, an Armenian, a naive old peasant, and an Othello. He is married to a young and very beautiful woman whom he rules with a rod of iron. He is friendly with Sultans, Shahs, and Amirs. He collaborated with Glinka in writing "Ruslan and Liudmila." He was a friend of Pushkin, but has never read him. He has not read a single book in his life. When it is suggested to him that he should read something he answers, "Why should I read when I have opinions of my own?" I spent a whole day in his house and had dinner there. The dinner was fearfully long, with endless toasts. By the way, at that dinner I was introduced to the lady doctor, wife of the well-known professor. She is a fat, bulky piece of flesh. If she were undressed and painted green she would look just like a frog. After talking to her I mentally scratched her off the list of women doctors. . . .

TO HIS BROTHER MIHAIL.

July 28, 1888.
  On the Seas Black, Caspian, and of Life.

. . . A wretched little cargo steamer, Dir, is racing full steam from Suhum to Poti. It is about midnight. The little cabin—the only one in the steamer—is insufferably hot and stuffy. There is a smell of burning, of rope, of fish and of the sea. One hears the engine going "Boom-boom-boom." . . . There are devils creaking up aloft and under the floor. The darkness is swaying in the cabin and the bed rocks up and down. . . . One's stomach's whole attention is concentrated on the bed, and, as though to find its level, it rolls the Seltzer water I had drunk right up to my throat and then lets it down to my heels. Not to be sick over my clothes in the dark I hastily put on my things and go out. . . . It is dark. My feet stumble against some invisible iron bars, a rope; wherever you step there are barrels, sacks, rags. There is coal dust under foot. In the dark I knock against a kind of grating: it is a cage with wild goats which I saw in the daytime. They are awake and anxiously listening to the rocking of the boat. By the cage sit two Turks who are not asleep either. . . . I grope my way up the stairs to the captain's bridge. . . . A warm but violent and unpleasant wind tries to blow away my cap. . . . The steamer rocks. The mast in front of the captain's bridge sways regularly and leisurely like a metronome; I try to look away from it, but my eyes will not obey me and, just like my stomach, insist on following moving objects. . . . The sky and the sea are dark, the shore is not in sight, the deck looks a dark blur . . . there is not a single light.

Behind me is a window . . . I look into it and see a man who looks attentively at something and turns a wheel with an expression as though he were playing the ninth symphony. . . . Next to me stands the little stout captain in tan shoes. . . . He talks to me of Caucasian emigrants, of the heat, of winter storms, and at the same time looks intently into the dark distance in the direction of the shore.

"You seem to be going too much to the left again," he says to someone; or, "There ought to be lights here.... Do you see them?"

"No, sir," someone answers from the dark.

"Climb up and look."

A dark figure appears on the bridge and leisurely climbs up. In a minute we hear:

"Yes, sir."

I look to the left where the lights of the lighthouse are supposed to be, borrow the captain's glasses, but see nothing.... Half an hour passes, then an hour. The mast sways regularly, the devils creak, the wind makes dashes at my cap.... It is not pitch dark, but one feels uneasy.

Suddenly the captain dashes off somewhere to the rear of the ship, crying, "You devil's doll!"

"To the left," he shouts anxiously at the top of his voice. "To the left! ... To the right! A-va-va-a!"

Incomprehensible words of command are heard. The steamer starts, the devils give a creak.... "A-va-va!" shouts the captain; at the bows a bell is rung, on the black deck there are sounds of running, knocking, cries of anxiety.... The Dir starts once more, puffs painfully, and apparently tries to move backwards.

"What is it?" I ask, and feel something like a faint terror. There is no answer.

"He'd like a collision, the devil's doll!" I hear the captain's harsh shout. "To the left!"

Red lights appear in front, and suddenly among the uproar is heard the whistling, not of the Dir, but of some other steamer.... Now I understand it: there is going to be a collision! The Dir puffs, trembles, and does not move, as though waiting for a signal to go down.... But just when I think all is lost, the red lights appear on the left of us, and the dark silhouette of a steamer can be discerned.... A long black body sails past us, guiltily blinks its red eyes, and gives a guilty whistle....

"Oof! What steamer is it?" I ask the captain.

The captain looks at the silhouette through his glasses and replies:

"It is the Tweedie."

After a pause we begin to talk of the Vesta, which collided with two steamers and went down. Under the influence of this conversation the sea, the night and the wind begin to seem hideous, created on purpose for man's undoing, and I feel sorry as I look at the fat little captain. . . . Something whispers to me that this poor man, too, will sooner or later sink to the bottom and be choked with salt water.

I go back to my cabin. . . . It is stuffy, and there is a smell of cooking. My travelling companion, Suvorin-fils, is asleep already. . . . I take off all my clothes and go to bed. . . . The darkness sways to and fro, the bed seems to breathe. . . . Boom-boom-boom! Bathed in perspiration, breathless, and feeling an oppression all over with the rocking, I ask myself, "What am I here for?"

I wake up. It is no longer dark. Wet all over, with a nasty taste in my mouth, I dress and go out. Everything is covered with dew. . . . The wild goats look with human eyes through the grating of their cage and seem to be asking "Why are we here?" The captain stands still as before and looks intently into the distance. . . .

A mountainous shore stretches on the left. . . . Elborus is seen from behind the mountains.

A blurred sun rises in the sky. . . . One can see the green valley of Rion and the Bay of Poti by the side of it.

TO N. A. LEIKIN.

SUMY, August 12.

. . . I have been to the Crimea. I spent twelve days at Suvorin's in Feodosia, bathed, idled about; I have been to Aivazovsky's estate. From Feodosia I went by steamer to Batum. On the way I spent half a day at Suhum—a charming little town buried in luxuriant, un-Russian greenery, and one day at the Monastery, at New Athos. It is so lovely there at New Athos that there is no describing it: waterfalls, eucalyptuses, tea-plants, cypresses, olive-trees, and, above all, sea and mountains, mountains, mountains. From Athos and Suhum I went to Poti; the River Rion, renowned for its valley and its sturgeons, is close by. The vegetation is luxuriant. All the streets are planted with poplars. Batum is a big commercial and military, foreign-looking, café'-chantant sort of town; you feel in it at every step that we have conquered the Turks. There is nothing special about it (except a great number of brothels), but the surrounding country is charming. Particularly fine is the road to Kars and the swift river Tchoraksu.

The road from Batum to Tiflis is poetical and original; you look all the time out of window and exclaim: there are mountains, tunnels, rocks, rivers, waterfalls, big and little. But the road from Tiflis to Baku is the abomination of desolation, a bald plain, covered with sand and created for Persians, tarantulas, and phalangas to live in. There is not a single tree, there is no grass ... dreary as hell.... Baku and the Caspian Sea are such rotten places that I would not agree to live there for a million. There are no roofs, there are no trees either; Persian faces everywhere, fifty degrees Reaumur of heat, a smell of kerosine, the naphtha-soaked mud squelches under one's feet, the drinking water is salt.

... You have seen the Caucasus. I believe you have seen the Georgian Military Road, too. If you have not been there yet, pawn your wives and children and the Oskolki [Translator's Note: Oskolki, (i.e., "Chips," "Bits") the paper of which Leikin was editor.] and go. I have never in my life seen anything like it. It is not a road, but unbroken poetry, a wonderful, fantastic story written by the Demon in love with Tamara.

TO A. S. SUVORIN.

SUMY, August 29, 1888.

... When as a boy I used to stay at my grandfather's on Count Platov's estate, I had to sit from sunrise to sunset by the thrashing machine and write down the number of poods and pounds of corn that had been thrashed; the whistling, the hissing, and the bass note, like the sound of a whirling top, that the machine makes at full speed, the creaking of the wheels, the lazy tread of the oxen, the clouds of dust, the grimy, perspiring faces of some three score of men—all this has stamped itself upon my memory like the Lord's Prayer. And now, too, I have been spending hours at the thrashing and felt intensely happy. When the thrashing engine is at work it looks as though alive; it has a cunning, playful expression, while the men and oxen look like machines. In the district of Mirgorod few have thrashing machines of their own, but everyone can hire one. The engine goes about the whole province drawn by six oxen and offers itself to all who can pay for it.

MOSCOW,
September 11.

... You advise me not to hunt after two hares, and not to think of medical work. I do not know why one should not hunt two hares even in the literal sense.... I feel more confident and more satisfied with myself when I reflect that I have two professions and not one. Medicine is my lawful wife and literature is my mistress. When I get tired of one I spend the night with the other. Though it's disorderly, it's not so dull, and besides neither of them loses anything from my infidelity. If I did not have my medical work I doubt if I could have given my leisure and my spare thoughts to literature. There is no discipline in me.

MOSCOW,
October 27, 1888.

... In conversation with my literary colleagues I always insist that it is not the artist's business to solve problems that require a specialist's knowledge. It is a bad thing if a writer tackles a subject he does not understand. We have specialists for dealing with special questions: it is their business to judge of the commune, of the future of capitalism, of the evils of drunkenness, of boots, of the diseases of women. An artist must only judge of what he understands, his field is just as limited as that of any other specialist—I repeat this and insist on it always. That in his sphere there are no questions, but only answers, can only be maintained by those who have never written and have had no experience of thinking in images. An artist observes, selects, guesses, combines—and this in itself presupposes a problem: unless he had set himself a problem from the very first there would be nothing to conjecture and nothing to select. To put it briefly, I will end by using the language of psychiatry: if one denies that creative work involves problems and purposes, one must admit that an artist creates without premeditation or intention, in a state of aberration; therefore, if an author boasted to me of having written a novel without a preconceived design, under a sudden inspiration, I should call him mad.

You are right in demanding that an artist should take an intelligent attitude to his work, but you confuse two things: solving a problem and stating a problem correctly. It is only the second that is obligatory for the artist. In "Anna Karenin" and "Evgeny Onyegin" not a single problem is solved, but they satisfy you completely because all the problems are correctly stated in them. It is the business of the judge to put the right questions, but the answers must be given by the jury according to their own lights.

... You say that the hero of my "Party" is a character worth developing. Good Lord! I am not a senseless brute, you know, I understand that. I understand that I cut the throats of my characters and spoil them, and that I waste good material. . . . To tell you the truth, I would gladly have spent six months over the "Party"; I like taking things easy, and see no attraction in publishing at headlong speed. I would willingly, with pleasure, with feeling, in a leisurely way, describe the whole of my hero, describe the state of his mind while his wife was in labour, his trial, the horrid feeling he has after he is acquitted; I would describe the midwife and the doctors having tea in the middle of the night, I would describe the rain. . . . It would give me nothing but pleasure because I like to rummage about and dawdle. But what am I to do? I begin a story on September 10th with the thought that I must finish it by October 5th at the latest; if I don't I shall fail the editor and be left without money. I let myself go at the beginning and write with an easy mind; but by the time I get to the middle I begin to grow timid and to fear that my story will be too long: I have to remember that the Syeverny Vyestnik has not much money, and that I am one of their expensive contributors. This is why the beginning of my stories is always very promising and looks as though I were starting on a novel, the middle is huddled and timid, and the end is, as in a short sketch, like fireworks. And so in planning a story one is bound to think first about its framework: from a crowd of leading or subordinate characters one selects one person only—wife or husband; one puts him on the canvas and paints him alone, making him prominent, while the others one scatters over the canvas like small coin, and the result is something like the vault of heaven: one big moon and a number of very small stars around it. But the moon is not a success because it can only be understood if the stars too are intelligible, and the stars are not worked out. And so what I produce is not literature, but something like the patching of Trishka's coat. What am I to do? I don't know, I don't know. I must trust to time which heals all things.

To tell the truth again, I have not yet begun my literary work, though I have received a literary prize. Subjects for five stories and two novels are languishing in my head. One of the novels was thought of long ago, and some of the characters have grown old without managing to be written. In my head there is a whole army of people asking to be let out and waiting for the word of command. All that I have written so far is rubbish in comparison with what I should like to write and should write with rapture. It is all the same to me whether I write "The Party" or "The Lights," or a vaudeville or a letter to a friend—it is all dull, spiritless, mechanical, and I get annoyed with critics who attach any importance to "The Lights," for instance. I fancy that I deceive him with my work just as I deceive many people with my face, which looks serious or over-cheerful. I don't like being successful; the subjects which sit in my head are annoyed and jealous of what has already been written. I am vexed that the rubbish has been done and the good things lie about in the lumber-room like old books. Of course, in thus lamenting I rather exaggerate, and much of what I say is only my fancy, but there is a part of the truth in it, a good big part of it. What do I call good? The images which seem best to me, which I love and jealously guard lest I spend and spoil them for the sake of some "Party" written against time. . . . If my love is mistaken, I am wrong, but then it may not be mistaken! I am either a fool and a conceited fellow or I really am an organism capable of being a good writer. All that I now write displeases and bores me, but what sits in my head interests, excites and moves me—from which I conclude that everybody does the wrong thing and I alone know the secret of doing the right one. Most likely all writers think that. But the devil himself would break his neck in these problems.

Money will not help me to decide what I am to do and how I am to act. An extra thousand roubles will not settle matters, and a hundred thousand is a castle in the air. Besides, when I have money—it may be from lack of habit, I don't know—I become extremely careless and idle; the sea seems only knee-deep to me then. . . . I need time and solitude.

November, 1888.

In the November number of the Syeverny Vyestnik there is an article by the poet Merezhkovsky about your humble servant. It is a long article. I commend to your attention the end of it; it is characteristic. Merezhkovsky is still very young, a student—of science I believe. Those who have assimilated the wisdom of the scientific method and learned to think scientifically experience many alluring temptations. Archimedes wanted to turn the earth round, and the present day hot-heads want by science to conceive the inconceivable, to discover the physical laws of creative art, to detect the laws and the formulae which are instinctively felt by the artist and are followed by him in creating music, novels, pictures, etc. Such formulae probably exist in nature. We know that A, B, C, do, re, mi, fa, sol, are found in nature, and so are curves, straight lines, circles, squares, green, blue, and red. . . . We know that in certain combinations all this produces a melody, or a poem or a picture, just as simple chemical substances in certain combinations produce a tree, or a stone, or the sea; but all we know is that the combination exists, while the law of it is hidden from us. Those who are masters of the scientific method feel in their souls that a piece of music and a tree have something in common, that both are built up in accordance with equally uniform and simple laws. Hence the question: What are these laws? And hence the temptation to work out a physiology of creative art (like Boborykin), or in the case of younger and more diffident writers, to base their arguments on nature and on the laws of nature (Merezhkovsky). There probably is such a thing as the physiology of creative art, but we must nip in the bud our dreams of discovering it. If the critics take up a scientific attitude no good will come of it: they will waste a dozen years, write a lot of rubbish, make the subject more obscure than ever—and nothing more. It is always a good thing to think scientifically, but the trouble is that scientific thinking about creative art will be bound to degenerate in the end into searching for the "cells" or the "centres" which control the creative faculty. Some stolid German will discover these cells somewhere in the occipital lobes, another German will agree with him, a third will disagree, and a Russian will glance through the article about the cells and reel off an essay about it to the Syeverny Vyestnik. The Vyestnik Evropi will criticize the essay, and for three years there will be in Russia an epidemic of nonsense which will give money and popularity to blockheads and do nothing but irritate intelligent people.

For those who are obsessed with the scientific method and to whom God has given the rare talent of thinking scientifically, there is to my mind only one way out—the philosophy of creative art. One might collect together all the best works of art that have been produced throughout the ages and, with the help of the scientific method, discover the common element in them which makes them like one another and conditions their value. That common element will be the law. There is a great deal that works which are called immortal have in common; if this common element were excluded from each of them, a work would lose its charm and its value. So that this universal something is necessary, and is the conditio sine qua non of every work that claims to be immortal. It is of more use to young people to write critical articles than poetry. Merezhkovsky writes smoothly and youthfully, but at every page he loses heart, makes reservations and concessions, and this means that he is not clear upon the subject. He calls me a poet, he styles my stories "novelli" and my heroes "failures"—that is, he follows the beaten track. It is time to give up these "failures," superfluous people, etc., and to think of something original. Merezhkovsky calls my monk [Translator's Note: "Easter Eve."] who composes the songs of praise a failure. But how is he a failure? God grant us all a life like his: he believed in God, and he had enough to eat and he had the gift of composing poetry. . . . To divide men into the successful and the unsuccessful is to look at human nature from a narrow, preconceived point of view. Are you a success or not? Am I? Was Napoleon? Is your servant Vassily? What is the criterion? One must be a god to be able to tell successes from failures without making a mistake.

MOSCOW,
November 7, 1888.

. . . It is not the public that is to blame for our theatres being so wretched. The public is always and everywhere the same: intelligent and stupid, sympathetic and pitiless according to mood. It has always been a flock which needs good shepherds and dogs, and it has always gone in the direction in which the shepherds and the dogs drove it. You are indignant that it laughs at flat witticisms and applauds sounding phrases; but then the very same stupid public fills the house to hear "Othello," and, listening to the opera "Evgeny Onyegin," weeps when Tatyana writes her letter.

. . . The water-carrier has stolen from somewhere a Siberian kitten with long white fur and black eyes, and brought it to us. This kitten takes people for mice: when it sees anyone it lies flat on its stomach, stalks one's feet and rushes at them. This morning as I was pacing up and down the room it several times stalked me, and a la tigre pounced at my boots. I imagine the thought of being more terrible than anyone in the house affords it the greatest delight.

November 11, 1888.

I finished to-day the story for the Garshin sbornik: it is such a load off my mind. In this story I have told my own opinion—which is of no interest to anyone—of such rare men as Garshin. I have run to almost 2,000 lines. I speak at length about prostitution, but settle nothing. Why do they write nothing about prostitution in your paper? It is the most fearful evil, you know. Our Sobolev street is a regular slave-market.

November 15, 1888.

My "Party" has pleased the ladies. They sing my praises wherever I go. It really isn't bad to be a doctor and to understand what one is writing about. The ladies say the description of the confinement is true. In the story for the Garshin sbornik I have described spiritual agony.

(No date), 1888.

. . . You say that writers are God's elect. I will not contradict you. Shtcheglov calls me the Potyomkin of literature, and so it is not for me to speak of the thorny path, of disappointments, and so on. I do not know whether I have ever suffered more than shoemakers, mathematicians, or railway guards do; I do not know who speaks through my lips—God or someone worse. I will allow myself to mention only one little drawback which I have experienced and you probably know from experience also. It is this. You and I are fond of ordinary people; but other people are fond of us because they think we are not ordinary. Me, for instance, they invite everywhere and regale me with food and drink like a general at a wedding. My sister is indignant that people on all sides invite her simply because she is a writer's sister. No one wants to love the ordinary people in us. Hence it follows that if in the eyes of our friends we should appear to-morrow as ordinary mortals, they will leave off loving us, and will only pity us. And that is horrid. It is horrid, too, that they like the very things in us which we often dislike and despise in ourselves. It is horrid that I was right when I wrote the story "The First-Class Passenger," in which an engineer and a professor talk about fame.

I am going away into the country. Hang them all! You have Feodosia. By the way, about Feodosia and the Tatars. The Tatars have been robbed of their land, but no one thinks of their welfare. There ought to be Tatar schools. Write and suggest that the money which is being spent on the sausage Dorpat University, where useless Germans are studying, should be devoted to schools for Tatars, who are of use to Russia. I would write about it myself, but I don't know how to.

December 23, 1888.

... There are moments when I completely lose heart. For whom and for what do I write? For the public? But I don't see it, and believe in it less than I do in spooks: it is uneducated, badly brought up, and its best elements are unfair and insincere to us. I cannot make out whether this public wants me or not. Burenin says that it does not, and that I waste my time on trifles; the Academy has given me a prize. The devil himself could not make head or tail of it. Write for the sake of money? But I never have any money, and not being used to having it I am almost indifferent to it. For the sake of money I work apathetically. Write for the sake of praise? But praise merely irritates me. Literary society, students, Pleshtcheyev, young ladies, etc., were enthusiastic in their praises of my "Nervous Breakdown," but Grigorovitch is the only one who has noticed the description of the first snow. And so on, and so on. If we had critics I should know that I provide material, whether good or bad does not matter—that to men who devote themselves to the study of life I am as necessary as a star is to an astronomer. And then I would take trouble over my work and should know what I was working for. But as it is you, I, Muravlin, and the rest are like lunatics who write books and plays to please themselves. To please oneself is, of course, an excellent thing; one feels the pleasure while one is writing, but afterwards? But . . . I will shut up. In short, I am sorry for Tatyana Repin, [Translator's Note: Suvorin's play.] not because she poisoned herself, but because she lived her life, died in agony, and was described absolutely to no purpose, without any good to anyone. A number of tribes, religions, languages, civilizations, have vanished without a trace—vanished because there were no historians or biologists. In the same way a number of lives and works of art disappear before our very eyes owing to the complete absence of criticism. It may be objected that critics would have nothing to do because all modern works are poor and insignificant. But this is a narrow way of looking at things. Life must be studied not from the pluses alone, but from the minuses too. The conviction that the "eighties" have not produced a single writer may in itself provide material for five volumes.

. . . I settled down last night to write a story for the Novoye Vremya, but a woman appeared and dragged me to see the poet Palmin who, when he was drunk, had fallen and cut his forehead to the bone. I was busy over the drunken fellow for nearly two hours, was tired out, began to smell of iodoform all over, felt cross, and came home exhausted. . . . Altogether my life is a dreary one, and I begin to get fits of hating people which used never to happen to me before. Long stupid conversations, visitors, people asking for help, and helping them to the extent of one or two or three roubles, spending money on cabs for the sake of patients who do not pay me a penny—altogether it is such a hotch-potch that I feel like running away from home. People borrow money from me and don't pay it back, they take my books, they waste my time. . . . Blighted love is the one thing that is missing.

December 26, 1888.

. . . You say that from compassion women fall in love, from compassion they get married. . . . And what about men? I don't like realistic writers to slander women, but I don't like it either when people put women on a pedestal and attempt to prove that even if they are worse than men, anyway they are angels and men scoundrels. Neither men nor women are worth a brass farthing, but men are more just and more intelligent.

December 30, 1888.

. . . This is how I understand my characters. [Translator's Note: In the play "Ivanov."] Ivanov is a gentleman, a University man, and not remarkable in any way. He is excitable, hotheaded, easily carried away, honest and straightforward like most people of his class. He has lived on his estate and served on the Zemstvo. What he has been doing and how he has behaved, what he has been interested in and enthusiastic over, can be seen from the following words of his, addressed to the doctor (Act I., Scene 5): "Don't marry Jewesses or neurotic women or blue-stockings . . . don't fight with thousands single-handed, don't wage war on windmills, don't batter your head against the wall . . . God preserve you from scientific farming, wonderful schools, enthusiastic speeches. . . ." This is what he has in his past. Sarra, who has seen his scientific farming and other crazes, says about him to the doctor: "He is a remarkable man, doctor, and I am sorry you did not meet him two or three years ago. Now he is depressed and melancholy, he doesn't talk or do anything, but in old days . . . how charming he was!" (Act I., Scene 7). His past is beautiful, as is generally the case with educated Russians. There is not, or there hardly is, a single Russian gentleman or University man who does not boast of his past. The present is always worse than the past. Why? Because Russian excitability has one specific characteristic: it is quickly followed by exhaustion. A man has scarcely left the class-room before he rushes to take up a burden beyond his strength; he tackles at once the schools, the peasants, scientific farming, and the Vyestnik Evropi, he makes speeches, writes to the minister, combats evil, applauds good, falls in love, not in an ordinary, simple way, but selects either a blue-stocking or a neurotic or a Jewess, or even a prostitute whom he tries to save, and so on, and so on. But by the time he is thirty or thirty-five he begins to feel tired and bored. He has not got decent moustaches yet, but he already says with authority:

"Don't marry, my dear fellow. . . . Trust my experience," or, "After all, what does Liberalism come to? Between ourselves Katkov was often right. . . ." He is ready to reject the Zemstvo and scientific farming, and science and love. My Ivanov says to the doctor (Act I., Scene 5): "You took your degree only last year, my dear friend, you are still young and vigorous, while I am thirty-five. I have a right to advise you. . . ." That is how these prematurely exhausted people talk. Further down, sighing authoritatively, he advises: "Don't you marry in this or that way (see above), but choose something commonplace, grey, with no vivid colours or superfluous flourishes. Altogether build your life according to the conventional pattern. The greyer and more monotonous the background the better. . . . The life that I have led—how tiring it is! Ah, how tiring!"

Conscious of physical exhaustion and boredom, he does not understand what is the matter with him, and what has happened.

Horrified, he says to the doctor (Act I., Scene 3): "Here you tell me she is soon going to die and I feel neither love nor pity, but a sort of emptiness and weariness. . . . If one looks at me from outside it must be horrible. I don't understand what is happening to my soul." Finding themselves in such a position, narrow and unconscientious people generally throw the whole blame on their environment, or write themselves down as Hamlets and superfluous people, and are satisfied with that. But Ivanov, a straightforward man, openly says to the doctor and to the public that he does not understand his own mind. "I don't understand! I don't understand!" That he really doesn't understand can be seen from his long monologue in Act III., where, tete-a-tete with the public, he opens his heart to it and even weeps.

The change that has taken place in him offends his sense of what is fitting. He looks for the causes outside himself and fails to find them; he begins to look for them inside and finds only an indefinite feeling of guilt. It is a Russian feeling. Whether there is a death or illness in his family, whether he owes money or lends it, a Russian always feels guilty. Ivanov talks all the time about being to blame in some way, and the feeling of guilt increases in him at every juncture. In Act I. he says: "Suppose I am terribly to blame, yet my thoughts are in a tangle, my soul is in bondage to a sort of sloth, and I am incapable of understanding myself. . . ." In Act II. he says to Sasha: "My conscience aches day and night, I feel that I am profoundly to blame, but in what exactly I have done wrong I cannot make out."

To exhaustion, boredom, and the feeling of guilt add one more enemy: loneliness. Were Ivanov an official, an actor, a priest, a professor, he would have grown used to his position. But he lives on his estate. He is in the country. His neighbours are either drunkards or fond of cards, or are of the same type as the doctor. None of them care about his feelings or the change that has taken place in him. He is lonely. Long winters, long evenings, an empty garden, empty rooms, the grumbling Count, the ailing wife. . . . He has nowhere to go. This is why he is every minute tortured by the question: what is he to do with himself?

Now about his fifth enemy. Ivanov is tired and does not understand himself, but life has nothing to do with that! It makes its legitimate demands upon him, and whether he will or no, he must settle problems. His sick wife is a problem, his numerous debts are a problem, Sasha flinging herself on his neck is a problem. The way in which he settles all these problems must be evident from his monologue in Act III., and from the contents of the last two acts. Men like Ivanov do not solve difficulties but collapse under their weight. They lose their heads, gesticulate, become nervous, complain, do silly things, and finally, giving rein to their flabby, undisciplined nerves, lose the ground under their feet and enter the class of the "broken down" and "misunderstood."

Disappointment, apathy, nervous limpness and exhaustion are the inevitable consequence of extreme excitability, and such excitability is extremely characteristic of our young people. Take literature. Take the present time.... Socialism is one of the forms of this excitement. But where is socialism? You see it in Tihomirov's letter to the Tsar. The socialists are married and are criticizing the Zemstvo. Where is Liberalism? Mihailovsky himself says that all the labels have been mixed up now. And what are all the Russian enthusiasms worth? The war has wearied us, Bulgaria has wearied us till we can only be ironical about it. Zucchi has wearied us and so has the comic opera.

Exhaustion (Dr. Bertensen will confirm this) finds expression not only in complaining or the sensation of boredom. The life of an over-tired man cannot be represented like this:

[Transcriber's note: The line graph in the print version depicts a wavy horizontal "line" with minimal variation in the vertical direction. The ASCII diagram below gives a rough approximation.]

~~~~~~~~~~~~~~~~~~~~~~~~~~~~~

It is very unequal. Over-tired people never lose the capacity for becoming extremely excited, but cannot keep it up for long, and each excitement is followed by still greater apathy.... Graphically, it could be represented like this:

[Transcriber's note: The line graph in the print version depicts a series of wavy horizontal segments punctuated by sharp "dips," each horizontal segment a little lower than the one before. The ASCII illustration below gives a rough approximation.]

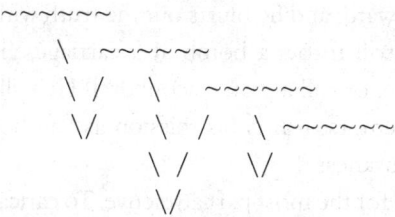

The fall, as you see, is not continuous but broken. Sasha declares her love and Ivanov cries out in ecstasy, "A new life!"—and next morning he believes in this new life as little as he does in spooks (the monologue in Act III.); his wife insults him, and, fearfully worked up and beside himself with anger, he flings a cruel insult at her. He is called a scoundrel. This is either fatal to his tottering brain, or stimulates him to a fresh paroxysm and he pronounces sentence on himself.

Not to tire you out altogether I pass now to Dr. Lvov. He is the type of an honest, straightforward, hotheaded, but narrow and uncompromising man. Clever people say of such men: "He is stupid but his heart is in the right place." Anything like width of outlook or unreflecting feeling is foreign to Lvov. He is the embodiment of a programme, a walking tendency. He looks through a narrow frame at every person and event, he judges everything according to preconceived notions. Those who shout, "Make way for honest labour!" are an object of worship to him; those who do not shout it are scoundrels and exploiters. There is no middle. He has been brought up on Mihailov's [Translator's Note: The author of second-rate works inculcating civic virtue with a revolutionary bias.] novels; at the theatre he has seen on the stage "new men," i.e., the exploiters and sons of our age, painted by the modern playwrights. He has stored it all up, and so much so, that when he reads "Rudin" he is sure to be asking himself, "Is Rudin a scoundrel or not?" Literature and the stage have so educated him that he approaches every character in real life and in fiction with this question. . . . It is not enough for him that all men are sinners. He wants saints and villains!

He was prejudiced before he came to the district. He at once classed all the rich peasants as exploiters, and Ivanov, whom he could not understand, as a scoundrel. Why, the man has a sick wife and he goes to see a rich lady neighbour—of course he is a scoundrel! It is obvious that he is killing his wife in order to marry an heiress.

Lvov is honest and straightforward, and he blurts out the truth without sparing himself. If necessary, he will throw a bomb at a carriage, give a school inspector a blow in the face, or call a man a scoundrel. He will not stop at anything. He never feels remorse—it is his mission as "an honest worker" to fight "the powers of darkness"!

Such people are useful, and are for the most part attractive. To caricature them, even in the interests of the play, is unfair and, indeed, unnecessary. True, a caricature is more striking, and therefore easier to understand, but it is better to put your colour on too faint than too strong.

Now about the women. What do they love Ivanov for? Sarra loves him because he is a fine man, because he has enthusiasm, because he is brilliant and speaks with as much heat as Lvov does (Act I., Scene 7). She loves him so long as he is excited and interesting; but when he begins to grow misty in her eyes, and to lose definiteness of outline, she ceases to understand him, and at the end of Act III. speaks out plainly and sharply.

Sasha is a young woman of the newest type. She is well-educated, intelligent, honest, and so on. In the realm of the blind a one-eyed man is king, and so she favours Ivanov in spite of his being thirty-five. He is better than anyone else. She knew him when she was a child and saw his work close at hand, at the period before he was exhausted. He is a friend of her father's.

She is a female who is not won by the vivid plumage of the male, not by their courage and dexterity, but by their complaints, whinings and failures. She is the sort of girl who loves a man when he is going downhill. The moment Ivanov loses heart the young lady is on the spot! That's just what she was waiting for. Just think of it, she now has such a holy, such a grateful task before her! She will raise up the fallen one, set him on his feet, make him happy. . . . It is not Ivanov she loves, but this task. Argenton in Daudet's book says, "Life is not a novel." Sasha does not know this. She does not know that for Ivanov love is only a fresh complication, an extra stab in the back. And what comes of it? She struggles with him for a whole year and, instead of being raised, he sinks lower and lower.

. . . In my description of Ivanov there often occurs the word "Russian." Don't be cross about it. When I was writing the play I had in mind only the things that really matter—that is, only the typical Russian characteristics. Thus the extreme excitability, the feeling of guilt, the liability to become exhausted are purely Russian. Germans are never excited, and that is why Germany knows nothing of disappointed, superfluous, or over-tired people. . . . The excitability of the French is always maintained at one and the same level, and makes no sudden bounds or falls, and so a Frenchman is normally excited down to a decrepit old age. In other words, the French do not have to waste their strength in over-excitement; they spend their powers sensibly, and do not go bankrupt.

. . . Ivanov and Lvov appear to my imagination to be living people. I tell you honestly, in all conscience, these men were born in my head, not by accident, not out of sea foam, or preconceived "intellectual" ideas. They are the result of observing and studying life. They stand in my brain, and I feel that I have not falsified the truth nor exaggerated it a jot. If on paper they have not come out clear and living, the fault is not in them but in me, for not being able to express my thoughts. It shows it is too early for me to begin writing plays.

January 7, 1889.

. . . I have been cherishing the bold dream of summing up all that has hitherto been written about whining, miserable people, and with my Ivanov saying the last word. It seemed to me that all Russian novelists and playwrights were drawn to depict despondent men, but that they all wrote instinctively, having no definite image or views on the subject. As far as my design goes I was on the right track, but the execution is good for nothing. I ought to have waited! I am glad I did not listen to Grigorovitch two or three years ago, and write a novel! I can just imagine what a lot of good material I should have spoiled. He says: "Talent and freshness overcome everything." It is more true to say that talent and freshness can spoil a great deal. In addition to plenty of material and talent, one wants something else which is no less important. One wants to be mature—that is one thing; and for another the feeling of personal freedom is essential, and that feeling has only recently begun to develop in me. I used not to have it before; its place was successfully filled by my frivolity, carelessness, and lack of respect for my work.

What writers belonging to the upper class have received from nature for nothing, plebeians acquire at the cost of their youth. Write a story of how a young man, the son of a serf, who has served in a shop, sung in a choir, been at a high school and a university, who has been brought up to respect everyone of higher rank and position, to kiss priests' hands, to reverence other people's ideas, to be thankful for every morsel of bread, who has been many times whipped, who has trudged from one pupil to another without goloshes, who has been used to fighting, and tormenting animals, who has liked dining with his rich relations, and been hypocritical before God and men from the mere consciousness of his own insignificance—write how this young man squeezes the slave out of himself, drop by drop, and how waking one beautiful morning he feels that he has no longer a slave's blood in his veins but a real man's. . . .

March 5, 1889.

. . . Last night I drove out of town and listened to the gypsies. They sing well, the wild creatures. Their singing reminds me of a train falling off a high bank in a violent snow-storm: there is a lot of turmoil, screeching and banging.

. . . I bought Dostoevsky in your shop and am now reading him. It is fine, but very long and indiscreet. It is over-pretentious.

SUMY,
LINTVARYOVS' ESTATE, May, 1889.

. . . Among other things I am reading Gontcharov and wondering. I wonder how I could have considered Gontcharov a first-rate writer. His "Oblomov" is not really good. Oblomov himself is exaggerated and is not so striking as to make it worth while to write a whole book about him. A flabby sluggard like so many, a commonplace, petty nature without any complexity in it: to raise this person to the rank of a social type is to make too much of him. I ask myself, what would Oblomov be if he had not been a sluggard? And I answer that he would not have been anything. And if so, let him snore in peace. The other characters are trivial, with a flavour of Leikin about them; they are taken at random, and are half unreal. They are not characteristic of the epoch and give one nothing new. Stoltz does not inspire me with any confidence. The author says he is a splendid fellow, but I don't believe him. He is a sly brute, who thinks very well of himself and is very complacent. He is half unreal, and three-quarters on stilts. Olga is unreal and is dragged in by the tail. And the chief trouble is that the whole novel is cold, cold, cold. I scratch out Gontcharov from the list of my demi-gods.

But how direct, how powerful is Gogol, and what an artist he is! His "Marriage" alone is worth two hundred thousand roubles. It is simply delicious, and that is all about it. He is the greatest of Russian writers. In "The Inspector General" the first act is the best, in "The Marriage" the third act is the worst. I am going to read it aloud to my people.

May 4, 1889.

. . . Nature is an excellent sedative. It pacifies—that is, it makes one indifferent. And it is essential in this world to be indifferent. Only those who are indifferent are able to see things clearly, to be just and to work. Of course, I am only speaking of intelligent people of fine natures; the empty and selfish are indifferent enough any way.

You say that I have grown lazy. That does not mean that I am now lazier than I used to be. I work now as much as I did three or five years ago. To work and to look as though I were working from nine in the morning till dinner, and from evening tea till bedtime has become a habit with me, and in that respect I am just like a government clerk. And if my work does not produce two novels a month or an income of ten thousand, it is not my laziness that is at fault, but my fundamental, psychological peculiarities. I do not care enough for money to succeed in medicine, and for literature I have not enough passion and therefore not enough talent. The fire burns in me slowly and evenly, without suddenly spluttering and flaring up, and this is why it does not happen to me to write three or four signatures a night, or to be so carried away by work as to prevent myself from going to bed if I am sleepy; this is why I commit no particular follies nor do anything particularly wise.

I am afraid that in this respect I resemble Gontcharov, whom I don't like, who is ten heads taller than I am in talent. I have not enough passion; add to that this sort of lunacy: for the last two years I have for no reason at all ceased to care about seeing my work in print, have become indifferent to reviews, to literary conversations, to gossip, to success and failure, to good pay—in short, I have gone downright silly. There is a sort of stagnation in my soul. I explain it by the stagnation in my personal life. I am not disappointed, I am not tired, I am not depressed, but simply everything has suddenly become less interesting. I must do something to rouse myself.

May 7.

I have read Bourget's "Disciple" in the Russian translation. This is how it strikes me. Bourget is a gifted, very intelligent and cultured man. He is as thoroughly acquainted with the method of the natural sciences, and as imbued with it as though he had taken a good degree in science or medicine. He is not a stranger in the domain he proposes to deal with—a merit absent in Russian writers both new and old.

... The novel is interesting. I have read it and understand why you were so absorbed by it. It is clever, interesting, in places witty, somewhat fantastic. As to its defects, the chief of them is his pretentious crusade against materialism. Forgive me, but I can't understand such crusades. They never lead to anything and only bring needless confusion into people's thoughts. Whom is the crusade against, and what is its object? Where is the enemy and what is there dangerous about him? In the first place, the materialistic movement is not a school or tendency in the narrow journalistic sense; it is not something passing or accidental; it is necessary, inevitable, and beyond the power of man. All that lives on earth is bound to be materialistic. In animals, in savages, in Moscow merchants, all that is higher and non-animal is conditioned by an unconscious instinct, while all the rest is material, and they of course cannot help it. Beings of a higher order, thinking men, are also bound to be materialists. They seek for truth in matter, for there is nowhere else to seek for it, since they see, hear, and sense matter alone. Of necessity they can only seek for truth where their microscopes, lancets, and knives are of use to them. To forbid a man to follow the materialistic line of thought is equivalent to forbidding him to seek truth. Outside matter there is neither knowledge nor experience, and consequently there is no truth. ...

I think that when dissecting a corpse, the most inveterate spiritualist will be bound to ask himself, "Where is the soul here?" And if one knows how great is the likeness between bodily and mental diseases, and that both are treated by the same remedies, one cannot help refusing to separate the soul from the body.

... To speak of the danger and harm of materialism, and even more to fight against it, is, to say the least, premature. We have not enough data to draw up an indictment. There are many theories and suppositions, but no facts. ... The priests complain of unbelief, immorality, and so on. There is no unbelief. People believe in something, whatever it may be. ...

As to immorality, it is not people like Mendeleyev but poets, abbots, and personages regularly attending Embassy churches, who have the reputation of being perverted debauchees, libertines, and drunkards.

In short, I cannot understand Bourget's crusade. If, in starting upon it, he had at the same time taken the trouble to point out to the materialists an incorporeal God in the sky, and to point to Him in such a way that they should see Him, that would be another matter, and I should understand what he is driving at.

May 14, 1889.

. . . You want to know if the lady doctor hates you as before. Alas! she has grown stouter and much more resigned, which I do not like at all. There are not many women doctors left on earth. They are disappearing and dying out like the branches in the Byelovyezhsky forest. Some die of consumption, others become mystics, some marry widowed squadron-commanders, some still try to stand firm, but are obviously losing heart. Probably the first tailors and the first astrologers also died out rapidly. Life is hard on those who have the temerity first to enter upon an unknown path. The vanguard always has a bad time of it.

May 15, 1889.

If you have not gone abroad yet, I will answer your letter about Bourget. . . . You are speaking of the "right to live" of this or that branch of knowledge; I am speaking of peace, not of rights. I want people not to see war where there is none. Different branches of knowledge have always lived together in peace. Anatomy and belles-lettres are of equally noble descent; they have the same purpose and the same enemy—the devil—and there is absolutely nothing for them to fight about. There is no struggle for existence between them. If a man knows about the circulation of the blood, he is rich; if he also learns the history of religion and the song "I remember a marvellous moment," he becomes richer, not poorer—that is to say, we are concerned with pluses alone. This is why geniuses have never fought, and in Goethe the poet lived amicably side by side with the scientist.

It is not branches of knowledge such as poetry and anatomy, but errors—that is to say, men—that fight with one another. When a man fails to understand something he is conscious of a discord, and seeks for the cause of it not in himself, as he should, but outside himself—hence the war with what he does not understand. In the middle ages alchemy was gradually in a natural, peaceful way changing into chemistry, and astrology into astronomy; the monks did not understand, saw a conflict and fought against it. Just such a belligerent Spanish monk was our Pisarev in the sixties.

Bourget, too, is fighting. You say he is not, and I say he is. Imagine his novel falling into the hands of a man whose children are studying in the faculty of science, or of a bishop who is looking for a subject for his Sunday sermon. Will the effect be anything like peace? It will not. Or imagine the novel catching the eye of an anatomist or a physiologist, or any such. It will not breathe peace into anyone's soul; it will irritate those who know and give false ideas to those who don't.

TO A. N. PLESHTCHEYEV.

MOSCOW, September 30, 1889.

... I do not think I ought to change the title of the story. The wags who will, as you foretell, make jokes about "A Dreary Story," are so dull that one need not fear them; and if someone makes a good joke I shall be glad to have given him the occasion for it. The professor could not write about Katya's husband because he did not know him, and Katya does not say anything about him; besides, one of my hero's chief characteristics is that he cares far too little about the inner life of those who surround him, and while people around him are weeping, making mistakes, telling lies, he calmly talks about the theatre or literature. Were he a different sort of man, Liza and Katya might not have come to grief.

October, 1889.

I am afraid of those who look for a tendency between the lines, and who are determined to regard me either as a liberal or as a conservative. I am not a liberal, not a conservative, not a believer in gradual progress, not a monk, not an indifferentist. I should like to be a free artist and nothing more, and I regret that God has not given me the power to be one. I hate lying and violence in all their forms, and am equally repelled by the secretaries of consistories and by Notovitch and Gradovsky. Pharisaism, stupidity and despotism reign not in merchants' houses and prisons alone. I see them in science, in literature, in the younger generation. . . . That is why I have no preference either for gendarmes, or for butchers, or for scientists, or for writers, or for the younger generation. I regard trade-marks and labels as a superstition. My holy of holies is the human body, health, intelligence, talent, inspiration, love, and the most absolute freedom—freedom from violence and lying, whatever forms they may take. This is the programme I would follow if I were a great artist.

MOSCOW,
February 15, 1890.

I answer you, dear Alexey Nikolaevitch, at once on receiving your letter. It was your name-day, and I forgot it!! Forgive me, dear friend, and accept my belated congratulations.

Did you really not like the "Kreutzer Sonata"? I don't say it is a work of genius for all time, of that I am no judge; but to my thinking, among the mass of all that is written now, here and abroad, one scarcely could find anything else as powerful both in the gravity of its conception and the beauty of its execution. To say nothing of its artistic merits, which in places are striking, one must be grateful to the novel, if only because it is keenly stimulating to thought. As one reads it, one can scarcely refrain from crying out: "That's true," or "That's absurd." It is true it has some very annoying defects. Apart from all those you enumerate, it has one for which one cannot readily forgive the author—that is, the audacity with which Tolstoy holds forth about what he doesn't know and is too obstinate to care to understand. Thus his statements about syphilis, foundling hospitals, the aversion of women for the sexual relation, and so on, are not merely open to dispute, but show him up as an ignoramus who has not, in the course of his long life, taken the trouble to read two or three books written by specialists. But yet these defects fly away like feathers in the wind; one simply does not notice them in face of the real worth of the story, or, if one notices them, it is only with a little vexation that the story has not escaped the fate of all the works of man, all imperfect and never free from blemish.

My Petersburg friends and acquaintances are angry with me? What for? For my not having bored them enough with my presence, which has for so long been a bore to myself! Soothe their minds. Tell them that in Petersburg I ate a great many dinners and a great many suppers, but did not fascinate one lady; that every day I was confident of leaving by the evening train, that I was detained by my friends and by The Marine Almanack, the whole of which I had to look through from the year 1852. While I was in Petersburg, I got through in one month more than my young friends would in a year. Let them be angry, though!

I sit all day long reading and making extracts. I have nothing in my head or on paper except Sahalin. Mental obsession. Mania Sachalinosa.

Not long ago I dined with Madame Yermolov. [Translator's Note: The celebrated actress.] A wild-flower thrust into the same nosegay with the carnation was the more fragrant for the good company it had kept. So I, after dining with the star, was aware of a halo round my head for two days afterwards . . .

Good-bye, my dear friend; come and see us. . . .

TO A. S. SUVORIN.

MOSCOW, February 23, 1890.

. . . My brother Alexandr is a slow-witted creature; he is enthusiastic over Ornatsky's missionary speech, in which he says that the natives do not become Christians because they are waiting for a special ukaz (that is, command) from the Tsar on the subject and are waiting for their chiefs to be baptized . . . (by force—be it understood). This eloquent pontifex says, too, that the native priests ought, in view of their ascetic manner of life, to be removed from the natives and put into special institutions somewhat after the fashion of monasteries. A nice set of people and no mistake! They have wasted two million roubles, they send out every year from the academy dozens of missionaries who cost the treasury and the people large sums, yet they cannot convert the natives, and what is more, want the police and the military to help them with fire and sword. . . .

If you have Madame Tsebrikov's article, do not trouble to send it. Such articles give no information and only waste time; I want facts. Indeed, in Russia there is a terrible poverty of facts, and a terrible abundance of reflections of all sorts.

February 28.

... To-morrow is spring, and within ten to fifteen days the larks will come back. But alas!—the coming spring seems strange to me, for I am going away from it.

In Sahalin there is very good fish, but there are no hot drinks. ...

Our geologists, ichthyologists, zoologists and so on, are fearfully uneducated people. They write such a vile jargon that it not only bores one to read it, but one actually has at times to remodel the sentences before one can understand them; on the other hand, they have solemnity and earnestness enough and to spare. It's really beastly. ...

March 4.

I have sent you to-day two stories: Filippov's (he was here yesterday) and Yezhov's. I have not had time to read the latter, and I think it is as well to say, once for all, that I am not responsible for what I send you. My handwriting on the address does not mean that I like the story.

Poor Yezhov has been to see me; he sat near the table crying: his young wife is in consumption. He must take her at once to the south. To my question whether he had money he answered that he had. ... It's vile catch-cold weather; the sky itself is sneezing. I can't bear to look at it. ... I have already begun writing of Sahalin. I have written five pages. It reads all right, as though written with intelligence and authority ... I quote foreign authors second-hand, but minutely and in a tone as though I could speak every foreign language perfectly. It's regular swindling.

Yezhov has upset me with his tears. He reminded me of something, and I was sorry for him too.

Don't forget us sinners.

TO N. M. LINTVARYOV.

MOSCOW, March 5, 1890.

... As for me, I have a cough too, but I am alive and I believe I'm well. I shan't be with you this summer, as I am going in April, on affairs of my own, to the island of Sahalin, and shall not be back till December. I am going across Siberia (eleven thousand versts) and shall come back by sea.

I believe Misha wrote to you as though someone were commissioning me to go, but that's nonsense. I am commissioning myself to go, on my own account. There are lots of bears and escaped convicts in Sahalin, so that in case messieurs the wild beasts dine off me or some tramp cuts my throat, I beg you not to remember evil against me.

Of course if I have the time and the skill to write what I want to about Sahalin, I shall send you the book immediately that it comes into the world; it will be dull, a specialist's book consisting of nothing but figures, but let me count upon your indulgence: you will suppress your yawns as you read it. . . .

TO A. S. SUVORIN.

MOSCOW, March 9.

About Sahalin we are both mistaken, but you probably more than I. I am going in the full conviction that my visit will furnish no contribution of value either to literature or science: I have neither the knowledge, nor the time, nor the ambition for that. I have neither the plans of a Humboldt nor of a Kennan. I want to write some 100 to 200 pages, and so do something, however little, for medical science, which, as you are aware, I have neglected shockingly. Possibly I shall not succeed in writing anything, but still the expedition does not lose its charm for me: reading, looking about me, and listening, I shall learn a great deal and gain experience. I have not yet travelled, but thanks to the books which I have been compelled to read, I have learned a great deal which anyone ought to be flogged for not knowing, and which I was so ignorant as not to have known before. Moreover, I imagine the journey will be six months of incessant hard work, physical and mental, and that is essential for me, for I am a Little Russian and have already begun to be lazy. I must take myself in hand. My expedition may be nonsense, obstinacy, a craze, but think a moment and tell me what I am losing if I go. Time? Money? Shall I suffer hardships? My time is worth nothing; money I never have anyway; as for hardships, I shall travel with horses, twenty-five to thirty days, not more, all the rest of the time I shall be sitting on the deck of a steamer or in a room, and shall be continually bombarding you with letters.

Suppose the expedition gives me nothing, yet surely there will be 2 or 3 days out of the whole journey which I shall remember all my life with ecstasy or bitterness, etc., etc. . . . So that's how it is, sir. All that is unconvincing, but you know you write just as unconvincingly. For instance, you say that Sahalin is of no use and no interest to anyone. Can that be true? Sahalin can be useless and uninteresting only to a society which does not exile thousands of people to it and does not spend millions of roubles on it. Except Australia in the past and Cayenne, Sahalin is the only place where one can study colonization by convicts; all Europe is interested in it, and is it no use to us? Not more than 25 to 30 years ago our Russians exploring Sahalin performed amazing feats which exalt them above humanity, and that's no use to us: we don't know what those men were, and simply sit within four walls and complain that God has made man amiss. Sahalin is a place of the most unbearable sufferings of which man, free and captive, is capable. Those who work near it and upon it have solved fearful, responsible problems, and are still solving them. I am not sentimental, or I would say that we ought to go to places like Sahalin to worship as the Turks go to Mecca, and that sailors and gaolers ought to think of the prison in Sahalin as military men think of Sevastopol. From the books I have read and am reading, it is evident that we have sent millions of men to rot in prison, have destroyed them—casually, without thinking, barbarously; we have driven men in fetters through the cold ten thousand versts, have infected them with syphilis, have depraved them, have multiplied criminals, and the blame for all this we have thrown upon the gaolers and red-nosed superintendents. Now all educated Europe knows that it is not the superintendents that are to blame, but all of us; yet that has nothing to do with us, it is not interesting. The vaunted sixties did nothing for the sick and for prisoners, so breaking the chief commandment of Christian civilization. In our day something is being done for the sick, nothing for prisoners; prison management is entirely without interest for our jurists. No, I assure you that Sahalin is of use and of interest to us, and the only thing to regret is that I am going there, and not someone else who knows more about it and would be more able to rouse public interest. Nothing much will come of my going there.

There have been disturbances among the students on a grand scale here. It began with the Petrovsky Academy, where the authorities forbade the students to take young ladies to their rooms, suspecting the ladies of politics as well as of prostitution. From the Academy it spread to the University, where now the students, surrounded by fully armed and mounted Hectors and Achilleses with lances, make the following demands:

1. Complete autonomy for the universities.
2. Complete freedom of teaching.
3. Free right of entrance to the university without distinction of religious denomination, nationality, sex, and social position.
4. Right of entrance to the university for the Jews without restriction, and equal rights for them with the other students.
5. Freedom of meeting and recognition of the students' associations.
6. The establishment of a university and students' tribunal.
7. The abolition of the police duties of the inspectors.
8. Lowering of the fees for instruction.

This I copied from a manifesto, with some abbreviations.

TO I. L. SHTCHEGLOV.

MOSCOW, March 22, 1890.

My greetings, dear Jean! Thanks for your long letter and for the good will of which it is full from beginning to end. I shall be delighted to read your military story. Will it come out in the Easter number? It is a long time since I read anything of yours or my own. You say that you want to give me a harsh scolding "especially on the score of morality and art," you speak vaguely of my crimes as deserving friendly censure, and threaten me with "an influential newspaper criticism." If you scratch out the word "art," the whole phrase in quotation marks becomes clearer, but gains a significance which, to tell the truth, perplexes me not a little. Jean, what is it? How is one to understand it? Can I really be different in my ideas of morality from people like you, and so much so as to deserve censure and even an influential article? I cannot take it that you mean some subtle higher morality, as there are no lower, higher, or medium moralities, but only one which Jesus Christ gave us, and which now prevents you and me and Barantsevitch from stealing, insulting, lying, and so on. If I can trust the ease of my conscience, I have never by word or deed, in thought, or in my stories, or in my farces, coveted my neighbour's wife, nor his man, nor his ox, nor any of his cattle, I have not stolen, nor been a hypocrite, I have not flattered the great nor sought their favour, I have not blackmailed, nor lived at other people's expense. It is true I have waxed wanton and slothful, have laughed heedlessly, have eaten too much and drunk too much and been profligate. But all that is a personal matter, and all that does not deprive me of the right to think that, as far as morals are concerned, I am nothing out of the ordinary, one way or the other. Nothing heroic and nothing scoundrelly—I am just like everyone else; I have many sins, but I am quits with morality, as I pay for those sins with interest in the discomforts they bring with them. If you want to abuse me cruelly because I am not a hero, you'd better throw your cruelty out of the window, and instead of abuse, let me hear your charming tragic laugh—that's better.

But of the word "art" I am terrified, as merchants' wives are terrified of "brimstone." When people talk to me of what is artistic and inartistic, of what is dramatic and not dramatic, of tendency, realism, and so on, I am bewildered, hesitatingly assent, and answer with banal half-truths not worth a brass farthing. I divide all works into two classes: those I like and those I don't. I have no other criterion, and if you ask me why I like Shakespeare and don't like Zlatovratsky, I don't venture to answer. Perhaps in time and as I grow wiser I may work out some criterion, but meanwhile all conversations about what is "artistic" only weary me, and seem to me like a continuation of the scholastic disputations with which people wearied themselves in the middle ages.

If criticism, on the authority of which you rely, knows what you and I don't know, why has it up till now not spoken? why does it not reveal the truth and the immutable laws? If it knew, believe me, it would long ago have shown us the true path and we should have known what to do, and Fofanov would not have been in a madhouse, Garshin would have been alive to-day, Barantsevitch would not have been so depressed and we should not be so dull and ill at ease as we are, and you would not feel drawn to the theatre and I to Sahalin. But criticism maintains a dignified silence or gets out of it with idle trashy babble. If it seems to you authoritative it is because it is stupid, conceited, impudent, and clamorous; because it is an empty barrel one cannot help hearing.

But let us have done with that and sing something out of a different opera. Please don't build any literary hopes on my Sahalin trip. I am not going for the sake of impressions or observations, but simply for the sake of living for six months differently from how I have lived hitherto. Don't rely on me, old man; if I am successful and clever enough to do something, so much the better; if not, don't blame me. I am going after Easter. I will send you in due time my Sahalin address and minute instructions. . . .

TO A. S. SUVORIN.

MOSCOW, March 22, 1890.

. . . Yesterday a young lady told me that Professor Storozhenko had related to her the following anecdote. The Sovereign liked the Kreutzer Sonata. Pobyedonostsev, Lubimov, and the other cherubim and seraphim, hastened to justify their attitude to Tolstoy by showing his Majesty "Nikolay Palkin." After reading it, his Majesty was so furious that he ordered measures to be taken. Prince Dolgorukov was informed. And so one fine day an adjutant from Dolgorukov comes to Tolstoy and invites him to go at once to the prince. The latter replies: "Tell the prince that I only visit the houses of my acquaintances." The adjutant, overcome with confusion, rides away, and next day brings Tolstoy the official notice demanding from him an explanation in regard to his "Nikolay Palkin." Tolstoy reads the document and says:

"Tell his excellency that I have not for a long time past written anything for publication; I write only for my friends, and if my friends spread my writings abroad, they are responsible and not I. Tell him that!"

"But I can't tell him that," cried the adjutant in horror, "the prince will not believe me!"

"The prince will not believe his subordinates? That's bad."

Two days later the adjutant comes again with a fresh document, and learns that Tolstoy has gone away to Yasnaya Polyana. That is the end of the anecdote.

Now about the new movements. They flog in our police stations; a rate has been fixed; from a peasant they take ten kopecks for a beating, from a workman twenty—that's for the rods and the trouble. Peasant women are flogged too. Not long ago, in their enthusiasm for beating in a police station, they thrashed a couple of budding lawyers, an incident upon which Russkiya Vyedomosti has a vague paragraph to-day; an investigation has begun.

Another sign of the times: the cabmen approve of the students' disturbances.

"They are making a riot for the poor to be taken in to study," they explain, "learning is not only for the rich." It is said that when a crowd of students were being taken by night to the prison the populace fell upon the gendarmes to rescue the students from them. The populace is said to have shouted: "You have set up flogging for us, but they stand up for us."

March 29.

. . . Fatigue is a relative matter. You say you used to work twenty hours out of the twenty-four and were not exhausted. But you know one may be exhausted lying all day long on the sofa. You used to write for twenty hours, but you know you were in perfect health all that time, you were stimulated by success, defiance, a sense of your talent; you liked your work, or you wouldn't have written. Your heir-apparent sits up late, not because he has a talent for journalism or a love for his work, but simply because his father is an editor of a newspaper. The difference is vast. He ought to have been a doctor or a lawyer, to have had an income of two thousand roubles a year, and published his articles not in Novoye Vremya and not in the spirit of Novoye Vremya. Only those young people can be accepted as healthy who refuse to be reconciled with the old order and foolishly or wisely struggle against it—such is the will of nature and it is the foundation of progress, while your son began by absorbing the old order. In our most intimate talks he has never once abused Tatistchev or Burenin, and that's a bad sign. You are a hundred times as liberal as he is, and it ought to be the other way. He utters a listless and indolent protest, he soon drops his voice and soon agrees, and altogether one has the impression that he has no interest whatever in the contest; that is, he looks on at the cock-fight like a spectator and has no cock of his own. And one ought to have one's own cock, else life is without interest. The unfortunate thing, too, is that he is intelligent, and great intelligence with little interest in life is like a great machine which produces nothing, yet requires a great deal of fuel and exhausts the owner. . . .

April 1.

You abuse me for objectivity, calling it indifference to good and evil, lack of ideals and ideas, and so on. You would have me, when I describe horse-stealers, say: "Stealing horses is an evil." But that has been known for ages without my saying so. Let the jury judge them, it's my job simply to show what sort of people they are. I write: you are dealing with horse-stealers, so let me tell you that they are not beggars but well-fed people, that they are people of a special cult, and that horse-stealing is not simply theft but a passion. Of course it would be pleasant to combine art with a sermon, but for me personally it is extremely difficult and almost impossible, owing to the conditions of technique. You see, to depict horse-stealers in seven hundred lines I must all the time speak and think in their tone and feel in their spirit, otherwise, if I introduce subjectivity, the image becomes blurred and the story will not be as compact as all short stories ought to be. When I write I reckon entirely upon the reader to add for himself the subjective elements that are lacking in the story.

April 11.

Madame N. who used at one time to live in your family is here now. She married the artist N., a nice but tedious man who wants at all costs to travel with me to Sahalin to sketch. To refuse him my company I haven't the courage, but to travel with him would be simple misery. He is going to Petersburg in a day or two to sell his pictures, and at his wife's request will call on you to ask your advice. With a view to this his wife came to ask me for a letter of introduction to you. Be my benefactor, tell N. that I am a drunkard, a swindler, a nihilist, a rowdy character, and that it is out of the question to travel with me, and that a journey in my company will do nothing but upset him. Tell him he will be wasting his time. Of course it would be very nice to have my book illustrated, but when I learned that N. was hoping to get not less than a thousand roubles for it, I lost all appetite for illustrations. My dear fellow, advise him against it!!! Why it is your advice he wants, the devil only knows.

April 15.

And so, my dear friend, I am setting off on Wednesday or Thursday at latest. Good-bye till December. Good luck in my absence. I received the money, thank you very much, though fifteen hundred roubles is a great deal; I don't know where to put it. . . . I feel as though I were preparing for the battlefield, though I see no dangers before me but toothache, which I am sure to have on the journey. As I am provided with nothing in the way of papers but a passport, I may have unpleasant encounters with the authorities, but that is a passing trouble. If they refuse to show me something, I shall simply write in my book that they wouldn't show it me, and that's all, and I won't worry. In case I am drowned or anything of that sort, you might keep it in mind that all I have or may have in the future belongs to my sister; she will pay my debts.

I am taking my mother with me and putting her down at the Troitsky Monastery; I am taking my sister too, and leaving her at Kostroma. I am telling them I shall be back in September.

I shall go over the university in Tomsk. As the only faculty there is medicine I shall not show myself an ignoramus.

I have bought myself a fur coat, an officer's waterproof leather coat, big boots, and a big knife for cutting sausage and hunting tigers. I am equipped from head to foot.

TO HIS SISTER.

STEAMER "ALEXANDR NEVSKY 23," April, 1890, early in the morning.

My dear Tunguses!
Did you have rain when Ivan was coming back from the monastery? In Yaroslavl there was such a downpour that I had to swathe myself in my leather chiton. My first impression of the Volga was poisoned by the rain, by the tear-stained windows of the cabin, and the wet nose of G., who came to meet me at the station. In the rain Yaroslavl looks like Zvenigorod, and its churches remind me of Perervinsky Monastery; there are lots of illiterate signboards, it's muddy, jackdaws with big heads strut about the pavement.

In the steamer I made it my first duty to indulge my talent—that is, to sleep. When I woke I beheld the sun. The Volga is not bad; water meadows, monasteries bathed in sunshine, white churches; the wide expanse is marvellous, wherever one looks it would be a nice place to sit down and begin fishing. Class ladies [Translator's Note: I.e., School chaperons, whose duty it is to sit in the classroom while the girls are receiving instruction from a master.] wander about on the banks, nipping at the green grass. The shepherd's horn can be heard now and then. White gulls, looking like the younger Drishka, hover over the water.

The steamer is not up to much. . . .

Kundasova is travelling with me. Where she is going and with what object I don't know. When I question her about it, she launches off into extremely misty allusions about someone who has appointed a tryst with her in a ravine near Kineshma, then goes off into a wild giggle and begins stamping her feet or prodding with her elbow whatever comes first. We have passed both Kineshma and the ravine, but she still goes on in the steamer, at which of course I am very much pleased; by the way, yesterday for the first time in my life I saw her eating. She eats no less than other people, but she eats mechanically, as though she were munching oats.

Kostroma is a nice town. I saw the stretch of river on which the languid Levitan used to live. I saw Kineshma, where I walked along the boulevard and watched the local beaus. Here I went into the chemist's shop to buy some Bertholet salts for my tongue, which was like leather after the medicine I had taken. The chemist, on seeing Olga Petrovna, was overcome with delight and confusion; she was the same. They were evidently old acquaintances, and judging from the conversation between them they had walked more than once about the ravines near Kineshma.

. . . It's rather cold and rather dull, but interesting on the whole. The steamer whistles every minute; its whistle is midway between the bray of an ass and an Aeolian harp. In five or six hours we shall be in Nizhni. The sun is rising. I slept last night artistically. My money is safe; that is because I am constantly pressing my hands on my stomach.

Very beautiful are the steam-tugs, dragging after them four or five barges each; they look like some fine young intellectual trying to run away while a plebeian wife, mother-in-law, sister-in-law, and wife's grandmother hold on to his coat-tails.

The sun is hiding behind the clouds, the sky is overcast, and the broad Volga looks gloomy. Levitan ought not to live on the Volga. It lays a weight of gloom on the soul. Though it would not be bad to have an estate on its banks.

If the waiter would wake I should ask him for some coffee; as it is, I have to drink water without any relish for it. My greetings to Maryushka and Olga.

Well, keep well and take care of yourselves. I will write regularly.

Your bored Volga-travelling
Homo Sachaliensis,
A. CHEKHOV.

FROM THE STEAMER,
Evening, April 24, 1890.

MY DEAR TUNGUSES!

I am floating on the Kama, but I can't fix the exact locality; I believe we are near Tchistopol. I cannot extol the beauties of the scenery either, as it is hellishly cold; the birches are not yet out, there are still patches of snow here and there, bits of ice float by—in short, the picturesque has gone to the dogs. I sit in the cabin, where people of all sorts and conditions sit at the table, and listen to the conversation, wondering whether it is not time for me to have tea. If I had my way I should do nothing all day but eat; as I haven't the money to be eating all day long I sleep and sleep. I don't go up on deck, it's cold. By night it rains and by day there is an unpleasant wind.

Oh, the caviare! I eat it and eat and never have enough.

. . . It is a pity I did not think to get myself a little bag for tea and sugar. I have to order it a glass at a time, which is tiresome and expensive. I meant to buy some tea and sugar to-day at Kazan, but I over-slept myself.

Rejoice, O mother! I believe I stop twenty-four hours at Ekaterinburg, and shall see the relations. Perhaps their hearts may be softened and they will give me three roubles and an ounce of tea.

From the conversation I am listening to at this moment, I gather that the members of a judicial tribunal are travelling with me. They are not gifted persons. The merchants, who put in their word from time to time seem, however, intelligent. One comes across fearfully rich people.

Sterlets are cheaper than mushrooms; you soon get sick of them. What more is there for me to write about? There is nothing. . . . There is a General, though, and a lean fair man. The former keeps dashing from his cabin to the deck and back again, and sending his photograph off somewhere; the latter is got up to look like Nadson, and tries thereby to give one to know that he is a writer. Today he was mendaciously telling a lady that he had a book published by Suvorin; I, of course, put on an expression of awe.

My money is all safe, except what I have eaten. They won't feed me for nothing, the scoundrels.

I am neither gay nor bored, but there is a sort of numbness in my soul. I like to sit without moving or speaking. To-day, for instance, I have scarcely uttered five words. That's not true, though: I talked to a priest on deck.

We begin to come across natives; there are lots of Tatars: they are a respectable and well-behaved people.

I beg Father and Mother not to worry, and not to imagine dangers which do not exist.

Excuse me for writing about nothing but food. If I did not write about food I should have to write about cold, for I have no other subjects.

April 29, 1890.
MY DEAR TUNGUSES!

The Kama is a very dull river. To realise its beauties one would have to be a native sitting motionless on a barge beside a barrel of naphtha, or a sack of dried fish, continually taking a pull at the bottle. The river banks are bare, the trees are bare, the earth is a dull brown, there are patches of snow, and there is such a wind that the devil himself could not blow as keenly and hatefully. When a cold wind blows and ruffles up the water, which now after the floods is the colour of coffee slops, one feels cold and bored and miserable; the strains of a concertina on the bank sound dejected, figures in tattered sheepskins standing motionless on the barges that meet us look as though they were petrified by some unending grief. The towns on the Kama are grey; one would think the inhabitants were employed in the manufacture of clouds, boredom, soaking fences and mud in the streets, as their sole occupation. The stopping-places are thronged with inhabitants of the educated class, for whom the arrival of a steamer is an event. . . .

. . . To judge from appearances not one of them earns more than thirty-five roubles, and all of them are ailing in some way.

I have told you already there are some legal gentlemen in the steamer: the president of the court, one of the judges, and the prosecutor. The president is a hale and hearty old German who has embraced Orthodoxy, is pious, a homoeopath, and evidently a devotee of the sex. The judge is an old man such as dear Nikolay used to draw; he walks bent double, coughs, and is fond of facetious subjects. The prosecutor is a man of forty-three, dissatisfied with life, a liberal, a sceptic, and a very good-natured fellow. All the journey these gentlemen have been occupied in eating, settling mighty questions and eating, reading and eating. There is a library on the steamer, and I saw the prosecutor reading my "In the Twilight." They began talking about me. Mamin-Sibiryak, who has described the Urals, is the author most liked in these parts. He is more talked of than Tolstoy.

I have been two and a half years sailing to Perm, so it seems to me. We reached there at two o'clock in the night. The train went at six o'clock in the evening. I had to wait. It rained. Rain, cold, mud . . . brrr! The Uralsky line is a good one. . . . That is due to the abundance of business-like people here, factories, mines, and so on, for whom time is precious.

Waking yesterday morning and looking out of the carriage window I felt an aversion for nature: the earth was white, trees covered with hoar-frost, and a regular blizzard pursuing the train. Now isn't it revolting? Isn't it disgusting? . . . I have no goloshes, I pulled on my big boots, and on my way to the refreshment-room for coffee I made the whole Ural region smell of tar. And when we got to Ekaterinburg there was rain, snow, and hail. I put on my leather coat. The cabs are something inconceivable, wretched, dirty, drenched, without springs, the horse's four legs straddling, huge hoofs, gaunt spines . . . the droshkies here are a clumsy parody of our britchkas. A tattered top is put on to a britchka, that is all. And the more exactly I describe the cabman here and his vehicle, the more it will seem like a caricature. They drive not on the middle of the road where it is jolting, but near the gutter where it is muddy and soft. All the cabmen are like Dobrolyubov.

In Russia all the towns are alike. Ekaterinburg is exactly the same as Perm or Tula. The note of the bells is magnificent, velvety. I stopped at the American Hotel (not at all bad), and at once sent word of my arrival to A. M. S., telling him I meant to stay in my hotel room for two days.

The people here inspire the newcomer with a feeling akin to horror. They are big-browed, big-jawed, broad-shouldered fellows with huge fists and tiny eyes. They are born in the local iron foundries, and at their birth a mechanic officiates instead of an accoucheur. A specimen comes into your room with a samovar or a bottle of water, and you expect him every minute to murder you. I stand aside. This morning just such a one came in, big-browed, big-jawed, huge, towering up to the ceiling, seven feet across the shoulders and wearing a fur coat too.

Well, I thought, this one will certainly murder me. It appeared that this was our relation A. M. S. We began to talk. He is a member of the local Zemstvo and manager of his cousin's mill, which is lighted by electric light; he is editor of the Ekaterinburg Week which is under the censorship of the police-master Baron Taube, is married and has two children, is growing rich and getting fat and elderly, and lives in a "substantial way." He says he has no time to be bored. He advised me to visit the museum, the factories, and the mines; I thanked him for his advice. He invited me to tea to-morrow evening; I invited him to dine with me. He did not invite me to dinner, and altogether did not press me very much to visit him. From this mother may conclude that the relations' heart is not softened. . . . Relations are a race in which I take no interest.

There is snow in the street, and I have purposely let down the blind over the windows so as not to see the Asiatic sight. I am sitting here waiting for an answer from Tyumen to my telegram. I telegraphed: "Tyumen. Kurbatov steamer line. Reply paid. Inform me when the passenger steamer starts Tomsk." It depends on the answer whether I go by steamer or gallop fifteen hundred versts in the slush of the thaw.

All night long they beat on sheets of iron at every corner here. You need a head of iron not to go crazy from the incessant clanging. To-day I tried to make myself coffee. The result was a horrid mess. I just drank it with a shrug. I looked at five sheets, handled them, and did not take one. I am going to-day to buy rubber overshoes.

Shall I find a letter from you at Irkutsk?

Ask Lika not to leave such big margins in her letters.

Your Homo Sachaliensis,
A. CHEKHOV.

TO MADAME KISELYOV.

THE BANK OF THE IRTYSH, May 7, 1890.

    My greetings, honoured Marya Vladimirovna! I meant to write you a farewell letter from Moscow, but I had not time; I write to you now sitting in a hut on the bank of the Irtysh.
    It is night. This is how I have come to be here. I am driving across the plain of Siberia. I have already driven 715 versts; I have been transformed from head to foot into a great martyr. This morning a keen cold wind began blowing, and it began drizzling with the most detestable rain. I must observe that there is no spring yet in Siberia. The earth is brown, the trees are bare, and there are white patches of snow wherever one looks; I wear my fur coat and felt overboots day and night. . . . Well, the wind has been blowing since early morning. . . . Heavy leaden clouds, dull brown earth, mud, rain, wind. . . . Brrr! I drive on and on. . . . I drive on endlessly, and the weather does not improve. Towards evening I am told at the station I can't go on further, as everything is under water, the bridges have been carried away, and so on. Knowing how fond these drivers are of frightening one with the elements so as to keep the traveller for the night (it is to their interest), I did not believe them, and ordered them to harness the three horses; and now—alas for me!—I had not driven more than five versts when I saw the land on the bank of the Irtysh all covered with great lakes, the road disappeared under water, and the bridges on the road really had been swept away or had decayed. I was prevented from turning back partly by obstinacy and partly by the desire to get out of these dreary parts as quickly as possible. We began driving through the lakes. . . . My God, I have never experienced anything like it in my life! The cutting wind, the cold, the loathsome rain, and one had to get out of the chaise (not a covered one), if you please, and hold the horses: at each little bridge one could only lead the horses over one at a time. . . . What had I come to? Where was I? All around, desert, dreariness; the bare sullen bank of the Irtysh in sight. . . . We drive into the very biggest lake. Now I should be glad to turn back, but it is not easy. . . . We drive on a long strip of land . . . the strip comes to an end—we go splash! Again a strip of land, again a splash. . . . My hands were numb, and the wild ducks seemed jeering at us and floated in huge flocks over our

heads. . . . It got dark. The driver said nothing—he was bewildered. But at last we reached the last strip that separated the Irtysh from the lake. . . . The sloping bank of the Irtysh was nearly three feet above the level; it was of clay, bare, hollowed out, and looked slippery. The water was muddy. . . . White waves splashed on the clay, but the Irtysh itself made no roar or din, but gave forth a strange sound as though someone were nailing up a coffin under the water. . . . The further bank was a flat, disconsolate plain. . . . You often dream of the Bozharovsky pool; in the same way now I shall dream of the Irtysh. . . .

But behold a ferry. We must be ferried across to the other side. A peasant shrinking from the rain comes out of a hut, and tells us that the ferry cannot cross now as it is too windy. . . . (The ferries are worked by oars). He advises us to wait for calm weather. . . .

And so I am sitting at night in a hut on a lake at the very edge of the Irtysh. I feel a penetrating dampness to the very marrow of my bones, and a loneliness in my soul; I hear my Irtysh banging on the coffins and the wind howling, and wonder where I am, why I am here.

In the next room the peasants who work the ferry and my driver are asleep. They are good-natured people. But if they were bad people they could perfectly well rob me and drown me in the Irtysh. The hut is the only one on the river bank; there would be no witnesses.

The road to Tomsk is absolutely free from danger as far as brigands are concerned. It isn't the fashion even to talk of robbery. There is no stealing even from travellers. When you go into a hut you can leave your things outside and they will all be safe.

But they very nearly did kill me all the same. Imagine the night just before dawn. . . . I was driving along in a chaise, thinking and thinking. . . . All at once I see coming flying towards us at full gallop a post-cart with three horses; my driver had hardly time to turn to the right, the three horses dashed by, and I noticed in it the driver who had to take it back. . . . Behind it came another, also at full speed; we had turned to the right, it turned to the left. "We shall smash into each other," flashed into my mind . . . one instant, and—there was a crash, the horses were mixed up in a black mass, my chaise was rearing in the air, and I was rolling on the ground with all my bags and boxes on the top of me. I leap up and see—a third troika dashing upon us. . . .

My mother must have been praying for me that night, I suppose. If I had been asleep, or if the third troika had come immediately after the second, I should have been crushed to death or maimed. It appeared the foremost driver lashed on the horses, while the drivers in the second and the third carts were asleep and did not see us. The collision was followed by the blankest amazement on both sides, then a storm of ferocious abuse. The traces were torn, the shafts were broken, the yokes were lying about on the road. . . . Ah, how the drivers swore! At night, in that swearing turbulent crew, I felt in utter solitude such as I have never felt before in my life. . . .

But my paper is running out.

TO HIS SISTER.

THE VILLAGE OF YAR,
45 VERSTS FROM TOMSK, May 14, 1890.

My glorious mother, my splendid Masha, my sweet Misha, and all my household! At Ekaterinburg I got my reply telegram from Tyumen. "The first steamer to Tomsk goes on the 18th May." This meant that, whether I liked it or not, I must do the journey with horses. So I did. I drove out of Tyumen on the third of May after spending in Ekaterinburg two or three days, which I devoted to the repair of my coughing and haemorrhoidal person. Besides the public posting service, one can get private drivers that take one across Siberia. I chose the latter: it is just the same. They put me, the servant of God, into a basketwork chaise and drove me with two horses; one sits in the basket like a goldfinch, looking at God's world and thinking of nothing. . . . The plain of Siberia begins, I think, from Ekaterinburg, and ends goodness knows where; I should say it is very like our South Russian Steppe, except for the little birch copses here and there and the cold wind that stings one's cheeks. Spring has not begun yet. There is no green at all, the woods are bare, the snow has not thawed everywhere. There is opaque ice on the lakes. On the ninth of May there was a hard frost, and to-day, the fourteenth, snow has fallen to the depth of three or four inches. No one speaks of spring but the ducks. Ah, what masses of ducks! Never in my life have I seen such abundance. They fly over one's head, they fly up close to the chaise, swim on the lakes and in the pools—

in short, with the poorest sort of gun I could have shot a thousand in one day. One can hear the wild geese calling. . . . There are lots of them here too. One often comes upon a string of cranes or swans. . . . Snipe and woodcock flutter about in the birch copses. The hares which are not eaten or shot here, stand on their hindlegs, and, pricking up their ears, watch the passer-by with an inquisitive stare without the slightest misgiving. They are so often running across the road that to see them doing so is not considered a bad omen.

It's cold driving . . .; I have my fur coat on. My body is all right, but my feet are freezing. I wrap them in the leather overcoat-but it is no use. . . . I have two pairs of breeches on. Well, one drives on and on. . . . Telegraph poles, pools, birch copses flash by. Here we overtake some emigrants, then an etape. . . . We meet tramps with pots on their back; these gentry promenade all over the plain of Siberia without hindrance. One time they will murder some poor old woman to take her petticoat for their leg-wrappers; at another they will strip from the verst post the metal plate with the number on it—it might be useful; at another will smash the head of some beggar or knock out the eyes of some brother exile; but they never touch travellers. Altogether, travelling here is absolutely safe as far as brigands are concerned. Neither the post-drivers nor the private ones from Tyumen to Tomsk remember an instance of any things being stolen from a traveller. When you reach a station you leave your things outside; if you ask whether they won't be stolen, they merely smile in answer. It is not the thing even to speak of robbery and murder on the road. I believe, if I were to lose my money in the station or in the chaise, the driver would certainly give it me if he found it, and would not boast of having done so. Altogether the people here are good and kindly, and have excellent traditions. Their rooms are simply furnished but clean, with claims to luxury; the beds are soft, all feather mattresses and big pillows. The floors are painted or covered with home-made linen rugs. The explanation of this, of course, is their prosperity, the fact that a family has sixteen dessyatins of black earth, and that excellent wheat grows in this black earth. (Wheaten flour costs thirty kopecks a pood here.) But it cannot all be put down to prosperity and being well fed. One must give some of the credit to their manner of life. When you go at night into a room where people are asleep, the nose is not aware of any stuffiness or "Russian smell." It is true one old woman when she handed me a teaspoon wiped it on the back of her skirt; but they don't set you down to drink tea without a tablecloth, and they don't search in each other's heads in your presence, they don't put their fingers inside the glass when they hand you milk or water; the crockery is clean, the kvass is transparent as beer—in fact, there is a cleanliness of which our Little Russians can only dream, yet the Little Russians are far and away cleaner than the Great Russians! They make the most delicious bread here—I overate myself with it at first. The pies and pancakes and fritters and the fancy rolls, which remind one of the spongy Little Russian ring rolls, are very good too. . . . But all the rest is not for the European stomach. For instance, I am regaled everywhere with "duck broth." It's perfectly disgusting, a muddy-looking liquid with bits of wild duck and uncooked onion floating in it. . . . I once asked them to make me some soup from meat and to fry me some perch. They gave me soup too salt, dirty, with hard bits of skin instead of meat; and the perch was cooked with the scales on it. They make their cabbage soup from salt meat; they roast it too. They have just served me some salt meat roasted: it's most repulsive; I chewed at it and gave it up. They drink brick tea. It is a decoction of sage and beetles—that's what it is like in taste and appearance.

By the way, I brought from Ekaterinburg a quarter of a pound of tea, five pounds of sugar, and three lemons. It was not enough tea and there is nowhere to buy any. In these scurvy little towns even the government officials drink brick tea, and even the best shops don't keep tea at more than one rouble fifty kopecks a pound. I have to drink the sage brew.

The distance apart of the posting stations depends on the distance of the nearest villages from each other—that is, 20 to 40 versts. The villages here are large, there are no little hamlets. There are churches and schools everywhere, the huts are of wood and there are some with two storeys.

Towards the evening the road and the puddles begin to freeze, and at night there is a regular frost, one wants an extra fur coat . . . Brrr! It's jolting, for the mud is transformed into hard lumps. One's soul is shaken inside out. . . . Towards daybreak one is fearfully exhausted by the cold, by the jolting and the jingle of the bells: one has a passionate longing for warmth and a bed. While they change horses one curls up in some corner and at once drops asleep, and a minute later the driver pulls at one's sleeve and says: "Get up, friend, it is time to start." On the second night I had acute toothache in my heels. It was unbearably painful. I wondered whether they were frostbitten.

I can't write more though. The "president," that is the district police inspector, has come. We have made acquaintance and are beginning to talk. Goodbye till to-morrow.

TOMSK,
May 16.

It seems my strong boots were the cause, being too tight at the back. My sweet Misha, if you ever have any children, which I have no doubt you will, the advice I bequeath to them is not to run after cheap goods. Cheapness in Russian goods is the label of worthlessness. To my mind it is better to go barefoot than to wear cheap boots. Picture my agony! I keep getting out of the chaise, sitting down on damp ground and taking off my boots to rest my heels. So comfortable in the frost! I had to buy felt over-boots in Ishim. . . . So I drove in felt boots till they collapsed from the mud and the damp.

In the morning between five and six o'clock one drinks tea at a hut. Tea on a journey is a great blessing. I know its value now, and drink it with the fury of a Yanov. It warms one through and drives away sleep; one eats a lot of bread with it, and in the absence of other nourishment, bread has to be eaten in great quantities; that is why peasants eat so much bread and farinaceous food. One drinks tea and talks with the peasant women, who are sensible, tenderhearted, industrious, as well as being devoted mothers and more free than in European Russia; their husbands don't abuse or beat them, because they are as tall, as strong, and as clever as their lords and masters are. They act as drivers when their husbands are away from home; they like making jokes. They are not severe with their children, they spoil them. The children sleep on soft beds and lie as long as they like, drink tea and eat with the men, and scold the latter when they laugh at them affectionately. There is no diphtheria. Malignant smallpox is prevalent here, but strange to say, it is less contagious than in other parts of the world; two or three catch it and die and that is the end of the epidemic. There are no hospitals or doctors. The doctoring is done by feldshers. Bleeding and cupping are done on a grandiose, brutal scale. I examined a Jew with cancer in the liver. The Jew was exhausted, hardly breathing, but that did not prevent the feldsher from cupping him twelve times. Apropos of the Jews. Here they till the land, work as drivers and ferry-men, trade and are called Krestyany, [Translator's Note: I.e., Peasants, literally "Christians."] because they are de jure and de facto Krestyany. They enjoy universal respect, and according to the "president" they are not infrequently chosen as village elders. I saw a tall thin Jew who scowled with disgust and spat when the "president" told indecent stories: a chaste soul; his wife makes splendid fish-soup. The wife of the Jew who had cancer regaled me with pike caviare and with most delicious white bread. One hears nothing of exploitation by the Jews. And, by the way, about the Poles. There are a few exiles here, sent from Poland in 1864. They are good, hospitable, and very refined people. Some of them live in a very wealthy way; others are very poor, and serve as clerks at the stations. Upon the amnesty the former went back to their own country, but soon returned to Siberia again—here they are better off; the latter dream of their native land, though they are old and infirm. At Ishim a wealthy Pole, Pan Zalyessky, who has a daughter like Sasha Kiselyov, for a rouble gave me an excellent dinner and a room to sleep in; he keeps an inn and has become a money-grubber to the marrow of his bones; he fleeces everyone, but yet one feels the Polish gentleman in his manner, in the way the meals are served, in everything. He does not go back to Poland through greed, and through greed endures snow till St. Nikolay's day; when he dies his daughter, who was born at Ishim, will remain here for ever and so will multiply the black eyes and soft features in Siberia! This casual intermixture of blood is to the good, for the Siberian people are not beautiful. There are no dark-haired people. Perhaps you would like me to write about the Tatars? Certainly. There are very few of them here. They are good people. In the province of Kazan everyone speaks well of them, even the priests, and in Siberia they are "better than the Russians" as the "president" said to me in the presence of Russians, who assented to this by their silence. My God, how rich Russia is in good people! If it were not for the cold which deprives Siberia of the summer, and if it were not for the officials who corrupt the peasants and the exiles, Siberia would be the richest and happiest of lands.

I have nothing for dinner. Sensible people usually take twenty pounds of provisions when they go to Tomsk. It seems I was a fool and so I have fed for a fortnight on nothing but milk and eggs, which are boiled so that the yolk is hard and the white is soft. One is sick of such fare in two days. I have only twice had dinner during the whole journey, not counting the Jewess's fish-soup, which I swallowed after I had had enough to eat with my tea. I have not had any vodka: the Siberian vodka is disgusting, and indeed, I got out of the habit of taking it while I was on the way to Ekaterinburg. One ought to drink vodka: it stimulates the brain, dull and apathetic from travelling, which makes one stupid and feeble.

Stop! I can't write: the editor of the Sibirsky Vyestnik, N., a local Nozdryov, a drunkard and a rake, has come to make my acquaintance.

N. has drunk some beer and gone away. I continue.

For the first three days of my journey my collarbones, my shoulders and my vertebrae ached from the shaking and jolting. I couldn't stand or sit or lie. . . . But on the other hand, all pains in my head and chest have vanished, my appetite has developed incredibly, and my haemorrhoids have subsided completely. The overstrain, the constant worry with luggage and so on, and perhaps the farewell drinking parties in Moscow, had brought on spitting of blood in the mornings, which induced something like depression, arousing gloomy thoughts, but towards the end of the journey it has left off; now I haven't even a cough. It is a long time since I have coughed so little as now, after being for a fortnight in the open air. After the first three days of travelling my body grew used to the jolting, and in time I did not notice the coming of midday and then of evening and night. The time flew by rapidly as it does in serious illness. You think it is scarcely midday when the peasants say—"You ought to put up for the night, sir, or we may lose our way in the dark"; you look at your watch, and it is actually eight o'clock.

They drive quickly, but the speed is nothing remarkable. Probably I have come upon the roads in bad condition, and in winter travelling would have been quicker. They dash uphill at a gallop, and before setting off and before the driver gets on the box, the horses need two or three men to hold them. The horses remind me of the fire brigade horses in Moscow. One day we nearly ran over an old woman, and another time almost dashed into an etape. Now, would you like an adventure for which I am indebted to Siberian driving? Only I beg mother not to wail and lament, for it all ended well. On the 6th of May towards daybreak I was being driven with two horses by a very nice old man. It was a little chaise, I was drowsy, and, to while away the time, watched the gleaming of zigzagging lights in the fields and birch copses—it was last year's grass on fire; it is their habit here to burn it. Suddenly I hear the swift rattle of wheels, a post-cart at full speed comes flying towards us like a bird, my old man hastens to move to the right, the three horses dash by, and I see in the dusk a huge heavy post-cart with a driver for the return journey in it. It was followed by a second cart also going at full speed. We made haste to move aside to the right. To my great amazement and alarm the approaching cart moved not to its right, but its left . . . I hardly had time to think, "Good heavens! we shall run into each other," when there was a desperate crash, the horses were mixed up in a dark blur, the yokes fell off, my chaise reared up into the air, and I flew to the ground, and my luggage on the top of me. But that was not all . . . A third cart was dashing upon us. This really ought to have smashed me and my luggage to atoms but, thank God! I was not asleep, I broke no bones in the fall, and managed to jump up so quickly that I was able to get out of the way. "Stop," I bawled to the third cart, "Stop!" The third dashed up to the second and stopped. Of course if I were able to sleep in a chaise, or if the third cart had followed instantly on the second, I should certainly have come back a cripple or a headless horseman. The results of the collision were broken shafts, torn traces, yokes and luggage scattered on the ground, the horses scared and harassed, and the alarming feeling that we had just been in danger. It turned out that the first driver had lashed up the horses; while in the other two carts the drivers were asleep, and the horses followed the first team with no one controlling them. On recovering from the shock, my old man and the other three men fell to abusing each other ferociously. Oh, how they swore! I thought it would end in a fight. You can't imagine the feeling of isolation in the middle of that savage swearing crew in the open country, just before dawn, in sight of the fires far and near consuming the grass, but not warming the cold night air! Oh, how heavy my heart was! One listened to the swearing, looked at the broken shafts and at one's tormented luggage, and it seemed as though one were cast away in another world, as though one would be crushed in a moment. . . . After an hour's abuse my old man began splicing together the shafts with cord and tying up the traces; my straps were forced into the service too. We got to the station somehow, crawling along and stopping from time to time.

After five or six days rain with high winds began. It rained day and night. The leather overcoat came to the rescue and kept me safe from rain and wind. It's a wonderful coat. The mud was almost impassable, the drivers began to be unwilling to go on at night. But what was worst of all, and what I shall never forget, was crossing the rivers. One reaches a river at night.... One begins shouting and so does the driver.... Rain, wind, pieces of ice glide down the river, there is a sound of splashing.... And to add to our gaiety there is the cry of a heron. Herons live on the Siberian rivers, so it seems they don't consider the climate but the geographical position.... Well, an hour later, in the darkness, a huge ferry-boat of the shape of a barge comes into sight with huge oars that look like the pincers of a crab. The ferry-men are a rowdy set, for the most part exiles banished here by the verdict of society for their vicious life. They use insufferably bad language, shout, and ask for money for vodka.... The ferrying across takes a long, long time ... an agonizingly long time. The ferryboat crawls. Again the feeling of loneliness, and the heron seems calling on purpose, as though he means to say: "Don't be frightened, old man, I am here, the Lintvaryovs have sent me here from the Psyol."

On the 7th of May when I asked for horses the driver said the Irtysh had overflowed its banks and flooded the meadows, that Kuzma had set off the day before and had difficulty in getting back, and that I could not go, but must wait.... I asked: "Wait till when?" Answer: "The Lord only knows!" That was vague. Besides, I had taken a vow to get rid on the journey of two of my vices which were a source of considerable expense, trouble, and inconvenience; I mean my readiness to give in, and be overpersuaded. I am quick to agree, and so I have had to travel anyhow, sometimes to pay double and to wait for hours at a time. I had taken to refusing to agree and to believe—and my sides have ached less. For instance, they bring out not a proper carriage but a common, jolting cart. I refuse to travel in the jolting cart, I insist, and the carriage is sure to appear, though they may have declared that there was no such thing in the whole village, and so on. Well, I suspected that the Irtysh floods were invented simply to avoid driving me by night through the mud. I protested and told them to start. The peasant who had heard of the floods from Kuzma, and had not himself seen them, scratched himself and consented; the old men encouraged him, saying that when they were young and used to drive, they were afraid of nothing. We set off. Much rain, a vicious wind, cold ... and felt boots on my feet. Do you know what felt boots are like when they are soaked? They are like boots of jelly. We drive on and on, and behold, there lies stretched before my eyes an immense lake from which the earth appears in patches here and there, and bushes stand out: these are the flooded meadows. In the distance stretches the steep bank of the Irtysh, on which there are white streaks of snow. . . . We begin driving through the lake. We might have turned back, but obstinacy prevented me, and an incomprehensible impulse of defiance mastered me—that impulse which made me bathe from the yacht in the middle of the Black Sea and has impelled me to not a few acts of folly . . . I suppose it is a special neurosis. We drive on and make for the little islands and strips of land. The direction is indicated by bridges and planks; they have been washed away. To cross by them we had to unharness the horses and lead them over one by one. . . . The driver unharnesses the horses, I jump out into the water in my felt boots and hold them. . . . A pleasant diversion! And the rain and wind. . . . Queen of Heaven! At last we get to a little island where there stands a hut without a roof. . . . Wet horses are wandering about in the wet dung. A peasant with a long stick comes out of the hut and undertakes to guide us. He measures the depth of the water with his stick, and tries the ground. He led us out—God bless him for it!—on to a long strip of ground which he called "the ridge." He instructs us that we must keep to the right—or perhaps it was to the left, I don't remember—and get on to another ridge. This we do. My felt boots are soaking and squelching, my socks are snuffling. The driver says nothing and clicks dejectedly to his horses. He would gladly turn back, but by now it was late, it was dark. . . . At last—oh, joy!—we reach the Irtysh. . . . The further bank is steep but the near bank is sloping. The near one is hollowed out, looks slippery, hateful, not a trace of vegetation. . . . The turbid water splashes upon it with crests of white foam, and dashes back again as though disgusted at touching the uncouth slippery bank on which it seems that none but toads and the souls of murderers could live. . . . The Irtysh makes no loud or roaring sound, but it sounds as though it were hammering on coffins in its depths. . . . A damnable impression! The further bank is steep, dark brown, desolate. . . .

There is a hut; the ferry-men live in it. One of them comes out and announces that it is impossible to work the ferry as a storm has come up. The river, they said, was wide, and the wind was strong. And so I had to stay the night at the hut. . . . I remember the night. The snoring of the ferry-men and my driver, the roar of the wind, the patter of the rain, the mutterings of the Irtysh. . . . Before going to sleep I wrote a letter to Marya Vladimirovna; I was reminded of the Bozharovsky pool.

In the morning they were unwilling to ferry me across: there was a high wind. We had to row across in the boat. I am rowed across the river, while the rain comes lashing down, the wind blows, my luggage is drenched and my felt boots, which had been dried overnight in the oven, become jelly again. Oh, the darling leather coat! If I did not catch cold I owe it entirely to that. When I come back you must reward it with an anointing of tallow or castor-oil. On the bank I sat for a whole hour on my portmanteau waiting for horses to come from the village. I remember it was very slippery clambering up the bank. In the village I warmed myself and had some tea. Some exiles came to beg for alms. Every family makes forty pounds of wheaten flour into bread for them every day. It's a kind of forced tribute.

The exiles take the bread and sell it for drink at the tavern. One exile, a tattered, closely shaven old man, whose eyes had been knocked out in the tavern by his fellow-exiles, hearing that there was a traveller in the room and taking me for a merchant, began singing and repeating the prayers. He recited the prayer for health and for the rest of the soul, and sang the Easter hymn, "Let the Lord arise," and "With thy Saints, O Lord"— goodness knows what he didn't sing! Then he began telling lies, saying that he was a Moscow merchant. I noticed how this drunken creature despised the peasants upon whom he was living.

On the 11th I drove with posting horses. I read the books of complaints at the posting station in my boredom.

. . . On the 12th of May they would not give me horses, saying that I could not drive, because the River Ob had overflowed its banks and flooded all the meadows. They advised me to turn off the track as far as Krasny Yar; then go by boat twelve versts to Dubrovin, and at Dubrovin you can get posting horses. . . . I drove with private horses as far as Krasny Yar. I arrive in the morning; I am told there is a boat, but that I must wait a little as the grandfather had sent the workman to row the president's secretary to Dubrovin in it. Very well, we will wait. . . . An hour passes, a second, a third. . . . Midday arrives, then evening. . . . Allah kerim, what a lot of tea I drank, what a lot of bread I ate, what a lot of thoughts I thought! And what a lot I slept! Night came on and still no boat. . . . Early morning came. . . . At last at nine o'clock the workmen returned. . . . Thank heaven, we are afloat at last! And how pleasant it is! The air is still, the oarsmen are good, the islands are beautiful. . . . The floods caught men and cattle unawares and I see peasant women rowing in boats to the islands to milk the cows. And the cows are lean and dejected. There is absolutely no grass for them, owing to the cold. I was rowed twelve versts. At the station of Dubrovin I had tea, and for tea they gave me, can you imagine! waffles. . . . I suppose the woman of the house was an exile or the wife of an exile. At the next station an old clerk, a Pole, to whom I gave some antipyrin for his headache, complained of his poverty, and said Count Sapyega, a Pole who was a gentleman-in-waiting at the Austrian Court, and who assisted his fellow-countrymen, had lately arrived there on his way to Siberia, "He stayed near the station," said the clerk, "and I didn't know it! Holy Mother! He would have helped me! I wrote to him at Vienna, but I got no answer, . . ." and so on. Why am I not a Sapyega? I would send this poor fellow to his own country.

On the 14th of May again they would not give me horses. The Tom was flooded. How vexatious! It meant not mere vexation but despair! Fifty versts from Tomsk and how unexpected! A woman in my place would have sobbed. Some kind-hearted people found a solution for me. "Drive on, sir, as far as the Tom, it is only six versts from here; there they will row you across to Yar, and Ilya Markovitch will take you on from there to Tomsk." I hired a horse and drove to the Tom, to the place where the boat was to be. I drove—there was no boat. They told me it had just set off with the post, and was hardly likely to return as there was such a wind. I began waiting. . . . The ground was covered with snow, it rained and hailed and the wind blew. . . . One hour passed, a second, and no boat. Fate was laughing at me. I returned to the station. There the driver of the mail with three posting horses was just setting off for the Tom. I told him there was no boat. He stayed. Fate rewarded me; the clerk in response to my hesitating inquiry whether there was anything to eat told me the woman of the house had some cabbage soup. Oh, rapture! Oh, radiant day! And the daughter of the house did in fact give me some excellent cabbage soup, with some capital meat with roast potatoes and cucumbers. I have not had such a dinner since I was at Pan Zalyessky's. After the potatoes I let myself go, and made myself some coffee.

Towards evening the mail driver, an elderly man who had evidently endured a good deal in his day, and who did not venture to sit down in my presence, began preparing to set off to the Tom. I did the same. We drove off. As soon as we reached the river the boat came into sight—a long boat: I have never dreamed of a boat so long. While the post was being loaded on to the boat I witnessed a strange phenomenon—there was a peal of thunder, a queer thing in a cold wind, with snow on the ground. They loaded up and rowed off. My sweet Misha, forgive me for being so rejoiced that I did not bring you with me! How sensible it was of me not to take anyone with me! At first our boat floated over a meadow near willow-bushes. . . . As is common before a storm or during a storm, a violent wind suddenly sprang up on the water and stirred up the waves. The boatman who was sitting at the helm advised our waiting in the willow-bushes till the storm was over. They answered him that if the storm grew worse, they might stay in the willow-bushes till night and be drowned all the same. They proceeded to settle it by majority of votes, and decided to row on. An evil mocking fate is mine. Oh, why these jests? We rowed on in silence, concentrating our thoughts. . . . I remember the figure of the mail-driver, a man of varied experiences. I remember the little soldier who suddenly became as crimson as cherry juice. I thought, if the boat upsets I will fling off my fur coat and my leather coat . . . then my felt boots, then . . . and so on. . . . But the bank came nearer and nearer, one's soul felt easier and easier, one's heart throbbed with joy, one heaved deep sighs as though one could breathe freely at last, and leapt on the wet slippery bank. . . . Thank God!

At Ilya Markovitch's, the converted Jew's, I was told that I could not drive at night; the road was bad; that I must remain till next day. Very good, I stayed. After tea I sat down to write you this letter, interrupted by the visit of the "president." The president is a rich mixture of Nozdryov, Hlestakov and a cur. A drunkard, a rake, a liar, a singer, a story-teller, and with all that a good-natured man. He had brought with him a big trunk stuffed full of business papers, a bedstead and mattress, a gun, and a secretary. The secretary is an excellent, well-educated man, a protesting liberal who has studied in Petersburg, and is free in his ideas; I don't know how he came to Siberia, he is infected to the marrow of his bones with every sort of disease, and is taking to drink, thanks to his principal, who calls him Kolya.

The representative of authority sends for a cordial. "Doctor," he bawls, "drink another glass, I beseech you humbly!" Of course, I drink it. The representative of authority drinks soundly, lies outrageously, uses shameless language. We go to bed. In the morning a cordial is sent for again. They swill the cordial till ten o'clock and at last they go. The converted Jew, Ilya Markovitch, whom the peasants here idolize—so I was told—gave me horses to drive to Tomsk.

The "president," the secretary and I got into the same conveyance. All the way the "president" told lies, drank out of the bottle, boasted that he did not take bribes, raved about the scenery, and shook his fist at the tramps that he met. We drove fifteen versts, then halt! The village of Brovkino.... We stop near a Jew's shop and go to take "rest and refreshment." The Jew runs to fetch us a cordial while his wife makes us some fish-soup, of which I have written to you already. The "president" gave orders that the sotsky, the desyatsky, and the road contractor should come to him, and in his drunkenness began reproving them, not the least restrained by my presence. He swore like a Tatar.

I soon parted from the "president," and on the evening of the 15th of May by an appalling road reached Tomsk. During the last two days I have only done seventy versts; you can imagine what the roads are like!

In Tomsk the mud was almost impassable. Of the town and the manner of living here I will write in a day or two, but good-bye for now—I am tired of writing.

There are no poplars. The Kuvshinnikov General was lying. I have seen no nightingales. There are magpies and cuckoos.

I received a telegram of eighty words from Suvorin to-day.

Excuse this letter's being like a hotch-potch. It's incoherent, but I can't help it. Sitting in an hotel room one can't write better. Excuse its being long, It's not my fault. My pen ran away with me—besides, I wanted to go on talking to you. It's three o'clock in the night. My hand is tired. The wick of the candle wants snuffing, I can hardly see. Write to me at Sahalin every four or five days. It seems that the post goes there, not only by sea but across Siberia, so I shall get letters frequently.

All the Tomsk people tell me that there has not been a spring so cold and rainy as this one since 1842. Half Tomsk is under water. My luck!

I am eating sweets.

I shall have to stay at Tomsk till the rains are over. They say the road to Irkutsk is awful.

TOMSK,
May 20.

It is Trinity Sunday with you, while with us even the willow has not yet come out, and there is still snow on the banks of the Tom. To-morrow I am starting for Irkutsk. I am rested. There is no need for hurry, as steam navigation on Lake Baikal does not begin till the 10th of June; but I shall go all the same.

I am alive and well, my money is safe; I have a slight pain in my right eye. It aches.

. . . Everyone advises me to go back across America, as they say one may die of boredom in the Volunteer Fleet; it's all military discipline and red tape regulations, and they don't often touch at a port.

To fill up my time I have been writing some impressions of my journey and sending them to Novoye Vremya; you will read them soon after the 10th of June. I write a little about everything, chit-chat. I don't write for glory but from a financial point of view, and in consideration of the money I have had in advance.

Tomsk is a very dull town. To judge from the drunkards whose acquaintance I have made, and from the intellectual people who have come to the hotel to pay their respects to me, the inhabitants are very dull too.

In two and a half days I shall be in Krasnoyarsk, and in seven or eight in Irkutsk. It's fifteen hundred versts to Irkutsk. I have made myself coffee and am just going to drink it.

. . . After Tomsk the Taiga begins. We shall see it.

My greeting to all the Lintvaryovs and to our old Maryushka. I beg mother not to worry and not to put faith in bad dreams. Have the radishes succeeded? There are none here at all.

Keep well, don't worry about money—there will be plenty; don't try to spend less and spoil the summer for yourselves.

Selected Letters

TO A. S. SUVORIN.

TOMSK, May 20, 1890.

Greetings to you at last from Siberia, dear Alexey Sergeyevitch! I have missed you and our correspondence terribly.

I will begin from the beginning, however. At Tyumen I was told the first steamer to Tomsk went on the 18th of May. I had to do the journey with horses. For the first three days every joint and sinew ached, but afterwards I got used to the jolting and felt no more aches. Only the lack of sleep, the continual worry over the luggage, the jolting and the fasting brought on spitting of blood when I coughed, and this depressed my spirits, which were none too grand before. For the first few days it was bearable but then a cold wind began to blow, the windows of heaven were opened, the rivers flooded the meadows and roads, I was continually having to change my chaise for a boat. You'll read of my struggles with the floods and the mud in the article I enclose. I did not mention in it that my big high boots were tight, and that I waded through the mud and the water in my felt boots, and that my felt boots were soaked to jelly. The road was so abominable that during the last two days of my journey I only did seventy versts.

When I set off I promised to send you notes of my journey after Tomsk, since the road between Tyumen and Tomsk has been described a thousand times already. But in your telegram you have expressed the desire to get my impressions of Siberia as quickly as possible, and have even had the cruelty, sir, to reproach me with lapse of memory, as though I had forgotten you. It was absolutely impossible to write on the road. I kept a brief diary in pencil and can offer you now only what is written in that diary. To avoid writing at great length and getting mixed up, I divided all my impressions into chapters. I am sending you six chapters. They are written for you personally. I wrote for you only, and so have not been afraid of being too subjective, and have not been afraid of there being more of Chekhov's feelings and thoughts than of Siberia in them. If you find some lines interesting and worth printing, give them a profitable publicity, signing them with my name and printing them in separate chapters, a tablespoonful once an hour. The general title can be From Siberia, then From Trans-Baikalia, then From the Amur, and so on.

You shall have another helping from Irkutsk, for which I am starting to-morrow. I shall not be less than ten days on the journey—the road is bad. I shall send you a few chapters again, and shall send them whether you intend to print them or not. Read them and when you are tired of them telegraph to me "Shut up!"

I have been as hungry as a dog the whole way. I stuffed myself with bread so as not to dream of turbot, asparagus, and suchlike. I even dreamed of buckwheat porridge. I have dreamed of it for hours at a time.

At Tyumen I bought some sausage for the journey, but what sausage! When you take a bit in your mouth there's a sniff as though you had gone into a stable at the very moment when the coachmen were taking off their leg-wrappers; when you begin chewing it, you feel as though you had fastened your teeth into a dog's tail defiled with pitch. Tfoo! I ate some once or twice, and threw it away.

I have had one telegram and the letter from you in which you write that you want to bring out an encyclopaedic dictionary. I don't know why, but the news of that dictionary rejoiced me greatly. Do, my dear friend! If I am any use for working on it, I will devote November and December to you, and will spend those months in Petersburg. I will sit at it from morning till night.

I made a fair copy of my notes at Tomsk in horrid hotel surroundings, but I took trouble about it and was not without a desire to please you. I thought, he must be bored and hot in Feodosia, let him read about the cold. These notes will come to you instead of a letter which has been taking shape in my head during the whole journey. In return you must send to me at Sahalin all your critical reviews except the first two, which I have read; have Peshel's "Ethnology" sent me there too, except the first two instalments, which I have already.

The post to Sahalin goes both by sea and across Siberia, so if people write to me I shall get letters often. Don't lose my address—Island of Sahalin, Alexandrovsky Post.

Oh, the expense! Gewalt! Thanks to the floods, I had to pay the drivers double and almost treble, for it has been fiendishly hard work. My trunk, a very charming article, has turned out unsuitable for the journey; it takes a lot of room, pokes one in the ribs, and rattles, and worst of all threatens to burst open. "Don't take boxes on long journeys!" good people said to me, but I remembered this advice only when I had gone half-way. Well, I am leaving my trunk to reside permanently at Tomsk, and am buying instead of it a sort of leather carcase, which has the advantage that it can be tied so as to form two halves at the bottom of the chaise as one likes. I paid sixteen roubles for it. Next point. To travel to the Amur, changing one's conveyance at every station, is torture. You shatter both yourself and all your luggage. I was advised to buy a trap. I bought one to-day for one hundred and thirty roubles. If I don't succeed in selling it at Sryetensk, where my horse journey ends, I shall be in a fix and shall howl aloud. To-day I dined with the editor of the Sibirsky Vyestnik, a local Nozdryov, a broad nature. . . . He drank to the tune of six roubles.

Stop! They announce that the deputy police master wants to see me. What can it be?!?

My alarm was unnecessary. The police officer turns out to be devoted to literature and himself an author; he has come to pay his respects to me. He went home to fetch his play, and I believe intends to regale me with it. He is just coming again and preventing me from writing to you. . . .

. . . My greetings to Nastyusha and Boris. I should be genuinely delighted for their satisfaction to fling myself into the jaws of a tiger and call them to my aid, but, alas! I haven't reached the tigers here: the only furry animals I have seen so far in Siberia are many hares and one mouse.

Stop! The police officer has returned. He has not read me his drama though he brought it, but regaled me with a story. It's not bad, only too local. He showed me a nugget of gold. He asked for some vodka. I don't remember a single educated Siberian who has not asked for vodka on coming to see me. He told me he had a mistress, a married woman; he gave me a petition to the Tsar about divorce to read. . . .

How glad I am when I am forced to stop somewhere for the night! I no sooner roll into bed than I am asleep. Here, travelling and not sleeping at night, one prizes sleep above everything. There is no greater enjoyment in life than sleep when one is sleepy. In Moscow, in Russia generally, I never was sleepy as I understand the word now. I went to bed simply because one had to. But now! Another observation. On a journey one has no desire for spirits. I can't drink. I smoke a great deal. One's mind does not work well. I cannot put my thoughts together. Time flies rapidly, so that one scarcely notices it, from ten o'clock in the morning to seven o'clock in the evening. Evening comes quickly after morning. It's just the same when one is seriously ill. The wind and the rain have made my face all scaly, and when I look in the looking-glass I don't recognize my once noble features.

I am not going to describe Tomsk. All the towns are alike in Russia. Tomsk is a dull and intemperate town. There are absolutely no good-looking women, and the disregard for justice is Asiatic. The town is remarkable for the fact that governors die in it.

If my letters are short, careless, or dry, don't be cross, for one cannot always be oneself on a journey and write as one wants to. The ink is bad, and there is always a hair or a splodge on one's pen.

TO HIS SISTER.

KRASNOYARSK, May 28, 1890.

What a deadly road! It was all we could do to crawl to Krasnoyarsk and my trap had to be repaired twice. The first thing to be broken was the vertical piece of iron connecting the front of the carriage with the axle; then the so-called circle under the front broke. I have never in all my life seen such a road—such impassable mud and such an utterly neglected road. I am going to write about its horrors to the Novoye Vremya, and so won't talk about it now.

The last three stations have been splendid; as one comes down to Krasnoyarsk one seems to be getting into a different world. You come out of the forest into a plain which is like our Donets steppe, but here the mountain ridges are grander. The sun shines its very best and the birch-trees are out, though three stations back the buds were not even bursting. Thank God, I have at last reached a summer in which there is neither rain nor a cold wind. Krasnoyarsk is a picturesque, cultured town; compared with it, Tomsk is "a pig in a skull-cap and the acme of mauvais ton." The streets are clean and paved, the houses are of stone and large, the churches are elegant.

I am alive and perfectly well. My money is all right, and so are my things; I lost my woollen stockings but soon found them again.

Apart from my trap, everything so far has been satisfactory and I have nothing to complain of. Only I am spending an awful lot of money.

Incompetence in the practical affairs of life is never felt so much as on a journey. I pay more than I need to, I do the wrong thing, and I say the wrong thing, and I am always expecting what does not happen.

... I shall be in Irkutsk in five or six days, shall spend as many days there, then drive on to Sryetensk—and that will be the end of my journey on land. For more than a fortnight I have been driving without a break, I think about nothing else, I live for nothing else; every morning I see the sunrise from beginning to end. I've grown so used to it that it seems as though all my life I had been driving and struggling with the muddy roads. When it does not rain, and there are no pits of mud on the road, one feels queer and even a little bored. And how filthy I am, what a rapscallion I look! What a state my luckless clothes are in!

... For mother's information: I have still a jar and a half of coffee; I feed on locusts and wild honey; I shall dine to-day at Irkutsk. The further east one gets the dearer everything is. Rye flour is seventy kopecks a pood, while on the other side of Tomsk it was twenty-five and twenty-seven kopecks per pood, and wheaten flour thirty kopecks. The tobacco sold in Siberia is vile and loathsome; I tremble because mine is nearly done.

... I am travelling with two lieutenants and an army doctor who are all on their way to the Amur. So my revolver is after all quite superfluous. In such company hell would have no terrors. We are just having tea at the station, and after tea we are going to have a look at the town.

I should have no objection to living in Krasnoyarsk. I can't think why this is a favourite place for sending exiles to.

Your Homo Sachaliensis,
A. CHEKHOV.

TO HIS BROTHER ALEXANDR.

IRKUTSK, June 5, 1890.

MY EUROPEAN BROTHER,

It is, of course, unpleasant to live in Siberia; but better to live in Siberia and feel oneself a man of moral worth, than to live in Petersburg with the reputation of a drunkard and a scoundrel. No reference to present company.

Siberia is a cold and long country. I drive on and on and see no end to it. I see little that is new or of interest, but I feel and experience a great deal. I have contended with flooded rivers, with cold, with impassable mud, hunger and sleepiness: such sensations as you could not get for a million in Moscow! You ought to come to Siberia. Ask the authorities to exile you.

The best of all Siberian towns is Irkutsk. Tomsk is not worth a brass farthing, and the district towns are no better than the Kryepkaya in which you were so heedlessly born. What is most provoking, there is nothing to eat in the district towns, and oh dear, how conscious one is of that on the journey! You get to a town and feel ready to eat a mountain; you arrive and—alack!—no sausage, no cheese, no meat, no herring even, but the same insipid eggs and milk as in the villages.

On the whole I am satisfied with my expedition, and don't regret having come. The travelling is hard, but the resting after it is delightful. I rest with enjoyment.

From Irkutsk I shall make for Baikal, which I shall cross by steamer; it's a thousand versts from the Baikal to the Amur, and thence I shall go by steamer to the Pacific, where the first thing I shall do is to have a bath and eat oysters.

I got here yesterday and went first of all to have a bath, then to bed. Oh, how I slept! I never understood what sleep meant till now.

I bless you with both hands.

Your Asiatic brother,
A. CHEKHOV.

TO A. N. PLESHTCHEYEV.

IRKUTSK, June 5, 1890.

A thousand greetings to you, dear Alexey Nikolaevitch. At last I have vanquished the most difficult three thousand versts; I am sitting in a decent hotel and can write. I have rigged myself out all in new things and, as far as possible, smart ones, for you cannot imagine how sick I was of my big muddy boots, of my sheepskin smelling of tar, of my overcoat covered with bits of hay, of dust and crumbs in my pockets, and of my extremely dirty linen. I looked such a ragamuffin on the journey that even the tramps eyed me askance; and then, as ill luck would have it, the cold winds and rain chapped my face and made it scaly like a fish. Now at last I am a European again, and I am conscious of it all over.

Well, what am I to write to you? It's all so long and so vast that one doesn't know where to begin. All my experiences in Siberia I divide into three periods. From Tyumen to Tomsk, fifteen hundred versts, terrible cold, day and night, sheepskin, felt boots, cold rains, winds and a desperate life-and-death struggle with the flooded rivers. The rivers had flooded the meadows and roads, and I was constantly exchanging my trap for a boat and floating like a Venetian on a gondola; the boats, the waiting on the bank for them, the rowing across, etc., all that took up so much time that during the last two days before reaching Tomsk, in spite of all my efforts, I only did seventy versts instead of four or five hundred. There were, moreover, some very uneasy and unpleasant moments, especially when the wind rose and began to buffet the boat. From Tomsk to Krasnoyarsk, five hundred versts, impassable mud, my chaise and I stuck in the mud like flies in thick jam. How many times I broke my chaise (it's my own property!) how many versts I walked! how bespattered my countenance and my clothes were! It was not driving but wading through mud. How I swore at it all! My brain would not work, I could do nothing but swear. I was utterly exhausted, and was very glad to reach the posting station at Krasnoyarsk. From Krasnoyarsk to Irkutsk, fifteen hundred and sixty-six versts, heat, smoke from the burning woods, and dust—dust in one's mouth, in one's nose, in one's pockets; when you look at yourself in the glass, you think your face has been painted. When, on reaching Irkutsk, I washed at the baths, the soapsuds off my head were not white but of an ashen brown colour, as though I were washing a horse.

When I get home I will tell you about the Yenissey and the Taiga—very interesting and curious, for it is something quite new to a European; everything else is ordinary and monotonous. Roughly speaking, the scenery of Siberia is not very different from that of European Russia; there are differences, but they are not very noticeable. Travelling is perfectly safe.

Robbers and highwaymen are all nonsense and fairy tales. A revolver is utterly unnecessary, and you are as safe at night in the forest as you are by day on the Nevsky Prospect. It's different for anyone travelling on foot. . . .

TO N. A. LEIKIN.

IRKUTSK, June 5, 1890.

    Greetings, dear Nikolay Alexandrovitch!

    I send you heartfelt good wishes from Irkutsk, from the depths of Siberia. I reached Irkutsk last night and was very glad to have arrived, as I was exhausted by the journey and missed friends and relations, to whom I had not written for ages. Well, what is there of interest to write to you? I will begin by telling you that the journey is extraordinarily long. From Tyumen to Irkutsk I have driven more than three thousand versts. From Tyumen to Tomsk I had cold and flooded rivers to contend with. The cold was awful; on Ascension Day there was frost and snow, so that I could not take off my sheepskin and felt boots until I reached the hotel at Tomsk. As for the floods, they were a veritable plague of Egypt. The rivers rose above their banks and overflowed the meadows, and with them the roads, for dozens of versts around. I was continually having to exchange my chaise for a boat, and one could not get a boat for nothing—for a good boat one had to pay with one's heart's blood, for one had to sit waiting on the bank for twenty-four hours at a stretch in the cold wind and the rain. . . . From Tomsk to Krasnoyarsk was a desperate struggle through impassable mud. My goodness, it frightens me to think of it! How often I had to mend my chaise, to walk, to swear, to get out of my chaise and get into it again, and so on! It sometimes happened that I was from six to ten hours getting from one station to another, and every time the chaise had to be mended it took from ten to fifteen hours. From Krasnoyarsk to Irkutsk was fearfully hot and dusty. Add to all that hunger, dust in one's nose, one's eyes glued together with sleep, the continual dread that something would get broken in the chaise (it is my own), and boredom. . . . Nevertheless I am well content, and I thank God that He has given me the strength and opportunity to make this journey. I have seen and experienced a great deal, and it has all been very new and interesting to me not as a literary man, but as a human being. The Yenissey, the Taiga, the stations, the drivers, the wild scenery, the wild life, the physical agonies caused by the discomforts of the journey, the enjoyment I got from rest—all taken together is so delightful that I can't describe it. The mere fact that I have been for more than a month in the open air is interesting and healthy; every day for a month I have seen the sunrise. . . .

TO HIS SISTER.

IRKUTSK, June 6, 1890.

    Greetings to you, dear mother, Ivan, Masha and Misha, and all of you! In my last long letter I wrote to you that the mountains near Krasnoyarsk are like the Donets Ridge, but that's not true; when I looked at them from the street I saw they were like high walls surrounding the city, and I was vividly reminded of the Caucasus. And when towards evening I left the town and was crossing the Yenissey, I saw on the other bank mountains that were exactly like the Caucasus, as misty and dreamy. The Yenissey is a broad, swift, winding river, beautiful, finer than the Volga. And the ferry across it is wonderful, ingeniously constructed, moving against the current; I will tell you when I am home about the construction of it. And so the mountains and the Yenissey are the first things original and new that I have met in Siberia. The mountains and the Yenissey have given me sensations which have made up to me a hundredfold for all the trials and troubles of the journey, and which have made me call Levitan a fool for being so stupid as not to come with me.

    The Taiga stretches unbroken from Krasnoyarsk to Irkutsk. The trees are not bigger than in Sokolniki, but not one driver knows how far it goes. There is no end to be seen to it. It stretches for hundreds of versts. No one knows who or what is in the Taiga, and it only happens in winter that people come through the Taiga from the far north with reindeer for bread. When you get to the top of a mountain and look down, you see a mountain before you, then another, mountains at the sides too—and all thickly covered with forest. It makes one feel almost frightened. That's the second thing original and new.

    From Krasnoyarsk it began to be hot and dusty. The heat was terrible. My sheepskin and cap lie buried away. The dust is in my mouth, in my nose, down my neck—tfoo! We were approaching Irkutsk—we had to cross the Angara by ferry. As though to mock us a high wind sprang up. My military companions and I, after dreaming for ten days of a bath, dinner, and sleep, stood on the bank and turned pale at the thought that we should have to spend the night not at Irkutsk, but in the village. The ferry could not succeed in reaching the bank. We stood an hour, a second, and—oh Heavens!—the ferry made an effort and reached the bank. Bravo, we shall have a bath, we shall have supper and sleep! Oh, how sweet to steam oneself, to eat, to sleep!

Irkutsk is a fine town. Quite a cultured town. There is a theatre, a museum, a town garden with a band, a good hotel. . . . No hideous fences, no absurd shop-signs, and no waste places with warming placards. There is a tavern called "Taganrog"; sugar costs twenty-four kopecks a pound, pine kernels six kopecks a pound.

I am quite well. My money is safe. I am saving up my coffee for Sahalin. I have splendid tea here, after which I am aware of an agreeable excitement. I see Chinamen. They are a good-natured and intelligent people. At the Siberian bank they gave me money at once, received me cordially, regaled me with cigarettes, and invited me to their summer villa. There is a magnificent confectioner's but everything is fiendishly dear. The pavements are of wood.

Last night I drove with the officers about the town. We heard someone cry "help" six times. It must have been someone being murdered. We went to look, but could not find anyone.

The cabs in Irkutsk have springs. It is a better town than Ekaterinburg or Tomsk. Quite European.

Have a Mass celebrated on June 17th, and keep the 29th as festively as you can; I shall be with you in thought and you must drink my health.

Everything I have is crumpled, dirty, torn! I look like a pickpocket.

I shall not bring you any furs most likely. I do not know where they are sold, and I am too lazy to ask.

One must take at least two big pillows for a journey and dark pillow cases are essential.

What is Ivan doing? Where has he been? Has he been to the south? I am going from Irkutsk to Baikal. My companions are preparing for seasickness.

My big boots have grown looser with wearing, and don't hurt my heels now.

I have ordered buckwheat porridge for to-morrow. On the journey here I thought of curds and began having them with milk at the stations.

Did you get my postcards from the little towns? Keep them: I shall be able to judge from them how long the post takes. The post here is in no hurry.

IRKUTSK,
June 7, 1890.

... The steamer from Sryetensk leaves on June 20th. Good Christians, what am I to do till the 20th? How am I to dispose of myself? The journey to Sryetensk will only take five or six days. I have greatly altered the route of my journey. From Habarovsk I am going not to Nikolaevsk, but by the Ussuri to Vladivostok, and from there to Sahalin. I must have a look at the Ussuri region. At Vladivostok I shall bathe in the sea and eat oysters.

It was cold till I reached Kansk; from Kansk (see map) I began to go down to the south. Everything is as green as with you, even the oaks are out. The birches here are darker than in Russia, the green is not so sentimental. There are masses of the Russian white service-tree, which here takes the place of both the lilac and the cherry. They say they make an excellent jam from the service-tree. I tasted some of the fruit pickled; it was not bad.

Two lieutenants and an army doctor are travelling with me. They have received their travelling expenses three times over, but have spent all the money, though they are travelling in one carriage. They are sitting without a farthing, waiting for the pay department to send them some money. They are nice fellows. They have had from fifteen hundred to two thousand roubles each for travelling expenses, and the journey will cost them next to nothing (excluding, of course, the cost of the stopping places). They do nothing but pitch into everybody at hotels and stations so that people are positively afraid to present their bills. In their company I pay less than usual. ... To-day for the first time in my life I saw a Siberian cat. It has long soft fur, and a gentle disposition.

... I felt homesick and sent you a telegram today asking you to subscribe together and send me a long telegram. It would be nothing to all of you, inhabitants of Luka, to fling away five roubles.

... With whom is Mishka in love? To what happy woman is Ivanenko telling stories of his uncle? ... I must be in love with Jamais as I dreamed of her yesterday. In comparison with all the "jeunes Siberiennes" with their Yakut-Buriat physiognomies, who do not know how to dress, to sing, and to laugh, our Jamais, Drishka, and Gundassiha are simply queens. The Siberian girls and women are like frozen fish; one would have to be a walrus or a seal to get up a flirtation with them.

I am tired of my companions. It is much nicer travelling alone. I like silence better than anything on the journey and my companions talk and sing without stopping, and they talk of nothing but women. They borrowed a hundred and thirty-six roubles from me till to-morrow and have already spent it. They are regular sieves.

. . . The stations are sometimes thirty to thirty-five versts apart. You drive by night, you drive and drive, till you feel silly and light-headed, and if you venture to ask the driver how far it is to the next station, he will never say less than seventeen versts. That's particularly agonizing when you have to go at a walking pace along a muddy road full of holes, and when you are thirsty. I have learned to do without sleep; I don't mind a bit when they wake me. As a rule one does not sleep for one day and night, and then the next day at dinner-time there is a strained feeling in one's eyelids; in the evening and in the night towards daybreak of the third day, one dozes in the chaise and sometimes falls asleep for a minute as one sits; at dinner and after dinner at the stations, while the horses are being harnessed, one lolls on the sofa, and the real torture only begins at night. In the evening, after drinking five glasses of tea, one's face begins to burn, one's body feels limp all over and longs to bend backwards; one's eyes close, one's feet ache in one's big boots, one's brain is in a tangle. If I allow myself to put up for the night I fall into a dead sleep at once; if I have strength of will to go on, I drop asleep in the chaise, however violent the jolting may be; at the stations the drivers wake one up, as one has to get out of the chaise and pay for the journey. They wake one not so much by shouting and tugging at one's sleeve, as by the stink of garlic that issues from their lips; they smell of garlic and onion till they make me sick. I only learned to sleep in the chaise after Krasnoyarsk. On the way to Irkutsk I slept for fifty-eight versts, and was only once woken up. But the sleep one gets as one drives makes one feel no better. It's not real sleep, but a sort of unconscious condition, after which one's head is muddled and there's a bad taste in one's mouth.

Chinamen are like those decrepit old gentlemen dear Nikolay used to like drawing. Some of them have splendid pigtails.

The police came to see me at Tomsk. Towards eleven o'clock the waiter suddenly announced to me that the assistant police-master wanted to see me. What was this for? Could it be politics? Could they suspect me of being a Voltairian? I said to the waiter, "Ask him in." A gentleman with long moustaches walks in and introduces himself. It appears he is devoted to literature, writes himself, and has come to me in my hotel room as though to Mahomed at Mecca to worship. I'll tell you why I thought of him. Late in the autumn he is going to Petersburg, and I have foisted my trunk upon him and asked him to leave it at the Novoye Vremya office. You might keep that in mind in case any one of us or our friends goes to Petersburg.

You might, by the way, look out for a place in the country. When I get back to Russia I shall take five years' rest—that is, stay in one place and twiddle my thumbs. A place in the country will come in very handy. I think the money will be found, for things don't look bad. If I work off the money I have had in advance (half of it is worked off already) I shall certainly borrow two or three thousand in the spring, to be paid off over a period of five years. That will not be against my conscience, as I have already let the publishing department of the Novoye Vremya make two or three thousand out of my books, and I shall let them make more.

I think I shall not begin on any serious work till I am five and thirty. . . . I want to try personal life, of which I have had some before, but have not noticed it owing to various circumstances.

To-day I rubbed my leather coat with grease. It's a splendid coat. It has saved me from catching cold. My sheepskin is a capital thing, too: it serves me as a coat and a mattress, both. One is as warm in it as on a stove. It's wretched without pillows. Hay does not take the place of them, and with the continual friction there's a lot of dust from it which tickles one's face and prevents one from dozing. I haven't a single sheet. That's horrid too. And I ought to have taken some more trousers. The more luggage one has the better—there's less jolting and more comfort.

Good-bye, though. I have got nothing more to write about. My greetings to all.

STATION LISTVENITCHNAYA,
ON LAKE BAIKAL, June 13.

I am having an idiotic time. On the evening of the 11th of June, the day before yesterday, we set off from Irkutsk, in the fond hope of catching the Baikal steamer, which leaves at four o'clock in the morning. From Irkutsk to Baikal there are only three stations. At the first station they informed us that all the horses were exhausted and that it was therefore impossible to go. We had to put up for the night. Yesterday morning we set off from that station, and by midday we reached Baikal. We went to the harbour, and in answer to our inquiries were told that the steamer did not go till Friday the fifteenth. This meant that we should have to sit on the bank and look at the water and wait. As there is nothing that does not end in time, I have no objection to waiting, and always wait patiently; but the point is the steamer leaves Sryetensk on the 20th and sails down the Amur: if we don't catch it we must wait for the next steamer, which does not go till the 30th. Merciful Heavens, when shall I get to Sahalin!

We drove to Baikal along the bank of the Angara, which rises out of Lake Baikal and flows into the Yenissey. Look at the map. The banks are picturesque. Mountains and mountains, and dense forests on the mountains. The weather was exquisite still, sunny and warm; as I drove I felt I was exceptionally well; I felt so happy that I cannot describe it. It was perhaps the contrast after the stay at Irkutsk, and because the scenery on the Angara is like Switzerland. It is something new and original. We drove along the river bank, came to the mouth of the river, and turned to the left; then we came upon the bank of Lake Baikal, which in Siberia is called the sea. It is like a mirror. The other side, of course, is out of sight; it is ninety versts away. The banks are high, steep, stony, and covered with forest, to right and to left there are promontories which jut into the sea like Au-dag or the Tohtebel at Feodosia. It's like the Crimea. The station of Listvenitchnaya lies at the water's edge, and is strikingly like Yalta: if the houses were white it would be exactly like Yalta. Only there are no buildings on the mountains, as they are too overhanging and it is impossible to build on them.

We have taken a little barn of a lodging that reminds one of any of the Kraskovsky summer villas. Just outside the window, two or three yards from the wall, is Lake Baikal. We pay a rouble a day. The mountains, the forests, the mirror-like Baikal are all poisoned for me by the thought that we shall have to stay here till the fifteenth. What are we to do here? What is more, we don't know what there is for us to eat. The inhabitants feed upon nothing but garlic. There is neither meat nor fish. They have given us no milk, but have promised it. For a little white loaf they demanded sixteen kopecks. I bought some buckwheat and a piece of smoked pork, and asked them to make a thin porridge of it: it was not nice, but there was nothing to be done, I had to eat it. All the evening we hunted about the village to find someone who would sell us a hen, and found no one. . . . But there is vodka. The Russian is a great pig. If you ask him why he doesn't eat meat and fish he justifies himself by the absence of transport, ways and communications, and so on, and yet vodka is to be found in the remotest villages and as much of it as you please. And yet one would have supposed that it would have been much easier to obtain meat and fish than vodka, which is more expensive and more difficult to transport. . . . Yes, drinking vodka must be much more interesting than fishing in Lake Baikal or rearing cattle.

At midnight a little steamer arrived; we went to look at it, and seized the opportunity to ask if there was anything to eat. We were told that to-morrow we should be able to get dinner, but that now it was late, the kitchen fire was out, and so on. We thanked them for "to-morrow"—it was something to look forward to anyway! But alas! the captain came in and told us that at four o'clock in the morning the steamer was setting off for Kultuk. We thanked him. In the refreshment bar, where there was not room to turn round, we drank a bottle of sour beer (thirty-five kopecks), and saw on a plate some amber beads—it was salmon caviare. We returned home, and to sleep. I am sick of sleeping. Every day one has to put down one's sheepskin with the wool upwards, under one's head one puts a folded greatcoat and a pillow, and one sleeps on this heap in one's waistcoat and trousers. . . . Civilization, where art thou?

To-day there is rain and Lake Baikal is plunged in mist. "Interesting," Semaskho would say. It's dull. One ought to sit down and write, but one can never work in bad weather. One has a foreboding of merciless boredom; if I were alone I should not mind but there are two lieutenants and an army doctor with me, who are fond of talking and arguing. They don't understand much but they talk about everything. One of the lieutenants, moreover, is a bit of a Hlestakov and a braggart. When one is travelling one absolutely must be alone. To sit in a chaise or in a room alone with one's thoughts is much more interesting than being with people.

Congratulate me: I sold my own carriage at Irkutsk. How much I gained on it I won't say, or mother would fall into a faint and not sleep for five nights.

Your Homo Sachaliensis,
A. CHEKHOV.

TO HIS MOTHER.

STEAMER "YERMAK," June 20, 1890.

Greeting, dear ones at home!

At last I can take off my heavy muddy boots, my shabby breeches, and my blue shirt which is shiny with dust and sweat; I can wash and dress like a human being. I am not sitting in a chaise but in a first-class cabin of the steamer Yermak. This change took place ten days ago, and this is how it happened. I wrote to you from Listvenitchnaya that I was late for the Baikal steamer, that I had to cross Lake Baikal on Friday instead of Tuesday, and that owing to this I should only be able to catch the Amur steamer on the 30th. But fate is capricious, and often plays us tricks we do not expect. On Thursday morning I went out for a walk on the shores of Lake Baikal; behold—the funnel of one of the little steamers is smoking. I inquire where the steamer is going. They tell me, "Across the sea" to Klyuevo; some merchant had hired it to take his waggons of goods across the Lake. We, too, wanted to cross "the sea" and to go to Boyarskaya station. I inquire how many versts from Klyuevo to Boyarskaya. They tell me twenty-seven. I run back to my companions and beg them to take the risk of going to Klyuevo. I say the "risk" because, going to Klyuevo where there is nothing but a harbour and a watchman's hut, we ran the risk of not finding horses, having to stay on at Klyuevo, and being late for Friday's steamer, which for us would be worse than Igor's death, as we should have to wait till Tuesday. My companions consented. We gathered together our belongings, with cheerful legs stepped on to the steamer and straight to the refreshment bar: soup, for the love of God! Half my kingdom for a plate of soup! The refreshment bar was very nasty and cramped; but the cook, Grigory Ivanitch, who had been a house-serf at Voronezh, turned out to be at the tip-top of his profession. He fed us magnificently. The weather was still and sunny. The water of Lake Baikal is the colour of turquoise, more transparent than the Black Sea. They say that in deep places you can see the bottom over a verst below; and I myself have seen to such a depth, with rocks and mountains plunged in the turquoise-blue, that it sent a shiver all over me. Our journey over Lake Baikal was wonderful. I shall never forget it as long as I live. But I will tell you what was not nice. We travelled third class, and the whole deck was occupied by the waggon-horses, which were wild as mad things. These horses gave a special character to our crossing: it seemed as though we were in a brigand's steamer. At Klyuevo the watchman undertook to convey our luggage to the station; he drove the cart while we walked along the very picturesque shore. Levitan was an ass not to come with me. The way was through woods: on the right, woods running uphill; on the left, woods running down to the Lake. Such ravines, such crags! The colouring of Lake Baikal is soft and warm. It was, by the way, very warm. After walking eight versts we reached the station of Myskan, where a Kyahtan official, who was also on his travels, regaled us with excellent tea, and where we got the horses for Boyarskaya; and so we set off on Thursday instead of Friday; what is more, we got twenty-four hours in advance of the post, which usually takes all the horses at the station. We began driving as fast as we could, cherishing a faint hope of reaching Sryetensk by the 20th. I will tell you when we meet about my journey along the bank of the Selenga and across Transbaikalia. Now I will only say that Selenga is one continuous loneliness, and in Transbaikalia I found everything I wanted: the Caucasus, and the valley of the Psyol, and the Zvenigorod district, and the Don. By day you gallop through the Caucasus, at night along the steppe of the Don; in the morning, rousing yourself from slumber, behold the province of Poltava—and so for the whole thousand versts. Verhneudinsk is a nice little town. Tchita is a wretched place, in the style of Sumy. I need hardly say that we had no time to think of sleep or dinner. One gallops on thinking of nothing but the chance that at the next station we might not get horses, and might be kept five or six hours. We did two hundred versts in twenty-four hours—one can't do more than that in the summer. We were stupefied. The heat was fearful by day, while at night it was so cold that I had to put on my leather coat over my cloth one. One night I even wore my sheepskin. Well, we drove on and on, and reached Sryetensk this morning just an hour before the steamer left, giving the drivers from the last two stations a rouble each for themselves.

And so my horse-journey is over. It has lasted two months (I set out on the 21st of April). If we exclude the time spent on the railway and the steamer, the three days spent in Ekaterinburg, the week in Tomsk, the day in Krasnoyarsk, the week in Irkutsk, the two days on the shores of Lake Baikal, and the days wasted in waiting for boats to cross the floods, you can judge of the rate at which I have driven. My journey has been most successful, I wish nothing better for anyone. I have not once been ill, and of the mass of things I had with me I have lost nothing but a penknife, the strap off my trunk, and a little jar of carbolic ointment. My money is safe. It is not often that anyone succeeds in travelling a thousand versts so well.

I have grown so used to driving that now I don't feel like myself, and cannot believe that I am not in a chaise and that I don't hear the rattling and the jingling of the bells. It seems strange that when I go to bed I can stretch out my legs full length, and that my face is not covered with dust. But what is stranger still is that the bottle of brandy Kuvshinnikov gave me has not been broken, and that the brandy is still in it, every drop of it. I have vowed not to uncork it except on the shore of the Pacific.

I am sailing down the Shilka, which runs into the Amur at the Pokrovskaya Stanitsa. The river is not broader than the Psyol, it is even narrower. The shores are stony: there are crags and forests. It is absolutely wild. . . . We tack about to avoid foundering on a sandbank, or running our helm into the banks: steamers and barges often do so in the rapids. It's stifling. We have just stopped at Ust-Kara, where we have landed five or six convicts. There are mines here and a convict prison.

Yesterday we were at Nertchinsk. The little town is nothing to boast of, but one could live there.

And how are you, messieurs and mesdames? I know positively nothing about you. You might subscribe twopence each and send me a full telegram.

The steamer will stay the night at Gorbitsa. The nights here are foggy, sailing is dangerous, I shall send off this letter at Gorbitsa.

... I am going first class because my companions are in the second. I have got away from them. We have driven together (three in one chaise), we have slept together and are sick of each other, especially I of them.

My handwriting is very bad, shaky. That is because the steamer rocks. It's difficult to write.

I broke off here. I went to my lieutenants and had tea. They have both had a long sleep and were in a very cordial mood. One of them, Lieutenant N. (the surname jars upon my ear), is in the infantry; he is a tall, well-fed, loud-voiced Courlander, a great braggart and Hlestakov, who sings songs from every opera, but has no more ear than a smoked herring, an unlucky fellow who has squandered all the money for his travelling expenses, knows all Mickiewicz by heart, is ill-bred, far too unreserved, and babbles till it makes you sick. Like me, he is fond of talking about his uncles and aunts. The other lieutenant, M., a geographer, is a quiet, modest, thoroughly well-educated fellow. If it were not for N., I could travel with the other for a million versts without being bored. But with N., who intrudes into every conversation, the other bores me too.... I believe we are reaching Gorbitsa.

To-morrow I will make up the form of a telegram which you must send me to Sahalin. I will try to put all I want to know in thirty words, and you must try and keep strictly to the pattern.

The gad-flies bite.

TO N. A. LEIKIN.

GORBITSA, June 20, 1890.

Greetings, dear Nikolay Alexandrovitch!

I wrote you this as I approached Gorbitsa, one of the Cossack settlements on the banks of the Shilka, a tributary of the Amur. This is where I have got to. I am sailing down the Amur.

I sent you a letter from Irkutsk. Did you get it? Since then more than a week has passed, in the course of which I have crossed Lake Baikal and driven through Transbaikalia. Lake Baikal is wonderful, and the Siberians may well call it a sea instead of a lake. The water is extraordinarily transparent, so that one can see through it as through air; the colour is a soft turquoise very agreeable to the eye. The banks are mountainous, and covered with forests; it is all impenetrable wildness without a break anywhere.

There are great numbers of bears, wild goats, and wild creatures of all sorts, who spend their time living in the Taiga and eating one another. I spent two days and nights on the shore of Lake Baikal.

It was still and hot when I was sailing.

Transbaikalia is splendid. It is a mixture of Switzerland, the Don, and Finland.

I have driven with horses more than four thousand versts. My journey was entirely successful. I was in good health all the time, and lost nothing of my luggage but a penknife. I can wish no one a better journey. The journey is absolutely free from danger, and all the tales of escaped convicts, of night attacks, and so on are nothing but legends, traditions of the remote past. A revolver is an entirely superfluous article. Now I am sitting in a first-class cabin, and feel as though I were in Europe. I feel in the mood one is in after passing an examination. A whistle!—that's Gorbitsa.

The banks of the Shilka are picturesque like stage scenes but, alas! there is something oppressive in this complete absence of human beings. It is like a cage without a bird.

TO HIS SISTER.

June 21, 1890.

6 o'clock in the evening, not far from the Stanitsa Pokrovskaya.

We ran upon a rock, stove a hole in the steamer, and are now undergoing repairs. We are aground on a sandbank and pumping out water. On the left is the Russian bank, on the right the Chinese. If I were back at home now I should have the right to boast: "Though I have not been in China I have seen China only twenty feet off." We are to stay the night in Pokrovskaya. We shall make up a party to see the place.

If I were a millionaire I should certainly have a steamer of my own on the Amur. It is a fine, interesting country. I advise Yegor Mihailovitch not to go to Tuapse but here; there are here by the way neither tarantulas nor phalangas. On the Chinese side there is a sentry post—a small hut; sacks of flour are piled up on the bank, ragged Chinamen are dragging the sacks on barrows to the hut. And beyond is the dense, endless forest.

Some schoolgirls are travelling with us from Irkutsk—Russian faces, but not good-looking.

POKROVSKAYA STANITSA,
June 23, 1890.

    I have told you already we are aground on a sandbank. At Ust-Stryelka, where the Shilka joins the Argun (see map), the steamer went aground in two and a half feet of water, struck a rock, and stove in several holes in its side and, the hold filling with water, the steamer sank to the bottom. They began pumping out water and putting on patches; a naked sailor crawled into the hold, stood up to his neck in water, and tried the holes with his heels. Each hole was covered on the inside with cloth smeared with grease: they lay a board on the top, and stuck a support upon the latter which pressed against the ceiling like a column. Such is the repairing. They were pumping from five o'clock in the evening till night, but still the water did not abate: they had to put off the work till morning. In the morning they discovered some more holes, and began patching and pumping again. The sailors pump while we, the general public, pace up and down the decks, criticize, eat, drink, and sleep; the captain and his mate do the same as the general public, and seem in no hurry. On the right is the Chinese bank, on the left is the stanitsa, Pokrovskaya, with the Cossacks of the Amur; if one likes one can stay in Russia, if one likes one can go into China, there is nothing to hinder one. It is insufferably hot in the daytime, so that one has to put on a silk shirt. They give us dinner at twelve o'clock, supper at seven.

    Unluckily the steamer Vyestnik coming the other way with a crowd of passengers is approaching the stanitsa. The Vyestnik cannot go on either, and both steamers stay stock-still. There is a military band on the Vyestnik, consequently there has been a regular festival. All yesterday the band was playing on deck to the entertainment of the captain and sailors, and consequently to the delay of the repairing. The feminine half of the public were highly delighted; a band, officers, naval men . . . oh! The schoolgirls were particularly pleased. Yesterday evening we walked about the Cossack settlement, where the same band, hired by the Cossacks, was playing. Today we are continuing the repairs.

The captain promises that we shall start after dinner, but he promises it listlessly, gazing away into space—obviously he does not mean it. We are in no haste. When I asked a passenger, "Whenever are we going on?" he asked, "Why, aren't you all right here!"

And that's true. Why not stay, as long as we are not bored?

The captain, his mate, and his agent are the acme of politeness. The Chinese in the third class are good-natured and funny. Yesterday a Chinaman sat on the deck and sang something very mournful in a falsetto voice; as he did so his profile was funnier than any caricature. Everybody looked at him and laughed, while he took not the slightest notice. He sang falsetto and then began singing tenor. My God, what a voice! It was like the bleat of a sheep or a calf. The Chinese remind me of good-natured tame animals, their pigtails are long and black like Natalya Mihailovna's. Apropos of tame animals, there's a tame fox cub living in the toilet-room. It sits and looks on as one washes. If it sees no one for a long time it begins to whine.

What strange conversations one hears! They talk of nothing but gold, the mines, the Volunteer Fleet and Japan. In Pokrovskaya all the peasants and even the priests mine for gold. The exiles follow the same occupation and grow rich as quickly as they grow poor. There are people who look like artizans and who never drink anything but champagne, and walk to the tavern on red baize which is laid down from their hut to the tavern.

The Amur country is exceedingly interesting. Highly original. The life here is such as people have no conception of in Europe. It reminds me of American stories. The shores of the Amur are so wild, original, and luxuriant that one longs to live there all one's life. I am writing these last few lines on the 25th of June. The steamer rocks and prevents my writing properly. We are moving again. I have come a thousand versts down the Amur already, and have seen a million gorgeous landscapes; I feel giddy with ecstasy. . . . It's marvellous scenery, and how hot! What warm nights! There is a mist in the mornings but it is warm.

I look through an opera-glass at the shore and see a prodigious number of ducks, geese, grebes, herons and all sorts of creatures with long beaks. This would be the place to take a summer villa in! At a little place called Reinov a goldminer asked me to see his sick wife. As I was leaving him he thrust into my hands a roll of notes. I felt ashamed. I was beginning to refuse and thrust it back, saying that I was very rich myself; we talked together for a long time trying to persuade each other, and yet in the end fifteen roubles remained in my hands. Yesterday a goldminer with the face of Petya Polevaev dined in my cabin; at dinner he drank champagne instead of water, and treated us to it.

The villages here are like those on the Don. There is a difference in the buildings but nothing to speak of. The inhabitants don't keep the fasts, and eat meat even in Holy Week; the girls smoke cigarettes, and old women smoke pipes—it is the correct thing. It's strange to see peasants with cigarettes! And what liberalism! Oh, what liberalism!

The air on the steamer is positively red-hot with the talk that goes on. People are not afraid to talk aloud here. There's no one to arrest them and nowhere to exile them to, so you can be as liberal as you like. The people for the most part are independent, self-reliant, and logical. If there is any misunderstanding at Ust-Kara, where the convicts work (among them many politicals who don't work), all the Amur region is in revolt. It is not the thing to tell tales. An escaped convict can travel freely on the steamer to the ocean, without any fear of the captain's giving him up. This is partly due to the absolute indifference to everything that is done in Russia. Everybody says: "What is it to do with me?"

I forgot to tell you that in Transbaikalia the drivers are not Russians but Buriats. A funny people! Their horses are regular vipers; they could never be harnessed without trouble—more furious than fire-brigade horses. While the trace-horse is being harnessed, its legs are hobbled; as soon as they are set free the chaise goes flying to the devil, so that one holds one's breath. If one does not hobble a horse while it is being harnessed, it kicks, knocks bits out of the shaft with its hoofs, tears the harness, and behaves like a young devil that has been caught by the horns.

June 26.

We are getting near Blagoveshtchensk. Be well and merry, and don't get used to being without me. No doubt you have already? Respectful greetings to all, and a friendly kiss.

I am perfectly well.

TO A. S. SUVORIN.

BLAGOVESHTCHENSK, June 27, 1890.

The Amur is a very fine river; I have gained more from it than I could have expected, and I have been wishing for a long time to share my transports with you, but the rascally steamer has been rocking all the seven days I have been on it, and prevents me writing properly. Moreover, I am quite incapable of describing anything so beautiful as the shores of the Amur; I am at a complete loss before them, and recognise my bankruptcy. How is one to describe them? . . . Rocks, crags, forests, thousands of ducks, herons and all sorts of beaked gentry, and absolute wilderness. On the left the Russian shore, on the right the Chinese. I can look at Russia or China as I please. China is as deserted and wild as Russia: villages and sentinels' huts are rare. Everything in my head is muddled; and no wonder, your Excellency! I have come more than a thousand versts down the Amur and seen a million landscapes, and you know before the Amur there was Lake Baikal, Transbaikalia. . . . Truly I have seen such riches and had so much enjoyment that death would have no terrors now. The people on the Amur are original, their life is interesting, unlike ours. They talk of gold, gold, gold, and nothing else. I am in a stupid state, I feel no inclination to write, and I write shortly, piggishly; to-day I sent you four papers about Yenissey and the Taiga, later on I will send you something about Lake Baikal, Transbaikalia, and the Amur. Don't throw away these sheets; I will collect them, and they will serve as notes from which I can tell you what I don't know how to put on paper.

To-day I changed into the steamer Muravyov, which they say does not rock; maybe I shall write.

I am in love with the Amur; I should be glad to spend a couple of years on it. There is beauty, space, freedom and warmth. Switzerland and France have never known such freedom. The lowest convict breathes more freely on the Amur than the highest general in Russia. If you lived here, you would write a great deal of good stuff and delight the public, but I am not equal to it.

One begins to meet Chinamen at Irkutsk, and here they are common as flies. They are the most good-natured people. If Nastya and Borya made the acquaintance of the Chinese, they would leave donkeys alone, and transfer their affection to the Chinese. They are charming tame animals.

... When I invited a Chinaman to the refreshment bar to treat him to vodka, before drinking it he held out the glass to me, the bar-keeper, the waiters, and said: "Taste." That's the Chinese ceremonial. He did not drink it off as we do, but drank it in sips, eating something between each sip, and then, to express his gratitude, gave me several Chinese coins. An awfully polite people. They are dressed poorly, but beautifully; they eat daintily, with ceremony....

TO HIS SISTER.

THE STEAMER "MURAVYOV," June 29, 1890.

Meteors are flying in my cabin—these are luminous beetles that look like electric sparks. Wild goats swim across the Amur in the day-time. The flies here are huge. I am sharing my cabin with a Chinaman—Son-Luli—who is constantly telling me how in China for the merest trifle it is "off with his head." Last night he got drunk with opium, and was talking in his sleep all night and preventing me from sleeping. On the 27th I walked about the Chinese town Aigun. Little by little I seem gradually to be stepping into a fantastic world. The steamer rocks, it is hard to write.

To-morrow I shall reach Habarovsk. The Chinaman began to sing from music written on his fan.

TELEGRAM TO HIS MOTHER.

SAHALIN, July 11, 1890.

Arrived well, telegraph Sahalin.—CHEKHOV.

TELEGRAM TO HIS MOTHER.

SAHALIN, September 27, 1890.

Well. Shall arrive shortly.—CHEKHOV.

TO A. S. SUVORIN.

THE STEAMER "BAIKAL," September 11, 1890.

Greetings! I am sailing on the Gulf of Tartary from the north of Sahalin to the south. I am writing; and don't know when this letter will reach you. I am well, though I see on all sides glaring at me the green eyes of cholera which has laid a trap for me. In Vladivostok, in Japan, in Shanghai, Tchifu, Suez, and even in the moon, I fancy—everywhere there is cholera, everywhere quarantine and terror.... They expect the cholera in Sahalin and keep all vessels in quarantine. In short, it is a bad lookout. Europeans are dying at Vladivostok, among others the wife of a general has died.

I have spent just two months in the north of Sahalin. I was received by the local administration very amicably, though Galkin had not written a single word about me. Neither Galkin nor the Baroness V., nor any of the other genii I was so foolish as to appeal to for help, turned out of the slightest use to me; I had to act on my own initiative.

The Sahalin general, Kononovitch, is a cultivated and gentlemanly man. We soon got on together, and everything went off well. I am bringing some papers with me from which you will see that I was put on the most agreeable footing from the first. I have seen everything, so that the question is not now what I have seen, but how I have seen it.

I don't know what will come of it, but I have done a good deal. I have got enough material for three dissertations. I got up every morning at five o'clock and went to bed late; and all day long was on the strain from the thought that there was still so much I hadn't done; and now that I have done with the convict system, I have the feeling that I have seen everything but have not noticed the elephants.

By the way, I had the patience to make a census of the whole Sahalin population. I made the round of all the settlements, went into every hut and talked to everyone; I made use of the card system in making the census, and I have already registered about ten thousand convicts and settlers. In other words, there is not in Sahalin one convict or settler who has not talked with me. I was particularly successful with the census of the children, on which I am building great hopes.

I dined at Landsberg's; I sat in the kitchen of the former Baroness Gembruk. . . . I visited all the celebrities. I was present at a flogging, after which I dreamed for three or four nights of the executioner and the revolting accessories. I have talked to men who were chained to trucks. Once when I was drinking tea in a mine, Borodavkin, once a Petersburg merchant who was convicted of arson, took a teaspoon out of his pocket and gave it to me, and the long and the short of it is that I have upset my nerves and have vowed not to come to Sahalin again.

I should write more to you, but there is a lady in the cabin who giggles and chatters unceasingly. I haven't the strength to write. She has been laughing and cackling ever since yesterday evening.

This letter will go across America, but I shall go probably not across America. Everyone says that the American way is duller and more expensive.

To-morrow I shall see Japan, the Island of Matsmai. Now it is twelve o'clock at night. It is dark on the sea, the wind is blowing. I don't understand how the steamer can go on and find its direction when one can't see a thing, and above all in such wild, little-known waters as those in the Gulf of Tartary.

When I remember that I am ten thousand versts away from my world I am overcome with apathy. It seems I shall not be home for a hundred years. . . . God give you health and all blessings. I feel dreary.

TO HIS MOTHER.

SAHALIN, October 6, 1890.

My greetings, dear mother!

I write you this letter almost on the eve of my departure for Russia. Every day we expect a steamer of the Volunteer Fleet, and cherish hopes that it will not come later than the 10th of October. I send this letter to Japan, whence it will go by Shanghai or America. I am living at the station of Korsakovo, where there is neither telegraph nor post, and which is not visited by ships oftener than once a fortnight. Yesterday a steamer arrived and brought me from the north a pile of letters and telegrams. From the letters I learn that Masha likes the Crimea, I believe she will like the Caucasus better still. . . .

Strange, with you it has been cold and rainy, while in Sahalin from the day of my arrival till to-day it has been bright warm weather: there is slight cold with hoar-frost in the mornings, the snow is white on one of the mountains, but the earth is still green, the leaves have not fallen, and all the vegetation is still as flourishing as at a summer villa in May. There you have Sahalin!

At midnight yesterday I heard the roar of a steamer. Everybody jumped out of bed: hurrah! the steamer has arrived! We dressed and went out with lanterns to the harbour; we gazed into the distance; there really was a steamer. . . . The majority of voices decided that it was the Petersburg, on which I am to go to Russia. I was overjoyed. We got into a boat and rowed to the steamer. We went on and on, till at last we saw in the mist the dark hulk of a steamer. One of us shouted in a hoarse voice asking the name of the vessel. And we received the answer "the Baikal." Tfoo! anathema! what a disappointment! I am I homesick, and weary of Sahalin. Here for the last three months I have seen no one but convicts or people who can talk of nothing but penal servitude, the lash, and the convicts. A depressing existence. One longs to get quickly to Japan and from there to India.

I am quite well, except for flashes in my eye from which I often suffer now, after which I always have a bad headache. I had the flashes in my eye yesterday and to-day, and so I am writing this with a headache and heaviness all over.

At the station the Japanese General Kuse-San lives with his two secretaries, good friends of mine. They live like Europeans. To-day the local authorities visited them in state to present decorations that had been conferred on them; and I, too, went with my headache and had to drink champagne.

Since I have been in the south I have three times driven to Nay Race where the real ocean waves break. Look at the map and you will see at once on the south coast that poor dismal Nay Race. The waves cast up a boat with six American whalefishers, who had been shipwrecked off the coast of Sahalin; they are living now at the station and solemnly walk about the streets. They are waiting for the Petersburg and will sail with me.

I am not bringing you furs, there are none in Sahalin. Keep well and Heaven guard you all.

I am bringing you all presents. The cholera in Vladivostok and Japan is over.

TO A. S. SUVORIN.

MALAYA DMITROVKA, MOSCOW, December 9.

... Hurrah! Here at last I am sitting at my table at home! I pray to my faded penates and write to you. I have now a happy feeling as though I had not been away from home at all. I am well and thriving to the marrow of my bones. Here's a very brief report for you. I was in Sahalin not two months, as you have printed, but three months plus two days. I worked at high pressure. I made a full and minute census of the whole of Sahalin's population, and saw everything except the death penalty. When we see each other I will show you a whole trunkful of stuff about the convicts which is very valuable as raw material. I know a very great deal now, but I have brought away a horrid feeling. While I was staying in Sahalin, I only had a bitter feeling in my inside as though from rancid butter; and now, as I remember it, Sahalin seems to me a perfect hell. For two months I worked intensely, putting my back into it; in the third month I began to feel ill from the bitterness I have spoken of, from boredom, and the thought that the cholera would come from Vladivostok to Sahalin, and that so I was in danger of having to winter in the convict settlement. But, thank God! the cholera ceased, and on the 13th of October the steamer bore me away from Sahalin. I have been in Vladivostok. About the Primorsky Region and our Eastern sea-coast with its fleets, its problems, and its Pacific dreams altogether, I have only one thing to tell of: its crying poverty! Poverty, ignorance, and worthlessness, that might drive one to despair. One honest man for ninety-nine thieves, that are blackening the name of Russia.... We passed Japan because the cholera was there, and so I have not bought you anything Japanese, and the five hundred you gave me for your purchases I have spent on my own needs, for which you have, by law, the right to send me to a settlement in Siberia. The first foreign port we reached was Hong Kong. It is an exquisite bay. The traffic on the sea was such as I had never seen before even in pictures; excellent roads, trams, a railway to the mountains, a museum, botanical gardens; wherever you look you see the tenderest solicitude on the part of the English for the men in their service; there is even a club for the sailors. I went about in a jinrickshaw—that is, carried by men—bought all sorts of rubbish of the Chinese, and was moved to indignation at hearing my Russian fellow-travellers abuse the English for exploiting the natives. I thought: Yes, the English exploit the Chinese, the Sepoys, the Hindoos, but they do give them roads, aqueducts, museums, Christianity, and what do you give them?

When we left Hong Kong the boat began to rock. The steamer was empty and lurched through an angle of thirty-eight degrees, so that we were afraid it would upset. I am not subject to sea-sickness: that discovery was very agreeable to me. On the way to Singapore we threw two corpses into the sea. When one sees a dead man, wrapped in sailcloth, fly, turning somersaults in the water, and remembers that it is several miles to the bottom, one feels frightened, and for some reason begins to fancy that one will die oneself and will be thrown into the sea. Our horned cattle have fallen sick. Through the united verdict of Dr. Stcherbak and your humble servant, the cattle have been killed and thrown into the sea.

I have no clear memory of Singapore as, for some reason, I felt very sad while I was driving about it, and was almost weeping. Next after it comes Ceylon—an earthly Paradise. There in that Paradise I went more than a hundred versts on the railway and gazed at palm forests and bronze women to my heart's content. . . . After Ceylon we sailed for thirteen days and nights without stopping and were all stupid from boredom. I bear the heat well. The Red Sea is depressing; I felt touched as I gazed at Sinai.

God's world is a good place. The one thing not good in it is we. How little justice and humility there is in us. How little we understand true patriotism! A drunken, broken-down debauchee of a husband loves his wife and children, but of what use is that love? We, so we are told in our own newspapers, love our great motherland, but how does that love express itself? Instead of knowledge—insolence and immeasurable conceit; instead of work—sloth and swinishness; there is no justice, the conception of honour does not go beyond "the honour of the uniform"—the uniform which is so commonly seen adorning the prisoner's dock in our courts. Work is what is wanted, and the rest can go to the devil. First of all we must be just, and all the rest will be added unto us,

I have a passionate desire to talk to you. My soul is in a ferment. I want no one else but you, for it is only with you I can talk.

How glad I am that everything was managed without Galkin-Vrasskoy's help. He didn't write one line about me, and I turned up in Sahalin utterly unknown.

MOSCOW,
December 24, 1890.

I believe in Koch and in spermine and praise God for it. All that—that is the kochines, spermines, and so on—seem to the public a kind of miracle that leaped forth from some brain, after the fashion of Pallas Athene; but people who have a closer acquaintance with the facts know that they are only the natural sequel of what has been done during the last twenty years. A great deal has been done, my dear fellow! Surgery alone has done so much that one is fairly dumbfounded at it. To one who is studying medicine now, the time before twenty years ago seems simply pitiable. My dear friend, if I were offered the choice between the "ideals" of the renowned "sixties," or the very poorest Zemstvo hospital of to-day, I should, without a moment's hesitation, choose the second.

Will kochine cure syphilis? It's possible. But as for cancer, you must allow me to have my doubts. Cancer is not a microbe; it's a tissue, growing in the wrong place, and like a noxious weed smothering all the neighbouring tissues. If N.'s uncle feels better, that is, because the microbes of erysipelas—that is, the elements that produce the disease of erysipelas—form a component part of kochine. It was observed long ago that with the development of erysipelas, the growth of malignant tumours is temporarily checked.

It's a strange business—while I was travelling to Sahalin and back I felt perfectly well, but now, at home, the devil knows what is happening to me. My head is continually aching, I have a feeling of languor all over, I am quickly exhausted, apathetic, and worst of all, my heart is not beating regularly. My heart is continually stopping for a few seconds....

MOSCOW,
January, 1891.

I shall probably come to Petersburg on the 8th of January.... Since by February I shall not have a farthing, I must make haste and finish the novel

I've begun. There is something in the novel about which I must talk to you and ask your advice.

I spent Christmas in a horrible way. To begin with, I had palpitations of the heart; secondly, my brother Ivan came to stay and was ill with typhoid, poor fellow; thirdly, after my Sahalin labours and the tropics, my Moscow life seems to me now so petty, so bourgeois, and so dull, that I feel ready to bite; fourthly, working for my daily bread prevents my giving up my time to Sahalin; fifthly, my acquaintances bother me, and so on.

The poet Merezhkovsky has been to see me twice; he is a very intelligent man.

How sorry I am you did not see my mongoose. It is a wonderful creature.

TO HIS SISTER.

ST. PETERSBURG, January 14, 1891.

Unforeseen circumstances have kept me a few days longer. I am alive and well. There is no news. I saw Tolstoy's "The Power of Darkness" the other day, though. I have been to Ryepin's studio. What else? Nothing else. It's dull, in fact.

I went to-day to a dog-show; I went there with Suvorin, who at the moment I am writing these lines is standing by the table and asking me to write and tell you that I have been to the dog-show with the famous dog Suvorin....

January, later.

I am alive and well, I have no palpitations, I've no money either, and everything is going well.

I am paying visits and seeing acquaintances. I have to talk about Sahalin and India. It's horribly boring.

... Anna Ivanovna is as nice as ever, Suvorin talks as incessantly as ever.

I receive the most boring invitations to the most boring dinners. It seems I must make haste and get back to Moscow, as they won't let me work here.

Hurrah, we are avenged! To make up for our being so bored, the cotton ball has yielded 1,500 roubles clear profit, in confirmation of which I enclose a cutting from a newspaper.

If anything is collected for the benefit of the Sahalin schools, let me know at once.

How is my mongoose? Don't forget to give him food and drink, and beat him without mercy when he jumps on the table. Does he eat people?

Write how Ivan is. . . .

January, later.

I am tired as a ballet dancer after five acts and eight tableaux. Dinners, letters which I am too lazy to answer, conversations and imbecilities of all sorts. I have to go immediately to dine in Vassilyevsky Ostrov, and I am bored and ought to work.

I'll stay another three days and see whether the ballet will go on the same, then I shall go home, or to see Ivan.

I am surrounded by a thick atmosphere of ill-feeling, extremely vague and to me incomprehensible. They feed me with dinners and pay me the vulgarest compliments, and at the same time they are ready to devour me. What for? The devil only knows. If I were to shoot myself I should thereby provide the greatest gratification to nine-tenths of my friends and admirers. And how pettily they express their petty feelings!

. . . My greetings to Lydia Yegorovna Mizinov. I expect a programme from her. Tell her not to eat farinaceous food and to avoid Levitan. A better admirer than me she will not find in her Town Council nor in higher society.

January 16, 1891.

I have the honour to congratulate you and the hero of the name-day; I wish you and him health and prosperity, and above all that the mongoose should not break the crockery or tear the wall-paper. I shall celebrate my name-day at the Maly Yaroslavets restaurant, from the restaurant to the benefit performance, from the benefit performance to the restaurant again.

I am working, but with very great difficulty. No sooner have I written a line than the bell rings and someone comes in to talk to me about Sahalin. It's simply awful! . . .

I have found Drishka. It appears that she is living in the same house as I am. She ran away from Moscow to Petersburg under romantic circumstances: she meant to marry a lawyer, plighted her troth to him, but an army captain turned up, and so on; she had to run away or the lawyer would have shot both Drishka and the captain with a pistol loaded with cranberries. She is prospering and is the same lively rogue as ever. I went to Svobodin's name-day party with her yesterday. She sang gipsy songs, and created such a sensation that all the great men kissed her hand.

Rumours have reached me that Lidia Stahievna is going to be married par depit. Is it true? Tell her that I shall carry her off from her husband par depit. I am a violent man.

Has not anything been collected for the benefit of the Sahalin schools? Let me know. . . .

TO A. F. KONI.

PETERSBURG, January 16, 1891.

DEAR SIR, ANATOLY FYODOROVITCH,

I did not hasten to answer your letter because I am not leaving Petersburg before next Saturday. I am sorry I have not been to see Madame Naryshkin, but I think I had better defer my visit till my book has come out, when I shall be able to turn more freely to the material I have. My brief Sahalin past looms so immense in my imagination that when I want to speak about it I don't know where to begin, and it always seems to me that I have not said what was wanted.

I will try and describe minutely the position of the children and young people in Sahalin. It is exceptional. I saw starving children, I saw girls of thirteen prostitutes, girls of fifteen with child. Girls begin to live by prostitution from twelve years old, sometimes before menstruation has begun. Church and school exist only on paper, the children are educated by their environment and the convict surroundings. Among other things I have noted down a conversation with a boy of ten years old. I was making the census of the settlement of Upper Armudano; all the inhabitants are poverty-stricken, every one of them, and have the reputation of being desperate gamblers at the game of shtoss. I go into a hut; the people are not at home; on a bench sits a white-haired, round-shouldered, bare-footed boy; he seems lost in thought. We begin to talk.

I. "What is your father's second name?"

He. "I don't know."

I. "How is that? You live with your father and don't know what his name is? Shame!"

He. "He is not my real father."

I. "How is that?"

He. "He is living with mother."

I. "Is your mother married or a widow?"

He. "A widow. She followed her husband here."

I. "What has become of her husband, then?"

He. "She killed him."

I. "Do you remember your father?"

He. "No, I don't, I am illegitimate. I was born when mother was at Kara."

On the Amur steamer going to Sahalin, there was a convict with fetters on his legs who had murdered his wife. His daughter, a little girl of six, was with him. I noticed wherever the convict moved the little girl scrambled after him, holding on to his fetters. At night the child slept with the convicts and soldiers all in a heap together. I remember I was at a funeral in Sahalin. Beside the newly dug grave stood four convict bearers ex officio; the treasury clerk and I, in the capacity of Hamlet and Horatio, wandering about the cemetery; the dead woman's lodger, a Circassian, who had come because he had nothing better to do; and a convict woman who had come out of pity and had brought the dead woman's two children, one a baby, and the other, Alyoshka, a boy of four, wearing a woman's jacket and blue breeches with bright-coloured patches on the knees. It was cold and damp, there was water in the grave, the convicts were laughing. The sea was in sight. Alyoshka looked into the grave with curiosity; he tried to wipe his chilly nose, but the long sleeve of his jacket got into his way. When they began to fill in the grave I asked him: "Alyoshka, where is your mother?" He waved his hand with the air of a gentleman who has lost at cards, laughed, and said: "They have buried her!"

The convicts laughed, the Circassian turned and asked what he was to do with the children, saying it was not his duty to feed them.

Infectious diseases I did not meet with in Sahalin. There is very little congenital syphilis, but I saw blind children, filthy, covered with eruptions—all diseases that are evidence of neglect. Of course I am not going to settle the problem of the children. I don't know what ought to be done. But it seems to me that one will do nothing by means of philanthropy and what little is left of prison and other funds. To my thinking, to make something of great importance dependent upon charity, which in Russia always has a casual character, and on funds which do not exist, is pernicious. I should prefer it to be financed out of the government treasury.

TO A. S. SUVORIN.

MOSCOW, January 31, 1891.

At home I found depression. My nicest and most intelligent mongoose had fallen ill and was lying very quietly under a quilt. The little beast eats and drinks nothing. The climate has already laid its cold claw on it and means to kill it. What for?

We have received a dismal letter. In Taganrog we were on friendly terms with a well-to-do Polish family. The cakes and jam I ate in their house when I was a boy at school arouse in me now the most touching reminiscences; there used to be music, young ladies, home-made liqueurs, and catching goldfinches in the immense courtyard. The father had a post in the Taganrog customs and got into trouble. The investigation and trial ruined the family. There were two daughters and a son. When the elder daughter married a rascal of a Greek, the family took an orphan girl into the house to bring up. This little girl was attacked by disease of the knee and they amputated the leg. Then the son died of consumption, a medical student in his fourth year, an excellent fellow, a perfect Hercules, the hope of the family. . . . Then came terrible poverty. . . . The father took to wandering about the cemetery, longed to take to drink but could not: vodka simply made his head ache cruelly while his thoughts remained the same, just as sober and revolting. Now they write that the younger daughter, a beautiful, plump young girl, is consumptive. . . . The father writes to me of that and writes to me for a loan of ten roubles. . . . Ach!

I felt awfully unwilling to leave you, but still I am glad I did not remain another day—I went away and showed that I had strength of will. I am writing already. By the time you come to Moscow my novel will be finished, and I will go back with you to Petersburg.

Tell Borya, Mitya, and Andrushka that I vituperate them. In the pocket of my greatcoat I found some notes on which was scrawled: "Anton Pavlovitch, for shame, for shame, for shame!" O pessimi discipuli! Utinam vos lupus devoret!

Last night I did not sleep, and I read through my "Motley Tales" for the second edition. I threw out about twenty stories.

MOSCOW,
February 5, 1891.

My mongoose has recovered and breaks crockery again with unfailing regularity.

I am writing and writing! I must own I was afraid that my Sahalin expedition would have put me out of the way of writing, but now I see that it is all right. I have written a great deal. I am writing diffusely a la Yasinsky. I want to get hold of a thousand roubles.

I shall soon begin to expect you. Are we going to Italy or not? We ought to.

In Petersburg I don't sleep at night, I drink and loaf about, but I feel immeasurably better than in Moscow. The devil only knows why it is so.

I am not depressed, because in the first place I am writing, and in the second, one feels that summer, which I love more than anything, is close at hand. I long to prepare my fishing tackle....

February 23.

Greetings, my dear friend.

Your telegram about the Tormidor upset me. I felt dreadfully attracted to Petersburg: now for the sake of Sardou and the Parisian visitors. But practical considerations pulled me up. I reflected that I must hurry on with my novel; that I don't know French, and so should only be taking up someone else's place in the box; that I have very little money, and so on. In short, as it seems to me now, I am a poor comrade, though apparently I acted sensibly.

My novel is progressing. It's all smooth, even, there is scarcely anything that is too long. But do you know what is very bad? There is no movement in my novel, and that frightens me. I am afraid it will be difficult to read to the middle, to say nothing of reading to the end. Anyway, I shall finish it. I shall bring Anna Pavlovna a copy on vellum paper to read in the bathroom. I should like something to sting her in the water, so that she would run out of the bathroom sobbing.

I was melancholy when you went away....

Send me some money. I have none and seem to have nowhere to borrow. By my reckoning I cannot under favourable circumstances get more than a thousand roubles from you before September. But don't send the money by post, as I can't bear going to post offices....

March 5.

We are going!!! I agree to go, where you like and when you like. My soul is leaping with delight. It would be stupid on my part not to go, for when would an opportunity come again? But, my dear friend, I leave you to weigh the following circumstances.

(1) My work is still far from being finished; if I put it by till May, I shall not be able to begin my Sahalin work before July, and that is risky. For my Sahalin impressions are already evaporating, and I run the risk of forgetting a great deal.

(2) I have absolutely no money. If without finishing my novel I take another thousand roubles for the tour abroad, and then for living after the tour, I shall get into such a tangle that the devil himself could not pull me out by the ears. I am not in a tangle yet because I am up to all sorts of dodges, and live more frugally than a mouse; but if I go abroad everything will go to the devil. My accounts will be in a mess and I shall get myself hopelessly in debt. The very thought of a debt of two thousand makes my heart sink.

There are other considerations, but they are all of small account beside that of money and work. And so, thoroughly digest my objections, put yourself into my skin for a moment, and decide, wouldn't it be better for me to stay at home? You will say all this is unimportant. But lay aside your point of view? and look at it from mine.

I await a speedy answer.
My novel is progressing, but I have not got far.
I have been to the Kiselyovs'. The rooks are already arriving.

TO MADAME KISELYOV.

MOSCOW, March 11, 1891.

As I depart for France, Spain, and Italy, I beseech you, oh, Heavens, keep Babkino in good health and prosperity!

Yes, Marya Vladimirovna! As it is written in the scripture: he had not time to cry out, before a bear devoured him. So I had not time to cry out before an unseen power has drawn me again to the mysterious distance. To-day I am going to Petersburg, from there to Berlin, and so further. Whether I climb Vesuvius or watch a bull-fight in Spain, I shall remember you in my holiest prayers. Good-bye.

I have been to a seminary and picked out a seminarist for Vassilisa. There were plenty with delicate feelings and responsive natures, but not one would consent. At first, especially when I told them that you sometimes had peas and radishes on your table, they consented; but when I accidentally let out that in the district captain's room there was a bedstead on which people were flogged, they scratched their heads and muttered that they must think it over. One, however, a pockmarked fellow called Gerasim Ivanovitch, with very delicate feelings and a responsive nature, is coming to see you in a day or two. I hope that Vassilisa and you will make him welcome. Snatch the chance: it's a brilliant match. You can flog Gerasim Ivanovitch, for he told me: "I am immensely fond of violent sensations;" when he is with you you had better lock the cupboard where the vodka is kept and keep the windows open, as the seminary inspiration and responsiveness is perceptible at every minute.

"What a happy girl is Vassilisa!"

Idiotik has not been to see me yet.

The hens peck the cock. They must be keeping Lent, or perhaps the virtuous widows don't care for their new suitor.

They have brought me a new overcoat with check lining.

Well, be in Heaven's keeping, happy, healthy and peaceful. God give you all everything good. I shall come back in Holy Week. Don't forget your truly devoted,

ANTON CHEKHOV.

TO HIS SISTER.

PETERSBURG, March 16. Midnight.

I have just seen the Italian actress Duse in Shakespeare's Cleopatra. I don't know Italian, but she acted so well that it seemed to me I understood every word. A remarkable actress! I have never seen anything like it before. I gazed at that Duse and felt overcome with misery at the thought that we have to educate our temperaments and tastes on such wooden actresses as N. and her like, whom we call great because we have seen nothing better. Looking at Duse I understood why it is that the Russian theatre is so dull.

I sent three hundred roubles to-day, did you get them?

After Duse it was amusing to read the address I enclose. My God, how low taste and a sense of justice have sunk! And these are the students—the devil take them! Whether it is Solovtsov or whether it is Salvini, it's all the same to them, both equally "stir a warm response in the hearts of the young." They are worth a farthing, all those hearts.

We set off for Warsaw at half-past one to-morrow. My greetings to all, even the mongooses, though they don't deserve it. I will write.

VIENNA,
March 20, 1891.

MY DEAR CZECHS,

I write to you from Vienna, which I reached yesterday at four o'clock in the afternoon. Everything went well on the journey. From Warsaw to Vienna I travelled like a railway Nana in a luxurious compartment of the "Societe Internationale des Wagons-Lits." Beds, looking-glasses, huge windows, rugs, and so on.

Ah, my dears, if you only knew how nice Vienna is! It can't be compared with any of the towns I have seen in my life. The streets are broad and elegantly paved, there are numbers of boulevards and squares, the houses have always six or seven storeys, and shops—they are not shops, but a perfect delirium, a dream! There are myriads of neckties alone in the windows! Such amazing things made of bronze, china, and leather! The churches are huge, but they do not oppress one by their hugeness; they caress the eye, for it seems as though they are woven of lace. St. Stephen and the Votiv-Kirche are particularly fine. They are not like buildings, but like cakes for tea. The parliament, the town hall, and the university are magnificent. It is all magnificent, and I have for the first time realized, yesterday and to-day, that architecture is really an art. And here the art is not seen in little bits, as with us, but stretches over several versts. There are numbers of monuments. In every side street there is sure to be a bookshop. In the windows of the bookshops there are Russian books to be seen—not, alas, the works of Albov, of Barantsevitch, and of Chekhov, but of all sorts of anonymous authors who write and publish abroad. I saw "Renan," "The Mysteries of the Winter Palace," and so on. It is strange that here one is free to read anything and to say what one likes. Understand, O ye peoples, what the cabs are like here! The devil take them! There are no droshkys, but they are all new, pretty carriages with one and often two horses. The horses are splendid. On the box sit dandies in top-hats and reefer jackets, reading the newspaper, all politeness and readiness to oblige.

The dinners are good. There is no vodka; they drink beer and fairly good wine. There is one thing that is nasty: they make you pay for bread. When they bring the bill they ask, Wie viel brodchen?—that is, how many rolls have you devoured? And you have to pay for every little roll.

The women are beautiful and elegant. Indeed, everything is diabolically elegant.

I have not quite forgotten German. I understand, and am understood.

When we crossed the frontier it was snowing. In Vienna there is no snow, but it is cold all the same.

I am homesick and miss you all, and indeed I am conscience-stricken, too, at deserting you all again. But there, never mind! I shall come back and stay at home for a whole year. I send my greetings to everyone, everyone.

I wish you all things good; don't forget me with my many transgressions. I embrace you, I bless you, send my greetings and remain,

Your loving
A. CHEKHOV.

Everyone who meets us recognises that we are Russians, and stares not at my face, but at my grizzled cap. Looking at my cap they probably think I am a very rich Russian Count.

TO HIS BROTHER IVAN.

VENICE, March 24, 1891.

I am now in Venice. I arrived here two days ago from Vienna. One thing I can say: I have never in my life seen a town more marvellous than Venice. It is perfectly enchanting, brilliance, joy, life. Instead of streets and roads there are canals; instead of cabs, gondolas. The architecture is amazing, and there is not a single spot that does not excite some historical or artistic interest. You float in a gondola and see the palace of the Doges, the house where Desdemona lived, homes of various painters, churches. And in the churches there are sculptures and paintings such as we have never dreamed of. In fact it is enchantment.

All day from morning till night I sit in a gondola and glide along the streets, or I saunter about the famous St. Mark's Square. The square is as level and clean as a parquet floor. Here there is St. Mark's—something impossible to describe—the Palace of the Doges, and other buildings which make me feel as I do listening to part singing—I feel the amazing beauty and revel in it.

And the evenings! My God! One might almost die of the strangeness of it. One goes in a gondola . . . warmth, stillness, stars. . . . There are no horses in Venice, and so there is a silence here as in the open country. Gondolas flit to and fro, . . . then a gondola glides by, hung with lanterns. In it are a double-bass, violins, a guitar, a mandolin and cornet, two or three ladies, several men, and one hears singing and music. They sing from operas. What voices! One goes on a little further and again meets a boat with singers, and then again, and the air is full, till midnight, of the mingled strains of violins and tenor voices, and all sorts of heart-stirring sounds.

Merezhkovsky, whom I have met here, is off his head with ecstasy. For us poor and oppressed Russians it is easy to go out of our minds here in a world of beauty, wealth, and freedom. One longs to remain here for ever, and when one stands in the churches and listens to the organ one longs to become a Catholic.

The tombs of Canova and Titian are magnificent. Here they bury great artists like kings in churches; here they do not despise art as with us; the churches provide a shelter for pictures and statues however naked they may be.

In the Palace of the Doges there is a picture in which there are about ten thousand human figures.

To-day is Sunday. There will be a band playing in St. Mark's Square. . . .

If you ever happen to come to Venice it will be the best thing in your life. You ought to see the glass here! Your bottles are so hideous compared with the things here, that it makes one sick to think of them.

I will write again; meanwhile, good-bye.

TO MADAME KISELYOV

VENICE, March 25.

I am in Venice. You may put me in a madhouse. Gondolas, St. Mark's Square, water, stars, Italian women, serenades, mandolins, Falernian wine—in fact all is lost!

Don't remember evil against me.

The shade of the lovely Desdemona sends a smile to the District Captain.

Greetings to all. ANTONIO.

The Jesuits send their love to you.

TO HIS SISTER,
VENICE, March 25, 1891.

Bewitching blue-eyed Venice sends her greetings to all of you. Oh, signori and signorine, what an exquisite town this Venice is! Imagine a town consisting of houses and churches such as you have never seen; an intoxicating architecture, everything as graceful and light as the birdlike gondola. Such houses and churches can only be built by people possessed of immense artistic and musical taste and endowed with a lion-like temperament. Now imagine in the streets and alleys, instead of pavement, water; imagine that there is not one horse in the town; that instead of cabmen you see gondoliers on their wonderful boats, light, delicate long-beaked birds which scarcely seem to touch the water and tremble at the tiniest wave. And all from earth to sky bathed in sunshine.

There are streets as broad as the Nevsky, and others in which you can bar the way by stretching out your arms. The centre of the town is St. Mark's Square with the celebrated cathedral of the same name. The cathedral is magnificent, especially on the outside. Beside it is the Palace of the Doges where Othello made his confession before the senators.

In short, there is not a spot that does not call up memories and touch the heart. For instance, the little house where Desdemona lived makes an impression that is difficult to shake off. The very best time in Venice is the evening. First the stars; secondly, the long canals in which the lights and stars are reflected; thirdly, gondolas, gondolas, and gondolas; when it is dark they seem to be alive. Fourthly, one wants to cry because on all sides one hears music and superb singing. A gondola glides up hung with many-coloured lanterns; there is light enough for one to distinguish a double-bass, a guitar, a mandolin, a violin.... Then another gondola like it.... Men and women sing, and how they sing! It's quite an opera.

Fifthly, it's warm.

In short, the man's a fool who does not go to Venice. Living is cheap here. Board and lodging costs eighteen francs a week—that is, six roubles each or twenty-five roubles a month. A gondolier asks a franc for an hour-that is, thirty kopecks. Admission to the academies, museums, and so on, is free. The Crimea is ten times as expensive, and the Crimea beside Venice is a cuttle-fish beside a whale.

I am afraid Father is angry with me for not having said good-bye to him. I ask his forgiveness.

What glass there is here! what mirrors! Why am I not a millionaire! . . . Next year let us all take a summer cottage in Venice.

The air is full of the vibration of church bells: my dear Tunguses, let us all embrace Catholicism. If only you knew how lovely the organs are in the churches, what sculptures there are here, what Italian women on their knees with prayer-books!

Keep well and don't forget me, a sinner.

A picturesque railway line, of which I have been told a great deal, runs from Vienna to Venice. But I was disappointed in the journey. The mountains, the precipices, and the snowy crests I have seen in the Caucasus and Ceylon are far more impressive than here. Addio.

VENICE,
March 26, 1891.

It is pelting cats and dogs. Venetia bella has ceased to be bella. The water excites a feeling of dejected dreariness, and one longs to hasten somewhere where there is sun.

The rain has reminded me of my raincoat (the leather one); I believe the rats have gnawed it a little. If they have, send it to be mended as soon as you can. . . .

How is Signor Mongoose? I am afraid every day of hearing that he is dead.

In describing the cheapness of Venetian life yesterday, I overdid it a bit. It is Madame Merezhkovsky's fault; she told me that she and her husband paid only six francs per week each. But instead of per week, read per day. Anyway, it is cheap. The franc here goes as far as a rouble.

We are going to Florence.

May the Holy Mother bless you.

I have seen Titian's Madonna. It's very fine. But it is a pity that here fine works are mixed up side by side with worthless things, that have been preserved and not flung away simply from the spirit of conservatism all-present in such creatures of habit as messieurs les hommes. There are many pictures the long life of which is quite incomprehensible.

The house where Desdemona used to live is to let.

BOLOGNA,
March 28, 1891.

I am in Bologna, a town remarkable for its arcades, slanting towers, and Raphael's pictures of "Cecilia." We are going on to-day to Florence.

FLORENCE,
March 29, 1891.

I am in Florence. I am worn out with racing about to museums and churches. I have seen the Venus of Medici, and I think that if she were dressed in modern clothes she would be hideous, especially about the waist.

The sky is overcast, and Italy without sun is like a face in a mask.

P. S.—Dante's monument is fine.

FLORENCE,
March 30, 1891.

I am in Florence. To-morrow we are going to Rome. It's cold. We have the spleen. You can't take a step in Florence without coming to a picture-shop or a statue-shop.

P. S.—Send my watch to be mended.

TO MADAME KISELYOV.

ROME, April 1, 1891.

The Pope of Rome charges me to congratulate you on your name-day and wish you as much money as he has rooms. He has eleven thousand! Strolling about the Vatican I was nearly dead with exhaustion, and when I got home I felt that my legs were made of cotton-wool.

I am dining at the table d'hote. Can you imagine just opposite me are sitting two Dutch girls: one of them is like Pushkin's Tatyana, and the other like her sister Olga. I watch them all through dinner, and imagine a neat, clean little house with a turret, excellent butter, superb Dutch cheese, Dutch herrings, a benevolent-looking pastor, a sedate teacher, . . . and I feel

I should like to marry a Dutch girl and be depicted with her on a tea-tray beside the little white house.

I have seen everything and dragged myself everywhere I was told to go. What was offered me to sniff at, I sniffed at. But meanwhile I feel nothing but exhaustion and a craving for cabbage-soup and buckwheat porridge. I was enchanted by Venice, beside myself; but since I have left it, it has been nothing but Baedeker and bad weather.

Good-bye for now, Marya Vladimirovna, and the Lord God keep you. Humble respects from me and the other Pope to his Honour, Vassilisa and Elizaveta Alexandrovna.

Neckties are marvellously cheap here. I think I may take to eating them. They are a franc a pair.

To-morrow I am going to Naples. Pray that I may meet there a beautiful Russian lady, if possible a widow or a divorced wife.

In the guide-books it says that a love affair is an essential condition for a tour in Italy. Well, hang them all! I am ready for anything. If there must be a love affair, so be it.

Don't forget your sinful, but sincerely devoted,

ANTON CHEKHOV,

My respects to the starlings.

TO HIS SISTER.

ROME, April 1, 1891.

When I got to Rome I went to the post-office and did not find a single letter. Suvorin has got several letters. I made up my mind to pay you out, not to write to you at all—but there, God bless you! I am not so very fond of letters, but when one is travelling nothing is so bad as uncertainty. How have you settled the summer villa question? Is the mongoose alive? And so on and so on.

I have been in St. Peter's, in the Capitol, in the Coliseum, in the Forum—I have even been in a cafe'-chantant, but did not derive from it the gratification I had expected. The weather is a drawback, it is raining. I am hot in my autumn overcoat, and cold in my summer one.

Travelling is very cheap. One may pay a visit to Italy with only four hundred roubles and go back with purchases. If I were travelling alone or with Ivan, I should have brought away the conviction that travelling in Italy was much cheaper than travelling in the Caucasus. But alas! I am with the Suvorins. . . . In Venice we lived in the best of hotels like Doges; here in Rome we live like Cardinals, for we have taken a salon of what was once the palace of Cardinal Conti, now the Hotel Minerva; two huge drawing-rooms, chandeliers, carpets, open fireplaces, and all sorts of useless rubbish, costing us forty francs a day.

My back aches, and the soles of my feet burn from tramping about. It's awful how we walk!

It seems odd to me that Levitan did not like Italy. It's a fascinating country. If I were a solitary person, an artist, and had money, I should live here in the winter. You see, Italy, apart from its natural scenery and warmth, is the one country in which you feel convinced that art is really supreme over everything, and that conviction gives one courage.

NAPLES,
April 4, 1891.

I arrived in Naples, went to the post-office and found there five letters from home, for which I am very grateful to you all. Well done, relations! Even Vesuvius is so touched it has gone out.

Vesuvius hides its top in clouds and can only be seen well in the evening. By day the sky is overcast. We are staying on the sea-front and have a view of everything: the sea, Vesuvius, Capri, Sorrento. . . . We drove in the daytime up to the monastery of St. Martini: the view from here is such as I have never seen before, a marvellous panorama. I saw something like it at Hong Kong when I went up the mountain in the railway.

In Naples there is a magnificent arcade. And the shops!! The shops make me quite giddy. What brilliance! You, Masha, and you, Lika, would be rabid with delight.

There is a wonderful aquarium in Naples. There are even sharks and squids. When a squid (an octopus) devours some animals it's a revolting sight.

I have been to a barber's and watched a young man having his beard clipped for a whole hour. He was probably engaged to be married or else a cardsharper. At the barber's the ceiling and all the four walls were made of looking-glass, so that you feel that you are not at a hairdresser's but at the Vatican where there are eleven thousand rooms. They cut your hair wonderfully.

I shan't bring you any presents, as you don't write to me about the summer villa and the mongoose. I bought you a watch, Masha, but I have cast it to the swine. But there, God forgive you!

P.S.—I shall be back by Easter, come and meet me at the station.

NAPLES,
April 7, 1891.

Yesterday I went to Pompeii and went over it. As you know, it is a Roman town buried under the lava and ashes of Vesuvius in 79 A.D. I walked about the streets of the town and saw the houses, the temples, the theatre, the squares. . . . I saw and marvelled at the faculty of the Romans for combining simplicity with convenience and beauty. After viewing Pompeii, I lunched at a restaurant and then decided to go to Vesuvius. The excellent red wine I had drunk had a great deal to do with this decision. I had to ride on horseback to the foot of Vesuvius. I have in consequence to-day a sensation in some parts of my mortal frame as though I had been in the Third Division, and had there been flogged. What an agonising business it is climbing up Vesuvius! Ashes, mountains of lava, solid waves of molten minerals, mounds of earth, and every sort of abomination. You take one step forward and fall half a step back, the soles of your feet hurt you, your breathing is oppressed. . . . You go on and on and on, and it is still a long way to the top. You wonder whether to turn back, but you are ashamed to turn back, you would be laughed at. The ascent began at half-past two, and ended at six. The crater of Vesuvius is a great many yards in diameter. I stood on its edge and looked down as into a cup. The soil around, covered by a layer of sulphur, was smoking vigorously. From the crater rose white stinking smoke; spurts of hot water and red-hot stones fly out while Satan lies snoring under cover of the smoke. The noise is rather mixed, you hear in it the beating of breakers and the roar of thunder, and the rumble of the railway line and the falling of planks. It is very terrible, and at the same time one has an impulse to jump right into the crater. I believe in hell now. The lava has such a high temperature that copper coins melt in it.

Coming down was as horrid as going up. You sink up to your knees in ashes. I was fearfully tired. I went back on horseback through a little village and by houses; there was a glorious fragrance and the moon was shining. I sniffed, gazed at the moon, and thought of her—that is, of Lika L.

All the summer, noble gentlemen, we shall have no money, and the thought of that spoils my appetite. I have got into debt for a thousand for a tour, which I could have made solo for three hundred roubles. All my hopes now are in the fools of amateurs who are going to act my "Bear."

Have you taken a house for the holidays, signori? You treat me piggishly, you write nothing to me, and I don't know what's going on, and how things are at home.

Humble respects to you all. Take care of yourselves, and don't completely forget me.

MONTE CARLO,
April 13, 1891.

I am writing to you from Monte Carlo, from the very place where they play roulette. I can't tell you how thrilling the game is. First of all I won eighty francs, then I lost, then I won again, and in the end was left with a loss of forty francs. I have twenty francs left, I shall go and try my luck again. I have been here since the morning, and it is twelve o'clock at night. If I had money to spare I believe I should spend the whole year gambling and walking about the magnificent halls of the casino. It is interesting to watch the ladies who lose thousands. This morning a young lady lost 5000 francs. The tables with piles of gold are interesting too. In fact it is beyond all words. This charming Monte Carlo is extremely like a fine . . . den of thieves. The suicide of losers is quite a regular thing.

Suvorin fils lost 300 francs.

We shall soon see each other. I am weary of wandering over the face of the earth. One must draw the line. My heels are sore as it is.

TO HIS BROTHER MIHAIL.

NICE, Monday in Holy Week, April, 1891.

We are staying in Nice, on the sea-front. The sun is shining, it is warm, green and fragrant, but windy. An hour's journey from Nice is the famous Monaco. There is Monte Carlo, where roulette is played. Imagine the rooms of the Hall of Nobility but handsomer, loftier and larger. There are big tables, and on the tables roulette—which I will describe to you when I get home. The day before yesterday I went over there, played and lost. The game is fearfully fascinating. After losing, Suvorin fils and I fell to thinking it over, and thought out a system which would ensure one's winning. We went yesterday, taking five hundred francs each; at the first staking I won two gold pieces, then again and again; my waistcoat pockets bulged with gold. I had in hand French money even of the year 1808, as well as Belgian, Italian, Greek, and Austrian coins. . . . I have never before seen so much gold and silver. I began playing at five o'clock and by ten I had not a single franc in my pocket, and the only thing left me was the satisfaction of knowing that I had my return ticket to Nice. So there it is, my friends! You will say, of course: "What a mean thing to do! We are so poor, while he out there plays roulette." Perfectly just, and I give you permission to slay me. But I personally am much pleased with myself. Anyway, now I can tell my grandchildren that I have played roulette, and know the feeling which is excited by gambling.

Beside the Casino where roulette is played there is another swindle—the restaurants. They fleece one frightfully and feed one magnificently. Every dish is a regular work of art, before which one is expected to bow one's knee in homage and to be too awe-stricken to eat it. Every morsel is rigged out with lots of artichokes, truffles, and nightingales' tongues of all sorts. And, good Lord! how contemptible and loathsome this life is with its artichokes, its palms, and its smell of orange blossoms! I love wealth and luxury, but the luxury here, the luxury of the gambling saloon, reminds one of a luxurious water-closet. There is something in the atmosphere that offends one's sense of decency and vulgarizes the scenery, the sound of the sea, the moon.

Yesterday—Sunday—I went to the Russian church here. What was peculiar was the use of palm-branches instead of willows; and instead of boy choristers a choir of ladies, which gives the singing an operatic effect. They put foreign money in the plate; the verger and beadle speak French, and so on....

Of all the places I have been in hitherto Venice has left me the loveliest memories. Rome on the whole is rather like Harkov, and Naples is filthy. And the sea does not attract me, as I got tired of it last November and December.

I feel as though I have been travelling for a whole year. I had scarcely got back from Sahalin when I went to Petersburg, and then to Petersburg again, and to Italy.....

If I don't manage to get home by Easter, when you break the fast, remember me in your prayers, and receive my congratulations from a distance, and my assurance that I shall miss you all horribly on Easter night.

TO HIS SISTER.

PARIS, April 21, 1891.

To-day is Easter. So Christ is risen! It's my first Easter away from home.

I arrived in Paris on Friday morning and at once went to the Exhibition. Yes, the Eiffel Tower is very very high. The other exhibition buildings I saw only from the outside, as they were occupied by cavalry brought there in anticipation of disorders. On Friday they expected riots. The people flocked in crowds about the streets, shouting and whistling, greatly excited, while the police kept dispersing them. To disperse a big crowd a dozen policemen are sufficient here. The police make a combined attack, and the crowd runs like mad. In one of these attacks the honour was vouchsafed to me—a policeman caught hold of me under my shoulder, and pushed me in front of him.

There was a great deal of movement, the streets were swarming and surging. Noise, hubbub. The pavements are filled with little tables, and at the tables sit Frenchmen who feel as though they were at home in the street. A magnificent people. There is no describing Paris, though; I will put off the description of it till I get home.

I heard the midnight service in the Church of the Embassy....

I am afraid you have no money.

Misha, get my pince-nez mended, for the salvation of your soul! I am simply a martyr without spectacles. I went to the Salon and couldn't see half the pictures, thanks to my short sight. By the way, the Russian artists are far more serious than the French. . . . In comparison with the landscape painters I saw here yesterday Levitan is a king. . . .

PARIS, April 24.

A change again. One of the Russian sculptors living in Paris has undertaken to do a bust of Suvorin, and this will keep us till Saturday.
. . . How are you managing without money? Bear it till Thursday.
Imagine my delight. I was in the Chamber of Deputies just at the time of the sitting when the Minister for Internal Affairs was called to account for the irregularities which the government had ventured upon in putting down the riots in Fourmis (there were many killed and wounded). It was a stormy and extremely interesting sitting.
Men who tie boa-constrictors round their bodies, ladies who kick up to the ceiling, flying people, lions, cafe'-chantants, dinners and lunches begin to sicken me. It is time I was home. I am longing to work.

TO A. S. SUVORIN.

ALEXIN, May 7, 1891.

The summer villa is all right. There are woods and the Oka: it is far away in the wilds, it is warm, nightingales sing, and so on. It is quiet and peaceful, and in bad weather it will be dull and depressing here. After travelling abroad, life at a summer villa seems a little mawkish. I feel as though I had been taken prisoner and put into a fortress. But I am contented all the same. In Moscow I received from the Society of Dramatic Authors not two hundred roubles, as I expected, but three hundred. It's very kind on the part of fortune.
Well, my dear sir, I owe you, even if we adopt your reckoning, not less than eight hundred roubles. In June or July, when my money will be at the shop, I will write to Zandrok to send all that comes to me to you in Feodosia, and do not try and prevent me. I give you my word of honour

that when I have paid my debts and settled with you, I'll accept a loan of 2,000 from you. Do not imagine that it is disagreeable to me to be in your debt. I lend other people money, and so I feel I have the right to borrow money, but I am afraid of getting into difficulties and the habit of being in debt. You know I owe your firm a devilish lot.

There is a fine view from my window. Trains are continually passing. There is a bridge across the Oka.

ALEXIN,
May 10, 1891.

Yes, you are right, my soul needs balsam. I should read now with pleasure, even with joy, something serious, not merely about myself but things in general. I pine for serious reading, and recent Russian criticism does not nourish but simply irritates me. I could read with enthusiasm something new about Pushkin or Tolstoy. That would be balsam for my idle mind.

I am homesick for Venice and Florence too, and am ready to climb Vesuvius again; Bologna has been effaced from my memory and grown dim. As for Nice and Paris, when I recall them "I look on my life with loathing."

In the last number of The Messenger of Foreign Literature there is a story by Ouida, translated from the English by our Mihail. Why don't I know foreign languages? It seems to me I could translate magnificently. When I read anyone else's translation I keep altering and transposing the words in my brain, and the result is something light, ethereal, like lacework.

On Mondays, Tuesdays, and Wednesdays I write my Sahalin book, on the other days, except Sunday, my novel, and on Sundays, short stories. I work with zest. The weather has been superb every day; the site of our summer villa is dry and healthy. There is a lot of woodland. There are a lot of fish and crayfish in the Oka. I see the trains and the steamers. Altogether if it were not for being somewhat cramped I should be very very much pleased with it.

I don't intend to get married. I should like to be a little bald old man sitting at a big table in a fine study. . . .

ALEXIN,
May 13, 1891.

I am going to write you a Christmas story—that's certain. Two, indeed, if you like. I sit and write and write . . .; at last I have set to work. I am only sorry that my cursed teeth are aching and my stomach is out of order.

I am a dilatory but productive author. By the time I am forty I shall have hundreds of volumes, so that I can open a bookshop with nothing but my own works. To have a lot of books and to have nothing else is a horrible disgrace.

My dear friend, haven't you in your library Tagantsev's "Criminal Law"? If you have, couldn't you send it me? I would buy it, but I am now "a poor relation"—a beggar and as poor as Sidor's goat. Would you telephone to your shop, too, to send me, on account of favours to come, two books: "The Laws relating to Exiles," and "The Laws relating to Persons under Police Control." Don't imagine that I want to become a procurator; I want these works for my Sahalin book. I am going to direct my attack chiefly against life sentences, in which I see the root of all the evils; and against the laws dealing with exiles, which are fearfully out of date and contradictory.

TO L. S. MIZINOV.

ALEXIN, May 17, 1891.

Golden, mother-of-pearl, and fil d'Ecosse Lika! The mongoose ran away the day before yesterday, and will never come back again. It is dead. That is the first thing.

The second thing is, that we are moving our residence to the upper storey of the house of B.K.—the man who gave you milk to drink and forgot to give you strawberries. We will let you know the day we move in due time. Come to smell the flowers, to walk, to fish, and to blubber. Ah, lovely Lika! When you bedewed my right shoulder with your tears (I have taken out the spots with benzine), and when slice after slice you ate our bread and meat, we greedily devoured your face and head with our eyes. Ah, Lika, Lika, diabolical beauty! . . .

When you are at the Alhambra with Trofimov I hope you may accidentally jab out his eye with your fork.

TO A. S. SUVORIN.

ALEXIN, May 18, 1891.

... I get up at five o'clock in the morning; evidently when I am old I shall get up at four. My forefathers all got up very early, before the cock. And I notice people who get up very early are horribly fussy. So I suppose I shall be a fussy, restless old man. ...

BOGIMOVO,
May 20.

... The carp bite capitally. I forgot all my sorrows yesterday; first I sat by the pond and caught carp, and then by the old mill and caught perch.

... The last two proclamations—about the Siberian railway and the exiles—pleased me very much. The Siberian railway is called a national concern, and the tone of the proclamation guarantees its speedy completion; and convicts who have completed such and such terms as settlers are allowed to return to Russia without the right to live in the provinces of Petersburg and Moscow. The newspapers have let this pass unnoticed, and yet it is something which has never been in Russia before—it is the first step towards abolishing the life sentence which has so long weighed on the public conscience as unjust and cruel in the extreme. ...

BOGIMOVO,
May 27, 4 o'clock in the Morning.

The mongoose has run away into the woods and has not come back. It is cold. I have no money. But nevertheless, I don't envy you. One cannot live in town now, it is both dreary and unwholesome. I should like you to be sitting from morning till dinner-time in this verandah, drinking tea and writing something artistic, a play or something; and after dinner till evening, fishing and thinking peaceful thoughts. You have long ago earned the right which is denied you now by all sorts of chance circumstances, and it seems to me shameful and unjust that I should live more peacefully than you. Is it possible that you will stay all June in town? It's really terrible. . . .

. . . By the way, read Grigorovitch's letter to my enemy Anna Ivanovna. Let her soul rejoice. "Chekhov belongs to the generation which has perceptibly begun to turn away from the West and concentrate more closely on their own world. . . ." "Venice and Florence are nothing else than dull towns for a man of any intelligence. . . ." Merci, but I don't understand persons of such intelligence. One would have to be a bull to "turn away from the West" on arriving for the first time in Venice or Florence. There is very little intelligence in doing so. But I should like to know who is taking the trouble to announce to the whole universe that I did not like foreign parts. Good Lord! I never let drop one word about it. I liked even Bologna. Whatever ought I to have done? Howled with rapture? Broken the windows? Embraced Frenchmen? Do they say I gained no ideas? But I fancy I did. . . .

We must see each other—or more correctly, I must see you. I am missing you already, although to-day I caught two hundred and fifty-two carp and one crayfish.

BOGIMOVO,
June 4, 1891.

Why did you go away so soon? I was very dull, and could not get back into my usual petty routine very quickly afterwards. As luck would have it, after you went away the weather became warm and magnificent, and the fish began to bite.

. . . The mongoose has been found. A sportsman with dogs found him on this side of the Oka in a quarry; if there had not been a crevice in the quarry the dogs would have torn the mongoose to pieces. It had been astray in the woods for eighteen days. In spite of the climatic conditions, which are awful for it, it had grown fat—such is the effect of freedom. Yes, my dear sir, freedom is a grand thing.

I advise you again to go to Feodosia by the Volga. Anna Ivanovna and you will enjoy it, and it will be new and interesting for the children. If I were free I would come with you. It's snug now on those Volga steamers, they feed you well and the passengers are interesting.

Forgive me for your having been so uncomfortable with us. When I am grown up and order furniture from Venice, as I certainly shall do, you won't have such a cold and rough time with me.

TO L. S. MIZINOV.

BOGIMOVO, June 12, 1891.

Enchanting, amazing Lika!

Captivated by the Circassian Levitan, you have completely forgotten that you promised my brother Ivan you would come on the 1st of June, and you do not answer my sister's letter at all. I wrote to you from Moscow to invite you, but my letter, too, remained a voice crying in the wilderness. Though you are received in aristocratic society, you have been badly brought up all the same, and I don't regret having once chastised you with a switch. You must understand that expecting your arrival from day to day not only wearies us, but puts us to expense. In an ordinary way we only have for dinner what is left of yesterday's soup, but when we expect visitors we have also a dish of boiled beef, which we buy from the neighbouring cooks.

We have a magnificent garden, dark avenues, snug corners, a river, a mill, a boat, moonlight, nightingales, turkeys. In the pond and river there are very intelligent frogs. We often go for walks, during which I usually close my eyes and crook my right arm in the shape of a bread-ring, imagining that you are walking by my side.

... Give my greetings to Levitan. Please ask him not to write about you in every letter. In the first place it is not magnanimous on his part, and in the second, I have no interest whatever in his happiness.

Be well and happy and don't forget us. I have just received your letter, it is filled from top to bottom with such charming expressions as: "The devil choke you!" "The devil flay you!" "Anathema!" "A good smack," "rabble," "overeaten myself." Your friends—such as Trophim—with their cabmen's talk certainly have an improving influence on you.

You may bathe and go for evening walks. That's all nonsense. All my inside is full of coughs, wet and dry, but I bathe and walk about, and yet I am alive. ...

TO L. S. MIZINOV.

(Enclosing a photograph of a young man inscribed "To Lida from Petya.")
PRECIOUS LIDA!

Why these reproaches! I send you my portrait. To-morrow we shall meet. Do not forget your Petya. A thousand kisses!!!

I have bought Chekhov's stories. How delightful! Mind you buy them. Remember me to Masha Chekhov. What a darling you are!

TO THE SAME.

I love you passionately like a tiger, and I offer you my hand.

Marshal of Nobility,
GOLOVIN RTISHTCHEV.
P.S.—Answer me by signs. You do squint.

TO HIS SISTER.

BOGIMOVO, June, 1891.

Masha! Make haste and come home, as without you our intensive culture is going to complete ruin. There is nothing to eat, the flies are sickening. The mongoose has broken a jar of jam, and so on, and so on.

All the summer visitors sigh and lament over your absence. There is no news.... The spiderman is busy from morning to night with his spiders. He has already described five of the spider's legs, and has only three left to do. When he has finished with spiders he will begin upon fleas, which he will catch on his aunt. The K's sit every evening at the club, and no hints from me will prevail on them to move from the spot.

It is hot, there are no mushrooms. Suvorin has not come yet....

Come soon for it is devilishly dull. We have just caught a frog and given it to the mongoose. It has eaten it.

TO MADAME KISELYOV.

ALEXIN, July 20, 1891.

Greetings, honoured Marya Vladimirovna.

For God's sake write what you are doing, whether you are all well and how things are in regard to mushrooms and gudgeon.

We are living at Bogimovo in the province of Kaluga. . . . It's a huge house, a fine park, the inevitable views, at the sight of which I am for some reason expected to say "Ach!" A river, a pond with hungry carp who love to get on to the hook, a mass of sick people, a smell of iodoform, and walks in the evenings. I am busy with my Sahalin; and in the intervals, that I may not let my family starve, I cherish the muse and write stories. Everything goes on in the old way, there is nothing new. I get up every day at five o'clock, and prepare my coffee with my own hands—a sign that I have already got into old bachelor habits and am resigned to them. Masha is painting, Misha wears his cockade creditably, father talks about bishops, mother bustles about the house, Ivan fishes. On the same estate with us there is living a zoologist called Wagner and his family, and some Kisilyovs—not the Kisilyovs, but others, not the real ones.

Wagner catches ladybirds and spiders, and Kisilyov the father sketches, as he is an artist. We get up performances, tableaux-vivants, and picnics. It is very gay and amusing, but I have only to catch a perch or find a mushroom for my head to droop, and my thoughts to be carried back to the past, and my brain and soul begin in a funereal voice to sing the duet "We are parted." The "deposed idol and the deserted temple" rise up before my imagination, and I think devoutly: "I would exchange all the zoologists and great artists in the world for one little Idiotik." The weather has all the while been hot and dry, and only to-day there has been a crash of thunder and the gates of heaven are open. One longs to get away somewhere—for instance, to America, or Norway. . . . Be well and happy, and may the good spirits, of whom there are so many at Babkino, have you in their keeping.

TO HIS BROTHER ALEXANDR.

ALEXIN, July, 1891.

MY PHOTOGRAPHIC AND PROLIFIC BROTHER!

I got a letter from you a long time ago with the photographs of Semashko, but I haven't answered till now, because I have been all the time trying to formulate the great thoughts befitting my answer. All our people are alive and well, we often talk of you, and regret that your prolificness prevents you from coming to us here where you would be very welcome. Father, as I have written to you already, has thrown up Ivanygortch, and is living with us. Suvorin has been here twice; he talked about you, and caught fish. I am up to my neck in work with Sahalin, and other things no less wearisome and hard labour. I dream of winning forty thousand, so as to cut myself off completely from writing, which I am sick of, to buy a little bit of land and live like a hermit in idle seclusion, with you and Ivan in the neighbourhood—I dream of presenting you with fifteen acres each as poor relations. Altogether I have a dreary existence, I am sick of toiling over lines and halfpence, and old age is creeping nearer and nearer.

Your last story, in my opinion, shared by Suvorin, is good. Why do you write so little?

The zoologist V. A. Wagner, who took his degree with you, is staying in the same courtyard. He is writing a very solid dissertation. Kisilyov, the artist, is living in the same yard too. We go walks together in the evenings and discuss philosophy....

TO A. S. SUVORIN.

BOGIMOVO, July 24, 1891.

... Thanks for the five kopecks addition. Alas, it will not settle my difficulties! To save up a reserve, as you write, and extricate myself from the abyss of halfpenny anxieties and petty terrors, there is only one resource left me—an immoral one. To marry a rich woman or give out Anna Karenin as my work. And as that is impossible I dismiss my difficulties in despair and let things go as they please.

You once praised Rod, a French writer, and told me Tolstoy liked him. The other day I happened to read a novel of his and flung up my hands in amazement. He is equivalent to our Matchtet, only a little more intelligent. There is a terrible deal of affectation, dreariness, straining after originality, and as little of anything artistic as there was salt in that porridge we cooked in the evening at Bogimovo. In the preface this Rod regrets that he was in the past a "naturalist," and rejoices that the spiritualism of the latest recruits of literature has replaced materialism. Boyish boastfulness which is at the same time coarse and clumsy.... "If we are not as talented as you, Monsieur Zola, to make up for it we believe in God."...

July 29.

Well, thank God! To-day I have received from the bookshop notice that there is 690 roubles 6 kopecks coming to me. I have written in answer that they are to send five hundred roubles to Feodosia and the other one hundred and ninety to me. And so I am left owing you only one hundred and seventy. That is comforting, it's an advance anyway. To meet the debt to the newspaper I am arming myself with an immense story which I shall finish in a day or two and send. I ought to knock three hundred roubles off the debt, and get as much for myself. Ough!...

August 6.

... The death of a servant in the house makes a strange impression, doesn't it? The man while he was alive attracted attention only so far as he was one's "man"; but when he is dead he suddenly engrosses the attention of all, lies like a weight on the whole house, and becomes the despotic master who is talked of to the exclusion of everything.

... I shall finish my story to-morrow or the day after, but not to-day, for it has exhausted me fiendishly towards the end. Thanks to the haste with which I have worked at it, I have wasted a pound of nerves over it. The composition of it is a little complicated. I got into difficulties and often tore up what I had written, and for days at a time was dissatisfied with my work—that is why I have not finished it till now. How awful it is! I must rewrite it! It's impossible to leave it, for it is in a devil of a mess. My God! if the public likes my works as little as I do those of other people which I am reading, what an ass I am! There is something asinine about our writing....

To my great pleasure the amazing astronomer has arrived. She is angry with you, and calls you for some reason an "eloquent gossip." To begin with, she is free and independent; and then she has a poor opinion of men; and further, according to her, everyone is a savage or a ninny—and you dared to give her my address with the words "the being you adore lives at . . .," and so on. Upon my word, as though one could suspect earthly feelings in astronomers who soar among the clouds! She talks and laughs all day, is a capital mushroom-gatherer, and dreams of the Caucasus to which she is departing today.

August 18.

At last I have finished my long, wearisome story and am sending it to you in Feodosia. Please read it. It is too long for the paper, and not suitable for dividing into parts. Do as you think best, however. . . .

There are more than four signatures of print in the story. It's awful. I am exhausted, and dragged the end, like a train of waggons on a muddy night in autumn, at a walking pace with halts—that is why I am late with it. . . .

August 18.

Speaking of Nikolay and the doctor who attends him, you emphasize that "all that is done without love, without self-sacrifice, even in regard to trifling conveniences." You are right, speaking of people generally, but what would you have the doctors do? If, as your old nurse says, "The bowel has burst," what's one to do, even if one is ready to give one's life to the sufferer? As a rule, while the family, the relations, and the servants are doing "everything they can" and are straining every nerve, the doctor sits and looks like a fool, with his hands folded, disconsolately ashamed of himself and his science, and trying to preserve external tranquillity. . . .

Doctors have loathsome days and hours, such as I would not wish my worst enemy. It is true that ignoramuses and coarse louts are no rarity among doctors, nor are they among writers, engineers, people in general; but those loathsome days and hours of which I speak fall to the lot of doctors only, and for that, truly, much may be forgiven them. . . .

The amazing astronomer is at Batum now. As I told her I should go to Batum too, she will send her address to Feodosia. She has grown cleverer than ever of late. One day I overheard a learned discussion between her and the zoologist Wagner, whom you know. It seemed to me that in comparison with her the learned professor was simply a schoolboy. She has excellent logic and plenty of good common sense, but no rudder, . . . so that she drifts and drifts, and doesn't know where she is going. . . .

A woman was carting rye, and she fell off the waggon head downwards. She was terribly injured: concussion of the brain, straining of the vertebrae of the neck, sickness, fearful pains, and so on. She was brought to me. She was moaning and groaning and praying for death, and yet she looked at the man who brought her and muttered: "Let the lentils go, Kirila, you can thresh them later, but thresh the oats now." I told her that she could talk about oats afterwards, that there was something more serious to talk about, but she said to me: "His oats are ever so good!" A managing, vigilant woman. Death comes easy to such people. . . .

August 28.

I send you Mihailovsky's article on Tolstoy. Read it and grow perfect. It's a good article, but it's strange; one might write a thousand such articles and things would not be one step forwarder, and it would still remain unintelligible why such articles are written. . . .

I am writing my Sahalin, and I am bored, I am bored. . . . I am utterly sick of life.

Judging from your telegram I have not satisfied you with my story. You should not have hesitated to send it back to me.

Oh, how weary I am of sick people! A neighbouring landowner had a nervous stroke and they trundled me off to him in a scurvy jolting britchka. Most of all I am sick of peasant women with babies, and of powders which it is so tedious to weigh out.

There is a famine year coming. I suppose there will be epidemics of all sorts and risings on a small scale. . . .

August 28.

So you like my story? Well, thank God! Of late I have become devilishly suspicious and uneasy. I am constantly fancying that my trousers are horrid, and that I am writing not as I want to, and that I am giving my patients the wrong powders. It must be a special neurosis.

If Ladzievsky's surname is really horrible, you can call him something else. Let him be Lagievsky, let von Koren remain von Koren. The multitude of Wagners, Brandts, and so on, in all the scientific world, make a Russian name out of the question for a zoologist—though there is Kovalevsky. And by the way, Russian life is so mixed up nowadays that any surnames will do.

Sahalin is progressing. There are times when I long to sit over it from three to five years, and work at it furiously; but at times, in moments of doubt, I could spit on it. It would be a good thing, by God! to devote three years to it. I shall write a great deal of rubbish, because I am not a specialist, but really I shall write something sensible too. It is such a good subject, because it would live for a hundred years after me, as it would be the literary source and aid for all who are studying prison organization, or are interested in it.

You are right, your Excellency, I have done a great deal this summer. Another such summer and I may perhaps have written a novel and bought an estate. I have not only paid my way, but even paid off a thousand roubles of debt.

... Tell your son that I envy him. And I envy you too, and not because your wives have gone away, but because you are bathing in the sea and living in a warm house. I am cold in my barn. I should like new carpets, an open fireplace, bronzes, and learned conversations. Alas! I shall never be a Tolstoyan. In women I love beauty above all things; and in the history of mankind, culture, expressed in carpets, carriages with springs, and keenness of wit. Ach! To make haste and become an old man and sit at a big table! ...

P.S.—If we were to cut the zoological conversations out of "The Duel" wouldn't it make it more living? ...

MOSCOW,
September 8.

I have returned to Moscow and am keeping indoors. My family is busy trying to find a new flat but I say nothing because I am too lazy to turn round. They want to move to Devitchye Polye for the sake of cheapness.

The title you recommend for my novel—"Deception"—will not do: it would only be appropriate if it were a question of conscious lying.

Unconscious lying is not deception but a mistake. Tolstoy calls our having money and eating meat lying—that's too much....

Death gathers men little by little, he knows what he is about. One might write a play: an old chemist invents the elixir of life—take fifteen drops and you live for ever; but he breaks the phial from terror, lest such carrion as himself and his wife might live for ever. Tolstoy denies mankind immortality, but my God! how much that is personal there is in it! The day before yesterday I read his "Afterword." Strike me dead! but it is stupider and stuffier than "Letters to a Governor's Wife," which I despise. The devil take the philosophy of the great ones of this world! All the great sages are as despotic as generals, and as ignorant and as indelicate as generals, because they feel secure of impunity. Diogenes spat in people's faces, knowing that he would not suffer for it. Tolstoy abuses doctors as scoundrels, and displays his ignorance in great questions because he's just such a Diogenes who won't be locked up or abused in the newspapers. And so to the devil with the philosophy of all the great ones of this world! The whole of it with its fanatical "Afterwords" and "Letters to a Governor's Wife" is not worth one little mare in his "Story of a Horse...."

TO E. M. S.

MOSCOW, September 16.

So we old bachelors smell of dogs? So be it. But as for specialists in feminine diseases being at heart rakes and cynics, allow me to differ. Gynaecologists have to do with deadly prose such as you have never dreamed of, and to which perhaps, if you knew it, you would, with the ferocity characteristic of your imagination, attribute a worse smell than that of dogs. One who is always swimming in the sea loves dry land; one who for ever is plunged in prose passionately longs for poetry. All gynaecologists are idealists. Your doctor reads poems, your instinct prompted you right; I would add that he is a great liberal, a bit of a mystic, and that he dreams of a wife in the style of the Nekrassov Russian woman. The famous Snyegirev cannot speak of the "Russian woman" without a quiver in his voice. Another gynaecologist whom I know is in love with a mysterious lady in a veil whom he has only seen from a distance. Another one goes to all the first performances at the theatre and then is loud in his abuse, declaring that authors ought to represent only ideal women, and so on. You have omitted to consider also that a good gynaecologist cannot be a stupid man or a mediocrity. Intellect has a brighter lustre than baldness, but you have noticed the baldness and emphasized it—and have flung the intellect overboard. You have noticed, too, and emphasized that a fat man—brrr!—exudes a sort of greasiness, but you completely lose sight of the fact that he is a professor—that is, that he has spent several years in thinking and doing something which sets him high above millions of men, high above all the Verotchkas and Taganrog Greek girls, high above dinners and wines of all sorts. Noah had three sons, Shem, Ham, and Japheth. Ham only noticed that his father was a drunkard, and completely lost sight of the fact that he was a genius, that he had built an ark and saved the world.

Writers must not imitate Ham, bear that in mind.

I do not venture to ask you to love the gynaecologist and the professor, but I venture to remind you of the justice which for an objective writer is more precious than the air he breathes.

The girl of the merchant class is admirably drawn. That is a good passage in the doctor's speech in which he speaks of his lack of faith in medicine, but there is no need to make him drink after every sentence. . . .

Then from the particular to the general! Let me warn you. This is not a story and not a novel and not a work of art, but a long row of heavy, gloomy barrack buildings. Where is your construction which at first so enchanted your humble servant? Where is the lightness, the freshness, the grace? Read your story through: a description of a dinner, then a description of passing ladies and girls, then a description of a company, then a description of a dinner, . . . and so on endlessly. Descriptions and descriptions and no action at all. You ought to begin straight away with the merchant's daughter, and keep to her, and chuck out Verotchka and the Greek girls and all the rest, except the doctor and the merchant family.

Excuse this long letter.

TO A. S. SUVORIN.

MOSCOW, October 16, 1891.

I congratulate you on your new cook, and wish you an excellent appetite. Wish me the same, for I am coming to see you soon—sooner than I had intended—and shall eat for three. I simply must get away from home, if only for a fortnight. From morning till night I am unpleasantly irritable, I feel as though someone were drawing a blunt knife over my soul, and this irritability finds external expression in my hurrying off to bed early and avoiding conversation. Nothing I do succeeds. I began a story for the Sbornik; I wrote half and threw it up, and then began another; I have been struggling for more than a week with this story, and the time when I shall finish it and when I shall set to work and finish the first story, for which I am to be paid, seems to me far away. I have not been to the province of Nizhni Novgorod yet, for reasons not under my control, and I don't know when I shall go. In fact it's a hopeless mess—a silly muddle and not life. And I desire nothing now so much as to win two hundred thousand....

Ah, I have such a subject for a novel! If I were in a tolerable humour I could begin it on the first of November and finish it on the first of December. I would make five signatures of print. And I long to write as I did at Bogimovo—i.e., from morning till night and in my sleep.

Don't tell anyone I am coming to Petersburg. I shall live incognito. In my letters I write vaguely that I am coming in November....

Shall I remind you of Kashtanka, or forget about her? Won't she lose her childhood and youth if we don't print her? However, you know best....

P. S.—If you see my brother Alexandr, tell him that our aunt is dying of consumption. Her days are numbered. She was a splendid woman, a saint.

If you want to visit the famine-stricken provinces, let us go together in January, it will be more conspicuous then....

MOSCOW,
October 19, 1891.

What a splendid little letter has come from you! It is warmly and eloquently written, and every thought in it is true. To talk now of laziness and drunkenness, and so on, is as strange and tactless as to lecture a man on the conduct of life at a moment when he is being sick or lying ill of typhus. There is always a certain element of insolence in being well-fed, as in every kind of force, and that element finds expression chiefly in the well-fed man preaching to the hungry. If consolation is revolting at a time of real sorrow, what must be the effect of preaching morality; and how stupid and insulting that preaching must seem. These moral people imagine that if a man is fifteen roubles in arrears with his taxes he must be a wastrel, and ought not to drink; but they ought to reckon up how much states are in debt, and prime ministers, and what the debts of all the marshals of nobility and all the bishops taken together come to. What do the Guards owe! Only their tailors could tell us that. . . .

You have told them to send me four hundred? Vivat dominus Suvorin! So I have already received from your firm 400 + 100 + 400. Altogether I shall get for "The Duel" as I calculated, about fourteen hundred, so five hundred will go towards my debt. Well, and for that thank God! By the spring I must pay off all my debt or I shall go into a decline, for in the spring I want another advance from all my editors. I shall take it and escape to Java. . . .

Ah, my friends, how bored I am! If I am a doctor I ought to have patients and a hospital; if I am a literary man I ought to live among people instead of in a flat with a mongoose, I ought to have at least a scrap of social and political life—but this life between four walls, without nature, without people, without a country, without health and appetite, is not life, but some sort of . . . and nothing more.

For the sake of all the perch and pike you are going to catch on your Zaraish estate, I entreat you to publish the English humorist Bernard. [Translator's Note: ? Bernard Shaw.] . . .

TO MADAME LINTVARYOV.

MOSCOW, October 25, 1891.

HONOURED NATALYA MIHAILOVNA,

I have not gone to Nizhni as I meant to, but am sitting at home, writing and sneezing. Madame Morozov has seen the Minister, he has absolutely prohibited private initiative in the work of famine relief, and actually waved her out of his presence. This has reduced me to apathy at once. Add to that, complete lack of money, sneezing, a mass of work, the illness of my aunt who died to-day, the indefiniteness, the uncertainty in fact—everything has come together to hinder a lazy person like me. I have put off my going away till the first of December.

We felt dull without you for a long time, and when the Shah of Persia went away it was duller still. I have given orders that no one is to be admitted, and sit in my room like a heron in the reeds; I see no one, and no one sees me. And it is better so, or the public would pull the bell off, and my study would be turned into a smoking and talking room. It's dull to live like this, but what am I to do? I shall wait till the summer and then let myself go.

I shall sell the mongoose by auction. I should be glad to sell N. and his poems too, but no one would buy him. He dashes in to see me almost every evening as he used to do, and bores me with his doubts, his struggles, his volcanoes, slit nostrils, atamans, the life of the free, and such tosh, for which God forgive him.

Russkiya Vyedomosti is printing a Sbornik for the famine fund. With your permission, I shall send you a copy.

Well, good health and happiness to you; respects and greetings to all yours from the Geographer,

A. CHEKHOV.

P. S.—All my family send their regards.

We are all well but sorrowful. Our aunt was a general favourite, and was considered among us the incarnation of goodness, kindness, and justice, if only all that can be incarnated. Of course we shall all die, but still it is sad.

In April I shall be in your parts. By the spring I hope I shall have heaps of money. I judge by the omen: no money is a sign of money coming.

TO A. S. SUVORIN.

MOSCOW, October 25, 1891.

Print "The Duel" not twice a week but only once. To print it twice is breaking a long-established custom of the paper, and it would seem as though I were robbing the other contributors of one day a week; and meanwhile it makes no difference to me or my novel whether it is printed once a week or twice. The literary brotherhood in Petersburg seems to talk of nothing but the uncleanness of my motives. I have just received the good news that I am to be married to the rich Madame Sibiryakov. I get a lot of agreeable news altogether.

I wake up every night and read "War and Peace." One reads it with the same interest and naive wonder as though one had never read it before. It's amazingly good. Only I don't like the passages in which Napoleon appears. As soon as Napoleon comes on the scene there are forced explanations and tricks of all sorts to prove that he was stupider than he really was. Everything that is said and done by Pierre, Prince Andrey, or the absolutely insignificant Nikolay Rostov—all that is good, clever, natural, and touching; everything that is thought and done by Napoleon is not natural, not clever, inflated and worthless.

When I live in the provinces (of which I dream now day and night), I shall practice as a doctor and read novels.

I am not coming to Petersburg.

If I had been by Prince Andrey I should have saved him. It is strange to read that the wound of a prince, a rich man spending his days and nights with a doctor and being nursed by Natasha and Sonya, should have smelt like a corpse. What a scurvy affair medicine was in those days! Tolstoy could not help getting soaked through with hatred for medicine while he was writing his thick novel. . . .

MOSCOW,
November 18, 1891.

... I have read your letter about the influenza and Solovyov. I was unexpectedly aware of a dash of cruelty in it. The phrase "I hate" does not suit you at all; and a public confession "I am a sinner, a sinner, a sinner," is such pride that it made me feel uncomfortable. When the pope took the title "holiness," the head of the Eastern church, in pique, called himself "The servant of God's servants." So you publicly expatiate on your sinfulness from pique of Solovyov, who has the impudence to call himself orthodox. But does a word like orthodoxy, Judaism, or Catholicism contain any implication of exceptional personal merit or virtue? To my thinking everybody is bound to call himself orthodox if he has that word inscribed on his passport. Whether you believe or not, whether you are a prince of this world or an exile in penal servitude, you are, for practical purposes, orthodox. And Solovyov made no sort of pretension when he said he was no Jew or Chaldean but orthodox. ...

I still feel dull, blighted, foolish, and indifferent, and I am still sneezing and coughing, and I am beginning to think I shall not get back to my former health. But that's all in God's hands. Medical treatment and anxiety about one's physical existence arouse in me a feeling not far from loathing. I am not going to be doctored. I will take water and quinine, but I am not going to let myself be sounded. ...

I had only just finished this letter when I received yours. You say that if I go into the wilds I shall be quite cut off from you. But I am going to live in the country in order to be nearer Petersburg. If I have no flat in Moscow you must understand, my dear sir, I shall spend November, December, and January in Petersburg: that will be possible then. I shall be able to be idle all the summer too; I shall look out for a house in the country for you, but you are wrong in disliking Little Russians, they are not children or actors in the province of Poltava, but genuine people, and cheerful and well-fed into the bargain.

Do you know what relieves my cough? When I am working I sprinkle the edge of the table with turpentine with a sprayer and inhale its vapour. When I go to bed I spray my little table and other objects near me. The fine drops evaporate sooner than the liquid itself. And the smell of turpentine is pleasant. I drink Obersalzbrunnen, avoid hot things, talk little, and blame myself for smoking so much. I repeat, dress as warmly as possible, even at home. Avoid draughts at the theatre. Treat yourself like a hothouse plant or you will not soon be rid of your cough. If you want to try turpentine, buy the French kind. Take quinine once a day, and be careful to avoid constipation. Influenza has completely taken away from me any desire to drink spirituous liquors. They are disgusting to my taste. I don't drink my two glasses at night, and so it is a long time before I can get to sleep. I want to take ether.

I await your story. In the summer let us each write a play. Yes, by God! why the devil should we waste our time. . . .

TO E. M. S.

MOSCOW, November 19, 1891.

HONOURED ELENA MIHAILOVNA,

I am at home to all commencing, continuing, and concluding authors—that is my rule, and apart from your authorship and mine, I regard a visit from you as a great honour to me. Even if it were not so, even if for some reason I did not desire your visit, even then I should have received you, as I have enjoyed the greatest hospitality from your family. I did not receive you, and at once asked my brother to go to you and explain the cause. At the moment your card was handed me I was ill and undressed—forgive these homely details—I was in my bedroom, while there were persons in my study whose presence would not have been welcome to you. And so—to see you was physically impossible, and this my brother was to have explained to you, and you, a decent and good-hearted person, ought to have understood it; but you were offended. Well, I can't help it. . . .

But can you really have written only fifteen stories?—at this rate you won't learn to write till you are fifty.

I am in bad health; for over a month I have had to keep indoors—influenza and cough.

All good wishes.

Write another twenty stories and send them. I shall always read them with pleasure, and practice is essential for you.

TO A. S. SUVORIN.

MOSCOW, November 22, 1891.

My health is on the road to improvement. My cough is less, my strength is greater. My mood is livelier, and there is sunrise in my head. I wake up in the morning in good spirits, go to bed without gloomy thoughts, and at dinner I am not ill-humoured and don't say nasty things to my mother.

I don't know when I shall come to you. I have heaps of work pour manger. Till the spring I must work—that is, at senseless grind. A ray of liberty has beamed upon my horizon. There has come a whiff of freedom. Yesterday I got a letter from the province of Poltava. They write they have found me a suitable place. A brick house of seven rooms with an iron roof, lately built and needing no repairs, a stable, a cellar, an icehouse, eighteen acres of land, an excellent meadow for hay, an old shady garden on the bank of the river Psyol. The river bank is mine; on that side there is a marvellous view over a wide expanse. The price is merciful. Three thousand, and two thousand deferred payment over several years. Five in all. If heaven has mercy upon me, and the purchase comes off, I shall move there in March for good, to live quietly in the lap of nature for nine months and the rest of the year in Petersburg. I am sending my sister to look at the place.

Ach! liberty, liberty! If I can live on not more than two thousand a year, which is only possible in the country, I shall be absolutely free from all anxieties over money coming in and going out. Then I shall work and read, read ... in a word it will be marmelad. [Translator's Note: A kind of sweetmeat made by boiling down fruit to the consistency of damson cheese.] ...

MOSCOW,
November 30, 1891.

I return you the two manuscripts you sent me. One story is an Indian Legend—The Lotus Flower, Wreaths of Laurel, A Summer Night, The Humming Bird—that in India! He begins with Faust thirsting for youth and ends with "the bliss of the true life," in the style of Tolstoy. I have cut out parts, polished it up, and the result is a legend of no great value, indeed, but light, and it may be read with interest. The other story is illiterate, clumsy, and womanish in structure, but there is a story and a certain raciness. I have cut it down to half as you see. Both stories could be printed. . . .

I keep dreaming and dreaming. I dream of moving from Moscow into the country in March, and in the autumn coming to Petersburg to stay till the spring. I long to spend at least one winter in Petersburg, and that's only possible on condition I have no perch in Moscow. And I dream of how I shall spend five months talking to you about literature, and do as I think best in the Novoye Vremya, while in the country I shall go in for medicine heart and soul.

Boborykin has been to see me. He is dreaming too. He told me that he wants to write something in the way of the physiology of the Russian novel, its origin among us, and the natural course of its development. While he was talking I could not get rid of the feeling that I had a maniac before me, but a literary maniac who put literature far above everything in life. I so rarely see genuine literary people at home in Moscow that a conversation with Boborykin seemed like heavenly manna, though I don't believe in the physiology of the novel and the natural course of its development—that is, there may exist such a physiology in nature, but I don't believe with existing methods it can be detected. Boborykin dismisses Gogol absolutely and refuses to recognize him as a forerunner of Turgenev, Gontcharov, and Tolstoy. . . . He puts him apart, outside the current in which the Russian novel has flowed. Well, I don't understand that. If one takes the standpoint of natural development, it's impossible to put not only Gogol, but even a dog barking, outside the current, for all things in nature influence one another, and even the fact that I have just sneezed is not without its influence on surrounding nature. . . .

Good health to you! I am reading Shtchedrin's "Diary of a Provincial." How long and boring it is! And at the same time how like real life!

TO N. A. LEIKIN.

MOSCOW, December 2, 1891.

I am writing to ask you a great favour, dear Nikolay Alexandrovitch. This is what it is. Until last year I have always lived with my university diploma, which by land and by sea has served me for a passport; but every time it has been vise the police have warned me that one cannot live with a diploma, and that I ought to get a passport from "the proper department." I have asked everyone what this "proper department" means, and no one has given me an answer. A year ago the Moscow head police officer gave me a passport on the condition that within a year I should get a passport from "the proper department." I can't make head or tail of it! The other day I learned that as I have never been in the government service and by education am a doctor, I ought to be registered in the class of professional citizens, and that a certain department, I believe the heraldic, will furnish me with a certificate which will serve me as a passport for all the days of my life. I remembered that you had lately received the grade of professional citizen, and with it a certificate, and that therefore you must have applied somewhere and to someone and so, in a sense, are an old campaigner. For God's sake advise me to what department I ought to apply. What petition ought I to write, and how many stamps ought I to put on it? What documents must be enclosed with the petition? and so on, and so on. In the town hall there is a "passport bureau." Could not that bureau reveal the mystery if it is not sufficiently clear to you?

Forgive me for troubling you, but I really don't know to whom to apply, and I am a very poor lawyer myself. . . .

Your "Medal" is often given at Korsh's Theatre, and with success. It is played together with Myasnitsky's "Hare." I haven't seen them, but friends tell me that a great difference is felt between the two plays: that "The Medal" in comparison with "The Hare" seems something clean, artistic, and having form and semblance. There you have it! Literary men are swept out of the theatre, and plays are written by nondescript people, old and young, while the journals and newspapers are edited by tradesmen, government clerks, and young ladies. But there, the devil take them! . . .

TO E. P. YEGOROV.

MOSCOW, December 11, 1891.

HONOURED EVGRAF PETROVITCH,

I write to explain why my journey to you did not come off. I was intending to come to you not as a special correspondent, but on a commission from, or more correctly by agreement with, a small circle of people who want to do something for the famine-stricken peasants. The point is that the public does not trust the administration and so is deterred from subscribing. There are a thousand legends and fables about the waste, the shameless theft, and so on. People hold aloof from the Episcopal department and are indignant with the Red Cross. The owner of our beloved Babkino, the Zemsky Natchalnik, rapped out to me, bluntly and definitely: "The Red Cross in Moscow are thieves." Such being the state of feeling, the government can scarcely expect serious help from the public. And yet the public wants to help and its conscience is uneasy. In September the educated and wealthy classes of Moscow formed themselves into circles, thought, talked, and applied for advice to leading persons; everyone was talking of how to get round the government and organize independently. They decided to send to the famine-stricken provinces their own agents, who should make acquaintance with the position on the spot, open feeding centres, and so on. Some of the leaders of these circles, persons of weight, went to Durnovo to ask permission, and Durnovo refused it, declaring that the organization of relief must be left to the Episcopal department and the Red Cross. In short, private initiative was suppressed at its first efforts. Everyone was cast down and dispirited; some were furious, some simply washed their hands of the whole business. One must have the courage and authority of Tolstoy to act in opposition to all prohibitions and prevailing sentiments, and to follow the dictates of duty.

Well, now about myself. I am in complete sympathy with individual initiative, for every man has the right to do good in the way he thinks best; but all the discussion concerning the government, the Red Cross, and so on, seemed to me inopportune and impractical. I imagined that with coolness and good humour, one might get round all the terrors and delicacy of the position, and that there was no need to go to the Minister about it. I went to Sahalin without a single letter of recommendation, and yet I did everything I wanted to. Why cannot I go to the famine-stricken provinces? I remembered, too, such representatives of the government as you, Kiselyov, and all the Zemsky Natchalniks and tax inspectors of my acquaintance—all extremely decent people, worthy of complete confidence. And I resolved—if only for a small region—to combine the two elements of officialdom and private initiative. I want to come and consult you as soon as I can. The public trusts me; it would trust you, too, and I might reckon on succeeding. Do you remember I wrote to you? Suvorin came to Moscow at the time; I complained to him that I did not know your address. He telegraphed to Baranov, and Baranov was so kind as to send it to me. Suvorin was ill with influenza; as a rule when he comes to Moscow we spend whole days together discussing literature, of which he has a wide knowledge; we did the same on this occasion, and in consequence I caught his influenza, was laid up, and had a raging cough. Korolenko was in Moscow, and he found me ill. Lung complications kept me ill for a whole month, confined to the house and unable to do anything. Now I am on the way to recovery, though I still cough and am thin. There is the whole story for you. If it had not been for the influenza we might together perhaps have succeeded in extracting two or three thousand or more from the public.

Your exasperation with the press I can quite understand. The lucubrations of the journalists annoy you who know the true position of affairs, in the same way as the lucubrations of the profane about diphtheria annoy me as a doctor. But what would you have? Russia is not England and is not France. Our newspapers are not rich and they have very few men at their disposal. To send to the Volga a professor of the Petrovsky Academy or an Engelhardt is expensive: to send a talented and business-like member of the staff is impossible too—he is wanted at home. The Times could organize a census in the famine-stricken provinces at its own expense, could settle a Kennan in every district, paying him forty roubles a day, and then something sensible could be done; but what can the Russkiya Vyedomosti or the Novoye Vremya do, who consider an income of a hundred thousand as the wealth of Croesus? As for the correspondents themselves, they are townsmen who know the country only from Glyeb Uspensky. Their position is an utterly false one, they must fly into a district, sniff about, write, and dash on further. The Russian correspondent has neither material resources, nor freedom, nor authority. For two hundred roubles a month he gallops on and on, and only prays they may not be angry with him for his involuntary and inevitable misrepresentations. He feels guilty—though it is not he that is to blame but Russian darkness. The newspaper correspondents of the west have excellent maps, encyclopaedias, and statistics; in the west they could write their reports, sitting at home, but among us a correspondent can extract information only from talk and rumour. Among us in Russia only three districts have been investigated: the Tcherepov district, the Tambov district, and one other. That is all in the whole of Russia. The newspapers tell lies, the correspondents are duffers, but what's to be done? If our press said nothing the position would be still more awful, you'll admit that.

Your letter and your scheme for buying the cattle from the peasants has stirred me up. I am ready with all my heart and all my strength to follow your lead and do whatever you think best. I have thought it over for a long time, and this is my opinion: it is no use to reckon upon the rich. It is too late. Every wealthy man has by now forked out as many thousands as he is destined to. Our one resource now is the middle-class man who subscribes by the rouble and the half-rouble. Those who in September were talking about private initiative will by now have found themselves a niche in various boards and committees and are already at work. So only the middle-class man is left. Let us open a subscription list. You shall write a letter to the editors, and I will get it printed in Russkiya Vyedomosti and Novoye Vremya. To combine the two elements above mentioned, we might both sign the letter. If that is inconvenient to you from an official point of view, one might write in the third person as a communication that in the fifth section of the Nizhni Novgorod district this and that had been organized, that things were, thank God! going successfully and that subscriptions could be sent to the Zemsky Natchalnik, E. P. Yegorov, or to A. P. Chekhov, or to the editor of such and such papers. We need only to write at some length. Write in full detail, I will add something, and the thing will be done. We must ask for subscriptions and not for loans. No one will come forward with a loan; it is uncomfortable. It is hard to give, but it is harder still to take back.

I have only one rich acquaintance in Moscow, V. A. Morozov, a lady well-known for her philanthropy. I went to see her yesterday with your letter. I talked with her and dined with her. She is absorbed now in the committee of education, which is organizing relief centres for the school-children, and is giving everything to that. As education and horses are incommensurables, V. A. promised me the co-operation of the committee if we would start centres for feeding the school-children and send detailed information about it. I felt it awkward to ask her for money on the spot, for people beg and beg of her and fleece her like a fox. I only asked her when she had any committees and board meetings not to forget us, and she promised she would not....

If any roubles or half-roubles come in I will send them on to you without delay. Dispose of me and believe me that it would be a real happiness to me to do at least something, for so far I have done absolutely nothing for the famine-stricken peasants and for those who are helping them.

TO A. I. SMAGIN.

MOSCOW, December 11, 1891.

... Well, now I have something to tell you, my good sir. I am sitting at home in Moscow, but meantime my enterprise in the Nizhni Novgorod province is in full swing already! Together with my friend the Zemsky Natchalnik, an excellent man, we are hatching a little scheme, on which we expect to spend a hundred thousand or so, in the most remote section of the province, where there are no landowners nor doctors, nor even well-educated young ladies who are now to be found in numbers even in hell. Apart from famine relief of all sorts, we are making it our chief object to save the crops of next year. Owing to the fact that the peasants are selling their horses for next to nothing, there is a grave danger that the fields will not be ploughed for the spring corn, so that the famine will be repeated next year. So we are going to buy up the horses and feed them, and in spring give them back to their owners; our work is already firmly established, and in January I am going there to behold its fruits. Here is my object in writing to you. If in the course of some noisy banquet you or anyone else should chance to collect, if only half a rouble, for the famine fund, or if some Korobotchka bequeaths a rouble for that object, or if you yourself should win a hundred roubles, remember us sinners in your prayers, and spare us a part of your wealth! Not at once but when you like, only not later than in the spring. ...

TO A. S. SUVORIN.

MOSCOW, December 11, 1891.

... I am coming to you. My lying is unintentional. I have no money at all. I shall come when I get the various sums owing to me. Yesterday I got one hundred and fifty roubles, I shall soon get more, then I shall fly to you.

In January I am going to Nizhni Novgorod province: there my scheme is working already. I am very, very glad. I am going to write to Anna Pavlovna.

Ah, if you knew how agonizingly my head aches to-day! I want to come to Petersburg if only to lie motionless indoors for two days and only go out to dinner. For some reason I feel utterly exhausted. It's all this cursed influenza.

How many persons could you and would you undertake to feed? Tolstoy! ah, Tolstoy! In these days he is not a man but a super-man, a Jupiter. In the Sbornik he has published an article about the relief centres, and the article consists of advice and practical instructions. So business-like, simple, and sensible that, as the editor of Russkiya Vyedomosti said, it ought to be printed in the Government Gazette, instead of in the Sbornik. ...

December 13, 1891.

Now I understand why you don't sleep well at night. If I had written a story like that I should not have slept for ten nights in succession. The most terrible passage is where Varya strangles the hero and initiates him into the mysteries of the life beyond the grave. It's terrifying and consistent with spiritualism. You mustn't cut out a single word from Varya's speeches, especially where they are both riding on horseback. Don't touch it. The idea of the story is good, and the incidents are fantastic and interesting. ...

But why do you talk of our "nervous age"? There really is no nervous age. As people lived in the past so they live now, and the nerves of to-day are no worse than the nerves of Abraham, Isaac, and Jacob. Since you have already written the ending I shall not put you out by sending you mine. I was inspired and could not resist writing it. You can read it if you like. Stories are good in this way, that one can sit over them, pen in hand, for days together, and not notice how time passes, and at the same time be conscious of life of a sort. That's from the hygienic point of view. And from the point of view of usefulness and so on, to write a fairly good story and give the reader ten to twenty interesting minutes—that, as Gilyarovsky says, is not a sheep sneezing. . . .

I have a horrible headache again to-day. I don't know what to do. Yes, I suppose it's old age, or if it's not that it's something worse.

A little old gentleman brought me one hundred roubles to-day for the famine.

TO A. I. SMAGIN.

MOSCOW, December 16, 1891.

. . . Alas! if I don't move into the country this year, and if the purchase of the house and land for some reason does not come off, I shall be playing the part of a great villain in regard to my health. It seems to me that I am dried and warped like an old cupboard, and that if I go on living in Moscow next season, and give myself up to scribbling excesses, Gilyarovsky will read an excellent poem to welcome my entrance into that country place where there is neither sitting nor standing nor sneezing, but only lying down and nothing more. Do you know why you have no success with women? Because you have the most hideous, heathenish, desperate, tragic handwriting. . . .

TO A. N. PLESHTCHEYEV.

MOSCOW, December 25, 1891.

DEAR ALEXEY NIKOLAEVITCH,

Yesterday I chanced to learn your address, and I write to you. If you have a free minute please write to me how you are in health, and how you are getting on altogether. Write, if only a couple of lines.

I have had influenza for the last six weeks. There has been a complication of the lungs and I have a cruel cough. In March I am going south to the province of Poltava, and shall stay there till my cough is gone. My sister has gone down there to buy a house and garden.

Literary doings here are quiet but life is bustling. There is a great deal of talk about the famine, and a great deal of work resulting from the said talk. The theatres are empty, the weather is wretched, there are no frosts at all. Jean Shteheglov is captivated by the Tolstoyans. Merezhkovsky sits at home as of old, lost in a labyrinth of deep researches, and as of old is very nice; of Chekhov they say he has married the heiress Sibiryakov and got five millions dowry—all Petersburg is talking of it. For whose benefit and for what object this slander, I am utterly unable to imagine. It's positively sickening to read letters from Petersburg.

I have not seen Ostrovsky this year. . . .

We shall probably not meet very soon, as I am going away in March and shall not return to the North before November. I shall not keep a flat in Moscow, as that pleasure is beyond my means. I shall stay in Petersburg.

I embrace you warmly. By the way, a little explanation in private. One day at dinner in Paris, persuading me to remain there, you offered to lend me money. I refused, and it seemed to me my refusal hurt and vexed you, and I fancied that when we parted there was a touch of coldness on your side. Possibly I am mistaken, but if I am right I assure you, my dear friend, on my word of honour, that I refused not because I did not care to be under an obligation to you, but simply from a feeling of self-preservation; I was behaving stupidly in Paris, and an extra thousand francs would only have been bad for my health. Believe me that if I had needed it, I would have asked you for a loan as readily as Suvorin.

God keep you.

TO V. A. TIHONOV.

MOSCOW, February 22, 1892.

. . . You are mistaken in thinking you were drunk at Shtcheglov's name-day party. You had had a drop, that was all. You danced when they all danced, and your jigitivka on the cabman's box excited nothing but general delight. As for your criticism, it was most likely far from severe, as I don't remember it. I only remember that Vvedensky and I for some reason roared with laughter as we listened to you.

Do you want my biography? Here it is. I was born in Taganrog in 1860. I finished the course at Taganrog high school in 1879. In 1884 I took my degree in medicine at the University of Moscow. In 1888 I gained the Pushkin prize. In 1890 I made a journey to Sahalin across Siberia and back by sea. In 1891 I made a tour in Europe, where I drank excellent wine and ate oysters. In 1892 I took part in an orgy in the company of V. A. Tihonov at a name-day party. I began writing in 1879. The published collections of my works are: "Motley Tales," "In the Twilight," "Stories," "Surly People," and a novel, "The Duel." I have sinned in the dramatic line too, though with moderation. I have been translated into all the languages with the exception of the foreign ones, though I have indeed long ago been translated by the Germans. The Czechs and the Serbs approve of me also, and the French are not indifferent. The mysteries of love I fathomed at the age of thirteen. With my colleagues, doctors, and literary men alike, I am on the best of terms. I am a bachelor. I should like to receive a pension. I practice medicine, and so much so that sometimes in the summer I perform post-mortems, though I have not done so for two or three years. Of authors my favourite is Tolstoy, of doctors Zaharin.

All that is nonsense though. Write what you like. If you haven't facts make up with lyricism.

TO A. S. KISELYOV.

MELIHOVO, STATION LOPASNYA,
MOSCOW-KURSK LINE. March 7, 1892.

This is our new address. And here are the details for you. If a peasant woman has no troubles she buys a pig. We have bought a pig, too, a big cumbersome estate, the owner of which would in Germany infallibly be made a herzog. Six hundred and thirty-nine acres in two parts with land not ours in between. Three hundred acres of young copse, which in twenty years will look like a wood, at present is a thicket of bushes. They call it "shaft wood," but to my mind the name of "switch wood" would be more appropriate, since one could make nothing of it at present but switches. There is a fruit-garden, a park, big trees, long avenues of limes. The barns and sheds have been recently built, and have a fairly presentable appearance.

The poultry house is made in accordance with the latest deductions of science, the well has an iron pump. The whole place is shut off from the world by a fence in the style of a palisade. The yard, the garden, the park, and the threshing-floor are shut off from each other in the same way. The house is good and bad. It's more roomy than our Moscow flat, it's light and warm, roofed with iron, and stands in a fine position, has a verandah into the garden, French windows, and so on, but it is bad in not being lofty, not sufficiently new, having outside a very stupid and naive appearance, and inside swarms with bugs and beetles which could only be got rid of by one means—a fire: nothing else would do for them.

There are flower-beds. In the garden fifteen paces from the house is a pond (thirty-five yards long, and thirty-five feet wide), with carp and tench in it, so that you can catch fish from the window. Beyond the yard there is another pond, which I have not yet seen. In the other part of the estate there is a river, probably a nasty one. Two miles away there is a broad river full of fish. We shall sow oats and clover. We have bought clover seed at ten roubles a pood, but we have no money left for oats. The estate has been bought for thirteen thousand. The legal formalities cost about seven hundred and fifty roubles, total fourteen thousand. The artist who sold it was paid four thousand down, and received a mortgage for five thousand at five per cent, for five years. The remaining four thousand the artist will receive from the Land Bank when in the spring I mortgage the estate to a bank. You see what a good arrangement. In two or three years I shall have five thousand, and shall pay off the mortgage, and shall be left with only the four thousand debt to the bank; but I have got to live those two of three years, hang it all! What matters is not the interest—that is small, not more than five hundred roubles a year—but that I shall be obliged all the time to think about quarter-days and all sorts of horrors attendant on being in debt. Moreover, your honour, as long as I am alive and earning four or five thousand a year, the debts will seem a trifle, and even a convenience, for to pay four hundred and seventy interest is much easier than to pay a thousand for a flat in Moscow; that is all true. But what if I depart from you sinners to another world—that is, give up the ghost? Then the ducal estate with the debts would seem to my parents in their green old age and to my sister such a burden that they would raise a wail to heaven.

I was completely cleaned out over the move.

Ah, if you could come and see us! In the first place it would be very delightful and interesting to see you; and in the second, your advice would save us from a thousand idiocies. You know we don't understand a thing about it. Like Raspluev, all I know about agriculture is that the earth is black, and nothing more. Write. How is it best to sow clover?—among the rye, or among the spring wheat? . . .

TO I. L. SHTCHEGLOV.

MELIHOVO, March 9, 1892.

. . . Yes, such men as Ratchinsky are very rare in this world. I understand your enthusiasm, my dear fellow. After the suffocation one feels in the proximity of A. and B.—and the world is full of them—Ratchinsky with his ideas, his humanity, and his purity, seems like a breath of spring. I am ready to lay down my life for Ratchinsky; but, dear friend,—allow me that "but" and don't be vexed—I would not send my children to his school. Why? I received a religious education in my childhood—with church singing, with reading of the "apostles" and the psalms in church, with regular attendance at matins, with obligation to assist at the altar and ring the bells. And, do you know, when I think now of my childhood, it seems to me rather gloomy. I have no religion now. Do you know, when my brothers and I used to stand in the middle of the church and sing the trio "May my prayer be exalted," or "The Archangel's Voice," everyone looked at us with emotion and envied our parents, but we at that moment felt like little convicts. Yes, dear boy! Ratchinsky I understand, but the children who are trained by him I don't know. Their souls are dark for me. If there is joy in their souls, then they are happier than I and my brothers, whose childhood was suffering.

It is nice to be a lord. There is plenty of room, it's warm, people are not continually pulling at the bell; and it is easy to descend from one's lordship and serve as concierge or porter. My estate, sir, cost thirteen thousand, and I have only paid a third, the rest is a debt which will keep me long years on the chain.

Come and see me, Jean, together with Suvorin. Make a plan with him. I have such a garden! Such a naive courtyard, such geese! Write a little oftener.

TO A. S. SUVORIN.

MELIHOVO, March 17, 1892.

... Ah, my dear fellow, if only you could take a holiday! Living in the country is inconvenient. The insufferable time of thaw and mud is beginning, but something marvellous and moving is taking place in nature, the poetry and novelty of which makes up for all the discomforts of life. Every day there are surprises, one better than another. The starlings have returned, everywhere there is the gurgling of water, in places where the snow has thawed the grass is already green. The day drags on like eternity. One lives as though in Australia, somewhere at the ends of the earth; one's mood is calm, contemplative, and animal, in the sense that one does not regret yesterday or look forward to tomorrow. From here, far away, people seem very good, and that is natural, for in going away into the country we are not hiding from people but from our vanity, which in town among people is unjust and active beyond measure. Looking at the spring, I have a dreadful longing that there should be paradise in the other world. In fact, at moments I am so happy that I superstitiously pull myself up and remind myself of my creditors, who will one day drive me out of the Australia I have so happily won. ...

TO MADAME AVILOV.

MELIHOVO, March 19, 1892.

HONOURED LIDYA ALEXYEVNA,

I have read your story "On the Road." If I were the editor of an illustrated magazine, I should publish the story with great pleasure; but here is my advice as a reader: when you depict sad or unlucky people, and want to touch the reader's heart, try to be colder—it gives their grief as it were a background, against which it stands out in greater relief. As it is, your heroes weep and you sigh. Yes, you must be cold.

But don't listen to me, I am a bad critic. I have not the faculty of forming my critical ideas clearly. Sometimes I make a regular hash of it. ...

TO A. S. SUVORIN.

MELIHOVO, March, 1892.

The cost of labour is almost nil, and so I am very well off. I begin to see the charms of capitalism. To pull down the stove in the servants' quarters and build up there a kitchen stove with all its accessories, then to pull down the kitchen stove in the house arid put up a Dutch stove instead, costs twenty roubles altogether. The price of two men to dig, twenty-five kopecks. To fill the ice cellar it costs thirty kopecks a day to the workmen. A young labourer who does not drink or smoke, and can read and write, whose duties are to work the land and clean the boots and look after the flower-garden, costs five roubles a month. Floors, partitions, papering walls—all that is cheaper than mushrooms. And I am at ease. But if I were to pay for labour a quarter of what I get for my leisure I should be ruined in a month, as the number of stove-builders, carpenters, joiners, and so on, threatens to go for ever after the fashion of a recurring decimal. A spacious life not cramped within four walls requires a spacious pocket too. I have bored you already, but I must tell you one thing more: the clover seed costs one hundred roubles a pood, and the oats needed for seed cost more than a hundred. Think of that! They prophesy a harvest and wealth for me, but what is that to me! Better five kopecks in the present than a rouble in the future. I must sit and work. I must earn at least five hundred roubles for all these trifles. I have earned half already. And the snow is melting, it is warm, the birds are singing, the sky is bright and spring-like.

I am reading a mass of things. I have read Lyeskov's "Legendary Characters," religious and piquant—a combination of virtue, piety, and lewdness, but very interesting. Read it if you haven't read it. I have read again Pisarev's "Criticism of Pushkin." Awfully naive. The man pulls Onyegin and Tatyana down from their pedestals, but Pushkin remains unhurt. Pisarev is the grandfather and father of all the critics of to-day, including Burenin—the same pettiness in disparagement, the same cold and conceited wit, and the same coarseness and indelicacy in their attitude to people. It is not Pisarev's ideas that are brutalizing, for he has none, but his coarse tone. His attitude to Tatyana, especially to her charming letter, which I love tenderly, seems to me simply abominable. The critic has the foul aroma of an insolent captious procurator.

We have almost finished furnishing; only the shelves for my books are not done yet. When we take out the double windows we shall begin painting everything afresh, and then the house will have a very presentable appearance.

There are avenues of lime-trees, apple-trees, cherries, plums, and raspberries in the garden. . . .

MELIHOVO,
April 6, 1892.

It is Easter. There is a church here, but no clergy. We collected eleven roubles from the whole parish and got a priest from the Davydov Monastery, who began celebrating the service on Friday. The church is very old and chilly, with lattice windows. We sang the Easter service—that is, my family and my visitors, young people. The effect was very good and harmonious, particularly the mass. The peasants were very much pleased, and they say they have never had such a grand service. Yesterday the sun shone all day, it was warm. In the morning I went into the fields, from which the snow has gone already, and spent half an hour in the happiest frame of mind: it was amazingly nice! The winter corn is green already, and there is grass in the copse.

You will not like Melihovo, at least at first. Here everything is in miniature; a little avenue of lime-trees, a pond the size of an aquarium, a little garden and park, little trees; but when you have walked about it once or twice the impression of littleness goes off. There is great feeling of space in spite of the village being so near. There is a great deal of forest around. There are numbers of starlings, and the starling has the right to say of itself: "I sing to my God all the days of my life." It sings all day long without stopping. . . .

MELIHOVO,
April 8, 1892.

If Shapiro were to present me with the gigantic photograph of which you write, I should not know what to do with it. A cumbersome present.

You say that I used to be younger. Yes, imagine! Strange as it may seem, I have passed thirty some time ago, and I already feel forty close at hand. I have grown old not in body only, but in spirit. I have become stupidly indifferent to everything in the world, and for some reason or other the beginning of this indifference coincided with my tour abroad. I get up and go to bed feeling as though interest in life had dried up in me. This is either the illness called in the newspapers nervous exhaustion, or some working of the spirit not clear to the consciousness, which is called in novels a spiritual revulsion. If it is the latter it is all for the best, I suppose.

The artist Levitan is staying with me. Yesterday evening I went out with him shooting. He shot at a snipe; the bird, shot in the wing, fell into a pool. I picked it up: a long beak, big black eyes, and beautiful plumage. It looked at me with surprise. What was I to do with it? Levitan scowled, shut his eyes, and begged me, with a quiver in his voice: "My dear fellow, hit him on the head with the butt-end of your gun." I said: "I can't." He went on nervously, shrugging his shoulders, twitching his head and begging me to; and the snipe went on looking at me in wonder. I had to obey Levitan and kill it. One beautiful creature in love the less, while two fools went home and sat down to supper.

Jean Shtcheglov, in whose company you were so bored for a whole evening, is a great opponent of every sort of heresy, and amongst others of feminine intellect; and yet if one compares him with K., for instance, beside her he seems like a foolish little monk. By the way, if you see K., give her my greetings, and tell her that we are expecting her here. She is very interesting in the open air and far more intelligent than in town. . . .

TO MADAME AVILOV.

MELIHOVO, April 29, 1892.

. . . Yes, it is nice now in the country, not only nice but positively amazing. It's real spring, the trees are coming out, it is hot. The nightingales are singing, and the frogs are croaking in all sorts of tones. I haven't a halfpenny, but the way I look at it is this: the rich man is not he who has plenty of money, but he who has the means to live now in the luxurious surroundings given us by early spring. Yesterday I was in Moscow, but I almost expired there of boredom and all manner of disasters. Would you believe it, a lady of my acquaintance, aged forty-two, recognized herself in the twenty-year-old heroine of my story, "The Grasshopper" and all Moscow is accusing me of libelling her. The chief proof is the external likeness. The lady paints, her husband is a doctor, and she is living with an artist.

I am finishing a story ("Ward No. 6"), a very dull one, owing to a complete absence of woman and the element of love. I can't endure such stories. I write it as it were by accident, thoughtlessly.

Yes, I wrote to you once that you must be unconcerned when you write pathetic stories. And you did not understand me. You may weep and moan over your stories, you may suffer together with your heroes, but I consider one must do this so that the reader does not notice it. The more objective, the stronger will be the effect.

TO A. S. SUVORIN.

MELIHOVO, May 15, 1892.

... I have got hold of the peasants and the shopkeepers here. One had a haemorrhage from the throat, another had his arm crushed by a tree, a third had his little daughter sick.... It seems they would be in a desperate case without me. They bow respectfully to me as Germans do to their pastor, I am friends with them, and all goes well....

May 28, 1892.

Life is short, and Chekhov, from whom you are expecting an answer, would like it to flash by brilliantly and with dash. He would go to Prince's Island, to Constantinople, and again to India and Sahalin.... But in the first place he is not free, he has a respectable family who need his protection. In the second, he has a large dose of cowardice. Looking towards the future I call nothing but cowardice. I am afraid of getting into a muddle, and every journey complicates my financial position. No, don't tempt me without need. Don't write to me of the sea.

It is hot here. There are warm rains, the evenings are enchanting. Three-quarters of a mile from here there is a good bathing place and good sport for picnics, but no time to bathe or go to picnics. Either I am writing and gnashing my teeth, or settling questions of halfpence with carpenters and labourers. Misha was cruelly reprimanded by his superiors for coming to me every week instead of staying at home, and now there is no one but me to look after the farming, in which I have no faith, as it is on a petty scale, and more like a gentlemanly hobby than real work. I have bought three mousetraps, and catch twenty-five mice a day and carry them away to the copse. It is lovely in the copse. . . .

Our starlings, old and young, suddenly flew away. This puzzled us, for it won't be time for their migration for ever so long; but suddenly we learn that the other day clouds of grasshoppers from the south, which were taken for locusts, flew over Moscow. One wonders how did our starlings find out that on precisely such a day and so many miles from Melihovo these insects would fly past? Who told them about it? Truly this is a great mystery. . . .

June 16.
. . . You want me to write my impressions to you.

My soul longs for breadth and altitude, but I am forced to lead a narrow life spent over trashy roubles and kopecks. There is nothing more vulgar than a petty bourgeois life with its halfpence, its victuals, its futile talk, and its useless conventional virtue; my heart aches from the consciousness that I am working for money, and money is the centre of all I do. This aching feeling, together with a sense of justice, makes my writing a contemptible pursuit in my eyes: I don't respect what I write, I am apathetic and bored with myself, and glad that I have medicine which, anyway, I practise not for the sake of money. I ought to have a bath in sulphuric acid and flay off my skin, and then grow a new hide. . . .

MELIHOVO,
August 1.

My letters chase you, but do not catch you. I have written to you often, and among other places to St. Moritz. Judging from your letters you have had nothing from me. In the first place, there is cholera in Moscow and about Moscow, and it will be in our parts some day soon. In the second place, I have been appointed cholera doctor, and my section includes twenty-five villages, four factories, and one monastery. I am organizing the building of barracks, and so on, and I feel lonely, for all the cholera business is alien to my heart, and the work, which involves continual driving about, talking, and attention to petty details, is exhausting for me. I have no time to write. Literature has been thrown aside for a long time now, and I am poverty-stricken, as I thought it convenient for myself and my independence to refuse the remuneration received by the section doctors. I am bored, but there is a great deal that is interesting in cholera if you look at it from a detached point of view. I am sorry you are not in Russia. Material for short letters is being wasted. There is more good than bad, and in that cholera is a great contrast to the famine which we watched in the winter. Now all are working—they are working furiously. At the fair at Nizhni they are doing marvels which might force even Tolstoy to take a respectful attitude to medicine and the intervention of cultured people generally in life. It seems as though they had got a hold on the cholera. They have not only decreased the number of cases, but also the percentage of deaths. In immense Moscow the cholera does not exceed fifty cases a week, while on the Don it is a thousand a day—an impressive difference. We district doctors are getting ready; our plan of action is definite, and there are grounds for supposing that in our parts we too shall decrease the percentage of mortality from cholera. We have no assistants, one has to be doctor and sanitary attendant at one and the same time. The peasants are rude, dirty in their habits, and mistrustful; but the thought that our labours are not thrown away makes all that scarcely noticeable. Of all the Serpuhovo doctors I am the most pitiable; I have a scurvy carriage and horses, I don't know the roads, I see nothing by evening light, I have no money, I am very quickly exhausted, and worst of all, I can never forget that I ought to be writing, and I long to spit on the cholera and sit down and write to you, and I long to talk to you. I am in absolute loneliness.

Our farming labours have been crowned with complete success. The harvest is considerable, and when we sell the corn Melihovo will bring us more than a thousand roubles. The kitchen garden is magnificent. There are perfect mountains of cucumbers and the cabbage is wonderful. If it were not for the accursed cholera I might say that I have never spent a summer so happily as this one.

Nothing has been heard of cholera riots yet. There is talk of some arrests, some manifestoes, and so on. They say that A., the writer, has been condemned to fifteen years' penal servitude. If the socialists are really going to exploit the cholera for their own ends I shall despise them. Revolting means for good ends make the ends themselves revolting. Let them get a lift on the backs of the doctors and feldshers, but why lie to the peasants? Why persuade them that they are right in their ignorance and that their coarse prejudices are the holy truth? If I were a politician I could never bring myself to disgrace my present for the sake of the future, even though I were promised tons of felicity for an ounce of mean lying. Write to me as often as possible in consideration of my exceptional position. I cannot be in a good mood now, and your letters snatch me away from cholera concerns, and carry me for a brief space to another world. . . .

August 16.

I'll be damned if I write to you again. I have written to Abbazzio, to St. Moritz. I have written a dozen times at least, so far you have not sent me one correct address, and so not one of my letters has reached and my long description and lectures about the cholera have been wasted. It's mortifying. But what is most mortifying is that after a whole series of letters from me about our exertions against the cholera, you all at once write me from gay Biarritz that you envy my leisure! Well, Allah forgive you!

Well, I am alive and in good health. The summer was a splendid one, dry, warm, abounding in the fruits of the earth, but its whole charm was from July onwards, spoilt by news of the cholera. While you were inviting me in your letters first to Vienna, and then to Abbazzio I was already one of the doctors of the Serpuhovo Zemstvo, was trying to catch the cholera by its tail and organizing a new section full steam. In the morning I have to see patients, and in the afternoon drive about. I drive, I give lectures to the natives, treat them, get angry with them, and as the Zemstvo has not granted me a single kopeck for organizing the medical centres I cadge from the wealthy, first from one and then from another. I turn out to be an excellent beggar; thanks to my beggarly eloquence, my section has two excellent barracks with all the necessaries, and five barracks that are not excellent, but horrid. I have saved the Zemstvo from expenditure even on disinfectants. Lime, vitriol, and all sorts of stinking stuff I have begged from the manufacturers for all my twenty-five villages. In fact Kolomin ought to be proud of having been at the same high school with me. My soul is exhausted. I am bored. Not to belong to oneself, to think about nothing but diarrhoea, to start up in the night at a dog's barking and a knock at the gate ("Haven't they come for me?"), to drive with disgusting horses along unknown roads; to read about nothing but cholera, and to expect nothing but cholera, and at the same time to be utterly uninterested in that disease, and in the people whom one is serving—that, my good sir, is a hash which wouldn't agree with anyone. The cholera is already in Moscow and in the Moscow district. One must expect it from hour to hour. Judging from its course in Moscow one must suppose that it is already declining and that the bacillus is losing its strength. One is bound to think, too, that it is powerfully affected by the measures that have been taken in Moscow and among us. The educated classes are working vigorously, sparing neither themselves nor their purses; I see them every day, and am touched, and when I remember how Zhitel and Burenin used to vent their acrid spleen on these same educated people I feel almost suffocated. In Nizhni the doctors and the cultured people generally have done marvels. I was overwhelmed with enthusiasm when I read about the cholera. In the good old times, when people were infected and died by thousands, the amazing conquests that are being made before our eyes could not even be dreamed of. It's a pity you are not a doctor and cannot share my delight—that is, fully feel and recognize and appreciate all that is being done. But one cannot tell about it briefly.

The treatment of cholera requires of the doctor deliberation before all things—that is, one has to devote to each patient from five to ten hours or even longer. As I mean to employ Kantani's treatment—that is clysters of tannin and sub-cutaneous injection of a solution of common salt—my position will be worse than foolish; while I am busying myself over one patient, a dozen can fall ill and die. You see I am the only man for twenty-five villages, apart from a feldsher who calls me "your honour," does not venture to smoke in my presence, and cannot take a step without me. If there are isolated cases I shall be capital; but if there is an epidemic of only five cases a day, then I shall do nothing but be irritable and exhausted and feel myself guilty.

Of course there is no time even to think of literature. I am writing nothing. I refused remuneration so as to preserve some little freedom of action for myself, and so I have not a halfpenny. I am waiting till they have threshed and sold the rye. Until then I shall be living on "The Bear" and mushrooms, of which there are endless masses here. By the way, I have never lived so cheaply as now. We have everything of our own, even our own bread. I believe in a couple of years all my household expenses will not exceed a thousand roubles a year.

When you learn from the newspapers that the cholera is over, you will know that I have gone back to writing again. Don't think of me as a literary man while I am in the service of the Zemstvo. One can't do two things at once.

You write that I have given up Sahalin. I cannot abandon that child of mine. When I am oppressed by the boredom of belles-lettres I am glad to turn to something else. The question when I shall finish Sahalin and when I shall print does not strike me as being important. While Galkin-Vrasskoy reigns over the prison system I feel very much disinclined to bring out my book. Of course if I am driven to it by need, that is a different matter.

In all my letters I have pertinaciously asked you one question, which of course you are not obliged to answer: "Where are you going to be in the autumn, and wouldn't you like to spend part of September and October with me in Feodosia or the Crimea?" I have an impatient desire to eat, drink, and sleep, and talk about literature—that is, do nothing, and at the same time feel like a decent person. However, if my idleness annoys you, I can promise to write with or beside you, a play or a story. . . . Eh? Won't you? Well, God be with you, then.

The astronomer has been here twice. I felt bored with her on both occasions. Svobodin has been here too. He grows better and better. His serious illness has made him pass through a spiritual metamorphosis.

See what a long letter I have written, even though I don't feel sure that the letter will reach you. Imagine my cholera-boredom, my cholera-loneliness, and compulsory literary inactivity, and write to me more, and oftener. Your contemptuous feeling for France I share. The Germans are far above them, though for some reason they are called stupid. And the Franco-Russian Entente Cordiale I am as fond of as Tolstoy is. There's something nastily suggestive about these cordialities. On the other hand I was awfully pleased at Virchow's visit to us.

We have raised a very nice potato and a divine cabbage. How do you manage to get on without cabbage-soup? I don't envy you your sea, nor your freedom, nor the happy frame of mind you are in abroad. The Russian summer is better than anything. And by the way, I don't feel any great longing to be abroad. After Singapore, Ceylon, and perhaps even our Amur, Italy and even the crater of Vesuvius do not seem fascinating. After being in India and China I did not see a great difference between other European countries and Russia.

A neighbour of ours, the owner of the renowned Otrad, Count X, is staying now at Biarritz, having run away from the cholera; he gave his doctor only five hundred roubles for the campaign against the cholera. His sister, the countess, who is living in my section, when I went to discuss the provision of barracks for her workmen, treated me as though I had come to apply for a situation. It mortified me, and I told her a lie, pretending to be a rich man. I told the same lie to the Archimandrite, who refuses to provide quarters for the cases which may occur in the monastery. To my question what would he do with the cases that might be taken ill in his hostel, he answered me: "They are persons of means and will pay you themselves. . . ." Do you understand? And I flared up, and said I did not care about payment, as I was well off, and that all I wanted was the security of the monastery. . . . There are sometimes very stupid and humiliating positions. . . . Before the count went away I met his wife. Huge diamonds in her ears, wearing a bustle, and not knowing how to hold herself. A millionaire. In the company of such persons one has a stupid schoolboy feeling of wanting to be rude.

The village priest often comes and pays me long visits; he is a very good fellow, a widower, and has some illegitimate children.

Write or there will be trouble. . . .

MELIHOVO,
October 10, 1892.

Your telegram telling me of Svobodin's death caught me just as I was going out of the yard to see patients. You can imagine my feelings. Svobodin stayed with me this summer; he was very sweet and gentle, in a serene and affectionate mood, and became very much attached to me. It was evident to me that he had not very long to live, it was evident to him too. He had the thirst of the aged for everyday peace and quiet, and had grown to detest the stage and everything to do with the stage and dreaded returning to Petersburg. Of course I ought to go to the funeral, but to begin with, your telegram came towards evening, and the funeral is most likely tomorrow, and secondly the cholera is twenty miles away, and I cannot leave my centre. There are seven cases in one village, and two have died already. The cholera may break out in my section. It is strange that with winter coming on the cholera is spreading over a wider and wider region.

I have undertaken to be the section doctor till the fifteenth of October—my section will be officially closed on that day. I shall dismiss my feldsher, close the barracks, and if the cholera comes, I shall cut rather a comic figure. Add to that the doctor of the next section is ill with pleurisy and so, if the cholera appears in his section, I shall be bound, from a feeling of comradeship, to undertake his section.

So far I have not had a single case of cholera, but I have had epidemics of typhus, diphtheria, scarlatina, and so on. At the beginning of summer I had a great deal of work, then towards the autumn less and less.

The sum of my literary achievement this summer, thanks to the cholera, has been almost nil. I have written little, and have thought about literature even less. However, I have written two small stories—one tolerable, one bad.

Life has been hard work this summer, but it seems to me now that I have never spent a summer so well as this one. In spite of the turmoil of the cholera, and the poverty which has kept tight hold of me all the summer, I have liked the life and wanted to live. How many trees I have planted! Thanks to our system of cultivation, Melihovo has become unrecognizable, and seems now extraordinarily snug and beautiful, though very likely it is good for nothing. Great is the power of habit and the sense of property. And it's marvellous how pleasant it is not to have to pay rent. We have made new acquaintances and formed new relations. Our old terrors in facing the peasants now seem ludicrous. I have served in the Zemstvo, have presided at the Sanitary Council and visited the factories, and I liked all that. They think of me now as one of themselves, and stay the night with me when they pass through Melihovo. Add to that, that we have bought ourselves a new comfortable covered carriage, have made a new road, so that now we don't drive through the village. We are digging a pond. . . . Anything else?

In fact hitherto everything has been new and interesting, but how it will be later on, I don't know. There is snow already, it is cold, but I don't feel drawn to Moscow. So far I have not had any feeling of dulness.

The educated people here are very charming and interesting. What matters most, they are honest. Only the police are unattractive.

We have seven horses, a broad-faced calf, and puppies, called Muir and Merrilees....

November 22, 1892.

Snow is falling by day, while at night the moon is shining its utmost, a gorgeous amazing moon. It is magnificent. But nevertheless, I marvel at the fortitude of landowners who spend the winter in the country; there's so little to do that if anyone is not in one way or another engaged in intellectual work, he is inevitably bound to become a glutton or a drunkard, or a man like Turgenev's Pigasov. The monotony of the snowdrifts and the bare trees, the long nights, the moonlight, the deathlike stillness day and night, the peasant women and the old ladies—all that disposes one to indolence, indifference, and an enlarged liver....

November 25, 1892.

It is easy to understand you, and there is no need for you to abuse yourself for obscurity of expression. You are a hard drinker, and I have regaled you with sweet lemonade, and you, after giving the lemonade its due, justly observe that there is no spirit in it. That is just what is lacking in our productions—the alcohol which could intoxicate and subjugate, and you state that very well. Why not? Putting aside "Ward No. 6" and myself, let us discuss the matter in general, for that is more interesting. Let me discuss the general causes, if that won't bore you, and let us include the whole age. Tell me honestly, who of my contemporaries—that is, men between thirty and forty-five—have given the world one single drop of alcohol? Are not Korolenko, Nadson, and all the playwrights of to-day, lemonade? Have Ryepin's or Shishkin's pictures turned your head? Charming, talented, you are enthusiastic; but at the same time you can't forget that you want to smoke. Science and technical knowledge are passing through a great period now, but for our sort it is a flabby, stale, and dull time. We are stale and dull ourselves, we can only beget gutta-percha boys, and the only person who does not see that is Stassov, to whom nature has given a rare faculty for getting drunk on slops. The causes of this are not to be found in our stupidity, our lack of talent, or our insolence, as Burenin imagines, but in a disease which for the artist is worse than syphilis or sexual exhaustion. We lack "something," that is true, and that means that, lift the robe of our muse, and you will find within an empty void. Let me remind you that the writers, who we say are for all time or are simply good, and who intoxicate us, have one common and very important characteristic; they are going towards something and are summoning you towards it, too, and you feel not with your mind, but with your whole being, that they have some object, just like the ghost of Hamlet's father, who did not come and disturb the imagination for nothing. Some have more immediate objects—the abolition of serfdom, the liberation of their country, politics, beauty, or simply vodka, like Denis Davydov; others have remote objects—God, life beyond the grave, the happiness of humanity, and so on. The best of them are realists and paint life as it is, but, through every line's being soaked in the consciousness of an object, you feel, besides life as it is, the life which ought to be, and that captivates you. And we? We! We paint life as it is, but beyond that—nothing at all. . . . Flog us and we can do no more! We have neither immediate nor remote aims, and in our soul there is a great empty space. We have no politics, we do not believe in revolution, we have no God, we are not afraid of ghosts, and I personally am not afraid even of death and blindness. One who wants nothing, hopes for nothing, and fears nothing, cannot be an artist. Whether it is a disease or not—what it is does not matter; but we ought to recognize that our position is worse than a governor's. I don't know how it will be with us in ten or twenty years—then circumstances may be different, but meanwhile it would be rash to expect of us anything of real value, apart from the question whether we have talent or not. We write mechanically, merely obeying the long-established arrangement in accordance with which some men go into the government service, others into trade, others write. . . . Grigorovitch and you think I am clever. Yes, I am at least so far clever as not to conceal from myself my disease, and not to deceive myself, and not to cover up my own emptiness with other people's rags, such as the ideas of the sixties, and so on. I am not going to throw myself like Garshin over the banisters, but I am not going to flatter myself with hopes of a better future either. I am not to blame for my disease, and it's not for me to cure myself, for this disease, it must be supposed, has some good purpose hidden from us, and is not sent in vain. . . .

February, 1893.

My God! What a glorious thing "Fathers and Children" is! It is positively terrifying. Bazarov's illness is so powerfully done that I felt ill and had a sensation as though I had caught the infection from him. And the end of Bazarov? And the old men? And Kukshina? It's beyond words. It's simply a work of genius. I don't like the whole of "On the Eve," only Elena's father and the end. The end is full of tragedy. "The Dog" is very good, the language is wonderful in it. Please read it if you have forgotten it. "Acia" is charming, "A Quiet Backwater" is too compressed and not satisfactory. I don't like "Smoke" at all. "The House of Gentlefolk" is weaker than "Fathers and Children," but the end is like a miracle, too. Except for the old woman in "Fathers and Children"—that is, Bazarov's mother—and the mothers as a rule, especially the society ladies, who are, however, all alike (Liza's mother, Elena's mother), and Lavretsky's mother, who had been a serf, and the humble peasant woman, all Turgenev's girls and women are insufferable in their artificiality, and—forgive my saying it—falsity. Liza and Elena are not Russian girls, but some sort of Pythian prophetesses, full of extravagant pretensions. Irina in "Smoke," Madame Odintsov in "Fathers and Children," all the lionesses, in fact, fiery, alluring, insatiable creatures for ever craving for something, are all nonsensical. When one thinks of Tolstoy's "Anna Karenin," all these young ladies of Turgenev's, with their seductive shoulders, fade away into nothing. The negative types of women where Turgenev is slightly caricaturing (Kukshina) or jesting (the descriptions of balls) are wonderfully drawn, and so successful, that, as the saying is, you can't pick a hole in it.

The descriptions of nature are fine, but . . . I feel that we have already got out of the way of such descriptions and that we need something different. . . .

April 26, 1893.

. . . I am reading Pisemsky. His is a great, very great talent! The best of his works is "The Carpenters' Guild." His novels are exhausting in their minute detail. Everything in him that has a temporary character, all his digs at the critics and liberals of the period, all his critical observations with their assumption of smartness and modernity, and all the so-called profound reflections scattered here and there—how petty and naive it all is to our modern ideas! The fact of the matter is this: a novelist, an artist, ought to pass by everything that has only a temporary value. Pisemsky's people are living, his temperament is vigorous. Skabitchevsky in his history attacks him for obscurantism and treachery, but, my God! of all contemporary writers I don't know a single one so passionately and earnestly liberal as Pisemsky. All his priests, officials, and generals are regular blackguards. No one was so down on the old legal and military set as he.

By the way, I have read also Bourget's "Cosmopolis." Rome and the Pope and Correggio and Michael Angelo and Titian and doges and a fifty-year-old beauty and Russians and Poles are all in Bourget, but how thin and strained and mawkish and false it is in comparison even with our coarse and simple Pisemsky! ...

What a good thing I gave up the town! Tell all the Fofanovs, Tchermnys, et tutti quanti who live by literature, that living in the country is immensely cheaper than living in the town. I experience this now every day. My family costs me nothing now, for lodging, bread, vegetables, milk, butter, horses, are all our own. And there is so much to do, there is not time to get through it all. Of the whole family of Chekhovs, I am the only one to lie down, or sit at the table: all the rest are working from morning till night. Drive the poets and literary men into the country. Why should they live in starvation and beggary? Town life cannot give a poor man rich material in the sense of poetry and art. He lives within four walls and sees people only at the editors' offices and in eating-shops. ...

MELIHOVO,
January 25, 1894.

I believe I am mentally sound. It is true I have no special desire to live, but that is not, so far, disease, but something probably passing and natural. It does not follow every time that an author describes someone mentally deranged, that he is himself deranged. I wrote "The Black Monk" without any melancholy ideas, through cool reflection. I simply had a desire to describe megalomania. The monk floating across the country was a dream, and when I woke I told Misha about it. So you can tell Anna Ivanovna that poor Anton Pavlovitch, thank God! has not gone out of his mind yet, but that he eats a great deal at supper and so he dreams of monks.

I keep forgetting to write to you: read Ertel's story "The Seers" in "Russkaya Mysl." There is poetry and something terrible in the old-fashioned fairy-tale style about it. It is one of the best new things that has come out in Moscow. . . .

YALTA,
March 27, 1894.

I am in good health generally, ill in certain parts. For instance, a cough, palpitations of the heart, haemorrhoids. I had palpitations of the heart incessantly for six days, and the sensation all the time was loathsome. Since I have quite given up smoking I have been free from gloomy and anxious moods. Perhaps because I am not smoking, Tolstoy's morality has ceased to touch me; at the bottom of my heart I take up a hostile attitude towards it, and that of course is not just. I have peasant blood in my veins, and you won't astonish me with peasant virtues. From my childhood I have believed in progress, and I could not help believing in it since the difference between the time when I used to be thrashed and when they gave up thrashing me was tremendous. . . . But Tolstoy's philosophy touched me profoundly and took possession of me for six or seven years, and what affected me was not its general propositions, with which I was familiar beforehand, but Tolstoy's manner of expressing it, his reasonableness, and probably a sort of hypnotism. Now something in me protests, reason and justice tell me that in the electricity and heat of love for man there is something greater than chastity and abstinence from meat. War is an evil and legal justice is an evil; but it does not follow from that that I ought to wear bark shoes and sleep on the stove with the labourer, and so on, and so on. But that is not the point, it is not a matter of pro and con; the thing is that in one way or another Tolstoy has passed for me, he is not in my soul, and he has departed from me, saying: "I leave this your house empty." I am untenanted. I am sick of theorizing of all sorts, and such bounders as Max Nordau I read with positive disgust.

Patients in a fever do not want food, but they do want something, and that vague craving they express as "longing for something sour." I, too, want something sour, and that's not a mere chance feeling, for I notice the same mood in others around me. It is just as if they had all been in love, had fallen out of love, and now were looking for some new distraction. It is very possible and very likely that the Russians will pass through another period of enthusiasm for the natural sciences, and that the materialistic movement will be fashionable. Natural science is performing miracles now. And it may act upon people like Mamay, and dominate them by its mass and grandeur. All that is in the hands of God, however. And theorizing about it makes one's head go round.

TO L. S. MIZINOV.

YALTA, March 27, 1894.

DEAR LIKA,

Thanks for your letter. Though you do scare me in your letter saying you are soon going to die, though you do taunt me with having rejected you, yet thank you all the same; I know perfectly well you are not going to die, and that no one has rejected you.

I am in Yalta and I am dreary, very dreary indeed. The aristocracy, so to call it, are performing "Faust," and I go to the rehearsals and there I enjoy the spectacle of a perfect flower-bed of black, red, flaxen, and brown heads; I listen to the singing and I eat. At the house of the principal of the high school I eat tchibureks, and saddle of lamb with boiled grain; in various estimable families I eat green soup; at the confectioner's I eat—in my hotel also. I go to bed at ten and I get up at ten, and after dinner I lie down and rest, and yet I am bored, dear Lika. I am not bored because "my ladies" are not with me, but because the northern spring is better than the spring here, and because the thought that I must, that I ought to write never leaves me for an instant. To write and write and write! It is my opinion that true happiness is impossible without idleness. My ideal is to be idle and to love a plump girl. My loftiest happiness is to walk or to sit doing nothing; my favourite occupation is to gather up what is not wanted (leaves, straws, and so on) and to do what is useless. Meanwhile, I am a literary man, and have to write here in Yalta. Dear Lika, when you become a great singer and are paid a handsome salary, then be charitable to me, marry me, and keep me at your expense, that I may be free to do nothing. If you really are going to die, it might be undertaken by Varya Eberly, whom, as you know, I love. I am so all to pieces with the perpetual thought of work I ought to do and can't avoid that for the last week I have been continually tormented with palpitations of the heart. It's a loathsome sensation.

I have sold my fox-skin greatcoat for twenty roubles! It cost sixty, but as forty roubles' worth of fur has peeled off it, twenty roubles was not too low a price. The gooseberries are not ripe here yet, but it is warm and bright, the trees are coming out, the sea looks like summer, the young ladies are yearning for sensations: but yet the north is better than the south of Russia, in spring at any rate. In our part nature is more melancholy, more lyrical, more Levitanesque; here it is neither one thing nor the other, like good, sonorous, but frigid verse. Thanks to my palpitations I haven't drunk wine for a week, and that makes the surroundings seem even poorer....

M. gave a concert here, and made one hundred and fifty roubles clear profit. He roared like a grampus but had an immense success. I am awfully sorry I did not study singing; I could have roared too, as my throat is rich in husky elements, and they say I have a real octave. I should have earned money, and been a favourite with the ladies....

TO HIS BROTHER ALEXANDR.

MELIHOVO, April 15, 1894.

... I have come back from the flaming Tavrida and am already sitting on the cool banks of my pond. It's very warm, however: the thermometer runs up to twenty-six....

I am busy looking after the land: I am making new avenues, planting flowers, chopping down dead trees, and chasing the hens and the dogs out of the garden. Literature plays the part of Erakit, who was always in the background. I don't want to write, and indeed, it's hard to combine a desire to live and a desire to write....

TO A. S. SUVORIN.

MELIHOVO, April 21, 1894.

Of course it is very nice in the country; in fine weather Russia is an extraordinarily beautiful and enchanting country, especially for those who have been born and spent their childhood in the country. But you will never buy yourself an estate, as you don't know what you want. To like an estate you must make up your mind to buy it; so long as it is not yours it will seem comfortless and full of defects. My cough is considerably better, I am sunburnt, and they tell me I am fatter, but the other day I almost fell down and I fancied for a minute that I was dying. I was walking along the avenue with the prince, our neighbour, and was talking when all at once something seemed to break in my chest, I had a feeling of warmth and suffocation, there was a singing in my ears, I remembered that I had been having palpitations for a long time and thought—"they must have meant something then." I went rapidly towards the verandah on which visitors were sitting, and had one thought—that it would be awkward to fall down and die before strangers; but I went into my bedroom, drank some water, and recovered.

So you are not the only one who suffers from staggering!

I am beginning to build a pretty lodge....

May 9.

I have no news. The weather is most exquisite, and in the foliage near the house a nightingale is building and shouting incessantly. About twelve miles from me there is the village of Pokrovskoe-Meshtcherskoe; the old manor house there is now the lunatic asylum of the province. The Zemsky doctors from the whole Moscow province met there on the fourth of May, to the number of about seventy-five; I was there too. There are a great many patients but all that is interesting material for alienists and not for psychologists. One patient, a mystic, preaches that the Holy Trinity has come upon earth in the form of the metropolitan of Kiev, Ioannikiy. "A limit of ten years has been given us; eight have passed, only two years are left. If we do not want Russia to fall into ruins like Sodom, all Russia must go in a procession with the Cross to Kiev, as Moscow went to Troitsa, and pray there to the divine martyr in the noble form of the metropolitan Ioannikiy." This queer fellow is convinced that the doctors in the asylum are poisoning him, and that he is being saved by the miraculous intervention of Christ in the form of the metropolitan. He is continually praying to the East and singing, and, addressing himself to God, invariably adds the words, "in the noble form of the metropolitan Ioannikiy." He has a lovely expression of face....

From the madhouse I returned late at night in my troika. Two-thirds of the way I had to drive through the forest in the moonlight, and I had a wonderful feeling such as I have not had for a long time, as though I had come back from a tryst. I think that nearness to nature and idleness are essential elements of happiness; without them it is impossible....

TO MADAME AVILOV.

MELIHOVO, July, 1894.

I have so many visitors that I cannot answer your last letter. I want to write at length but am pulled up at the thought that any minute they may come in and hinder me. And in fact while I write the word "hinder," a girl has come in and announced that a patient has arrived; I must go.... I have grown to detest writing, and I don't know what to do. I would gladly take up medicine and would accept any sort of post, but I no longer have the physical elasticity for it. When I write now or think I ought to write I feel as much disgust as though I were eating soup from which I had just removed a beetle—forgive the comparison. What I hate is not the writing itself, but the literary entourage from which one cannot escape, and which one takes everywhere as the earth takes its atmosphere....

TO A. S. SUVORIN.

MELIHOVO, August 15, 1894.

Our trip on the Volga turned out rather a queer one in the end. Potapenko and I went to Yaroslav to take a steamer from there to Tsaritsyn, then to Kalatch, from there by the Don to Taganrog. The journey from Yaroslav to Nizhni is beautiful, but I had seen it before. Moreover, it was very hot in the cabin and the wind lashed in our faces on deck. The passengers were an uneducated set, whose presence was irritating. At Nizhni we were met by N., Tolstoy's friend. The heat, the dry wind, the noise of the fair and the conversation of N. suddenly made me feel so suffocated, so ill at ease, and so sick, that I took my portmanteau and ignominiously fled to the railway station. . . . Potapenko followed me. We took the train for Moscow, but we were ashamed to go home without having done anything, and we decided to go somewhere if it had to be to Lapland. If it had not been for his wife our choice would have fallen on Feodosia, but . . . alas! we have a wife living at Feodosia. We thought it over, we talked it over, we counted over our money, and came to the Psyol to Suma, which you know. . . . Well, the Psyol is magnificent. There is warmth, there is space, an immensity of water and of greenery and delightful people. We spent six days on the Psyol, ate and drank, walked and did nothing: my ideal of happiness, as you know, is idleness. Now I am at Melihovo again. There is a cold rain, a leaden sky, mud.

It sometimes happens that one passes a third-class refreshment room and sees a cold fish, cooked long before, and wonders carelessly who wants that unappetising fish. And yet undoubtedly that fish is wanted, and will be eaten, and there are people who will think it nice. One may say the same of the works of N. He is a bourgeois writer, writing for the unsophisticated public who travel third class. For that public Tolstoy and Turgenev are too luxurious, too aristocratic, somewhat alien and not easily digested. There is a public which eats salt beef and horse-radish sauce with relish, and does not care for artichokes and asparagus. Put yourself at its point of view, imagine the grey, dreary courtyard, the educated ladies who look like cooks, the smell of paraffin, the scantiness of interests and tasks—and you will understand N. and his readers. He is colourless; that is partly because the life he describes lacks colour. He is false because bourgeois writers cannot help being false. They are vulgar writers perfected. The vulgarians sin together with their public, while the bourgeois are hypocritical with them and flatter their narrow virtue.

MELIHOVO,
February 25, 1895.

. . . I should like to meet a philosopher like Nietzsche somewhere in a train or a steamer, and to spend the whole night talking to him. I consider his philosophy won't last long, however. It's more showy than convincing. . . .

MELIHOVO,
March 16, 1895.

Instead of you, heaven has sent me N., who has come to see me with E. and Z., two young duffers who never miss a single word but induce in the whole household a desperate boredom. N. looks flabby and physically slack; he has gone off, but has become warmer and more good-natured; he must be going to die. When my mother was ordering meat from the butcher, she said he must let us have better meat, as N. was staying with us from Petersburg.

"What N.?" asked the butcher in surprise—"the one who writes books?" and he sent us excellent meat. So the butcher does not know that I write books, for he never sends anything but gristle for my benefit. . . .

Your little letter about physical games for students will do good if only you will go on insisting on the subject. Games are absolutely essential. Playing games is good for health and beauty and liberalism, since nothing is so conducive to the blending of classes, et cetera, as public games. Games would give our solitary young people acquaintances; young people would more frequently fall in love; but games should not be instituted before the Russian student ceases to be hungry. No skating, no croquet, can keep the student cheerful and confident on an empty stomach.

MELIHOVO,
March 23, 1895.

I told you that Potapenko was a man very full of life, but you did not believe me. In the entrails of every Little Russian lie hidden many treasures. I fancy when our generation grows old, Potapenko will be the gayest and jolliest old man of us all.

By all means I will be married if you wish it. But on these conditions: everything must be as it has been hitherto—that is, she must live in Moscow while I live in the country, and I will come and see her. Happiness continued from day to day, from morning to morning, I cannot stand. When every day I am told of the same thing, in the same tone of voice, I become furious. I am furious, for instance, in the society of S., because he is very much like a woman ("a clever and responsive woman") and because in his presence the idea occurs to me that my wife might be like him. I promise you to be a splendid husband, but give me a wife who, like the moon, won't appear in my sky every day; I shan't write any better for being married....

Mamin-Sibiryak is a very nice fellow and an excellent writer. His last novel "Bread" is praised; Lyeskov was particularly enthusiastic about it. There are undoubtedly fine things in his work, and in his more successful stories the peasants are depicted every bit as well as in "Master and Man."

This is the fourth year I have been living at Melihovo. My calves have turned into cows, my copse has grown at least a yard higher, my heirs will make a capital bargain over the timber and will call me an ass, for heirs are never satisfied.

MELIHOVO,
March 30, 1895.

... We have spring here but there are regular mountains of snow, and there is no knowing when it will thaw. As soon as the sun hides behind a cloud there begins to be a chill breath from the snow, and it is horrible. Masha is already busy in the flower-beds and borders. She tires herself out and is constantly cross, so there is no need for her to read Madame Smirnov's article. The advice given is excellent; the young ladies will read it, and it will be their salvation. Only one point is not clear: how are they going to get rid of the apples and cabbages if the estate is far from the town, and of what stuff are they going to make their own dresses if their rye does not sell at all, and they have not a halfpenny? To live on one's land by the labour of one's own hands and the sweat of one's brow is only possible on one condition; that is, if one works oneself like a peasant, without regard for class or sex. There is no making use of slaves nowadays, one must take the scythe and axe oneself, and if one can't do that, no gardens will help one. Even the smallest success in farming is only gained in Russia at the price of a cruel struggle with nature, and wishing is not enough for the struggle, you need bodily strength and grit, you want traditions—and have young ladies all that? To advise young ladies to take up farming is much the same as to advise them to be bears, and to bend yokes. . . .

I have no money, but I live in the country: there are no restaurants and no cabmen, and money does not seem to be needed.

MELIHOVO,
April 13, 1895.

I am sick of Sienkiewicz's "The Family of the Polonetskys." It's the Polish Easter cake with saffron. Add Potapenko to Paul Bourget, sprinkle with Warsaw eau-de-Cologne, divide in two, and you get Sienkiewicz. "The Polonetskys" is unmistakably inspired by Bourget's "Cosmopolis," by Rome and by marriage (Sienkiewicz has lately got married). We have the catacombs and a queer old professor sighing after idealism, and Leo XIII, with the unearthly face among the saints, and the advice to return to the prayer-book, and the libel on the decadent who dies of morphinism after confessing and taking the sacrament—that is, after repenting of his errors in the name of the Church. There is a devilish lot of family happiness and talking about love, and the hero's wife is so faithful to her husband and so subtly comprehends "with her heart" the mysteries of God and life, that in the end one feels mawkish and uncomfortable as after a slobbering kiss. Sienkiewicz has evidently not read Tolstoy, and does not know Nietzsche, he talks about hypnotism like a shopman; on the other hand every page is positively sprinkled with Rubens, Borghesi, Correggio, Botticelli—and that is done to show off his culture to the bourgeois reader and make a long nose on the sly at materialism. The object of the novel is to lull the bourgeoisie to sleep in its golden dreams. Be faithful to your wife, pray with her over the prayer-book, save money, love sport, and all is well with you in this world and the next. The bourgeoisie is very fond of so-called practical types and novels with happy endings, since they soothe it with the idea that one can both accumulate capital and preserve innocence, be a beast and at the same time be happy. . . .

I wish you every sort of blessing. I congratulate you on the peace between Japan and China, and hope we may quickly obtain a Feodosia free from ice on the East Coast, and may make a railway to it.

The peasant woman had not troubles enough so she bought a pig. And I fancy we are saving up a lot of trouble for ourselves with this ice-free port. It will cost us dearer than if we were to take it into our heads to wage war on all Japan. However, futura sunt in manibus deorum.

MELIHOVO,
October 21, 1895.

Thanks for your letter, for your warm words and your invitation. I will come, but most likely not before the end of November, as I have a devilish lot to do. First in the spring I am going to build a new school in the village where I am school warden; before beginning I have to make a plan and calculations, and to drive off here and there, and so on. Secondly—can you imagine it—I am writing a play which I shall probably not finish before the end of November. I am writing it not without pleasure, though I swear fearfully at the conventions of the stage. It's a comedy, there are three women's parts, six men's, four acts, landscapes (view over a lake); a great deal of conversation about literature, little action, tons of love. I read of Ozerova's failure and was sorry, for nothing is more painful than failing. . . . I have read of the success of the "Powers of Darkness" in your theatre. . . . When I was at Tolstoy's in August, he told me, as he was wiping his hands after washing, that he wouldn't alter his play. And now, remembering that, I fancy that he knew even then that his play would be passed by the censor in toto. I spent two days and a night with him. He made a delightful impression, I felt as much at ease as though I were at home, and our talks were easy. . . .

MOSCOW,
October 26, 1895.

Tolstoy's daughters are very nice. They adore their father and have a fanatical faith in him and that means that Tolstoy really is a great moral force, for if he were insincere and not irreproachable his daughters would be the first to take up a sceptical attitude to him, for daughters are like sparrows: you don't catch them with empty chaff. . . . A man can deceive his fiancee or his mistress as much as he likes, and, in the eyes of a woman he loves, an ass may pass for a philosopher; but a daughter is a different matter. . . .

MELIHOVO,
November 21, 1895.

Well, I have finished with the play. I began it forte and ended it pianissimo—contrary to all the rules of dramatic art. It has turned into a novel. I am rather dissatisfied than satisfied with it, and reading over my new-born play, I am more convinced than ever that I am not a dramatist. The acts are very short. There are four of them. Though it is so far only the skeleton of a play, a plan which will be altered a million times before the coming season, I have ordered two copies to be typed and will send you one, only don't let anyone read it. . . .

TO HIS BROTHER MIHAIL.

PETERSBURG, October 15, 1896.

. . . My "Seagull" comes on on the seventeenth of October. Madame Kommissarzhevsky acts amazingly. There is no news. I am alive and well. I shall be at Melihovo about the twenty-fifth or towards the end of October. On the twenty-ninth is the meeting of the Zemstvo, at which I must be present as there will be a discussion about roads. . . .

TO A. S. SUVORIN.

PETERSBURG, October 18, 1896.

I am off to Melihovo. All good wishes. . . . Stop the printing of the plays. I shall never forget yesterday evening, but still I slept well, and am setting off in a very tolerable good humour.

Write to me. . . . I have received your letter. I am not going to produce the play in Moscow. I shall never either write plays or have them acted.

TO HIS SISTER.

PETERSBURG, October 18, 1896.

I am setting off to Melihovo. I shall be there tomorrow between one or two o'clock in the afternoon. Yesterday's adventure did not astonish or greatly disappoint me, for I was prepared for it by the rehearsals—and I don't feel particularly bad.

When you come to Melihovo bring Lika with you.

TO HIS BROTHER MIHAIL.

PETERSBURG, October 18, 1896.

The play has fallen flat, and come down with a crash. There was an oppressive strained feeling of disgrace and bewilderment in the theatre. The actors played abominably stupidly. The moral of it is, one ought not to write plays.

TO A. S. SUVORIN.

MELIHOVO, October 22, 1896.

In your last letter (of October 18) you three times call me womanish, and say that I was in a funk. Why this libel? After the performance I had supper at Romanov's. On my word of honour. Then I went to bed, slept soundly, and next day went home without uttering a sound of complaint. If I had been in a funk I should have run from editor to editor and actor to actor, should have nervously entreated them to be considerate, should nervously have inserted useless corrections and should have spent two or three weeks in Petersburg fussing over my "Seagull," in excitement, in a cold perspiration, in lamentation. . . . When you were with me the night after the performance you told me yourself that it would be the best thing for me to go away; and next morning I got a letter from you to say goodbye. How did I show funk? I acted as coldly and reasonably as a man who has made an offer, received a refusal, and has nothing left but to go. Yes, my vanity was stung, but you know it was not a bolt from the blue; I was expecting a failure, and was prepared for it, as I warned you with perfect sincerity beforehand.

When I got home I took a dose of castor oil, and had a cold bath, and now I am ready to write another play. I no longer feel exhausted and irritable, and am not afraid that Davydov and Jean will come to me and talk about the play. I agree with your corrections, and a thousand thanks for them. Only please don't regret that you were not at the rehearsals. You know there was in reality only one rehearsal, at which one could make out nothing. One could not see the play at all through the loathsome acting.

I have got a telegram from Potapenko—"A colossal success." I have had a letter from Mlle. Veselitsky (Mikulitch) whom I don't know. She expresses her sympathy in a tone as if one of my family were dead. It's really quite inappropriate; that's all nonsense, though.

My sister is delighted with you and Anna Ivanovna, and I am inexpressibly glad of it, for I love your family like my own. She hastened home from Petersburg, possibly imagining that I would hang myself....

TO E. M. S.

MELIHOVO, November, 1896.

If, O honoured "One of the Audience", you are writing of the first performance, then allow—oh, allow me to doubt your sincerity. You hasten to pour healing balsam on the author's wounds, supposing that, under the circumstances, that is more necessary and better than sincerity; you are kind, very kind, and it does credit to your heart. At the first performance I did not see all, but what I did see was dingy, grey, dismal and wooden. I did not distribute the parts and was not given new scenery. There were only two rehearsals, the actors did not know their parts—and the result was a general panic and utter depression; even Madame Kommissarzhevsky's acting was not up to much, though at one of the rehearsals she acted marvellously, so that people sitting in the stalls wept with bowed heads.

In any case I am grateful and very, very much touched. All my plays are being printed, and as soon as they are ready I shall send you a copy....

TO A. F. KONI.

MELIHOVO, November 11, 1896.

You cannot imagine how your letter rejoiced me. I saw from the front only the two first acts of my play. Afterwards I sat behind the scenes and felt the whole time that "The Seagull" was a failure. After the performance that night and next day, I was assured that I had hatched out nothing but idiots, that my play was clumsy from the stage point of view, that it was not clever, that it was unintelligible, even senseless, and so on and so on. You can imagine my position—it was a collapse such as I had never dreamed of! I felt ashamed and vexed, and I went away from Petersburg full of doubts of all sorts. I thought that if I had written and put on the stage a play so obviously brimming over with monstrous defects, I had lost all instinct and that, therefore, my machinery must have gone wrong for good. After I had reached home, they wrote to me from Petersburg that the second and third performances were a success; several letters, some signed, some anonymous, came praising the play and abusing the critics. I read them with pleasure, but still I felt vexed and ashamed, and the idea forced itself upon me that if kind-hearted people thought it was necessary to comfort me, it meant that I was in a bad way. But your letter has acted upon me in a most definite way. I have known you a long time, I have a deep respect for you, and I believe in you more than in all the critics taken together—you felt that when you wrote your letter, and that is why it is so excellent and convincing. My mind is at rest now, and I can think of the play and the performance without loathing. Kommissarzhevskaia is a wonderful actress. At one of the rehearsals many people were moved to tears as they looked at her, and said that she was the first actress in Russia to-day; but at the first performance she was affected by the general attitude of hostility to my "Seagull," and was, as it were, intimidated by it and lost her voice. Our press takes a cold tone to her that doesn't do justice to her merits, and I am sorry for her. Allow me to thank you with all my heart for your letter. Believe me, I value the feelings that prompted you to write it far more than I can express in words, and the sympathy you call "unnecessary" at the end of your letter I shall never never forget, whatever happens.

TO V. I. NEMIROVITCH-DANTCHENKO.

MELIHOVO, November 26, 1896.

DEAR FRIEND,
    I am answering the chief substance of your letter—the question why we so rarely talk of serious subjects. When people are silent, it is because they have nothing to talk about or because they are ill at ease. What is there to talk about? We have no politics, we have neither public life nor club life, nor even a life of the streets; our civic existence is poor, monotonous, burdensome, and uninteresting—and to talk is as boring as corresponding with L. You say that we are literary men, and that of itself makes our life a rich one. Is that so? We are stuck in our profession up to our ears, it has gradually isolated us from the external world, and the upshot of it is that we have little free time, little money, few books, we read little and reluctantly, we hear little, we rarely go anywhere. Should we talk about literature? . . . But we have talked about it already. Every year it's the same thing again and again, and all we usually say about literature may be reduced to discussing who write better, and who write worse. Conversations upon wider and more general topics never catch on, because when you have tundras and Esquimaux all round you, general ideas, being so inappropriate to the reality, quickly lose shape and slip away like thoughts of eternal bliss. Should we talk of personal life? Yes, that may sometimes be interesting and we might perhaps talk about it; but there again we are constrained, we are reserved and insincere: we are restrained by an instinct of self-preservation and we are afraid. We are afraid of being overheard by some uncultured Esquimaux who does not like us, and whom we don't like either. I personally am afraid that my acquaintance, N., whose cleverness attracts us, will hold forth with raised finger, in every railway carriage and every house about me, settling the question why I became so intimate with X. while I was beloved by Z. I am afraid of our morals, I am afraid of our ladies. . . . In short, for our silence, for the frivolity and dulness of our conversations, don't blame yourself or me, blame what the critics call "the age," blame the climate, the vast distances, what you will, and let circumstances go on their own fateful, relentless course, hoping for a better future.

TO A. S. SUVORIN.

MELIHOVO, January 11, 1897.

We are having a census. They have served out to the numerators detestable inkpots, detestable clumsy badges like the labels of a brewery, and portfolios into which the census forms will not fit—giving the effect of a sword that won't go into its sheath. It is a disgrace. From early morning I go from hut to hut, and knock my head in the low doorways which I can't get used to, and as ill-luck will have it my head aches hellishly; I have migraine and influenza. In one hut a little girl of nine years old, boarded out from the foundling hospital, wept bitterly because all the other little girls in the hut were Mihailovnas while she was called Lvovna after her godfather. I said call yourself Mihailovna. They were all highly delighted, and began thanking me. That's what's called making friends with the Mammon of Unrighteousness.

The "Journal of Surgery" has been sanctioned by the Censor. We are beginning to bring it out. Be so good as to do us a service—have the enclosed advertisement printed on your front page and charge it to my account. The journal will be a very good one, and this advertisement can lead to nothing but unmistakable and solid benefit. It's a great benefit, you know, to cut off people's legs.

While we are on medical topics—a remedy for cancer has been found. For almost a year past, thanks to a Russian doctor Denisenko, they have been trying the juice of the celandine, and one reads of astonishing results. Cancer is a terrible unbearable disease, the death from it is agonizing; you can imagine how pleasant it is for a man initiated into the secrets of Aesculapius to read of such results. . . .

MOSCOW,
February 8, 1897.

The census is over. I was pretty sick of the business, as I had both to enumerate and to write till my fingers ached, and to give lectures to fifteen numerators. The numerators worked excellently, with a pedantic exactitude almost absurd. On the other hand the Zemsky Natchalniks, to whom the census was entrusted in the districts, behaved disgustingly. They did nothing, understood little, and at the most difficult moments used to report themselves sick. The best of them turned out to be a man who drinks and draws the long bow a la Hlestakov [Translator's Note: A character in Gogol's "Inspector General."]—but was all the same a character, if only from the point of view of comedy, while the others were colourless beyond words, and it was annoying beyond words to have anything to do with them.

I am in Moscow at the Great Moscow Hotel. I am staying a short time, ten days, and then going home. The whole of Lent and the whole of April after it, I shall have to be busy again with carpenters and so on. I am building a school again. A deputation came to me from the peasants begging me for it, and I had not the courage to refuse. The Zemstvo is giving a thousand roubles, the peasants have collected three hundred, and that is all, while the school will not cost less than three thousand. So again I shall have all the summer to be thinking about money, and scraping it together here and there. Altogether life in the country is full of work and care. . . .

The police have made a raid upon Tchertkov, the well-known Tolstoyan, have carried off all that the Tolstoyans had collected relating to the Duhobors and sectarians—and so all at once as though by magic all evidence against Pobyedonostsev and his angels has vanished. Goremykin called upon Tchertkov's mother and said: "Your son must make the choice—either the Baltic Province where Prince Hilkov is already living in exile, or a foreign country." Tchertkov has chosen London.

He is setting off on the thirteenth of February. L. N. Tolstoy has gone to Petersburg to see him off; and yesterday they sent his winter overcoat after him. A great many are going to see him off, even Sytin, and I am sorry that I cannot do the same. I don't cherish tender sentiments for Tchertkov, but the way he has been treated fills me with intense, intense indignation. . . .

MOSCOW,
April 1, 1897.

The doctors have diagnosed tuberculosis in the upper part of the lungs, and have ordered me to change my manner of life. I understand their diagnosis but I don't understand their prescription, because it is almost impossible. They tell me I must live in the country, but you know living permanently in the country involves continual worry with peasants, with animals, with elementary forces of all kinds, and to escape from worries and anxieties in the country is as difficult as to escape burns in hell. But still I will try to change my life as far as possible, and have already, through Masha, announced that I shall give up medical practice in the country. This will be at the same time a great relief and a great deprivation to me. I shall drop all public duties in the district, shall buy a dressing-gown, bask in the sun, and eat a great deal. They tell me to eat six times a day and are indignant with me for eating, as they think, very little. I am forbidden to talk much, to swim, and so on, and so on.

Except my lungs, all my organs were found to be healthy. Hitherto I fancied I drank just so much as not to do harm; now it turns out on investigation that I was drinking less than I was entitled to. What a pity!

The author of "Ward No. 6" has been moved from Ward No. 16 to Ward No. 14. There is plenty of room here, two windows, lighting à la Potapenko, three tables. There is very little haemorrhage. After the evening when Tolstoy was here (we talked for a long time) at four o'clock in the morning I had violent haemorrhage again.

Melihovo is a healthy place; it stands exactly on a watershed, on high ground, so that there is never fever or diphtheria in it. They have decided, after general consultation, that I am not to go away anywhere but to go on living at Melihovo. I must only arrange the house somewhat more comfortably. . . .

MOSCOW,
April 7, 1897.

. . . You write that my ideal is laziness. No, it is not laziness. I despise laziness as I despise weakness and lack of mental and moral energy. I was not talking of laziness but of leisure, and I did not say leisure was an ideal but only one of the essential conditions of personal happiness.

If the experiments with Koch's new serum give favourable results, I shall go of course to Berlin. Feeding is absolutely no use to me. Here for the last fortnight they have been feeding me zealously, but it's no use, I have not gained weight.

I ought to get married. Perhaps a cross wife would cut down the number of my visitors by at least a half. Yesterday they were coming all day long, it was simply awful. They came two at a time—and each one begs me not to speak and at the same time asks me questions. . . .

TO A. I. ERTEL.

MELIHOVO, April 17, 1897.

DEAR FRIEND ALEXANDR IVANOVITCH,

I am now at home. For a fortnight before Easter I was lying in Ostroumov's clinic and was spitting blood. The doctor diagnosed tuberculosis in the lungs. I feel splendid, nothing aches, nothing is uneasy inside, but the doctors have forbidden me vinum, movement, and conversation, they have ordered me to eat a great deal, and forbidden me to practise—and I feel as it were dreary.

I hear nothing about the People's Theatre. At the congress it was spoken of apathetically, without interest, and the circle that had undertaken to write its constitution and set to work have evidently cooled off a little. It is due to the spring, I suppose. The only one of the circle I saw was Goltsev, and I had not time to talk to him about the theatre.

There is nothing new. A dead calm in literature. In the editor's offices they are drinking tea and cheap wine, drinking it without relish as they walk about, evidently from having nothing to do. Tolstoy is writing a little book about Art. He came to see me in the clinic, and said that he had flung aside his novel "Resurrection" as he did not like it, and was writing only about Art, and had read sixty books about Art. His idea is not a new one; all intelligent old men in all the ages have sung the same tune in different keys. Old men have always been prone to see the end of the world, and have always declared that morality was degenerating to the uttermost point, that Art was growing shallow and wearing thin, that people were growing feebler, and so on, and so on.

Lyov Nikolaevitch wants to persuade us in his little book that at the present time Art has entered upon its final phase, that it is in a blind alley, from which it has no outlet (except retreat).

I am doing nothing, I feed the sparrows with hemp-seed and prune a rose-tree a day. After my pruning, the roses flower magnificently. I am not looking after the farming.

Keep well, dear Alexandr Ivanovitch, thank you for your letter and friendly sympathy. Write to me for the sake of my infirmity, and don't blame me too much for my carelessness in correspondence.

In future I am going to try and answer your letters as soon as I have read them. Warmest greetings.

TO SUVORIN.

MELIHOVO, July 12, 1897.

... I am reading Maeterlinck, I have read his "Les Aveugles," "L'Intrus," and am reading "Aglavaine et Selysette." They are all strange wonderful things, but they make an immense impression, and if I had a theatre I should certainly stage "Les Aveugles." There is, by the way, a magnificent scenic effect in it, with the sea and a lighthouse in the distance. The public is semi-idiotic, but one might avoid the play's failing by writing the contents of the play—in brief, of course—on the programme, saying the play is the work of Maeterlinck, a Belgian author and decadent, and that what happens in it is that an old man, who leads about some blind men, has died in silence and that the blind men, not knowing this, are sitting and waiting for his return. ...

TO MADAME AVILOV.

NICE, October 6, 1897.

... You complain that my heroes are gloomy—alas! that's not my fault. This happens apart from my will, and when I write it does not seem to me that I am writing gloomily; in any case, as I work I am always in excellent spirits. It has been observed that gloomy, melancholy people always write cheerfully, while those who enjoy life put their depression into their writings. And I am a man who enjoys life; the first thirty years of my life I have lived as they say in pleasure and content. ...

TO F. D. BATYUSHKOV.

NICE, December 15, 1897.

... In one of your letters you expressed a desire that I should send you an international story, taking for my subject something from the life here. Such a story I can write only in Russia from reminiscences. I can only write from reminiscences, and I have never written directly from Nature. I have let my memory sift the subject, so that only what is important or typical is left in it as in a filter. ...

TO A. S. SUVORIN.

NICE, January 4, 1898.

... Judging from the extract printed in Novoye Vremya, Tolstoy's article on Art does not seem interesting. All that is old. He says about Art that it is decrepit, that it has got into a blind alley, that it is not what it ought to be, and so on, and so on. That's just like saying the desire to eat and drink has grown old, has outlived its day, and is not what it ought to be. Of course hunger is an old story, in the desire to eat we have got into a blind alley, but still eating is necessary, and we shall go on eating however the philosophers and irate old men moralise. ...

TO F. D. BATYUSHKOV.

NICE, January 28, 1898.

... We talk of nothing here but Zola and Dreyfus. The immense majority of educated people are on Zola's side and believe that Dreyfus is innocent. Zola has gained immensely in public esteem; his letters of protest are like a breath of fresh air, and every Frenchman has felt that, thank God! there is still justice in the world, and that if an innocent man is condemned there is still someone to champion him. The French papers are extremely interesting while the Russian are worthless. Novoye Vremya is simply loathsome. ...

TO A. S. SUVORIN.

NICE, February 6, 1898.

... You write that you are annoyed with Zola, and here everyone has a feeling as though a new, better Zola had arisen. In his trial he has been cleansed as though in turpentine from grease-spots, and now shines before the French in his true brilliance. There is a purity and moral elevation that was not suspected in him. You should follow the whole scandal from the very beginning. The degradation of Dreyfus, whether it was just or not, made on all (you were of the number I remember) a painful and depressing impression. It was noticed that at the time of the sentence Dreyfus behaved like a decent well-disciplined officer, while those present at the sentence, the journalists for instance, shouted at him, "Hold your tongue, Judas,"—that is, behaved badly and indecently. Everyone came back from the sentence dissatisfied and with a troubled conscience. Dreyfus' counsel Demange, an honest man, who even during the preliminary stages of the trial felt that something shifty was being done behind the scenes, was particularly dissatisfied—and then the experts who, to convince themselves that they had not made a mistake, kept talking of nothing but Dreyfus, of his being guilty, and kept wandering all over Paris! ...

Of the experts one turned out to be mad, the author of a monstrously absurd project; two were eccentric creatures.

People could not help talking of the Intelligence Department at the War Office, that military consistory which is employed in hunting for spies and reading other people's letters; it began to be said that the head of that Department, Sandhen, was suffering from progressive paralysis; Paty de Clam has shown himself to be something after the style of Tausch of Berlin; Picquart suddenly took his departure mysteriously, causing a lot of talk. All at once a series of gross judicial blunders came to light. By degrees people became convinced that Dreyfus had been condemned on the strength of a secret document, which had been shown neither to the accused man nor his defending counsel, and decent law-abiding people saw in this a fundamental breach of justice. If the latter were the work not simply of Wilhelm, but of the centre of the solar system, it ought to have been shown to Demange. All sorts of guesses were made as to the contents of this letter, the most impossible stories circulated. Dreyfus was an officer, the military were suspect; Dreyfus was a Jew, the Jews were suspect. People began talking about militarism, about the Jews. Such utterly disreputable people as Drumont held up their heads; little by little they stirred up a regular pother on a substratum of anti-semitism, on a substratum that smelt of the shambles. When something is wrong with us we look for the causes outside ourselves, and readily find them. "It's the Frenchman's nastiness, it's the Jews', it's Wilhelm's." Capital, brimstone, the freemasons, the Syndicate, the Jesuits—they are all bogeys, but how they relieve our uneasiness! They are of course a bad sign. Since the French have begun talking about the Jews, about the Syndicate, it shows they are feeling uncomfortable, that there is a worm gnawing at them, that they feel the need of these bogeys to soothe their over-excited conscience.

Then this Esterhazy, a duellist, in the style of Turgenev's duellists, an insolent ruffian, who had long been an object of suspicion, and was not respected by his comrades; the striking resemblance of his handwriting with that of the bordereau, the Uhlan's letters, his threats which for some reason he does not carry out; finally the judgment, utterly mysterious, strangely deciding that the bordereau was written in Esterhazy's handwriting but not by his hand! . . . And the gas has been continually accumulating, there has come to be a feeling of acute tension, of overwhelming oppression. The fighting in the court was a purely nervous manifestation, simply the hysterical result of that tension, and Zola's letter and his trial are a manifestation of the same kind. What would you have? The best people, always in advance of the nation, were bound to be the first to raise an agitation—and so it has been. The first to speak was Scherer-Kestner, of whom Frenchmen who know him intimately (according to Kovalevsky) say that he is a "sword-blade," so spotless and without blemish is he. The second is Zola, and now he is being tried.

Yes, Zola is not Voltaire, and we are none of us Voltaires, but there are in life conjunctions of circumstances when the reproach that we are not Voltaires is least of all appropriate. Think of Korolenko, who defended the Multanovsky natives and saved them from penal servitude. Dr. Haas is not a Voltaire either, and yet his wonderful life has been well spent up to the end.

I am well acquainted with the case from the stenographers' report, which is utterly different from what is in the newspapers, and I have a clear view of Zola. The chief point is that he is sincere—that is, he bases his judgments simply on what he sees, and not on phantoms like the others. And sincere people can be mistaken, no doubt of it, but such mistakes do less harm than calculated insincerity, prejudgments, or political considerations. Let Dreyfus be guilty, and Zola is still right, since it is the duty of writers not to accuse, not to prosecute, but to champion even the guilty once they have been condemned and are enduring punishment. I shall be told: "What of the political position? The interests of the State?" But great writers and artists ought to take part in politics only so far as they have to protect themselves from politics. There are plenty of accusers, prosecutors, and gendarmes without them, and in any case, the role of Paul suits them better than that of Saul. Whatever the verdict may be, Zola will anyway experience a vivid delight after the trial, his old age will be a fine old age, and he will die with a conscience at peace, or at any rate greatly solaced. The French are very sick. They clutch at every word of comfort and at every genuine reproach coming to them from outside. That is why Bernstein's letter and our Zakrevsky's article (which was read here in the Novosti) have had such a great success here, and why they are so disgusted by abuse of Zola, such as the gutter press, which they despise, flings at him every day. However neurotic Zola may be, still he stands before the court of French common sense, and the French love him for it and are proud of him, even though they do applaud the Generals who, in the simplicity of their hearts, scare them first with the honour of the army, then with war. . . .

TO HIS BROTHER ALEXANDR.

NICE, February 23, 1898.

. . . Novoye Vremya has behaved simply abominably about the Zola case. The old man and I have exchanged letters on the subject (in a tone of great moderation, however), and have both dropped the subject.

I don't want to write and I don't want his letters, in which he keeps justifying the tactlessness of his paper by saying he loves the military: I don't want them because I have been thoroughly sick of it all for a long time past. I love the military too, but I would not if I had a newspaper allow the cactuses to print Zola's novel for nothing in the Supplement, while they pour dirty water over this same Zola in the paper—and what for? For what not one of the cactuses has ever known—for a noble impulse and moral purity. And in any case to abuse Zola when he is on his trial—that is unworthy of literature. . . .

TO HIS BROTHER MIHAIL.

YALTA, October 26, 1898.

. . . I am buying a piece of land in Yalta and am going to build so as to have a place in which to spend the winters. The prospect of continual wandering with hotel rooms, hotel porters, chance cooking, and so on, and so on, alarms my imagination. Mother will spend the winter with me. There is no winter here; it's the end of October, but the roses and other flowers are blooming freely, the trees are green and it is warm.

There is a great deal of water. Nothing will be needed apart from the house, no outbuildings of any sort; it will all be under one roof. The coal, wood and everything will be in the basement. The hens lay the whole year round, and no special house is needed for them, an enclosure is enough. Close by there is a baker's shop and the bazaar, so that it will be very cosy for Mother and very convenient. By the way, there are chanterelles and boletuses to be gathered all the autumn, and that will be an amusement for Mother. I am not doing the building myself, the architect is doing it all. The houses will be ready by April. The grounds, for a town house, are considerable. There will be a garden and flowerbeds, and a vegetable garden. The railway will come to Yalta next year. . . .

As for getting married, upon which you are so urgent—what am I to say to you? To marry is interesting only for love; to marry a girl simply because she is nice is like buying something one does not want at the bazaar solely because it is of good quality.

The most important screw in family life is love, sexual attraction, one flesh, all the rest is dreary and cannot be reckoned upon, however cleverly we make our calculations. So the point is not in the girl's being nice but in her being loved; putting it off as you see counts for little. . . .

My "Uncle Vanya" is being done all over the province, and everywhere with success. So one never knows where one will gain and where one will lose; I had not reckoned on that play at all. . . .

TO GORKY.

YALTA, December 3, 1898.

Your last letter has given me great pleasure. I thank you with all my heart. "Uncle Vanya" was written long, long ago; I have never seen it on the stage. Of late years it has often been produced at provincial theatres. I feel cold about my plays as a rule; I gave up the theatre long ago, and feel no desire now to write for the stage.

You ask what is my opinion of your stories. My opinion? The talent is unmistakable and it is a real, great talent. For instance, in the story "In the Steppe" it is expressed with extraordinary vigour, and I actually felt a pang of envy that it was not I who had written it. You are an artist, a clever man, you feel superbly, you are plastic—that is, when you describe a thing you see it and you touch it with your hands. That is real art. There is my opinion for you, and I am very glad I can express it to you. I am, I repeat, very glad, and if we could meet and talk for an hour or two you would be convinced of my high appreciation of you and of the hopes I am building on your gifts.

Shall I speak now of defects? But that is not so easy. To speak of the defects of a talent is like speaking of the defects of a great tree growing in the garden; what is chiefly in question, you see, is not the tree itself but the tastes of the man who is looking at it. Is not that so?

I will begin by saying that to my mind you have not enough restraint. You are like a spectator at the theatre who expresses his transports with so little restraint that he prevents himself and other people from listening. This lack of restraint is particularly felt in the descriptions of nature with which you interrupt your dialogues; when one reads those descriptions one wishes they were more compact, shorter, put into two or three lines. The frequent mention of tenderness, whispering, velvetiness, and so on, give those descriptions a rhetorical and monotonous character—and they make one feel cold and almost exhaust one. The lack of restraint is felt also in the descriptions of women ("Malva," "On the Raft") and love scenes.

It is not vigour, not breadth of touch, but just lack of restraint. Then there is the frequent use of words quite unsuitable in stories of your type. "Accompaniment," "disc," "harmony," such words spoil the effect. You often talk of waves. There is a strained feeling and a sort of circumspection in your descriptions of educated people; that is not because you have not observed educated people sufficiently, you know them, but you don't seem to know from what side to approach them.

How old are you? I don't know you, I don't know where you came from or who you are, but it seems to me that while you are still young you ought to leave Nizhni and spend two or three years rubbing shoulders with literature and literary people; not to learn to crow like the rest of us and to sharpen your wits, but to take the final plunge head first into literature and to grow to love it. Besides, the provinces age a man early. Korolenko, Potapenko, Mamin, Ertel, are first-rate men; you would perhaps at first feel their company rather boring, but in a year or two you would grow used to them and appreciate them as they deserve, and their society would more than repay you for the disagreeableness and inconvenience of life in the capital. . . .

YALTA,
January 3, 1899.

. . . Apparently you have misunderstood me a little. I did not write to you of coarseness of style, but only of the incongruity of foreign, not genuinely Russian, or rarely used words. In other authors such words as, for instance, "fatalistically," pass unnoticed, but your things are musical, harmonious, and every crude touch jars fearfully. Of course it is a question of taste, and perhaps this is only a sign of excessive fastidiousness in me, or the conservatism of a man who has adopted definite habits for himself long ago. I am resigned to "a collegiate assessor," and "a captain of the second rank" in descriptions, but "flirt" and "champion" when they occur in descriptions excite repulsion in me.

Are you self-educated? In your stories you are completely an artist and at the same time an "educated" man in the truest sense.

Nothing is less characteristic of you than coarseness, you are clever and subtle and delicate in your feelings. Your best things are "In the Steppe," and "On the Raft,"—did I write to you about that? They are splendid things, masterpieces, they show the artist who has passed through a very good school. I don't think that I am mistaken. The only defect is the lack of restraint, the lack of grace. When a man spends the least possible number of movements over some definite action, that is grace. One is conscious of superfluity in your expenditure.

The descriptions of nature are the work of an artist; you are a real landscape painter. Only the frequent personification (anthropomorphism) when the sea breathes, the sky gazes, the steppe barks, nature whispers, speaks, mourns, and so on—such metaphors make your descriptions somewhat monotonous, sometimes sweetish, sometimes not clear; beauty and expressiveness in nature are attained only by simplicity, by such simple phrases as "The sun set," "It was dark," "It began to rain," and so on—and that simplicity is characteristic of you in the highest degree, more so perhaps than of any other writer. . . .

TO A. S. SUVORIN.

YALTA, January 17, 1899.

. . . I have been reading Tolstoy's son's story: "The Folly of the Mir." The construction of the story is poor, indeed it would have been better to write it simply as an article, but the thought is treated with justice and passion. I am against the Commune myself. There is sense in the Commune when one has to deal with external enemies who make frequent invasions, and with wild animals; but now it is a crowd artificially held together, like a crowd of convicts. They will tell us Russia is an agricultural country. That is so, but the Commune has nothing to do with that, at any rate at the present time. The commune exists by husbandry, but once husbandry begins to pass into scientific agriculture the commune begins to crack at every seam, as the commune and culture are not compatible ideas. Our national drunkenness and profound ignorance are, by the way, sins of the commune system. . . .

TO HIS BROTHER MIHAIL.

YALTA, February 6, 1899.

. . . Being bored, I am reading "The Book of my Life" by Bishop Porfiry. This passage about war occurs in it:

"Standing armies in time of peace are locusts devouring the people's bread and leaving a vile stench in society, while in time of war they are artificial fighting machines, and when they grow and develop, farewell to freedom, security, and national glory! . . . They are the lawless defenders of unjust and partial laws, of privilege and of tyranny." . . .

That was written in the forties. . . .

TO I. I. ORLOV.

YALTA, February 22, 1899.

. . . In your letter there is a text from Scripture. To your complaint in regard to the tutor and failures of all sorts I will reply by another text: "Put not thy trust in princes nor in any sons of man" . . . and I recall another expression in regard to the sons of man, those in particular who so annoy you: they are the sons of their age.

Not the tutor but the whole educated class—that is to blame, my dear sir. While the young men and women are students they are a good honest set, they are our hope, they are the future of Russia, but no sooner do those students enter upon independent life and become grown up than our hope and the future of Russia vanishes in smoke, and all that is left in the filter is doctors owning house property, hungry government clerks, and thieving engineers. Remember that Katkov, Pobyedonostsev, Vishnegradsky, were nurselings of the Universities, that they were our Professors—not military despots, but professors, luminaries. . . . I don't believe in our educated class, which is hypocritical, false, hysterical, badly educated and indolent. I don't believe in it even when it's suffering and complaining, for its oppressors come from its own entrails. I believe in individual people, I see salvation in individual personalities scattered here and there all over Russia—educated people or peasants—they have strength though they are few. No prophet is honoured in his own country, but the individual personalities of whom I am speaking play an unnoticed part in society, they are not domineering, but their work can be seen; anyway, science is advancing and advancing, social self-consciousness is growing, moral questions begin to take an uneasy character, and so on, and so on-and all this is being done in spite of the prosecutors, the engineers, and the tutors, in spite of the intellectual class en masse and in spite of everything....

TO MADAME AVILOV.

YALTA, March 9, 1899.

I shall not be at the writers' congress. In the autumn I shall be in the Crimea or abroad—that is, of course, if I am alive and free. I am going to spend the whole summer on my own place in the Serpuhov district.

By the way, in what district of the Tula province have you bought your estate? For the first two years after buying an estate one has a hard time, at moments it is very bad indeed, but by degrees one is led to Nirvana, by sweet habit. I bought an estate and mortgaged it, I had a very hard time the first years (famine, cholera). Afterwards everything went well, and now it is pleasant to remember that I have somewhere near the Oka a nook of my own. I live in peace with the peasants, they never steal anything from me, and when I walk through the village the old women smile and cross themselves. I use the formal address to all except children, and never shout at them; but what has done most to build up our good relations is medicine. You will be happy on your estate, only please don't listen to anyone's advice and gloomy prognostications, and don't at first be disappointed, or form an opinion about the peasants. The peasants behave sullenly and not genuinely to all new-comers, and especially so in the Tula province. There is indeed a saying: "He's a good man though he is from Tula."

So here's something like a sermon for you, you see, madam. Are you satisfied?

Do you know L. N. Tolstoy? Will your estate be far from Tolstoy's? If it is near I shall envy you. I like Tolstoy very much.

Speaking of new writers, you throw Melshin in with a whole lot. That's not right. Melshin stands apart. He is a great and unappreciated writer, an intelligent, powerful writer, though perhaps he will not write more than he has written already. Kuprin I have not read at all. Gorky I like, but of late he has taken to writing rubbish, revolting rubbish, so that I shall soon give up reading him. "Humble People" is good, though one could have done without Buhvostov, whose presence brings into the story an element of strain, of tiresomeness and even falsity. Korolenko is a delightful writer. He is loved—and with good reason. Apart from all the rest there is sobriety and purity in him.

You ask whether I am sorry for Suvorin. Of course I am. He is paying heavily for his mistakes. But I'm not at all sorry for those who are surrounding him....

TO GORKY.

MOSCOW, April 25, 1899.

... The day before yesterday I was at L. N. Tolstoy's; he praised you very highly and said that you were "a remarkable writer." He likes your "The Fair" and "In the Steppe" and does not like "Malva." He said: "You can invent anything you like, but you can't invent psychology, and in Gorky one comes across just psychological inventions: he describes what he has never felt." So much for you! I said that when you were next in Moscow we would go together to see him.

When will you be in Moscow? On Thursday there will be a private performance—for me—of "The Seagull." If you come to Moscow I will give you a seat....

From Petersburg I get painful letters, as it were from the damned, and it's painful to me as I don't know what to answer, how to behave. Yes, life when it is not a psychological invention is a difficult business....

TO O. L. KNIPPER.

YALTA, September 30, 1899.

At your command I hasten to answer your letter in which you ask me about Astrov's last scene with Elena.

You write that Astrov addresses Elena in that scene like the most ardent lover, "clutches at his feeling like a drowning man at a straw."

But that's not right, not right at all! Astrov likes Elena, she attracts him by her beauty; but in the last act he knows already that nothing will come of it, and he talks to her in that scene in the same tone as of the heat in Africa, and kisses her quite casually, to pass the time. If Astrov takes that scene violently, the whole mood of the fourth act—quiet and despondent—is lost....

TO G. I. ROSSOLIMO.

YALTA, October 11, 1899.

... Autobiography? I have a disease—Auto-biographophobia. To read any sort of details about myself, and still more to write them for print, is a veritable torture to me. On a separate sheet I send a few facts, very bald, but I can do no more....

I, A. P. Chekhov, was born on the 17th of January, 1860, at Taganrog. I was educated first in the Greek School near the church of Tsar Constantine; then in the Taganrog high school. In 1879 I entered the Moscow University in the Faculty of Medicine. I had at the time only a slight idea of the Faculties in general, and chose the Faculty of Medicine I don't remember on what grounds, but did not regret my choice afterwards. I began in my first year to publish stories in the weekly journals and newspapers, and these literary pursuits had, early in the eighties, acquired a permanent professional character. In 1888 I took the Pushkin prize. In 1890 I travelled to the Island of Sahalin, to write afterwards a book upon our penal colony and prisons there. Not counting reviews, feuilletons, paragraphs, and all that I have written from day to day for the newspapers, which it would be difficult now to seek out and collect, I have, during my twenty years of literary work, published more than three hundred signatures of print, of tales, and novels. I have also written plays for the stage.

I have no doubt that the study of medicine has had an important influence on my literary work; it has considerably enlarged the sphere of my observation, has enriched me with knowledge the true value of which for me as a writer can only be understood by one who is himself a doctor. It has also had a guiding influence, and it is probably due to my close association with medicine that I have succeeded in avoiding many mistakes.

Familiarity with the natural sciences and with scientific method has always kept me on my guard, and I have always tried where it was possible to be consistent with the facts of science, and where it was impossible I have preferred not to write at all. I may observe in passing that the conditions of artistic creation do not always admit of complete harmony with the facts of science. It is impossible to represent upon the stage a death from poisoning exactly as it takes place in reality. But harmony with the facts of science must be felt even under those conditions—i.e., it must be clear to the reader or spectator that this is only due to the conditions of art, and that he has to do with a writer who understands.

I do not belong to the class of literary men who take up a sceptical attitude towards science; and to the class of those who rush into everything with only their own imagination to go upon, I should not like to belong....

TO O. L. KNIPPER.

YALTA, October 30, 1899.

... You ask whether I shall be excited, but you see I only heard properly that "Uncle Vanya" was to be given on the twenty-sixth from your letter which I got on the twenty-seventh. The telegrams began coming on the evening of the twenty-seventh when I was in bed. They send them on to me by telephone. I woke up every time and ran with bare feet to the telephone, and got very much chilled; then I had scarcely dozed off when the bell rang again and again. It's the first time that my own fame has kept me awake. The next evening when I went to bed I put my slippers and dressing-gown beside my bed, but there were no more telegrams.

The telegrams were full of nothing but the number of calls and the brilliant success, but there was a subtle, almost elusive something in them from which I could conclude that the state of mind of all of you was not exactly of the very best. The newspapers I have got to-day confirm my conjectures.

Yes, dear actress, ordinary medium success is not enough now for all you artistic players: you want an uproar, big guns, dynamite. You have been spoiled at last, deafened by constant talk about successes, full and not full houses: you are already poisoned with that drug, and in another two or three years you will be good for nothing! So much for you!

How are you getting on? How are you feeling? I am still in the same place, and am still the same; I am working and planting trees.

But visitors have come, I can't go on writing. Visitors have been sitting here for more than an hour. They have asked for tea. They have sent for the samovar. Oh, how dreary!

Don't forget me, and don't let your friendship for me die away, so that we may go away together somewhere again this summer. Good-bye for the present. We shall most likely not meet before April. If you would all come in the spring to Yalta, would act here and rest—that would be wonderfully artistic. A visitor will take this letter and drop it into the post-box. . . .

P.S.—Dear actress, write for the sake of all that's holy, I am so dull and depressed. I might be in prison and I rage and rage. . . .

YALTA,
November 1, 1899.

I understand your mood, dear actress, I understand it very well; but yet in your place I would not be so desperately upset. Both the part of Anna and the play itself are not worth wasting so much feeling and nerves over. It is an old play. It is already out of date, and there are a great many defects in it; if more than half the performers have not fallen into the right tone, then naturally it is the fault of the play. That's one thing, and the second is, you must once and for all give up being worried about successes and failures. Don't let that concern you. It's your duty to go on working steadily day by day, quite quietly, to be prepared for mistakes which are inevitable, for failures—in short, to do your job as actress and let other people count the calls before the curtain. To write or to act, and to be conscious at the time that one is not doing the right thing—that is so usual, and for beginners so profitable!

The third thing is that the director has telegraphed that the second performance went magnificently, that everyone played splendidly, and that he was completely satisfied....

TO GORKY.

YALTA, January 2, 1900.

PRECIOUS ALEXEY MAXIMOVITCH,

I wish you a happy New Year! How are you getting on? How are you feeling? When are you coming to Yalta? Write fully. I have received the photograph, it is very good; many thanks for it.

Thank you, too, for the trouble you have taken in regard to our committee for assisting invalids coming here. Send any money there is or will be to me, or to the executive of the Benevolent Society, no matter which.

My story (i.e., "In the Ravine") has already been sent off to Zhizn. Did I tell you that I liked your story "An Orphan" extremely, and sent it to Moscow to first-rate readers? There is a certain Professor Foht in the Medical Faculty in Moscow who reads Slyeptsov capitally. I don't know a better reader. So I have sent your "Orphan" to him. Did I tell you how much I liked a story in your third volume, "My Travelling Companion"? There is the same strength in it as "In the Steppe." If I were you, I would take the best things out of your three volumes and republish them in one volume at a rouble—and that would be something really remarkable for vigour and harmony. As it is, everything seems shaken up together in the three volumes; there are no weak things, but it leaves an impression as though the three volumes were not the work of one author but of seven.

Scribble me a line or two.

TO O. L. KNIPPER.

YALTA, January 2, 1900.

My greetings, dear actress! Are you angry that I haven't written for so long? I used to write often, but you didn't get my letters because our common acquaintance intercepted them in the post.

I wish you all happiness in the New Year. I really do wish you happiness and bow down to your little feet. Be happy, wealthy, healthy, and gay.

We are getting on pretty well, we eat a great deal, chatter a great deal, laugh a great deal, and often talk of you. Masha will tell you when she goes back to Moscow how we spent Christmas.

I have not congratulated you on the success of "Lonely Lives." I still dream that you will all come to Yalta, that I shall see "Lonely Lives" on the stage, and congratulate you really from my heart. I wrote to Meierhold, and urged him in my letter not to be too violent in the part of a nervous man. The immense majority of people are nervous, you know: the greater number suffer, and a small proportion feel acute pain; but where—in streets and in houses—do you see people tearing about, leaping up, and clutching at their heads? Suffering ought to be expressed as it is expressed in life—that is, not by the arms and legs, but by the tone and expression; not by gesticulation, but by grace. Subtle emotions of the soul in educated people must be subtly expressed in an external way. You will say—stage conditions. No conditions allow falsity.

My sister tells me that you played "Anna" exquisitely. Ah, if only the Art Theatre would come to Yalta! Novoye Vremya highly praised your company. There is a change of tactics in that quarter; evidently they are going to praise you all even in Lent. My story, a very queer one, will be in the February number of Zhizn. There are a great number of characters, there is scenery too, there's a crescent moon, there's a bittern that cries far, far away: "Boo-oo! boo-oo!" like a cow shut up in a shed. There's everything in it.

Levitan is with us. Over my fireplace he has painted a moonlight night in the hayfield, cocks of hay, forest in the distance, a moon reigning on high above it all.

Well, the best of health to you, dear, wonderful actress. I have been pining for you.

And when are you going to send me your photograph? What treachery!

TO A. S. SUVORIN.

YALTA, January 8, 1900.

... My health is not so bad. I feel better than I did last year, but yet the doctors won't let me leave Yalta. I am as tired and sick of this charming town as of a disagreeable wife. It's curing me of tuberculosis, but it's making me ten years older. If I go to Nice it won't be before February. I am writing a little; not long ago I sent a long story to Zhizn. Money is short, all I have received so far from Marks for the plays is gone by now. ...

If Prince Baryatinsky is to be judged by his paper, I must own I was unjust to him, for I imagined him very different from what he is. They will shut up his paper, of course, but he will long maintain his reputation as a good journalist. You ask me why the Syeverny Kurier is successful? Because our society is exhausted, hatred has turned it as rank and rotten as grass in a bog, and it has a longing for something fresh, free, light—a desperate longing.

I often see the academician Kondakov here. We talk of the Pushkin section of belles-lettres. As Kondakov will take part in the elections of future academicians, I am trying to hypnotize him, and suggest that they should elect Barantsevitch and Mihailovsky. The former is broken down and worn out. He is unquestionably a literary man, is poverty-stricken in his old age. ... An income and rest would be the very thing for him. The latter—that is Mihailovsky—would make a good foundation for the new section, and his election would satisfy three-quarters of the brotherhood. But my hypnotism failed, my efforts came to nothing. The supplementary clauses to the statute are like Tolstoy's After-word to the Kreutzer Sonata. The academicians have done all they can to protect themselves from literary men, whose society shocks them as the society of the Russian academicians shocked the Germans. Literary men can only be honorary academicians, and that means nothing—it is just the same as being an honorary citizen of the town of Vyazma or Tcherepovets, there is no salary and no vote attached. A clever way out of it! The professors will be elected real academicians, and those of the writers will be elected honorary academicians who do not live in Petersburg, and so cannot be present at the sittings and abuse the professors.

I hear the muezzin calling in the minaret. The Turks are very religious; it's their fast now, they eat nothing the whole day. They have no religious ladies, that element which makes religion shallow as the sand does the Volga.

You do well to print the martyrology of Russian towns avoided by the extortionate railway contractors. Here is what the famous author Chekhov wrote on the subject in his story "My Life." Railway contractors are revengeful people; refuse them a trifle, and they will punish you for it all your life—and it's their tradition.

Thanks for your letter, thanks for your indulgence.

TO P. I. KURKIN.

YALTA, January 18, 1900.

DEAR PYOTR IVANOVITCH,

Thank you for your letter. I have long been wanting to write to you, but have never had time, under the load of business and official correspondence. Yesterday was the 17th of January—my name-day, and the day of my election to the Academy. What a lot of telegrams! And what a lot of letters still to come! And I must answer all of them, or posterity will accuse me of not knowing the laws of good manners.

There is news, but I won't tell you it now (no time), but later on. I am not very well. I was ailing all yesterday. I press your hand heartily. Keep well.

TO V. M. SOBOLEVSKY.

YALTA, January 19, 1900.

DEAR VASSILY MIHAILOVITCH,

In November I wrote a story fully intending to send it to Russkiya Vyedomosti, but the story lengthened out beyond the sixteen pages, and

I had to send it elsewhere. Then Elpatyevsky and I decided to send you a telegram on New Year's Eve, but there was such a rush and a whirl that we let the right moment slip, and now I send you my New Year wishes. Forgive me my many transgressions. You know how deeply I love and respect you, and if the intervals in our correspondence are prolonged it's merely external causes that are to blame.

I am alive and almost well. I am often ill, but not for long at a time; and I haven't once been kept in bed this winter, I keep about though I am ill. I am working harder than I did last year, and I am more bored. It's bad being without Russia in every way.... All the evergreen trees look as though they were made of tin, and one gets no joy out of them. And one sees nothing interesting, as one has no taste for the local life.

Elpatyevsky and Kondakov are here. The former has run up a huge house for himself which towers above all Yalta; the latter is going to Petersburg to take his seat in the Academy—and is glad to go. Elpatyevsky is cheerful and hearty, always in good spirits, goes out in all weathers, in a summer overcoat; Kondakov is irritably sarcastic, and goes about in a fur coat. Both often come and see me and we speak of you.

V. A. wrote that she had bought a piece of land in Tuapse. Oy-oy! but the boredom there is awful, you know. There are Tchetchentsi and scorpions, and worst of all there are no roads, and there won't be any for a long time. Of all warm places in Russia the best are on the south coast of the Crimea, there is no doubt of that, whatever they may say about the natural beauties of the Caucasus. I have been lately to Gurzufa, near Pushkin's rock, and admired the view, although it rained and although I am sick to death of views. In the Crimea it is snugger and nearer to Russia. Let V. A. sell her place in Tuapse or make a present of it to someone, and I will find her a bit of the sea-front with bathing, and a bay, in the Crimea.

When you are in Vosdvizhenka give my respects and greetings to Varvara Alexyevna, Varya, Natasha, and Glyeb. I can fancy how Glyeb and Natasha have grown. Now if only you would all come here for Easter, I could have a look at you all. Don't forget me, please, and don't be angry with me. I send you my warmest good wishes. I press your hand heartily and embrace you.

TO G. I. ROSSOLIMO.

YALTA, January 21, 1900.

DEAR GRIGORY IVANOVITCH,

... I send you in a registered parcel what I have that seems suitable for children—two stories of the life of a dog. And I think I have nothing else of the sort. I don't know how to write for children; I write for them once in ten years, and so-called children's books I don't like and don't believe in. Children ought only to be given what is suitable also for grown-up people. Andersen, "The Frigate Pallada," Gogol, are easily read by children and also by grown-up people. Books should not be written for children, but one ought to know how to choose from what has been written for grown-up people—that is, from real works of art. To be able to select among drugs, and to administer them in suitable doses, is more direct and consistent than trying to invent a special remedy for the patient because he is a child. Forgive the medical comparison. It's in keeping with the moment, perhaps, as for the last four days I have been occupied with medicine, doctoring my mother and myself. Influenza no doubt. Fever and headache.

If I write anything, I will let you know in due time, but anything I write can only be published by one man—Marks! For anything published by anyone else I have to pay a fine of 5,000 roubles (per signature). ...

TO O. L. KNIPPER.

YALTA, January 22, 1900.

DEAR ACTRESS,

On January 17th I had telegrams from your mother and your brother, from your uncle Alexandr Ivanovitch (signed Uncle Sasha), and from N. N. Sokolovsky. Be so good as to give them my warm thanks and the expression of my sincere feeling for them.

Why don't you write?—what has happened? Or are you already so fascinated? ... Well, there is no help for it. God be with you!

I am told that in May you will be in Yalta. If that is settled, why shouldn't you make inquiries beforehand about the theatre? The theatre here is let on lease, and you could not get hold of it without negotiating with the tenant, Novikov the actor. If you commission me to do so I would perhaps talk to him about it.

The 17th, my name-day and the day of my election to the Academy, passed dingily and gloomily, as I was unwell. Now I am better, but my mother is ailing. And these little troubles completely took away all taste and inclination for a name-day or election to the Academy, and they, too, have hindered me from writing to you and answering your telegram at the proper time.

Mother is getting better now.

I see the Sredins at times. They come to see us, and I go to them very, very rarely, but still I do go. . . .

So, then, you are not writing to me and not intending to write very soon either. . . . X. is to blame for all that. I understand you!

I kiss your little hand.

TO F. D. BATYUSHKOV.

YALTA, January 24, 1900.

MUCH RESPECTED F. D.,

Roche asks me to send him the passages from "Peasants" which were cut out by the Censor, but there were no such passages. There is one chapter which has not appeared in the magazine, nor in the book. It was a conversation of the peasants about religion and government. But there is no need to send that chapter to Paris, as indeed there was no need to translate "Peasants" into French at all.

I thank you most sincerely for the photograph; Ryepin's illustration is an honour I had not expected or dreamed of. It will be very pleasant to have the original; tell Ilya Efimovitch that I shall expect it with impatience, and that he cannot change his mind now, as I have already bequeathed the original to the town of Taganrog—in which, by the way, I was born.

In your letter you speak of Gorky: how do you like Gorky? I don't like everything he writes, but there are things I like very, very much, and to my mind there is not a shadow of doubt that Gorky is made of the dough of which artists are made. He is the real thing. He's a fine man, clever, thinking, and thoughtful. But there is a lot of unnecessary ballast upon him and in him—for example, his provincialism. . . .

Thanks very much for your letter, for remembering me. I am dull here, I am sick of it, and I have a feeling as though I have been thrown overboard. And the weather's bad too, and I am not well. I still go on coughing. All good wishes.

TO M. O. MENSHIKOV.

YALTA, January 28, 1900.

. . . I can't make out what Tolstoy's illness is. Tcherinov has sent me no answer, and from what I read in the papers and what you write me now I can draw no conclusion. Ulcers in the stomach and intestines would give different indications: they are not present, or there have been a few bleeding wounds caused by gall-stones which have passed and lacerated the walls. There is no cancer either. It would have shown itself first in the appetite, in the general condition, and above all the face would have betrayed cancer if he had had it. The most likely thing is that L. N. is in good health (apart from the gall-stones), and will live another twenty years. His illness frightened me, and kept me on tenter-hooks. I am afraid of Tolstoy's death. If he were to die there would be a big empty place in my life. To begin with, because I have never loved any man as much as him. I am not a believing man, but of all beliefs I consider his the nearest and most akin to me. Secondly, while Tolstoy is in literature it is easy and pleasant to be a literary man; even recognizing that one has done nothing and never will do anything is not so dreadful, since Tolstoy will do enough for all. His work is the justification of the enthusiasms and expectations built upon literature. Thirdly, Tolstoy takes a firm stand, he has an immense authority, and so long as he is alive, bad tastes in literature, vulgarity of every kind, insolent and lachrymose, all the bristling, exasperated vanities will be in the far background, in the shade. Nothing but his moral authority is capable of maintaining a certain elevation in the moods and tendencies of literature so called. Without him they would be a flock without a shepherd, or a hotch-potch, in which it would be difficult to discriminate anything.

To finish with Tolstoy, I have something to say about "Resurrection," which I have read not piecemeal, in parts, but as a whole, at one go. It is a remarkable artistic production. The least interesting part is all that is said of Nehludov's relations with Katusha; and the most interesting the princes, the generals, the aunts, the peasants, the convicts, the warders. The scene in the house of the General in command of the Peter-Paul Fortress, the spiritualist, I read with a throbbing heart—it is so good! And Madame Kortchagin in the easy chair; and the peasant, the husband of Fedosya! The peasant calls his grandmother "an artful one." That's just what Tolstoy's pen is—an artful one. There's no end to the novel, what there is you can't call an end. To write and write, and then to throw the whole weight of it on a text from the Gospel, that is quite in the theological style. To settle it all by a text from the Gospel is as arbitrary as dividing the convicts into five classes. Why into five and not into ten? He must make us believe in the Gospel, in its being the truth, and then settle it all by texts.

... They write about Tolstoy as old women talk about a crazy saint, all sorts of unctuous nonsense; it's a mistake for him to talk to those people....

They have elected Tolstoy—against the grain. According to notions there, he is a Nihilist. Anyway, that's what he was called by a lady, the wife of an actual privy councillor, and I heartily congratulate him upon it....

TO L. S. MIZINOV.

YALTA, January 29, 1900.

DEAR LIRA,

They have written to me that you have grown very fat and become dignified, and I did not expect that you would remember me and write to me. But you have remembered me—and thank you very much for it, dear. You write nothing about your health: evidently it's not bad, and I am glad. I hope your mother is well and that everything is going on all right. I am nearly well; I am ill from time to time, but not often, and only because I am old—the bacilli have nothing to do with it. And when I see a lovely woman now I smile in an aged way, and drop my lower lip—that's all.

Lika, I am dreadfully bored in Yalta. My life does not run or flow, but crawls along. Don't forget me; write to me now and then, anyway. In your letters just as in your life you are a very interesting woman. I press your hand warmly.

TO GORKY.

YALTA, February 3, 1900.

DEAR ALEXEY MAXIMOVITCH,

Thank you for your letter, for the lines about Tolstoy and about "Uncle Vanya," which I haven't seen on the stage; thanks altogether for not forgetting me. Here in this blessed Yalta one could hardly keep alive without letters. The idleness, the idiotic winter with the temperature always above freezing-point, the complete absence of interesting women, the pig-faces on the sea-front—all this may spoil a man and wear him out in a very short time. I am tired of it; it seems to me as though the winter had been going on for ten years.

You have pleurisy. If so, why do you stay on in Nizhni. Why? What do you want with that Nizhni, by the way? What glue keeps you sticking to that town? If you like Moscow, as you write, why don't you live in Moscow? In Moscow there are theatres and all the rest of it, and, what matters most of all, Moscow is handy for going abroad; while living in Nizhni you'll stick in Nizhni, and never go further than Vasilsursk. You want to see more, to know more, to have a wider range. Your imagination is quick to seize and hold, but it is like a big oven which is not provided with fuel enough. One feels this in general, and in particular in the stories: you present two or three figures in a story, but these figures stand apart, outside the mass; one sees that these figures are living in your imagination, but only these figures—the mass is not grasped. I except from this criticism your Crimean things (for instance, "My Travelling Companion"), in which, besides the figures, there is a feeling of the human mass out of which they have come, and atmosphere and background—everything, in fact. See what a lecture I am giving you—and all that you may not go on staying in Nizhni. You are a young man, strong and tough; if I were you I should make a tour in India and all sorts of places. I would take my degree in two or more faculties—I would, yes, I would! You laugh, but I do feel so badly treated at being forty already, at having asthma and all sorts of horrid things which prevent my living freely. Anyway, be a good fellow and a good comrade, and don't be angry with me for preaching at you like a head priest.

Write to me. I look forward to "Foma Gordeyev," which I haven't yet read properly.

There is no news. Keep well, I press your hand warmly.

TO O. L. KNIPPER.

YALTA, February 10, 1900.

DEAR ACTRESS,

The winter is very cold, I am not well, no one has written to me for nearly a whole month—and I had made up my mind that there was nothing left for me but to go abroad, where it is not so dull; but now it has begun to be warmer, and it's better, and I have decided that I shall go abroad only at the end of the summer, for the exhibition.

And you, why are you depressed? What are you depressed about? You are living, working, hoping, drinking; you laugh when your uncle reads aloud to you—what more do you want? I am a different matter. I am torn up by the roots, I am not living a full life, I don't drink, though I am fond of drinking; I love noise and don't hear it—in fact, I am in the condition of a transplanted tree which is hesitating whether to take root or to begin to wither. If I sometimes allow myself to complain of boredom, I have some grounds for doing so—but you? And Meierhold is complaining of the dulness of his life too. Aie, aie!

By the way, about Meierhold—he ought to spend the whole summer in the Crimea. His health needs it. Only it must be for the whole summer.

Well, now I am all right again. I am doing nothing because I intend to set to work. I dig in the garden. You write that for you, little people, the future is wrapped in mystery. I had a letter from your chief Nemirovitch not long ago. He writes that the company is going to be in Sevastopol, then in Yalta at the beginning of May: in Yalta there will be five performances, then evening rehearsals. Only the precious members of the company will remain for the rehearsals, the others can have a holiday where they please.

I trust that you are precious. To the director you are precious, to the author you are priceless. There is a pun for a titbit for you. I won't write another word to you till you send me your portrait.

Thank you for your good wishes in regard to my marriage. I have informed my fiancee of your design of coming to Yalta in order to cut her out a little. She said that if "that horrid woman" comes to Yalta, she will hold me tight in her embrace. I observed that to be embraced for so long in hot weather was not hygienic. She was offended and grew thoughtful, as though she were trying to guess in what surroundings I had picked up this facon de parler, and after a little while said that the theatre was an evil and that my intention of writing no more plays was extremely laudable—and asked me to kiss her. To this I replied that it was not proper for me to be so free with my kisses now that I am an academician. She burst into tears, and I went away.

In the spring the company will be in Harkov too. I will come and meet you then, only don't talk of that to anyone. Nadyezhda Ivanovna has gone off to Moscow.

TO A. S. SUVORIN.

YALTA, February 12, 1900.

I have been racking my brains over your fourth act, and have come to no conclusion except, perhaps, that you must not end it up with Nihilists. It's too turbulent and screaming; a quiet, lyrical, touching ending would be more in keeping with your play. When your heroine begins to grow old without arriving at anything or deciding anything for herself, and sees that she is forsaken by all, that she is uninteresting and superfluous, when she understands that the people around her were idle, useless, bad people (her father too), and that she has let her life slip—is not that more dreadful than the Nihilists?

Your letters about "The Russalka" and Korsh are very good. The tone is brilliant, and they are wonderfully written. But about Konovalov and the jury, I think you ought not to have written, however alluring the subject. Let A——t write as much as he likes about it, but not you, for it is not your affair. To treat such questions boldly and with conviction, one must be a man with a single purpose, while you would go off at a tangent halfway through the letter—as you have done—saying suddenly that we all sometimes desire to kill someone, and desire the death of our neighbours. When a daughter-in-law feels sick and tired of an invalid mother-in-law, a spiteful old woman, she, the daughter-in-law, feels easier at the thought that the old woman will soon die: but that's not desiring her death, but weariness, an exhausted spirit, vexation, longing for peace. If that daughter-in-law were ordered to kill the old woman, she would sooner kill herself, whatever desire might have been brooding in her heart.

Why, of course jurymen may make a mistake, but what of that? It does happen by mistake that help is given to the well-fed instead of to the hungry, but whatever you write on that subject, you will reach no result but harm to the hungry. Whether from our point of view the jury are mistaken or not mistaken, we ought to recognize that in each individual case they form a conscious judgment and make an effort to do so conscientiously; and if a captain steers his steamer conscientiously, continually consulting the chart and the compass, and if the steamer is shipwrecked all the same, would it not be more correct to put down the shipwreck not to the captain, but to something else—for instance, to think that the chart is out of date or that the bottom of the sea has changed? Yes, there are three points the jury have to take into consideration: (1) Apart from the criminal law, the penal code and legal procedure, there is a moral law which is always in advance of the established law, and which defines our actions precisely when we try to act on our conscience; thus, for instance, the heritage of a daughter is laid down by law as a seventh part. But you, acting on the dictates of purely moral principle, go beyond the law and in opposition to it, and bequeath her the same share as your sons, for you know that to act otherwise would be acting against your conscience. In the same way it sometimes happens to the jury to be put in a position in which they feel that their conscience is not satisfied by the established law, that in the case they are judging there are fine shades and subtleties which cannot be brought under the provisions of the penal code, and that obviously something else is needed for a just judgment, and that for the lack of that "something" they will be forced to give a judgment in which something is lacking. (2) The jury know that acquittal is not pardon, and that acquittal does not deliver the prisoner from the day of judgment in the other world, from the judgment of his conscience, from the judgment of public opinion; they decide the question only so far as it is a judicial question, and leave A———t to decide whether it is good to kill children or bad. (3) The prisoner comes to the court already exhausted by prison and examination, and he is in an agonizing position at his trial, so that even if he is acquitted he does not leave the court unpunished.

Well, be that as it may, my letter is almost finished, and I seem to have written nothing. We have the spring here in Yalta, no news of interest. . . .

"Resurrection" is a remarkable novel, I liked it very much, but it ought to be read straight off at one sitting. The end is uninteresting and false—false in a technical sense.

TO O. L. KNIPPER.

YALTA, February 14, 1900.

DEAR ACTRESS,

The photographs are very, very good, especially the one in which you are leaning in dejection with your elbows on the back of a chair, which gives you a discreetly mournful, gentle expression under which there lies hid a little demon. The other is good too, but it looks a little like a Jewess, a very musical person who attends a conservatoire, but at the same time is studying dentistry on the sly as a second string, and is engaged to be married to a young man in Mogilev, and whose fiance is a person like M———. Are you angry? Really, really angry? It's my revenge for your not signing them.

Of the seventy roses I planted in the autumn only three have not taken root. Lilies, irises, tulips, tuberoses, hyacinths, are all pushing out of the ground. The willow is already green. By the little seat in the corner the grass is luxuriant already. The almond-tree is in blossom. I have put little seats all over the garden, not grand ones with iron legs, but wooden ones which I paint green. I have made three bridges over the stream. I am planting palms. In fact, there are all sorts of novelties, so much so that you won't know the house, or the garden, or the street. Only the owner has not changed, he is just the same moping creature and devoted worshipper of the talents that reside at Nikitsky Gate. I have heard no music nor singing since the autumn, I have not seen one interesting woman. How can I help being melancholy?

I had made up my mind not to write to you, but since you have sent the photographs I have taken off the ban, and here you see I am writing. I will even come to Sevastopol, only I repeat, don't tell that to anyone, especially not to Vishnevsky. I shall be there incognito, I shall put myself down in the hotel-book Count Blackphiz.

I was joking when I said that you were like a Jewess in your photograph. Don't be angry, precious one. Well, herewith I kiss your little hand, and remain unalterably yours.

TO GORKY.

YALTA, February 15, 1900.

DEAR ALEXEY MAXIMOVITCH,

Your article in the Nizhni-Novgorod Listok was balm to my soul. What a talented person you are! I can't write anything but belles-lettres, you possess the pen of a journalist as well. I thought at first I liked the article so much because you praise me in it; afterwards it came out that Sredin and his family and Yartsev were all delighted with it. So peg away at journalism. God bless you!

Why don't they send me "Foma Gordeyev"? I have read it only in bits, and one ought to read it straight through at a sitting as I have just read "Resurrection." Except the relations of Nehludov and Katusha, which are somewhat obscure and made up, everything in the novel made the impression of strength, richness, and breadth, and the insincerity of a man afraid of death and refusing to admit it and clutching at texts and holy Scripture.

Write to them to send me "Foma."

"Twenty-six Men and a Girl" is a good story. There is a strong feeling of the environment. One smells the hot rolls.

They have just brought your letter. So you don't want to go to India? That's a pity. When India is in the past, a long sea voyage, you have something to think about when you can't get to sleep. And a tour abroad takes very little time, it need not prevent your going about in Russia on foot.

I am bored, not in the sense of weltschmerz, not in the sense of being weary of existence, but simply bored from want of people, from want of music which I love, and from want of women, of whom there are none in Yalta. I am bored without caviare and pickled cabbage.

I am very sorry that apparently you have given up the idea of coming to Yalta. The Art Theatre from Moscow will be here in May. It will give five performances and then remain for rehearsals. So you come, study the stage at the rehearsals, and then in five to eight days write a play, which I should welcome joyfully with my whole heart.

Yes, I have the right now to insist on the fact that I am forty, that I am a man no longer young. I used to be the youngest literary man, but you have appeared on the scene and I became more dignified at once, and no one calls me the youngest now.

TO V. A. POSSE.

YALTA, February 15, 1900.

MUCH RESPECTED VLADIMIR ALEXANDROVITCH,

"Foma Gordeyev" and in a superb binding too is a precious and touching present; I thank you from the bottom of my heart. A thousand thanks! I have read "Foma" only in bits, now I shall read it properly. Gorky should not be published in parts; either he must write more briefly, or you must put him in whole as the Vyestnik Evropy does with Boborykin. "Foma," by the way, is very successful, but only with intelligent well-read people—with the young also. I once overheard in a garden the conversation of a lady (from Petersburg) with her daughter: the mother was abusing the book, the daughter was praising it. . . .

YALTA,
February 29, 1900.

"Foma Gordeyev" is written all in one tone like a dissertation. All the characters speak alike, and their way of thinking is alike too. They all speak not simply but intentionally; they all have some idea in the background; as though there is something they know they don't speak out: but in reality there is nothing they know, and it is simply their facon de parler.

There are wonderful passages in "Foma." Gorky will make a very great writer if only he does not weary, does not grow cold and lazy.

TO A. S. SUVORIN,

YALTA, March 10, 1900.

No winter has ever dragged on so long for me as this one, and time merely drags and does not move, and now I realize how stupid it was of me to leave Moscow. I have lost touch with the north without getting into touch with the south, and one can think of nothing in my position but to go abroad. After the spring, winter has begun here again in Yalta—snow, rain, cold, mud—simply disgusting.

The Moscow Art Theatre will be in Yalta in April; it will bring its scenery and decorations. All the tickets for the four days advertised were sold in one day, although the prices have been considerably raised. They will give among other things Hauptmann's "Lonely Lives," a magnificent play in my opinion. I read it with great pleasure, although I am not fond of plays, and the production at the Art Theatre they say is marvellous.

There is no news. There is one great event, though: N.'s "Socrates" is printed in the Neva Supplement. I have read it, but with great effort. It is not Socrates but a dull-witted, captious, opinionated man, the whole of whose wisdom and interest is confined to tripping people up over words. There is not a trace or vestige of talent in it, but it is quite possible that the play might be successful because there are words in it such as "amphora," and Karpov says it would stage well.

How many consumptives there are here! What poverty, and how worried one is with them! The hotels and lodging-houses here won't take in those who are seriously ill. You can imagine the awful cases that may be seen here. People are dying from exhaustion, from their surroundings, from complete neglect, and this in blessed Taurida!

One loses all relish for the sun and the sea. . . .

TO O. L. KNIPPER.

YALTA, March 26, 1900.

There is a feeling of black melancholy about your letter, dear actress; you are gloomy, you are fearfully unhappy—but not for long, one may imagine, as soon, very soon, you will be sitting in the train, eating your lunch with a very good appetite. It is very nice that you are coming first with Masha before all the others; we shall at least have time to talk a little, walk a little, see things, drink and eat. But please don't bring with you . . .

I haven't a new play, it's a lie of the newspapers. The newspapers never do tell the truth about me. If I did begin a play, of course the first thing I should do would be to inform you of the fact.

There is a great wind here; the spring has not begun properly yet, but we go about without our goloshes and fur caps. The tulips will soon be out. I have a nice garden but it is untidy, moss-grown—a dilettante garden.

Gorky is here. He is warm in his praises of you and your theatre. I will introduce you to him.

Oh dear! Someone has arrived. A visitor has come in. Good-bye for now, actress!

TO HIS SISTER.

YALTA, March 26, 1900.

DEAR MASHA,

. . . There is no news, there is no water in the pipes either. I am sick to death of visitors. Yesterday, March 25, they came in an incessant stream all day; doctors keep sending people from Moscow and the provinces with letters asking me to find lodgings, to "make arrangements," as though I were a house-agent! Mother is well. Mind you keep well too, and make haste and come home.

TO O. L. KNIPPER.

YALTA, May 20, 1900.

Greetings to you, dear enchanting actress! How are you? How are you feeling? I was very unwell on the way back to Yalta. I had a bad headache and temperature before I left Moscow. I was wicked enough to conceal it from you, now I am all right.

How is Levitan? I feel dreadfully worried at not knowing. If you have heard, please write to me.

Keep well and be happy. I heard Masha was sending you a letter, and so I hasten to write these few lines.

TO HIS SISTER.

YALTA, September 9, 1900.

DEAR MASHA,

I answer the letter in which you write about Mother. To my thinking it would be better for her to go to Moscow now in the autumn and not after December. She will be tired of Moscow and pining for Yalta in a month, you know, and if you take her to Moscow in the autumn she will be back in Yalta before Christmas. That's how it seems to me, but possibly I am mistaken; in any case you must take into consideration that it is much drearier in Yalta before Christmas than it is after—infinitely drearier.

Most likely I will be in Moscow after the 20th of September, and then we will decide. From Moscow I shall go I don't know where—first to Paris, and then probably to Nice, from Nice to Africa. I shall hang on somehow to the spring, all April or May, when I shall come to Moscow again.

There is no news. There's no rain either, everything is dried up. At home here it is quiet, peaceful, satisfactory, and of course dull.

"Three Sisters" is very difficult to write, more difficult than my other plays. Oh well, it doesn't matter, perhaps something will come of it, next season if not this. It's very hard to write in Yalta, by the way: I am interrupted, and I feel as though I had no object in writing; what I wrote yesterday I don't like to-day. . . .

Well, take care of yourself.

My humblest greetings to Olga Leonardovna, to Vishnevsky, and all the rest of them too.

If Gorky is in Moscow, tell him that I have sent a letter to him in Nizhni-Novgorod.

TO GORKY.

YALTA, October 16, 1900.

DEAR ALEXEY MAXIMOVITCH,

... On the 21st of this month I am going to Moscow, and from there abroad. Can you imagine—I have written a play; but as it will be produced not now, but next season, I have not made a fair copy of it yet. It can lie as it is. It was very difficult to write "Three Sisters." Three heroines, you see, each a separate type and all the daughters of a general. The action is laid in a provincial town, as it might be Perm, the surroundings military, artillery.

The weather in Yalta is exquisite and fresh, my health is improving. I don't even want to go away to Moscow. I am working so well, and it is so pleasant to be free from the irritation I suffered from all the summer. I am not coughing, and am even eating meat. I am living alone, quite alone. My mother is in Moscow.

Thanks for your letters, my dear fellow, thanks very much. I read them over twice. My warmest greetings to your wife and Maxim. And so, till we meet in Moscow. I hope you won't play me false, and we shall see each other.

God keep you.

MOSCOW,
October 22, 1901.

Five days have passed since I read your play ("The Petty Bourgeois"). I have not written to you till now because I could not get hold of the fourth act; I have kept waiting for it, and—I still have not got it. And so I have only read three acts, but that I think is enough to judge of the play. It is, as I expected, very good, written a la Gorky, original, very interesting;

and, to begin by talking of the defects, I have noticed only one, a defect incorrigible as red hair in a red-haired man—the conservatism of the form. You make new and original people sing new songs to an accompaniment that looks second-hand, you have four acts, the characters deliver edifying discourses, there is a feeling of alarm before long speeches, and so on, and so on. But all that is not important, and it is all, so to speak, drowned in the good points of the play. Pertchihin—how living! His daughter is enchanting, Tatyana and Pyotr are also, and their mother is a splendid old woman. The central figure of the play, Nil, is vigorously drawn and extremely interesting! In fact, the play takes hold of one from the first act. Only God preserve you from letting anyone act Pertchihin except Artyom, while Alexeyev-Stanislavsky must certainly play Nil. Those two figures will do just what's needed; Pyotr—Meierhold. Only Nil's part, a wonderful part, must be made two or three times as long. You ought to end the play with it, to make it the leading part. Only do not contrast him with Pyotr and Tatyana, let him be by himself and them by themselves, all wonderful, splendid people independently of each other. When Nil tries to seem superior to Pyotr and Tatyana, and says of himself that he is a fine fellow, the element so characteristic of our decent working man, the element of modesty, is lost. He boasts, he argues, but you know one can see what sort of man he is without that. Let him be merry, let him play pranks through the whole four acts, let him eat a great deal after his work—and that will be enough for him to conquer the audience with. Pyotr, I repeat, is good. Most likely you don't even suspect how good he is. Tatyana, too, is a finished figure, only (a) she ought really to be a schoolmistress, ought to be teaching children, ought to come home from school, ought to be taken up with her pupils and exercise-books, and (b) it ought to be mentioned in the first or second act that she has attempted to poison herself; then, after that hint, the poisoning in the third act will not seem so startling and will be more in place. Telerev talks too much: such characters ought to be shown bit by bit between others, for in any case such people are everywhere merely incidental—both in life and on the stage. Make Elena dine with all the rest in the first act, let her sit and make jokes, or else there is very little of her, and she is not clear. Her avowal to Pyotr is too abrupt, on the stage it would come out in too high relief. Make her a passionate woman, if not loving at least apt to fall in love. . . .

July 29, 1902.

I have read your play. It is new and unmistakably fine. The second act is very good, it is the best, the strongest, and when I was reading it, especially the end, I almost danced with joy. The tone is gloomy, oppressive; the audience unaccustomed to such subjects will walk out of the theatre, and you may well say good-bye to your reputation as an optimist in any case. My wife will play Vassilisa, the immoral and spiteful woman; Vishnevsky walks about the house and imagines himself the Tatar—he is convinced that it is the part for him. Luka, alas! you must not give to Artyom. He will repeat himself in that part and be exhausted; but he would do the policeman wonderfully, it is his part. The part of the actor, in which you have been very successful (it is a magnificent part), should be given to an experienced actor, Stanislavsky perhaps. Katchalev will play the baron.

You have left out of the fourth act all the most interesting characters (except the actor), and you must mind now that there is no ill effect from it. The act may seem boring and unnecessary, especially if, with the exit of the strongest and most interesting actors, there are left only the mediocrities. The death of the actor is awful; it is as though you gave the spectator a sudden box on the ear apropos of nothing without preparing him in any way. How the baron got into the doss-house and why he is a baron is also not sufficiently clear.

Andreyev's "Thought" is something pretentious, difficult to understand, and apparently no good, but it is worked out with talent. Andreyev has no simplicity, and his talent reminds me of an artificial nightingale. Skitalets now is a sparrow, but he is a real living sparrow. . . .

TO S. P. DYAGILEV.

YALTA, December 30, 1902.

. . . You write that we talked of a serious religious movement in Russia. We talked of a movement not in Russia but in the intellectual class. I won't say anything about Russia; the intellectuals so far are only playing at religion, and for the most part from having nothing to do. One may say of the cultured part of our public that it has moved away from religion, and is moving further and further away from it, whatever people may say and however many philosophical and religious societies may be formed. Whether it is a good or a bad thing I cannot undertake to decide; I will only say that the religious movement of which you write is one thing, and the whole trend of modern culture is another, and one cannot place the second in any causal connection with the first. Modern culture is only the first beginning of work for a great future, work which will perhaps go on for tens of thousands of years, in order that man may if only in the remote future come to know the truth of the real God—that is not, I conjecture, by seeking in Dostoevsky, but by clear knowledge, as one knows twice two are four. Modern culture is the first beginning of the work, while the religious movement of which we talked is a survival, almost the end of what has ceased, or is ceasing to exist. But it is a long story, one can't put it all into a letter. . . .

TO A. S. SUVORIN.

MOSCOW, June 29, 1903.

. . . One feels a warm sympathy, of course, for Gorky's letter about the Kishinev pogrom, as one does for everything he writes; the letter is not written though, but put together, there is neither youthfulness in it nor confidence, like Tolstoy's.

July 1, 1903.

You are reading belles-lettres now, so read Veresaev's stories. Begin with a little story in the second volume called "Lizar." I think you will be very much pleased with it. Veresaev is a doctor; I have got to know him lately. He makes a very good impression. . . .

TO S. P. DYAGILEV.

YALTA, July 12, 1903.

. . . I have been thinking over your letter for a long time, and alluring as your suggestion or offer is, yet in the end I must answer it as neither you nor I would wish.

I cannot be the editor of The World of Art, as I cannot live in Petersburg, . . . that's the first point. And the second is that just as a picture must be painted by one artist and a speech delivered by one orator, so a magazine must be edited by one man. Of course I am not a critic, and I dare say I shouldn't make a very good job of the reviews; but on the other hand, how could I get on in the same boat with Merezhkovsky, who definitely believes, didactically believes, while I lost my faith years ago and can only look with perplexity at any "intellectual" who does believe? I respect Merezhkovsky, and think highly of him both as a man and as a writer, but we should be pulling in opposite directions. . . .

Don't be cross with me, dear Sergey Pavlovitch: it seems to me that if you go on editing the magazine for another five years you will come to agree with me. A magazine, like a picture or a poem, must bear the stamp of one personality and one will must be felt in it. This has been hitherto the case in the World of Art, and it was a good thing. And it must be kept up. . . .

TO K. S. STANISLAVSKY.

YALTA, July 28, 1903.

. . . My play "The Cherry Orchard" is not yet finished; it makes slow progress, which I put down to laziness, fine weather, and the difficulty of the subject. . . .

I think your part [Translator's Note: Stanislavsky acted Lopahin.] is all right, though I can't undertake to decide, as I can judge very little of a play by reading it. . . .

TO MADAME STANISLAVSKY.

YALTA, September 15, 1903.

. . . Don't believe anybody—no living soul has read my play yet; I have written for you not the part of a "canting hypocrite," but of a very nice girl, with which you will, I hope, be satisfied. I have almost finished the play, but eight or ten days ago I was taken ill, with coughing and weakness—in fact, last year's business over again. Now—that is to-day—it is warmer and I feel better, but still I cannot write, as my head is aching. Olga will not bring the play; I will send the four acts together as soon as it is possible for me to set to work for a whole day. It has turned out not a drama, but a comedy, in parts a farce, indeed, and I am afraid I shall catch it from Vladimir Ivanitch

I can't come for the opening of your season, I must stay in Yalta till November. Olga, who has grown fatter and stronger in the summer, will probably come to Moscow on Sunday. I shall remain alone, and of course shall take advantage of that. As a writer it is essential for me to observe women, to study them, and so, I regret to say, I cannot be a faithful husband. As I observe women chiefly for the sake of my plays, in my opinion the Art Theatre ought to increase my wife's salary or give her a pension! . . .

TO K. S. STANISLAVSKY.

YALTA, October 30, 1903.

. . . Many thanks for your letter and telegram. Letters are very precious to me now—in the first place, because I am utterly alone here; and in the second, because I sent the play three weeks ago and only got your letter yesterday, and if it were not for my wife, I should know nothing at all and might imagine any mortal thing. When I was writing Lopahin, I thought of it as a part for you. If for any reason you don't care for it, take the part of Gaev. Lopahin is a merchant, of course, but he is a very decent person in every sense. He must behave with perfect decorum, like an educated man, with no petty ways or tricks of any sort, and it seemed to me this part, the central one of the play, would come out brilliantly in your hands. . . . In choosing an actor for the part you must remember that Varya, a serious and religious girl, is in love with Lopahin; she wouldn't be in love with a mere money-grubber. . . .

TO V. I. NEMIROVITCH DANTCHENKO.

YALTA, November 2, 1903.

... About the play.

(1) Anya can be played by anyone you like, even by a quite unknown actress, so long as she is young and looks like a girl, and speaks in a youthful singing voice. It is not an important part.

(2) Varya is a more serious part. ... She is a character in a black dress, something of a nun, foolish, tearful, etc.

... Gorky is younger than you or I, he has his life before him. ... As for the Nizhni theatre, that's a mere episode; Gorky will try it, "sniff it and reject it." And while we are on this subject, the whole idea of a "people's" theatre and "people's" literature is foolishness and lollipops for the people. We mustn't bring Gogol down to the people but raise the people up to Gogol. ...

TO A. L. VISHNEVSKY.

YALTA, November 7, 1903.

... As I am soon coming to Moscow, please keep a ticket for me for "The Pillars of Society"; I want to see the marvellous Norwegian acting, and I will even pay for my seat. You know Ibsen is my favourite writer. ...

TO K. S. STANISLAVSKY.

YALTA, November 10, 1903.

DEAR KONSTANTIN SERGEYITCH,

Of course the scenery for III. and IV. can be the same, the hall and the staircase. Please do just as you like about the scenery, I leave it entirely to you; I am amazed and generally sit with my mouth wide open at your theatre. There can be no question about it, whatever you do will be excellent, a hundred times better than anything I could invent. ...

TO F. D. BATYUSHKOV.

MOSCOW, January 19, 1904.

... At the first performance of "The Cherry Orchard" on the 17th of January, they gave me an ovation, so lavish, warm, and really so unexpected, that I can't get over it even now. ...

TO MADAME AVILOV.

MOSCOW, February 14, 1904.

... All good wishes. Above all, be cheerful; don't look at life so much as a problem—it is, most likely, far simpler. And whether it—life, of which we know nothing—is worth all the agonizing reflections which wear out our Russian wits, is a question.

TO FATHER SERGEY SHTCHUKIN.

MOSCOW, May 27, 1904.

DEAR FATHER SERGEY,

Yesterday I talked to a very well-known lawyer about the case in which you are interested, and I will tell you his opinion. Let Mr. N. immediately put together all the necessary documents, let his fiancee do the same, and go off to another province, such as Kherson, and there get married. When they are married let them come home and live quietly, saying nothing about it. It is not a crime (there is no consanguinity), but only a breach of a long established tradition. If in another two or three years someone informs against them, or finds out and interferes, and the case is brought into court, anyway the children would be legitimate. And when there is a lawsuit (a trivial one anyway), then they can send in a petition to the Sovereign. The Sovereign does not sanction what is forbidden by law (so it is no use to petition for permission for the marriage), but the Sovereign enjoys the fullest privilege of pardon and does as a rule pardon what is inevitable.

I don't know whether I am putting it properly. You must forgive me, I am in bed, ill, and have been since the second of May, I have not been able to get up once all this time. I cannot execute your other commissions. . . .

TO HIS SISTER.

BERLIN, Sunday, June 6, 1904.

. . . I write to you from Berlin, where I have been now for twenty-four hours. It turned very cold in Moscow after you went away; we had snow, and it was most likely through that that I caught cold. I began to have rheumatic pains in my arms and legs, I did not sleep for nights, got very thin, had injections of morphia, took thousands of medicines of all sorts, and remember none of them with gratitude except heroin, which was once prescribed me by Altschuller. . . .

On Thursday I set off for foreign parts, very thin, with very lean skinny legs. We had a good and pleasant journey. Here in Berlin we have taken a comfortable room in the best hotel. I am enjoying being here, and it is a long time since I have eaten so well, with such appetite. The bread here is wonderful, I eat too much of it. The coffee is excellent and the dinners beyond description. Anyone who has not been abroad does not know what good bread means. There is no decent tea here (we have our own), there are no hors d'oeuvres, but all the rest is magnificent, though cheaper than with us. I am already the better for it, and to-day I even took a long drive in the Thiergarten, though it was cool. And so tell Mother and everyone who is interested that I am getting better, or indeed have already got better; my legs no longer ache, I have no diarrhoea, I am beginning to get fat, and am all day long on my legs, not lying down. . . .

BERLIN,
June 8.

. . . The worst thing here which catches the eye at once is the dress of the ladies. Fearfully bad taste, nowhere do women dress so abominably, with such utter lack of taste. I have not seen one beautiful woman, nor one who was not trimmed with some kind of absurd braid. Now I understand why taste is so slowly developed in Germans in Moscow. On the other hand, here in Berlin life is very comfortable. The food is good, things are not dear, the horses are well fed—the dogs, who are here harnessed to little carts, are well fed too. There is order and cleanliness in the streets. . . .

BADENWEILER,
June 12.

 I have been for three days settled here, this is my address—Germany, Badenweiler, Villa Fredericke. This Villa Fredericke, like all the houses and villas here, stands apart in a luxuriant garden in the sun, which shines and warms us till seven o'clock in the evening (after which I go indoors). We are boarding in the house; for fourteen or sixteen marks a day we have a double room flooded with sunshine, with washing-stands, bedsteads, etc., with a writing-table, and, best of all, with excellent water, like Seltzer water. The general impression: a big garden, beyond the garden, mountains covered with forest, few people, little movement in the street. The garden and the flowers are splendidly cared for. But to-day, apropos of nothing, it has begun raining; I sit in our room, and already begin to feel that in another two or three days I shall be thinking of how to escape.

 I am still eating butter in enormous quantities and with no effect. I can't take milk. The doctor here, Schworer, married to a Moscow woman, turns out to be skilful and nice.

 We shall perhaps return to Yalta by sea from Trieste or some other port. Health is coming back to me not by ounces but by stones. Anyway, I have learned here how to feed. Coffee is forbidden to me absolutely, it is supposed to be relaxing; I am beginning by degrees to eat eggs. Oh, how badly the German women dress!

 I live on the ground floor. If only you knew what the sun is here! It does not scorch, but caresses. I have a comfortable low chair in which I can sit or lie down. I will certainly buy the watch, I haven't forgotten it. How is Mother? Is she in good spirits? Write to me. Give her my love. Olga is going to a dentist here. . . .

June 16.

I am living amongst the Germans and have already got used to my room and to the regime, but can never get used to the German peace and quiet. Not a sound in the house or outside it; only at seven o'clock in the morning and at midday there is an expensive but very poor band playing in the garden. One feels there is not a single drop of talent in anything nor a single drop of taste; but, on the other hand, there is order and honesty to spare. Our Russian life is far more talented, and as for the Italian or the French, it is beyond comparison.

My health has improved. I don't notice now as I go about that I am ill; my asthma is better, nothing is aching. The only trace left of my illness is extreme thinness; my legs are thin as they have never been. The German doctors have turned all my life upside down. At seven o'clock in the morning I drink tea in bed—for some reason it must be in bed; at half-past seven a German by way of a masseur comes and rubs me all over with water, and this seems not at all bad. Then I have to lie still a little, get up at eight o'clock, drink acorn cocoa and eat an immense quantity of butter. At ten o'clock, oatmeal porridge, extremely nice to taste and to smell, not like our Russian. Fresh air and sunshine. Reading the newspaper. At one o'clock, dinner, at which I must not taste everything but only the things Olga chooses for me, according to the German doctor's prescription. At four o'clock the cocoa again. At seven o'clock supper. At bedtime a cup of strawberry tea—that is as a sleeping draught. In all this there is a lot of quackery, but a lot of what is really good and useful—for instance, the porridge. I shall bring some oatmeal from here with me. . . .

June 21.

Things are going all right with me, only I have begun to get sick of Badenweiler. There is so much German peace and order here. It was different in Italy. To-day at dinner they gave us boiled mutton—what a dish! The whole dinner is magnificent, but the maitres d'hotel look so important that it makes one uneasy.

June 28.

. . . It has begun to be terribly hot here. The heat caught me unawares, as I have only winter suits here. I am gasping and dreaming of getting away. But where to go? I should like to go to Italy, to Como, but everyone is running away from the heat there. It is hot everywhere in the south of Europe. I should like to go from Trieste to Odessa by steamer, but I don't know how far it is possible now, in June and July.... If it should be rather hot it doesn't matter; I should have a flannel suit. I confess I dread the railway journey. It is stifling in the train now, particularly with my asthma, which is made worse by the slightest thing. Besides, there are no sleeping carriages from Vienna right up to Odessa; it would be uncomfortable. And we should get home by railway sooner than we need, and I have not had enough holiday yet. It is so hot one can't bear one's clothes, I don't know what to do. Olga has gone to Freiburg to order a flannel suit for me, there are neither tailors nor shoemakers in Badenweiler. She has taken the suit Dushar made me as a pattern.

I like the food here very much, but it does not seem to suit me; my stomach is constantly being upset. I can't eat the butter here. Evidently my digestion is hopelessly ruined. It is scarcely possible to cure it by anything but fasting—that is, eating nothing—and that's the end of it. And the only remedy for the asthma is not moving.

There is not a single decently dressed German woman. The lack of taste makes one depressed.

Well, keep well and happy. My love to Mother, Vanya, George, and all the rest. Write!

I kiss you and press your hand.

Yours,
A.

[Transcriber's Note: In the Biographical Sketch, "Chekhov was found of hearing Potapenko" was changed to "Chekhov was fond of hearing Potapenko".]